I0782265

Tomb of the Sun King

BOOK 2 *of the* RAIDERS OF THE ARCANA

Tomb of the Sun King

BOOK II

RAIDERS OF THE ARCANA

JACQUELYN BENSON

Copyright © 2024 by Jacquelyn Benson
Cover design by Selkkie Designs
Character illustrations by Elsa Kroese
Aten chapter header modified from a vector by AtonX C9C BY 2.5
Cover copyright © 2024 by Jacquelyn Benson
Typeset in Garamond and Adorn Garland

First edition: October 2024
Second edition: March 2025

Library of Congress Catalog Number: 2024910415
ISBNs: 978-1-959050-19-3 (hardcover), 978-1-959050-18-6 (paperback), 978-1-959050-14-8 (ebook), 978-1-959050-17-9 (audiobook)

Published by Vaughan Woods Publishing
Originally published by Crimson Fox Publishing

Stay up-to-date on new book releases by subscribing to Jacquelyn's newsletter at JacquelynBenson.com.

Content warnings for Tomb of the Sun King:
Contains instances of martial arts fighting, collapsing earth, gunfire, difficulty swimming, restraint.
Contains references to sex and parental emotional abuse..

For all the laborers, scholars, and dreamers who were excluded from taking ownership of their own history.

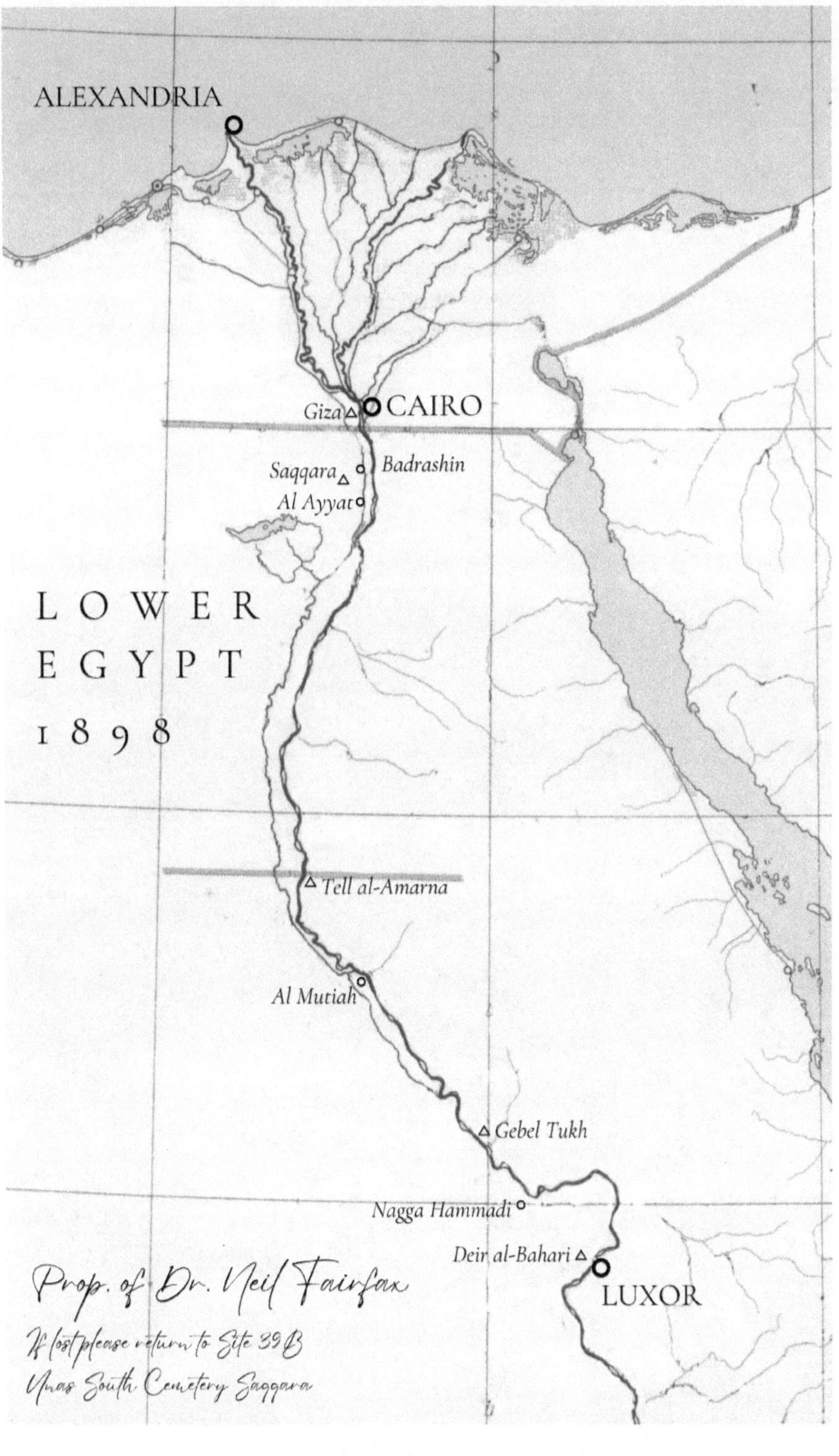

ALEXANDRIA
CAIRO
Giza
Saqqara
Badrashin
Al Ayyat
LOWER
EGYPT
1898
Tell al-Amarna
Al Mutiah
Gebel Tukh
Nagga Hammadi
Deir al-Bahari
LUXOR
Prop. of Dr. Neil Fairfax
If lost please return to Site 39 B
Unas South Cemetery Saqqara

*How manifold it is, what thou hast made ... O sole god, like whom there is
no other! Thou didst create the world according to thy desire, whilst thou wert
alone: All men, cattle, and wild beasts ... When thou hast risen they live, when
thou settest they die.*

THE GREAT HYMN TO THE ATEN
ATTRIBUTED TO NEFERKHEPERURE WAENRE AKHENATEN
TRANSLATION BY JOHN A. WILSON

*Oh Lord, how manifold are your works! In wisdom hast thou made them all: the earth
is full of thy riches.
Thou openest thine hands, they are filled with good. Thou hidest thy face, they are
troubled: thou takest away their breath, they die, and return to their dust..*

PSALM 104 V. 24, 28-29
KING JAMES VERSION

PROLOGUE

Nightfall
Seventh Day of the Month of Blossoming
1248 BCE
Near Mt. Nebo, Land of Moab

THE NIGHT WIND tasted of rain and smelled of the resinous fragrance of cypress flowers. It blew through the scrubby grass beyond the taut black fabric of the tent, hinting at the promise of a rare spring storm.

In the dim lamplight, Kaleb sat beside the pallet where his master lay dying. A scrawny gray cat with black spots dozed at the wheezing old man's feet.

The solid, powerful figure that Kaleb remembered was diminished, withered to stick-like proportions by age and illness. His face and head were clean-shaved, a habit Kaleb's master had brought with him from the land of his youth. He had never broken it, even though the people of Kaleb's tribe grew beards and had therefore found it strange.

Much about Kaleb's master was strange. He spoke foreign tongues with easy fluency and stamped clay with clusters of lines and wedges that could be read by men in far-away lands. The old man had taught Kaleb the secret of that frozen language so that he, too, could stamp the clay when his master's hands became too unsteady for the work.

The messages were sent to the emissaries of kings as Kaleb's master searched for a land where his people could set up their tents without fear of the raids that might turn them into slaves once again.

Kaleb did not remember that time of subjugation, but he had heard the stories of how his forebears sweated and died as they cut limestone talatat bricks for the new city of a tall, long-faced pharaoh whose eyes glittered with

"

the passion of a heretic.

The dying man before him had lived through those dark days. He had delivered Kaleb's people from them by the grace of another pharaoh, one with a gentler heart… and with the help of the object of miraculous power that now leaned against the pole of the tent.

Kaleb's eyes drifted past the pallet to rest on that blessed object. The oddly shaped staff was just visible in the dim lamplight as it leaned beside the rest of the old man's few belongings.

A simple bone comb rested on top of a neatly folded robe and a spare set of sandals. Stranger things lay within the woven reed baskets nearby—a golden amulet in the shape of a kohl-lined eye, an elaborate jeweled dagger, and a statue of a woman of astonishing grace and beauty, carved from the finest alabaster.

They were things from another world—one very far from the woven goat-hair tents and quietly grazing sheep of Kaleb's people.

"You must take it."

His master's words rasped in his throat like sand across the rocks of the desert. The cat on the pallet lifted its head, blinking lazy green eyes.

"Master?" Kaleb startled, feeling an uncertain pang of guilt at the thought that the old man might have seen him looking at his possessions.

"The staff," his master breathed with obvious effort.

As always, he used the word *mattah* instead of *mish'enah*—the term one might more likely apply to a walking stick. But then, the weapon of gleaming wood and tarnished bronze that seemed to gaze at Kaleb from the corner of the tent was clearly something more than a mere walking stick.

Kaleb had heard stories of its wonders—how it had called down bread from the sky when the people of his tribe were weak with hunger and punished Egypt with rains of frogs and storms of locusts.

They said that it had drowned an army in an impossible sweep of the sea. Turned daylight into a darkness that might never have ended.

"It is too dangerous," the old man rasped. "It must be hidden."

"But where am I to hide it?" Kaleb burst out as his chest tightened with fear.

His master's head fell back against the pallet, weak with exhaustion. "Bring it back to her."

"To whom?" Kaleb demanded.

The old man's face tightened with pain—and the memory of an old rage. "They took her name," he bit out harshly, though each word cost him dearly. "They tried to erase her from the memory of the world."

A hand rose from the bed and clamped around Kaleb's wrist, gripping him with a palpable echo of the immense power the man had once possessed.

"*Do not let them,*" Kaleb's master croaked.

Breath whistled painfully in his chest. The silence of the tent settled around Kaleb like a yoke across his shoulders.

"I… I won't. I promise," Kaleb vowed uneasily. "But where will I find this woman of whom you speak?"

"More… than a woman…" the old man wheezed. "So much more…"

Wind softly billowed the sides of the tent, making the flame of the oil lamp flicker. Shadows danced across the cloth like ghosts arranging them-selves into a tableau—a noble figure in a high blue crown. A grieving wife. A frightened child.

The figure on the pallet seemed to sink, his spark of life guttering like a spent candle.

"Master?" Kaleb prompted as imminent grief and the fear of unfulfilled promises twisted inside his chest.

The gray cat darted away as the dying man drew in a hoarse, hollow breath and gave Kaleb's wrist another squeeze.

"I will tell you," declared the leader and deliverer of Kaleb's people. "I will tell you all of it."

An hour later, the storm had passed. Kaleb stepped from the tent to see the early light of dawn streak through the sky, painting the plains of distant Ammon in streaks of gold.

He carried a cloth-wrapped bundle in his arms, holding it like something achingly fragile—or terribly dangerous.

His heart heavy with grief and purpose, Kaleb set off for Egypt.

ONE

Mid-afternoon
Thursday, June 9, 1898
Cairo, Egypt

THE FORECOURT OF the grand, modern Cairo railway station bustled with carriages, donkeys, street vendors, and the odd rattling, backfiring motorcar. The air rang with a mix of languages—English, French, Greek, and Masri, the Egyptian dialect of Arabic.

Ellie Mallory hovered at the edge of the chaos, squinting over a sea of black headscarves, bright red fezzes, and the occasional bowler hat for any sign of the ride that should be waiting for her.

The air was hot. Golden sun shone down on her from a hazily cloudless sky. She adjusted the brim of her straw boater hat to shield her eyes, grateful that she was dressed sensibly in a white blouse and practical tan waistcoat over her olive-hued summer skirt.

A stray cat lounged in the shade by her worn leather boots, as did a small brown valise. The bag was the same one that Ellie had carried with her when she had made a precipitous departure from London two months before. It was mostly stuffed with exactly the same rushed and somewhat random collection of belongings.

Between dodging nefarious antiquities thieves, discovering a lost civilization in the unexplored wilds of British Honduras, and then fleeing the colony after she'd inadvertently dropped said civilization into a sinkhole, she hadn't exactly found the time to update her traveling gear.

It had been a rather busy few weeks.

The circumstances that had brought her from British Honduras to Cairo were… *unanticipated*, to say the least, but Ellie still thrilled at the notion that the ancient, storied earth of Egypt lay beneath her boots. Towering date palms lined the canal that lay between the railroad station and the city's weathered medieval walls. From her current vantage, Ellie had an excellent view of the famous gate of Bab El Had. Its round, crenelated towers and arrow-slit windows dated back to the time of the Crusades. Beyond it rose the tightly clustered rooftops of Cairo proper, pierced by the elegant needles of the minarets from which the city's muezzins issued the five daily calls to prayer.

Within the city, Ellie would find the famous mosque and university of Al-Azhar, home to one of the oldest libraries in the world. On the far side of the Nile stood the pyramids of Giza along with the current home of the Egyptian Museum, which was stuffed with the most fascinating and important artifacts of the Ancient Egyptian civilization.

The City of the Dead. The palaces of the Fatamid caliphs. Ellie inwardly buzzed with the desire to explore it all, filling in the gaps in her knowledge of both Medieval Islamic culture and the ancient world.

And she would, she promised herself… just as soon as she stopped a pair of dastardly villains—the sweaty, self-important Professor Dawson and his menacing handler, Mr. Jacobs.

Ellie knew that both Dawson and Jacobs had survived the somewhat *explosive* conclusion of her adventures in British Honduras. She had seen them picking their way along a precarious mountainside as she and Adam made their escape from the cataclysm.

Thanks to Adam's snooping when they were Jacobs' captives, Ellie also knew where the two ne'er-do-wells had planned to go next—to Egypt, to seek yet another historic object with legendary powers… one that sounded even more dangerous than the dark force that she had encountered in the caves beneath the lost city of Tulan.

The impact of that encounter, and of her other experiences in British Honduras, continued to linger. Ordinary mirrors now made her feel uneasy—though she recognized that to be an entirely irrational response, as they were innocuous and useful pieces of household furnishing that would under no circumstances begin to whisper haunting and dangerous things to her. Though her bruises had faded, her guilt about the fate of the legendary civilization that she had discovered and then destroyed was still strong enough to tighten her throat.

Then there were her memories of that *other* Tulan—the living, breathing city that she had never seen, but which still somehow lurked inside of her brain as though impossibly planted there in the matter of an instant.

Ellie couldn't draw upon that vast well of knowledge at will. If she had been able to, she might at least have tried to write some of it down—for all the good that would do in the complete absence of any surviving physical proof of the city's existence. She had only little bits and pieces that popped into her mind by way of some bizarre association, like looking at the pattern on a scarf in Jamaica and thinking, *yes, that's rather like the ladies of Tulan used to do it.* Or when she tracked the flight of a falcon and found herself calculating auguries using the methods of a civilization that had died two hundred years before she was born.

Those fragments were as frustrating as they were tantalizing. She was the last living resource on a people and a way of life that had shaped the Mesoamerican world… and there was absolutely nothing she could *do* about it.

Now it looked as though she was going to have to do it all again here in Egypt. Ellie couldn't possibly allow another powerful arcanum to fall into Dawson and Jacobs' clutches—or those of whatever organization had hired them.

She knew next to nothing about who pulled the two villains' strings, but any group that would hire a man as ruthless as Jacobs to do their work for them certainly couldn't be trusted with the artifact they sought here in Egypt—namely the Staff of Moses, the Biblical relic with the power to turn water to blood and sink the world into an eternal night.

Never mind the plagues of locusts.

Ellie had raced from British Honduras with barely a stop to pick up her valise. She didn't see how Dawson and Jacobs could possibly have gotten a lead on her—but she had also learned the danger of underestimating the resources at their disposal. She had been on guard for their reappearance from the moment she stepped off the boat in Alexandria. It wasn't a question of whether Dawson and Jacobs would turn up—but *when*.

Ellie's only advantage lay in surprise. Dawson and Jacobs had no reason to suspect that she and Adam knew where they were headed next.

That was good—because to defeat them, she was going to need every edge she could scrape together.

"Nice hotel?"

The voice chirped up from beside her with startling volume. Ellie jolted as she looked around for the speaker—and then down.

The words had come from a boy of around eight who stood roughly the height of Ellie's shoulder, dressed in a skullcap and a galabeya with a tattered hem. His dark hair fell over his eyes, which fixed on her with an intimidating determination.

"Bag carrier? Donkey ride?" the boy pressed forcefully.

"No, thank you," Ellie replied.

"Pyramid tour? Dancing girls?" the boy tried.

"Dancing girls!" Ellie narrowed her eyes in disapproval.

The boy glared right back at her. "For your gentleman," he pressed.

Ellie stiffened. "I am sure I don't know what you mean."

The boy pointed to the valise at her feet. "That bag is yours," he said confidently. He shifted his finger to jab at the bag that slouched beside it—a battered, stained canvas rucksack. "*That* bag is not."

The stray cat by the two pieces of baggage rolled over, stretching out luxuriantly to expose its white and orange belly.

"How do you know?" Ellie challenged crossly.

"It smells like old donkey," the boy returned authoritatively. "If you carry it, you smell like the donkey too."

Ellie had to admire the perspicacity of his deduction. The truth was, the bag's owner was occasionally capable of smelling a little… well, less than perfectly fresh. He had freely admitted as much on more than one occasion, including a memorable morning where he had remedied the situation by cannon-balling into Ellie's bathing area.

She found herself vividly recalling a splash of water, an excess of bare male skin, and an irrepressible grin.

Trust me, Princess. You'll be glad I did this.

The memory brought a telling flush to her cheeks.

"That one belongs to my… traveling companion," she conceded.

"Aywa." The boy crossed his arms over his chest. "I ask *him*."

Ellie's jaw dropped slightly at the child's sheer audacity, but her frustration was offset by a grudging note of respect. The little monster was nothing if not determined.

She readied herself to give him a stern talking-to about reinforcing patriarchal notions of a woman's subservience to whatever man might happen to be a member of her party. Before she could begin, a call from the milling crowd of animals and travelers nearby caught her ear as one of the vendors switched from rapid Masri to simple, practiced English.

"Authentic artifacts! Ancient treasures! Best Egyptian souvenir!"

Ellie's gaze locked unerringly on a burly figure with a great black beard and a striped galabeya. The gentleman stood beside a bored-looking donkey tied to a wheeled display, which was thickly packed with trinkets.

"On second thought," Ellie said, "why don't you watch my bags for a moment?"

She plucked a pair of silver milliemes from her pocket and tossed them to the boy, who caught them deftly. He promptly took up an intimidating pose over the battered valise and slightly smelly rucksack, the unbothered cat lounging at his feet.

Her belongings secured, Ellie pushed through the shifting bodies to the hawker, where she cast an assessing gaze over the assembled objects that lined his cart. Her attention snagged on a row of identical statuettes roughly six inches in height, crafted from a softly gleaming blue ceramic.

"Salâmu 'alaykum, Sitt el Kol," the large fellow said as he noticed Ellie's presence. "You want very fine Egyptian artifact? Take home with you? These are very nice." He picked up one of the figurines and held it out for her inspection. A gold tooth winked from within his grin.

The little statues had all the appearance of being shabtis—representations of servants and courtiers that were meant to offer service to the Ancient Egyptian dead during their afterlives. Shabtis were depicted in the form of mummies, with crossed arms holding the crook and flail of Osiris and bodies covered in hieroglyphic inscriptions.

They were found in great numbers in tombs dating from the New Kingdom to the Ptolemaic period. Ellie had previously studied several specimens that had found their way to England. The small blue statue that the hawker held in his hand looked like a perfectly reasonable example of the type.

"Authentic Ancient Egyptian," he said proudly, offering the figure to her.

"I should certainly hope not," Ellie retorted.

At Ellie's words, the vendor's face blanked.

"Because selling Ancient Egyptian objects is, of course, *illegal*." Ellie paused, her mouth creasing into a frown. "Unless one is the director of the Antiquities Service of Egypt, of course, in which case one may pick any artifacts that one deems extraneous and offer them up for sale like a common street hawker." She caught herself as she glanced up at the common street hawker in front of her. "No offense intended, of course."

"Sitt?" the hawker said.

"It is only that no respectable gentleman can claim to be rigorously upholding his responsibility to preserve Egypt's ancient heritage while at the same time offering mummy pieces and amulets for sale like a Portobello Road pawnbroker!" Ellie continued pointedly.

Ellie had strong feelings about the Service des Antiquités d'Egypte. For one thing, it wasn't Egyptian at all. The department was directed by a bespectacled Frenchman and run under the auspices of the British Consul General—the English civil servant who had been ruling the country in everything but name for the last fifteen years.

The Antiquities Service claimed half of all the artifacts excavated in Egypt, allowing the rest to be carted back to whatever country the archaeologist—or the wealthy fellows who funded him—happened to hail from.

But even the relics retained by Egypt weren't safe. The director of the Antiquities Service was also empowered to declare artifacts 'duplicates' of others in the collection, in which case they were put on sale in a designated room within the museum, where they might be bought as trinkets by any tourist who happened to pass through.

Like most aspects of Britain's unofficial rule in Egypt, the system was designed to benefit privileged Europeans and Americans at the cost of the Egyptians—who likely had a thing or two to say about which parts of their heritage ought to be hawked off to the highest bidder.

Ellie plucked the shabti from the vendor's hands and gave it a careful examination.

"It appears to be made from blue faience—a commonly used material for such objects," she explained to a white-haired Turkish gentleman who had stopped beside her.

At her words, the gentleman cast an uneasy look up at the looming, narrow-eyed vendor, and then fled.

"The figure is in a traditional Osirian pose with crossed arms, tripartite wig, and false beard," Ellie continued. "All typical for a New Kingdom funeral shabti. The faience also exhibits the patina one would expect for an artifact of this age."

A crowd had gathered around Ellie, looking with nervous interest from her to the glowering street hawker. Ignoring her onlookers, Ellie flipped the shabti over for a peek under its feet. Her examination was interrupted by the cry of a familiar voice.

"There you are!"

Ellie turned to see a lacy peach parasol barreling through the crowd. The sunshade tilted back as it reached the souvenir cart, revealing the smiling face of Constance Tyrrell.

Ellie's childhood best friend barely topped five feet in height, her petite figure currently shown off by an elegantly tailored summer dress in the same rosy hue as her parasol. Her rich black hair was pinned up under an expansive hat flush with soft feathers, while the white arc of her smile contrasted prettily with her warmly brown complexion.

Behind her, a motorcar beeped an irritated horn at a well-appointed carriage bearing Constance's family crest, the door of which hung open.

"Eleanora!" Constance squealed happily as she threw her arms around Ellie. A pair of bystanders ducked back to avoid the sweep of her parasol. "But what are you *doing* here? How on earth have you come to be in Egypt? And why am I only hearing about it in a telegram reading 'Arrived Alexandria. Three-ten train to Cairo. Transport appreciated.'"

"They charge by the word," Ellie countered reasonably as she frowned at the tiny lines of painted hieroglyphs on the base of the shabti.

Ellie had known Constance since they were schoolgirls. Their paths had parted after that, as Ellie fought her way into university and Constance was shipped to finishing school to be polished up for a future husband. She had so far managed to avoid acquiring one, shaking off all the would-be suitors that her well-meaning parents threw at her.

When Ellie had last seen Constance two months before, she had been packing for the family's move to Egypt, where her father, Sir Robert, served as the new Comptroller General charged with auditing the budgets and economic policies put together by the country's British administrators.

As Sir Robert was cheerfully, obliviously, *painstakingly* good at his job, it would undoubtedly make him a burr in the side of any government officials who hoped to rig the books in their own favor.

Constance had always been eagerly willing to assist in any adventures that might involve trespassing, fisticuffs, or a bit of light burglary. Ellie's current race against Professor Dawson and Mr. Jacobs would most likely entail all of the above, making Constance a useful ally.

"As to what I am doing—at the moment, I am trying to determine whether this fellow is attempting to sell me a genuine New Kingdom funeral shabti, which would be a blatant violation of Egyptian law." Ellie flashed the looming vendor a disapproving glare.

"Are you quite certain that's a good idea?" Constance craned her neck back to give the large fellow an assessing look.

"Now let me see," Ellie continued, returning her attention to the shabti. "The figure is inscribed with an excerpt from Chapter Six of the Book of the Dead, as one would expect. And then there is a nice little spell that empowers Paw-er—that would be the name of the servant this shabti is meant to represent—to do all the necessary works for his master in the Beyond."

A pair of women nearby whispered behind their face veils, casting a nervous look at the increasingly red-faced hawker before hurrying away through a growing crowd. Ellie paid them only half a mind as she plucked up another shabti from the line of solemn-faced figures in the vendor's cart.

"Let's see." She twisted the second figure in her hand and raised an eyebrow. "This one is Paw-er as well. Our Paw-er really gets around, doesn't he?"

The hawker's jaw twitched.

"I knew I should have come armed," Constance sighed, snapping closed her parasol.

Back at the carriage, the motorcar blared its irritated horn a second time. In response, a long figure ducked through the carriage door and unfolded to a substantial height.

The imposingly tall fellow was dressed in an excellently tailored French linen suit with a crisp black bow tie and an elegant silk pocket square. A dapper red fez topped his close-cropped hair. The appearance of unimpeachable respectability was only slightly offset by the three deliberate horizontal scars that marked his mahogany cheeks.

He tugged on the ends of his jacket as he straightened, setting his suit back into perfect order, and then strode purposefully toward them with an air of resigned exasperation, seemingly oblivious to the crowd that parted around him like a shoal of fish.

Ellie stared up at the newcomer in surprise, the shabtis in her hands momentarily forgotten.

"Oh—Hello, Mr. Mahjoud," Constance said cheerfully. "Ellie, this is Aai's dragoman, whom she insists accompany me when I am out in the city to make sure I don't run into any trouble."

Ellie was familiar with the Turkish term, *dragoman*, which referred to a general guide, translator, and facilitator for foreign travel. It did not surprise her that Constance's grandmother would assign someone in that position to herd Constance about. The noble lady in question gave her granddaughter a longer leash than most grandmothers might, but she was still an extremely practical sort of person.

"I might even succeed in keeping you from running into trouble," Mr. Mahjoud declared in precise English, "if you refrained from leaping out of moving carriages."

"It wasn't moving very fast," Constance pointed out before returning her attention to Ellie. "Mr. Mahjoud is from the Sudan, where I have heard all the boys are raised fighting with lances and swords on horseback."

Constance shot Mr. Mahjoud a challenging look as though daring him to either confirm or deny the assertion.

Mr. Mahjoud raised a disdainful eyebrow.

"Miss Eleanora Mallory. Pleased to make your acquaintance." Ellie went to extend a hand to the dragoman and realized that she still held a shabti in it.

"Charmed," Mr. Mahjoud replied flatly. He shifted an assessing gaze to the glowering vendor. "And were we hoping to start a riot?"

"Oh, don't be dramatic," Constance scolded.

Ellie glanced back at the figurine in her hand. "Oh! But they are numbered! I had heard that many sets of funerary shabtis came in sequences." She looked closer. "This one is seven of forty-six. And this one…" She flipped over the statue in her other hand and squinted down at the tiny characters painted into the glaze by its feet. "This one is *also* seven of forty-six!" She waved the figurine playfully at the simmering hawker. "Why, you very nearly had me! These are excellent reproductions. Really, I don't know why you are misrepresenting them as originals. You ought to simply promote them as very high quality copies. I am sure that you would find even more customers eager to purchase them as souvenirs if they knew that in doing so, they were not removing part of Egypt's cultural heritage from her borders without permission."

"Somehow I doubt that," Constance cut in dryly. She plucked the two shabtis from Ellie's hands and thrust them at the vendor, who fumblingly managed to catch them. "Thank you. Excellent work. Best of luck to you."

With the shabtis disposed of, Constance hooked Ellie by her elbow and unceremoniously hauled her away from the cart with a strength that belied her diminutive size.

Mr. Mahjoud gave a deliberately audible sigh of relief as he followed after them, his long legs needing only a stroll to keep up.

"Now that we've settled the matter of those dolls—" Constance began.

"Dolls!" Ellie protested, stiffening. "Egyptian funerary shabtis, authentic or otherwise, can hardly be categorized as—"

"—it is high time that you explained what you are doing here in Egypt!"

Constance steered Ellie to the edge of the pavement. They stopped near the boy who still stood over Ellie's bags. He had been watching her exchange with the hawker with morbid interest.

The orange-and-white cat looked less horrified, calmly cleaning an extended leg.

"…*and* what happened with that dastardly Mr. Jacobs and your map!" Constance continued relentlessly. "Did you find your lost city? Was it full of ghosts and hidden occult treasure?"

"Ha ha ha," Ellie laughed uncomfortably. "You are quite letting your imagination run away with you, Connie." She deliberately shifted her attention to the boy. "Here's another millieme for you, young man, and I think we can quite manage for ourselves now."

The boy took the coin and gave it a brief inspection. He cast an appraising look up—and up—at Mr. Mahjoud, who glanced down his nose at the child with a disapproving frown.

The coin disappeared into a ragged pocket. "Salâm bye-bye." The boy scampered off into the crowd.

"Now *that's* settled," Mr. Mahjoud cut in, "might we return to the carriage as soon as we have collected your…"

Mr. Mahjoud's gaze moved to the luggage by Ellie's boots. It halted on the smellier of the two pieces, and his expression shifted to one of quiet horror.

"You *will* catch me up on everything that has happened," Constance pressed Ellie darkly. "But don't tell me that you really came all this way on your own!"

"I suppose one might…" Ellie began, flashing an involuntary and guilty look at the slightly malodorous rucksack still resting by her valise. "That is to say, I have not been *entirely*—"

"Hey Princess!" a boldly masculine voice called out from across the crowd. "How about some camels?"

Ellie turned at the sound. Beside her, Constance's eyes widened.

Adam Bates pushed through the shifting mass of bodies. He was still wearing a coat over his braces and shirtsleeves—which was a small miracle in itself, as Adam was not very good at keeping coats on… or shirts, for that matter. In a somewhat less respectable twist, he had pushed up the sleeves to expose his well-muscled forearms. His sun-kissed blond hair peeked out from under a battered, flat-brimmed fedora that Ellie had watched him yank out from under his bed two weeks before. His wide grin and piercing blue eyes contrasted with his deeply tanned skin.

Ellie's pulse automatically and inconveniently kicked up at the sight—just as it had insisted on doing for the better part of the last month and a half.

Familiarity, in the case of Adam Bates, had not bred contempt. In fact, it seemed to be doing the opposite, and over the course of their two-week voyage from British Honduras to Egypt, Ellie had come very close to doing things with him that would make their torrid embrace in a cenote in the tropical wilderness look like a church society dinner.

The memory of those stolen and entirely inappropriate encounters on the boat to Egypt flared to life inside her mind. She closed her hands into fists. It felt like the only reliable way to make sure that she did not reach out and run them over Adam's remarkable pectorals.

She should not be putting her hands on pectorals—or any other part of Adam Bates, for that matter. Not when their situation remained decidedly... complicated.

"Who... is... *that?*" Constance demanded in a low voice.

"That is my... er... traveling companion, Mr. Bates," Ellie replied.

"Delightful," Mr. Mahjoud said in a tone that sounded distinctly unenthusiastic.

"He is an old college friend of Neil's," Ellie added hopefully—as though the fact might make her situation slightly less awkward.

"Is he," Constance returned flatly as her eyes roved appreciatively over Adam's figure. They hitched on the eighteen-inch sheath strapped to his belt. "Your brother's *college friend* appears to be wearing a sword."

Mr. Mahjoud scoffed. Ellie glanced back at him in surprise. By the sound, one might almost have thought that the neatly dressed fellow was both familiar with swords and accustomed to ones larger than Adam's blade.

"It's a machete, actually," Ellie weakly corrected her. "It's very... useful."

Constance fixed Ellie with an alarmingly focused gaze. "And what uses have you found for the rest of it?"

Ellie clamped her mouth shut even as her cheeks flared with heat.

Constance's eyes narrowed to a dangerously knowing glare. "You have a great deal of explaining to do, Eleanora Mallory."

Ellie was saved from further interrogation by Adam's arrival as he popped through the press of rail travelers.

"He said we can have them for a week for a reduced rate." Adam pointed through the crowd to where Ellie could now see a wizened old man holding a pair of enormous dromedaries by their leads.

"How nice," Ellie said weakly.

Adam turned to her petite companion. "You must be Constance. I've heard all about you."

"And I have clearly *not* heard enough about you, which I hope will be remedied shortly." Constance flashed Ellie a dagger-pointed look before returning her attention to Adam. She assessed the firm curves of his biceps like an art scholar might a Greek statue.

Adam extended his hand to Mr. Mahjoud. "I'm Adam."

The hand was work-roughened, the palm of it crossed by the still-red line of a recent cut. The wound was accented by a frankly uneven row of pinpricks from a line of stitches that had only recently been removed.

Ellie felt just a little bad about those pinpricks. Then again, she had never been exceptionally handy with a needle.

Mr. Mahjoud eyed the hand skeptically as though worried that it might smell like the bag beside his flawlessly polished shoes. He finally accepted it with an air of resignation. "Abubakr Osman Mahjoud."

Adam bent down and gave the stray cat a rub between its orange ears as though loath to leave it out of the introductions. "Hi Kitty."

Ellie hurried to regain control over the situation.

"Constance, I am afraid that I have not come to Egypt purely for social reasons," she announced. "Mr. Bates and I do hope to impose upon your hospitality for the evening, but we must arrange travel to my brother's excavation at Saqqara at the first opportunity. It is imperative that I speak to Neil as soon as possible."

Thanks to Adam's snoop through Professor Dawson's notebook, Ellie had deduced that he and Mr. Jacobs had an interest in her stepbrother's dig… and yet, it was not the thought of convincing her brother of the threat posed by those two villains that left her nerves feeling rattled. She was rather *more* intimidated by the prospect of informing Dr. Neil Fairfax that she had spent the last six weeks traveling across half the world in the sole company of his best friend—a man who had once convinced Neil to put a stuffed emu on top of the King's College Chapel.

For a good portion of the voyage to Egypt, Ellie had puzzled over how to explain her connection to Adam in a way that would not send her brother into hysterics. But how could she—when she wasn't at all certain of the nature of their relationship herself?

"We can take the morning train to Saqqara," Constance declared. "That will get us there before lunch."

Adam flashed a disappointed look back at the old man with the camels, one of which promptly spat onto the pavement.

"It will give us a little time to catch up," Constance finished—and shifted a pointed look to where Adam gazed longingly back at the dromedaries.

Ellie swallowed thickly and wondered just how much more complicated things were about to become.

"Shall we, then?" Constance prompted, flashing Ellie a smile as threatening as a knife blade.

TWO

$\mathcal{A}$S THEY RODE through the streets of Cairo, Adam Bates found himself squished onto the carriage bench next to Constance's extremely well-dressed bodyguard. Mr. Mahjoud managed to look both fussy and intimidating at the same time. The man was tall enough that Adam actually had to look up a bit to meet his eyes, which was pretty unusual for someone of his own not-insubstantial size. Couple that with Mr. Mahjoud's air of pained disapproval, and Adam felt like he was back at Cambridge telling his tutor that he had once again accidentally set his exams on fire.

On the other side of the carriage, Ellie sat with her face plastered to the open window. Her eyes were wide, drinking up every bit of the city that she could see through streets crowded with donkeys, horses, carts, and other conveyances. She was probably picking out the respective ages and architectural styles of every building they passed. Adam would likely hear all about it the next time they had a quiet minute together, unless they got… *distracted*.

Then other things would happen. Things Adam definitely wasn't supposed to be doing with the sister of his best friend.

That he hadn't done even *more* of those things was entirely due to the fact that he and Ellie had barely had a moment alone together since they left the Cayo District.

After collecting their bags from the hotel Adam called home, he'd hitched them a ride on a fishing boat from Belize Town to Jamaica, where they slept out on the open deck with the captain and his eleven-year-old nephew. It'd rained the whole time. Adam put that down to the fact that it had been his first time on a boat since Ellie had tossed his lucky rock into a waterfall.

He supposed he ought to be grateful the drizzle hadn't turned into a hurricane.

On the steamer from Kingston to Alexandria, they'd stayed in separate cabins. Adam had shared his with a pair of German engineers who spent the whole trip arguing about struts. Ellie had been paired up with an elderly widow who'd gone to the islands to alleviate her rheumatism.

Adam now knew more about steel alloys than he had ever wanted, but he counted himself lucky, missing rock notwithstanding… because the minute Adam *did* find himself alone with Ellie, pure and unadulterated lust took over his brain.

When he'd run into her in the empty hallway outside his room on the boat to Egypt, he'd just stopped to ask her if she wanted to try playing some deck skittles—and before he knew what was happening, he had her up against the wall with his hands on… well, things he definitely wasn't supposed to have his hands on. They'd only barely disentangled themselves before the Germans turned the corner, shouting at each other about wind shear.

Then there had been that little incident in Ellie's stateroom. Adam had poked his head in to let her know it was time for lunch, since she had a habit of forgetting about things like the fact that food was a requirement for survival once she started scribbling in her notebook. Only he had happened to notice that Ellie's elderly roommate was sound asleep on her bunk, snoring lightly and evenly.

Somehow, Adam found himself taking a step inside the room as the door fell quietly shut behind him. Ellie rose from her desk, eyeing him like a starving man might look at a hunk of steak… and then he was kissing her furiously and silently in the middle of the stateroom with an old lady dozing two steps away.

Ellie had her fingers in his hair, tugging and tangling there as she devoured his bottom lip. Adam's hands gripped her hips, kneading the firm, smooth flesh he could feel through the fabric of her skirt. He didn't even realize he was pushing her backwards until she bumped up against the desk.

The resulting friction sent a bolt of explosive, mind-numbing pleasure shooting up into Adam's brain—and also knocked over Ellie's ink bottle. It had thankfully been capped, but it still rolled off the desk and onto the floor.

The bottle landed with a sharp little bang. The old lady snorted, smacking her lips as she stirred. Adam froze… with his waist between Ellie's thighs, his tongue in her mouth, and his hands on her rear end.

Which was not a position one ought to stay frozen in.

He jumped back, putting a shred of respectable distance between them. The roommate rolled over, drawing in another snorting breath before she went quiet again… at which point, part of Adam's brain had evilly suggested that he should go right back to what he'd been doing.

He resisted it, dragging his eyes from Ellie's heaving, flushed neckline.

"Lunch," he whispered hoarsely and fled from the room.

Neil was going to kill him.

Adam hadn't seen Ellie's stepbrother in person since their time together at Cambridge—but Neil was still one of his closest friends. They'd been exchanging letters every two weeks for years now. Neil's were pages stuffed with details about his studies, pet theories, job prospects, what he had for breakfast…

Adam's were shorter. He wasn't much of a wordsmith, if the words weren't coming out of his mouth. Adam's letters usually read something along the lines of *weather's fine & tried some tapir jerky*, or *tripped on a mudslide but I found a lucky rock.*

Neil hadn't minded. Neil had never minded Adam being… well, Adam.

Neil was definitely going to mind Adam being Adam when it came to his baby stepsister. He was really going to get his socks in a twist over the fact that Ellie and Adam had spent a solid week alone together in the wilderness of British Honduras.

As for what they'd gotten up to in the hall, or on the desk, or in that cenote back in Tulan…

Adam felt awful about all of it. There was a right way of going about this sort of business—and it wasn't throwing Ellie up against a wall while he nibbled her earlobe every time they found themselves alone together.

He wasn't precisely sure what the *right* way would have looked like, given Ellie's opposition to the whole notion of marriage… but it definitely involved coming clean to her brother and refraining from taking further liberties with her person until they'd sorted everything out.

Which he'd so far utterly failed to do.

He could almost hear his father's voice in his head.

It's not just that you're lazy. It's that you don't think about the consequences.

The memory of those words—and of George Bates's tired, disdainful expression—cut at Adam like a knife.

You can't cruise through the world on a whim and call that being a man.

He'd spent the last decade telling himself that he wasn't the person his father had always accused him of being—*irresponsible, self-indulgent, undisciplined.* But everything he'd been doing with Ellie seemed to fall right into those categories, and it left him burning with shame.

He had to make it right. Since he couldn't do that by dragging her to the nearest altar, he was going to have to talk to her—like a reasonable, responsible adult—and let her know he was sorry and that it wouldn't happen again.

Adam would do just that as soon as he got a chance… which wasn't now, as he rode through Cairo in a stuffy carriage, sandwiched between the door and the exasperated dragoman.

Instead, Adam found his gaze drifting down to the place where Ellie's thigh pushed against the light fabric of her skirt as she sat across from him.

He could easily have picked up her ankle, set it on his lap, and pushed that practical green twill up to expose one of her nicely-shaped calves…

Adam stifled a groan, dropping his head back against the seat as he fought to push the notion of Ellie's calves out of his head… and realized that Ellie's friend was staring at him.

Constance Tyrrell reminded him of one of those small, well-bred dogs that were fully capable of hamstringing you if you crossed them. The look she gave Adam left him certain that the woman wouldn't rest until she had squeezed every last bit of dirt out of Ellie about their travels together over the last six weeks.

The prospect made Adam feel distinctly nervous.

The carriage rolled to a stop. Mr. Mahjoud held the door for the ladies, Adam following behind them.

They stood on a narrow street fronted by tall featureless houses. Any windows that Adam could see were relatively small and completely veiled by elaborately carved wooden screens, which allowed no view of the interior. It made the area's wealth seem fairly subtle until you noticed the polished brass lanterns and elegant stained glass accents by the doors.

Constance led them inside, and the impression of plainness vanished. Adam found himself in a luxurious entryway lined with beautifully carved panels and a richly tiled floor.

More importantly, he could smell something cooking. His stomach rumbled in appreciative anticipation.

"I will see about arranging rooms for the… unexpected addition to our party," Mr. Mahjoud declared with a pointed look at Adam and an air of long-suffering endurance. "You will find Lady Sabita in the courtyard."

"Thank you, Mr. Mahjoud." Constance tugged off her gloves and hat. She thrust both of them at the dragoman, who caught them with a grimace and immediately passed them to a small, stout Egyptian servant who waited beside him. Then she hooked a hand through Ellie's arm and hauled her forward, leaving Adam to follow.

Around a sharp turn and a short passage, Adam stepped into a courtyard that felt like an oasis hidden within the heart of the city. The space was roughly square, framed on all sides by the three high stories of the house, which were lined with balconies and more of those elegantly carved wooden screens. The building blocked out any noise that might have clattered in from the street. All Adam could hear was the tinkling of an elegant fountain and the quiet chittering of birds.

That, and the grating bray of an Englishman laughing.

"Oh drat," Constance muttered as she glared over at a wrought-iron table where three people reclined in obvious leisure.

The first was a woman who looked a little shy of fifty, her dark hair marked by an elegant streak of silver. The resemblance between her and the petite hellion beside Adam was obvious, marking her as Constance's mother. Beside her sat an older lady with similar features and a darker complexion. She was wrapped in a stunning rose-hued Tussar silk sari embroidered with tiny birds, her neck dripping with jewels.

The source of the donkey-like chortle was a pale-skinned guy about Adam's age with a blond mustache and an expensive summer suit. The Mustache rose as they entered, his gaze snapping immediately to Constance. It stuck there with a look of fawning appreciation as he sketched a courtly bow.

"Miss Tyrrell!" he exclaimed. "And here I was beginning to fear that I might miss you entirely!"

If the custom-tailored trousers hadn't already led Adam to peg the stranger as an aristocrat, the 'good show, old sport' accent would definitely have given him up.

Adam suppressed a sigh and hoped that fancy-trousers wasn't going to do something that would make him want to throw the guy into the fountain. It wasn't that he minded treating some entitled prat to a dunk—after all, he'd done it before—but indulging the habit in the home of a bunch of people he'd just met wasn't the most *responsible* choice.

Plus, it'd probably get him booted before he'd had a chance to eat dinner.

The aristocrat was a hair shorter than Adam. He had the slender physique of someone who spent his Saturdays fencing at the gym before popping off for a round of polo.

"Julian! What a lovely surprise," Constance returned with a distinct lack of enthusiasm.

If the welcome was something less than entirely genuine, The Mustache didn't seem to notice. He plucked up Constance's hand and brushed a pretentious kiss over the back of it.

Adam resisted the urge to roll his eyes.

"Constance!" the middle-aged woman said in lightly accented English as she rose from the table to join them. "Julian was hoping that he would find you at home—but of course, I am relieved to see that you collected Miss Mallory safely." She turned her gaze to Adam. "And perhaps you will introduce me to your... other friend?"

"Oh, this is Mr. Bates," Constance explained with forceful cheer. "Mr. Bates, meet my mother, Lady Sabita Tyrrell. And this is my Aai—Her Highness Maharajkumari Padma Devi of Nandapur."

"Royal princess," Ellie muttered at him. "Maybe a bow instead of a handshake."

"Yup," Adam agreed as the stunningly dressed older woman—*princess*, he mentally corrected himself—rose from her chair. He bent at the waist. "Your Highness."

"Yes, Jhia—but where did he come from?" Lady Sabita demanded, waving an impatient hand at Adam.

He wondered if the answer to that question would end up with *him* being the one dunked in the fountain.

"About that..." he started.

"Ellie ran into him on the train," Constance cut in. "Mr. Bates is a professional badminton player who has come here to Cairo for training. As he hadn't yet made any arrangements for his accommodations, I invited him to stay with us for a day or two until he gets settled."

Adam opened his mouth to respond to this patently ludicrous story—and then snapped it shut again. What was he going to do—tell everybody he was actually a colonial surveyor who'd spent the last several weeks gallivanting around the globe unchaperoned with their daughter's best friend?

Badminton it was.

"Oh!" Lady Sabita said with a blink of surprise. "But of course, you're very welcome."

"Professional badminton?" Kumari Padma echoed dryly.

Adam could feel Constance's urgent glare, though he refrained from actually looking at her as he answered.

"Nothing I love more than whacking a few birdies around." He worked to keep his expression serious. At least he'd remembered it was birdies and not balls.

"Bates, did you say?" The Mustache asked. "And you're obviously an American. You're not one of the San Francisco Bateses, are you?"

Adam's back teeth ground together. "Nope," he replied, turning a grimace into a thin smile.

At least that one wasn't an outright lie. He *wasn't* a member of the wealthy and powerful San Francisco Bateses—not since his father George Bates, the head of that expansive insurance empire, had formally disowned him.

If you don't start taking things seriously, you'll spend the rest of your life letting people down.

Thankfully, Lady Sabita saved Adam from the need for any further elaboration. "I must say—I am very cross with you, Eleanora!" she exclaimed. "Why would you choose to journey to Egypt all on your own when you might have come along with us only a little earlier?"

"I told you, Mum!" Constance shot Ellie a quelling look. "Ellie was tied up with work, and she was able to join a very nice family from Essex for the trip. The Nitherscott-Watbys."

At the sound of Ellie's ridiculous former alias, Adam choked. He managed to turn it into something approximating a cough.

"Sorry," he rasped when he realized everyone was staring at him. "Just, ah… ate a bug."

"That was certainly very kind of the Nitherscott-Watbys," Lady Sabita said, though her tone still indicated a careful disapproval. "You must provide me with their address so that I can thank them for seeing after your friend."

"I'm sure that's not necessary," Constance assured her. "And anyway, they've gone on to… er, India."

"Oh?" Constance's Indian princess grandmother smiled a little dangerously. "And where in India have they gone?"

"Kolkata?" Constance offered back hopefully.

"Well, we are all here now, at any rate," Lady Sabita concluded. "So we shall make a little party of it."

"Indeed," Kumari Padma agreed blandly. "Your mother has only just invited Mr. Forster-Mowbray to join us for dinner."

Forster-Mowbray. Of course The Mustache would have a double-barreled surname.

"I wouldn't want to impose." Mr. Forster-Mowbray flashed Constance an ingratiating smile.

"You wouldn't be imposing," Lady Sabita hurriedly assured him.

"But Mum," Constance said a little desperately. "Surely you can see that Ellie is exhausted. She's only just come from a very trying journey and clearly needs a quiet evening to recover."

"That's thoughtful of her," Adam murmured.

"No, it's not," Ellie hissed back under her breath. "She's just impatient to interrogate me."

Adam blanched at the notion of precisely what information Constance hoped to grill out of Ellie.

"Ellie is very welcome to a quiet evening," Lady Sabita returned shortly with a sharp look at her daughter. "She might even take advantage of the sauna—I know Sir Robert finds it most refreshing after a long journey."

Adam's ears perked up at the mention of a sauna. He loved saunas.

"But that would leave *you* at odds and ends for the evening, wouldn't it?" Lady Sabita continued with a dire look at her daughter. "If I had not invited some charming company to dinner."

Adam had been a San Francisco Bates long enough to know an upper class courtship ritual when he saw one—if only so he could avoid them like the plague. It was pretty clear that Lady Sabita hoped to turn Julian Double-Barrels into a suitor for Constance's hand.

Given her princess grandma, her dad's high-ranking position in the local government, and the seeming lack of any siblings, Adam guessed that Ellie's intimidating peanut of a friend was most likely a substantial heiress.

The Mustache was clearly interested enough to play along. Constance seemed less enthusiastic—but Lady Sabita was obviously determined to encourage the match regardless.

At least Lady Sabita's maneuvering meant that Constance's interrogation of Ellie would have to wait. Her dinner invitation had been less *request* and more *direct order*.

Constance clearly recognized the difference. "Of course, Mother," she agreed, flashing a thin, steely smile.

THREE

$\mathcal{I}$N THE END, none of them escaped dinner, which Lady Sabita insisted they would keep 'terribly informal.' That apparently meant sitting at an elegantly laid table in the open air of the courtyard, ringed by lanterns and candles.

At least nobody asked Adam to put on an evening jacket. He tried to remember the last time he had even worn an evening jacket… failed… and decided that was a good thing.

At least sitting next to Julian Forster-Mowbray helped keep Adam's mind off his other problems. He couldn't spend much time worrying about the talk he needed to have with Ellie, or what her brother was going to say about their relationship, when he was actively resisting the temptation to dump a bowl of yogurt over The Mustache's perfect hair.

As one of the household staff set a platter of tasty-looking pastries down on the table, Adam even started to relax—until his dining buddy turned to address him.

"I must say, I've been known to swing a racket on occasion," Julian chummily offered. "When did you acquire your taste for badminton?"

Adam had just popped a ball of fried cheese soaked in cardamom-scented syrup into his mouth. He nearly choked on it.

"Are you all right?" Lady Sabita asked with alarm.

"Fine," Adam wheezed after he managed to swallow. "Great cheese balls."

Constance glared at him from across the table, and Adam realized that everyone was still waiting for him to answer.

"Uh… just kind of fell into it, I suppose," he awkwardly lied.

"Right, right," Julian obliviously agreed. "I must say, swordplay found me in much the same way."

"Fond of a spot of fencing at the gymkhana, are we?" Adam offered, inwardly congratulating himself on his lucky guess.

Ellie shot him a warning look from Julian's other side.

"Something a bit more than that, actually," Julian replied with a little chuckle. "I compete with an épée, but I also practice with a rapier."

"A *rapier*?" Adam burst out. "Why?"

As opposed to a traditional fencing weapon like an épée, which was light, flexible, and never intended to hack anybody's limbs off, a rapier was—well, more or less a proper sword. It was far too heavy and dangerous for any sort of competition, but also pretty useless in any modern defensive context. High society didn't exactly countenance men like Julian Forster-Mowbray strutting around with swords hanging from their belts.

Which was yet another reason why Adam had little time for high society. He gave the hilt of his machete a comforting pat under the flap of his jacket.

"Let's just say… it relates to my historical interests." Julian flashed a secretive smile.

"Yes, of course!" Lady Sabita piped in forcefully. "I forgot to mention that our Mr. Forster-Mowbray is quite active in Cairo's Egyptological circles."

"I wouldn't say *active*," Julian charmingly corrected her as he leaned back in his chair. "I am hardly running about digging things up myself. My role is more… administrative."

"But really, administrative work would be much less likely to take one away for months at a time," Lady Sabita chirped enthusiastically. "Which I am sure your future wife will find most preferable. Don't you think, Jhia?" she added with a rapier-pointed look at her daughter.

Adam paused with his second cheese ball halfway to his mouth, glancing from the innocent-eyed Lady Sabita to the smug Julian Forster-Mowbray and a glaring Constance.

Lady Sabita seemed to realize she was laying it on pretty thick, because she shifted her attention over to Ellie. "You're fond of history as well—aren't you, Miss Mallory?"

Ellie's fork paused in midair as her eyes narrowed. "If by 'fond,' you mean that I possess a degree specializing in the subject from University College, London…"

Adam could hear the warning in her tone.

"Have *you* a degree, then?" Julian cut in. "Isn't that jolly?"

"Jolly?" Ellie echoed flatly.

Uh-oh, Adam thought, casting an alarmed look at Ellie's left hand, which had tightened on her butter knife.

How much would it hurt to get stabbed in the thigh with a butter knife?

Adam wondered if Mr. Forster-Mowbray was about to find out.

"Don't you mean 'very impressive?'" he blurted awkwardly. "I know *I'm* impressed. I couldn't even manage to finish college."

Constance's face blanched across from him.

"Were you there on a badminton scholarship?" her grandmother asked smoothly.

Padma sat to Constance's left in all her finery, a serene expression on her face.

"Huh?" Adam replied.

Something kicked his shin under the table. He would've thought Constance's legs were too short to reach that far.

"I mean—not really," Adam coughed out. "I was… I didn't have any scholarships."

"I see." Padma smiled a bit like the Cheshire cat and took an unhurried sip of her tea.

Adam felt a distinct sense of danger. Constance's grandma probably wasn't big enough to rise to his collarbone, but something about the woman was frankly terrifying. He'd spent enough time in the uncharted wilderness to know that it wasn't the largest threats that you needed to worry about. The small critters were the ones that could take you down with a bite and leave you writhing in a puddle of your own sweat on the ground until your heart stopped.

A clear voice echoed out through the evening air, drifting into the courtyard in rhythmic, practiced tones from a sky soft with the pale pinks and violet of sunset. Adam figured it must be a call to one of the daily Islamic prayers. It sounded nice.

"Goodness, is that muezzin at it again already?" Julian piped up. "I'm afraid that means I have to be getting on—I have an appointment this evening that I can't shake, as much as I would prefer to spend more time with you charming ladies."

"How unfortunate," Ellie returned flatly.

"Your Highness." Julian rose to bow to Kumari Padma. "And Lady Sabita—always a pleasure. Constance, darling—I'm afraid I have a bit of business outside town tomorrow, but perhaps I might call on you again on Saturday?"

"Constance would be very happy to receive you." Lady Sabita cast a warning look at her daughter. "Isn't that right, Jhia?"

"Of course." Constance's reply was perfectly courteous—but Adam still found himself checking her hands for potential weapons as she rose to extend one to Julian.

The Mustache planted a well-practiced kiss onto the back of it. "I'll look forward to it, then," he concluded.

To Adam's surprise, Julian turned to him next. "Mr. Bates, why don't you leave the ladies to their gossip and join me outside for a smoke before I go?" He tossed the women around the table a saccharine smile.

Adam saw Ellie's hand tighten around the butter knife again.

He didn't want to join Julian Forster-Mowbray for a smoke. In fact, there were few things he found less enticing—but one of them was seeing what kind of trouble they'd get into if Ellie gave into the temptation to stab the man.

"Sure. Great." He pushed back his chair. "Why don't we head right on out and do that?"

One of the house's cadre of servants opened the door to let Adam outside. The quiet street had grown darker since their arrival that afternoon. The shadows lengthened with the evening as lights flickered to life behind the finely carved window screens.

Another muezzin had taken up the call to prayer from a minaret to the east. The sound drifted softly down into the narrow space between the buildings.

Julian took a holder from his pocket and slipped a cigarette out of it, offering it to Adam. Adam took it without a whole lot of optimism. He'd been pretty spoiled as far as tobacco went, living on the coast of the Caribbean for the past seven years.

The Mustache passed him a lighter, and Adam took a draw. He suppressed a grimace and thought longingly of Padre Kuyoc's cigars.

"I couldn't help but notice that you carry a knife." Julian nodded to the sheath at Adam's belt.

"Uh… yeah," Adam confirmed awkwardly.

His machete had definitely been attracting more attention in Egypt than it ever had in British Honduras—where anybody who spent more than five minutes outside of town kept a blade on hand as a matter of course.

Not that a few odd looks would stop Adam from wearing it. Nobody was ever going to take his knife away from him again—not if they wanted to keep all five of their fingers.

"I appreciate the value of a good blade—not that I make a habit of carrying one about," Julian amended. "I'm afraid it wouldn't be entirely seemly in the circles I move in. I gather that your own background is perhaps a bit more… eccentric?"

Adam hadn't been outside of high society so long that he'd forgotten what a sideways insult sounded like—and since he wasn't in the house any longer, he didn't feel quite as obligated to keep playing nice.

"How'd you like to hear what I think of guys who concern themselves with my background?" he offered easily.

"Not that I'm passing any judgment, of course," Julian went on as though Adam hadn't spoken—probably because he hadn't bothered to listen. "To each his own, I say. I only ask because it occurs to me that you might value a little—friendly assistance, shall we say?—with how things stand in Sir Robert's household."

Adam considered telling the man exactly where he could stuff his friendly assistance, but he doubted The Mustache would bother listening to that, either. He was obviously a guy who exclusively appreciated the sound of his own voice.

Unfortunately, Adam had more than his fair share of experience with the type.

Julian didn't bother to wait for Adam to respond anyway. He was still talking—which more or less proved Adam's point.

"It is only that Miss Tyrrell and I are on the verge of reaching an understanding with each other." Julian watched the smoke curl up from his mediocre cigarette. "One that I feel quite confident in saying her family fully support and encourage. And I should hate to see any… *investment* on your part if that effort is destined to be wasted."

"Huh?" Adam blinked at him. "Hold on—you think I'm interested in *Constance?*"

"I should hardly presume," Julian smoothly replied with a wave of his cigarette. "You have only just arrived in Egypt, after all. I suppose I merely aim to do you the service of deterring any ambitions you might develop in her direction. She is quite the choice plum, after all," he added with a little chuckle.

Adam decided it was probably a good thing there weren't any fountains on Constance's street. He was increasingly tempted to give this self-important ass a dunk, and to hell with the consequences.

"Don't worry about it," he said instead. "I'm not interested in plums."

Julian's cigarette went still as the man raised a curious eyebrow. "Not interested in plums… at all?" he asked carefully, frowning with obvious surprise.

Adam suppressed a choice adjective. "I mean… you're fine. With your… whatever the hell you're doing."

The Mustache brightened, making a jab toward Adam with his cigarette. Adam was starting to wonder whether the guy actually smoked them or just used them as accessories to wave around. Not that he could blame him if that was the case. They were godawful smokes.

"Aha!" Julian exclaimed. "I think I see now. It's not Miss Tyrrell you've set your cap on, is it? It's that delectable little bluestocking. She must have caught your eye on the train."

"The… what?" Adam's mind blanked at the audacity of the man's description of Ellie.

"You'll have your hands full with that one," Julian cautioned chummily. "Of course, Connie's quite the spirited little thing herself. I know that would put some gentlemen off, but I've grown quite fond of her. And of course, it's an entirely sensible match, whatever others might have to say about her less than entirely English pedigree."

Adam's fingers clenched. "Oh?" he prompted dangerously.

The Mustache waved his cigarette dismissively again. "It's of no matter to me," he assured Adam. "As a younger son, there's not a great deal set aside for my portion. My father's Lord Aldbury, you see, but as one would expect, the greater part of his estate is entailed to my brother Heathcliffe. It'd be the army for me if I had any aptitude for military life, or seconding that—perish the thought—the church. Thankfully, Constance brings more than enough fortune to settle us comfortably. And my pedigree—Daddy's an earl, after all, and my grandfather on my mother's side was a duke—will nicely raise her children's station in life."

"Isn't her grandma a princess?" Adam pointed out.

"In English terms, I mean." Julian finally took a draw on his cigarette, blowing the smoke out in a pale gray stream. "I dare say I think the two of us are quite compatible, and her parents obviously approve, so it's just a matter of winning the girl over to the idea. I've no doubt I can manage that in another month or two."

Adam briefly considered whether he ought to simply punch the man, fountains and consequences be damned. But then he thought about what he'd seen so far of The Mustache's 'spirited little plum,' and decided he'd sit back and let Constance eviscerate him herself. He had no doubt she was fully capable of it.

Julian flicked his cigarette down to the paving stones. "Glad we could sort all that out." He ground the ember to dust under his gleaming Oxford shoe.

"Best of luck with your bluestocking," he added, punctuating it with a friendly pat on Adam's shoulder.

At the touch, Julian's eyes widened with surprise. He poked Adam's shoulder a little more firmly.

"Goodness," he noted. "I didn't realize badminton was quite so strenuous."

"You have no idea," Adam replied evenly, glaring at him.

"Ha ha!" The Mustache laughed awkwardly. "I see I have to watch out for you! Very well, then—I'm off. Cheerio, Bates."

Adam watched him go, fiercely resisting the urge to throw something at the back of his pomaded head.

Once he had turned the corner, Adam crushed out the burning end of his own lousy cigarette. He picked The Mustache's butt from the stones and carried both ends inside.

He was gonna trash them, and then find that sauna Lady Sabita had mentioned. Talking to Julian Forster-Mowbray left him feeling like he needed to wash something off.

FOUR

$\mathcal{E}$LLIE LEANED BACK in her chair as three ladies from Lady Sabita's household staff cleared the table and set out little dishes of sweetened fennel seeds. As the light overhead fell into dusk, the courtyard around her warmed with lamplight.

"Mr. Forster-Mowbray is such a nice young man," Sabita said with a significant look at her daughter.

Constance had just thrown a pinch of candied seeds into her mouth. She spoke through them in an aggrieved tone. *"Mother!"*

"No, Jhia—you mustn't dismiss this one out of hand like all the others, especially now that we are here in Egypt," Sabita retorted. "There are not so many eligible gentlemen here as there are in London, and I do not think that you have forgotten our little talk about the importance of putting some thought into *settling down*—now have you?"

Constance's mouth clamped shut at her mother's words. The lack of response was so uncharacteristic, it left Ellie arching her eyebrows with surprise.

Across the table, Kumari Padma's expression was serenely unreadable— but there was a keen, careful glint in her eyes as she watched her daughter and granddaughter.

"He has a very nice family," Sabita continued in a more reasonable tone. "Very respectable, and none of the ladies here speak of him spending too much on the horses or—" She cast an awkward look over at Ellie. "Frequenting less reputable establishments."

Ellie figured that 'less reputable establishments' was Lady Sabita's polite way of referencing Cairo's brothels. That Julian Forster-Mowbray didn't utilize them or engage in an inveterate degree of gambling seemed a low bar for considering him a prospective son-in-law.

A door closed firmly from the direction of the entry. Heavy footsteps thudded along the balcony that lined the nearest wing of the house. Ellie looked up to see Adam Bates stalking past the open spaces between the meshrabiyeh screens, a snippet of his muttered monologue catching her ear.

"…dunno how a guy's supposed to find a damned fountain when he needs one…" he grumbled before disappearing around the corner.

Another impatiently closing door punctuated his departure.

The three other women at the table stared up in the direction of Adam's irritable parade. Lady Sabita was the first to recover. "All that I am saying is that you should not dismiss Mr. Forster-Mowbray out of hand."

"Whatever would I do that for?" Constance's words seemed casual, but Ellie could hear a note of steel running through them.

"Why indeed?" Padma fixed a thoughtful, diamond-sharp look on her granddaughter.

Constance paled a little. Ellie couldn't entirely blame her for it. The silver-haired, jewel-draped princess at the table was not a force to be trifled with—and something in the kumari's tone had held a thrill of danger.

"Now why don't you show Ellie Jhia to her room?" Padma continued smoothly. "I am sure that she must be tired. She has had a *very* long journey to get to us."

Padma punctuated her suggestion by shifting that dangerously astute look to Ellie—leaving her with the uncomfortable notion that somehow Constance's grandmother knew exactly how long her journey had really been.

"Oh yes, Aai." Constance hurriedly rose from her seat and hooked her arm through Ellie's elbow, half-hauling her to her feet. "I'm sure she's absolutely bushed. We'll get you settled right in, won't we?" She steered Ellie forcefully toward the stairs to the balcony. "Goodnight, Mum! Shubha ratri, Aai!"

Constance more or less shoved Ellie into the stairwell to the upper floors.

"I really am rather tired," Ellie offered hopefully as Constance propelled her up the steps.

"Oh no, you don't," Constance retorted. "You're not going anywhere until I'm finished with you."

"I'm sure that I have no idea what you mean," Ellie protested a little desperately as Constance wheeled her past the opening to the floor with the guest rooms and compelled her upward.

"Yes, you bloody well do," Constance returned. "Ah! Here we are."

They popped through a doorway onto the flat rooftop of the house, which was furnished much like one of the sitting rooms below. Long benches thickly covered in colorful cushions lined a recess set into the floor. Intricately carved meshrabiyeh screens framed the space, topped by wooden awnings that granted it privacy from any peering eyes from the neighboring buildings. Potted palms, night-blooming jasmine, and even a lemon tree, all warmed by the glow of the scattered glass lanterns, gave the space a lush atmosphere.

Over it all hung the enormous, dusk-streaked sky. The sun had dipped below the horizon in the west, painting the cloudless expanse overhead in hues of rich purple and fuchsia.

From this high perch, Ellie could see the needles of the minarets and the great dome of a nearby mosque. Further on, glimpses of the dark ribbon of the Nile were just visible between the buildings. She took it all in as the warm night breeze danced over her skin, soft as a caress.

A speckled tortoiseshell tabby slept comfortably on the cushions. Constance tossed herself down beside it and reclined there like a tiny, dangerous goddess.

"Is that your cat?" Ellie asked, stalling for time.

"No." Constance gave the animal a cozy scratch. "This is Egypt. There are cats everywhere. And now you are going to tell me *exactly* what you have been up to."

"Well," Ellie said a little nervously, "since we last spoke, I have discovered the remnants of a mythical city, come up against the most dastardly cabal of villains—"

"Not that," Constance cut in. "I want to know about you and Mr. Bates."

Ellie bristled. "How is my connection to a man more important than the discovery of a secret civilization that completely upends our understanding of the Mesoamerican world?"

"You know full well why," Constance retorted. "Now spill."

The cat blinked at Ellie unsympathetically. She sensed the mouth of an inevitable trap closing over her.

"I haven't the foggiest idea where to begin," she protested weakly.

"Try the beginning, then," Constance replied impatiently.

"I met Mr. Bates in British Honduras, where after a few… less than fortuitous encounters, he was kind enough to agree to serve as my guide to the interior of the country. In that capacity, we engaged in a somewhat precipitous expedition to the Cayo District, which is the area of the colony least cataloged by modern survey—"

"Have you kissed him?" Constance demanded.

"What?" Ellie's cheeks flushed. "What would make you think… How is that the most important…"

"That's a yes, then," Constance declared with a wicked note of triumph. "Have you done anything *more* than kissing?"

"I haven't even admitted to kissing!"

"You didn't have to." Constance made an airy wave. "It was clearly implied. But has he actually made love to you yet?"

"Constance Tyrrell!" Ellie retorted in scandalized tones.

"Don't act like I'd judge you for it," Constance returned breezily. "I've been considering taking a lover myself."

"You—*what?"* Ellie burst out, forgetting her own embarrassment.

Constance flipped over onto her back, the tabby moving irritably and unhurriedly out of her way. Her hand flashed out, unerringly plucking a date from a platter that had been left out on the little table nearby. "It's hardly unreasonable. You see, Mum and Bapa have begun to insist that, as I am approaching the age of twenty-four, I must more seriously consider the matter of marriage. In fact, if I have not agreed to a choice of husband by my next birthday, they say there must be… *consequences."*

She contemplated the date in her hand as though the plump, sweet fruit were a jewel she was thinking of purchasing.

"Consequences?" Ellie echoed. "What does that mean, exactly?"

"Well, of course they can't technically marry me off against my will," Constance replied. "But if they were to lock me up inside until I relented, I am sure I'd go mad and take the next man who came knocking simply to escape, even if he was some dried up old buzzard." Constance paused, considering. "Perhaps I *should* pick a dried up old buzzard. Then I might outlive him and enjoy myself in the full bloom of young widowhood. I have always thought I would be best suited to a life of independent adventure. It is not as though I haven't the money for it, and I feel certain that traveling the globe while engaging in a series of wild and temporary affaires du coeur would keep me quite content with my lot." She frowned. "Though that plan would be ruined if my elderly husband turned out to have unusually robust health and live to a hundred."

"I suspect an old buzzard might prove more trouble than he was worth, even if he did turn out to be fortuitously short-lived," Ellie offered. "But what does your Aai have to say about all this?"

Sir Robert and Lady Sabita were both generally kind-hearted people whom Ellie knew lacked any real gift for torment, however much they might be driven to extreme measures out of concern for their daughter's well-being. Constance's grandmother, on the other hand, was a five-foot force to be reckoned with. When Maharajkumari Padma Devi chose a battle, she won it—without exception.

"So far, she has supported my determination not to settle for a man I do not think fully suits me," Constance replied. "Aai has always professed the belief that a lady ought to know herself first before she chooses a partner… but lately she has dropped a hint or two that perhaps I am taking longer about the matter than I ought to be."

Constance's breezy expression dropped, replaced by a flash of fear.

"If Aai decides that I have delayed for too long, there will be no getting around it," Constance admitted. "She is fully capable of devising the most dire consequences for me… and that is without even considering those thirty-nine favors I owe her."

Ellie was familiar with Padma's policy of counting the incidents in which she intervened to save Constance from trouble or help her get away with something she should not have been doing as 'favors.' Constance had been accumulating them for years now, with Padma calling in only a handful over that time.

But when the favors *were* called in, there could be no refusing them—not least because Padma now had a veritable pile of dirt on Constance's past adventures… and Ellie had no doubt that Constance's grandmother knew *exactly* how to use it.

"Thirty-nine!" Ellie repeated, aghast. The number sounded like a curse.

"Indeed," Constance confirmed direly. "And so, if she comes to agree that I have taken too long to choose, I am frankly terrified to think of what it will mean for me. Ugh!" She threw her hands out, sprawling across the cushions. "Not one of them is capable of conceiving that I might live a perfectly full and happy life without the burden of a husband!"

"I should like to see how long they continued to hold that opinion when faced with the countless women subjected to confinement, neglect, or outright abuse on the part of their spouses, without any viable legal recourse to escape it!" Ellie shot back. "Never mind the others who are forced to submit themselves to a man they hardly know because the sole alternatives available to them—"

"—are impoverishment or prostitution," Constance recited automatically with a wave of her hand. "Yes, yes. Do give me some credit, Ellie. I am hardly going to ally myself with a fellow who'd try to lock me in a cellar. And besides, even if he did, I'd just pick the lock. I have been continuing to refine my skills in that department." She popped a date into her mouth, chewing it enthusiastically. "It's not as though I'm opposed to the very notion of marriage—though of course I have nothing but respect for your own principled objections to it as an institution. I would be glad enough to marry if I could find someone who didn't bore me to tears. It's only that so many of these gentlemen are completely lacking in imagination! They might shower me with flattery and admiration for a little while, but then they will wander off to their clubs without sparing a thought as to how I am supposed to retain my sanity when I have only a bit of shopping and charity work to keep me entertained."

Constance plucked out her hairpins and sat up forcefully, her black curls tumbling around her shoulders. "I want a man with a healthy spark of adventure… but who also isn't an obvious cad. You wouldn't think that is such a hard thing to find—but trust me, I have looked."

"Don't tell me that Sir Robert and Lady Sabita are considering Mr. Forster-Mowbray as a potential match for you." Ellie grimaced with distaste.

"Oh, Julian is not so bad as some of them," Constance replied tiredly. "I might even be tempted to accept him if my circumstances were slightly more desperate."

"You can't possibly mean that!" Ellie protested as she recalled their obliviously self-important dinner companion.

"At least his presence here in Egypt shows that he's amenable to travel," Constance countered. "But you needn't worry. I won't marry Julian, or anyone else for that matter—not until I have first seized a little romantic experience for myself."

"Tell me we aren't back to that notion of taking a lover again," Ellie burst out with a thrill of alarm.

"We never left it!" Constance exclaimed. "That was the point! My parents insist that I must marry—but *I* insist that I will not have my amorous horizons so precipitously constrained. Men are outright encouraged to do as much, after all. Who hasn't heard young gentlemen being exhorted to sow their wild oats before settling down? If they are not held to the same standard, why should we women be?"

"Men are not at risk of becoming ruined and socially outcast if they take lovers," Ellie pointed out. "And what about pregnancy?"

"There are ways to avoid that," Constance asserted with a dismissive wave of her hand.

Ellie paused. "And… what might those be?" she asked with careful nonchalance.

"I am still gathering information about the best options." Constance picked up another date. "But I do know that there are a number of physical activities one might engage in that do not entail the risk of conception. Bapa has a *very* interesting book on the topic hidden in the bottom of his wardrobe that he does not think I know about. It is in Urdu, of course, but the illustrations are most… illustrative." She popped the date into her mouth. "I should be happy to lend it to you if you like."

With effort, Ellie worked to keep her expression bland.

"I might possibly be interested in examining it," she replied carefully, "for historical and cultural reasons."

Constance fixed Ellie with a dangerously astute look. "You are now going to tell me *exactly* what you have been getting up to with Mr. Bates."

"I don't think you want to know *all* that we've been getting up to," Ellie blurted out in wild protest.

"Yes," Constance countered flatly. "I most certainly do."

Ellie's cheeks burned. "Well, I am not going to tell you all of it. Suffice to say that Mr. Bates and I… That we have… What I mean to say is…" She raised a hand to her temple, where she felt the start of a headache coming on. "It's *complicated.*"

"Has he asked you to marry him?" Constance pressed curiously.

"Of course, he *asked*," Ellie admitted, and then quickly caught herself. "But only because he was trying to do the honorable thing."

Constance's eyes widened.

"After he learned that I was not in fact a widow!" Ellie continued hurriedly. "Because we had been traveling in the wilderness together."

"And how firmly is he insisting on it now that you've…" Constance let her voice trail off expectantly.

Ellie pointedly refused to take up her bait. "The matter has not come up in recent weeks," she primly returned.

"Might he have dropped the subject after you lectured him about how marriage is built on the exploitation of women and enforced by their complete exclusion from any other legitimate means of self-support?" Constance offered dryly.

Ellie drew in a breath, striving to keep her response reasonable. "I may have elaborated somewhat on the injustice of matrimony as a legal and social institution. But why should we be talking of marriage at all? We have only known each other for a matter of weeks! To throw ourselves into a permanent legal arrangement after such a short acquaintance would be an act of sheer madness!"

Constance shrugged. "People do it."

"That is hardly an endorsement."

Constance fixed Ellie with a canny stare. "Just out of curiosity, what exactly are you planning to do with yourself after you leave Egypt?"

"Leave Egypt?" Ellie echoed helplessly.

"You have lost your job. Your family think you are on a very extended holiday in Bournemouth—but I should imagine after two months they might be starting to worry that you've run off to join a carnival," Constance noted wryly. "So what is your plan, exactly? Unless you intend to stay here in Cairo with me indefinitely."

Ellie stiffened. "I am not interested in living on anyone's charity."

"It's not charity if it's among friends, Eleanora," Constance reminded her tiredly.

Ellie lifted her chin. "When I have finished what I need to do here, I will return to England and seek other employment."

"What sort of employment?" Constance lounged back against the colorful pillows.

Ellie's shoulders fell. "The only employment available to a university-educated woman without a reference is most likely to be… *teaching*."

She ground out the word like a curse.

Constance studied her fingernails. "Probably at some backwater school for girls. And you abhor children."

"I don't *abhor* them," Ellie returned defensively. "I just find them exceptionally tedious and believe they serve as tiny anchors binding a woman further into the virtual slavery that is the reality behind modern marriage—"

"Yes, yes. Tiny anchors," Constance interrupted quickly. "But tell me, now… where exactly is Mr. Bates in this scenario?"

Ellie opened her mouth to respond… and realized she hadn't the foggiest idea what to say.

Fear swept over her, numbing her skin despite the soft warmth of the Egyptian evening. Her hands clenched, gripping the sturdy folds of her twill skirt.

"Mr. Bates has taken a leave of absence from his position in British Honduras," she elaborated carefully. "He can extend it for perhaps another month, but after that he must either return or give up his position. Of course, as he is a man, he has far more options for employment at his disposal," she grumbled.

"But would he go back to England with you?" Constance pressed, her expression serious.

Ellie closed her eyes as the weight of Constance's gentle question swept through her.

Would Adam go back to England with her?

She thought of the rich, powerful current of affection she could see in his eyes when he looked at her. The warmth in his voice when he spoke her name.

He hadn't hesitated for a breath before agreeing to accompany her to Egypt—but that was Egypt, as part of a desperate quest to thwart a pack of villainous thieves. Would he feel the same way about following her to some backwater English village?

Ellie tried to imagine Adam in a place like Netherwallop or Upton Snodsbury—and failed. He was too big and wild to fit into some remote little hamlet. Asking him to confine himself to a place like that felt like an enormous sacrifice.

Constance spoke carefully into the silence where Ellie's answer should have been. "You know, you wouldn't necessarily have to teach—or work at all—if the two of you stayed together."

Ellie latched on to the far more comfortable feeling of indignation that Constance's suggestion aroused. "I am not interested in making myself a dependent, even upon a man whom I trust entirely not to take undue advantage of the situation! And anyway, such an arrangement would only really make sense within the confines of a marriage."

"You are forgetting the most obvious alternative," Constance pressed.

"And what is that?" Ellie returned skeptically.

"Just take him as your lover!"

"*What?*" Ellie squeaked. "I couldn't possibly!"

"Why not?"

"For all of the reasons we talked about before! Never mind that the gentleman involved would need to agree to it."

"That is not usually a major obstacle, as I understand it," Constance declared authoritatively.

"You don't know Adam," Ellie pushed back. "I'm afraid that despite all appearances, he is desperately honorable. He was already insisting on telling Neil about our travels together, and that was before we'd even—"

Ellie caught herself and bit off the rest.

Constance's eyes glittered with avid interest as she plucked another date from the dish. "Before you'd even…" she prompted.

"It isn't important," Ellie dismissed.

Constance tossed the date at her.

"What was that for!" Ellie exclaimed.

"You know perfectly well," Constance returned easily, then frowned. "It must be nearly a decade since I've seen your brother, but I can't imagine Stuffy has changed *that* much. Finding out you've been running about with his best friend will go over about as well as that time we tied all his socks into a rope for our makeshift hot air balloon."

"Neil was rather upset about that one," Ellie recalled—and then straightened. "But it's no matter, because I have been giving the situation a great deal of thought, and there *is* a perfectly logical solution to the problem of my connection to Mr. Bates—one that even Neil could not possibly object to. And that is for us to be…"

"Yes?" Constance prompted, leaning closer.

"Colleagues," Ellie finished.

"*Colleagues?*" Constance echoed in tones of disbelief. "You mean like a pair of solicitors skipping out for the occasional luncheon?"

"I mean devoted companions in scholarship and intellectual inquiry!" Ellie countered. "Really, when I gave it a bit more thought, it seems the perfect term to describe my relationship with Mr. Bates. The Latin word 'collega' suggests being deputized together in the service of a greater cause. It could be almost like a marriage, only without all of that… erm…"

"Physical intercourse?" Constance offered mercilessly.

Ellie's cheeks flushed. "Connie!" She drew in a breath, recovering herself. "I know that such an arrangement between a gentleman and a lady is not strictly the 'done' thing, but if it was clear to all the gossips that our connection was purely one of mutual respect and admiration…"

Constance frowned. "Are you saying you're not interested in physical intercourse with Mr. Bates?"

Ellie's cheeks heated even further. "That would not be… strictly accurate to say," she replied carefully. "But I am quite capable of controlling myself! It is hardly the most important aspect of a relationship, even a very close one! It is the meeting of minds that matters—the intellectual sympathy and shared curiosity of two scholars out to discover the true inner workings of the world and its history!"

"Right," Constance agreed skeptically. "And how would Mr. Bates feel about following you to England to be part of this meeting of intellectual minds?"

Ellie deflated. "I… am not entirely sure."

"Well, perhaps you ought to ask him about it." Constance dropped back onto the cushions and reached for another date.

Constance's entirely reasonable suggestion sparked a roiling, uncomfortable feeling in Ellie's chest.

"At any rate, it sounds as though you might have more immediate concerns," Constance continued. "What is this terribly urgent business at your brother's excavation in Saqqara? And are you certain it can't wait for another day or two? I should love to show you more of Cairo. We might even make an excursion to the bazaar! There is a wonderful lane completely lined with booksellers that I am certain you would happily get lost in."

Ellie gratefully accepted the change in the subject. She thought longingly of how very much she would enjoy browsing through countless stalls of jumbled books in the shadow of an ancient mosque.

"I am afraid the bazaar will have to wait," she asserted with a note of regret. "Do you recall our mutual acquaintance, Mr. Jacobs?"

"How could I forget?" Constance returned. "You led him on quite the merry chase back in London. Don't tell me that he's turned back up?"

"In fact, he followed me to British Honduras, and Mr. Bates and I had quite a bit of trouble with him while we were there. I have reason to believe that he is now on his way to Egypt—if he isn't here already—and that he has an interest in Neil's excavation."

"That *is* serious," Constance agreed. "But what could Mr. Jacobs possibly want with your brother's dig?"

"I suspect Jacobs, or whomever it is that he works for, is using the dig at Saqqara as a means of pursuing a very important and dangerous artifact."

Constance frowned. "How can an artifact be dangerous?"

Ellie reached into the pocket of her skirt and removed a battered tin cigar tube. The paper label, which read *The Belize Tobacco Company*, was faded with age.

"Have you taken up smoking, Ellie?" Constance eyed the tube skeptically.

Ellie didn't reply. Instead, she opened the lid and slid the contents of the tube into her palm.

"Is that a finger bone?" Constance asked with gruesome delight, scooting closer.

"It's from a wing, actually," Ellie corrected her. "It is inscribed with Glagolitic characters—an early Slavic script. I am afraid I haven't yet been able to translate it. There is some resemblance to modern Cyrillic but..."

"Why are you showing me the bird bone, Eleanora?" Constance cut in.

Ellie gave up her scholarly explanation with a sigh. "Because it does this."

She made a neat snap of her wrist—a maneuver she had discovered after days of frustrated experimentation inside her cabin on the boat from the Caribbean. The movement was quicker and certainly more elegant than the vigorous shaking that the previous owner of the bone had subjected it to.

The bone—the *firebird arcanum*—flared to life, spilling a fierce, moonlike illumination out across the rooftop. Rays of it pierced through the delicate filigree of the meshrabiyeh screens.

"Oh, but this is *marvelous!*" Constance said wonderingly.

"The object—the *arcanum*—that Mr. Jacobs' masters are seeking here in Egypt is *far* more powerful," Ellie pressed. "Should it fall into their hands, the consequences for the world could be devastating. I cannot allow that to happen!"

Constance met Ellie's gaze across the ferocious glare of the bone, her eyes bright with determination. "Then we shall simply have to stop them."

The words filled Ellie with a surprising sense of relief. She knew that she shouldn't feel that way about the notion of her friend being exposed to the threat of Mr. Jacobs—but the truth was, the prospect of facing him alone, or even with only Adam at her side, had filled Ellie with dread.

She would *need* help if she was to succeed at this—and Constance was a formidable ally.

But even as she soaked up that mix of both relief and worry, Ellie's thoughts pulled back to the tangled puzzle of her relationship with Adam Bates. She didn't realize that she had gone quiet until Constance slipped an arm around her shoulder, giving her a squeeze.

"It will all work out, you know," she said confidently.

"How?" Ellie demanded as the firebird bone continued to blaze, bright and silent, in her hand.

"I haven't the foggiest idea," Constance replied easily. "But it will. You'll see."

Ellie tried to let herself be reassured—but still felt as though the future loomed with peril like the rising cloud of a storm.

FIVE

$\mathscr{S}$OME FOOLS MAINTAINED that a sauna couldn't possibly be refreshing in a hot climate. They'd obviously never felt the pleasure of sweating out the grit of travel and then dumping a cold bucket of water over their heads.

Adam strode from the washroom feeling like a million bucks.

The warm night air kissed his skin as he emerged. It would've felt even better if he'd kept his shirt off—but somehow he doubted that Lady Sabita and Kumari Padma shared his somewhat lackadaisical policies when it came to proper dress.

He'd restored the shirt along with his trousers, though both clung to his still-damp skin. His feet remained bare as he stepped out into the soft light of the courtyard.

The fountain splashed gently to his right, the sound mingling with the quiet rustle of breeze-tossed palms and ferns. A few scattered oil lamps had been left out to illuminate the pathways.

Adam's attention was snagged by the sound of voices from above him.

"Don't stay up too late," Constance warned.

His gaze rose to one of the balconies that framed the courtyard, where he saw Constance give Ellie a hug.

"I won't," Ellie promised her.

Constance moved away, and Ellie remained behind. She gazed out over the fountain and the palms as though not really seeing any of it. The space between her eyebrows was creased with little furrowed lines—the *I'm thinking too much* look that Adam was coming to recognize.

Without quite realizing he was doing it, he moved toward her, stepping into the lamplight on the path that ran beneath her perch.

He wanted to nudge those worry lines out of her forehead. The scene suggested a perfect way for him to do it.

"'But soft! What light through yonder window breaks?'" he called up.

Ellie's eyes dropped to where he stood and widened with warm recognition, even as her mouth twisted skeptically. "Shakespeare? Really?"

Adam flashed her a grin. The next lines were ready on his lips—and he knew exactly how they would be received. "'Wert thou as far as that vast shore washed with the farthest sea, I would adventure for such merchandise.'"

"*Merchandise?*" Ellie echoed indignantly.

He pressed a hand to his chest. "'O speak again, bright angel.'"

"Perhaps I shall speak on the insidious impact of referring to women poetically as pieces of physical property," Ellie offered. "How have you the entire balcony scene from Romeo and Juliet memorized? I didn't take you for a thespian."

Adam shrugged. "It's the iambic. Sticks in your brain."

A taut silence fell, accented by the soft rush of the fountain and the distant sound of someone laughing.

Ellie's gaze dropped, tracing the line of water he could feel trickling from his hair down his neck. It slipped to the open buttons at the top of his shirt, where his skin was still damp from the sauna.

Her gaze locked there with a look that set Adam's nerves tingling.

She swallowed tightly. "Why are you wet?"

Adam's own attention was a little less focused than it ought to be. He kept studying the tendrils of hair that had come loose from her practical bun, thinking how much nicer they'd look if he just pulled all those pins out and then ran his hands through the thick chestnut waves of it.

"Sauna," Adam replied a little densely.

Ellie was still staring at him like he was a tall glass of lemonade on a hot day. "There's a sauna?" she pressed a little numbly.

"Had to try it after dealing with The Mustache," Adam replied with somewhat less than his own usual eloquence. He was thinking of how after he'd taken her hair down, it'd be awful nice to give it a gentle pull to guide her head back and then kiss his way down her throat to her—

"The Mustache?" Ellie echoed with a confused frown.

"Frosty-Mothballs," Adam rambled back, trying to push the image of tugging aside the open collar of her blouse from his brain. "Fusty-Mouseberry. Whatever the hell his name was. He thought I had designs on your friend. Wanted me to know his grandad's a duke."

Ellie stiffened with indignation. "As though that gives him the right to lay claim to a woman like a horse at an auctioneer?"

The sight of her righteous anger made Adam feel pleasantly warm. He liked it when Ellie got righteously angry. "I was close to tossing him into a fountain over it, only I didn't want to get us kicked out of the house."

Ellie's look heated with quiet approval. "Pity," she noted as she gazed down at him through the soft gold of the lamplight.

The silence returned, and their eyes locked. The night air gained a subtle electricity that danced across Adam's skin as he looked up at her, his mind racing with everything they might get up to in the twilight intimacy of the silent courtyard.

No, he told himself firmly as he fought for control. He couldn't kiss Ellie senseless on Constance's family's balcony. He needed to stop acting like an impulsive idiot and take control.

"Could I come up there for a second? Just to talk," he added quickly.

Ellie's eyes flashed with surprise and confusion, but she nodded.

Adam crossed over to the entryway beneath her perch and mounted the cool, dark stairs. He stepped out onto the balcony—and there she was, waiting for him. Still looking a little travel-rumpled with those tendrils of hair curling over her shoulders, lips practically begging for just the right kind of bite.

Talk, he told his brain firmly.

"I owe you an apology," he said.

Ellie frowned, clearly taken off guard. "For what?"

"For the… *liberties* I've taken with your…" Adam waved an awkward hand over Ellie's softly curved form. "…Person. Since we started traveling together."

"Liberties?" Ellie stared at him as though struggling to keep up with the turn in the conversation.

"You know," Adam elaborated. "In the cenote. And the hall on the boat. And that bit in your stateroom with the table and…"

"Oh!" Ellie exclaimed, finally catching on. Her cheeks flushed—which did not help Adam's concentration. "But why are you apologizing for that? I was hardly an unwilling participant."

"Maybe that's true," Adam returned stubbornly. "But it's still not right. I was being… *irresponsible.* And selfish. I've just been blundering along without thinking of the consequences."

Ellie seemed surprised by the sharp change in his tone. "I see," she said carefully.

"I wanted to let you know that it's not going to happen again," Adam declared firmly. "I'm going to stop acting like a cad and give you whatever time you need to figure things out."

Ellie went still. "Figure things out?" she echoed quietly. "What does that mean, exactly?"

Adam shifted uncomfortably where he stood on the paving stones. Something about her tone didn't sound right, but not in a way he could pin down.

This was the responsible thing to do, he reminded himself firmly. He owed it to her.

"You know," he explained awkwardly. "Just… where you want all this to go."

Ellie hugged her arms over her chest. "Where I want this to go?" she repeated tightly. "Is that… what this is about? Have you just been waiting for me to come to my senses and be reasonable about things?"

"Huh?" Adam replied, thrown.

Ellie's tone sharpened, hurt flashing behind her hazel eyes. "Because it's reasonable, of course, to just smile and go along with an institution that oppresses an entire gender—that has caused untold harm to countless women for *centuries*…"

Her tone sparked a quick flare of panic. This wasn't how Adam had expected the conversation to go. He was trying to do the right thing. Why was she getting mad at him for it?

And then his brain caught up with his gut as certain words from her tirade cut through the fog of his fear.

Institution. Harm. Centuries.

"Wait a minute," Adam cut in quickly. "Are you talking about marriage?"

Ellie frowned at him. "Yes. Aren't you? Isn't that what you were asking? When I was going to change my mind?"

"No!" Adam burst out in return. "I don't want you to change your mind about marriage!"

"You don't?" Ellie echoed, clearly confused.

"I *like* your mind!" Adam pushed back forcefully. "I like that you don't just pretend everything's okay when it's not! That takes a hell of a lot of courage and integrity. Why would I want to *change* that about you?"

"But if that doesn't change, we're never going to get married!" Ellie threw up her hands.

"So?" Adam retorted.

She stilled again, her eyes going wide and vulnerable. "Is that not…? I mean, I suppose I had just assumed that you…"

Her voice trailed off, and Adam could hear the hurt in it. It cut at him like a knife.

He was screwing this up again—fumbling into a disaster like someone who couldn't get out of his own goddamned way. He moved closer to her on instinct as though physical proximity could make up for the fact that he couldn't seem to get his foot out of his mouth.

"No!" he insisted, and then flinched. "I mean—yes! But..."

"Because you mentioned something about seeing it as a necessity back in British Honduras," Ellie hurried on tightly. "And that was before we had engaged in certain..."

"I did!" Adam confirmed quickly. "And I would still—absolutely!—if that was what you—"

Ellie stiffened. "I told you before, I have no interest in being someone's obligation."

"You're not my obligation!" Adam burst out.

"Then what am I, exactly?" Ellie pressed, her voice uneven.

This was all going wrong. The words weren't doing what Adam needed them to do. They twisted back on him like snakes, striking where he meant them to help.

He was screwing it up—again. Just like he'd done so many times before.

"You're..." he started, his voice strangled as he fought for a way to salvage this—to make her understand. "I..."

Her shoulders drew in on themselves as her eyes swam with hurt. "I see," she said softly.

Adam felt a crack as though a piece of something vital inside of him threatened to break loose and fall away. Fear roared up in response, along with a sudden rush of determination.

"No, you don't, dammit," he shot back—and grabbed her.

He tugged her to his body until he could feel every firm, shapely line of her pressed against his skin. Then he kissed her.

The embrace was fierce—claiming, devouring. She stilled for only a heartbeat with surprise before her hands rose to his hair, tangling in the wet locks of it as she pushed up on her toes to meet him.

She tasted like black tea and honey. Smelled of rustling old paper in the silence of a library, woven through with something wilder—ancient forests and the promise of lightening before a storm.

Adam dropped his hands to her thighs, gripping them through the layers of practical twill. He lifted, then pivoted to press her up against the wall.

Ellie let out a gasp at the impact, her head tilting back. He took it as an invitation to set his mouth to her throat, gliding up to catch her sensitive earlobe between his teeth.

She groaned, clutching him more tightly between her thighs. Somehow his shirt had come loose from his belt, and Ellie's hands were inside of it, gliding up the muscular ridges of his flanks.

Adam cursed into her mouth as his desire rose, sweeping in like a tide—fierce, implacable, insatiable. He wanted her closer. He wanted her bare. His hands slid beneath the fabric of her skirt, and the notions of what he was going to do with her burst through his mind like a fireworks display on the Fourth of July.

"You'll make it up to me, will you?" Lady Sabita chirped brightly from below.

Adam froze. He lifted his head from the opened front of Ellie's blouse to see Constance's mother dart playfully out of one of the doorways to the courtyard, turning back to smile at her husband.

Reality crashed in like a falling boulder. Ellie's hair was undone, pins scattered on the paving stones. Her shirt was open to expose the pale curves at the top of her practical corset. Adam's hands gripped the round curve of her rear beneath her skirt, holding her flush to the unmistakable evidence of his arousal.

Lady Sabita's giggle drifted up to their shadowy perch.

"Maybe I should be late more often," Sir Robert quipped playfully, giving a darting chase to his wife around the fountain.

Adam looked down into Ellie's eyes. Her pupils were dilated to black, her cheeks flushed. Lips red and bitten.

"I'm sorry," he breathed out desperately.

She blinked back at him, bewildered and pleasure-fogged. "You're sorry?"

He drew his hands away, letting her legs slip back down to the ground—where they belonged, he reminded himself furiously. He stepped back—one idiot stumble, just far enough to put a breath of space between them.

The distance only let him see that much more clearly how her chest heaved with her wild breath, her clothes in obvious disarray as her hair tumbled down over her shoulders.

He could knot his fingers in it, tug it back as she gasped…

"I have to go," he blurted out in a harsh whisper.

As Ellie gaped at him, he whirled on his heel and ran away.

SIX

*E*LLIE WATCHED THE outskirts of Cairo blur past the windows of the train as she perched on the comfortable bench of the first-class compartment Constance had booked for their journey.

She had woken awkwardly that morning to Constance pounding at her bedroom door, exhorting her to hurry. The high angle of the sunlight streaming through the slender openings in the meshrabiyeh screen over her window had indicated how late she had slept—probably because she had not slept particularly well at all, her mind still racing over the bewildering conversation she'd had with Adam the night before.

I don't want you to change your mind about marriage.

You're not my obligation!

She still hadn't the foggiest idea what he'd meant by it all—or by his fervent and obviously deeply felt apology after he had kissed her utterly senseless against the wall of the alcove.

They clearly needed to talk—again—but she was hardly going to manage that while sharing a train compartment with both Constance and Mr. Mahjoud, who had been given the duty of accompanying them to Neil's dig site.

Adam sat across from her, his tan worsted trousers tucked into his work boots. He'd deigned to put on a jacket again but had skipped donning a waistcoat. His battered fedora rested on the seat beside him.

He was unusually quiet, his brow furrowed and stormy as he frowned down at the notebook he held in his big capable hands.

Hands that had slid up the fabric of her drawers last night as he had pressed her against the wall.

Ellie awkwardly smoothed folds of her gray poplin skirt over her knees as the carriage seemed to grow a little hotter. "Have we any lemonade, by any chance?" she asked a little desperately.

Mr. Mahjoud—dressed in a perfectly tailored suit with a natty red waistcoat and bow tie—plucked a flask from the hamper at his feet and poured some into a tin cup.

Ellie took a grateful gulp—and then nearly dropped the cup as the houses outside the window gave way to an open stretch of desert punctuated by a trio of enormous sun-gilded peaks.

"Pyramids!" she squeaked.

Constance glanced up from her magazine. "Oh! There they are," she noted mildly before going back to reading.

With a sigh, Mr. Mahjoud reached out and plucked the cup from Ellie's nerveless fingers. She hardly noticed. Instead, she pressed herself to the frame of the open window as though it could bring her closer to those noble four-thousand-year-old monuments to power and kingly divinity.

"Khufu," she recited. Her gaze locked on the largest and nearest of the gilded peaks before sliding to the others. "Khafre. Menkaure."

She looked back to her traveling companions, burning with the need to share her wonder and excitement at actually *seeing* the immortal Pyramids of Giza in the flesh.

Constance was lifting the lid of the hamper for a peek. Mr. Mahjoud cleared his throat, flashing her a quelling look, and she sat back with a dissatisfied huff.

Adam's eyes were on Ellie.

His look flared with emotion—admiration, frustration, and a thundering heat that set Ellie's pulse racing before he quickly glanced away again.

"Couldn't I just—" Constance reached for the hamper again.

"Not until lunch," Mr. Mahjoud cut in, turning the page of his newspaper.

Shortly afterward, as the last clustered outbuildings of Cairo's sprawl fully gave way to farmland and desert, the train came to a sudden and unexpected halt. Ellie heard the screech of brakes and jolted against her seat.

"Wonderful," Mr. Mahjoud commented dourly.

"I'm guessing this isn't a regular stop," Adam commented.

"It isn't," Constance confirmed. "There's nothing here."

Ellie pressed herself back as Constance lurched into her lap to stick her neatly coiffed head through the window. Her derriere shifted as she craned her neck for a better angle.

"It looks like the engineers are out, but I can't see what they're looking at," she announced.

"Would you please refrain from throwing yourself out the window?" Mr. Mahjoud requested tiredly.

Ellie grasped Constance's skirts and tugged her back into the carriage.

"At any rate, *something* has clearly disrupted the tracks." Constance's eyes glittered with excitement. "My money is on sabotage!"

"It's sand," Mr. Mahjoud countered flatly, turning another page of his paper.

"Sand!" Constance protested, flashing him a glare.

"The tracks run up against the desert here," Mr. Mahjoud elaborated blithely. "And sand is prone to moving about."

"It isn't sand." Constance gave him a quelling look. "It's the nationalists! Sabotaging the railway is exactly the sort of strategy they would use. There have been quite a few suspicious incidents along the lines over the last several months. Herds of stray cattle, unexpected washouts…"

Ellie considered Constance's theory. Egypt's most well-known dalliance with a nationalist movement had ended over a decade ago when the revolutionary leader Urabi Pasha had been overcome at Tell El Kabir. That uprising had led Britain to impose its Consul General as the de facto head of the Egyptian government.

While there were plenty of Egyptians who continued to advocate—carefully—for a more representative government, she hadn't heard of any major organized opposition to British rule.

Of course, that didn't mean that one didn't exist.

"There was even one breakdown that almost certainly involved the use of explosives," Constance added significantly.

Ellie perked up. "Explosives, did you say?"

Mr. Mahjoud stilled, flashing her an alarmed look over the top of his paper.

"Not that any of us have any interest in that sort of thing," Ellie assured him.

With a sigh, Mr. Mahjoud crisply folded the paper. He set it down on the bench and placed his fez onto his head. The color perfectly matched his waistcoat and bow tie, the hat nearly brushing the ceiling of the compartment thanks to the dragoman's exceptional height.

"If you would all do me the extreme kindness of staying where I have put you?" he suggested—punctuating it with a pointed look at Constance.

"Wherever would we go?" Constance returned, batting her eyes at him innocently.

"Antarctica, perhaps?" Mr. Mahjoud suggested. "Or off with the nearest circus?"

Ellie was quietly impressed by the perspicacity of his suggestions.

"There aren't any circuses about," Constance pointed out.

With a skeptical glare, he stepped from the compartment.

Constance waited for a breath, then darted to the door herself—only to pull it open and find Mr. Mahjoud standing before it.

"*Please,*" he added with exaggerated patience.

Constance rolled her eyes. "Fine." She flopped back against her seat with dissatisfaction. "Sand!"

"Perhaps the nationalists shoveled it all there overnight?" Ellie suggested helpfully.

"You needn't patronize me," Constance returned haughtily.

Ellie glanced over at Adam. He had been uncharacteristically quiet about the interruption—and her passing mention of combustible materials. He still held his notebook in his hands but wasn't writing anything in it. Instead, he frowned down at the carpet as though contemplating how to wrestle it.

The compartment door slid back open, revealing Mr. Mahjoud's long and impeccably dressed frame. "It would seem that there is a great deal of sand on the tracks," he reported with only the slightest note of triumph.

"Hmph." Constance crossed her arms over her chest.

"It will take the railway staff several hours to clear it sufficiently for us to pass." The dragoman sat down, neatly picking up his paper and shaking it out. "I do hope everyone brought something to read, as I suggested?"

Adam stood, startling everyone with the sudden movement. "I'm going to help."

He shrugged out of his jacket, tossing it on the seat. Before Ellie could make any sort of comment, his shirt followed.

Her mind blanked as her perception was overwhelmed by an abundance of hard, tanned masculine flesh.

He tossed the shirt aside roughly. It landed half in her lap, Ellie's hands automatically catching at the fabric.

Without another word, he stalked from the compartment.

Mr. Mahjoud made a single eloquent blink, then pointedly raised up his newspaper.

Constance's frankly assessing gaze moved from the open door to Ellie, where it locked onto her helplessly dazed expression.

"Colleagues, is it?" Constance noted mercilessly.

The sand proved substantial. The afternoon was well progressed by the time the train started moving again, at which point Constance had worked her way through most of the contents of Mr. Mahjoud's hamper.

Adam returned to their compartment a little later. His golden hair was still dusty from the work, though he'd clearly managed a light wash, perhaps in one of the sleeper cabins. He pulled his shirt back on, slipped his braces over his shoulders, and settled into his seat without another word.

They stopped at the small but modern railway station that sat a short walk from the rustic village of Badrashin. New telegraph wires soared overhead, following the tracks south along the river. The Nile's flood plain was broad, flush with plantations of date palms and bright green fields crisscrossed by irrigation canals.

Behind Ellie lay the broad expanse of the great river itself, peppered with little single-sail feluccas and a slow, elegant dahabeeyah. On that larger boat, a cluster of pale Europeans played cards under a canopy in an open-air salon while an Egyptian crewman worked the rope for an overhead fan.

Mr. Mahjoud checked his pocket watch. "It is nearly four," he announced, snapping it shut and slipping it back into his waistcoat. "The necropolis at Saqqara is an hour's ride from here, and the return service to Cairo passes through at ten after five. We cannot make it there and back in time for the train. We will have to return home and try again tomorrow."

Ellie felt a pinch of panic at Mr. Mahjoud's announcement. They couldn't afford a further delay—not when Dawson and Jacobs might turn up at any moment. "Could we find a place to stay locally for the evening?"

"In *Badrashin?*" Mr. Mahjoud said with a look of horror, as though Ellie had just suggested they bed down in a nest of porcupines rather than a quaint mud-brick village shaded by tall palms.

"Don't they let visitors overnight at Mariette's House?" Constance offered brightly, using a long white scarf to tie her enormous and very fashionable straw hat into place. "That's right next to the pyramids."

Mr. Mahjoud straightened, making himself a bit taller—perhaps in order to sharpen the angle at which he looked down his nose at her. "Mariette's House is not appropriate for ladies. It is entirely too rustic."

"Are there any Bedouin about, then?" Constance pressed with an air of studied innocence. "I have heard they are most accommodating to guests."

With some alarm, Ellie recalled Constance's ambition to acquire a handsome sheikh as a lover. "Mariette's House will do nicely," she cut in quickly. "Both Mr. Bates and I are accustomed to 'rustic,' and I am sure Constance doesn't mind."

Constance flashed Ellie a narrow-eyed look as though perfectly aware of why Ellie had made her intervention. "Oh, very well," she agreed a little crossly. "Mariette's House it shall be."

Mr. Mahjoud blinked—a simple motion that somehow still exuded disapproval. "I will see about arranging transportation," he concluded, sounding as though he were accepting a prison sentence. He shifted a seemingly bland gaze to Constance. "And restocking the hamper."

"Oh yes!" Constance agreed, brightening. "Do see if there are any kofta sellers about. And perhaps you can find a few of those lovely little semolina cakes."

Mr. Mahjoud's posture was an eloquent display of dignified resignation as he walked away.

He returned a quarter hour later with kofta, semolina cakes, and a slightly pudgy boy towing a line of donkeys.

"Are you quite sure we can't walk?" Ellie asked, eyeing the animals skeptically. She still had vivid memories of her sore rear from spending all day on mule-back in the wilderness of British Honduras.

"What would we do that for?" Constance returned as she nimbly mounted her beast with a hand from the boy.

Ellie's donkey snorted.

"Need a lift?" Adam offered.

She startled as she realized that he had come to stand beside her.

"That… would be lovely," she replied awkwardly. "Thank you."

The exchange felt oddly formal. Adam had been so distant and quietly stormy since their bizarre conversation the night before that Ellie found herself uncertain quite how to act around him.

He offered her his knee and a hand. The gesture had an unconsciously courtly air—for all that she was standing next to a bored-looking donkey and not a noble steed.

Ellie accepted his grip. The calloused texture of his palm sent a shiver through her skin as she awkwardly planted herself in the saddle.

The donkey shifted beneath her, and she nearly fell backwards.

"Tuck your knees up by his neck," Adam instructed. "It'll help you stay balanced. They get nervous when you wobble."

He stroked a hand down the donkey's flank, then gave it a scratch behind the ears. The donkey huffed with approval.

Then he turned and walked away without another word. Ellie stared after him, utterly at a loss.

"Yalla! Yalla!" the donkey boy cried, jarring her out of the confused whirlwind of her thoughts. "Mâshi!"

The beast beneath her lurched into motion. Ellie jolted back in the saddle and then clung on for dear life as they trotted down the road.

The flat, fertile fields were verdant with sprouts of new wheat, tended by fellahin who tucked their long galabeyas into their loose cotton breeches to keep them from the mud. The donkey boy continued to call out cheerful Masri imprecations at their mounts as they rode along the narrow packed-earth pathways. To Ellie's ears, the boy's words sounded like a mix of routine commands and more personal and affectionate compliments.

The fields gave way to tall, orderly rows of date palms interspersed here and there by the occasional tidy farmhouse—and then the fertile land abruptly turned to desert.

The change was like a line drawn across the earth, an immediate and dramatic shift from towering trees to arid, rock-strewn ground. As the date plantation fell away, Ellie finally saw the ragged, humped shapes of the less-well-known pyramids of Dahshur.

Though nowhere near the size of the famous monuments at Giza, they were significantly older, and therefore perhaps even more fascinating. Ellie picked the tiered form of the Pyramid of Djoser from the clustered structures. The tower of stone was nearly five thousand years old and was most likely the first pyramid ever built in Egypt.

The crumbling monuments represented only a fraction of the history that had accumulated at the necropolis of Saqqara, which had been in use for over three thousand years, from the third dynasty to the Ptolemaic period. The arid landscape was peppered with tumbles of ancient mud-brick and scattered debris. Ellie's eyes immediately picked out the patterns in it—the straight line of a wall, the flat surface of an ancient road. The ground was littered with relics of Egypt's ancient past.

Ellie had been furiously, painfully jealous when she had learned that Neil had been hired to oversee an excavation here—and at a very promising New Kingdom tomb site, no less. That ache had only deepened when Neil's initial survey produced strong indications that the tomb had been built for Horemheb, the Eighteenth Dynasty general who had risen to become a pharaoh in his own right despite his lack of royal blood.

Horemheb was a fascinating figure, and the Eighteenth Dynasty was Ellie's favorite period of Egyptian history. She would have given almost anything to have been able to join in uncovering a new chapter of it.

Not that she had been invited.

The impact of finally being in this storied landscape was somewhat compromised by the hawkers and would-be guides who clustered at the end of the lane.

"Tour guide!" one shouted. "Climb the pyramid of the great pharaoh!"

"Authentic Saqqara souvenirs!" another called out.

Ellie gave the wares on his blanket a careful glare as they rode past, looking out for any genuine artifacts he might be trying to sell.

Mr. Mahjoud dismissed all the would-be helpers with a disapproving glare as he led their party past the entrance and into the necropolis.

As they rode past the pitted openings to abandoned tomb shafts, Ellie thought uneasily of her upcoming reunion with her brother, who had been in Egypt for just over two years now.

When Ellie had still been a schoolgirl, Neil had happily indulged her curiosity about his books and studies. That comfortable intellectual banter had changed when he left for university. Neil had grown more distant. He had always been a bit over-serious, but it began to feel as though his mind was somewhere else when he returned home for holidays.

After Ellie managed to fight her way into university herself, there had been sparks of that old dynamic between them—moments where Ellie had lured Neil into a debate about the antecedents of Ancient Greek or the fall of the Byzantine Empire. But after a little while, Neil always pulled away again, pleading another paper he needed to write or books he had neglected.

There was nothing wrong with that, of course—not in any way that Ellie could point her finger at—and yet something about it had left her feeling oddly frustrated… and perhaps just a bit let down.

She was fairly certain Neil would *not* be excited to learn that she had come to Egypt—even without the added complication of Adam Bates. The thought made her hands clench a little tighter on the reins of her donkey as they followed the winding path deeper into the desert.

Adam rode just behind her. He was still oddly quiet as his blue eyes carefully scanned the desert.

Ellie let her donkey fall back a bit until she was bobbing uncomfortably beside him. "Is something wrong?"

"Hard to say till we get there," Adam replied automatically, still not looking at her. "Might be a good idea to have Mr. M question the workers and see if anyone matching Dawson or Jacobs' description has been sniffing about. It'd give us a better notion of how to approach your brother about the whole business. I can't say I'm at all sure he's going to be happy to learn that a bunch of artifact thieves have an interest in his dig."

"No," Ellie agreed. "But that wasn't what I meant."

Adam finally met her gaze—only to quickly look away again. "Oh?"

Ellie repressed a sigh of exasperation. "Maybe I was asking why you kissed me last night and then apologized as though you'd just run over my cat. And why you've been avoiding me for most of the day."

"I haven't been avoiding you," Adam countered stubbornly. "I'm right here."

"But you can barely bring yourself to look at me!" Ellie exclaimed.

Constance turned on her donkey where she rode ahead of them, glancing back with a concerned frown.

Ellie flashed her a reassuring smile and a wave.

Constance's eyes narrowed, shifting from her to Adam, but she finally turned back around.

"I'm just trying to do the right thing," Adam pushed back, keeping his voice low and his eyes on the road ahead of them.

"The right thing about what?" Ellie fought to keep the exasperation from her tone.

Adam turned his head to stare down at her. "You, Ellie."

The intensity of his look—fierce with tumultuous but unnameable feeling—took her breath.

"But what does that mean?" Ellie pressed a little unevenly.

Mr. Mahjoud's voice cut through the evening air before Adam could respond.

"We have arrived," the dragoman announced, drawing his donkey up short at the edge of a sprawling pit.

SEVEN

*T*HE GROUND IN front of Ellie fell away steeply, the layers of earth peeled away to expose the roofless walls of Horemheb's ruined funerary temple.

The paving stones of the ancient floor lay about seven feet down from where she stood. A few Egyptian workers carried buckets of debris up a steep ramp to where a cluster of women in dark blue cloaks and headscarves sifted the rubble. Younger boys hauled the processed spoil to a heap further away.

Other men set down their picks, shovels, and buckets to close out their day's work, chatting together comfortably. It was nearly time for supper, and they would soon return to their homes in the village for the evening.

The sun had fallen in the west, and the air cooled ever-so-slightly from the burning heat of the day.

"Well?" Constance prompted as she hopped off her donkey. "Are we going down?"

Ellie instinctively glanced back at Adam. His eyes narrowed as he scanned the roofless maze of the temple like a potential battlefield.

Carefully dismounting, she followed Constance down the ramp to a narrow opening framed by a pair of pylons—thick walls filled with rubble that served as impressive gateways to sacred Egyptian sites. The two that flanked her were no longer tall, having crumbled down to waist height when their materials were scavenged by later builders for other projects at the necropolis.

Beyond the pylons lay a wide antechamber marked out by more half-tumbled walls, where a cluster of workers eyed Ellie and the others with surprise and a touch of discomfort.

"Very sorry!" one of them called over. "No tourist!"

"Wait here," Mr. Mahjoud ordered.

He strode over to the men, engaging in a rapid and authoritative exchange of Masri. One of the workers detached himself from the group to dart back up the ramp to ground level, obviously set on some errand.

Nothing about the scene spoke of the sort of tension Ellie might expect if the excavation was under siege. But then again, why would it? Adam's snooping had only revealed that Dawson and Jacobs thought Neil's site might contain some clue to the location of the next arcana they hoped to acquire. They might come in with guns blazing to snatch it—or with a smile and a letter of recommendation from one of Neil's sponsors. Ellie still hadn't a clue who Dawson and Jacobs worked for, but she did know the pair were exceptionally well-funded and connected, which meant that the latter possibility couldn't be ruled out. The scribble Adam had spotted in Dawson's notebook had simply mentioned *receiving another update*. Who was to say whether that update came through official channels or by way of a spy or informant on the excavation's staff?

Still, it was hard to imagine that any group of workers would look this relaxed if someone like Jacobs was lurking about.

Somewhat reassured, but still wary, Ellie let her attention drift to the temple itself while Mr. Mahjoud chatted with the staff.

Beyond the antechamber lay another roofless room, this one framed by a row of tumbled columns. The pieces of debris were all neatly tagged and labeled, the fragments set into tidy piles.

More of the walls had survived here than in the antechamber, including some limestone panels covered in carved text and images. A worker squatted comfortably beside one of the larger murals, making a neat, careful copy in his sketchbook. The piece was done in bas relief, with the surrounding stone shallowly cut away from the image.

The heads of the larger figures on the panel were lost, as they fell above the level of the surviving portion of the wall. Smaller forms had survived mostly intact, save for a few places where details had flaked away.

The more diminutive people were kneeling with their heads bowed in supplication. Their arms were bound and linked together with ropes. From the distinctive curls of their hair and the fact that their faces were bearded, Ellie suspected they represented members of some Semitic tribe that the great general Horemheb had conquered.

She pulled her attention from the bas relief to the worker's sketchbook. His page was lined with neat rows of the hieroglyphs that he had already copied from the wall. Ellie's mind instinctively leapt to translate them, though the knowledge was somewhat rusty. She hadn't found much cause to read hieroglyphs while working at the Public Record Office.

"*Flame… Isis… speaks…*" she read.

The writing system of the Ancient Egyptian language combined ideograms—symbols meant to represent entire concepts—with symbols that stood for the phonemes of ancient words… at least, in as much as anyone knew what those had been. The sounds of the Ancient Egyptian tongue had been lost for centuries, and scholars were still struggling to reconstruct it.

"*Surround…*" Ellie muttered, lifting her eyes from the worker's sketchbook to pick out the relevant section from the text on the wall. "*Hidden… tomb…*"

"Are you reading those hieroglyphs, Eleanora?" Constance pressed with delighted interest.

"I am trying to," Ellie retorted, frowning at the symbols, "once I recall what this figure with the stick on his head is meant to be. Oh wait! Not a stick—an ax!"

"Why does he have an ax on his head?" Constance asked.

"Because that's the sign for *enemy*," Ellie replied dismissively as she focused on the text. "It's meant to be sticking out of his brain."

"Is it really?" Constance pressed with obvious relish, moving in for a closer look.

"Now then," Ellie continued, excitement driving her onward. "That would make the whole of it, *The Flame of Isis says—I surround the hidden tomb with sand and drive thy enemy away.*" She smiled brightly. "How splendid! I am quite certain that's from one of the later chapters of the Book of the Dead. I wonder if I can remember which one…"

"I see we have done a marvelous job of *waiting*," Mr. Mahjoud commented blandly.

Ellie turned to see the dragoman approach, followed by an Egyptian gentleman with a neat silver beard and a fine black quftan. A clean white turban crowned his head.

"Mr. Abdelrahman says that Dr. Fairfax went down the shaft," Mr. Mahjoud reported.

Ellie sparked with scholarly interest. "Shaft, did you say? Do you mean he found the entrance to Horemheb's actual tomb? But how far have they excavated? Did they survey the entirety or have they been proceeding chamber-by-chamber?"

"Have there been any other recent visitors to the site?" Adam cut in, his tone serious. His eyes were on the doorway while his hand rested on the hilt of his machete.

Mr. Mahjoud exchanged a few more words with the Egyptian.

"No," the dragoman reported. "Not for the last six weeks, since the tourist season died down."

Ellie felt a quick wave of relief. "Where is the shaft?"

Mr. Abdelrahman waved toward the next chamber.

Ellie couldn't see what lay there, as the walls in that portion of the ruins had survived to a height of over ten feet, but it must be the inner and most sacred chapel of Horemheb's funeral temple—an entirely sensible place for the ancient priests to have situated the vertical tunnel that would lead to the great general's tomb.

She picked up the hem of her skirts and stalked inside, the others following as Mr. Abdelrahman let out a stream of protests.

The sanctum was smaller than the other chambers. The walls of it rose high and close. There were more surviving bas reliefs here, though Ellie could also see places where the panels of limestone had been sheared off— probably stolen by earlier visitors to Saqqara, like the soldiers of Napoleon who had come here a century before.

On the right side of the room lay a perfectly rectangular hole in the floor, revealed by the removal of one of the paving stones. The opening was clearly a tomb shaft.

"Of course, my beastly brother didn't write to tell me that he had found this!" Ellie exclaimed. She dropped to her knees at the edge of the hole and peered down. The tunnel descended straight into the rock for roughly ten yards. Someone had left a lantern at the bottom.

Adam came up to the opposite side of it—and then promptly stepped back. "That's... farther down than I thought it'd be."

"Is this setting off your vertigo?" Ellie demanded, surprised. "But it's going *into* the ground, not out of it."

"Ss' good," Adam replied queasily. "I'm good. Just gonna... stand over here."

Constance took his place and studied the wooden scaffold that hung over the shaft. A rope dangled from the pulley rigged to the top of it. Ellie could just see the bucket tied to the far end of it at the bottom of the hole.

"Is this how we get down?" Constance suggested.

Ellie felt a dart of hopeful interest. Though descending thirty feet into the ground in a bucket was a moderately daunting prospect, she would happily attempt it for the chance to venture into a bona fide Eighteenth Dynasty tomb built by one of the most important figures in Egypt's New Kingdom period.

"You are not going down," Mr. Mahjoud calmly and flatly informed her. "Mr. Abdelrahman will descend and inform Dr. Fairfax that you are here."

"Hmph," Constance replied with a dissatisfied frown.

One of the other workers called down to them from where he stood on the high ground outside the dig site.

"Abdelrahman! Ya amir hena!"

"Mâshi. Ana gai," Mr. Abdelrahman shouted back. He gave the three foreigners a narrow-eyed look. "You stay," he ordered firmly before striding back toward the entrance.

"What's all that about?" Adam's eyes narrowed. He seemed to have recovered from his brief encounter with the pit.

"He said their amir has come." Mr. Mahjoud watched the older man depart with a thoughtful frown.

"Their amir?" Ellie echoed.

"It means boss," Constance clarified as she gave the winch for the bucket a thoughtful, deliberate turn.

"But Neil is in the tomb," Ellie said, pointing down the shaft.

"Then they must mean the man with the money," Constance replied.

"Oh. Of course," Ellie agreed uneasily.

The funds for Neil's excavation had been provided by the British Athenaeum for Egyptological Studies, a well-established and respectable scholarly organization. This newly arrived amir must be their local representative.

The sky above them was streaked orange with the decline into evening. It was a bit late for someone like that to be paying the excavation a casual visit.

Adam moved to the doorway of the chapel, standing in the shadow of the remaining wall as he cast a wary look over the rest of the funerary complex.

His body tensed like a jaguar before a pounce as his voice went low with warning. "We've got company."

A moment later, Ellie heard the cause of his alarm for herself.

"I don't care what time it is," a familiar voice complained in pretentious, Scots-accented tones. "I will speak to Dr. Fairfax immediately!"

The sound tossed a bucket of ice water over Ellie's brain.

"Dawson!" she hissed.

He couldn't be any further than the next chamber.

"Looks like it's just the idiot," Adam reported warily from his post by the entrance. "There's no sign of Jacobs—*yet.*"

Ellie quickly assessed their options. Though the chapel was roofless, the walls that framed the space were still over ten feet high. Adam stood by the only door—which led right to where Dawson approached.

"Should we go over the top?" Constance prompted in an eager whisper. "I'm sure Mr. Mahjoud can vault us up there."

"I beg your pardon?" Mr. Mahjoud retorted, aghast.

Ellie's mind whirled furiously. She had accounted for the possibility that Dawson and Jacobs might have already beaten them here—but not for the chance that her enemies would arrive right at the same time.

Adam's gaze met hers from across the chapel, his hand still ready on the hilt of the machete. "We gonna run? Or fight?"

Ellie fought for an answer. "If we run, we risk Neil telling Dawson about anything he might have already found. We have to at least *try* to warn him before Dawson gets here."

Adam yanked the machete from its sheath. "Sounds like fight," he concluded.

"You are forgetting a third option," Constance hissed, grasping Adam by the elbow and pulling him back from the doorway. "The one where both of you go into the tomb while Mr. Mahjoud and I remain behind as a distraction!"

"We what?!" Mr. Mahjoud protested, stiffening with alarm.

"This professor of yours doesn't know who we are," Constance pressed. "As long as he isn't aware that you are here, his guard will be down. We'll just... er, *inconvenience* him until you can fetch Neil and get him out of there," she finished with an awkward look at the obviously disapproving dragoman.

Adam met Constance's eyes, his blue gaze narrowly assessing. "Fine," he concluded, shoving the machete back into its place at his belt. "But you see one sign of a snake-eyed, black-haired English bastard—"

"We won't do anything foolish," Constance assured him, already reeling up the bucket.

"This is already foolish!" Mr. Mahjoud pointed out.

"Well, what do *you* think we should do?" Constance retorted.

"Go home?" Mr. Mahjoud suggested.

"Would you be telling my grandmother to *go home?*" Constance pushed back.

Mr. Mahjoud blanched at the thought.

Constance pointed into the tomb shaft. "Get in the bucket, Eleanora."

The makeshift elevator hung just inside the mouth of the thirty-foot drop. The notion of balancing in it while clinging to a rope made Ellie's stomach tighten.

The grating tones of Dawson's voice were growing louder as he approached. She hesitated, looking to Adam.

He nodded.

With an exasperated sigh, Mr. Mahjoud firmly cut in front of Constance to take hold of the winch. Constance crossed her arms and shot him a glare at the intervention.

Gingerly, Ellie set her boot into the bucket. The opening only had enough room for one of her feet. The other was left to dangle uncomfortably as she wobbled. She managed to straighten herself, then went into a slow, awkward spin.

"La sahla illa ma ja 'altahu sahla," Mr. Mahjoud muttered.

"What does that mean?" Ellie pressed curiously.

"It is a dua for trying circumstances," Mr. Mahjoud retorted with a pointed look at her and turned the winch.

With a jolt, Ellie descended, bumping awkwardly against the tight, evenly cut sides of the shaft. She looked up to see Constance's face framed in the pale square of the opening.

Adam joined her there, immediately turning a bit green.

The bucket thumped to the ground with an impact that made Ellie's teeth clack. She scrambled out and tucked herself up against the wall by the lantern as Mr. Mahjoud reeled the bucket back up again.

"It's perfectly fine," Ellie lied, hissing up at Adam. "You'll hardly mind it at all."

"You should probably scoot," Adam replied as the bucket reached the top of the shaft again, and he wearily moved to set his foot in it. "In case I puke."

A narrow opening stood in the wall nearby, just large enough for Ellie to crawl through. She plucked up the lantern—lest Adam's fear of heights do it any untoward damage—and brought it with her. She emerged in a narrow, unadorned passageway.

A scrape and a muttered curse from behind her marked Adam's arrival. He spilled through the opening, landed on the floor, and sprawled out his arms as he stared up at the ceiling.

"Maybe it'll be better on the way up," he offered without much confidence.

"I'm sure that it will," Ellie assured him awkwardly. "But now, we'd best get moving. We haven't any time to waste."

Adam staggered to his feet, bracing himself with a hand to the wall for a moment before he straightened.

"Guess it's time to find your brother," he concluded wearily.

EIGHT

$\mathcal{D}$USTY AND SWEATING in the depths of an Eighteenth Dynasty tomb, Dr. Neil Fairfax put his extensive education in Egyptology and ancient history to work by holding up a piece of wood.

Playing human scaffold for a sturdily built frame covered in stretched canvas was not what Neil had imagined himself doing when he had received his doctorate from Cambridge—but somebody needed to keep it upright until the braces were constructed, and Neil's foreman, Sayyid Al-Ahmed, was better at building things than Neil was.

Neil's arms jarred as Sayyid hammered in another nail. "There!" the foreman declared, scrambling to his feet and dusting off his hands.

Sayyid was roughly the same height as Neil but sturdier in build. His neatly trimmed beard was normally the hue of honeyed burnt wood, but at the moment it looked more silver with dust. Instead of the tailored suit and dapper fez that he wore when out and about in Cairo, he was stripped to his waistcoat and bareheaded, his shirt smudged with dirt.

Neil almost certainly looked worse. His tweed waistcoat and bow tie might have been dapper enough when he'd risen that morning but were now amply disheveled. His light brown hair was messy. He plucked off his round gold-rimmed spectacles and gave them a rub on his handkerchief, trying to remove a day's worth of fingerprints.

The excavation of Horemheb's funerary chapel had been executed with painstaking attention to conservation and documentation. That included the tomb beneath it, even though the gaps in the rubble-filled doorways told Neil that he wasn't the first one to penetrate the complex's secrets. At least one set of thieves had beaten him to it, probably around the time that Caesar had been flirting with Cleopatra.

Neil knew better than to expect to find Horemheb himself at the end of the series of underground chambers and passages. The great general-turned-pharaoh would have been put to rest somewhere in the Valley of the Kings, where archaeologists with more experience—or posher connections—than Neil were granted permission to excavate.

That was fine with Neil. He was happy to be at Saqqara, where three thousand years of occupation offered a unique opportunity to explore the evolution of Egypt's funerary practices.

He released the wooden frame with a sigh of relief, shaking out his arms. The canvas-covered box was sized to cover the wall of the narrow antechamber in which they stood. It would serve to protect a delicate painting there from damage as they cleared the passage to the next chamber of the tomb.

The way onward was currently blocked with rubble, save for a hole those centuries-old thieves had made in an upper corner. If Neil stood up on his toes, he could peer through it into a passage scattered with debris and distinguished by four evenly spaced columns.

Neil itched to discover what the rest of the tomb would reveal about Horemheb's early life and the history of the late Eighteenth Dynasty. He would get his chance after they cleared the doorway, which they would begin working on tomorrow. Right now, his stomach was telling him that it was time to call it a day.

"Can we have supper now?" Neil asked.

"One more moment," Sayyid said, scooting the frame aside to take another look at the painting on the wall.

The mural was a very fine example of late Eighteenth Dynasty bas relief, a find well worth protecting when so much of the artistic material above ground had been destroyed in antiquity or carried off by previous 'explorers.' In the relief, Horemheb made offerings to Osiris, who was wrapped in the shroud of a mummy and holding his traditional crook and flail. The god of the dead's complexion was a rich blue. The black of Horemheb's wig and the dark umber of his skin had survived as well.

Sayyid had spent the day before stabilizing the ancient painting by applying a light, clear adhesive to any areas where the surviving fragments of color were at risk of flaking away.

Conserving artwork was another thing Sayyid did far better than Neil.

Sayyid had learned his trade at the knees of his father Kamal, who had been possibly the most respected foreman in Egypt during his time. Before he had passed away six years earlier, Kamal had worked under some of the most influential Egyptologists of the last thirty years in digs at Giza and Luxor—managing the day-to-day operations of an excavation for men like

Flinders Petrie, Mariette, and Karl Lepsius.

Neil had to admit that Sayyid's education in Egyptology at his father's hands had been as comprehensive as anything he might have received at Oxford or the Sorbonne—maybe even better. Neil was often humbled by Sayyid's detailed knowledge of the latest methods for stabilizing fragile artifacts and his extensive understanding of the various dialects of the Ancient Egyptian language.

As this was Neil's first Egyptian excavation, he had been relying heavily on Sayyid's more extensive experience—especially as he frequently had cause to discover that the archaeological methods and 'best practices' that he had been taught at Cambridge fell apart in the face of real conditions at the excavation.

All in all, he felt desperately lucky that Sayyid had been available to work on the dig—even if he did keep poking fun at Neil's mustache.

Neil's hand rose to the facial hair in question. He had been trying to grow it out since the Eid holiday. Neil had been cursed with a face that perpetually looked younger than it actually was. With his smooth skin and round spectacles, he was regularly mistaken for a student until someone got around to introducing him as 'doctor.'

He hoped the mustache would help… just as soon as it filled in a bit more. He rubbed awkwardly at the thin growth.

"Poking at it isn't going to make it any better," Sayyid noted helpfully as he added another dab of adhesive to a bit of cracked charcoal under Horemheb's eye.

Neil self-consciously dropped his hand. "It's still growing in."

"I have seen better mustaches on donkey boys," Sayyid returned cheerfully. "Perhaps instead of worrying over your not-a-mustache, you might copy down another section of those hieroglyphs."

"I'm not worrying over my mustache," Neil retorted. "I am waiting for you to finish up so we can eat." His stomach punctuated the thought with an audible growl.

"I will stop soon enough—it is nearly time to pray." Sayyid made another delicate line with his brush. "Just one more section."

With a sigh, Neil pulled out his notebook and pencil. He moved to the part of the wall where he had left off transcribing earlier that day.

Sometimes, despite the Cambridge-certified letters after his name, Neil felt as though Sayyid were really the one in charge, and he was the assistant. He might have found that slightly mortifying—if it wasn't far *less* mortifying than the thought of bungling things because he insisted on being in charge while Sayyid painfully looked on.

He knew that point of view wasn't one that many of his fellow archaeologists would share. He'd heard the disdainful way they talked about their Egyptian excavation workers back at Cambridge. But maybe they had never had someone like Sayyid on their digs… or perhaps they were simply so sure of their own superiority, it had never occurred to them to look for talent anywhere else.

Neil had never been particularly sure of his superiority at much of anything.

He pushed his attention to the hieroglyphs, carefully copying down the next line.

"Make sure you don't mix up the ideogram for ear with a measure of grain again," Sayyid helpfully suggested.

Neil's cheeks burned. "It's a perfectly reasonable mistake. They both consist of the exact same curling line from the eye of Horus."

"Yes, but the ear retains the vertical line, and the grain does not," Sayyid pointed out.

"You Egyptians talk about grain far more than you talk about ears," Neil grumbled.

"Ah yes," Sayyid easily replied. "I'm sure that is it."

"Sometimes I wonder why I'm even here," Neil complained.

"To be fair, you are the one who found the tomb," Sayyid cheerfully allowed. "If you hadn't changed the site location, we'd still be sifting through sand thirty meters away."

Neil supposed he could take credit for that. When he had arrived at Saqqara two years earlier to start the dig, one look at the landscape where they were meant to excavate had left him with the nagging sense that they were in the wrong place.

He'd been terrified to push his funders to move everything ninety feet to the east—but the notion of spending months churning through dirt in a spot he knew in his bones was wrong had been even more unbearable.

Not that Neil could have told anyone *why* the site was wrong. When asked, he had rattled off an elaborate justification based on Ancient Egyptian measurement systems and the relative ranking of known courtiers during the reign of Tutankhamun—all of which was entirely true. But none of it had actually passed through his thoughts when he had looked at the stretch of rubble-strewn desert and known, *No—it's over there.*

That hadn't been the first time some itching instinct had pushed Neil in a particular historical direction. He had come to think of those seemingly out-of-the-blue notions as the result of some unconscious mental process. It wasn't that they came from nowhere or were mere 'lucky guesses,' but rather that his mind coughed up a conclusion after surreptitiously rifling through the extensive library of all the theses, excavation reports, and journal articles that Neil had consumed over his years of study.

Whatever lay behind his hunches, he had learned to trust them—and that if he didn't, he'd be left feeling uncomfortable and dissatisfied, like a man forced into a wool coat without a shirt.

Neil's hunch about Saqqara had proved accurate when they had uncovered the upper extent of the funerary temple pylon in the first week of digging. He'd received a hearty pat on the back from his funders, and with Sayyid's capable help, the temple had revealed its secrets—including the passages and chambers of the subterranean tomb complex where Neil now worked to copy down more of the characters carved into the wall.

"*Person… disturb… tomb…*" he muttered aloud, working through the translation as he marked down the hieroglyphs. "*No life… enemies… me?*"

"Looks like you found a curse," Sayyid noted.

Neil mentally translated the rest and hid a smile. "I don't think you're going to like it," he replied, his tone deceptively mild.

"Oh?" Sayyid returned distractedly.

With a hint of wicked delight, Neil read the words out loud in Egyptian. "*Keper ir'ef… her tah…*"

"Not keh," Sayyid automatically corrected him. "*Khaa.*" The syllable rasped in the back of his throat. "Like the Arabic."

"Khuuargh," Neil tried.

"No," Sayyid replied.

"Carrrgh."

"Khaa," Sayyid replied, making the sound again. "Khaa."

"Auuugch."

Sayyid's understanding of the Ancient Egyptian language was exceptional—which was saying something, since the original pronunciation of the words had been lost for over a thousand years. Scholars had been working to reconstruct it—most of them Americans or Europeans. It was a true challenge, since the Egyptian hieroglyphs that represented sounds only covered consonants, leaving out the vowels.

Sayyid's father, Kamal, had quietly devoted himself to the task in his later years. While many academics had identified Coptic as the surviving tongue that likely came closest to resembling Ancient Egyptian, Kamal had drawn on his knowledge of several other languages in the region, including various dialects of Arabic, to inform his work. After all, it made far more sense that the phonemes of Ancient Egyptian would align with those of other languages of the Levant and North Africa than with Latin-based languages like English and French.

Kamal had been working on a lexicon, which was left unfinished when he died. Neil had never been able to examine it himself—it had been written in Arabic, of course, a language he was barely learning to speak, never mind read—but his conversations with Sayyid had convinced him that, even incomplete, the book must be an exceptional piece of scholarship.

"I could use a bit of help with this," Neil prodded, suppressing any note of mischief from his voice.

With a sigh, Sayyid pulled his attention from the painting, shifting his gaze to Neil's hieroglyphs.

"*Kheper ir'ef her tah*," he read easily, making a perfect *khaa* in the back of his throat. "*In kheper wanam'ef sen.*"

Reaching the end of the line, Sayyid blanched.

"'As for the person who disturbs this tomb,'" Neil translated with a hint of devilish glee. "'The scarab is set against him on land. It is the scarab who will eat.'"

"Eat *him*," Sayyid corrected him a little queasily. "You're forgetting the pronoun, ef."

"Ah yes," Neil agreed brightly. "Let me see now. That would make it… 'It is the scarab who will eat him.' Isn't that colorful?"

Neil might have noticed that his foreman had a bit of a phobia of bugs.

"Scarabs are meant to be very… er, lucky," Sayyid countered weakly.

"I don't think they're meant to be lucky for this fellow," Neil countered. He read off the next line. "*It will destroy you. You will perish completely.*"

Sayyid cleared his throat. "This section looks very stable, anyway," he concluded deliberately and turned away.

Neil suppressed a snort, moving on to the next line in the inscription. It was a tricky one, using glyph combinations that were somewhat less conventional for the period.

"Dashed Late Egyptian creeping in already," he grumbled, half aware of the sound of footsteps hurrying down the stairs to the antechamber. With his concentration locked on the wall, he only vaguely registered that the figure that popped into view out of the corner of his eye wasn't one of the workers from above but rather a young woman in a gray poplin skirt and waistcoat. Unruly chestnut hair escaped from under her straw boater hat and a spray of freckles danced across her nose.

Just Ellie, Neil thought automatically as he frowned at a chipped section of the text. "Hold on a minute, Peanut," he said absently. "I need to figure out if this is a viper or a cobra."

Behind him, Sayyid straightened, blinking with surprise as he looked from Neil to the woman in the doorway.

Ellie came closer, peering at the hieroglyphs over Neil's shoulder. "Cobra," she concluded. "It's being used as the 'f' pronoun, for the masculine third person."

"Pronouns again!" Neil grumbled—and then it clicked.

Ellie interrupting his work wasn't unusual… in England.

But Neil wasn't *in* England.

His eyes went wide as he whirled to face his baby stepsister, his pencil falling from his fingers. "Ellie!" he exclaimed, pulling her into a hug and then immediately pushing her back to blink at her. "But this is Egypt! You're not supposed to be in Egypt! What are you doing here?"

"I am sorry to ambush you like this," Ellie admitted uncomfortably as she stood right in front of him, where she absolutely should not have been. "There have been some… unexpected developments since I last wrote. I shall fill you in on all of them in just a little while, I promise, but at this precise moment I am afraid we have a slightly more urgent matter to attend to—namely whether you have uncovered any… er…" Ellie trailed off, frowning as she stared at Neil's face. "I'm sorry. Is there something on your lip?"

"What? No!" Neil released her to rub uncomfortably at the fine growth of his nascent mustache.

"This is all very surprising," Sayyid commented.

"Oh! I'm terribly sorry." Ellie extended her hand. "Miss Eleanora Mallory. I'm Dr. Fairfax's sister."

"Sayyid Al-Ahmed," Sayyid replied.

"But what I meant to ask is—have you come across any artifacts in your recent work here that might have referenced something… well, a little Biblical?" Ellie pressed.

"Biblical?" Neil echoed dumbly.

His impossibly present little sister took in his bewildered expression. "I suppose that's a no, then." She cast an assessing look at the blocked doorway to the next passage. "But you've only gone into part of the tomb?"

"We are working our way through one chamber at a time," Neil retorted a little defensively. "There is a great deal of conservation work to be done along the way, and…" He paused, shaking himself as if waking once again from a dream. "But do our parents know you're here? What about your job? How did you even get here?!"

"Not exactly. I don't have one anymore. And on a boat," Ellie replied in neat sequence. "Now, if we could please save the rest for later. We only have a few minutes at most before that villain and your amir reach the tomb shaft."

"*Villain?*" Neil echoed, paling.

"Is your Peanut always this exciting?" Sayyid asked with a touch of awe.

"What? No. She's… Well, I suppose maybe a bit…" Neil hedged thoughtfully, and then caught himself. "Hold on—what villain?"

"He is after a clue which will point to the location of an extremely important artifact—one which he cannot be allowed to find." Ellie looked around the antechamber, her boot tapping thoughtfully on the ground. She eyed the rubble blocking the way to the passage. "Anything of importance to the Egyptians would have been placed with the interred remains of the deceased. If it were possible to find and secure it before Dawson arrived…" She turned to face him, her expression a little apologetic. "How much trouble would it be if we were to push directly through to the burial chamber?"

"What—now?" Neil blurted back, his sense of alarm rising. "But you haven't explained anything! How are you here? Who are these villains you're raving about? What does any of this have to do with the Bible?"

Before Ellie could answer, a second intruder hopped into Neil's tomb, his boots clumping heavily against the floor at the foot of the stairs.

The new arrival had the broad-shouldered physique of a wrestler. He straightened, pushing back the brim of his battered fedora to reveal a sun-kissed complexion—and a pair of very familiar bright blue eyes.

"Hey, Fairfax," Adam Bates said uneasily.

Neil stared slack-jawed at his friend… who was supposed to be living on the other side of the world. "How are you…" he began helplessly.

"It's kind of a long story…" Adam started.

Neil whirled to Sayyid. "Do you see him?"

"The large American with the very blue eyes?" Sayyid carefully returned.

Neil put his fingers to his temples. "I am not going mad," he determined. "But this is… this is too much! First Ellie—who's supposed to be in London cataloging government documents, and now you—who ought to be in British Honduras surveying land grants! Is everyone I've ever met going to turn up in this tomb today? Either one of you would have been an utter surprise, but the sheer coincidence that the two of you show up here at the exact same time…"

Sayyid's eyebrows lifted skeptically. Ellie and Adam exchanged an uncomfortable look.

"Right, sorry," Neil said, catching himself. "You haven't actually met. Ellie, this is Adam Bates, my old friend from Cambridge. Bates, this is my sister, Ellie."

All three of them—Adam, Ellie, and Sayyid—stared at Neil as if he'd just announced that he was going to marry a badger.

"What?" Neil asked a little irritably. "What did I say?"

"Should I, uh…" Adam began awkwardly, his words addressed to Ellie.

"I suppose we had better," Ellie agreed grimly. "If we can find a way to do it quickly."

An odd silence followed. Adam's gaze drifted to the ceiling of the antechamber.

"Nice crocodile lady you've got there," he commented, nodding at one of the figures painted on the plaster.

"That would be the goddess Ammit," Ellie explained thinly without looking up. "The devourer of the hearts of the dead."

Sayyid coughed suspiciously.

At that moment, as if to prove that the day could in fact get even more mad than it already was, a *third* intruder burst into the antechamber.

Neil's latest uninvited visitor wore a fashionable white lawn dress and appeared by way of sliding down the steeply inclined frame of the stairs on her neatly laced kid boots. She landed in the midst of Neil and the others with a violent grace and a puff of dust.

With a neat tug, she loosened the scarf tied under her chin and plucked off her enormous hat. Neil found himself looking down into a heart-shaped face punctuated by bottomless brown eyes and a thick mane of dark chocolate hair, which had been whipped into an elegant Gibson tuck.

It was an exceptionally pretty face, and Neil stood up a little straighter.

"Oh!" he said, self-consciously adjusting his bow tie. "I'm sorry. You've arrived in the middle of…" His throat tightened with nerves, and he changed tactics. "Er, that is to say, this tomb isn't currently open to tourists, as we are still in the process of—"

"I'm afraid you'll have to save the lecture," the extremely attractive woman cut in authoritatively. "That professor has spotted the tomb shaft, and Mr. Mahjoud won't be able to delay him for much longer."

The sound of her voice sparked a bolt of recognition through Neil's brain, memory painting itself over the womanly features before him—of a small face dwarfed by the same pair of enormous brown eyes, which shone devilishly at him as they popped up from behind his desk, nearly making him spill his tea. Of his notes on Greco-Roman trade routes being turned into paper airplanes. New marginalia appearing in his textbooks, mostly depicting battle scenes drenched in red ink.

Of the sense of sheer horror that had swept over him every time he heard a particular set of unnaturally heavy footfalls on the stairs—and knew that Ellie had invited her most terrifying friend over to play.

The danger gnome, Neil had called her.

Now the danger gnome was here. In his tomb. Looking… gorgeous.

"Connie?!" Neil burst out, the words tight with confusion.

"Hello, Stuffy." Constance cast a considering gaze over Neil's person. "You're looking well." Her assessment stopped at his mustache, and she frowned. "But have you got a bit of soot on your lip?"

Neil wondered if it might be possible for him to sink into his shoes and disappear.

"Are you certain this one is not the Peanut?" Sayyid pressed, blinking at the diminutive new arrival.

"But did you see who was with Professor Dawson?" Ellie demanded urgently. "Was Jacobs there?"

"Tall? Dark hair? Expression kinda like that crocodile lady on the ceiling?" Adam offered helpfully.

"I didn't get a chance to look," Constance replied. "It all happened rather quickly. Mr. Mahjoud was set on boosting me over the temple walls, and I only barely managed to get into the tomb shaft instead."

"But why would you do that?" Neil exclaimed. "Why would you climb into the shaft?"

"To warn the rest of you," Constance returned.

"About what?" Neil's volume had risen again.

"The imminent arrival of the villains, of course," Constance said as though the answer ought to have been perfectly obvious.

Neil began to feel dizzy.

"Should we go?" Adam asked.

Bizarrely, he appeared to be directing the question to Ellie.

"We would be leaving whatever is here in Dawson's hands," Ellie replied with a tight desperation.

"I am afraid there is most likely not much here at all—at least that would be of interest to thieves," Sayyid informed her. "Though the entrance to this tomb complex was still intact, it is already quite clear the entirety of it was looted in antiquity. There is still plenty left of scholarly interest, of course, but anything of more obvious value would have been taken from here nearly two thousand years ago. If your Dawson is a treasure hunter, he will most likely be disappointed."

"Dawson is after a different sort of treasure," Ellie retorted grimly.

"Hold on!" Neil pressed his hands to his temples. "If this Dawson person you all keep going on about is some kind of tomb robber, our men will stop him. None of this is necessary!"

"Didn't you hear me?" Constance returned. "Dawson is here with your amir! Your men aren't going to go up against the fellow who provides the funds for their pay, are they?"

"But that doesn't make any sense!" Neil protested wildly. "Why would my amir bring a thief to the tomb?"

"More importantly, how shall we get whatever we find past him?" Constance pressed with an unsettling excitement. "We will need to stage an ambush. Mr. Bates has his machete, and I took the precaution of securing a few knives about my person in the usual spots—"

"Knives?!" Neil echoed, blanching.

"I am more interested to learn that there are 'usual spots,'" Sayyid added, looking both impressed and intimidated.

"We must be able to think of a better plan than a knife-fighting melee!" Ellie protested. Her look shifted, turning to one of avaricious interest. "Perhaps there is something chemically volatile down here…"

"No explosions," Adam cut in quickly. "Or plans. If we wanna stop Dawson from getting whatever's down here, we're gonna have to wing it."

"I suppose you are right." Ellie crossed to the crumbling gap in the rubble that blocked the doorway to the next chamber. "Could I get a leg up?"

Adam… *blushed.*

Neil wasn't sure he had ever seen Adam blush before.

"I mean—might I have a boost to the opening?" Ellie amended primly.

Her cheeks had turned a little pink.

"Boost. Right," Adam returned, crossing over and forming his hands into a stirrup. "Here you go, Princess."

Ellie set her boot into his grip and squirmed through the opening, her sturdy walking boots disappearing from his view.

Neil gaped at the place where they had been. "Did my sister just crawl into the unsurveyed portion of the tomb?"

"It would appear so," Sayyid said from beside him, looking pale.

"Lend another lady a hand?" Constance asked cheerfully.

"Of course," Adam agreed, launching her up behind Ellie.

"And why did Bates call my sister 'Princess?'" Neil asked, bewildered.

Sayyid gave him a long, surprised blink. "Have you not… Did it not seem to you that…"

Neil stared at him blankly, waiting for him to elaborate.

Sayyid clamped his mouth shut.

"Either of you need a lift?" Adam called over, sounding a little tired.

"Allahumma la sahla illa maa ja'altahu sahlan," Sayyid recited with a shake of his head. "At least I can try to make sure they do not damage the paintings."

Without waiting for Neil, he crossed over and wriggled through the gap.

"But procedure…" Neil began helplessly. "Proper survey methods… Stabilization…"

Adam scooped a coil of rope up from the dig supplies on the floor. His eyes flashed with sympathy as he clamped a warm hand on Neil's shoulder—and then used it to steer Neil toward the door. "Come on, Fairfax. Looks like we're gonna raid your tomb."

NINE

$\mathcal{W}$ITH HER BOOT braced on a loop of rope, Ellie dropped awkwardly down the dark, narrow length of another shaft. At least this one was shorter than the first they had descended, so it was less likely that Adam would reach the bottom of it and need to lie down.

She bumped against the tight stone walls as she haltingly descended. Above her, Adam reeled the rope out around one of the big columns in the pillared hall, a handkerchief tied around his palm to keep the fibers from irritating his scar.

Ellie had spotted a scattering of blue faience shabtis—real ones this time—among the rubble on the floor of that chamber. The find strongly indicated that Neil's foreman, Mr. Al-Ahmed, was right. The tomb had almost certainly been looted in ancient times. A Roman-era thief wouldn't have found much value in the little statues, but a modern one would have been able to fetch a good price for them on the black market.

Ellie didn't let that dissuade her. She had a theory about the nature of the clue Dawson was seeking in the tomb. If she was right, what they were looking for wouldn't have been of interest to a Roman thief, either. It would take the form of something more humble—something meant to be kept hidden.

Her rope slipped lower, bumping her against the wall of the shaft again, and finally her boots swung out into the open air. The rest of her followed, bringing the final sacred room of the tomb complex into view.

The burial chamber was perhaps twelve feet long and a little less wide. It was also a mess.

Plaster boxes of ox bones lay smashed in piles, mingling with rotted bundles of linen. Broken sticks of furniture stuck up from the debris beside sharp-edged shards of shattered vases. The destruction was mounded in piles halfway up the walls—and yet Ellie could already pick out treasures that had survived.

A beautifully carved ebony walking stick. A huntsman's bow, still strung, beside an overturned quiver of arrows. More shabtis, their placid faces gazing out at her from amid the dusty tatters of old robes.

The tomb was covered with artwork. Murals of scenes from Horemheb's life—then a general in the service of Tutankhamun—intermingled with the usual excerpts from the Book of the Dead.

One of the walls featured a grand depiction of the twelve great gods of the afterlife overseeing the weighing of the heart of the deceased. The great black mouth of a tunnel braced with ancient, unsteady-looking beams had been cut into the heart of the mural.

"I suppose we know how the thieves got in," Ellie observed as she released the rope and dusted off her skirt.

"And who they robbed," Mr. Al-Ahmed added, his tone reverent.

Neil's foreman had quietly but firmly insisted on being the first to descend into the burial chamber, hoping to identify any vulnerable objects and keep the rest of them from coming too close. Thankfully, the ancient thieves had left an area of the center of the floor fairly clear of debris, which meant that they were able to enter the room without crushing priceless pieces of the historical record under their boots.

Neil had followed after Mr. Al-Ahmed, and the two men now crouched over an area of rubble to Ellie's left. As she joined them, she realized that they were gazing down at a jumbled set of bones.

The remains were terribly old and looked as though they had been unceremoniously dumped from their coffin, pieces of which lay in a splintered, dusty mess nearby. The skeleton was still partially articulated. Enough scraps of the wrappings remained to show that the body had been mummified. The rest had been callously unwound, likely by looters searching for the charms and amulets that would have been carefully positioned around the deceased.

"It's not Horemheb, presumably," Ellie deduced. When the great general was made pharaoh, he would have abandoned this tomb at Saqqara to build a new one among the other royals in the Valley of the Kings.

"It's Mutnedjmet," Neil replied automatically without taking his eyes from the bones. "His wife."

"We suspected she might be here," Mr. Al-Ahmed filled in. "The Valley of the Queens only routinely came into use for the burial of great royal wives during the Nineteenth Dynasty."

"But how do you know it's really her and not someone else?" Constance pressed, peering over Ellie's shoulder.

Ellie had been so focused on the bones, she hadn't heard her friend climb down.

Neil blinked as though coming out of a daze. "I…"

Mr. Al-Ahmed reached out with the tip of his pen and tilted up a piece of the shattered coffin. "There's her cartouche," he said, peering at the circled hieroglyphs on the underside of the wood.

"Well, those thieves were a batch of cads, tossing her around like that." Constance straightened, brightening. "What are we looking for?"

Neil stiffened, and Mr. Al-Ahmed looked uncomfortable. Ellie couldn't blame them. She was feeling rather uncomfortable herself. She was too much of a scholar not to sense the wrongness of what they were doing—barreling into a vulnerable and important archaeological site without taking the time to properly survey and catalog each step of the way. It made her feel far too much like the Roman bounders who had tossed Mutnedjmet's bones onto the floor.

But there simply wasn't any time to do things properly—not with Dawson on their heels. Too much was at stake for Ellie to let the professor and his handler get their hands on whatever secrets this tomb held.

"I… can't say exactly," Ellie admitted awkwardly. "But I do have a theory."

Behind her, Adam slid down the rope from the shaft, his boots landing solidly on the carved stone of the burial chamber floor. He cast an assessing look over the jumble of toppled furniture and broken artifacts stuffed against the walls of the room.

"Hold on!" Neil stiffened, turning on her. "This burial chamber was only meant to be entered after careful clearing and documentation of all the proceeding chambers—and even then, I was explicitly instructed not to open it without the presence of the designated representative of the British Athenaeum, the organization that is providing *every cent* of the funding that makes this excavation possible! This entire dig depends upon maintaining their approval and goodwill, and now you tell me that I am risking all of that on a *theory?*"

"Well, it's *your* theory!" Ellie snapped back.

Neil's eyes widened with surprise. "It is?"

"The one about the possible connection between the Egyptian cult of the Aten and the later emergence of monotheistic religion in the Levant?" Ellie clarified impatiently.

"What's an Aten?" Constance asked, leaning down for a closer look at an ancient beaded sandal.

"Well, it was originally another aspect of the god Ra, represented by the golden sun disk," Ellie eagerly rattled off. "But it began to rise in prominence as a deity in its own right during the reign of—"

"What do you mean?" Neil cut in urgently. "What does this have to do with monotheism and the Aten?"

"You mentioned in your letters that you thought this site might have Atenist connections. Because of her." Ellie pointed to the bones of the dead queen by their boots.

Adam caught her eye. He raised a questioning eyebrow, but Ellie pressed on, knowing any more detailed explanation would have to wait.

"If your theories about the cult of the Aten and the move toward monotheism among the Hebrews during the time of the Exodus are correct…" she continued.

"What does your invasion of my tomb have to do with the Exodus?!" Neil burst out, throwing up his hands.

"Because we're looking for the Staff of Moses!" Ellie retorted, her patience snapping.

Sayyid's eyes widened. Neil's jaw dropped—and then snapped shut again, his eyes blazing with anger and bewilderment.

"This is barking!" he burst out. "First you show up in my tomb out of nowhere, and then Bates pops up like a bad penny—which makes absolutely no sense at all…"

Ellie shot a guilty look over at Adam, who grimaced.

"And then *she's* here," Neil jabbed a finger toward Constance, "rambling on about clues and villains like we've plunged into some tawdry dime novel! And the next thing I know, we're breaking into an extremely important New Kingdom site against the entirely reasonable wishes of my funders, and you're ranting about the parting of the Red Sea!"

"Goodness!" Constance said, pulling her attention from a miraculously upright Eighteenth Dynasty table covered in debris. "I haven't seen him this worked up since that time I glued all his textbooks to his desk."

Neil made a strangled sound in the back of his throat.

"Might want to save the rest of the lecture for later," Adam suggested. "Last we heard, that jackass professor was headed for the tomb shaft—and he doesn't usually travel alone."

"So will the clue be round?" Constance returned her gaze to the rubbish on the table. "Or stick-like?"

She picked up the neck of a smashed vase to give it a better look.

Ellie, Neil, and Mr. Al-Ahmed all lurched forward.

"Don't touch that!" Neil cried out.

"Connie, you really oughtn't…" Ellie started.

"If you could please refrain from handling…" Mr. Al-Ahmed began, his voice strangled.

"Oh!" Constance said. "Sorry."

She quickly set the vase back down on the table.

The table promptly collapsed.

The small mountain of damaged artifacts cluttering its surface tumbled to the ground. Mr. Al-Ahmed let out a groan of dismay as he rushed toward the catastrophe, Ellie close on his heels.

She sneezed against the dust that filled the air, waving it aside for a better look. The tabletop hung askew, slanted over two broken legs, while its contents lay in a heap at her feet. It was hard to tell what was newly damaged and what had already been broken.

"We should clear the fallen objects first," Mr. Al-Ahmed recited as though on instinct as he gazed forlornly at the pile, "after documenting their positions. Then we can see if the table can be stabilized or whether it must be carefully disassembled."

Ellie's gaze snagged on something that protruded from a nest of papyrus matting—an arc of gold like the first glimpse of the rising sun catching her eye. Instinct tugged at her, and she reached out, carefully withdrawing the artifact from the shredded material.

The slender, square wooden box was a little larger than her hand. Its lines were still plumb, the wood grain reasonably tight even after three thousand years. The only ornamentation on its surface was a single, perfectly round disk of thinly inlaid gold, set into the narrow front face.

"It's a jewelry box," she said wonderingly.

The lid consisted of a panel that slid against grooves carefully carved into the sides. It was partially open, left that way by the thieves who had rifled the piece for treasure.

"Please," Mr. Al-Ahmed said worriedly. "May I see that?"

He sounded like a mother asking for the return of her child. Ellie obliged him, hovering close by as he examined the relic. His immediate panic settled as he took in the box's relatively sound condition.

"Cypress wood," Mr. Al-Ahmed observed. "Naturally resistant to pests and humidity."

"It's empty," Constance noted, poking her head over Ellie's shoulder to peer down at the artifact.

It was still a lovely find—just a wooden shell to the looters who had ravaged the tomb over a millennium before, but to a scholar, the jewelry box offered a poignant glimpse into the everyday life of the woman who lay on the floor behind them. Ellie could picture Mutnedjmet carefully sliding it open to pick out a set of earrings to wear for the day.

"That's it," Neil declared behind them. "I'm going back up to do the best I can to save this dig."

He grasped the rope that still hung down from the shaft opening in the ceiling.

"Oh, no, you don't!" Constance whirled after him.

Mr. Al-Ahmed turned the box gently in his hands as though unable to resist the urge to appreciate its details. Ellie hovered near him.

Adam stood at her back. "Am I gonna need to hogtie your brother?"

"I think Constance has the situation under control," Ellie replied distractedly.

"Stay away from the rope, Stuffy," Constance warned menacingly from behind them. "Or I may be forced to resort to violence."

"*Violence?*" Neil spluttered. "What on earth does that mean?"

"Is it just me, or is there something off about the depth?" Ellie leaned closer to Mr. Al-Ahmed as she studied the box.

"It seems more shallow than it ought to be," he confirmed thoughtfully.

He tilted the angle of the artifact for a better look—and Ellie heard a soft but distinct rattle.

Both she and Mr. Al-Ahmed went still, their eyes locking with a matched look of significance.

Neil's voice called out stridently behind her. "I will not be threatened inside my own—"

"Quiet," Adam ordered, his voice low and serious as he looked up at the tomb shaft. "We've got company."

Ellie's gaze snapped to the dark opening in the ceiling… and the clamor of distance voices echoed down to her from above.

TEN

*B*ESIDE ELLIE, MR. AL-AHMED still frowned thoughtfully at the wooden box, seemingly oblivious to the chaos blooming behind him. With a muttered prayer, he set his thumb to the gold disk inlaid into the narrow front face—and pressed.

The gold sank into the cypress with a distinct click.

"We should prepare for battle!" Constance declared in a stout whisper.

"Battle?" Neil's eyes widened with panic, even as he continued to keep his voice low. "There's no battling in archaeology!"

A thin, dark gap opened along one of the edges of the interior floor of the box.

"Pick," Mr. Al-Ahmed ordered automatically, holding out his hand. Ellie startled, then spotted his opened box of tools nearby. She plucked out a slender metal instrument with a hooked end.

Mr. Al-Ahmed accepted it, carefully sliding it beneath the base of the box.

"I've got an idea." Adam grasped the rope to the shaft and started to climb.

Ellie hurried over to the opening in the ceiling, looking up at the bottom of Adam's battered work boots. "Please tell me that your idea isn't to try to fend them off single-handedly!"

"I'm not that crazy," Adam muttered down to her. "But you might want to step back."

He yanked the machete from his belt and neatly cut the rope.

Ellie took a quick stumble away as the severed length snaked down in front of her, coming to rest in the long coil of woven hemp. Adam followed, dropping from the tomb shaft and landing in a crouch.

"That'll buy us a little more time," he said, shaking off his recently wounded hand with a wince.

"But you… you cut the rope!" Neil stammered, paling. "How are we supposed to get out of here without a rope?"

"Tunnel," Adam replied, shoving his machete back into its sheath.

"That tunnel," Neil whispered desperately, stabbing a finger back at the precarious black opening in the wall behind him. "The one that is two thousand years old. The one that looks as though it is about to collapse. And which most likely leads to nowhere."

Mr. Al-Ahmed paused in his careful work on the interior of the jewelry box. "That would… not be an entirely accurate statement."

"Why not?" Neil demanded.

"A few months ago, one of the workers found an opening under a slab near one of the spoil dumps to the southeast of the temple complex," Mr. Al-Ahmed replied, keeping his voice low. "Which turned out to be a very simple late Twentieth Dynasty tomb shaft—entirely cleared out, of course, by looters or Frenchmen."

"For all the difference there is between them," Ellie grumbled.

"I mean to say that it was not a site of any interest," Mr. Al-Ahmed hurried on. "But when I descended into it—"

"Descended?!" Neil cut in with a hiss.

"I could not know that it was not a site of value until I had seen it, could I?" Mr. Al-Ahmed protested uncomfortably, then went back to his work at the interior of the wooden box. "But while I was inside, it is possible that I might have seen an opening to a thieves' tunnel in the northern wall, the orientation of which would roughly align with the location for the burial chamber in this complex."

"But did you go into the tunnel?" Constance pressed excitedly.

"Absolutely not!" Mr. Al-Ahmed was clearly aghast at the notion. "It is almost certainly a death trap!"

"So's going upstairs," Adam pointed out.

"But Dawson won't know there's anything wrong—not yet," Ellie reasoned.

He met her eyes, his expression grim. "And just how long do you think it's gonna take him to figure it out once he sees us?"

With a soft click, the interior floor of the jewelry box came loose. Mr. Al-Ahmed looked down at it in surprise, as though he had nearly forgotten that he was still working at it. Carefully, he lifted the delicate wooden panel away, exposing a narrow compartment that lay hidden beneath it.

The compartment was not empty. It held a finely made loop of glimmering electrum, the alloy hued a subtle bronze. A flat bezel at the top was inscribed with a cluster of hieroglyphs.

"It's a seal ring!" Ellie breathed wonderingly.

Mr. Al-Ahmed carefully plucked it from the box, shifting it toward the lamplight to illuminate the symbols.

"*True servant, beloved of his lord,*" he read off easily.

"*The king's scribe, Ahmose,*" Ellie filled in, leaning over him for a closer look.

"The proper pronunciation is 'Yahmoseh,'" Mr. Al-Ahmed corrected her distractedly.

A chill danced over Ellie's skin despite the warm air. "But something has been done to one of the glyphs. The crescent moon symbol—it's filled in with plaster."

"That's the glyph for Yah," Mr. Al-Ahmed clarified. "The god of the moon."

Neil whirled back toward them, his gaze sharpening with sudden interest. "Hold on—did you say the name of the god was *deliberately* filled in?"

The chill electrifying Ellie's skin intensified, raising the hairs on her arms. "But if the glyph was filled, that sound wouldn't have imprinted itself into the wax when the seal was used."

Neil held out his hand. "Could I... *please?*" he asked, the word tinged with desperation.

Mr. Al-Ahmed carefully passed him the ring, which Neil cradled reverently in his hand.

"The god's name was *intentionally* removed from this seal..." Neil began urgently.

Ellie had already started talking as well. "But the elimination of the phoneme for Yah would have made the name..."

"...which means that this artifact must be..." Neil continued.

"Moseh," Ellie finished.

"Atenist," Neil blurted.

She and Neil turned to each other, eyes locking with a mirrored astonishment at the significance of their mutual revelations.

Mr. Al-Ahmed didn't seem to hear any of it. His attention was locked on the jewelry box. "Do you know—I think there is an inscription under this false floor," he observed with obvious delight. "It appears to be in a form of hieratic."

"Sorry to cut in," Adam said darkly, his hand moving to the hilt of his machete. "But I think we're out of time."

The muffled voices from above grew louder—and the outraged tones of Professor Dawson echoed clearly down the shaft.

"I thought you said this site was secure!"

"Of course, it's secure," came the easy, confident reply… in a voice that Ellie recognized from Lady Sabita's dinner party the night before.

"But that's Mr. Forster-Mowbray!" she hissed.

Adam pinched the bridge of his nose as though fighting the sudden onset of a headache. "The Mustache is the amir," he muttered flatly. "Just my goddamned luck."

"Lady Sabita did say he moved in Egyptological circles," Ellie offered weakly.

"Mr. Forster-Mowbray is the local representative of the British Athenaeum," Neil said distractedly, still intently studying the seal ring.

"I am shocked to find him involved in anything so interesting as your Athenaeum, never mind an international ring of magical artifact thieves," Constance mused in a conspiratorial whisper.

"*Magical?*" Neil's gaze snapped up to Constance and Ellie as he fumbled his hold on the artifact.

"Fiddlesticks," Ellie muttered.

"Is that you, Fairfax?" Julian shouted down through the darkness of the shaft. "You all right down there?"

"M-maybe?" Neil stammered back, clutching the ring to his chest. "I mean—yes! Perfectly jolly! Ha ha ha!"

"Are you quite sure?" Julian pressed. "You seem to be short half a rope."

Neil had begun to sweat. "Oh, that! Oddest thing, really. Just—ah—broke on us, you see. But we're already working on a… er, solution to the, uh…"

His panicked gaze roved over the rest of them, leaping from a machete-wielding Adam to a dust-smeared Constance, and then Mr. Al-Ahmed, who was frowning over a three-thousand-year-old jewelry box.

His eyes finally slid to Ellie with a look of desperation.

"I must say, I'm surprised to find you down here." Julian's tone was lightly admonishing as it echoed down from the chamber above. "I had thought you were to notify me when you cleared the next entrance so that I could join you."

Neil paled further and slowly closed his eyes.

"But no need to worry," Julian finished cheerfully. "We'll sort you out in a jiffy."

The silence that followed felt like a ticking clock.

"*That the true story be known…*" Mr. Al-Ahmed read.

"What?" Ellie rasped, her throat dry.

"The inscription in the box," Mr. Al-Ahmed replied impatiently, as though the answer should have been obvious. "It begins, *That the true story be known.*"

"The true story of what?" Ellie pressed urgently.

"I haven't gotten far enough to say," Mr. Al-Ahmed replied with a quelling look that reminded Ellie of one of her old professors. "There are a significant number of ligatures and abbreviations, which likely means that it is a more informal variety of hieratic."

"Princess…" Adam said warningly from where he stood ready below the dark mouth of the tomb shaft.

Ellie let her eyes roam over the mountains of unexamined debris piled against the walls of the room.

A box with an Atenist ring. The name Moseh. An ancient text that promised a *true story*.

That was all she had. She prayed it was enough.

At the top of the shaft, Julian Forster-Mowbray laughed again.

Ellie set a hand on Mr. Al-Ahmed's shoulder, capturing his attention. "I know it is not at all in keeping with proper archaeological practices, but if we should find ourselves needing to make an immediate removal from this chamber—say through an unstable two-thousand-year-old thieves' tunnel— what would be the safest way to transport that box without damaging it?"

Mr. Al-Ahmed's eyes widened. He looked from Ellie to the box with the air of a frightened parent. Then his shoulders sagged. "Might I have your scarf, Miss Tyrrell?" he asked politely.

"Oh!" Constance returned. "Certainly."

She tugged the length of frothy fabric from her neck and handed it over. Mr. Al-Ahmed gently wound it around the box.

"Hold this—carefully!" he ordered as he passed the bundle to Ellie.

With a sigh of grim resignation, he dumped out the contents of his slender leather tool case.

"What are you doing?!" Neil looked urgently from the mouth of the shaft overhead to the place where his foreman knelt on the floor.

"I am not entirely sure," Mr. Al-Ahmed calmly admitted, holding out his hands.

Ellie set the box into them, and Mr. Al-Ahmed carefully placed it in his case. He snapped the lid shut. After a moment's hesitation, he shoved the whole thing down the front of his waistcoat.

He trudged to the hole in the tomb wall, where he paused to glance back at her. "I look forward to hearing the full story behind your business here, Miss Mallory," he said significantly.

"I promise you that I will provide it, Mr. Al-Ahmed," Ellie vowed.

He gave her a nod. Picking up one of their two lanterns, he drew in an unhappy breath—and crawled into the tunnel.

"Sayyid, where are you—!" Neil exclaimed, wide-eyed. "You can't possibly be—!"

"Neil," Ellie said calmly, holding out her hand. "The ring."

Neil looked from her to the gold-hued relic he still held in his palm, his expression twisted with conflict. "But we haven't recorded the context!" he protested forlornly.

"I know," Ellie said sympathetically. "And I am sorry for it. But we need to go."

"No!" Neil burst out. He caught himself, containing his volume with obvious effort. "Why should we throw ourselves into a potentially deadly tunnel when the only thing at risk here is that I am about to *lose my job?*"

"Afraid it might be a bit more than that," Adam cautioned as he watched the entrance to the shaft, his knife still ready in his hand.

Ellie grasped her brother's shoulders, forcing him to face her. "I understand that this is all terribly hard to accept, but if you have ever had any faith in my intelligence and judgment, I am begging you to do what I am asking."

Neil gazed at her helplessly. "I… I'm not… I don't…"

Something inside of Ellie started to crack like a delicate fault in the surface of an old vase.

"Bugger it," Constance declared.

She tossed up the light froth of her skirts. Neil's eyes snapped to the exposed skin of her knee, his jaw dropping.

His expression turned to a different sort of shock as Constance whipped a neat little dagger from a sheath at her thigh.

"Into the tunnel, Stuffy," she ordered, pointing the blade at him.

"You can't seriously mean to—yeek!" Neil's words dissolved into a truncated shriek as Constance gave him a little jab.

He looked desperately to Ellie and Adam—neither of whom made any move to intercede.

"Quickly, now," Constance cheerfully urged.

With an expression of horrified betrayal, Neil shoved the ring into his pocket and scrambled into the tunnel. Constance agilely followed behind him.

"Your turn," Adam ordered with a pointed look back at Ellie as he wound the long coil of their severed rope around his shoulder.

Ellie knew better than to argue. She quickly crawled into the dark mouth in the wall, uncomfortably conscious of the dusty age of the timber supports that framed it.

A new rope unfurled through the tomb shaft. It hit the floor of the burial chamber with a soft slap… and immediately started to twitch.

Adam's look darkened. "And get ready to yank on me."

"Yank on you?" Ellie echoed. "Why on earth would I need to—"

Before she could finish, a stranger dropped into the room—a lanky Egyptian fellow in a turban and galabeya, his narrow chin marred by the white slash of a scar. At the sight of Adam and the machete, he grinned and swung a rifle from his shoulder up into his hands.

Another intruder descended behind him. He looked remarkably like the first man, with the same pointed chin and beak-like nose, except that he was stouter in build and sported an enormous black beard.

He hefted a big cudgel in his hands, eyes glinting threateningly.

Behind them, Julian Forster-Mowbray slid into view. He straightened and brushed off his tailored khaki suit. Dust settled onto his gleaming jodhpurs. "Goodness! Mr. Bates and Miss Mallory? I hardly expected to see *you* here."

"Mr. Forster-Mowbray," Ellie cautiously acknowledged from where she crouched in the mouth of the tunnel, conscious of Constance, Neil, and Mr. Al-Ahmed hiding in the darkness behind her.

The rope jerked again, more awkwardly and frantically, and Professor Dawson fell into the tomb. He landed roughly on his rear, scrambling back up and tugging to adjust his tweed suit and pith helmet.

"Please tell me we haven't any more climbing to—*What?!*" he exclaimed, eyes bulging at the sight of Ellie and Adam. "Not you two again!"

"Miss us?" Adam drawled, his tone deceptively lazy.

"Shoot them!" Dawson dashed behind the bearded thug. "Shoot them before they collapse this entire tomb on us!"

"Wasn't planning on collapsing any tombs," Adam noted casually. "Were you, Princess?"

"I hardly *planned* on collapsing anything back in British Honduras," Ellie retorted. "Sometimes one is confronted with unexpected circumstances where an explosion simply becomes inevitable."

Dawson made a strangled noise of terror from his hiding place behind the confused-looking Egyptian.

"Hold on!" Julian said with a look of surprise, jabbing a finger toward Ellie and Adam. "*This* is the couple you were telling me about?"

"Less talking!" Dawson squawked. "More shooting!"

"Surely we can discuss this like reasonable people," Julian pressed uncomfortably. "It seems a bit much to go straight into tossing bullets around."

"You have no idea what sort of menace you are up against!" Dawson pleaded.

"I'm actually feeling kinda flattered," Adam said with a hint of surprise.

"You will be feeling less flattered if they actually shoot you," Ellie retorted tersely.

Julian put his fingertips to his temple, looking harried. "I suppose needs must," he concluded tightly. He flapped a hand at the two Egyptians. "Get on with it, then."

The scarred man and the bearded one exchanged a confused look.

"Remember what I said a minute ago?" Adam muttered back at Ellie without looking away from the cluster of men by the shaft.

"That bit about the yanking?" Ellie pressed back uncertainly.

"Go on!" Julian ordered impatiently, then huffed out a sigh. "Right. Dashed Arabic. Al-Saboor!" he shouted up the shaft.

"Yes, Amir!" an Egyptian-accented voice called down.

"Tell your cousins to shoot the people in the tomb!" Julian shouted up irritably.

A line of Masri echoed down from the opening to the tomb shaft. The bearded Egyptian pulled a pistol from the sash of his belt as his cousin leveled his rifle.

Adam leapt into the tunnel, landing halfway across Ellie's lap.

A pair of gunshots thundered into the opening. Clods of loose earth rained down onto her face from the impact of the bullets.

Flipping nimbly onto his back, Adam set his boots to the half-rotted wooden supports to either side of the tunnel mouth.

"Time for that yank," he informed her—and kicked.

As another gunshot cracked across the silence, the ancient beams exploded into dust—and the mouth of the tunnel collapsed.

ELEVEN

*E*LLIE HAULED ON Adam as the tunnel caved in around them, dirt pelting down against her face. The dull thunder of another gunshot was nearly lost in the thick rush of falling earth—until the avalanche finally slowed.

She lay on her back with Adam sprawled halfway on top of her. Carefully, she drew in a breath. She was surprised to find that she *could* breathe.

The splintering pillars of another two-thousand-year-old wooden brace stood to either side of her head. The frame had somehow halted the progress of the collapse—though it creaked ominously above her, sending a little shower of dust down onto her forehead.

Ellie sneezed. At the sound, Neil let out a strangled gurgle of terror from behind her.

In the light of Mr. Al-Ahmed's lantern, Neil's face was streaked with dirt, his spectacles sitting crooked on his nose. Beside him, Constance's curls were coming loose from the precarious bundle of her bun, her white lawn dress marred with mud.

Mr. Al-Ahmed crouched behind them, gazing at the blocked tunnel with wide eyes.

"Wh-what was that?" Neil demanded in choked tones, blinking at the new wall of earth that blocked off the tunnel and buried Adam to his knees.

"Afraid we had to make this a one-way," Adam replied, attempting to wriggle his foot. "What with the gunshots and all."

Neil gaped at the wall of dirt. "No, no, no," he stammered wildly. "You must have heard that wrong. Mr. Forster-Mowbray would never have shot at us."

"Because he's your boss?" Adam drawled back.

"Because he's the official Cairo liaison of the British Athenaeum for Egyptological Studies, and a well-bred gentleman!"

"Well-bred gentlemen do awful things all the time!" Ellie retorted.

"I heard three gunshots, at least," Constance offered cheerfully. "This is all dreadfully exciting!"

Neil gaped at her with horrified dismay. "*Exciting?*" he echoed, and then threw up his hands—at least as far as he could within the confines of the tunnel. "Well, why not? Why wouldn't you think someone shooting at you is exciting? You thought starting a fire in the back garden was exciting, too!"

"A fire in the back garden?" Ellie frowned. "I'm not sure I remember that one."

"It was when we were playing The Sack of Troy," Constance replied.

"Perhaps the more important question is whether we have actually escaped these men who may or may not have been shooting at us," Mr. Al-Ahmed offered a little weakly.

"It would appear that we have," Ellie returned uncertainly.

"At least until they start digging." Adam addressed the words to the ceiling, as he was still lying across her lap.

"But the tunnel isn't stable!" Mr. Al-Ahmed ran a frantic hand through his dusty hair. "If they disturb the fill, they could bring the rest of it down on us!"

"Mr. Forster-Mowbray wouldn't—" Neil began.

"He most certainly would!" Ellie shot back crossly.

"In either case, it would seem prudent that we exit this place as soon as possible," Mr. Al-Ahmed urged.

"I'm with him." Adam sat up, freeing Ellie of his weight, and then looked down. "Just as soon as I dig out my legs."

He started shoveling with his hands.

Ellie squirmed the rest of the way free—and cast an uneasy gaze past him at the cave-in. "I didn't see Jacobs back there."

"No," Adam agreed grimly, digging at his left knee.

"Could he have stayed behind in British Honduras?" she offered hopefully.

"Would be pretty great if he had." Adam yanked a leg loose. "But I'm betting that's too much to hope for."

He tugged at his still-buried right side. It stayed stuck. With a frown, he braced his free boot against the piled earth and shoved. He popped free, sprawling back into Ellie again and revealing a foot clad only with a very dirty sock. "Dammit. Lost my boot."

He reached into the place where his leg had been, fishing around in the dirt.

"Ellie, maybe he could use a bit more light," Constance suggested meaningfully.

"Oh!" Ellie jolted as she realized what Constance was talking about. She fumbled for her pocket and pulled out the cigar tube.

"Have you taken up *smoking* now as well?" Neil exclaimed with obvious dismay.

"Oh, do be quiet!" Ellie snapped, her nerves frazzled beyond the point of making a more tactful response.

She slipped the firebird bone out into her hand.

"Got it!" Adam announced.

He yanked a filthy boot from the dirt—and the walls around them fell in.

Constance grabbed the back of Neil's shirt, yanking him with her as she launched herself deeper into the tunnel. Mr. Al-Ahmed caught Ellie by the arm, hauling at her as Adam scrambled back and the dirt cascaded down around them.

They burst past the crooked frame of another old support, where Ellie fell onto Mr. Al-Ahmed's shoes.

Her ears rang with the delicate patter of loose earth as the newly collapsed section settled a few inches from her heels.

"I've just lost my job, haven't I?" Neil asked mournfully from where he lay sprawled beneath Constance.

"Is that really your greatest concern right now?" Ellie pressed irritably from between Mr. Al-Ahmed's ankles.

"I'm sure you can clear it all up with a nicely-worded letter," Constance offered sarcastically.

"Do you think so?" Neil asked hopefully.

Constance rolled her eyes, then braced her hands against Neil's tweed waistcoat and shoved herself up into a seated position.

She paused as she thoughtfully pushed against his chest. Her gaze down at Ellie's brother shifted to one of dangerous interest. "Well, that's a surprise."

"What is?" Neil asked weakly, his eyes wide.

"If any other shoes have been swallowed," Mr. Al-Ahmed begged, "let us please leave them where they are?"

"Fine by me," Adam replied. He held his boot in one hand and very carefully pulled his feet free of the loose debris at the edge of the collapse.

Ellie sat up—and realized that her own hand was empty. With a worried jolt, she patted at her muddy blouse and skirt, then the ground around her. "I've lost it!" she burst out.

"What—your bone?" Constance lurched across Neil to grab the lantern, then pivoted to straddle him before crawling free.

Neil sucked in a whoosh of breath, staring after her with shock.

Constance held the light up to the wall of splintered wood and earth. "Here it is!" she announced cheerfully.

She reached for the white stick of the bone where it protruded from the pile.

"No!" Mr. Al-Ahmed and Ellie both shouted at once—but Constance had already plucked it loose.

Nothing happened.

"Here." Constance handed the arcanum over.

Ellie accepted it with a wash of relief and gave it a flick. The bone whispered with a subtle spark of illumination—and nothing more.

She tried it again, using the same practiced snap of her wrist. The arcanum stayed dark.

"What is she doing?" Mr. Al-Ahmed asked quietly, staring at her with worry.

"Maybe try it the other way," Adam suggested sympathetically.

Ellie repressed a scowl at the thought of how ridiculous she was about to look—but shook the bone like an angry toddler.

Mr. Al-Ahmed's eyes went wide. Constance's lips pursed into a puzzled frown.

Neil stared aghast as though he had just concluded that his sister was, in fact, a lunatic.

"It isn't working," Ellie concluded desperately when the arcanum didn't so much as flicker.

Adam took it from her and gave it a casually vigorous shake of his own.

Neil looked queasy.

"Huh." Adam moved the bone into the light of the lantern. "Something dinged it—right here."

Ellie took it back from him. She examined it urgently, and her stomach dropped. "It looks like a stone chipped off one of the Glagolitic characters."

"Can't you just draw it back on?" Constance suggested.

"I don't know if that would fix it," Ellie said woefully. "And my Glagolitic is terrible!"

"What does the bone in your cigar tube have to do with an early Slavic writing system?" Neil asked with an excessive, nervous care.

Ellie stared at him. How could she possibly explain to her skeptical brother that she was holding a piece of a legend in her hand—now that she'd lost her only means of convincing him that such things actually existed?

"How about we talk it all over once we figure out whether this tunnel really has an 'out' hole?" Adam cut in. "You know—before the bad guys dig us out of here or the whole thing comes crashing down on our heads?"

"We had best go… the only way we can, then," Mr. Al-Ahmed concluded helplessly, then led them forward in a bedraggled, crawling parade.

A thankfully short time later, they spilled out into the narrow confines of another burial chamber. The light of the lantern revealed it to be a simple tomb without the rich ornamentation of Horemheb's complex—a mere box carved from the ground, empty of everything but rubble and scattered bones, most of them animals. Ellie spotted a little Napoleonic graffiti on the walls.

Neil's eyes widened happily at the sight. He stopped short, gazing around the humble, narrow space with obvious admiration. "This is actually an excellent example of Ramesside administrative tomb building! Note the positioning of the sarcophagus pit, and that cut portion of the wall was almost certainly a funeral stele—"

"The sarcophagus pit is very nice." Constance hooked a hand through Neil's elbow. "And I'm sure you can come back and examine it in detail when we are no longer being pursued by people who mean to kill us."

She hauled him up the steep ramp that led out of the burial chamber. Ellie trailed behind them. It really was a very fine example of Ramesside administrative tomb building, even if it had been entirely cleared out.

At the top of the ramp, she joined the others in a claustrophobic antechamber. Another square black tomb shaft was cut into the ceiling. Ellie peered up at it.

"It looks blocked," she noted uneasily.

"That's because I set a pair of pavers over it," Mr. Al-Ahmed replied. "They ought to be simple enough to push aside—assuming that we can get up there."

"I can do it," Adam announced as he tugged on his loose boot. "So long as one of you guys can play ladder."

Ellie looked to her brother, but he was gazing back down the ramp to the burial chamber. "Some of those pot shards might allow for a more precise dating…" he said forlornly.

With a sigh, Mr. Al-Ahmed handed Ellie the lantern. He pulled his tool case from his waistcoat as though afraid to see what damage it had sustained, but the slender leather box appeared to be intact.

Ellie held out her other hand for it. Mr. Al-Ahmed passed it to her carefully and then planted himself under the mouth of the shaft.

"Oh drat," Ellie blurted as she realized what Adam intended. "Are you sure that's a good idea?"

"It's fine," Adam assured her as he stepped onto Mr. Al-Ahmed's knee.

"But that shaft must be—" Ellie began.

Adam cut her off with a quickly raised hand. "—Nice and dark," he finished for her pointedly. "Which makes it real hard to see how high it is. And that means it's probably not so high at all. Right, Sayyid?"

"Er…" Mr. Al-Ahmed began awkwardly.

"There you go," Adam concluded.

He stepped from Mr. Al-Ahmed's knee to his shoulder and boosted himself into the opening of the shaft—the foreman coughing out a mouthful of Masri as he lurched under Adam's weight.

The opening was roughly three feet across. Adam wedged himself into it, planting his boots against one wall with his back braced against the opposite side. The coil of rope that he had salvaged from Mutnedjmet's burial chamber was looped around his neck.

Constance joined Ellie and Mr. Al-Ahmed under the opening as they watched Adam's ascending form.

"Is your gentleman always this… vigorous?" Mr. Al-Ahmed asked.

"It really is quite impressive," Constance agreed with obvious and slightly wicked appreciation.

"He's not my…" Ellie began, and then sighed. "Well—yes. But you might also wish to move, in case he realizes how high up he is."

"I might not have to realize it at all," Adam called down with forced cheer, "if you'd stop bringing it up."

"What happens if he realizes how high up he is?" Constance asked.

The scuffling noises of Adam's ascent paused. "Hoooh boy," he said, his voice distinctly queasy.

Mr. Al-Ahmed's eyes widened with understanding, and he took a quick, substantial step back from the opening in the ceiling, courteously bringing Constance with him.

"Do you need assistance?" Ellie called up through the tomb shaft—though at a careful pace away.

"Nope," Adam said tightly. "Just… gonna breathe here for a minute."

With a string of muttered curses that raised Constance's eyebrows and made Mr. Al-Ahmed blush, the sounds of Adam's ascent resumed.

"Made it up," he reported back, his breath a little tight. "Just… need to clear the slabs."

A loud scrape indicated the movement of the paving stones laid over the shaft's mouth. Ellie risked another look and saw Adam haul himself through the new-formed gap—and immediately flop over out of view.

"Told you I wasssn't gonna puke," he called down triumphantly from above, the words a little slurred. "Imma man of m'word."

"You most certainly are," Ellie said in return. "Now could you send down the rope?"

"Sure," Adam promised. "Just as soon as the sky stops spinning."

Adam hauled each of them up in turn. Constance went first, Ellie following to emerge into a splendid desert twilight. The sky had turned to a deep purple, casting the rubble-strewn plain of the necropolis into gloom and shadows. Ellie could just make out the lumpy silhouettes of a few small Old Kingdom pyramids and the ragged walls of funerary temples.

She had only a moment to take it in before Constance tugged her down behind the knee-high remnants of a Twentieth Dynasty chapel wall. Her white lawn dress was smudged with dirt, as was her face. Her hair had come mostly unraveled, dark curls falling around her shoulders.

"Looks like they're on the hunt," Constance reported in a slightly gleeful whisper.

Neil's excavation lay about forty yards to the north. The pit that held Horemheb's funerary temple sparked with escaping flares of lantern light. Voices called out urgently as more lights fanned out across the surrounding ruins.

Neil squirmed from the tomb shaft with an awkward groan and staggered free of it, half slumping against another pile of rubble. Mr. Al-Ahmed ascended last, Adam lending an arm to lever him free. The foreman brushed at his trousers in a futile attempt to tidy himself, but he remained as hopelessly disheveled as the rest of them.

Adam worked to shove the slabs back into place over the opening.

Neil staggered to where Ellie and Constance hid. He stared out at the lights of the dig with a forlorn expression. "I had recommendations from four Cambridge deans."

"What's that?" Ellie prompted, confused.

"One even wrote to his cousin at the Royal Geographical Society to put in a word for me," Neil continued mournfully. "How is anyone from the Royal Geographical Society going to put in a word for me after this?"

Constance rolled her eyes. Ellie felt a dart of guilt.

"I've lost all of it, haven't I?" Neil said, a note of panic entering his voice. "My position. My reputation. My prospects for future employment. It's all gone."

"I am sorry, Neil." Ellie's heart sank like a lead weight. "I promise you that was never my intention. The timing just turned out to be awful in a way none of us could have predicted."

"Wouldn't have happened," Adam cut in with a grunt as he shoved the final slab into place, "if I still had my lucky rock."

Ellie barely suppressed her huff of frustration. "Your lucky rock must've weighed eight pounds," she pointed out impatiently. "Were you going to carry it around the whole of Egypt with you?"

"It still would've worked if I'd left it with my stuff," Adam returned authoritatively as he came over to join her.

Ellie threw up her hands. "How does that make any sort of sense?"

"But why do you know about Bates's lucky rock?" Neil asked helplessly.

Ellie went still—and Neil's eyes widened with a dawning and terrible understanding.

"You… you didn't just arrive at my tomb at the same time. Did you?" he demanded. "You came here together! Why did you come here together? How… *How* did you come here together?!"

Constance popped down to sit on a block of limestone, making herself comfortable. "I won't say I haven't been looking forward to this," she admitted conspiratorially to Mr. Al-Ahmed.

"Mr. Bates and I have been traveling together," Ellie replied carefully, her pulse fluttering nervously, "after a series of unforeseen circumstances necessitated that I undertake a journey to British Honduras, where by pure chance—"

"British Honduras?" Neil's face paled. "Why were you in British Honduras?!"

Ellie fought to maintain her equanimity. "Rather a lot has happened since we last exchanged letters, but I believe you will agree that we handled the situation as rationally and reasonably as possible, given the circumstances, once I have had a chance to fully explain—"

"But how long has this been going on?" Neil's gaze shot wildly between them.

"Six weeks," Adam replied flatly, meeting Neil's gaze.

"Six weeks?!" Neil squawked, his voice rising. "The two of you have been traveling together for *six weeks*?!"

"As I said," Ellie pressed on firmly, "circumstances were—"

"It's not Ellie's fault," Adam cut in sharply.

"But were you *alone* together?" Neil squawked.

"Well, I was hardly going to drag a chaperone into the wilds of the Cayo District…" Ellie's tone sharpened as her patience thinned.

"Yes," Adam replied.

Ellie shot him an uncomfortable look.

"Have you…" Neil flapped a hand helplessly, then coughed out the word. "…*Touched* each other?"

"Really, this is getting quite patriarchal!" Ellie protested stoutly.

"Ellie…" Adam started, his look pleading.

"But did you…" Neil frankly choked on the rest—not that he needed to say it.

"Neil Fairfax!" Ellie scolded.

"It's not like that," Adam shot back.

Neil's shoulders slumped with relief. He rubbed a tired hand over his features. "So you two haven't kissed?" he offered hopefully.

Ellie's mouth clamped shut. Her cheeks burned.

Adam turned his gaze to the sprawling evening sky as he let out a long, low breath.

Neil's face was drawn into lines of horror. He tried to speak. All that came out was a strangled gurgle in the back of his throat.

"That was very nearly a *khaa*," Mr. Al-Ahmed observed helpfully from where he had joined Constance to watch the show.

"You should challenge him to a duel, Stuffy," Constance gleefully suggested.

Mr. Al-Ahmed looked both alarmed and intrigued. "Do Englishmen still do that?"

"I'm not English," Adam quickly pointed out.

"And what do they do in America when you dishonor someone's sister?" Mr. Al-Ahmed prompted mercilessly.

"We, uh…" Adam began uncomfortably, "maybe talk it all over. Give them a little time to explain things, and…"

Ellie put her hand on his arm to silence him. "We don't have *time* for any of this! In case you have forgotten, the better part of your own workforce is currently hunting for us at the behest of your murderous employer!"

Neil put his face in his hands. "Thiff iff the worft day of mwy wiffe!" he moaned, the words muffled by his palms.

"We need to find someplace safe to regroup and make a plan," Ellie declared.

Adam nodded toward the dig site. "What about Mr. M? Is he gonna need a rescue?"

"Mr. Mahjoud? Need a rescue?" Constance scoffed. "I am quite certain he is capable of skewering the whole lot of them if he chooses."

"Is he?" Ellie frowned, thinking of the exceptionally well-dressed and tiredly disapproving dragoman.

"He's Sudanese," Constance said as though the answer were self-explanatory. "So where do we go? Mariette's House is out of the question, as is any public accommodation in Badrashin—those are the first places they will think we have gone." Her eyes glittered excitedly. "Perhaps we can find a troop of river pirates and convince them to join our cause!"

Mr. Al-Ahmed rubbed his face. The gesture only made it even more dirty. He let out a sigh. "I know where we can go."

Without waiting for a response, he trudged toward the shadowy line of distant date palms that marked the edge of the inundation zone.

Constance gave Ellie a surprised look, then hurried after him, her footsteps light.

Ellie glanced back at her brother.

Neil was staring once more at the lights and noise of his former excavation. With a slow and eloquent sigh of dismay, he turned and slumped wearily after Mr. Al-Ahmed and Constance like a man condemned.

Adam lingered behind, his posture stiff as he gazed out over the shadowy expanse of the desert.

"Adam?" Ellie prompted softly.

He tore himself from his silent study to join her, but remained unusually quiet. Through the shadows of the evening, his expression looked like a closed door. "We should catch up."

Silence fell after his words, thick and uneasy. Ellie realized that he was waiting for her—that even in this odd, brooding state, he still wouldn't go unless he knew she was coming with him.

"Why won't you tell me what's wrong?" she pressed stubbornly.

He finally looked down at her. His expression was pained. "I…" He stopped, rubbing at the bridge of his nose as though fighting a headache. "This isn't a good time."

Ellie's heart twisted nervously in her chest, tight with unexpected fear. Part of her flinched back in response, wanting to close up—to protect herself before she could get hurt.

She drew in a careful, deliberate breath—and reached out to take his hand instead.

His expression softened as he looked down at the place where her fingers clasped the handkerchief wrapped over his wounded palm.

"But you *will* tell me," Ellie insisted.

For just a moment, his warm, strong grip tightened around her own. He gave her an uncertain nod, then let her go.

"Come on, Princess," he said solemnly and led her after the others.

TWELVE

$\mathcal{M}$R. AL-AHMED LED THEM along a winding trail that was barely discernible from the rocky ground of the desert necropolis. Overhead, the last vestiges of twilight slipped below the horizon, bringing a greater array of stars out against the rich darkness overhead.

They passed into the tidy rows of towering date palms that loomed silently against the sand like watching sentinels. Mr. Al-Ahmed steered them unerringly along a dirt path through knee-high fields of rice and sorghum threaded with the shimmering lines of canals. Here and there, low mud-brick houses punctuated the scene, lamplight flickering from behind their window screens.

A mile later, Ellie's guide took a turn onto a narrower track that led them to a tidy single-story house of whitewashed mud-brick framed by flowering shrubs and palms. The building was set on a little rise safely above the level of the inundation. A cluster of humbler homes stood a little distance away, but the spot was otherwise quite private, with views across both the green fields and the broad, still sands of the desert.

Light glimmered through the meshrabiyeh screens over the windows, framing a freshly painted door.

"Whose house is this?" Ellie asked quietly.

"Mine, for now," Mr. Al-Ahmed replied.

"Hold on!" Neil stopped short in the path. "You have a *house* here?"

Mr. Al-Ahmed sighed and turned back to him. "Yes?"

"I thought you slept in one of the tents!" Neil protested.

"Why would I sleep in a tent when I can stay in a nice house?" Mr. Al-Ahmed countered.

"But *I'm* sleeping in a tent! I thought that was the way it was done!"

Mr. Al-Ahmed made a dismissive noise. "Pssh. My abba always rented a house for his excavations if there was one available nearby for a reasonable rate."

Ellie hadn't thought it was possible for her brother to look even more dejected, but somehow he managed it.

They reached the door. Mr. Al-Ahmed paused at the threshold with an awkward look back at the rest of them. "Could you… wait here for a moment?"

A little spill of lamplight fell across the path as he slipped inside.

Ellie could just make out a rapid and tense exchange from beyond the door. Mr. Al-Ahmed's tones were apologetic. A strong female voice answered him. It sounded frustrated and disapproving.

"I thought he stayed in a tent," Neil voiced in low, mournful tones as he stared bewilderingly at the house.

The door swung open, framing both Mr. Al-Ahmed and the woman Ellie had heard speaking. She was an Egyptian lady dressed in a fitted yelek gown slit at the sides to reveal loose trousers. The fabric was an emerald hue that set off the green tones in her eyes. The hijab that covered her hair was elegantly embroidered.

She was studying them with obvious irritation.

"Please, come in," Mr. Al-Ahmed said with an uncomfortable smile.

Past the crooked entryway, Mr. Al-Ahmed led them through a small courtyard into a comfortably appointed sitting room. The furnishings were in a mix of Egyptian and European styles, with a low divan, a few over-stuffed chairs, and a coffee table. A pile of books with titles in English, French, and Arabic sat beside a wooden desk clock.

The green-eyed woman planted herself in one of the chairs in a manner that clearly indicated she had no intention of being moved from it.

"Ya habibti," Sayyid said a little nervously. "I believe you remember Dr. Fairfax. This is his sister, Miss Mallory, and her friends Mr. Bates and Miss Tyrrell. Everyone, this is my wife, Zeinab."

"Do sit down." Mrs. Al-Ahmed's words were ostensibly polite, but they had the air of a general issuing an order. "I am, of course, eager for my dear husband to further explain what brought this *unexpected* visit about."

Ellie plopped down onto the nearest piece of furniture, which happened to be the divan. Mr. Al-Ahmed took the chair beside his wife, eyeing her nervously, while Constance cheerfully made herself at home on an ottoman.

Neil stopped behind a sofa, staring at all of them blankly as though he couldn't quite fathom how he had come to be there.

Adam crossed to the window, leaning against the wall as he gazed out through the screen, his posture one of careful readiness.

Checking to make sure they hadn't been followed, Ellie realized.

An awkward silence followed. Ellie took it upon herself to break it. "Do you live here throughout the dig season, Mrs. Al-Ahmed?"

"No," Mrs. Al-Ahmed replied shortly. "My work is in Cairo. Fridays are the one day of the week when I can visit my husband."

"Zeinab is a daya—a midwife," Mr. Al-Ahmed explained with a note of pride. "She is very sought after for her skills."

"A midwife, did you say?" Constance perked up.

"Yes?" Mrs. Al-Ahmed replied cautiously.

"And you don't veil or retire to the haramlek when there are guests," Constance noted. "So you must be fairly modern."

At Constance's look of razor-sharp interest, Ellie recalled her curiosity about methods for avoiding pregnancy—to better facilitate her plan of taking a lover.

"Oh drat," she muttered under her breath.

Adam cast her a curious look.

"As modern as the word of Allah," Mrs. Al-Ahmed retorted, "which I happen to have read for myself, and which does not require any such practice on the part of faithful women. Not that I can fault some of us for wishing for space to ourselves."

She punctuated this with a pointed look at her husband, who blanched and sank down in his chair a bit.

Ellie couldn't entirely blame her for being irritated with the poor man. She didn't imagine that she would be terribly pleased herself if she had only one day a week with her spouse, and he turned up to it with a load of bedraggled foreigners in tow.

"Ha ha ha," Mr. Al-Ahmed said nervously. "Very funny, ya habibti."

Neil slumped forward in his chair, pressing his face into his hands. "This is a disaster!" He lifted his head again, wide-eyed with dismay. His glasses were still a bit crooked and his mouse-brown hair was wildly askew. "We just stomped through the burial chamber of one of the most important figures of the late Eighteenth Dynasty! Plundered artifacts! Collapsed a two-thousand-year-old looters' tunnel—an important archaeological find in its own right, as it happens! And lost both Sayyid and I our jobs!"

Mrs. Al-Ahmed slowly turned a sharp green-eyed gaze on her husband.

"Technically we have not been formally dismissed," Mr. Al-Ahmed pointed out a little weakly.

"At least nobody was shot," Constance offered cheerfully. Her fashionable dress was very dirty.

"*Shot?*" Mrs. Al-Ahmed echoed dangerously.

"We are not entirely sure that there were gunshots," Mr. Al-Ahmed hurriedly assured her. "Perhaps someone simply dropped a boot… or three."

With her eyes still fixed on her husband, Mrs. Al-Ahmed slowly arched a single eloquent eyebrow.

Ellie felt a burst of guilt. None of what Neil had said was wrong. She *had* burst into his tomb, plundered an artifact, and probably lost him his job.

Never mind the gunshots.

Looking back, it was hard to see what else she could have done—not without leaving the field wide open to Professor Dawson. But that didn't change the fact that Mr. Al-Ahmed and her brother hadn't asked to be involved in this. Ellie had inflicted it on them without giving them any say in the matter.

She raised her chin. "The situation is my fault and my responsibility, Mrs. Al-Ahmed. I deeply regret that it brought your husband into any danger. I did not expect our circumstances to become quite so—er, complicated—but I assure you, it was prompted by a matter of the utmost seriousness and importance."

"What matter?" Mrs. Al-Ahmed demanded flatly.

Ellie looked at Adam, a little helpless as to where to begin. He met her gaze steadily. The quiet confidence in his look bolstered her—at least enough for her to draw a breath and dive in.

"Last month, Mr. Bates and I were involved in an incident in British Honduras. One that brought to our attention a particular… *quality*… of certain artifacts mentioned in the historical documents and folklore of various parts of the world."

"Quality?" Neil echoed anxiously. "What quality?"

"That they are… well…" Ellie began.

"Magic," Adam finished for her from his place by the window. He swept a gaze over the rest of the room as though daring anyone there to object. "All that stuff in those old books you spend so much time with," he elaborated, fixing his eyes on Neil. "Invisibility bracelets and flying boots. They're real." He paused. "At least, some of them are," he hedged less comfortably.

Mr. Al-Ahmed's expression was darkly thoughtful. His wife raised a careful, surprised eyebrow—and then turned a penetrating glance at her husband.

Neil's expression was one of utter horror. "Are you—" he spluttered. "Have you completely lost your—"

"I've seen it!" Constance bounced on her ottoman with excitement. "On our roof in Cairo, Ellie's bone lit up like a comet!"

Neil's pale cheeks flushed. "Show me."

"I… can't," Ellie replied uncomfortably. "It's broken."

Neil laughed, the sound a little mad. He dropped onto the sofa as though someone had cut his strings, putting his head in his hands. "Of course it is."

Adam's eyes narrowed on his friend—and then he sharply looked away again, as though torn between his temper and an even less comfortable emotion.

"I… may have heard of something like this," Mr. Al-Ahmed said carefully.

"*What?!*" Neil gaped at his foreman with dismay.

Mr. Al-Ahmed bristled, holding up a defensive hand. "I am not saying that I have seen any… glowing bones. Only that my father might have mentioned such things to me before, when I was a boy."

"Your father?" Ellie pressed.

"Kamal Hussein Al-Ahmed. He was…" Mr. Al-Ahmed drew in a breath as though struggling to think of how best to complete the sentence. "He served as a foreman on digs throughout both Upper and Lower Egypt. He told me once that he had found artifacts that held flashes of the old powers described in the ancient stories."

He cast a quick, uncomfortable glance at his audience, clearly nervous as to how his revelation was being received. Constance had set her elbows on her knees, leaning forward eagerly. Mrs. Al-Ahmed's expression was more hooded—enough that Ellie found it hard to guess what she was thinking.

Neil looked betrayed, gaping at his foreman from behind his smudged spectacles.

Mr. Al-Ahmed's jaw tightened at the look. "They were just a few things in glass cases in the museum. I remember a bronze amulet inscribed with a spell of protection against snakes, along with a senet board. My abba… claimed it might receive messages from the dead."

"But that's a load of superstitious nonsense," Neil blurted, obviously bewildered. "I thought your father was a scholar."

"He *was* a scholar." Mr. Al-Ahmed's eyes briefly flashed with hurt. "A scholar, linguist, and scientist. And he was not the sort of man who teased children with a bit of fancy. He was not fanciful."

He looked at the rest of them as though challenging anyone else to echo Neil's accusation. "My father told me that he had worked very hard to make sure those pieces stayed here in Egypt instead of going to the partage share and disappearing into Germany or America. He would not have taken that risk out of *superstition*."

Ellie was familiar with the system of partage—the law that dictated which of the artifacts found in Egypt stayed there and which belonged to the foreign museums or investors who funded the various excavations.

Any artifacts of significant historical or archaeological value were supposed to go to Egypt's share, with duplicates or less-important pieces granted to the excavators and their sponsors—but that wasn't always how it worked. The network of powerful men who dominated Egypt's archaeological scene was small and close-knit, and those sorts of ties could result in 'favors' being done… or there was always bureaucratic incompetence or deliberate fraud to help a desired artifact escape the country.

For an Egyptian foreman to go up against that system and win spoke of careful brilliance and a great deal of quiet ingenuity.

Mr. Al-Ahmed looked to Ellie—and almost defiantly *not* at Neil. "I cannot dismiss what you claim as impossible."

Neil stood. He crossed over to the door, looking into the open-air courtyard with his arms crossed over his chest as he oozed silent frustration.

"In British Honduras," Ellie continued, "Mr. Bates and I were drawn into an effort to prevent one such artifact from falling into the hands of the gentleman you briefly met this evening, Professor Dawson, and his… rather unsavory colleague, Mr. Jacobs."

"I had a brief run-in with Mr. Jacobs in London before Ellie left," Constance added with a note of relish. "I can confirm that he is desperately intimidating, even when one has only seen the top of his head."

"And he is thankfully not here," Ellie added. "If he had been, our escape from the tomb would have been far more… *complicated*," she finished with an awkward look at the obviously disapproving Mrs. Al-Ahmed.

"That guy turns up like a bad penny," Adam cut in grimly. "I wouldn't count on having seen the last of him."

"In British Honduras, we were able to keep Dawson and Jacobs from acquiring the object they sought, but it was destroyed in the process. Along with… a great deal more," Ellie admitted with a wince and a burst of guilt.

It still horrified her to remember the sight of the city of Tulan crumbling into oblivion—as a direct result of her own actions. She had spent many nights lying awake as she wondered whether there might have been a different way for her to stop the Smoking Mirror from falling into Dawson and Jacobs' hands. Surely she should have been able to think of something— though she couldn't entirely take credit for the course of action that she *had* taken.

The words of an old priest echoed through her mind.

You followed the path the mirror set for you. You buried it with the bones of all its dead.

"This Dawson," Mr. Al-Ahmed asked slowly. "What does he mean to use these…"

"Arcana," Ellie filled in, even though it irked her to have to use Dawson's word for it. She hadn't been able to think of a better one.

"…these *arcana* for?" he finished.

"That jackass isn't using them for anything," Adam replied. "He works for somebody else."

"We don't know who," Ellie quickly added, anticipating the next question. "Only that it's some sort of secretive organization… one that doesn't mind resorting to theft or murder to achieve their goals."

"I suppose that assessment is confirmed by the… er, very slim possible presence of perhaps a gunshot or two in the tomb this evening," Mr. Al-Ahmed said, flashing an uncomfortable look at his wife.

Her mouth thinned.

"And clearly, Julian Forster-Mowbray is working with them," Constance noted. "Though I still find it hard to believe that Julian is half so interesting as all that."

Neil stiffened. "You can't possibly be implying that the British Athenaeum for Egyptological Studies has anything to do with this!" He threw out his arms. "It's a scholarly organization that has existed for nearly *two hundred years,* with an impeccable reputation for supporting the most respected research into Ancient Egyptian history. It publishes papers! And an annual journal! The members are all retired university lecturers, for goodness' sake! They get into arguments about translations. They do not hire thugs to steal supposedly magical artifacts at gunpoint!"

Mr. Al-Ahmed cleared his throat a little. "They do take artifacts, strictly speaking."

"That's partage!" Neil burst out. "It's a perfectly legal share of the finds, overseen by the Egyptian Antiquities Service! It's not *stealing*!"

"That is a matter of one's perspective," Mrs. Al-Ahmed countered with razor-edged crispness.

"And it may do to recall that the Antiquities Service is run by a Frenchman who continues to operate a sale room out of the Egyptian Museum, where he hawks artifacts to tourists," Ellie added with a familiar burst of indignation. "Which is also *perfectly legal.*"

"But t-those are… They're extras. They're items that are already… already represented in the…" Neil trailed off, his shoulders slumping.

Mr. Al-Ahmed sighed tiredly.

Adam cast Ellie a significant look. "The Mustache isn't a retired professor."

"No," Constance agreed wryly. "He most certainly is not."

"Mr. Mustache—I mean Mowbray—*Forster-Mowbray*," Neil spluttered, "is not a member of the Athenaeum. He's a… well, you know. He… represents them."

"If that fellow knows hieratic from demotic, I will eat my hat," Ellie asserted firmly. "He is entirely a dilettante. Why would the Athenaeum trust someone like Julian Forster-Mowbray as their liaison?"

"Money," Mrs. Al-Ahmed asserted flatly. "If he is not a scholar, then he is connected to the money. That is why he oversees your work."

Adam looked at Neil. "So where's the money come from?"

"The money?" Neil echoed helplessly.

"You know—the stuff that pays your salary?" Adam elaborated in a drawl. "If your Athenaeum is all a bunch of retired professors, where's the cash for your dig come from?"

"Oh!" Neil said. "Well, there's a small endowment, of course, but most of the funds come through private investment."

"Of course!" Constance straightened, eyes bright. "Your nefarious mystery organization must be funding the Athenaeum. That's why they were able to make Julian their Johnny-on-the-spot for Neil's dig—though why they chose *him* is anyone's guess."

"He's probably related to somebody," Adam sighed tiredly. "Where he comes from, they're always handing out easy jobs to idiot nephews."

"Where he comes from?" Ellie asked. "You mean England?"

"I mean rich people," Adam corrected her. "That guy's got idiot nephew written all over him."

"And now they are after the Staff of Moses," Mr. Al-Ahmed said flatly.

"You are speaking of the prophet Musa?" his wife cut in, her eyebrows arching with surprise.

"Dropped into the bulrushes. Adopted by an Egyptian Princess," Constance recited easily. "Cursed Egypt with ten terrible plagues, freed the Hebrew slaves, and drowned Pharaoh's army in the parting of the Red Sea."

The others stared at her.

"What?" Constance returned blithely. "I don't *always* use church as a chance to catch up on my adventure novels."

"That would be the one," Mrs. Al-Ahmed confirmed dryly.

"Let me see if I can remember all the plagues he brought with his staff,"

Constance mused. "There were frogs, gnats, locusts, flies… er, pestilence?"

"Boils," Ellie automatically corrected her.

"Turning water into blood," Constance added. "Eternal darkness… well, a few days or so anyway… and the wholesale slaughter of helpless infants!"

An uncomfortable silence followed her words.

"*Then we inspired him to throw down his rod,*" Mrs. Al-Ahmed recited quietly. "*And it swallowed their illusions.* It is in our book, too."

A chill danced across Ellie's skin that defied the warmth of the night, and she remembered black stone smooth as water and the scarred face of a ghost.

"I've seen… *felt,*" she corrected herself, "what an arcanum can do." She raised her eyes to the rest of them. "I can't let them find this one."

"This is madness," Neil announced, looking at them all with a dazed, shocked expression. "All of you are mad."

"Where do we start?" Constance eagerly rubbed her hands together.

"How about with the ring?" Ellie looked pointedly at her brother.

Neil's face was drawn, but his hand moved automatically to the pocket of his battered tweed waistcoat. He pulled out the electrum ring, and the others gathered around him—all but Adam, who remained by the window, and Mrs. Al-Ahmed, who watched in thoughtful silence from her chair.

"So these hieroglyphs spell the name Moseh," Constance mused. "Which sounds an awful lot like Moses."

"Moses *is* Moseh," Neil grumbled. "It's an Egyptian name—Moseh. We're the ones who say it wrong."

"To the Arabs, he is Musa," Mr. Al-Ahmed offered. "For the Hebrews, Moshe."

"It means 'son of,' and is generally preceded by the name of a patron deity," Ellie added with a pointed look at her brother. "It's an Egyptian name *element.*"

"Not when the rest of the name has been blanked out," Mr. Al-Ahmed noted distractedly, studying the ring as Neil held it out in the lamplight.

"It's been blanked out because it's Atenist," Neil declared.

He shoved himself off the sofa with a new energy, pacing the room with the ring in his hand. "I knew it! I *knew* the connection would be there! But of course, she would have had to downplay it—to pretend loyalty to the regime that was defacing Akhenaten's image from the walls of every temple from here to Aswan. But how could we not find some evidence of her continued sympathy for the cult that had been of such vital interest to her beloved…"

Neil trailed off as he realized the rest of the room had gone silent. Ellie was fighting to suppress a smile.

Constance arched an eyebrow. "You realize your sister is possibly the only other person in the room who knows what you're talking about," she pointed out, and then caught herself. "And Mr. Al-Ahmed, I should imagine."

Mr. Al-Ahmed had carefully removed the jewelry box from his tool case, unwrapping it from the white froth of Constance's scarf. He flashed her an indulgent smile before peering down once more at the inscription.

Ellie waded into the breach, as Neil was rotten at providing simple explanations for his favorite historical topics.

"Throughout the history of Egypt, the Egyptians worshiped an extensive pantheon of deities," she explained. "There were sun gods and moon gods, gods that oversaw childbirth, gods of vegetation and farming, gods of death—"

"Loads of gods," Constance said, sitting up straight and looking the part of the eager student. "Got it."

"Then midway through the Eighteenth Dynasty, along comes a pharaoh named Akhenaten," Ellie started.

"Actually, at the time he was made co-regent, he was Amenhotep IV," Neil interrupted her quickly. "It was only after his father, Amenhotep III, had passed to the Field of Reeds that—"

"*Akhenaten,*" Ellie continued deliberately, cutting him short, "worshiped only one god—the Aten. As I mentioned back in the tomb, the Aten had originally been a relatively obscure form of the god of the sun, represented by the solar disk. But when Akhenaten became the sole king, he made the Aten the preeminent god of all of Egypt. A few years later, he went even further. He ruled that the Aten wasn't just the most important of all the gods—it was the *only* god."

"What did he do—outlaw all the others?" Constance suggested.

"No," Neil replied defensively. He caught himself, his tone shifting. "I mean—possibly. It's not entirely clear. But what *is* clear is that Akhenaten proclaimed the Aten not just as the chief among the gods, but as the *only true god* in existence."

"You have to understand how revolutionary this was," Ellie jumped in to explain. "This was thousands of years before the emergence of Judaism. The people who would later become the Israelites weren't monotheists at this point in history. Their Yahweh was a tribal god—one that they thought was superior to all others, but his rivals were no less real than he was. It was only much later that the likes of Baal and Asherah came to be thought of as demons instead of deities. Akhenaten was the first person that we know of in history to say that there was only *one*."

"'Oh sole god, like whom there is no other,'" Neil recited, "'you created the world according to your desire, while you were alone.'"

A shiver flashed over Ellie's skin at the sound of Neil's solemn words.

"What's that from?" Adam pressed, frowning. "Psalms?"

"Ha!" Neil declared triumphantly. "One might think so, but it's from The Hymn to the Aten, written by Akhenaten himself!"

"Not all of us have memorized the Hymn to the Aten," Ellie reminded him.

Mr. Al-Ahmed snorted lightly without looking up from his study of the jewelry box.

Constance leaned forward on her ottoman with a glimmer of unusual interest. "How very… *intriguing*."

Ellie felt a quick dart of alarm. There was something less than purely scholarly about the glint in Constance's eyes.

"At any rate," Neil went on obliviously, holding the ring out in front of him, "*that* is how I know this ring belonged to an Atenist. It was common during Akhenaten's reign for his courtiers and supporters to change their names, replacing references to other gods with the Aten or just dropping them entirely. The Amarna period is the only logical point of origin for an artifact with these characteristics."

"Amarna?" Constance echoed.

Ellie repressed a sigh, cutting in yet again to clarify her brother's scholarly excesses. "It's the term scholars use for the period of Akhenaten's reign. It refers to the modern name for the location where he built his capital city—Tell al-Amarna."

"Akhenaten didn't want to rule from the city of Thebes, like his father had," Neil eagerly elaborated. "Thebes was a city rife with the influence of other cults, like those of Hathor, Isis, and Amun. He built an entirely new capital devoted to the worship of his god and called it Akhetaten—Horizon of the Aten. But this?" He shook the ring again and let out a slightly wild laugh. "I have speculated for *years* that Moses' origins lay in the heart of the Amarna period! After all, Moses' story in the Book of Exodus more or less describes how he was first raised as an Egyptian, and then guided the Hebrews to worship a single god above all others."

"The whole golden calf bit," Adam offered, finally pulling his attention from the window.

"Exactly!" Neil agreed excitedly. "Now—what makes more sense? That a shift toward monotheism happened spontaneously and independently among two disparate cultures—proto-Hebrew and Egyptian—at roughly the same period of history? Or that one culture exerted an influence over the other? For the love of God, Moses is an Egyptian name!"

Neil caught himself, shooting a nervous look at Ellie, whose mouth had already pulled down into a disapproving frown. "Or *name element*," he corrected quickly, and then pressed on. "I have been working on this theory for years now. The only thing I have been missing is an explicit link between the Hebrews and the Atenists. But if hard evidence exists that Moses was in fact an official in Akhenaten's court—"

"Hold on," Constance cut in. "Are you saying that the Egyptians invented God?"

Neil's mouth clamped shut. His gaze shifted from Constance to the others—and stopped on Mrs. Al-Ahmed, who had crossed her arms over her chest as she regarded him with a challengingly raised eyebrow.

"When you put it that way, I suppose it sounds rather…" He cleared his throat. "That is to say—we are talking about historical theory, not a theological argument…"

"It is a very compelling historical theory," Mr. Al-Ahmed offered, pulling his attention away from the jewelry box. "If one allows for a historical basis behind the Exodus story at all."

His wife cast him a wry and affectionate look. "And only a little blasphemous."

Mr. Al-Ahmed stiffened with quick alarm.

"I *did* know I was marrying a scholar and not an imam," Mrs. Al-Ahmed reminded him warmly.

Her husband flashed her a slightly rueful smile before going back to his study of the inscription.

"So your only-a-little-blasphemous theory is that Moses learned about God from this Akhenaten character," Constance filled in. "And then carried that off and taught it to the Hebrews. But how did his ring end up in Mutnedjmet's tomb? Was she an Atenist too?"

"Mutnedjmet was Nefertiti's sister," Neil replied, as though the answer ought to have been obvious.

"You're jumping ahead again, buddy," Adam noted with a hint of wry affection.

"Nefertiti was the great royal wife of Akhenaten—his queen," Ellie filled in. "And one with an unusually prominent role in Egyptian life. Most of the time, the wives of pharaohs are shown as smaller, secondary figures to their husbands. But Nefertiti is given equal size in the art of the Amarna period—as though she were his partner, sharing his high status as they made offerings to the Aten or accepted tribute from lesser kings."

"It is even possible that Nefertiti inspired Akhenaten to invent an entirely new form of Egyptian art," Neil jumped in to add, eyes bright with scholarly excitement. "One that was incredibly lifelike and intimate, as opposed to the more stylized and formal scenes we find both before and after the period. You can actually see the flaws and imperfections, like Akhenaten's rounded belly or the wrinkles around Nefertiti's eyes. Instead of conventional scenes of the pharaoh marching along with the gods, Akhenaten and Nefertiti are shown playing with their children or sharing a meal. Grieving for a dying daughter. It's… It looks like…"

"Love?" Constance filled in when Neil's voice trailed off.

"But we do not know for certain that the Mutnedjmet who was Horemheb's queen is the same Mutnedjmet mentioned in the tombs of Amarna as Nefertiti's sister." Mr. Al-Ahmed's words had the air of an old argument.

"We know it for certain *now*," Neil retorted, waving the ring at him. "I did tell you that we would find a connection!"

Mr. Al-Ahmed sighed. "Sometimes I wonder if I would like you more if you were not such an obnoxiously lucky guesser."

Neil frowned. "It's not guessing. It's—"

"But is this a well-known theory?" Adam pressed a little impatiently. "All this stuff about Moses and Akhenaten, and the queen in your tomb being Nefertiti's sister? I'm just wondering how the hell Dawson would've thought to look for a clue to the location of Moses' staff at your Eighteenth Dynasty excavation."

"It's… possible that I might have engaged in a little theoretical speculation in some of my reports to the British Athenaeum," Neil admitted uneasily.

Adam's tone went dry. "In other words, you wrote your bosses a nice report about all of it."

"It *is* my job," Neil pushed back crossly, and then caught himself, his shoulders sagging. "*Was* my job."

"But does any of this tell us where we can actually find the damned thing?" Adam pressed. "You know—the dangerous artifact that can unleash plagues of boils and locusts on the world if the wrong guys get hold of it?"

At the mention of the staff's purported magical powers, Neil stiffened.

"Perhaps the inscription in the box will help with that," Ellie suggested uncertainly.

Mr. Al-Ahmed sighed with a note of frustration. "This hieratic is a variety mostly seen in letter-writing, and it is positively rife with abbreviations and shortcuts—a bit like your English shorthand. I will need to consult some of my father's old notes before I can hope to make any sense of it beyond those first few words."

"If you wouldn't mind, Mr. Al-Ahmed," Ellie pleaded. "We must know whether there is anything else in that text that might help us."

"Call me Sayyid," he corrected her tiredly. "If we are to be working together on the mystery behind the life of one of the world's greatest prophets, we might as well dispense with the formalities."

"Of course, Sayyid," Ellie agreed gratefully.

"I will see what I can do with the hieratic." Sayyid cradled the box as carefully as he might an infant as he rose and headed for his study.

His wife stood as well, casting a ruefully assessing look over the rest of them. "And I will find you all somewhere to sleep."

"Is there anything to eat?" Constance asked, yawning. "All of this history has made me a bit peckish."

"I will put on some rice," Mrs. Al-Ahmed conceded, flashing another irritated look at her husband as he settled down at his desk in the next room.

"I can help!" Constance brightly offered, hopping to her feet.

Constance looked at Ellie expectantly.

Ellie's stomach sank at the thought of being asked to assist. She was an absolutely rotten cook. "I can… er…"

"I got it, Princess," Adam cut in a little dryly.

At the sound of that comfortable nickname—*Princess*—Neil stiffened. He put his fingers to his temples as though fighting a wave of dizziness.

"I need some air," he declared abruptly.

He pivoted on his heel and hurried out of the house at a pace that was barely short of a run—as if he might somehow escape all the various ways that his life had taken a turn over the last two hours.

Adam watched him go, his expression flashing with guilt and unease.

Ellie was feeling much the same herself.

Constance hooked a hand under each of their elbows, steering them after Mrs. Al-Ahmed. "Come on, then, you two. Let's see if Sayyid has any dates."

THIRTEEN

With two bowls of lentils in his hands, Adam set out to face the music.

Neil hadn't come back to the house since he'd run out an hour before. The lion's share of Neil's angst seemed to be coming from the whole busting-into-his-tomb and possibly-costing-him-his-job thing… but Adam knew the revelation that he'd been running around with Neil's sister hadn't helped.

At all.

When Adam had first shown up at Cambridge University, he'd been a big, awkward American who couldn't spend more than ten minutes staring at a book before he realized he'd just read the same sentence six times and gave up. He hadn't fit in with the guys who didn't bother even trying to read, because they were mostly stuck-up rich kids in need of a good dunking. And he'd figured the ones who actually did read were probably a lost cause, since it wouldn't take them long to figure out that all Adam knew about history was what he managed to pick up during lectures when his mind wasn't wandering.

Neil had definitely been one of the reading guys, but he'd started sitting next to Adam in their Greek class, asking him questions about America or what his thoughts were on the historicity of the Iliad. Before Adam quite knew what was happening, Neil had absorbed him into a friendship like some kind of osmosis.

He still wasn't sure why Neil had picked him, of all people. Adam certainly hadn't asked for it, but he'd been grateful all the same. Neil—whose mind was practically exploding with things he'd read in books—had never once made Adam feel like an idiot or a failure. He'd just start rambling at Adam about the reliability of Roman accounts of early Celtic culture, and before Adam knew it, he'd be theorizing about ancient British kinship structures right alongside him.

He liked to think he'd given something back to Neil as well. Fairfax definitely wasn't the kind of kid who jumped at the chance for an adventure, but Adam was pretty sure Neil had enjoyed that prank with the stuffed emu and the incident with the soda canister and the Dean's miniature schnauzer more than he'd let on.

To Adam's even greater surprise, he and Neil had actually stayed close even after Adam blew off his final exams and ran away to Central America. Neil had asked for Adam's address, but Adam hadn't actually expected to hear from him. He'd figured the whole 'quitting university out of spite' thing would've made star-student Neil realize how little they really had in common—but then the letters had started coming, and they'd come like clockwork every two weeks for seven years. Hell, there were probably three of them waiting for him back in Belize Town even now, full of ramblings about Middle Egyptian grammar and how Neil missed plum tarts—and had Adam seen the latest excavation report from Teotihuacan?

Adam hadn't, but it wouldn't matter. Just like Adam never made Neil feel bad for being bookish, Neil had never made Adam feel lousy for using books as paperweights—even when he really did *intend* to try to read them.

Maybe that was the real secret to why they'd stuck together. They'd never made each other feel less for being who they were.

It was pretty lousy for Adam to repay all that by ruining the guy's sister.

Not that he'd *meant* to... but even after he'd found out that Ellie was Neil's Peanut, he'd kept making bad decisions.

Hot, passionate bad decisions with his hands and his lips and his... well.

Friends didn't do that, and Neil would have every right to cut Adam out of his life over it. But Adam couldn't let that happen, because Neil was Ellie's brother. He was always going to be a part of her world, and if Adam had any hope of sticking with her—whatever the hell that might end up looking like—he owed it to her to try to make things right, no matter what he had to do to earn that.

He figured the effort would at least involve getting verbally torn up, down, and sideways. Maybe even taking a solid punch to the face... not that Neil could hit all that hard.

So that was the plan. Face the music, get what he deserved, and hope that on the other side of it there were still enough fragments of their friendship left to come to some sort of peace.

He found Neil on the path by the canal. The narrow waterway lay maybe a dozen yards from the house, but it was far enough to be out of earshot and past any fall of light through the meshrabiyeh screens over Sayyid's windows.

Tall, slender palms rose around them. Beyond the narrow, gleaming water at Neil's feet, the landscape turned from shaded garden to sprawling, starlit fields.

It wasn't the smartest spot to hang around in the dark. In fact, it looked to Adam like exactly the sort of place where you might expect to find a lurking crocodile.

Adam wondered if maybe Neil didn't know about crocodiles—though you'd think a guy who had been in Egypt for two years now might've learned at least the raw basics of survival.

Then again, Neil had never had a particularly strong instinct for self-preservation.

Adam would've felt a little better about walking into a potential encounter with a croc if he'd had his machete in his hand instead of two bowls of dinner. Thankfully, he had a solution for that problem.

"Take this, would you?" Adam pushed one of the bowls at Neil.

"What?!" Neil exclaimed, whirling in surprise and nearly stumbling into the canal.

Adam wondered if he'd have to drop a bowl in order to catch him, but Neil managed to right himself, arms wheeling.

"Why did you sneak up on me like that?" Neil demanded.

"Pretty sure I was making plenty of noise," Adam offered back. "It's a hell of a lot better to scare a crocodile off than come up on it unawares."

"Crocodile? What crocodile?" Neil looked around wildly.

"You're standing in a swamp." Adam glanced over the edge of the canal. "Looks all right for the moment. Still, wanna take one of these?"

Neil awkwardly accepted his dinner, which freed up Adam's hand. The bowl he still held was stuffed with rice and lentils topped with chunks of ripe tomato, salty olives, briny cheese, and a big folded hunk of flatbread to scoop it up with. Adam would've normally dived into that kind of meal with relish—but his appetite was lacking.

With a sigh, he set the bowl into the crook of a tree branch.

Neil's own supper remained forgotten in his hand as he continued to stare morosely out at the fields.

Adam wondered how to broach the subject that had brought him out there.

So about your sister…

It wasn't his finest turn of phrase, but it was the best he'd been able to come up with.

"So…" Adam started.

"This is all patently ridiculous!" Neil burst out. "We've paraded into unsurveyed burial chambers, crawled through unstable tunnels—and now we're hiding in the house Sayyid didn't even tell me he had—and for what? Because Ellie thinks the British Athenaeum for Egyptological Studies is in the pocket of some cabal of dastardly villains looking for magical artifacts?"

"That's... well, not entirely inaccurate," Adam awkwardly admitted. "But the way you're putting it..."

"My funders aren't *unreasonable*." Neil paced along the bank of the canal, gesturing with his bowl still in his hand. "They certainly won't be happy that we entered the burial chamber contrary to their instructions, but I'm sure that if I... if I just explain..." He stopped short, his face pale with panic. "Mr. Forster-Mowbray is perhaps not the *most* scholarly in his inclinations, but I'm sure if I tell him that it was all a terrible... Or scorpions!" he burst out, clutching the bowl to his chest. "I could say that we were assaulted by a... a whole... flock?"

"Nest," Adam filled in tiredly.

"—A whole nest of scorpions! So of course we had to retreat to the burial chamber for safety reasons!" Neil closed his eyes and let out a moan. "Oh, blast it. This is a mess! And you—you, of all people! Showing up on the wrong bloody continent, waving around enormous knives and talking about gunshots and glowing bones... I know you enjoy a good prank, Bates, but this is really beyond the pale!"

"Prank?" Adam echoed.

The word sounded a little dangerous. He hadn't intended for it to come out that way. After all, he was there to apologize to Neil, whatever that ended up requiring of him—not get his hackles up in the first two minutes.

"What else could it be?!" Neil waved his arms—one hand still precariously clutching the bowl. "Unless it's all part of some bizarre scheme to win over my sister—and I haven't even begun to share my thoughts on *that* subject. What are you *doing* here with her? I can't imagine what I'm going to tell David and my mother about all of this. 'I'm sorry, sir, but my best friend has *ruined your daughter* and dragged her off to the other side of the world where she is now invading people's tombs and raving about magical artifacts!'"

Part of Adam distantly recognized that this was the point at which he should start apologizing. Unfortunately, that part was rapidly drowned out by a fierce and indignant burst of temper.

"Ellie's not raving," Adam shot back.

"She thinks she has a *glowing bone!*" Neil raved back.

"That's because *we found one!*" Adam yelled. "Along with a four-foot-wide, creepy as hell, extremely magical mirror! And before you start calling Ellie crazy, you'd better know that I touched the damned thing too, and it showed me exactly where to find my knife! So what—you gonna think both of us are lunatics?!"

Neil gaped at him as though that were precisely what he was thinking, but he was just prudent enough not to blurt it out.

"And how did you and my sister find this magic mirror, then?" he retorted instead on what he clearly thought was safer ground. "When you were gallivanting around the wilderness together, completely unchaperoned, with no mind at all for the utter havoc that would wreak on her reputation? How did she even end up in British Honduras in the first place? Was that your fault, too?"

"Ellie made it to British Honduras all on her own," Adam snapped back, anger heating his skin.

Neil blanched. "How is that better? That's not better! That's... that's *terrifying!* How am I going to explain this to our parents? This is Egypt—it's not the middle of nowhere! Somebody is bound to recognize her, and then what? If word gets back to London of what the two of you have been up to..." He stopped, eyes widening. "What *have* the two of you been up to?"

Adam's anger deflated.

"Er... about that..." he started awkwardly.

Neil gaped at him with a new level of horror. "But you did say you hadn't yet... yerrgh," he finished, choking on the rest of the words.

"We haven't!" Adam quickly assured him. "There hasn't—yet—been any... of that..." He caught himself, pulling in an uncomfortable breath. "I mean—if we're talking about the thing that I think we're talking about."

"That... That's..." Neil backed up a step, stammering. "Do you realize that implies that there are *other things* we aren't talking about?"

Adam shifted uncomfortably in his boots. "I mean, in a purely rhetorical sense, there are always going to be things other than the things that we're talking about..."

He trailed off weakly.

"Just tell me what you've been doing with my sister!" Neil demanded.

Adam drew in a breath. This was what he had come out here for, after all. He owed it to Neil—and to Ellie. He needed to tell the truth, and then take whatever hell broke loose as a result.

Now he just had to figure out where to start.

"Well," he began carefully, "first there was some... boating. And then we had this little problem with a waterfall. Some... kissing might have happened after that. And then some more kissing on another boat—the one to Egypt—and, uh…"

"Is that all, then? Just kissing?" Neil pressed hopefully.

"Yes," Adam assured him with a brief rush of relief.

Neil's expression flashed with a reluctant unease. "What sort of kissing?"

Adam was glad that he had already set his bowl down. He was pretty sure that the time had come for him to take that punch in the face. At least now, he wouldn't end up both punched and splattered with lentils.

He drew in a breath and spat out the rest. "The kind where she's got her legs around my waist, and I'm holding on to her—"

"*Stop!*" Neil shouted, throwing his free hand over his eyes as though it would make the visions of what Adam had just described disappear from his brain. "Just… please… Have you… Do you even have the *foggiest* notion…"

The words struck like something sharp in Adam's guts. "Of what?" he pushed back unevenly.

"Of the *damage* that you've done!" Neil shot back loudly. "Of how completely *irresponsible* this is! Had you no thought at all about her reputation? To the impact that would have on my mother and David? Did you think for even a moment about what you were doing?"

The words dug deeper, striking at Adam like stones—*irresponsible, damage. Had you no thought at all?*

He felt as though he were standing on the edge of a precipice. Before it lay the cold glass of a mirror, reflecting back everything about himself he'd been afraid of. That he *was* irresponsible and thoughtless. That he never considered the consequences.

His father's voice echoed through his brain. *Impulsive, reckless, selfish…*

Neil was still talking. "And as to how I'm supposed to explain this to our parents, I can't even *begin* to fathom… She's my *sister*, Bates!"

At Neil's words, the pressure building up inside of Adam suddenly snapped—and something else poured out of him, hot and powerful as a geyser unleashing.

"*I know!*" he roared back. "I know exactly who she is, and she's a hell of a lot more than just *your sister!* She's a scholar and a rebel—and the smartest damned person that I've ever met, and that includes you, along with everybody else at that damned university. She's resourceful, and clever, and braver than she's got any right to be. She's principled and passionate, and the last thing she needs is somebody—brother or otherwise—telling her what the hell she's supposed to do with herself! I know I screwed up, all right? But what do you think—that I'm some scoundrel dragging her down the path to ruin? Ellie's about as easy to drag as an elephant! I'm not dragging her anywhere! I'm… I'm…"

Adam trailed off—because the truth was, he had absolutely no idea what he was doing with Ellie.

That was precisely the problem.

Nothing about this conversation was helping to fix it. Adam had come out there to apologize, not get into a shouting match.

With a herculean effort, he reined his temper in and tried to go back to something at least remotely approaching reasonable.

"Look," he said carefully, pinching the bridge of his nose, where he could feel a headache threatening to pound in. "I'm just trying to explain…"

"And *I'm* just trying to protect her!" Neil shot back angrily. "Because that's my *job*, Bates!"

Adam's temporary victory over his anger fizzled out like a dud firecracker. "What do you think this is? Do you think I set out to seduce your sister and then leave her in a ditch? You've known me for over *ten years*, Fairfax! We're supposed to be friends! Do you honestly believe I'm that kind of person?"

"Friends don't spend god-knows-how-long running around in the wilderness with each other's sisters!" Neil retorted. "Or… or kissing them with… with leg-wrapping! Or…"

A colder, sharper emotion washed over Adam—one that felt uncomfortably like hurt. It mingled with the hefty dose of guilt that had taken up proprietary residence in his gut, right next to the one mouthful of lentils he'd managed to eat. "Right," he bit out shortly. "Got it."

He pivoted on his heel and began to walk away. He made it three steps before another impulsive and almost certainly bad idea took hold of him, forcing him to whirl back.

"You say it's your *job* to protect your sister?" Adam snapped. "Then where were you when she was trying to get into university and the scholarship people kept telling her that she was a waste of money because she's a girl? Or when her classmates told her she should stop 'taking up space' in the library?"

Adam took a step closer, the anger whipping through him like the winds of a storm. He jabbed a finger into Neil's chest, forcing him to stumble back a step. "Or how about when she got out of school and the whole world slammed the door in her face when she dared to tell them what she wanted to do with her life? That's right—you were waltzing down your own gold-paved path to exactly what you always knew you would do. And you didn't once look back over your shoulder to see her standing there behind you—

your sister, who's as smart as you are, if not smarter—and who could do that job you were so damned worried about ten minutes ago as well as you can, if not better. But she'll never get a chance, will she? Because she's shut out of it on account of her being a woman—and because people like you keep pretending there's absolutely nothing wrong with that!"

Neil paled with a different emotion. "I… I didn't…"

But Adam wasn't waiting for him. "You know what probably matters a hell of a lot more to Ellie than her virtue in the eyes of society?" he burned on relentlessly. "Maybe knowing she has a brother who actually believes in her. One who might use his oh-so-important position in the world to do something to help her live the life she's always dreamed of—the life *you* got handed on a damned platter!—instead of worrying about where the hell she's been putting her legs!"

Adam's words rang out over the flat, still silence of the fields. He felt the shocking weight of them even as he slowly absorbed that he'd probably just blown any chance he had at earning Neil's forgiveness.

He couldn't entirely regret it. None of what he'd said was wrong, even if he'd left out all the other things he'd meant to own up to when he came out here.

I knew better, and I did it anyway. I'm going to do whatever I have to in order to make it right.

I'm sorry.

Beside him, Neil emptied of anger like a deflated balloon, his face drawn into lines of dismay.

"What can I do?" he demanded helplessly. "*Hire* her? You think I wouldn't? I know what she can do! I'd do it in a minute, but the funders would never have it! They'd call it nepotism, or… or—I don't know— something even worse, and then we'd both be out!" He held his bowl of lentils in both hands. It trembled furiously. "I can't change the world for her just because it's unfair!"

Adam's joints ached as though from the steady pressure of some unseen weight. "The world doesn't change. Not unless we make it—you, me, everybody. We've got to keep rattling the bars, even though they feel like they could never possibly break. Because maybe if enough of us do, something'll finally give."

He drew in a long breath. The night air tasted of river. Crickets chirped into the silence around them.

"I'm the last one in any position to stand here and moralize," he continued quietly. "But Ellie really could've used a brother who rattled the bars for her."

Neil slumped back against the trunk of a palm tree. He looked exhausted. A breeze whispered through the fronds overhead, setting them rustling as the water rippled softly against the banks of the canal.

"Are you going to marry her?" Neil finally asked without looking at him.

Adam found the other side of the palm trunk and leaned against it. He looked up. Through the lace of the leaves, he glimpsed a sky thickly scattered with stars. "Ellie's got… strong opinions about marriage."

"That's one way of putting it," Neil replied dryly. "But… surely she must see… I mean, given the situation…"

"That it's the most reasonable thing to do?" Adam filled in thinly.

"Isn't it?" Neil asked desperately.

Adam didn't answer. Was it reasonable to ask someone to take part in an institution they hated—and with pretty damned good reasons?

He'd told Ellie before that he didn't want her to change her mind about marriage, and he'd meant it. But where did that leave them?

Maybe some small, miserable part of him had been hoping that somehow Ellie would find a way to be okay with the whole marriage thing. That the problem would just go away.

He felt worse about that part of himself than he did about the part that'd gone out and taken all those *irresponsible liberties* with Ellie's legs.

But if he truly took marriage out of the equation, what did that leave them? Was there a path to the future that they both could walk together— and still be who they were at the end of it?

"I'm…" Neil started tentatively. "I'm trying, Bates. But this… all this…"

His voice trailed off. Adam nodded, even though Neil—on the far side of the trunk—couldn't see it. "Yeah," he agreed—as though it were the answer to everything and nothing, all at the same time. He closed his eyes, sinking back against the tree. "For whatever it's worth, I'm sorry. I'm trying not to cause any more hurt. I'm… not always all that good at it. But I'm trying."

"I know," Neil replied quietly. "And for whatever it's worth, I'm not sure I'm really any better."

Something about his quiet admission, floating to Adam through the whispering darkness of the night, lifted just a little bit of the weight from Adam's shoulders.

"Thanks, Fairfax." The words came out rough and uneven, tight with something that felt close to tears.

"We should probably head inside," Neil offered back, his tone unexpectedly tense. "As it occurs to me that log on the other side of the canal might not actually be a log."

Adam spun around the tree for a better look. A pair of beady yellow eyes gazed back at him, glinting in the dim light of the moon.

"Yup," Adam concluded. "Definitely time to go."

Light flashed to them from the bright rectangle of an open doorway on the far side of the garden. It framed Constance's petite figure.

"Adam!" she called out, voice ringing like a bell. "Bring Stuffy! Sayyid has translated the box!"

"Shall we?" Adam offered.

Without waiting for a response, he hooked a hand through Neil's elbow and hauled him toward the house.

FOURTEEN

NEIL LET ADAM drag him along, his pace hurried by the sound of a terrifying croak from across the canal. He lagged back once Adam released him, less than enthusiastic about joining the party gathered in Sayyid's office.

It felt as though someone had tossed him from the comfortable perch of his ordinary life into a dark and possibly bottomless rabbit hole. Only a few hours earlier, Neil had been happily translating curses in a properly documented tomb antechamber with Sayyid. Now he was hiding in a house he hadn't known existed, worrying about the future of both his excavation and his employment, and all over a magical staff he was fairly certain he didn't believe in.

The thought made him want to turn right around and march back out into the night... only he was feeling utterly wrung out, and a crocodile lurked outside. One that might even now be enjoying the supper he had left behind.

The thought made him want to cry.

He forced himself to keep going. After all, what was worse—pushing forward with the lunatic plan everyone had been cheerfully discussing earlier, or being left out of it entirely to wonder what sort of madness was going to be inflicted upon him next?

That, and there was the desperately intriguing matter of the Atenist ring.

Neil had been working on his theory about the connection between the Aten cult and the rise of monotheism among the Hebrews for nearly a decade. To have finally found a piece of concrete evidence for his hypothesis was earth-shattering. If there was a chance that the hieratic inscription in the jewelry box might shed more light on Moses' true identity, he couldn't possibly bring himself to miss it—even if he had to swallow his thoughts on the matter of magical staffs to do it.

He followed Bates into Sayyid's office. The space was another unsettling revelation—a cozy nest with a cluttered desk and a comfortable armchair where Neil would have happily whiled away quiet hours of research. There were shelves stuffed with books. A thickly woven carpet with just the right amount of wear covered the floor. A few scattered artifacts—items from Sayyid's father's personal collection—punctuated the walls and cases.

Neil could vividly imagine Sayyid holed up in here after a long day at the excavation, consolidating his notes from the dig or picking away at a bit of his linguistic work.

At the sound of Neil's footsteps in the doorway, Mrs. Al-Ahmed flashed him a distinctly disapproving look, making it abundantly clear who she blamed for both the unexpected interruption of her evening with her husband and the fact that he'd been possibly-perhaps shot at.

Ellie stood by the bookshelves, studying the titles on the spines. Adam joined her there, and the warm look she gave him as he arrived made Neil feel both guilty and utterly dismayed at the same time.

Constance perched on the edge of the desk, shamelessly spying over Sayyid's notes. Neil was still reeling from the discovery that the exasperating little ball of energy once hell-bent on disturbing his study habits had turned into this creature of thick eyelashes and feminine curves.

Danger gnome, he thought to himself furiously. If he could keep reminding himself of how she used to play MacBeth in the attic—complete with weapons and screaming—perhaps it might keep him from thinking about what her legs looked like under that lawn dress… where she kept her knife hidden.

He suppressed the urge to groan.

"So what's this inscription tell us about the Moseh from the ring?" Adam leaned against the built-in bookcase with a naturally leonine grace that Neil couldn't have imitated if he tried.

"Nothing, as it happens," Sayyid replied a little distractedly, rubbing at the thinning hair at the top of his head.

"Nothing?" Ellie echoed with obvious dismay.

"The inscription does not mention *Moseh,*" Sayyid explained.

"Who does it mention?" Neil pressed, picking up on Sayyid's suggestive tone.

Sayyid glanced significantly at Neil and recited his response from his sheet of notes. *"That the true story be known of the King of Upper and Lower Egypt, Living in Truth, Lord of the Two Lands, Lord of Crowns… The Most Beautiful of the Beautiful Ones of the Aten."*

Recognition burst to glorious life in Neil's head at the sound of that final phrase.

The Most Beautiful of the Beautiful Ones of the Aten.

The words weren't just another royal title. They were a name—one of the most intriguing names in Egyptian history.

"Neferneferuaten!" Neil blurted out.

Sayyid grinned back at him with boyish excitement. "Neferneferuaten," he confirmed.

"Oh!" Ellie's eyes widened with understanding.

"That's…" Neil began, stammering with excitement. "Have you any notion… I mean, of course you do! But Sayyid… This is…"

"Utterly meaningless to the rest of us," Constance filled in with a note of exasperation. "Really, you Egyptologists!"

"I'm sorry," Ellie piped in, shaking herself out of her shock. "It's only that Neferneferuaten is… well, possibly the biggest mystery of the Amarna Period, if not the entire Eighteenth Dynasty!"

She shifted her gaze to Neil as though waiting for him to take over… probably because he'd been nattering to her about Neferneferuaten for years now. In fact, the only reason he'd done his dissertation on Eighteenth Dynasty administrative units in Lower Egypt was because basing a thesis on his theories about Neferneferuaten would have been considered positively fringe.

Ellie continued talking, and Neil realized he'd been staring back at her speechless instead of picking up the opening she had been trying to hand him.

"The name Neferneferuaten appears within a royal cartouche on a few artifacts recovered from the ruins of Akhetaten—Akhenaten's capital city at Tell al-Amarna," Ellie pressed on helpfully.

"So this Neferneferuaten was a pharaoh," Adam filled in.

"He must have been," Ellie agreed, "but there's so little evidence, we haven't the foggiest idea who he was or how he ended up sitting on the throne. It's an utter mystery—so much so that some scholars question whether Neferneferuaten actually existed."

"Of course he existed!" Neil burst out, crossing over to the desk, where Constance had hopped up to sit. "One doesn't run about making up imaginary pharaohs and putting their names in cartouches. Neferneferuaten must have ruled sometime during the three years between the death of Akhenaten and the ascension of King Tutankhamun." He looked helplessly over Sayyid's notes—all of which were in Arabic. "Akhenaten died suddenly and unexpectedly, and—"

"How?" Constance demanded.

Neil realized that in his hurry to see what Sayyid had found, he had ended up leaning across her lap. He snapped upright. A furious rush of blood pinked the tips of his ears.

The danger gnome blinked at him innocently.

"A plague, actually," Neil replied awkwardly.

Her eyes widened. They really were the most remarkably rich brown.

"Like the sort that a Biblical staff might toss at you?" she pressed.

"No!" Neil protested. "Just… an entirely ordinary sort of plague. The perfectly non-magical variety. It killed a great many slaves and courtiers as well as members of the royal family, like Akhenaten's mother and possibly one or two of his daughters—and he only had daughters," he added pointedly. "When he got ill himself, he must have been left scrambling to appoint an heir to his throne—someone he trusted to keep his greatest achievement, the cult of the Aten, alive after he was gone."

"Only that didn't work out very well, because the heir he chose—Neferneferuaten—could only have survived for perhaps three years after Akhenaten's death," Ellie added. "After that, the boy Tutankhamun was named king."

"Now, we know Tut was of royal blood." Neil started to pace as he fell into the alluring rhythm of this familiar story. "He was probably descended from Akhenaten in some less obvious way—perhaps the child of a concubine or a grandson by one of his daughters. He was most likely placed on the throne by some of Akhenaten's most powerful courtiers, who continued to serve prominently within Tut's administration… courtiers who had absolutely *no* interest in maintaining Akhenaten's monotheistic experiment," Neil added with a note of bitterness. "They waited just long enough to make sure Tutankhamun was firmly settled in as pharaoh, and then they abandoned the capital Akhenaten had built at Amarna. The Aten temples were left to fall into ruin while support and tribute swung back to the priests of all Egypt's other gods."

"So these court guys were just there in the background waiting for this Neferneferuaten to get out of the way?" Adam suggested. "And then they put a kid on the throne and rule through him to put stuff back the way they wanted?"

"They might have done a bit more than wait," Neil cut back—and hesitated. He was about to venture off the archaeological record and into the realm of speculation. Neil tried to make it a point never to speculate. He was a scholar, after all—not a spiritualist. His theories and conclusions were always based on hard data... even if he occasionally came to them by way of a tiny jolt of intuition to begin with.

"In possible support of that theory," Sayyid said carefully, "we know that Tutankhamun must have died only shortly after reaching manhood. And the pharaoh who succeeded him was not a member of the royal line at all, but rather Ay, who had been one of Akhenaten's leading viziers."

"So this Ay is some big shot adviser," Adam drawled, tapping the points out on his fingers. "The radical religious nut of a king dies. You get a couple years with this other person—the mysterious Neferneferuaten—and then Ay puts a baby king on the throne. Only the baby king mysteriously dies just when he's getting old enough to have his own ideas about things, and Ay conveniently takes it all over for himself. That about right?"

"That is... a fairly accurate summary," Neil admitted. "As pharaoh, Ay goes even further to dismantle the Aten cult. He actually started scraping Akhenaten's image off of monuments and temples all over Egypt—as though Ay hoped to erase his former master from history."

"Probably because Ay's rise to power was supported by the high priests of the other gods," Sayyid added, "who had been starved for income and patronage during Akhenaten's reign. It is not an unreasonable theory, as Dr. Fairfax and I have previously discussed."

Neil felt a little burst of warmth at his words. They *had* discussed it, of course—Neil rattling on about one of his favorite subjects while Sayyid interrupted him with pointed observations or challenging questions, bringing his own detailed knowledge of the period to bear. It had been an infinitely satisfying experience.

"All these other priests wanted things to go back to the good old days, then," Adam summarized.

"Oh, almost certainly," Sayyid agreed.

"And what about the rest of the inscription?" Mrs. Al-Ahmed prompted.

Neil startled. For a moment, he'd forgotten that Sayyid's wife was in the room—sitting quietly in the armchair in the corner like a waiting queen disdainfully eyeing her squabbling subjects.

"You know, the one that we have all gathered to hear translated?" she added wryly.

Sayyid unerringly plucked a piece of paper from the clutter on his desk. *"That the true story be known of the King of Upper and Lower Egypt, Living in Truth, Lord of the Two Lands, Lord of Crowns Neferneferuaten, last bearer of the Power of Khemenu,"* he read, *"seek behind the sun disk in the Holy of Holies of Maat-ka-re Khnemet Amun Hatshepsut."* He set the paper down. "Except that the word isn't exactly *power,*" he added pointedly.

Ellie straightened in her seat, her attention on the foreman sharpening. A feeling of uncomfortable suspicion crept over Neil's skin.

"It's *was,*" Sayyid finished significantly.

"Was?" Adam asked. "What was?"

"Not was," Neil replied tightly as the significance of Sayyid's words bloomed inside his skull. "*Was.*"

"'Was' is an Egyptian word," Ellie explained with growing excitement. "It can mean power—divine or supernatural power. Or it can refer to an object that *represents* that power."

Adam met her gaze, obviously sensing the breathless promise in her voice. "And what object would that be?"

"A staff," Neil answered hollowly as he felt the ground start to give way beneath him.

Constance gasped with delight. Ellie and Adam shared a look that was dark with import.

Mrs. Al-Ahmed's gaze was as sharp and careful as glass.

"The was-scepter," Sayyid elaborated. "It is a ritual object with a distinct shape modeled after the Set beast."

"Slender nose," Neil recited automatically. "Long ears. Forked tail."

"You see them depicted all over Egyptian art," Ellie added. "Was-scepters are held by gods, or pharaohs, or very high-ranking priests."

"Where there is a was-scepter," Sayyid noted deliberately, "there is an intimation that the bearer possesses power over the spiritual essence that shapes and animates all living things."

"So it's a magic wand!" Constance declared brightly.

Neil stared at her in horror.

"Er… I suppose one *could* frame it that way," Ellie hedged uncomfortably.

"So we've got a ring that says Moses and an inscription about a magic staff." Adam raised an eyebrow. "The rest of you thinking what I'm thinking?"

Neil felt trapped. The thrilling, comfortable academic space he had inhabited a moment before seemed to suddenly dissolve into a swamp that threatened to swallow him.

Magic. They were talking about magic.

"But the staff in the inscription is Neferneferuaten's!" he protested. "What does Neferneferuaten have to do with Moses?"

"Do you really not know a proper clue when it's staring you in the face?" Constance pressed with a note of exasperation. "His ring was in the same box as the inscription. Really—one would think you had never read an adventure novel in your life!"

"I haven't!" Neil exclaimed, bewildered.

"We can't know for certain that they *are* connected," Ellie reasoned firmly. "Not yet. But that's exactly what we need to find out."

"The Holy of Holies of the pharaoh Hatshepsut," Sayyid mused. "That will be her funerary temple at Deir al-Bahari in Luxor."

"Her?" Constance brightened with interest.

"Hatshepsut was a woman," Ellie explained. "She claimed the throne after the death of her husband and ruled for nearly twenty years."

"Her funerary temple has been thoroughly excavated," Sayyid informed them. "I have never heard of any mention of Neferneferuaten being found there."

"Then they must have done a good job of hiding it," Ellie retorted stubbornly.

"Well, then." Adam pushed back from the bookcase, straightening. "Sounds like we're going to Luxor."

Neil's growing dismay descended into panic. "*What?!*"

The word came out at a more potent volume than he had strictly intended.

"Where else would we go?" Constance retorted as though Neil were being a bit thick.

He clamped his mouth shut, momentarily speechless.

"Or…" Ellie countered grimly. "If we could know for certain that this is the only clue left behind in Mutnedjmet's tomb, then we might simply destroy it now and be done with it."

"*Destroy it?*" Neil burst back wildly.

Ellie met his eyes. Her hazel gaze looked hollow. "I know it sounds terrible. But you have no idea what's at stake here."

"If Fairfax's theories are right, and the lady in that tomb today was Nefertiti's sister, she would have been part of Akhenaten's court at the same time as this Moseh," Adam pointed out. "There's no way to know whether some other reference to him might still be lying around in there—however long it might take an idiot like Dawson to make sense of it," he finished wryly.

Ellie's gaze dropped to the jewelry box. A telltale crease marked the space between her eyebrows. Years ago, Neil would've reached out and skimmed his thumb over it.

What are you doing?

Just rubbing the worry out.

He hadn't done that in a very long time.

"You're right," Ellie finally admitted. Her expression firmed into one of determination. "The only way we can be certain the staff doesn't fall into Dawson's hands is to find it first ourselves."

"That settles it, then," Constance concluded confidently. "Luxor it is."

Nothing about this felt settled to Neil. He looked around the room frantically for someone else who might recognize the lunacy of what they were talking about.

Adam looked worried—but also determined. Sayyid's mouth was creased into a thoughtful frown, but he wasn't protesting. Neil's frantic gaze moved past him—and stopped with a startled jolt as he realized that Mrs. Al-Ahmed was staring at him. Her green eyes were narrowed as though Neil were a dubious insect squirming under a microscope.

Neil swallowed thickly, forcing out one last final desperate attempt to make them see reason. "But… but shouldn't we at least consider…"

Everyone turned to look at him as though surprised that he was speaking.

"…Perhaps just trying to speak with Mr. Forster-Mowbray?" Neil's words threatened to devolve into a squeak. "It is only that he has always presented himself as a respectable sort of person, and it's possible that he simply doesn't realize that this Dawson fellow is some sort of… nefarious…" He swallowed thickly against a throat made dry by desperation. "If… if we just tried to explain…"

They were all staring at him as though *he* were the lunatic in the room.

He was Dr. Neil Fairfax, the Cambridge-trained archaeologist entrusted with the excavation of Horemheb's Saqqara tomb. He was supposed to be *in charge*.

The thought made Neil stiffen his spine. "If we simply explained what all this is about," he continued more firmly, "we might clear up a very big misunderstanding and make everything a great deal simpler. Perhaps Mr. Forster-Mowbray and the Athenaeum would even grant us the funds to follow up on this… er, academic detour."

"That won't be necessary. We're quite all right for cash." Constance plunged her hand into the bosom of her dirt-streaked lawn dress and pulled out a wad of banknotes. "I brought a modest emergency fund with me, as I usually do when headed on an adventure."

Neil realized that his jaw was hanging open. He snapped it shut.

"M-modest…" he echoed helplessly.

He forced his eyes to fix on the pile of bills. It kept them from shifting back to Constance's nicely rounded bosom.

"Pfft. This is only part of it," Constance said dismissively. "I'm hardly going to keep it all hidden in one place, am I?"

"But where else could you hide it?" Neil blurted out.

"Wouldn't *you* like to know?" Constance returned with a wink.

Neil's ears reddened again. *Danger gnome*, he reminded himself frantically.

"So—Luxor," Adam cut in. "We'll need to catch the train, but we can't leave out of Badrashin. Dawson and his cronies will certainly look for us there."

"The next station south is at Al-Ayyat," Sayyid offered. "It's a little over twenty-five kilometers. If you ride, you can be there in about four hours. But to catch the Luxor service, you would have to leave early—no later than five." He looked at his wife. "Do you think Mr. Jabari would be willing to lend his animals for the trip at that hour?"

"He'll be up," Mrs. Al-Ahmed asserted confidently. "He has gout."

Constance clapped her hands with delight. "We can disguise ourselves as a Bedouin sheikh and his harem!"

"Nobody is going to believe that you lot are Bedouin." Mrs. Al-Ahmed looked as though she were barely resisting the urge to roll her eyes.

"What if we have camels?" Constance pressed.

Adam's eyes lit up at the mention of dromedaries.

"No camels," Sayyid replied with a hint of sympathy. "There are only donkeys."

"Be tourists," Mrs. Al-Ahmed instructed flatly. "There are enough of you about even at this time of year, like a plague of locusts."

"Then that is what we shall do." Ellie rose to her feet. "I'm afraid we can't take the risk of allowing Mr. Forster-Mowbray to have any notion of where we have gone. If he's associated with Dawson, trusting him is simply too dangerous. I'm sorry," she added with an uncomfortable look at Neil.

"And he did order his lackeys to shoot at us," Constance pointed out helpfully.

"He couldn't…" Neil spluttered. "He wouldn't possibly have…"

"I heard at least three bullets," she asserted breezily as she tucked the cash back into her corset.

"I am not precisely certain whether I heard anything at all," Sayyid said quickly with an uncomfortable glance at his wife.

"I do need to get a message back home," Constance conceded. "My family are sure to be frantic otherwise. Well—they will most likely be frantic either way, but at least if I send a telegram, they will be less quick to send the police and the army after us. And something will need to be done about Mr. Mahjoud. He must still be back at Saqqara and is certain to be worried."

"I find it kinda hard to imagine Mr. M worried," Adam said. "Exasperated and vaguely annoyed? Sure."

"We can send Mr. Jabari's grandson," Mrs. Al-Ahmed declared. "He can deliver a note to the telegram operator at the Badrashin station to send on to Cairo and then locate your dragoman to let him know that you are safe."

In the silence that followed, Ellie cast an awkward and hopeful look at Sayyid… one that filled Neil with a sudden sense of dread.

"I know it is a tremendous imposition, Sayyid… but would you consider joining us?" Ellie asked. "I cannot promise you that the endeavor would be without risk, but your skills would make you an invaluable addition to our party."

Neil wanted to protest. The words demanding that Sayyid refuse were on the tip of his tongue… because he very much did not *want* Sayyid to go. He *wanted* to turn the clock back five hours and return to teasing his foreman about his fear of bugs in the quiet of the antechamber—before he had learned that his best friend had all-but-ruined his sister, seen his brainless boss accused of throwing in with a cabal of thieves, and been calmly informed that the world was full of dangerous magical artifacts.

In the waiting stillness of the office, it seemed as though Sayyid's next words would be the key to all of that—the pivot on which Neil's entire future balanced. He desperately wanted to protest, but stayed quiet. Despite the storm that raged in his gut, Neil knew he had no right to make Sayyid's decision for him.

Sayyid shot Neil an uncomfortable glance, and then looked at his wife. Mrs. Al-Ahmed gave her husband a small, clear nod.

"Yes," he finally answered. "I will come."

Neil felt the last remaining fragments of his comfortable world quietly shatter.

"Well! That settles that, then," Constance said cheerfully.

"Five o'clock's gonna come around early," Adam observed tiredly.

"We should all get some sleep," Ellie agreed.

"I will gather you blankets," Mrs. Al-Ahmed offered. "This way."

She led them out. Ellie and the others followed—all except Sayyid.

"Will you come as well?" Sayyid tentatively asked.

Neil realized with a horrified jolt that no one else had bothered to pose the question. The others had all simply assumed that he would join them, hauled along in their wake like a recalcitrant dog.

But what else could he do? Go back to the dig? He ached to, but even he had to admit that things weren't simply going to fall back into their comfortable old arrangement. That, and he'd be leaving his sister and his best friend—as well as Sayyid and Constance—to stumble into who-knew-what trouble without him.

Which seemed like a wretchedly cowardly thing to do.

Nor could Neil forget that they were setting out after a possible clue to the identity of the most mysterious and intriguing pharaohs of the Eighteenth Dynasty—one that lay at the center of Neil's own passionate research interests. The allure of learning even some small part of the truth about Neferneferuaten—never mind any possible connection to Moses—was powerful, tugging at Neil like a fishing line even though he felt as though he were being swept out into a wind-tossed sea.

He hated it, and yet he couldn't possibly walk away.

Sayyid was still waiting for his answer.

"I wish you hadn't encouraged them," Neil returned tightly.

Sayyid's mouth thinned, his eyes flashing with a quick snap of emotion that left Neil wondering what he was trying not to say.

"Goodnight, Dr. Fairfax," Sayyid replied—and then left Neil to the deserted office and his own uncomfortable thoughts.

FIFTEEN

ORNING SUNLIGHT SPILLED over the scattered villages that punctuated the green ribbon of fertile land outside the windows of the train. Ellie watched them pass from her seat in another first-class compartment, paid for with bills from the pile of money in Constance's corset.

Their departure early that morning had been uneventful. There had been no sign of pursuit as they trotted along the paths through the fields on the backs of Sayyid's neighbor's donkeys. Ellie felt confident that they had slipped away from Professor Dawson and his hired guns—and yet she knew better than to let her guard down. Jacobs had been conspicuously missing from the group that attacked them at Mutnedjmet's tomb, but it would be a mistake to assume that meant he was no longer a threat.

With nothing outside the window to distract her, Ellie cast an uncomfortable look over the rest of her traveling party.

Sayyid sat nearest to the door. He was dressed in a tailored gray suit with a bright red fez crowning his head, which made him look very much the part of a refined Egyptian effendi as he browsed an Arabic newspaper. He was there because Ellie had asked him to come—but did he truly understand the risks of their journey? The scarred and bearded Al-Saboor cousins that they had encountered in Horemheb's tomb had been bad enough, but they were nothing compared to the terrifying competence of Mr. Jacobs.

Ellie thought of the intense, unreadable look in Mrs. Al-Ahmed's eyes as she stood on the path outside the house and watched Sayyid ride away with them that morning. She felt an uncomfortable twist of guilt.

Constance sat beside Ellie and was practically bouncing with excitement in her seat. Yesterday, they had set out from Cairo on a straightforward mission to beg Ellie's brother to withhold a little information from his employers. Since then, they had been shot at, nearly buried alive, and were now headed halfway across the length of Egypt in pursuit of a clue from a three-thousand-year-old inscription.

None of that had deterred Constance in the slightest. Ellie wondered whether even a run-in with Jacobs would make Constance truly understand the risks she was taking.

At least Adam fully comprehended what he was getting into… but he came with a host of his own complications. Even with the others sharing the close confines of their compartment, Ellie could feel her pulse skip at the easy way his legs sprawled across the floor as he crossed his arms over the broad expanse of his chest. Every quiet minute where she found herself near him, her brain snapped back to the vivid, tantalizing memory of what his hands felt like on her skin.

He was still acting unusually quiet, his mouth creased into a thoughtful frown when he didn't think anyone was looking at him. Ellie knew she needed to find a way to talk to him about whatever was making him act so strange—but she found herself uneasy about where that conversation might lead.

Finally, there was Neil. He sat between Adam and Sayyid on the opposite bench like a prisoner in the middle of an unwelcome transfer, his shoulders slumped in his uncharacteristically rumpled tweed suit.

For a moment that morning, Ellie had actually wondered whether her brother had reached his limit and simply deserted them. Ellie noticed that he'd vanished right around the time they were all loading onto the donkeys that Sayyid had borrowed from his gouty neighbor. For a beat, her heart had sunk in her chest, weighed down with the knowledge that she must have pushed her brother too far.

Then he had rounded the corner, hurrying back toward the house along the path. When Adam asked him where he'd been, Neil had flushed and bit out something about needing a walk.

Ellie couldn't blame him for wanting space. Neil hadn't asked for any of this and clearly wasn't happy about having it forced on him. Even the tantalizing possibility of solving some part of the mystery of Neferneferuaten wasn't enough to overcome his obvious frustration and dismay.

The only bright note was that Neil had done away with that embarrassing excuse for a mustache. He really ought to have known better than to even attempt it. After all, the man was nearly thirty. Surely he should have realized by now that he was fundamentally impaired when it came to the cultivation of facial hair.

"Ellie, you are missing another batch of pyramids." Constance poked her in the arm.

Ellie forced herself out of her guilty reverie. Outside the window, another cluster of dusty, weathered lumps of stone drifted past them, punctuated by a fringe of date palms.

"Dahshur," Ellie concluded distantly, recognizing their forms from books she had read in the past.

The pyramids of Dahshur were of immense scholarly importance… but Ellie struggled to muster interest. She was simply too bogged down by worry and uncertainty.

"Well, then," Constance offered brightly. "Who wants to play charades?"

It was well into the afternoon when the call Ellie had been waiting for finally sounded from the corridor outside their compartment.

"Al-uqsur!" the conductor announced. "Luxor! Le dernier arrêt!"

Luxor.

Ellie snapped out of her tired fog. Past a slow turn in the tracks, she could make out the modern town, a mix of low mud-brick houses and tall, finer buildings framed by palms and leafy trees that clustered along the broad, glittering length of the Nile. Closer by, the sand-blasted columns of an ancient temple rose from the sand.

Ellie recognized those columns. They were possibly the most important columns in the Egyptian archaeological landscape.

She leapt from her seat to press herself to the window. "That's Karnak! There's Hatshepsut's obelisk! And the Avenue of the Sphinxes!"

She was too far away. Ellie gripped the sill and stuck her head out of the opening. Wind tugged at her hair, peppering her skin with tiny grains of sand.

"I think I can see the Temple of Mut!" she shouted, the stiff breeze trying to steal her voice.

A pair of small but sturdy hands gripped the back of her waistcoat and gave it a firm yank. Ellie popped back into the carriage, half falling into her seat.

"You will see it better when you get there," Constance said. "Which will happen faster if you refrain from tumbling out the window."

"It is only one of the most important ritual sites in all of Egypt," Ellie grumbled in her defense, smoothing out the folds of her skirt.

Sayyid flashed her an understanding smile. Neil frowned down at a newspaper—one that he had been holding for the better part of an hour without turning a page.

Ellie shifted her gaze to Adam. It locked there, captured by the intense, admiring heat she saw in his eyes. Warmth pinked her cheeks, and Adam cleared his throat and looked away awkwardly.

Her heart beating just a little faster, she restrained herself to only slightly craning her neck as Karnak drifted past them.

A few minutes later, the train slowed for the approach to Luxor station. On the platform, Ellie found herself submerged in a crowd of travelers. Voices in Masri, Greek, Armenian, and Turkish clamored through the air, echoing off the high ceiling of the obviously modern building, which was accented by garishly painted faux-Egyptian columns like some dreamy French architect's tribute to an ancient palace.

Their party was immediately swarmed by local fellows in a mix of galabeyas and second-hand suits shouting about hotels and carriages.

Sayyid slipped into the lead. With a careful look, he picked an older gentleman out from the buzzing crowd. After peppering him with quick, determined questions, Sayyid authoritatively waved the others away.

In the chaos, Ellie idly glanced over the bustling lines of passengers both embarking and disembarking from the steaming train. Something caught her eye through the shifting mass of bodies—a flash of pale skin, dark eyes, and coal-black hair around the merest glimpse of cold, aquiline, terrifyingly familiar features.

Her skin chilled despite the dry Egyptian heat as a name blazed across her mind like an alarm.

Jacobs.

"Adam!" she gasped, her hand instinctively flashing out to grip his arm.

"What is it?" he asked, suddenly serious.

"I…" she began—but she had blinked, and the crowd had moved. In the place where she thought she had seen Jacobs was only a light-skinned Turkish gentleman in a dark suit, glaring as he shooed away a ragged boy angling for baksheesh.

She supposed something about the lean, sharp lines of the man's face somewhat recalled those of Mr. Jacobs.

Adam was still waiting for her to answer.

"It's nothing," Ellie concluded. "Sorry. Just my imagination running away with me."

Adam frowned down at her, then directed a sharp blue gaze out over the crowd, a protective hand still resting against her lower back.

"This way," Sayyid called over. He waved them toward the exit, where the guide he had been talking to waited for them.

With a final uneasy look over the busy station, Ellie let Adam guide her away.

They were loaded into a worn carriage for what turned out to be a very short drive to where fine limestone buildings and leafy trees parted to reveal a glimpse of the river. Just before the water, the driver turned them onto a straight driveway that led through an elegant garden accented by exceptionally tall palms.

Their conveyance stopped at a fine two-story structure fronted by a shady veranda. Painted letters on the wall just below the roof line read *Luxor Hotel.* The building looked well-kept and freshly painted. A pale-skinned gentleman in a cream suit hurried through the entrance to greet them.

With a tired sigh, Neil crossed over to accept the man's enthusiastic handshake.

"Dr. Fairfax is already acquainted with Mr. Oliver, the manager," Sayyid explained beside her. "He'll make the arrangements."

"Can Neil do that?" Ellie prompted with a flash of worry at the thought of her brother's non-existent negotiation skills.

Sayyid did a reasonable job of turning his chuckle into a polite cough. "This is a Cooks' hotel, and they have a special rate for Egyptologists," he replied. "So he cannot muck it up too badly."

While her brother chatted awkwardly with the hotel manager, Ellie took a moment to soak up the fact that she was actually standing in the city that lay at the heart of the Ancient Egyptian world. Luxor sat on the ruins of Thebes, the capital city of many of Egypt's greatest dynasties and home to some of its most important temples. To the west sprawled the steep canyons riddled with the tombs of the noble dead.

She couldn't see a great deal of that from where she stood, as the hotel's garden was framed by a plastered wall roughly her own height, but her surroundings were far from unpleasant. Bushy, flowering shrubs and a lovely fountain filled the space between the enormous palm trees—but Ellie's appreciation of the landscaping came to an abrupt halt at a pair of basalt sculptures that framed the walkway to the hotel door.

The statues were a matched pair that took the form of a noble woman seated on a square throne—only instead of a human face, she had the head of a lioness topped by the round disk of the full moon.

Or at least, one iteration of her did. The other moon-disk crown had broken off.

Ellie stiffened with recognition. She knew who that lion-headed woman was—Sekhmet, the Ancient Egyptian goddess of war and healing.

She gripped Sayyid's arm. "Please tell me those are reproductions!"

Sayyid's gaze shifted nervously to the statues. "Er… I am afraid they may have been removed from the ruins at Karnak."

"*Removed?!*" Ellie echoed, her voice squeaking with outrage. "You mean they were taken from their original context so that they could serve as *garden furniture* for a tourists' hotel?"

Adam strolled over to join them. "Wanna steal them back?"

"They must weigh over a thousand pounds," Constance noted. It was not so much an objection as a statement of fact. Her thoughtful gaze at the sculptures indicated that she was seriously considering Adam's suggestion.

"It's not *that* hard to move a thousand pounds," Adam pushed back. "It's all about leverage."

"They would only find them at the temple and bring them back here." Sayyid sounded resigned.

"Then perhaps we should position them outside the manager's bedroom window," Ellie suggested darkly, "so that he thinks they are cursed and determined to haunt him."

Sayyid stared at her with surprise.

"I say—that's a properly Gothic idea!" Constance remarked admiringly.

Adam's blue gaze dropped to her, his mouth quirking with approval.

Neil finally freed himself from the manager and came to join them. "Mr. Oliver is arranging rooms for us."

"Does he have someone he could send to the shops?" Constance brushed off her dress, which was looking decidedly less pristine than it had the previous morning.

"I… didn't think to ask," Neil admitted, flushing.

"Of course you didn't." Constance gave him a sympathetic pat on the arm. "I'll make a little list and pass it to the concierge. Shall we, then?"

She marched into the hotel like a general in a dingy lawn dress, head high. Ellie trailed along in her wake with a reluctant look at the sculptures.

There would be time to settle the matter of the misappropriated Sekhmets later. First, she had a mystery to solve—and a staff to save.

From the open window of her upper-floor room, Ellie could see past the hotel gardens to the Nile. The broad river gleamed with hints of gold as sunset painted the sky in vibrant streaks of pink and purple. On its banks stood another famous temple of Luxor, this one devoted to the worship of the divine kings of Upper and Lower Egypt. The mosque that rose from the center of the ruins was hundreds of years old but still in use. Ellie could hear the call of the muezzin from its minaret as the time for another of the daily prayers approached.

Past the line of fertile green on the far side of the river, she picked out the hazy shapes of half-crumbled walls and scattered columns that marked out more of the ruins of ancient Thebes. Beyond them were the steep cliffs of the range that held the famous tombs of the Valley of the Kings, the ragged stones quickly falling into rich purple shadow.

It still felt unreal to Ellie that tomorrow, she would cross that river to search those ruins for a secret that might have remained concealed for three thousand years.

The peace and wonder of the moment was broken by the sound of a door being thrown open.

"Goodness, did I need that bath!" Constance declared as she strode into the room.

She kicked the door shut behind her with a bang.

Ellie's petite friend tossed her towel over the back of the room's only armchair with a practiced motion. She collapsed into the seat, lifting and then flopping the thick black waves of her hair over the cloth, where they dripped onto the carpet.

"Shouldn't you wrap your hair?" Ellie asked.

"What do you think I am—a savage? Have you any idea what would happen to these curls if I tried that? In this heat? No." Constance leaned back, wriggling her rear a bit to settle more comfortably into the chair as she closed her eyes. "I am going to air dry, slowly, as God intended me to do. I just wish I had a magazine." She opened her eyes, looking to Ellie hopefully. "Are there any magazines?"

"Just a Bible," Ellie informed her, plucking the book in question from the table beside her. "Shall I bring it over?"

Constance considered the question, torn between obvious distaste and boredom. "No," she concluded with a sigh.

Ellie had enjoyed the luxury of a wash herself a little earlier. She was now dressed in a comfortable galabeya and loose trousers that one of the chambermaids had delivered to the room—items from the shopping list Constance had scribbled out for the hotel manager, Mr. Oliver. Ellie's own things were being laundered. They had thoroughly required it after being worn for two straight days that included a tomb raid, a crawl through a collapsing tunnel, and a ten-hour train ride.

Her skin was still damp from her bath. The soft breeze that tossed the pale, light curtains by the window felt deliciously cool.

Ellie turned her eyes back to the distant ruins across the river. "We need to make our arrangements to get to Hatshepsut's temple."

"Already done," Constance replied with a breezy wave of her hand, still leaning back against her towel.

"Already done?" Ellie echoed in surprise.

"We are leaving at ten o'clock. Mr. Oliver is seeing to it," Constance explained. "It's the sort of thing he does all the time."

The Luxor Hotel was owned by the Thomas Cook company, which also ran tourist steamboats and luxury dahabeeyahs up and down the Nile. They had built the establishment as a spot where their passengers could overnight while exploring the many famous sites of Thebes. It made perfect sense that the manager would know how to book the boats, animals, and guides needed to make an expedition to the ruins.

The fact that their own excursion had less to do with sightseeing and more to do with preventing the theft of an extremely dangerous arcanum likely made little difference in purely practical terms. With the matter of tomorrow's mission more or less settled, Ellie turned her attention once more to the wonders that lay just outside her window.

"It really is quite splendid, isn't it?" Constance prompted comfortably from her chair. The dripping of her hair had slowed a bit.

"I don't think I really believed I'd ever see it," Ellie admitted quietly, her eyes still on the shadowy cliffs.

"Whyever not?" Constance frowned. "It isn't as though it's on the other side of the world. And your brother lives here."

"Neil never extended an invitation," Ellie returned.

"Stuffy is even more of a curmudgeon than I remember." Constance swung her legs happily. Her feet didn't quite reach the floor. "I had to give him a solid poke in the kidney with one of my knives just to get him into that tunnel! What did he think was going to happen if he kept standing around— that the baddies would give him a handshake and apologize for the interruption? One would think he had never had an actual adventure before!"

"I am fairly certain he hasn't," Ellie admitted.

"Well, if we are really going to chase down a mysterious pharaoh and uncover the location of the long-lost Staff of Moses, he is going to need to lighten up," Constance concluded firmly.

The lazy kicking of her legs stilled. Her expression became unsettlingly contemplative.

Ellie pulled her gaze from the window and gave her friend a wary look. "What are you thinking about?"

"Oh—only that it has just occurred to me that I might know a way to help with that."

"And what might that be?"

"Taking him for a lover, of course," Constance replied distractedly.

Ellie dropped the Bible. "You... *what?!*"

"It's as much a surprise to me as it is to you, I can assure you," Constance confessed brightly. "I have certainly never thought of your brother in that way before, and he isn't at all the type I was imagining for myself, as you know. I was really more in mind for a mysterious desert prince or perhaps the master of a den of dangerous thieves. But Neil is already here, and I needn't get myself kidnapped or don trousers and run away from home to find him."

Ellie tried to protest—though she hadn't the foggiest notion of what to say. Only a soft, strangled noise managed to escape from her throat.

"I think I half expected that when I saw him again, he'd still be that scrawny stick-in-the-mud who was always shouting at me to stop sprinkling confetti between his bedsheets—but he has actually turned out rather well," Constance continued, oblivious. "He's quite attractive in a vaguely helpless sort of way—especially since he has done away with that wretched attempt at a mustache. He's always been clever, and those spectacles have a certain charm. And you might not believe this, Ellie, but I have discovered that he's actually quite fit under all that tweed! Who would have ever thought?"

"His... *tweed...*" Ellie began. Horror trapped the words in her throat.

"Most importantly, he is *not* in the market for a fortune," Constance added. "I couldn't possibly choose a lover who has actual ambitions of trying to marry me. That would be a disaster! But with Neil, I am certain that he would prefer our affair remain incognito. After all, it would hardly reflect well on his career prospects as an academic if he gained a reputation for seducing heiresses!"

Ellie was feeling dizzy. She grabbed the side of the window frame for support.

Constance's eyes narrowed, glinting with an even more frightening spark of interest. "I suspect he might even be a bit wild once you peel off all those scholarly pretensions."

"No!" Ellie finally croaked out, shaking her head. "You can't possibly...

Neil isn't… There's no *wild* under his… his tweed! His *anything!*"

Constance folded her hands comfortably on the curve of her belly, her feet swinging happily as she gazed up at the ceiling. "Really, the more I think about it, the more he seems like the perfect candidate."

"Please…" Ellie forced herself to breathe. "Please tell me that you aren't serious."

"Of course not!" Constance retorted.

Ellie let out a low, desperate sigh of relief.

"I am merely considering the idea," Constance went on, casually obliterating Ellie's moment of calm. "After all, I have it on good authority that scholarly men make for far more attentive and generous lovers than athletic types."

Ellie vividly recalled the sensation of strong, calloused hands gliding up the skin of her thighs.

"I… do not think that is necessarily true," she picked out awkwardly.

"It would be good for both of us," Constance declared authoritatively. "I would be able to engage in a bit of much-needed oat-sowing before my inevitable marriage, and Stuffy could loosen up a bit. Maybe learn how to go along with things instead of always looking as though he's about to faint." Constance flashed Ellie a measuring glance. "You know—a bit like how you're looking right now."

Ellie coughed, her throat suddenly dry.

Constance sprang upright. She went to the pitcher on the nightstand and poured a glass of water.

"I understand that we are engaged in an urgent enterprise." Constance pushed the cup into Ellie's hand. "But once that's all settled, I'm sure I can find an opportunity to turn my wiles on him."

Ellie choked on the water.

"Well, you can hardly imagine that *Neil's* going to take the initiative, can you?" Constance replied as though Ellie's gasping were a question. "He's hardly the type for *that*. I mean, he nearly had a fit back in London over that incident with the taxidermy mermaid and the museum, and that was only a bit of fun!"

Constance's damp, glossy waves fell in abundance around her shoulders. Her Egyptian garments hugged her generously curved figure in all the right places. Her big brown eyes were framed by a rich, thick fringe of lashes, while her skin was the warm, flawless gold of a desert evening.

If Constance set her mind on getting Neil into her bed, she'd pursue it with the fearless tenacity of a terrier… and Neil wouldn't stand a chance.

Trying to talk Constance out of the notion using cool logic and rationality wasn't going to work. In fact, in Ellie's experience, it would only serve to make Constance even more determined.

If Ellie had any hope of preventing Constance from enacting her horrifying scheme, she would have to take a different approach. Swallowing her shock and mortification, she crossed to the vanity, plucked up a brush, and yanked it through a length of her hair.

"If that's all," she said, keeping her tone forcefully casual, "do let me know when you've made up your mind about it."

Constance gave her a deeply skeptical look through the mirror. "You are going to give yourself a terrible frizz. And is that all you really have to say about it?"

"What else would I have to say?" Ellie slapped the brush back down on the table. Plucking the Bible up from the floor, she dropped onto her bed with it, holding it up like a shield. "You're both intelligent people," she concluded from behind the safety of the pages. "I'm sure you'll sort it out."

Constance gave her a suspicious look as Ellie pointedly fixed her attention on Leviticus.

"Well, then," Constance finally replied. "If that's the case, I shall."

"Shall what?" Ellie demanded as she fumblingly turned the page.

Constance's smile curved like a scimitar. "Let you know if I decide to seduce your brother," she replied dangerously.

SIXTEEN

$\mathcal{E}$LLIE FOLLOWED a cat across a softly undulating desert. The empty landscape around her was painted in the orange, peach, and shadowy violet of dusk.

The cat's gray coat was peppered with black spots like the pelt of a leopard, its body long and sleek with pointed ears. Ellie trudged in its wake as it padded lightly up the shifting sands of a low, sprawling dune.

She crested the rise, and the cat was gone. Instead, a woman stood in the deserted hollow. She was slight in stature but radiated a quiet strength in her simple white gown. Her umber skin glowed warmly in the golden light, framed by braids of thick black hair.

Ellie knew her. She knew the gold-flecked eyes that watched as she approached and the lightning bolt of a scar that marred the surface of her cheek.

She knew the sound of her voice. The blood that had stained her hands. The memory of the face of her lover.

Her name.

"Ixb'ahjun," Ellie breathed out in surprise. "But I… I haven't seen you since…"

She trailed off, her throat tightening with guilt at the memory of white pyramids falling with ancient roads and towering forests into a vast black pit.

One that she had opened.

"How are you here?" Ellie caught herself with a lurch of dismay. "*Are* you here? Is this just a dream, or…"

The priestess from the other side of the world did not answer. She gazed at Ellie with a quiet knowing, then turned and led her across the desert.

They climbed another dune. On the far side, the flowing sand gave way to a flat, rocky plain.

A long, slender box sat isolated in the center of the open ground, covered in lines of hieroglyphs between accents of shimmering gold.

Ellie recognized it as a coffin.

Ixb'ahjun stopped at the head of it. She looked at Ellie as though waiting.

Ellie slowly approached. The coffin was a typical example of Egyptian New Kingdom royal funerary arts, with a stylized face framed by a striped nemes headdress. Carved arms were crossed over its breast, holding the crook and flail of Egypt.

A gust of wind tugged at Ellie's skirts, tossing the loose tendrils of her hair. A storm was rising to the north, visible as a dark, obscure haze marring the line of the horizon. The first grains of blowing sand pecked at her skin with a subtle sting.

"She is waiting for you," Ixb'ahjun declared from her place at the head of the beautiful coffin.

"Who?" Ellie demanded.

"The Stranger," Ixb'ahjun replied. "The Lady of a Hundred Names."

The breeze strengthened. The air around Ellie dulled with dust tossed in wild little swirls and eddies.

"But what can I possibly do for her?" Ellie pitched her voice to be heard over the wind as she raised up her arm to protect her eyes.

"Learn." Ixb'ahjun's fiery gaze was steady through the growing hiss of the storm. "*Remember.*"

Ellie opened her mouth to reply—and the desert swept in, blinding her in a maelstrom of burning sand.

She woke with a gasp to a thick black night, the weight of Leviticus resting heavily on her chest.

Constance snored softly in the other bed. Through the open windows of the hotel, Luxor was quiet. Ellie could hear only the trill of night birds and the distant, gentle creak of the wharves.

Her mind was troubled and restless, spinning with the remnants of unsettled dreams.

The light fabric of the curtains hung still, without so much as a ripple of a breeze. Constance let out a dreamy mumble.

"Never win… dastardly…" Constance rolled over, twisting in her sheets. "…Devilish kisses…"

Ellie was filled with the need to escape the room and feel open air on her skin. Throwing back the blankets, she swung her legs off the bed.

The concierge had left her and Constance a pair of the loose dark cloaks that Egyptian women typically wore to cover their regular clothes when they left home. Ellie slipped hers on over her galabeya and tiptoed out, pulling the door quietly shut behind her.

She found her way down to the veranda that ran along the front of the hotel, where she gave the twin statues of Sekhmet a commiserating glare. Leaving the stolen monuments behind, she moved to the end of the covered walkway, near to where the garden wall blocked her view of the black, still waters of the Nile.

She wished the wall was not there. She itched to go further, stealing up to the banks of the great river to sink her bare toes into its mud.

"Bad dreams?"

The voice rumbled softly from behind her. Ellie turned to see Adam leaning against the wall of the hotel, his lanky form swathed in shadows. His sleeves were rolled up to his elbows. His feet were bare. The clothes he wore looked reasonably clean, which meant they had most likely been borrowed from someone else.

"What are you doing out here?" Her voice sounded hoarse—like a man in a desert who'd just spotted a drink of water.

Adam flashed her a slightly rueful smile and lifted his hand to reveal the orange ember of a cigar.

"Of course you are," Ellie noted dryly. "And who is responsible for supplying you with those?"

"Hotel guy pointed me to the street with the shops," Adam replied. "Probably because he could guess what the state of my socks would be in the morning without a swap. Might've happened to stumble across a tobacconist on my way to the socks."

"Tripped right over it, I imagine." Ellie's gaze dropped to his exposed toes. "And where are the socks now?"

"My feet were hot." Adam grinned at her.

The sight of that crooked, boyish smile sent a warm, heady feeling rushing through her. Ellie found herself exquisitely aware that they were alone together at an hour when they might remain uninterrupted and unobserved for quite some time. It invited notions that had her skin feeling hot despite the comfortable temperature of the night air—thoughts of how Adam's lips would taste like cigar. Of what it would feel like for him to press her up against the wall of the hotel or make some wicked use of the sturdy wrought-iron table beside her.

The force of the desire rocked through her like lightning. She *wanted* to feel it. She wanted to feel *him*—every precious, infuriating inch of him.

"So I had a little… er, *chat* with your brother back in Saqqara," Adam offered awkwardly.

His words hit like a splash of cold water, breaking the dangerous spell that had been weaving around her.

"Fiddlesticks," Ellie blurted.

"It wasn't *that* bad," Adam countered.

"It wasn't?" Ellie returned skeptically.

Adam shifted uncomfortably. "I mean… maybe it was a little bit that bad. But not… as bad as it could've been." His expression firmed. "I did make it damned clear that none of this is your fault."

A sense of exhaustion crept up around her like tendrils vining out from the paving stones.

"Adam, why are you using that word?" Ellie asked quietly.

"What word?" he pressed back, confused.

"Fault."

He went still, the gold ember of the cigar continuing to burn in his hand. After a moment, he reached over to set it down on the ashtray that stood by the table. "I'm just trying to do the right thing, Ellie."

"You said that before," Ellie pointed out, even as the first silent wisps of fear tightened her throat. "But I don't know what it means."

Adam met her eyes from across the shadows of the veranda, the blue of his irises shaded to cobalt. "It means that only an irresponsible cad would keep kissing you when he hasn't figured out where all of this is going."

"You're not an irresponsible cad," Ellie pushed back, bewildered.

"I've sure as hell been acting like one."

"Why?" she pressed firmly. "Because you kissed me? You're not the only one who initiated those encounters, if I might remind you. Does that make me a cad as well?"

"Of course not!" Adam protested.

"Why not?"

"Because you're…"

"A woman?" she prompted thinly.

"No!" he burst out, and then caught himself. "I mean—you are. But that's not what I meant!"

"Then what did you mean?" Ellie's voice was tinged with a hint of exasperation.

"Adam's expression hardened. "You aren't just… cruising through your life without taking responsibility for things," he bit out sharply.

Ellie stilled as she took in the stiffness of his form—the tension that infused every line of him.

"Is that what you think you're doing?" she asked carefully.

"I didn't think it before!" Adam shot back, throwing out his hand. "But now I'm kissing you in caves, or on boats, or balconies, and completely mortifying your brother—all without having the first goddamned idea how all of this is supposed to turn out. And I'm not sure what the hell else you're supposed to call that!"

His voice had risen almost to a shout. Ellie held herself carefully still. Something about their conversation felt dangerous, like a vase poised on the very edge of a table.

"Would all of this be easier if I was open to the idea of marriage?"

"No," Adam retorted shortly, and then hedged, his expression falling into one of helplessness. "Yes? I don't know, Ellie!" He treaded across the stones of the veranda like a caged lion. "Maybe it would be—but that doesn't mean it's what I want! I told you—I like you the way you are. Maybe if you were more open to the idea of marriage, I wouldn't have already fallen half in love with you!"

Ellie froze for a different reason. A sudden and dizzying warmth swept through her. "Do you really mean that?"

Adam looked over at her in confusion. "Which part?"

"The part about being half in love with me," she returned with careful patience.

His look burned through the darkness that separated them. "Yeah."

Ellie closed her eyes as the word washed over her. It felt as though her feet had rooted themselves to the ground—as though nothing in the world could have moved her if she didn't want it to.

The night air stretched around her, warm and delicate with the sound of softly chirping insects and the fluttering of black-winged birds.

"But I'm not doing a very good job of it, Princess," Adam continued softly, his tone aching with regret.

Ellie pinned him with a glare as a bolt of sudden fury shot through her. "Says who?"

"Huh?" Adam returned, frowning.

Ellie took a step toward him, closing the distance between them. She pushed a finger against the solid wall of his chest. "Who says you aren't doing a good job of it? Whose voice are you hearing in your head, telling you that?"

Adam was quiet—but he didn't flinch back as he gazed down at her through the shadows. "My father," he admitted.

Ellie's heart twisted painfully in her chest. She brushed a hand softly over the stubble on his cheek. "Adam, your father disowned you."

"I'm aware," he returned with a wry twist of his lips.

"No," Ellie pushed back, shaking her head. "I mean—you don't do that to someone you truly care about. To someone you *love*." Her tone firmed as her resolve hardened. "I don't know everything that passed between the two of you, but George Bates gave up the right to live in your head the day he signed those papers and cut you out of his life."

"You don't know what I did to push him to it," Adam countered.

"Be yourself? Make your own choices in life? Refuse to become the person he thought you ought to be instead of who you really are? That's not pushing, Adam! That's... that's what you have to do in order to *survive!*" Ellie raised her other hand to frame his face gently with her palms, forcing him to meet her gaze. "Who would you be right now if you had buttoned up the real Adam Bates and done everything your father asked of you? Not the man who's saved my life three times over! Who took a chance on me for a medallion and a fairy tale, and stuck by me even when I didn't deserve it!"

Her voice was raw with feeling. The cool track of a tear slipped from the corner of her eye to glide down her cheek.

"I don't need to see that other Adam Bates—that one your father would've made you into—to know that I would never have chosen him over the one that's standing right in front of me," she finished roughly.

Adam was very still. "The other me probably would've read more books," he said quietly.

"So?" Ellie protested.

A warm, firm hand slipped around the small of her back, drawing her a half step closer.

"He wouldn't have just run off from his job," he continued. "Probably smell a little better."

Ellie dashed a hand against the damp that stained her cheeks. "I *like* the way you smell."

Adam raised a skeptical eyebrow. "That's because you haven't really got me at my worst yet. Lemme tell you, after two weeks in the bush with no—"

Ellie pushed up on her toes to kiss him. Her lips were tender, her hand steady as she slipped it up the nape of his neck to tangle in his hair. He met her with something softer than the fiery heat that had threatened to consume them every time they'd touched before.

She brushed her other hand over his cheek, where a drop of betraying moisture broke against his unshaven jaw.

He carefully pulled back to gaze down at her. For the first time, Ellie could see the fear and vulnerability written plain on his rugged features. "I don't know if I'm good enough for you," he confessed roughly.

Ellie gently pushed a lock of hair back from his forehead. "Don't you dare try to decide that for me," she declared softly.

He let his head fall forward until it came to rest against her own. His eyes closed. His arms were warm around her back as he held her. "Still don't know quite where that leaves us."

"Well, I *had* thought the obvious solution was for us to become colleagues," Ellie began.

Adam lifted his head, frowning down at her. "Colleagues?"

"Extremely close, deeply committed colleagues!" Ellie protested. "After all, the Latin root of the word strongly suggests…" She trailed off, sensing that now was not the time for etymology. "At any rate, I have realized that solution fails to address all of the key aspects of our relationship… such as the fact that I can't seem to stop wanting to touch you."

Adam's lip quirked into a slightly satisfied smirk. "Find me pretty touchable, huh?"

Ellie gave a wry smile of her own, but resisted entirely succumbing to Adam's considerable charm until she had finished. "So I have been working on alternate options for addressing our situation. And it has not failed to occur to me that the most obvious of them is for me to… amend my stance on the question of marriage," she finished awkwardly.

Adam's expression grew serious once more. The lines of his face were shadowed by the gloom of the veranda. "Don't, Ellie."

"Don't?" Ellie echoed uncertainly.

"I meant what I said," Adam continued. "I don't want you to change your mind. Fighting for what's important to you is who you are. If I tried to shake that out of you for my convenience, I'd be no better than my dad."

Ellie raised her hands to the beard-roughened sides of his face again as she infused her voice with as much certainty as she could muster. "You are *nothing* like your father."

He gave her a sad smile. "How do you know? You've never met him."

Ellie let her thumb caress the strong line of his cheek, her gaze softening. "I don't have to."

Adam moved in a little closer—near enough that she could feel the subtle heat of his body a breath from her own. "See, when you say things like that, it makes me want to lay you out on this patio table."

The words sparked a vivid image of what it would feel like for Adam to do exactly that. Ellie's cheeks heated. "Oh?"

"Which is why…" He lowered his head so that his breath tickled warmly against the line of her jaw. "…I'm going to have to insist that you get back to bed."

Ellie fought back a frustrated sigh. The patio table sounded *much* more enticing than her room upstairs and the rest of Leviticus, but it would be deeply unfair of her to push Adam's limits—not now that she understood what that might cost him far better than she had an hour before.

"Yes." She mustered the willpower to take a deliberate step back from him. "I'll do that."

She lingered another moment, achingly conscious of the delicate breeze, the distant lap of the river—and the lean, powerful form of the man who stood before her, his midnight gaze like an electric current that cut through the darkness that divided them.

"Goodnight, Princess," Adam said, his voice rich with heat, respect, and affection.

"Goodnight, *my* Adam Bates," Ellie replied forcefully—and then slipped away.

SEVENTEEN

$\mathcal{E}$LLIE WOKE TO daylight streaming through the open window and a pillow thumping her in the face.

"Get up, you slug!" Constance called out cheerfully. "We have a temple to raid!"

Constance tossed the pillow aside and popped back over to the vanity to check on her hair, which was twisted into a perfectly tousled Gibson, every strand gleaming.

Ellie forced herself upright. Every movement took effort. It had taken her hours to fall back asleep after she'd returned to her room in the middle of the night, tossed between worry about Adam and thoughts of what use they might have made of that shadowed patio table.

She winced against the glare of the sun and forced herself to remember why she had come to Luxor in the first place.

That the true story be known… seek behind the sun disk in the Holy of Holies of Maat-ka-re Khnemet Amun Hatshepsut.

Ellie was wildly intrigued by the mention of Neferneferuaten in the inscription in Mutnedjmet's jewelry box. That mysterious figure had captured her imagination ever since Neil had started rattling on to her about it years before. But how did the identity of Akhenaten's obscure successor connect to the story of the Exodus—if at all? And did the inscription's reference of a was-scepter—a staff the Ancient Egyptians believed imbued with magical power—have any connection to the Staff of Moses?

As she readied herself, Ellie wondered how many of those questions might be answered by today's endeavor.

A maid had dropped off their laundered clothes earlier. Constance was already in her lawn dress, which had survived its ordeal at Saqqara with aplomb. She leaned toward the mirror as she set a new hat in place. It was significantly less ostentatious than the last one, but Constance set it at just the right angle to make it look eminently fashionable.

Ellie had been furnished with another perfectly serviceable straw boater. She pinned it on after Constance had vacated the mirror, only to find herself staring at the dark circles that shadowed her eyes.

Constance popped into the frame of the glass beside her. "You need cucumbers," she declared authoritatively. "But we haven't any time for them now. Come on!"

She hurried Ellie out of the room. As they headed for the stairs to the lobby, Ellie's brain finally stuttered back to life.

"We'll need a ferry to cross the river. Animals for transportation to the ruins," she recited. "Some sort of hamper for lunch."

"Yes, yes," Constance said dismissively. "I told you. The hotel has taken care of all of that. Deir al-Bahari is one of their regular excursions."

"*Excursions?*" The word set off a low note of alarm in Ellie's mind.

Constance tugged Ellie into the lobby, and the nightmare of her situation became instantly clear.

The space in front of the welcome desk was packed with practically every other guest who was staying at the hotel. A morose Welsh painter juggled a bundle of canvases and an easel. A pair of German brothers were picking through a wicker case stuffed with provisions.

"But there ought to be at least two types of pickles!" the first complained.

"Wo ist die Wurst?" exclaimed the other.

"I can't eat wurst in this climate," complained an American woman with pearls as she fanned herself. "I need cold chicken. Can't somebody bring an icebox? Dick, tell Chester to stop stabbing the florals."

The boy in question—Chester—was still in short pants. With a flat, blank look at his parents, he drew back the fountain pen he had been using to poke holes in the potted tropical shrubbery.

Ellie stared aghast at the scene. "This is a disaster."

"What—you mean the sausages?" Constance asked.

Ellie yanked Constance partially behind a leafy palm. "This!" she replied with an urgent wave at the crowd. "How are we supposed to find the sign of the sun disk somewhere in the funerary temple of Hatshepsut while we are on a *tourist* expedition?"

"We'll just sneak off," Constance returned easily. "Don't worry about it. I'm going to go make sure they packed some dates."

She abandoned Ellie to take a peek into the lunch basket.

Adam stepped into the lobby. His eyes found Ellie from the other side of the complaining crowd, and he crossed to her side.

His shoulders were broad under his white shirt and suspenders. After a moment, Ellie realized that instead of speaking to him, she was staring up at him like a drowning woman looking at land. She cleared her throat, forcing herself to act like a reasonable person. "No jacket?"

Adam shrugged. "It's an outdoor excursion."

"That's just an excuse," Ellie pointed out.

"Complaining?" He flashed her a grin. "At least I haven't lost my shirt yet."

Ellie flushed at the memory of precisely what lay beneath Adam's shirt. "You might do with a hat."

"Forgot to put it on the shopping list," Adam replied.

"What if you get a sunburn?"

"I gave up worrying about sunburns a long time ago."

"That is because you still have all of your hair." Sayyid sighed as he joined them, his dashing red fez perched on top of his close-cropped curls. "If you were starting to look like a monk on the top of your head, you might feel differently."

"I think bald men can be very dashing," Constance asserted as she came back over and slipped her hand gallantly through Sayyid's arm.

Neil stepped into the lobby, his jaw dropping as he looked over the tourist-cluttered scene. "Who are all these people?"

Constance's mouth widened into a dangerous smile as her eyes locked onto Neil's figure. "Were you hoping for something more *intimate?*"

Ellie blanched with horror as she recalled Constance's illicit designs on her brother. She opened her mouth to protest, but only a strangled noise came out.

Adam frowned down at her with a flash of concern.

"Oh, there's the horn for the ferry!" Constance innocently blinked her long, thick lashes. "We'd best load up."

She blithely strolled away, tugging Sayyid along with her. Neil morosely followed, blinking with dismay at the noisy crowd.

"Did I miss something just then?" Adam asked, lingering behind.

Ellie closed her eyes. "I would really, *really* rather not talk about it."

Adam raised an eyebrow, and Ellie forced herself to follow after their friends.

The heat of the day was already beginning to rise as they walked to the nearby quay, and for the first time since her arrival in Egypt, Ellie found herself actually standing on the banks of the Nile. The river was broad at Luxor and busy with boats, from quickly darting single-sail feluccas to an elegantly appointed sixty-foot dahabeeyah that lay at anchor a little way off the shore. The columns of the Luxor Temple rose beside her, and beyond that, she could see the modern, Western-style facades of the American, French, and English consulate buildings, flying their colorful respective flags.

The hotel's ferry was a brightly painted steam launch. Ellie found herself comparing it to the much smaller and more rugged *Mary Lee*... which she had last seen plummeting over a waterfall.

She and Constance boarded just ahead of the American family.

"I sure am excited to see another one of those pagan tombs," the gentleman drawled as he walked up the gangplank, his pearl-wearing wife trailing in his wake. "I bought a real nice little statue off some kid at the last one."

"Is that right, Mr. Swingley?" Constance cast a nervous look at Ellie, whose knuckles whitened where she gripped the railing.

Adam joined them as the Swingleys moved on. "Pretty hot," he noted.

Though it was still morning, the desert sun already beat down mercilessly from above.

"Might need to go for a swim later," he added with just a hint of a smirk as he deliberately glanced over at Ellie.

Ellie felt the air get a little warmer. "You are incorrigible."

"Who, me?"

"Just do try to keep your shirt on," Ellie ordered in a slightly hopeless whisper.

Adam grinned at her before stepping back to make way for another passenger.

"Your cheeks are pink," Constance observed.

"It's the heat," Ellie grumbled back.

"Sure it is," Constance returned dryly.

On the far side of the Nile, an assortment of donkeys awaited them. There was a great deal of shuffling and complaining as the Swingleys and the Habenschuss brothers wrangled for the best mount.

"But I need one for my canvases!" complained Mr. Beddoe, the Welsh artist.

"Why is this taking so long?" Neil demanded desperately.

"I was hoping for camels," Adam noted a little sadly.

Finally, they were all mounted. Ellie's ride lurched forward at the shouts of the donkey boy and trotted quickly up the road.

They passed through verdant cotton fields dotted with simple farmhouses as they headed north along the Nile. Women walked the tracks along the canals balancing urns of water on their heads. Farmers drove their oxen through the newly plowed rows.

A pair of odd, dark shapes emerged from the haze ahead of them where the fertile land gave way to desert. As Ellie drew closer, they resolved themselves into the sun-gilded forms of two enormous statues.

The monuments towered over the landscape, utterly out of proportion with the rows of cucumbers and the little stone ring of an old well. They were weathered and wind-scoured, leaving only the rough shape of crowned forms seated on giant thrones.

History called them the Colossi of Memnon. The faces were entirely gone, chipped and scoured away by time, but Ellie already knew whose features she would have seen a few thousand years before—those of Amenhotep III, the father of Akhenaten.

She stopped her donkey just before the twin figures, craning back her neck to gaze at a feat of engineering that would have challenged even modern builders.

"Awe-inspiring, aren't they?" Sayyid said from beside her.

Ellie flashed him an apologetic smile. "I must be gawking at them like the worst sort of tourist."

"The worst sort of tourist stops to take a Kodak and then rides past without another thought," Sayyid replied.

Ellie took his comment as permission to gape up at the massive statues for a little longer, thrumming with excitement at their sheer, time-weathered splendor. The impact was so great, she barely found herself thinking about how they compared to other monumental sculptures of the mid-Eighteenth Dynasty.

When she finally pulled her eyes away, she was startled to realize that the rest of the party had ridden some distance ahead. Adam turned in his saddle to look back at her. Ellie gave him a quick, reassuring wave and nudged her donkey back into motion as Sayyid fell into place beside her.

"Have you spent much time in Luxor?" Ellie asked.

"I have." He flashed her a smile tinged with nostalgia. "It will always remind me of my father. He served as a foreman on a number of excavations here and often talked my mother into letting me join him, even when I really ought to have been in school."

"That must have been wonderful," Ellie said meaningfully, feeling a little pang of envy. "And more than worth making up a bit of missed study."

"Oh, that wasn't necessary," Sayyid countered. "My father was more than capable of tutoring me in whatever I missed. He was university educated himself."

"He was?" Ellie frowned. "But if he had a degree, why was he working as a foreman?"

Sayyid cast Ellie a careful look. "You know what a concession is?"

"An official permit granting the right to excavate at a particular site here in Egypt," she replied automatically. "They're acquired by applying to the Antiquities Service."

"Unless one is an Egyptian," Sayyid added with a tired smile.

Ellie stilled as the import of Sayyid's words sunk into her brain.

She had been reading about Ancient Egypt for ages. She had soaked up piles of excavation reports written by the likes of Flinders Petrie and Mariette… and she had never *once* stopped to wonder why none of the names on those reports had been Egyptian.

Her donkey stopped beneath her as her cheeks flushed with humiliation. Hadn't she dreamed of acquiring just such a concession for herself? Had it never occurred to her that if by some miracle she had received one, it might have been granted to her at the expense of an equally qualified Egyptian?

Dismay washed over her. "I feel like such a wretched fool!"

"It is not as though you would have found it printed in a book," Sayyid offered with a note of sympathy. "It is not an official policy."

"I still ought to have noticed before now," Ellie returned forcefully. "As someone who is routinely excluded from opportunities for professional and academic advancement myself, I might have paid better attention to who else was being left out! There is no excuse for it, and I can only offer a most sincere apology."

"You needn't apologize to me," Sayyid returned quickly, his cheeks flushing.

"To Egypt, then," Ellie determined firmly. "I will not allow myself to be so self-absorbed in the future. One cannot claim to be committed to righting injustice and then abandon that principle when it is not a matter that impacts one personally."

"You can hardly expect yourself to know of every injustice in the world." Sayyid looked a little alarmed at the notion.

"Perhaps not," Ellie agreed a little reluctantly. "But I must certainly do a better job than I have been. Tell me, then—is it simple prejudice that lies behind the denial of excavation rights to Egyptians, or are the gentlemen at the Antiquities Service perhaps afraid that if you begin digging up your own history, you might question why you need the rest of us outsiders at all? You might even start to wonder whether it is right that half your heritage is routinely carted off to foreign museums and collectors!"

She added that last point with an extra note of fervor. Ellie's opinions about the distribution of archaeological finds to Europe and America had changed the moment she stepped into a cave in British Honduras and saw the devastation wreaked by looters searching for artifacts they could sell on the black market. She could still vividly recall the resigned, hollow look in Adam's eyes as he had taken in the scene.

I'm lying about what's out there. And the worst part is, I'm not even sure it matters.

"I am not entirely certain," Sayyid replied awkwardly. "I have never applied."

"But if you were to even try, they would look at you as though you were mad," Ellie filled in with feeling. "And your request would be turned down for some reason or another, if they even bothered to respond at all!"

Sayyid's eyes flashed with an unnameable emotion—and Ellie knew that she had found the nub of it. And why wouldn't she? She knew precisely how these things went.

Adam threw another worried look back at her. The rest of the party had ridden even further ahead. Ellie forced her donkey to trot along after them before she and Sayyid fell too conspicuously behind.

"Where did your father go to school?" she asked, searching for a less infuriating and painful topic of conversation.

"The English name for it would be 'The School of the Ancient Egyptian Tongue.'"

There was something a little careful in how Sayyid said it.

Ellie's interest perked at the intriguing name. "Is it here in Egypt?"

"Was," Sayyid replied shortly.

"What happened?" Ellie felt another quick flash of anger, already anticipating Sayyid's answer.

"The British Consul General closed it down. It was not just my father's school," Sayyid continued hurriedly. "Lord Cromer is suspicious of all higher education for Egyptians." He held back for a moment, but then burst out with the rest of his thought, which came in a distinctly wry tone. "He thinks it turns us into revolutionaries."

Ellie decided to keep her resulting thoughts about Lord Cromer to herself, lest the sound of her ranting reach the others and send Adam back to check on her.

"That must have been terribly hard for your father," she said instead. "To know that he was just as well educated as the men he worked for but could only ever play a supporting role."

"He had a reputation for being an extremely knowledgeable and capable foreman—the best, really," Sayyid replied carefully. "And the foreign archaeologists all wanted the best. There was never any shortage of work."

"But it was not the work he deserved," Ellie declared firmly.

"No." Sayyid met her eyes. "It was not."

They had left the fields behind for an arid path through rubble-strewn desert. The Colossi of Memnon receded behind them. The ruins of an empire sprawled across the dry ground to either side in little more than tumbled piles of rubble.

Ellie's chest still seethed with a tight mix of conflicted feeling. It prompted her to be more frank than she might normally have been with a relatively new acquaintance.

"Are you ever so angry that you feel like you could just... *explode?*"

Sayyid's smile was both sympathetic and a little sad. "You sound like my wife."

Ellie tapped her donkey back into motion, conscious once more of their distance from the rest of the party. "I like your wife."

Sayyid burst out with a laugh. He looked a little surprised by it, and shook his head as he rode beside her.

They rejoined the party just as the rugged track turned onto a wide, well-paved road.

Not a road, Ellie corrected herself with a sense of wonder. She was looking at a processional way built thousands of years ago for the enormous structure nestled at the foot of the soaring cliffs—the funerary temple of the pharaoh Hatshepsut.

A soaring tribute to a woman who had turned herself into a king, the temple was partially ruined but still impressive, rising like an elaborate wedding cake in three grand tiers that framed a broad central staircase. Shadowy enclaves to either side of the steps were fronted by surviving rows of elegant columns.

"Does anyone have any perfume?" Mrs. Swingley complained. "My donkey smells absolutely awful."

"I don't want to hire one of those grifters to talk about the art again," her husband complained. "Half of them don't speak English properly, and I bet they're just making up who all the animal-headed people are."

Ellie realized her teeth were grinding together.

"Heeeey." Adam deliberately let his donkey fall back beside her. "Those big statues back there were pretty great. Want to tell me all the things you know about them?"

Ellie shot him a grateful look as her burst of temper diffused.

Constance slowed to join them. "We only have to put up with them until we reach the temple," she whispered loudly.

The structure grew in scale and impressiveness the nearer they came to it. Once they reached the base of the steps, the tourists drifted over to a makeshift souvenir shop nearby. It was more or less a rug thrown down by the stairs, which was covered with an assortment of cheap trinkets. A group of women sat beside it, gossiping with each other as they ignored the foreigners. They wore the black cloaks and headscarves that Ellie had seen all over Egypt, along with niqab veils that covered the lower half of their faces.

It looked like she and the others were the first visitors to reach the temple that day, but Ellie could see a closed carriage approaching on the processional way behind them, likely carrying another batch of sightseers.

She supposed she should be grateful there weren't more of them. During the peak of Egypt's tourist season in the winter, the temple would have been crawling with tourists, making her mission far more complicated.

Adam studied the three enormous levels of the building a little ruefully. "Looks a lot bigger up close than it does from a distance."

"Should we expect to run into any *official forces*?" Constance asked.

"She means archaeologists," Ellie clarified at Sayyid's confused look.

"Édouard Naville has been leading the work here for the last several years," Sayyid offered. "But his season ended in April. I shouldn't expect to see any of his people about."

Ellie glanced at Neil, who stood a little apart from the rest of them. He had been unusually quiet all morning—or since they had left Saqqara, really. Not that she could blame him. Neil hadn't asked for any of this—not losing his job and being railroaded into a trip to Luxor… or learning that his sister was involved with his trouble-making best friend.

Adam might have talked things through with Neil back at Saqqara—for better or worse—but Ellie knew her own reckoning with her brother still awaited her. She'd frankly been avoiding it because Neil was sure to have questions that she had no idea how to answer.

"We should split up," Constance declared authoritatively, "so that we can cover the temple more efficiently. Ellie, why don't you and Adam examine the lower level? Sayyid could take the center while Stuffy and I manage the top. That way, we are maximizing our Egyptologists."

The lower level of the temple was lined with colonnades framing shadowy, intimate recesses. Ellie's thoughts snapped irresistibly to just what she and Adam might get up to while searching those hidden alcoves for clues.

No, she thought quickly, suppressing a groan. She couldn't explore any shadowy recesses with Adam—not when he remained so conflicted about the liberties they had already taken with each other.

If Ellie had given any outward sign of her confusion, Constance didn't notice. Her gaze had locked onto Ellie's brother, darkening with a special—and *deeply* alarming—glint of interest.

There were plenty of shadowy recesses at the top of the temple as well.

"Wait!" Ellie blurted out in protest as she searched frantically for a reasonable excuse to overturn Constance's plan.

Before she could manage it, Sayyid danced back from the steps, biting out an alarmed yelp.

"Is something wrong?" Constance pressed.

"Beetle!" Sayyid managed, his voice strangled. "Shoe!"

Neil rolled his eyes. "It's just a bug!"

"A bug intent on climbing the leg of my trousers!" Sayyid whipped out a handkerchief, wiping his forehead with it nervously.

"Goodness! It is rather large." Constance bent over to study the insect with gruesome interest. It was an inch or so long with big black pincers and an iridescent sheen to its carapace.

"It had nearly reached my laces." Sayyid barely repressed a shudder.

"But it's a scarab!" Ellie said, recognizing the distinct form of the insect. "I should think an Egyptologist would be fond of them, considering how sacred they were to the ancient people here."

"They can be perfectly sacred, and one can still prefer that they remain very far away," Sayyid retorted.

Constance cast another interested look at Neil, who had turned away to gaze at the temple with a slightly mournful air. "Well!" she said brightly. "Now that's settled..."

Ellie hurried to cut her off before she could cement her plan. "I believe both Sayyid and my brother are already familiar with the temple structure. Clearly, it makes the most sense for the rest of us to form teams around them."

Constance shot Ellie a dangerous glare. "Oh, really?"

"I can explore the upper level with Neil," Ellie continued deliberately. "You, Adam, and Sayyid can check these lower colonnades."

"Or I can explore the upper level," Constance returned evenly, knives flashing behind her eyes. "And you may do the colonnades."

"Why are they arguing about this?" Sayyid asked, clearly bewildered.

"Think I'm starting to have an idea," Adam replied, "and I'm pretty sure you don't want to know."

He cast a sympathetic glance at Neil, who was obliviously polishing his spectacles on a handkerchief.

In the end, Ellie was saved by the American, Mr. Swingley, who strolled over to join them.

"Does your Egyptian fellow speak English?" he demanded.

It took Ellie a moment to realize that he was talking about Sayyid, who stared back at the man with blank astonishment.

"Not a word," Adam cut in. He looped his arm through Sayyid's elbow, hauling him toward the colonnade. "Come on, Connie," he called back.

Constance shot Ellie a glare ripe with the threat of revenge before stalking after him.

Ellie made her way over to Neil. "Shall we, then?"

"Shall we what?" Neil blinked at her with confusion behind his spectacles.

"Explore the upper level," Ellie explained tiredly. "Or weren't you listening to any of that?"

"I… That is… my mind might've been wandering a bit," Neil replied uncomfortably.

Ellie wondered if she should be frustrated or grateful for that.

"Goodness!" Constance exclaimed as she peered past Adam and Sayyid at the recessed wall behind one of the nearby colonnades. "That's a remarkably large—"

"—ithyphallic representation of the god Amun," Sayyid quickly and awkwardly finished for her, patting his forehead with his handkerchief once more. "Perhaps we should move on to the next one?"

Ellie barely suppressed a snort. Adam glanced over at her with a wryly raised eyebrow, and their gazes locked.

Ithyphallic representations. Shadowy alcoves.

A flush of heat that had nothing to do with the rising ambient temperature rose into her cheeks.

No, she thought forcefully. She had to stop letting her unruly thoughts run wild when it came to Adam Bates—not until they had sorted things out between them like reasonable, rational people.

Adam cleared his throat and turned his eyes deliberately to the ceiling of the colonnade. Ellie pivoted back to her oblivious brother, hooking her hand through his arm. "Come on," she ordered and hauled him toward the stairs.

EIGHTEEN

$\mathcal{E}$LLIE CLIMBED TO the top of the grand temple stairway, dragging Neil along with her. The highest tier of the enormous structure would once have housed its most sacred precincts. Back then, a grand colonnade would have fronted the level, interspersed with statues of the pharaoh and her gods. That facade was nothing but tumbled rubble now, footings and fragments that lined the edge of the floor like a row of jagged teeth.

Beyond the broken columns lay a private open-air courtyard. Chapels and annexes branched off from it, including one carved directly into the face of the cliff, which rose from the back of the courtyard to a dizzying height overhead.

Ellie puzzled over the most likely place where she might find the sun disk mentioned in the inscription from the jewelry box. Could it be something painted on the remaining walls that lined the courtyard? Or might it be hidden in one of the chapels?

The truth was that it could be anywhere.

Instinctively, she turned to Neil for input—but he was looking back over his shoulder at the processional way and the distant glimmer of the Nile. The carriage she had seen earlier had reached the base of the temple, promising the imminent invasion of more tourists. Ellie suppressed a sigh.

"Ist das ein schöner Ort für ein Picknick?" one of the Germans from the hotel announced as he skipped up the steps to the courtyard.

Ellie did not want to search for ancient clues while being watched by a pair of Deutschlanders munching on pickles.

"How about this way?" She tugged Neil through the opening in the cliff.

The heat outside had been rising with the day, but in the shadowy confines of the carved chapel, Ellie was instantly cooler. The space was also quiet. The chatter of the tourists fell away as they moved deeper inside.

She tingled with excitement as she breathed in the smell of stone and dust. In this protected space, more of the temple's original artwork had survived the centuries. The blue-tinted wings of a ba-bird extended over lines of hieroglyphs and graceful figures draped in royal finery.

"It's a shrine to Amun." She spotted the name of one of the pre-eminent deities of Thebes above an empty niche cut into the wall.

"That's Hatshepsut and her father, Thutmose I, making offerings to the gods," Neil pointed out from behind her, wiping his mouth after taking a pull from his canteen.

Ellie turned to look. The woman who had made herself king was crowned with the uraeus cobra of a pharaoh. A false beard extended in a column from her chin. Her skin was a ruddy ocher, and she was depicted bare-chested, wearing a man's white kilt.

She studied the image as Neil stood beside her. The silence between them began to feel awkward.

This was the first moment Ellie had been alone with her brother since she had ambushed him in his tomb in Saqqara, and the weight of everything they had not yet talked about hung over her.

Part of Ellie loathed the idea of bringing up her relationship with Adam when so much remained unsettled between them, but she owed Neil better than that. He was her brother, after all, and Adam was his best friend. She ought to at least *try* to clear the air between them on the subject, and she couldn't know when she might get a better opportunity to do it—which meant that she had best stiffen up and get on with it.

She drew in a breath. "I suppose I ought to…"

"So about you and…" Neil began at the same time.

They both stopped, exchanging an awkward look.

"Of course," Ellie continued hurriedly, "the whole situation was entirely unexpected…"

"And as your older brother," Neil pressed on simultaneously, "I feel a certain obligation…"

"I mean, we were halfway through the wilderness before I even realized!" Ellie protested.

"But you're a grown woman," Neil said stoutly. "It's hardly my place to…"

He trailed off, and they both stared at each other.

"Good chat," Ellie concluded.

"Yes," Neil agreed, adjusting his spectacles as he turned back to the image of the pharaoh.

Ellie cleared her throat, pushing her attention to the mural as well.

She had always found Hatshepsut desperately intriguing. She wasn't the only woman to hold the role of pharaoh, but the list was exceedingly short. Hatshepsut had claimed the throne for herself against all precedent and proceeded to rule over Egypt through a period of great prosperity. The notion that Ellie was actually looking upon that ancient ruler's face—or even a stylized representation of it—struck her powerfully.

"It's impressive this wasn't destroyed," Neil noted.

"What do you mean?"

"Thutmose III, her successor, had most representations of Hatshepsut defaced." Neil frowned. "Didn't you know?"

Ellie hadn't. The realization made her cheeks flush. "But why?"

"It was probably meant as some sort of divine punishment," Neil replied distractedly, leaning in to study a cartouche.

"Punishment," Ellie echoed. "For being pharaoh… and a woman."

Neil cast her an uncomfortable look.

Ellie gazed at the noble, powerful features on the wall, her heart aching with a tumbled mix of emotion she wasn't quite sure how to name.

"There's nothing here," her brother declared.

He was right. As intriguing as the chapel was, it lacked any promising sun disks. Ellie turned to go, even though part of her itched to linger and study every aspect of the artwork.

Outside, the glare of midday blinded her. She shielded her eyes with the brim of her hat until they adjusted.

The upper level of the temple was a sprawl of low ruins. The Germans had spread a blanket out in the center of the sacred courtyard and were snacking on sandwiches.

Where should they look next?

"That message was left in the jewelry box by someone who wanted Nefer-neferuaten's story to survive," Ellie mused aloud. "They would have put it somewhere they thought it would remain safe indefinitely."

Neil waved a hand over the ruins. "Three-quarters of the superstructure of this temple has been destroyed. Even if they'd put it in a location they thought would be permanent, there's no guarantee it's actually still here."

"The people of the Eighteenth Dynasty would have seen plenty of ruined monuments at places like Saqqara, where relics of the Old Kingdom were already crumbling," Ellie countered, thinking furiously. "Whoever left that message would know to hide what we're looking for somewhere that wasn't going to fall down."

"We already checked the chapel in the cliff," Neil reminded her. "And there aren't any burial shafts here contemporary with Horemheb's time. Look, I'm as intrigued as you are by the notion of finding another Atenist relic, but you've got to at least consider the possibility that this is a dead end."

Ellie tried not to let his skepticism sting, even though the task of finding what they were looking for felt immense when faced with the sprawl of the temple.

"Hatshepsut wasn't an Atenist," Ellie pushed back. "Whoever hid this next clue must have brought it here over a hundred years after her death. If you were hiding an Atenist clue in this temple, where would you have put it?"

Neil frowned, his eyes going a bit distant. "Well—in the sun chapel, I suppose."

Ellie stared at him in surprise. "What sun chapel?"

"That one over there." Neil pointed across the courtyard to a narrow opening that framed a set of descending stairs. A flicker of movement at its base caught Ellie's eye as a skinny, sand-hued cat darted inside.

Ellie didn't recall seeing anything about a sun chapel in her readings about Hatshepsut's funerary temple—and Ellie was very good at recalling what she had read. "Was that in one of the excavation reports?"

Neil blinked at her as though coming out of a daydream. "Where else would I have found it?"

The question sounded slightly more bewildered than rhetorical. Ellie frowned thoughtfully at her brother.

"What?" he asked, surreptitiously adjusting his spectacles again.

"Nothing." Ellie turned her attention back to their mission. "A sun chapel would be situated in an open-air courtyard to catch the light of the rising dawn each day. If there's no ceiling, it can't fall down."

"Let's go have a look, then," Neil concluded tiredly.

The doorway only appeared narrow from a distance because it was so very tall. Ellie craned her neck back to look up at it as they passed through, filled with a sense of quiet awe at its monumental scale.

A set of stairs descended a half-story to a space that would once have been a covered vestibule. Bas relief art on the walls had been scoured clean of all but a few remnants of old paint, but Ellie could still make out a few lines of hieroglyphs and the kilted figure of the pharaoh.

Her face had been chipped away.

Another doorway framed by half-ruined walls opened from the vestibule to the sun chapel. As Ellie had expected, the space was open to the sky. Even though the walls that framed it were partially fallen into rubble, they were still high enough to reach well above Ellie's head, making the space a private secret closed away from the rest of the temple.

The Ancient Egyptians had worshiped the sun in many forms, stretching back thousands of years. Ellie shouldn't be surprised to find a space dedicated to that practice inside Hatshepsut's mortuary temple—though she still wondered how Neil had known about it.

The open-air chapel would have been built several generations before Akhenaten transformed the sun cult into a faith in the Aten as the sole god of Egypt and creator of all life—but it still felt plausible that an Atenist might have found this an appropriate place to conceal a clue to the secret history of the mysterious pharaoh Neferneferuaten.

The sun altar itself dominated the small courtyard. The square platform, roughly four feet in height, was where the ancient priests would have stood when making prayers and offerings to the rising sun.

Ellie circled it, carefully studying the stones as Neil frowned at some of the surviving fragments of artwork on the courtyard walls.

It didn't take her long to fully explore the space. The sun chapel was really just a rectangular box, open to the air and entirely lacking in distinctive features. Besides the altar, there were only two little nooks in the walls that once held votive statues. They were now empty except for the sandy-colored cat, which had hopped up into one of them to lick at a paw.

"I don't see any disks," Ellie admitted.

"This space wasn't as heavily decorated as other areas of the temple," Neil replied a little distractedly, still studying the walls.

"But it has to be here," Ellie insisted. "This is the only place that makes sense."

"I don't know what to tell you, Peanut." Neil pulled his attention from the stones and gave a little shrug. "It's just a courtyard and a rebuilt altar."

"Rebuilt?" Ellie echoed, confused. She looked back to the stone platform that dominated the center of the space. Its perfectly squared blocks all looked unbroken and original—which she would not have expected with a structure that had been recently restored. "By whom? Mr. Naville?"

"Not Naville," Neil returned with a hint of exasperation as he poked his head into one of the votive nooks. "The priests."

Ellie stared once more at the box of neatly quarried limestone. "Neil, how do you know this was rebuilt by the ancient priests?"

"Just look at it," Neil ordered with a dismissive wave of his hand.

"I *am*," Ellie insisted—and then she saw it.

The altar was built of a finer sort of limestone with a light, even grade… but the color of the blocks was slightly different on part of the staircase. It looked as though one type of stone had been layered over the top of another—as if the original stairs had been lengthened and increased in height to accommodate a larger altar.

The difference was almost indistinguishable unless you were up close and looking for it… which Neil hadn't been, as he was standing on the opposite side of the platform.

Ellie fought back a wave of frustration and admiration. This was just the sort of thing that had always driven her batty about her brother. Neil was handy with facts and figures—but Ellie could out-memorize him any day of the week. His startling leaps of intuition were what took his scholarship to the next level and made it feel nearly impossible to compete with him. They came out of nowhere, though Neil always managed to rattle off some explanation for how he'd arrived at them when pressed on the matter.

Yet those explanations had never felt quite right to Ellie. They were always just a little short of what they ought to be to explain how he came to his conclusions.

Were she a more superstitious sort of person, Ellie might have called it uncanny.

She pushed her attention back to the sun altar—because Neil's revelation, however he arrived at it, raised an intriguing possibility.

"Ancient builders wouldn't have wanted to waste high quality limestone by making these facing blocks any thicker than needed," she mused aloud. "I would bet my left foot that they're only panels, supported by struts laid over the structure of the older, smaller altar, with rubble filled in for added stability."

Ellie buzzed with excitement at the discovery—but Neil didn't seem to hear her. He gazed at her from the other side of the altar, his shoulders slumped into lines of dismay.

"Peanut…" he began.

He looked so forlorn that for once his use of Ellie's wretched nickname failed to infuriate her.

"What is it?" she demanded instead. "What's wrong?"

Neil looked down at his shoes and drew in a breath. "It has recently come to my attention that I have not been as good a brother to you as I ought to have been," he confessed awkwardly.

"What do you mean?" Ellie pressed, confused.

"Only that you are so dashed good at this!" Neil burst out, pacing. "When you were sitting under my desk, stealing my textbooks to read—well, I encouraged it, didn't I? Because you were so terribly clever. But I was treating it all like a game, and then I realized that you were serious. And why wouldn't you be?" He threw up his hands. "You have the knowledge, the skills, the drive, the intelligence—but I..."

His words choked off.

"What?" Ellie set her hands on her hips.

Her brother stared at her helplessly. His hair was mussed and his eyeglasses were a little crooked. "I hoped you would give it up." He closed his eyes. "Because I didn't see how you could do this—how it could possibly happen. And I didn't think you could ever be happy if you had your mind set on a life that was impossible!"

Ellie felt as though the ground beneath her trembled, threatening to give way. Any response she might have made to him caught in her throat.

"But I *know* you have just as much right to it as I do!" Neil protested, throwing out his arms. "That the rest of the world is mad when they say a woman can't do this sort of work! I just went along with it because I couldn't see how I could change it. And I still can't! I haven't the foggiest idea where I could even start! But I... I..."

He trailed off, his eyes pleading.

"...feel like you ought to have tried," Ellie filled in softly.

His words stirred up a storm—a whirling tumult of frustration, disappointment, sadness, and rage. Or perhaps the storm had been there for years, only Ellie had always held it at bay—staving it off with discipline and stubbornness, principle and determination.

She felt it all now in the face of her brother's words. The brother she hadn't been born with. The brother who had appeared in her life far enough along that Ellie could remember what it had been like *not* to have one.

Neil had dropped into the empty landscape of her childhood like a miracle. Once she had been alone, and then Neil had come, who was clever, and kind, and deeply passionate about the same history that captured Ellie's own imagination and set it afire. She had believed that the pair of them shared a camaraderie—two scholars under the same roof who could serve as partners and companions in their explorations of the lost mysteries of the past.

That had changed. The change had hurt. Ellie had managed to lock that hurt away inside of her, but now it rose from the secret place where she had hidden it.

"When you went to Cambridge," she began. "You... you left... and when you came back, you were..."

She swallowed painfully, fighting for the words.

He had gone to university, and when he returned home for his first holiday, Ellie had found a new distance between them. She had stumbled into it like an invisible wall set in her path. They hadn't been comrades anymore. Neil played the part of the serious scholar, and Ellie was simply his pesky little sister. When she attempted to draw him into discussions about a new excavation report or a linguistic anomaly, at first it would be as though she had lit a spark. Neil's interest would catch, and he would pepper her with questions, throwing back his thoughts and ideas… until something shifted. His expression would shutter, the enthusiastic light falling from his eyes. *It's nice you're keeping up with your reading,* he would say distantly, and then turn back to his work as though he had just been caught doing something he shouldn't have been.

It had only been Neil moving on, stepping further into the realm of growing up—but Ellie had never been able to understand why it felt like in doing so, he had left her behind.

"You were going to get hurt if you kept at it," Neil said quietly. "And I… I didn't know how to…"

Ellie's hands were shaking. She tucked them under her arms to keep them still. She was very afraid that if she let herself truly think about what Neil was saying, she might start to cry, and she didn't want to do that—not here, not now.

She was so angry—and so wretchedly sad. The sadness piled onto her quiet fear and worry about the conundrum of her relationship with Adam Bates, and it was simply too much—a dam that threatened to break right there in the middle of the sun court at Deir al-Bahari, where at any moment one of the tourists from the hotel might wander in to see them.

"I can't do this right now." Ellie raised a hand to her face, furiously shoving away a tear that had somehow started streaking down her cheek.

Neil's face drew into deeper lines of dismay. "I'm making it worse, aren't I? I'm just buggering things up again. I… I'm…"

He caught himself at the desperate look on her face and bit back whatever he was going to say next. Instead, he paced across the courtyard to the vestibule and drew in a breath.

When he turned, he pushed his spectacles back into place. "So do you think the sun disk might be somewhere on the altar?" he asked deliberately.

He was giving her a way out—an escape from the painful maelstrom of hurt and memory he had stumbled them into. Ellie accepted it, fighting back the rest of the tears that threatened to spill out.

"It's a logical place for it," she agreed carefully. "And it's the only space here that has a 'behind' for any sun disk we might find—though of course, we can't know for certain at what point in the past the altar was expanded."

She shot Neil a look as though daring him to contradict that by blurting out a date he couldn't possibly have read about.

"The work might conceivably have been done before Akhenaten's time," he said more carefully instead.

Ellie studied the regular blocks of the altar. Neil did the same, running his fingers lightly and carefully over the stones to feel for anything his eyes might miss.

He shot an awkward and slightly guilty look over at her. "Peanut—all of that other business aside, there is… well, something else I really ought to tell you."

Ellie only half heard him as she studied the stones on the east side of the altar, which would face the rising sun. "Oh?"

"You have to understand, your arrival in Mutnedjmet's tomb took me entirely off guard," Neil hurriedly explained. "And then all of a sudden, we were barreling into the burial chamber, which I'd expressly promised the Athenaeum I wouldn't do, and it just seemed to me that I couldn't possibly run off without… without trying in *some* way to explain things…"

A cat jumped up onto the stones in front of her. Ellie startled at the sudden movement.

It was the sandy-hued stray. It laid down on the altar, flopped over, and stretched out, exposing its pale belly to the sunlight.

When Ellie did not immediately reach out to rub its tummy—knowing cats well enough to recognize she could well subject herself to a mauling if she tried—the cat rolled back over and settled in for a nap, blinking at her.

Something about the slab of limestone directly under the bored-looking animal caught Ellie's eye.

"Am I mad," she said, "or does this look like a hand?"

She set her finger delicately to the corner of the block, where a slight divot in the limestone appeared, on closer inspection, to take the shape of a cupped palm and gently curved fingers.

"I… what?" Neil leaned over the altar to give the spot a closer look. "I say—I believe it does!"

Ellie moved her finger along the surface of the altar around the cat, which remained entirely nonplussed. The limestone was washed with midday sunlight, which made it hard to pick out irregularities that might be more easily seen in the gentler wash of morning or dusk, but now that Ellie knew what she was looking for, more shapes leapt out at her.

"There's another one!" she declared with a spark of excitement. Her finger moved left. "And a third!"

The little marks were very subtle. From a distance, they would seem like natural chips or faults in the limestone. It was only up close that one could make out the tiny curve of a thumb and the delicate lines that delineated fingers.

A tickling suspicion prodded at Ellie's mind.

"Neil—remind me again how Akhenaten depicted the Aten," she pressed without taking her eyes from the marks.

"As a sun disk surrounded by extended rays." Neil's voice was tight. "Each one ending in an upturned hand. There are—ah—ten of them here, by the way."

His finger swept across the pale surface of the altar, and Ellie saw them—an array of tiny hands, spread out in a perfect arc.

Ellie grabbed the strap of Neil's canteen where it crossed his chest. Catching the tin container, she splashed a little water into her cupped palm.

"That's for drinking, not washing your hands!" Neil protested.

Ellie ignored him as she dipped a finger into the water and used it to draw across the stones, painting straight lines from each of the hands to where they met.

The spot was directly under the cat.

She picked the animal up and deposited it onto the ground as it made a halfhearted yowl of protest. Where it had been sitting, she used a little more water to draw the shape of a circle—of a *sun disk*—and then pointed to it, raising her eyebrow at Neil and waiting.

"It's… I mean, I suppose it could be…" Neil stammered, still clutching the canteen. "At least, one must admit the possibility that…"

"It's the Aten," Ellie concluded firmly.

The water-painted shape sat in the center of the slab one block back from the edge of the altar.

"But it's just another piece of limestone," Neil protested.

Ellie studied the block with a critical eye. "We won't get that out on its own. We should take the block at the edge first and then work our way in." She flapped an impatient hand at Neil. "I need something I can pry with."

"Pry?!" Neil echoed.

Ellie glared at him. Neil gave in, patting his pockets wildly. "I have… a pen?" he offered weakly, pulling the writing implement from his jacket.

She felt a little pang of remorse. "I'll quite ruin it."

"I don't have anything else!" Neil protested.

With a sigh, Ellie plucked the pen from his hand. She jabbed the nib into the seam under the slab at the edge of the altar.

"You can't just go taking apart pieces of sun altars!" Neil protested.

At Ellie's rueful look, he flushed.

"What I mean to say is, it would be shockingly irresponsible to simply…" Neil trailed off awkwardly. "There are proper procedures for this sort of thing and… Obviously, someone ought to be informed before we…"

As she continued to wait, his shoulders slumped.

Ellie went back to work with the pen, twisting and wrenching it.

Neil groaned beside her. She wasn't sure if he was more upset that she was attempting to take apart an important Eighteenth Dynasty monument or that she was utterly destroying his nib.

The block wriggled up a bit, and Ellie worked the pen further into the gap. She left it there and scrambled up onto the top of the altar, taking hold of the edge of the stone. She waved impatiently at the pen, which still stuck out from underneath the slab. "Lend me a hand, would you?"

With a reluctant groan, Neil levered at the pen as Ellie worked to get a better grip. There was a good bit of muttering and complaining—and the limestone block came free.

The piece was about eleven inches square and perhaps one and a half inches thick. Ellie hauled it out and shoved it aside.

She stuck her head over the opening to peer in. Neil did the same, pressing in beside her.

"Rubble," he concluded.

The jumbled fill was packed into the space between the facing stones and the old altar, which Ellie could pick out here and there beneath.

"But there's a strut at the edge of the stones, just as I predicted," Ellie noted. "And we can pull up the proper slab now."

With a sigh, Neil climbed up to join her, and the pair of them made quick work of yanking out the stone where Ellie had painted the sun disk.

The altar was looking properly ravaged now. Ellie felt a spark of guilt at the sight.

"Well, then?" Neil pressed in to peer at the new space they had opened.

"I don't know!" Ellie retorted crossly. "I can't see anything with your head blocking my light!"

"I'm not blocking the light any more than you are!" Neil retorted.

Ellie shoved back on her brother's shoulders, then shifted her own position. Sunlight spilled down into the dark mouth left by the displaced stone.

The space was not filled with rubble. Instead, it formed a little hollow framed by the struts that supported the limestone, with the surface of the old altar serving as the floor.

Nor was it empty. Ellie reached into it and carefully lifted out a thin slab of baked clay. The object was perhaps six inches square, and its surface was covered in close-packed, stick-like characters.

"That's a tablet." Neil's voice was numb with surprise.

"Stamped with cuneiform." Ellie traced a delicate finger over the intricate arrangements of triangular-headed wedges and lines.

"A piece of diplomatic correspondence, perhaps?" Neil pressed closer to peer down at it. "Akkadian was the lingua franca during the New Kingdom period for communication between Egypt and other empires." He grimaced a little ruefully. "I might have a go at translating it if I had my library along, but I'm afraid I'm hopeless if I'm working off the top of my—."

"*King*," Ellie read, pointing to one of the symbols on the tablet's surface.

She shifted her finger over as Neil stared at her. "*Grave*," she translated, and then stilled. "Though that could also be read as *tomb*."

"You know Akkadian?" Neil asked weakly.

"I haven't yet made a proper study of it," Ellie replied distantly, still focused on the text. "I only have a handful of words memorized, along with the phonetic characters. I do have a good number of the logograms, though."

"You know Akkadian." Neil's tone sounded as though he ought to add a slightly overwrought *and why not?*

"*Tomb… horizon… sun…*" Ellie read out carefully, and then brightened. "Tomb at the Horizon of the Sun."

"Whose tomb?" Neil pressed more urgently, peering over her shoulder.

"That part is in syllabic characters," Ellie replied. "Let me see… that's *Ne*, then *Per*. Then those two repeat again, and we have *Yu… Ha… Ten*." She paused, cheerfully reading it back. "*Ne per ne per yu ha ten*."

The sound of the syllables ringing through the courtyard in her own voice made her go still.

"But there's no 'f' phoneme in Akkadian." She suddenly felt breathless. Her hand flashed out, clamping onto her brother's arm and giving it a shake. "There's no 'f,' Neil!"

She thrust the tablet at him, beginning to pace as the words spilled out.

"Of course, we can't know for certain what the original Egyptian pronunciation would have been," she rattled on. "But if an Akkadian writer had used the 'p' sign in place of the 'f' phoneme from the Egyptian language, then that would make the true name…"

"Neferneferuaten," Neil blurted, blinking at her in shock. He dropped his eyes wonderingly to the tablet. "It's talking about the tomb of Neferneferu-aten."

"There has never been any hint of where Neferneferuaten was buried!" Ellie reminded him excitedly. "You told me yourself that the absence of artifacts with his name in private and museum collections strongly indicates that wherever he was entombed, the site was never looted—at least not within recent memory."

Neil looked helplessly down at the tablet. "Are you saying this might tell us where to find the tomb of Neferneferuaten?"

Their eyes met in a look of startled shared significance, and Ellie pressed herself to Neil's side, peering down at the text once more.

"That's *king* again," she read, her finger hovering over the cuneiform lines. "And there's *divine*. That makes it *Neferneferuaten, Beloved of the Divine King*," she declared triumphantly—and then frowned. "But that's odd."

"What is?"

"*Beloved* is right here. *Ḥibtu.*" Ellie pointed to the cluster of lines and wedges. "But *tu* is the feminine ending."

Neil stared at her in shock, even as Ellie's own mind spun with the wild significance of what she had just translated.

"The feminine ending?" he echoed. "But that would imply that…"

The shocking, paradigm-shattering epiphany pouring through her mind was abruptly halted by the sound of a smooth, dangerously familiar voice from behind her.

"How terribly interesting," Mr. Jacobs said.

NINETEEN

Overall, Adam figured the day was going pretty well.

His conversation with Ellie the night before had grabbed his heart and wrung it out like an old dishcloth… but there'd been something almost like relief in that. He'd actually slept after he went back up to his room—more soundly than he had in a long time, even though he'd woke up halfway through the night with thoughts of patio tables and Ellie's flushed cheeks in his head.

Adam had dealt with that in another way his father wouldn't have approved of, then crashed like a fallen tree.

He still had no idea how he and Ellie were going to find their way through the muddled morass of his morals and her principles, but he simply felt less *scared* of it now than he had before. It wasn't just George Bates's voice he was hearing in his brain. Now Ellie's was right there with it. And where George Bates's voice made Adam feel like an irredeemable ass, Ellie's made him feel as big as one of those statues they'd passed on the way here.

I don't need to see that other Adam Bates—that one your father would've made you into—to know that I would never have chosen him over this one that's standing right in front of me.

The memory warmed Adam up from the inside like a torch. Maybe he'd even keep feeling that way—so long as he kept from screwing things up.

He was mostly trailing behind Constance and Sayyid as they searched the temple for Ellie's sun disk. Sayyid knew the layout of the place and took the lead. Adam had heard him mention that he'd been here before with his dad, who sounded like he'd been as much of an archaeologist as any of the guys who'd taught Adam's classes back at Cambridge.

Adam just kept his eyes peeled for big orange circles. He actually spotted a good few of them—sun disks with falcon wings sprouting out from the sides of them and sun disks on gods' heads—but they were carved onto columns or faces of solid rock, not something with a *behind* where someone might've hidden a clue.

They had reached the second level of the temple, where a big plaza was framed by tumbled columns. They'd surveyed the open square of ground pretty quickly, and Sayyid led them to a small enclosed chapel hidden on the north side.

As Adam stepped into it, his nose was filled with the scent of dry stone and dust. Then his eyes adjusted, and he reeled at the beautifully preserved paintings that completely covered the walls and ceiling.

"Hell," he commented eloquently.

"Now this is intriguing!" Sayyid's tone quickened with excitement. "These hieroglyphs here are part of the King as Sun Priest text, which celebrates the pharaoh's role as the heir and servant of the sun god—which perhaps demonstrates an early movement toward the conception of the Aten as a sole creator of the universe."

"I don't see any suns." Constance frowned.

"Oh—that's this fellow, right here." Sayyid looked a little embarrassed. "In this depiction, the sun is being represented by the form of the god Ra."

As Sayyid rattled on, something tickled at the back of Adam's awareness. It was just a whisper of warning instinct… but he'd had that instinct before, and doing what it told him had saved his hide more times than he could count.

By the time he actually heard the soft scrape of a boot on stone, he was already turning.

He met the first intruder with a fist, taking the guy in the ribs.

With a twist and a grunt, he tossed him into the chapel, where he rolled to collapse at Constance's feet.

Adam had only enough time to register that the groaning villain was Scarface, one of the Al-Saboor cousins from the tomb at Saqqara, before a guy who looked almost identical to him, save for the scar, barreled into the room with a cudgel in his hand.

Adam welcomed the newer Al-Saboor with a friendly kick to the shin. He went down too, yelping out a string of Masri imprecations as he clutched his leg.

"Oh no, you don't!" Adam heard Constance reprimand behind him. Out of the corner of his eye, he saw Ellie's petite friend catch Scarface as he tried to scramble to his feet. With a tidy maneuver, she twisted his arm behind his back at a painful angle and forced him to the floor. She pinned him there with a fashionable kid boot between his shoulder blades as Sayyid gaped at her.

Two more Al-Saboors burst into the chapel.

Adam treated the guy he'd just kicked to a further punch in the gut, leaving him wheezing.

The next one came at Adam with a right hook. Adam caught it in an echo of Constance's pivot a moment before with Scarface. With a powerful twist, he wrenched the thug's arm behind his back—and felt his shoulder pop.

The man collapsed against the wall, holding his limp arm and railing at Adam. He spoke in Masri, but that hardly mattered. Adam knew what it sounded like when he was being cursed out.

He still hadn't taken out his machete. It was close-quarters fighting in the chapel, with Constance and Sayyid right behind him—Sayyid pressed back against the walls like he was trying to disappear through them, and Constance still pinning Scarface to the floor, even as she eyed Adam's attackers with a dangerous determination.

The knife would make quicker work of the Al-Saboors—but some of them would probably end up dead.

Adam didn't much like killing if he didn't have to.

The next fool to come running into the tomb sported the Al-Saboor pointed chin and prominent nose with the added charm of a missing front tooth. He held a sword in his hands and screamed out a battle cry.

Adam whirled to the man whose right arm he had just dislocated. He grabbed him by the front of his galabeya and threw him at his gap-toothed cousin.

Lefty went down, tangling up with the guy Adam had hobbled earlier, who was just staggering to his feet. Hobbles toppled like a bowling pin, and Gaps fell over the pair of them, the sword clattering from his hand.

All in all, things were going swell—until the next two Al-Saboors burst into the chapel with rifles in their hands.

They leveled both of the guns at Adam, who recognized bad odds when he saw them. He raised his hands over his head.

Out of the corner of his eye, he saw Constance's face firm into lines of furious determination as she reached for something under her skirt.

Knives, Adam recalled dimly, remembering how she had threatened Neil back in the tomb.

"Don't," he ordered sharply.

Constance didn't look happy about it—but she listened.

The thugs with the rifles parted to make way for someone else who shared the family features but on a frankly enormous scale. His thick shoulders pulled at the seams of his robe, hands like ham hocks clenched at his sides.

Adam tilted his head back to look up at him as the big man took in the tangled pile of his groaning cousins at Adam's feet.

"I think I'll call you Muscles," Adam commented.

Muscles replied with a fist to Adam's face.

———

Adam ended up with about four Al-Saboors piled on top of him. He scored a few more blows to his jaw and ribs before someone who sounded like they were in charge barreled into the chapel and hollered. Adam was hauled up off the floor, and his hands were roughly tied behind his back as the senior Al-Saboor—distinguished by the threads of gray in his dark hair—grimaced with unhappy exasperation at the scene.

With an irritated wave of his hand, Al-Saboor the First ordered them out of the chapel. Adam followed Constance and Sayyid in a grim procession as they were led through the shadows of the colonnade to where a spill of rubble formed a precarious track up to the top level of the temple.

His face hurt. So did his ribs. The cut on his still-healing hand was sore—and his brain was working furiously. This was no chance robbery. The men who surrounded him were hired thugs—which meant the guy who had hired them couldn't be far away.

There was still no sign of Ellie and Neil. Adam dared to hope that the two of them might have escaped… until he was shoved down a crumbling half-flight of stairs and heard their voices from around the corner ahead of him.

"I'm terribly sorry, but we are professional archaeologists in the middle of a survey and this chapel is meant to be closed."

That was Neil—and he sounded nervous as hell.

He heard Ellie next, and her words sent a frisson of fear through his blood.

"I had wondered where you were in Saqqara."

Adam closed his eyes, already knowing whose tones he would hear in response.

"An unfortunate but necessary detour," came the familiar, implacable reply.

Jacobs.

Constance and Sayyid were herded around the turn ahead of him. Muscles planted a hand between Adam's shoulder blades, shoving him into stumbling down the last steps, off-balance thanks to his bound hands.

Sun glared down over a limestone courtyard framed by thick stone walls. Ellie crouched on a square platform that dominated the center of the space, with Neil hovering uneasily beside her.

Jacobs stood before them, looking for all the world as though he hadn't nearly been buried alive in the catastrophic collapse of a legendary city a couple weeks before.

Muscles propelled Adam the rest of the way into the courtyard, then shoved him to his knees.

Neil's jaw dropped with shock and dismay. Ellie's gaze danced over him worriedly, cataloging the bruises Adam could feel forming on his jaw and cheek before stopping to linger on the blood dripping from his split lip.

He flashed her a determined smile before his view was cut off by a pair of black trousers.

Adam looked up to meet Jacobs' cold stare. "I was wondering when you'd turn up."

"Mr. Bates," Jacobs returned smoothly. His gaze dropped to Adam's belt, and Adam let out a groan.

"Come on!" he protested. "It's not like I can even…"

His voice trailed off as Jacobs plucked the machete from Adam's belt.

"…Use it," Adam finished mournfully.

Jacobs really was a bastard.

"Excuse me! Pardon! Coming through!" Dawson's voice immediately grated on Adam's nerves. The professor awkwardly pushed his way through the crowd of Al-Saboors, stumbling to a halt at Adam's side.

He put his hands on his knees, panting slightly. He was already sweating.

The professor turned his head—and noticed Adam kneeling beside him. He stumbled back with alarm, reaching up to catch his pith helmet before it fell off his head.

"You…! He…!" he stammered, pointing at Adam wildly until he noticed the ropes around his wrists.

Dawson visibly relaxed, though he still took a careful step back from where Adam knelt on the paving stones.

Jacobs turned away from Adam to focus his implacable attention on Ellie and Neil.

"Why don't you show me what your little excavation turned up?" Jacobs prompted silkily, nodding to something Neil held in his hand. "And then we can all have a nice little chat with your employer."

Neil clutched the object to his chest. It looked like a small slab of clay. He stared at Jacobs nervously.

At least he had the instinct to recognize the man was a threat.

"Don't give it to him," Ellie ordered, her eyes still locked on Jacobs. "And don't go anywhere with him, either."

Jacobs flashed her a thin smile. "Neither of you has anywhere else to go, Miss Mallory."

Ellie's fists clenched at her sides. "Then I'll take my chances with a fight."

Adam's heart twisted with a burst of mingled fear and admiration.

That's my girl, he thought warmly… and then hoped desperately she wasn't about to get herself killed.

She wouldn't, Adam determined grimly. Because he'd take out the whole Al-Saboor family and Jacobs with them if they touched so much as a hair on her head, rifles be damned.

No matter what it cost him.

He made a silent assessment of where things stood. Lefty and Hobbles had split off from them outside the chapel, clearly not much use after what Adam had done to them in the brawl. The two Al-Saboors with the rifles had become Ears and Ralph in Adam's head—one because he looked like a horse-toothed guy Adam had known back in San Francisco, and the other because… well, *ears*. Beardy had his cudgel. Gaps had retrieved his sword. Scarface pulled a pair of daggers from his sleeves, and Muscles had… well, himself, which seemed like more than enough.

Sayyid and Constance hung back by the wall of the courtyard, half hidden from his view by Scarface and Beardy. Adam hadn't pegged Sayyid as a fighting type. Constance had her knives, but the notion of her having to use them made Adam feel a little queasy.

And then there was Jacobs.

Adam didn't love the way it all added up.

Jacobs was studying Ellie, his look coldly thoughtful. Quick as a snake, his hand flashed out—and set the blade of Adam's machete against his neck.

Adam swallowed, and the steel rasped against the stubble of his throat. The knife was damned sharp. Adam always made sure of that.

Ellie's gaze flashed with fear—and then she grabbed Neil's wrist, forcing both it and the clay artifact up over their heads.

"Hurt him, and I'll smash it," she snarled. "And you know that's not an idle threat."

"Nobody needs to hurt anybody!" Neil protested, pulling against Ellie's grip. "We don't even know what it is yet!"

Ellie's eyes met Adam's from across the courtyard. She flinched with worry.

Adam looked back at her steadily, willing her not to break.

We'll get through this, he thought at her. *Trust me.*

Not that he had any idea how just yet.

"Out of the way. Coming through."

The supercilious tones of Julian Forster-Mowbray sounded from behind Adam as The Mustache pushed his way through the clustered Al-Saboors. He was dressed in a pristine suit of pale linen with a stylish flat-brimmed hat in a matching hue.

"Well! I see we're all here," he declared brightly—until his blue eyes fell to the knife Jacobs held at Adam's throat.

Julian startled, then hedged his way around Adam's bound figure as he made a nervous adjustment to the line of his blond mustache. "Fairfax, old bean. This is quite the merry chase you've led us on—though I did appreciate your note."

Adam's ears began to buzz. Across the courtyard, Neil's face fell into lines of guilty dismay.

Ellie's grip on his arm slackened. Her eyes widened as if the ground were opening up at her feet.

"Note?" she echoed, shock dulling her voice.

Adam groaned, already sensing where things were going.

"I…" Neil stammered, looking pale and uneasy. "I was trying to tell you. I just… It all happened so quickly! And you weren't making any sense! So it seemed the reasonable thing to do was to… to write an explanation for what had happened. That the incident in the tomb was just a… a slight…" He swallowed thickly. "And that I would be taking a brief leave of absence…"

"And you told them where you were going," Adam filled in.

He could feel the scrape of the machete blade against his skin as he spoke.

"I… I wanted him to know it was all in good faith!" Neil protested, clutching the tablet to his chest.

"Hold on," Constance cut in sharply, stepping out from behind the substantial bulk of Muscles. "Are you saying you wrote the baddies an *apology letter?*"

Mr. Forster-Mowbray whirled around. "*Connie?!* What on earth are you doing here?"

Adam cocked a surprised eyebrow—but then, Constance had been inside the tunnel by the time Julian entered Mutnedjmet's tomb. He'd had no reason to suspect she was involved—until now.

The Mustache looked like he'd just got caught with his hand in a cookie jar. Adam couldn't help but feel a certain sort of satisfaction at the expression.

"I'm with them, obviously!" Constance waved a hand that took in Ellie, Neil, Adam, and Sayyid.

Julian's jaw dropped.

Ellie barely noticed the exchange. She was staring at her brother with a look of hurt and disappointment. It twisted Adam's heart to see it.

"Why?" she said softly.

"I'd been employed by the fellow for two years!" Neil burst out. "As the representative of a respected scholarly organization! I thought all of you must be getting yourselves worked up over a big misunderstanding!"

"Big misunderstanding, huh?" Adam commented flatly.

Sunlight glinted off the blade of the machete at the corner of his eye.

Neil's color drained even further. His face fell into lines of obvious dismay. He stumbled a half step back, nearly falling off the raised platform of the altar. "I didn't mean…" His gaze whirled from Ellie to Adam, then landed helplessly on Sayyid. "I… I'm…"

At Neil's look, Sayyid's eyes blazed with an uncharacteristic, angry heat. His lips thinned as though he were biting back whatever wanted to spill from his mouth.

Neil winced, then pivoted, stalking to the front of the altar and holding the tablet out to Julian and Jacobs. "Take the bloody thing. It doesn't matter." He half shouted the rest back at Ellie. "*It doesn't matter!* Whatever this is, it can't possibly be worth dying over!"

"Don't do it, Fairfax," Adam warned lowly.

"He has a knife at your throat! Those fellows have guns!" Neil burst out, waving frantically at Ears and Ralph. "I'm sorry! I buggered everything up. I just don't want anybody to get hurt."

"Of course not, Fairfax, old bean," Julian assured him soothingly. "I'm sure we can all settle this like reasonable people." He waved a dismissive hand at Jacobs. "Do stop threatening that fellow quite so menacingly. It's not like he can do anything with his hands tied."

Jacobs' jaw tightened. Dark emotion flickered through his eyes before it was reined in behind his usual placid expression.

Now *that* was interesting, Adam noted silently.

There was no way Jacobs would've deferred to an idiot like Julian Forster-Mowbray by choice, which meant that The Mustache was actually the guy in charge of all this… maybe because Jacobs had failed to bring back the artifact his mysterious bosses had wanted so badly in British Honduras.

Adam wondered uneasily if Jacobs blamed him and Ellie for that. More than likely, he did. After all, they'd been the ones to blow the whole place up.

The notion didn't bode particularly well for their current prospects.

Sayyid had used the distraction of Neil's outburst to inch out from behind the cluster of Al-Saboors. Nobody seemed to notice. The thugs had clearly decided the scholarly Egyptian wasn't a threat. He took another careful step along the wall toward Ellie as Neil climbed down from the platform of the altar and held the tablet out to Julian.

Julian took it, gave it a disinterested glance, and thrust it blindly back behind him. "Sort that out, will you, Mr. Dawson?"

Dawson scampered forward to catch the block of clay, fumblingly clutching it to his chest. He cleared his throat. "Actually, it's 'professor.' Professor Da—"

Julian turned to Constance. "I'm dreadfully sorry about this, Connie! I don't know what these people told you to get you mixed up in this, but we'll sort it out in a jiffy."

Constance blinked with surprise and quick comprehension, and then her expression shifted to one of benign confusion.

"I should certainly hope so!" she exclaimed charmingly. "Really, Julian— waving knives and guns about? What would my Aai say to that, do you think?"

Julian blanched a bit at the mention of Constance's grandmother. Adam couldn't entirely blame him. The woman was mildly terrifying.

"I'm sure we don't need to worry her about it." Julian flashed Constance a nervous smile. "Well! Now that we have all that sorted… Fairfax, I'm afraid we'll have to delay your return to Saqqara for just a tick. I'll need you along for this next bit, if you don't mind."

"Next bit?" Neil echoed uncomfortably.

Sayyid was still moving. He had reached the wall of the sun court and picked his way along it, closer to where Ellie still stood on top of the far side of the altar.

Jacobs' head swiveled, and Sayyid froze like a bug on a windowpane. Jacobs gave him a look of bland consideration—and then turned away again, clearly dismissing the foreman as beneath his consideration.

Adam slightly adjusted his mental calculations. Not that they amounted to anything remotely approaching a plan at this point.

"What do you need *him* for?" Dawson protested, still clutching the tablet possessively. "This is in Akkadian, and my Akkadian is excellent! Well—with just a little consultation of some of the books I brought along, of course," he hedged.

"I… *We*," Neil corrected himself with a pleading look back at Ellie, "really ought to be getting back to the dig at Saqqara. We left things in an awful muddle, and there's a great deal of very urgent… er, conservation work…"

He trailed off in the face of Jacobs' amused gaze and Julian's cross frown.

"I'm afraid I must insist," Julian countered. "And I do hope we can keep this all civilized." He caught himself with a nervous glance back at Constance. "I mean, of course we'll all be civilized. We are all civilized people here, aren't we? Mr. Al-Saboor, why don't you have your cousins… er, very politely escort Dr. Fairfax back to our conveyance."

Constance looked as though she could barely contain the urge to roll her eyes. Adam was right there with her.

Jacobs had let the machete fall to his side—but his hand was still tense and ready on the hilt.

Mr. Al-Saboor jerked his head at Scarface and Gaps, who took hold of Neil's arms. They propelled him forward through the crowd of their cousins as he bleated out protests.

"But I really must… You can't just… This is outrageous! Peanut!" he called out, his expression tight with worry as he twisted to look back at his sister.

Ellie watched him go, her mouth drawn into a grim line.

Constance's gaze followed Neil as well, sharp as one of the knives she had strapped to her body. Adam could practically see the wheels turning in her head.

They clicked into place—and she looked to Adam.

He could read the question in her eyes. He answered it with a subtle nod.

Determination flashed through Constance's expression—and then a blindingly bright smile lit up her face as she hooked her hand possessively around Julian's arm.

"Well, now all that nonsense is out of the way," she cut in as Julian startled. "How long will you be staying in Luxor?"

"I'm… er, afraid we must be moving right along, darling," Julian returned awkwardly.

"Splendid, then," Constance replied. "I'll join you."

"W-what?!" Dawson jumped with surprise, nearly dropping the tablet.

Constance looked from the obviously horrified professor to Julian. "Unless you would rather not have me?" She widened her eyes with every appearance of dismayed surprise.

Clever girl, Adam thought, admiration mingling with worry.

Constance had recognized her unique opportunity to force herself into Julian's party—and get a shot at foiling his plans and saving Neil's hide.

Adam just hoped she stayed clever enough not to get herself killed.

Sayyid used the distraction to dart the rest of the way to the altar, stopping just below the place where Ellie stood. He gripped the surface as though readying himself to dive behind it.

"Er… of course, we should like nothing better! Isn't that right?" Julian added with a challenging look at the rest of his crew.

Dawson snapped his gaping jaw shut. Ears and Ralph exchanged a confused glance over their rifles.

Another flash of irritation twisted through Jacobs' expression. It slid away a moment later, replaced by his usual mask.

"Whatever you say, ya Amir," Mr. Al-Saboor commented tiredly.

"Marvelous!" Constance snuggled into Julian's side.

"Right, then!" Julian turned for the stairs.

Dawson startled. "What about… But where do you want me to…"

Julian didn't look back. Dawson scurried after him like a rat, still clutching the tablet.

The courtyard was silent as the sound of their footsteps faded.

"What do we do with these ones?" Mr. Al-Saboor asked, looking at Jacobs. "Should we… let them go?"

The senior Al-Saboor sounded a little hopeful about the prospect. Adam felt hopeful about it too—at least until he saw a snarl twist Jacobs' lip.

"Absolutely not," Jacobs bit out sharply.

Adam couldn't really blame Jacobs for that. After all, the last time he and Ellie had turned up in the man's life, they'd spoiled every one of his plans—and dropped a city on top of the magical artifact that he'd been tasked to find.

Jacobs had once told Adam that he got his job by being a guy who *does whatever needs to be done.*

Somebody who prided himself on competence likely didn't appreciate being made to look like a screw-up. Nor was he likely to make the same mistake twice—by letting the people who'd mucked everything up for him last time go free to do it all over again.

Which meant that things were probably about to get unpleasantly messy.

Adam waited for Jacobs to give the order he knew had to be coming… and waited.

Jacobs was silent.

Adam finally took a moment to really look at the man. He was… *seething.*

His gaze shifted to Ellie and Adam as though he was vividly imagining how good it would feel to take the pair of them out with two tidy gunshots—which he might easily have done.

And yet, he didn't. Instead, his expression twisted with frustration. The look was uncharacteristically raw for the usually calm and uncannily collected Jacobs.

Something was holding him back from executing the violence he obviously wanted, and which Adam knew must have looked entirely justified from Jacobs' point of view. But what could it possibly be? It sure as hell wasn't moral conviction—a man who would've unflinchingly cut Ellie to pieces to ensure Adam's obedience back in British Honduras was hardly going to shrink from a run-of-the-mill execution. Had Julian given him some sort of blanket order not to kill?

Or was something else going on?

Ellie had caught on to Jacobs' tension and hesitation as well. She shot Adam a puzzled glance, even as she looked ready to dive behind the sun altar with Sayyid.

"Ya Reis?" Al-Saboor the First prompted with an uneasy look at his boss.

Before Jacobs could answer, the shadows in the antechamber came to life.

Black-cloaked forms spilled from behind piles of ruined stone. Others leapt down from the lower portions of the sun chapel walls. One of the first to appear spun from behind a column to grab a handful of Jacobs' hair and press a small, thin silver blade to his jugular.

Adam realized that all of them were women—and not just any women. It was the ladies from the souvenir stand at the base of the temple, cloaked from head to toe in Egypt's ubiquitous black abayas. Their faces were veiled, but the one holding a scalpel to Jacobs' throat sported a pair of angry green eyes that struck Adam as oddly… familiar.

She muttered something at Jacobs' ear, her voice too low for Adam to make out—but whatever she said must've been damned threatening, because it made Jacobs drop Adam's machete.

The other black-cloaked women were armed with what looked mostly like an assortment of kitchen knives—damned sharp kitchen knives.

Faced with three blades leveled at various parts of his body, Beardy dropped his cudgel. Ears let a tall, slender woman pull his rifle from his hands, prompted by another who stood at his back, prodding her knife into his spine. The taller one immediately leveled the gun at Muscles, cocking it with clear expertise.

Though Adam couldn't see her face behind her black half-veil, he was oddly certain that she was smiling.

Muscles slowly raised his hands over his head.

Ralph had already thrown his own arms up, flashing his veiled ambushers a nervous smile as he held his rifle over his head.

Adam counted nine ladies all together. They held themselves with a silent, determined readiness.

A short, stout woman stepped out from behind the others. Based on the deep lines around her near-black eyes, she was probably someone's grandma. She spoke a line of quick Masri that had the air of an order.

"She says to go stand against the wall," Al-Saboor the First called out in translation.

He had somehow scrambled into the antechamber, where he crouched behind a jumble of rock like someone expecting an explosion.

Jacobs was stiff with seething, dangerous frustration—but the scalpel at his jugular didn't waver. "Do it," he barked flatly.

The rest of the Al-Saboors shuffled morosely over to the wall of the courtyard, where the women engaged in a quick, huddled conversation that resulted in the sudden appearance of a small pile of scarves and belts from under their black cloaks.

The Al-Saboors were rapidly bound. All the while, the green-eyed woman kept her blade at Jacobs' throat, her body as poised and ready as a cat.

At another murmured prompt from her, Jacobs held out his wrists. The gesture was calm—but Adam could see the wicked tension that seethed through his figure.

The grandma tied Jacobs with a fisherman's expertise, and then the willowy girl with the rifle was there, directing him to stand by the Al-Saboors with a casual wiggle of the muzzle.

Jacobs joined his thugs, black eyes flashing with rage—and Adam found himself swept up in a sea of quick-moving women. They hurried Sayyid and Ellie along as well, carrying them to the stairs like a flood of black water.

TWENTY

$\mathcal{C}$ARRIED ALONG IN a current of cloaked ladies, Ellie stumbled into the open air of the temple. The German picnickers had thankfully moved on, leaving the space deserted.

The harsh bark of Jacobs' voice sounded from the sun court. The green-eyed woman who had held the scalpel to his throat hissed out a command to the others, pointing across the courtyard.

"Yalla!" one of the nearest women said, waving at Ellie urgently.

They dashed past the piles of rubble and the broken columns into the ruins of another chapel, where Ellie could see signs of past excavation work. Beyond that, Hatshepsut's temple ended in a steep, rocky slope scattered with red-brown scree. The women shooed Ellie onto it, and she half-skidded down into the shadow of the enormous cliff that loomed over the site.

A cluster of donkeys and four impatient-looking horses waited for them at the bottom, minded by a diminutive woman in another niqab and black cloak, who popped up urgently as they appeared.

Ellie's rescuers hurried over to join her in the shadows of the cliff, holding a rapid conference in Masri. Their urgent tones and hand gestures left Ellie wondering just how well-planned their actions had been.

She turned to Adam, taking in his split lip and bruised jaw. She could vividly recall the way the light had glinted off his machete as Jacobs held the blade to his throat. Had Jacobs not hesitated—had he moved just a few seconds faster…

"I could have lost you!" Ellie burst out as she threw her arms around Adam's chest. She clutched him tightly around his bound arms as she buried her face in the warmth of his shoulder.

"Not that I mind this," Adam commented with a wince, "but could you make it just a little less tight?"

Ellie held him back as she made an urgent assessment of his person. "What is it? Where are you hurt?"

"Arms. Face. Probably bruised a couple of ribs," Adam replied.

"Are you certain they're bruised and not broken?" Ellie pressed worriedly.

"Sure."

Ellie narrowed her eyes skeptically. "How can you know that?"

"Because I've done both a few times before," he replied. "We can take a full inventory later. Right now, can you help me get these damned ropes off?"

Ellie thought about what such an inventory might entail were she to conduct it on him. The notion set her toes tingling—but Adam was still waiting for her, frowning with impatience.

"Oh! Right!" She came behind him to tug at the ropes. "They won't budge!"

"Maybe I can slide out of them," Adam countered, wriggling again.

"You're making it worse!"

"I'm pretty sure I've got it," Adam assured her.

"You pulling on them is why they are so dashed tight!" Ellie shot back.

"Why don't you use this?" asked the tall, slender young woman from their team of rescuers. Her English was musically accented, and she still had a stolen rifle slung over her shoulder.

At the sound of her voice, Sayyid's head snapped up from where he had slumped down with exhausted shock by the rocks. His eyes widened with uncomfortable recognition.

"Just a moment…" he began—and then dropped his jaw as the girl whipped an enormous blade from beneath her cloak.

"You got my knife!" Adam exclaimed happily.

"Thank you," Ellie said as the young woman handed her Adam's machete. She sliced it through the ropes around Adam's wrists, and Adam shook out his arms with a groan.

He took his blade back with a look of sublime relief, then shoved the knife into its sheath and pulled her into a slightly gentler hug.

Ellie soaked up the sheer relief of his arms before looking past him to their clustered rescuers. "But who *are* all of you?"

The green-eyed woman who had threatened Jacobs stepped forward and unhooked her niqab. The fabric fell away from her face, revealing the features of Zeinab Al-Ahmed.

"Habibti?!" Sayyid blurted in shock as he stared at his wife. "But how are you… What is this… Who are all these…"

"Hello, Mr. Al-Ahmed!" the tall young woman with the stolen rifle announced happily. She plucked off her veil to reveal the features of a girl of perhaps nineteen with a long, straight nose and a wide smile.

"Jemmahor?!" Sayyid blurted, staring aghast at her before shifting his horrified gaze back to his wife. "You brought your *apprentice* to a knife fight?"

"We may discuss all of this when we are not running for our lives," Zeinab snapped in reply. "Those ropes will not hold that cold-eyed snake for long. Get on that horse. Mr. Bates, I assume you can ride as well?"

Adam's expression was stubborn. "What about Constance and Fairfax? Somebody's gotta find out where they've been taken."

"And it will not be you," Zeinab retorted flatly. "Umm Waseem will see to it."

She gestured to the short, sturdy older woman who had bossed Jacobs around in the courtyard—likely so that Zeinab would not reveal herself by her voice and provoke an outburst from her husband, Ellie realized.

"Aywa, aywa," Umm Waseem replied with a dismissive wave. She went back to chatting to a cluster of the other veiled women with no apparent display of urgency.

"Umm Waseem's family are fishermen," Jemmahor reported in a conspiratorial tone. "Which is a nicer way of saying that they are smugglers. These other ladies are her cousins here in Luxor. She has cousins everywhere and is very good at sneaking about. She will be able to find where they have taken your friends."

"Oh!" Ellie replied, unsure how to respond. She wondered who else besides a sharp-eyed old smuggler Zeinab had been consorting with—and why she had followed them to Luxor.

Based on the blanched, dismayed way that Sayyid continued to stare at his wife, he hadn't the foggiest notion of the answers to those questions, either.

Umm Waseem's cousins broke up, mounting the assortment of donkeys. The women perched on the animals with their legs tucked neatly to one side, and then scattered, slipping off in various directions.

Umm Waseem trotted over, comfortably settled on her own donkey. She had slung a black canvas satchel over the back of her saddle. Stopping beside them, she raised an expectant eyebrow.

Zeinab and her apprentice had already mounted, as had Sayyid—though he looked far from happy about it. Only Ellie and Adam remained standing, with a single horse waiting nearby.

"Go with Jemmahor," Zeinab ordered, motioning Ellie sharply toward the tall apprentice midwife.

"She rides with me," Adam shot back, fixing Zeinab with a glare.

Zeinab rolled her eyes. "Wear out the horse if you like—just do it quickly!"

"Get up, Princess." Adam offered Ellie his hand.

Ellie let him boost her into the saddle, perching on it sideways and clinging to the horn for dear life. Adam hauled himself up behind her. Ellie heard him let out a hiss of discomfort at the movement.

His substantial weight slid into place at her back, landing her more or less on his lap. An iron arm clamped firmly around her waist. With his other hand, he reached around her for the reins. He urged the animal into motion, and the horse jolted beneath them as it followed the others.

They climbed a trail that looked like little more than an ancient, dusty runoff. It wended steeply up into the range of ragged hills and deep wadis that sprawled across the desert. Adam's warm hold on Ellie took away some of the nervousness she would normally feel at riding. She let herself melt back against the solid wall of his chest with a wash of relief.

There was no sign of pursuit from Jacobs and his men. It seemed that the rescue party had managed to slip away before their enemies cut themselves loose.

They reached the top of the trail and rode out onto a narrow path that offered a sprawling view of the surrounding countryside. Ellie glanced down to her left, where the mountain fell away precipitously into a long, arid valley. A packed-earth road ran along the base. A scattering of dark, gated rectangles set into the walls of the cliffs sparked her recognition.

"That's the Valley of the Kings!" Ellie burst out. "We're riding right above the *Valley of the Kings!* Adam, look!"

She leaned forward for a better view, heedless of how it compromised her balance in the saddle. The horse huffed in protest, and Adam hauled her back into place.

"I'd rather not, if it's all the same," he replied uncomfortably.

Ellie glanced back at him. He was looking a bit green, his knuckles white where they clutched the reins.

"Oh dear!" she exclaimed with sudden understanding. "We are just a tad high up, aren't we?"

"Kinda trying not to think about that," Adam noted. "I don't want to fall out of the saddle." He paused. "Or puke down your shirt."

Ellie flashed him a sympathetic smile before leaning back against him once more, studying the wonders of the valley more sedately as they rode past.

"What do you think that was all about back in the temple?" she asked. "I can't say I know Jacobs particularly well, but I'm not sure I would ever have thought him the sort to… well, hesitate at the use of violence to achieve his aims."

"Maybe his bosses told him he can't kill anybody this time around," Adam offered. "He could be on some kind of probation for things going south back in British Honduras."

"But being willing to kill people seems like precisely the reason one would hire a man like Jacobs in the first place," Ellie pointed out. "What could he possibly offer on the hunt for a powerful arcanum if he's forbidden from using violence?"

"I don't know, Princess," Adam replied with a frown she could hear in his voice. "The whole thing just seemed a little… weird."

Even with Jacobs' inexplicable reluctance to shoot them, they had still come far too close to disaster. The notion of just how bad things might have gone swept over Ellie and left her feeling a little shaky.

She soaked up the reassuring warmth of Adam's presence, which was strong and steady despite his bruises.

"I still can't quite believe that Neil gave us away," she said after a little while.

"I can," Adam replied.

Ellie twisted back to frown at him.

"Not like that," Adam corrected. "I meant… Fairfax has always been a bit of a homebody. You can tempt him into the odd adventure, but he likes knowing he's got someplace steady to go back to." He paused as he guided the horse through a turn. "I think that dig was his steady place here in Egypt, and we kinda blew it up on him. It doesn't surprise me that he'd scramble a bit to get it back."

"But I *told* him that Julian was involved," Ellie countered, unable to keep the hurt from her tone.

"For a smart guy," Adam replied, "your brother can be a real idiot sometimes."

Ellie leaned back against him once more as the ruddy peaks and rifts of the mountains unfolded around them.

"If it's any consolation," Adam added, "*I* know you're pretty much always right."

"Only 'pretty much?'"

"You've got dubious taste in surveyors." Adam spread his strong fingers out across her stomach in a caress that belied his light tone.

Ellie wove her grip with his own, holding his hand tightly. "I have the *best* taste in surveyors," she countered firmly.

TWENTY-ONE

$\mathcal{T}$HEIR WINDING PATH slowly descended through the sprawling hills, and they emerged on a windswept desert plain. The green of the inundation was just visible in the distance. The sprawling, arid landscape closer by was interrupted only by a squat, thick-walled cluster of buildings marked by low arches and an elegant dome. An iron cross over the gate revealed that the structures must belong to a community of Egypt's Christian minority, the Copts.

The buildings were obviously old. A wooden door set by the gate cracked open as they approached, and a young woman in a black headscarf and robes peered out at them wide-eyed. Her attire was near enough to what one might see in a Catholic convent for Ellie to recognize her as a nun.

"Ya Jemmahor!" Zeinab called impatiently.

"Wait here," Jemmahor instructed.

As she swung down from her horse, the sleeve of her cloak slipped up, revealing a small blue tattoo of an even-sided cross on the inside of her wrist. The mark identified the young woman as a Copt herself.

Zeinab's apprentice exchanged a few quick words with the nun at the door, speaking a language that sounded quite different from Masri. The tongue of Egypt's Copts was thought to be the nearest living language to that of Ancient Egypt, and this was the first time Ellie had the privilege of hearing it spoken aloud.

She was hearing it quite loudly, as Jemmahor was gesticulating enthusiastically while the nun squeaked out replies with obvious surprise and alarm. Zeinab looked on the verge of rolling her eyes.

The exchange apparently reached a satisfactory conclusion, as the nun ducked back inside and the big gate swung slowly open on heavy iron hinges.

The rescue party paraded into a simple packed-earth courtyard framed by the convent buildings and a low stable. Other nuns popped into the narrow doorways set into the thick walls or peered from small windows.

An older woman hurried out to meet them, the lines at the corners of her eyes creased with worry.

"That's my aunt," Jemmahor announced cheerfully from beside Ellie and Adam's horse. "She is abbess here at the convent of St. Hilaria. Don't worry—she will be very happy to see me."

The abbess did not look particularly happy. She looked more as though she was wondering where she was going to put an assortment of unexpected guests, including two strange men and a foreign woman.

Jemmahor ran over to her and enthusiastically kissed her cheeks, rattling on in excited Coptic.

Adam slipped down from the saddle in a maneuver that would have had Ellie plummeting backwards over the rear of the horse. He managed it with grace, save for a slight wince as the twist pulled at his bruised ribs, then turned and offered his arms to Ellie.

She hesitated. "Isn't it going to hurt if you try to catch me?"

Adam raised an eloquent eyebrow.

Ellie frowned back at him with barely concealed frustration. "I ought to be capable of getting down from a horse on my own!"

"You don't ride," Adam pointed out.

"I'm from London!" Ellie protested. "Why would I ride when I can take a perfectly docile tram?"

Adam set his hands to her waist and plucked her from the saddle.

She landed with her hands on his shoulders, only a breath from sliding down the front of his body. His exceptionally blue eyes twinkled at her with amusement, and the temptation to haul him down to her for a kiss electrified her nerves.

You are standing in a convent, she reminded herself forcibly. At roughly the same time, Adam cleared his throat and stepped back to put a modest distance between them.

Ellie did the same—and promptly bumped up against the horse.

The horse huffed in protest, and Ellie quickly skipped away.

Zeinab appeared beside them. "We need to talk." Her gaze drifted from Ellie and Adam to Sayyid, who was standing off to the side, looking forlorn and bewildered. "Follow me."

Jemmahor detached herself from the abbess to join them as Zeinab led them into the cool, dim interior of the building. Umm Waseem strolled at their heels with her black satchel slung over her shoulder.

They emerged in a quiet chapel lit by narrow windows set in thick walls. Tidy rows of worn wooden pews faced a stone altar, while the dome overhead was decorated with time-worn paintings of colorful saints.

Zeinab dropped into one of the pews. For a moment, her facade of authority fell away, revealing the tired, overwhelmed woman who hid beneath it. "Can we be certain we were not followed?"

"I saw no one on the trail," Jemmahor reported. "If they did mean to follow us, they would have to see our tracks, and the wind is blowing. The mountains won't leave any sign that we came through."

"Then let us get down to business," Zeinab concluded.

"No!" Sayyid burst out.

He had not taken a seat, but had rather remained standing, pacing uncomfortably across the narrow space between the pews and the steps to the altar. Tension radiated off of him.

"We aren't doing anything until you tell me what is going on!" he continued. "Why are you ambushing villains? Threatening dangerous people with scalpels? You help people have babies! You don't maraud around the countryside like some kind of bandit!"

A flash of hurt flickered through Zeinab's expression. It was quickly swallowed by a cold, simmering anger. "You don't approve?"

"*Approve?!*" Sayyid echoed with a wild laugh. "Of course I don't approve! I'm absolutely terrified! What if you had been caught? What if one of those men had *shot* you?!"

"They could not shoot her," Jemmahor cheerfully interjected. "One of Umm Waseem's cousins pinned down that fellow with the big ears, and I stole the other gun." She lifted her rifle and gave it a little wave. "Not that I would actually shoot anyone with it. I am not a barbarian."

Her explanation did not seem to relieve Sayyid. "And now your apprentice is stealing guns!" he exclaimed, throwing up his hands. "*Guns*, ya habibti! This is… Any one of you might have… Have you no sense of… of…"

The rest of whatever he intended to say was choked off by a rising panic. With a grumbling sigh, Umm Waseem pushed up from her seat and crossed over to him. She shoved him down into a pew.

"Hot rasak ben rokbetak," the older woman ordered authoritatively before pushing his head down over his lap.

Sayyid more or less collapsed under her ministrations, dropping his head onto his arms. "I think I might be sick," he groaned.

"But why *did* you come?" Ellie demanded.

"To watch you," Zeinab returned shortly with an uncomfortable glance at her husband. "To see whether you succeeded in finding the Staff of Musa."

"And if we did?" Ellie prompted with a thrill of suspicion.

Zeinab's look was hard. "To take it from you, if it should prove necessary."

"What would've made it necessary?" Adam asked.

He had taken a seat beside Ellie, draping his arm comfortably over the back of the pew as he stretched his crossed legs out in front of him.

"She means if you intended to use it to keep Egypt under your boots," Jemmahor piped in helpfully, her dark eyes glittering.

"And is that something you do often?" Adam prompted dryly. "Menace bad guys and rescue magic artifacts?"

Zeinab looked to Umm Waseem, who chuckled darkly as she settled herself back into one of the pews.

Jemmahor plastered an innocent expression on her face—which only succeeded in making her seem entirely suspicious. "We are part of an informal ladies' association devoted to protecting the interests of the Egyptian people. Ostazah Zeinab is our leader, and Umm Waseem is our…"

Jemmahor's voice trailed off awkwardly as she flashed a guilty look at Sayyid.

"Munitions expert," Zeinab filled in tiredly from where she sat slumped in her pew.

Sayyid made a choked sound. He lifted his head from his lap, staring at his wife and her friends with dismay.

Ellie shifted her gaze to the wrinkled woman in the back row. "Munitions expert, did you say?" She felt a spark of excited interest at the notion of finding someone with whom she could discuss practical chemistry—and then caught herself. "But why does a ladies' association need a munitions expert?"

"Pretty sure it's because they're revolutionaries," Adam offered from beside her.

"Nobody notices the women," Jemmahor explained eagerly, now that it appeared Zeinab had more or less let her off the leash with their secret. "But we are quiet, and we are clever. We can show the British that Egypt will not lie docile while they set their heels to our throats. Er… begging your pardon," she added with an apologetic look at Ellie.

"Oh, don't worry about me," Ellie assured her, still reeling from the revelations.

"How long?" Sayyid's question came out in a desperate croak.

Zeinab met his eyes as she answered it. "Since before we were wed."

"But why didn't you *say* anything?" he pleaded.

"It was better that you did not know," Zeinab replied firmly. "It was safer that way."

"Safer?!" Sayyid's agitation snapped back up to the surface as he threw out his arms. "How is any of this *safe?!* In the last two hours, I have been kidnapped, marched around at gunpoint, nearly stabbed, and then rescued by my wife waving her scalpel at one of the most terrifying men I have ever seen!" He caught himself, pinching the bridge of his nose as he fought to bring his emotions under control. "Did you think that I would stop you?"

"You could not." Zeinab's eyes flashed dangerously. "It is in our marriage contract."

"Marriage contract?" Ellie felt a spark of intrigue at the unfamiliar term.

"When two parties are wed in our faith, they put their terms for the marriage into the contract, so that there can be no misunderstandings in the future." Zeinab offered the explanation without looking at Ellie, keeping her gaze locked meaningfully on her husband.

Ellie's suffragist instincts perked up with interest at her description. "Can you put anything you like in there?" she prompted. "And is it legally binding?"

"Half the time such contracts are written by fathers or brothers," Jemmahor replied wryly. "And the judges are all men."

"It is binding before Allah," Zeinab replied fiercely. "And our contract states that my husband will not prohibit me from traveling where I will and associating with whom I choose while in pursuit of my professional endeavors or work of principle."

"I didn't know that meant you would be a revolutionary!" Sayyid protested.

"Would it have changed things between us if you had?" Zeinab snapped back.

Sayyid met his wife's eyes with a look of quiet devastation. "Of course not," he replied hoarsely.

An exquisite vulnerability flashed across Zeinab's hard features. The revealing expression was there for only a moment before she drew it away, hiding it as though behind the cloak she had used to disguise herself in the temple.

"Didn't you trust me?" Hurt and confusion were written plainly on Sayyid's features.

"You are a scholar, my love." Zeinab's eyes softened. "Not a warrior."

Sayyid closed his mouth, his eyes hollow.

With a deliberate effort, his wife straightened and put a calm authority back into her tone, fixing her attention on Ellie. "Were you able to read any of that tablet before it was taken?"

Ellie hesitated, instinctively glancing at Adam.

He read the question in her eyes as clearly as if she had spoken it aloud. "It seems to me that these ladies just saved our hides. For which we're genuinely grateful." He deliberately looked at Zeinab, who accepted his words with a regal nod. "I think we can trust them. And frankly, if we're gonna get Constance, Fairfax, or that damned tablet back, we'll need help."

"They just said they meant to take the staff from us!" Ellie pushed back uncomfortably.

"We never wanted it," Adam countered. "We just don't want it going to the wrong people."

The wrong people…

At Adam's words, memory flooded back to Ellie.

A mirror like a great black eye waiting in the darkness. Visions of blood-splattered victory. A voice that whispered through her dreams.

What do you want?

A wrenching temptation—and a choice.

A different fear gripped her, and Ellie surged to her feet, facing the three revolutionaries. "The Staff of Moses—would you use it?"

Jemmahor cast a wide-eyed look at her teacher. Umm Waseem comfortably folded her hands over her belly.

Zeinab's green eyes were unreadable.

"You say you are fighting to free Egypt from tyranny," Ellie pressed, her voice breaking with urgency. "The staff would put untold power in your hands to accomplish those aims. You could darken the skies. Turn the waters of England to blood. Curse us all with pestilence. Kill." Her hands shook. Ellie clenched them into fists. "*Would you use it?*"

Adam's face flashed with comprehension. His hand came around her back in a silent gesture of comfort as he rose.

Ellie needed it. She let herself lean against him.

Zeinab paced to the altar. She gripped the rail and bowed her head, her frame tight with a quiet agitation. "You have seen something like this before."

Ellie remembered the smell of blood and smoke. The fierce gaze of a woman with a scar on her cheek. The war that had raged inside her heart, pitting her dreams against the things that she had known in her deepest heart were right.

"Yes," she replied hoarsely, watching Zeinab from the steady circle of Adam's arms.

Zeinab raised her head. "They have bound us in debt. Strangled our livelihoods to turn us into cogs for their own industry." She looked at the stricken face of her husband, and her eyes flashed with both sympathy and a quiet rage. "They close our schools and force our people into ignorance. Rape our history and carry it off to their museums. We are Egypt. We were the greatest empire on the earth. And we suffocate under the rule of an unelected foreign dictator who holds ultimate power over every aspect of our lives."

The words were taut with pain and anger. Then her eyes fell closed, a different emotion sweeping over her expression. "But even Musa had to learn of the inscrutability of the will of Allah from His messenger in the desert. Wa kaifa tasbiru 'alaa maa lam tuhit bihee khubraa—*How can you patiently bear with that which you do not understand?* He failed three times. And I am not a prophet."

Sayyid's expression shifted as he gazed at his wife. An aching compassion and complicated admiration broke through the shock and dismay that he had been feeling since Zeinab's revelation, though Ellie could still see the hurt in the tight lines around his eyes.

Zeinab pushed back from the altar, her figure straightening as she turned to face them.

"No." She lifted her chin and met Ellie's eyes. "I would not use it." A tear slipped down her cheek, and her hands remained clenched into fists. "I am too angry to trust myself with the power of God."

At Zeinab's declaration, the tension twisting inside of Ellie broke like a weight slipping softly from her shoulders.

"The tablet was in Akkadian," she said quietly, stepping from the shelter of Adam's arm to drop back down in the pew. "I was only able to decipher a few words before we were interrupted. It spoke of the location of the tomb of a king—one with a name phonetically similar to Neferneferuaten. But..." She cast an uncomfortable glance at Sayyid, knowing he was the only other person in the room likely to recognize the significance of what she was about to reveal. "The verb forms were feminine."

Sayyid frowned thoughtfully as his attention sharpened. "Which verb?"

"Beloved," Ellie replied significantly. "The description was *beloved of the divine king.*"

"The female form? *Beloved?*" Sayyid rose to his feet, pacing in the aisle as his mind whirled. "Of course, there could be cultural differences, as Akkadian was used by everyone from Egyptian royal administrators to Mitanni princes..."

"But it seems to imply that Neferneferuaten was a *woman*," Ellie filled in. "A woman beloved by a king."

"Presumably the king that she succeeded," Sayyid added with wide-eyed reverence. "And the king who died before Neferneferuaten's reign was *Akhenaten*."

"And his beloved was his *queen*. That's what it's saying, isn't it?" Ellie pressed, anxious for someone with a true Egyptological mind to confirm the wild theory that had burst into her brain back in the sun chapel. "It's saying that the pharaoh Neferneferuaten, who took the throne after Akhenaten's death, was none other than the woman he had married—Nefertiti!"

"A lady pharaoh?" Jemmahor perked with interest.

"It makes perfect sense," Ellie continued excitedly. "It would have been of the utmost importance to Akhenaten to pass his crown to someone who would uphold the faith of the Aten, and Nefertiti was his partner in that from the beginning."

"It would not be entirely unheard of," Sayyid replied thoughtfully. "During the Twelfth Dynasty, Sobekneferu took the throne after the death of her husband, Amenemhat IV. She is included on several of the king lists. And of course, we were at Hatshepsut's temple today. She claimed the throne for herself after her husband died, instead of ruling as a regent for her stepson."

"But what about the staff?" Zeinab pressed.

Ellie cast an uneasy glance at Sayyid. "The tablet mentioned a tomb at the Horizon of the Sun."

"Akhetaten!" Sayyid exclaimed. "The new capital city Akhenaten and Nefertiti built at Tell al-Amarna. That's what the name means—Horizon of the Aten, the god of the sun. Of course, the cliffs behind Tell al-Amarna are peppered with tombs—those of Akhenaten himself as well as many of his leading courtiers. The necropolis was abandoned along with his capital sometime around the beginning of the reign of Tutankhamun."

"But has anyone ever found Nefertiti's tomb?" Jemmahor's eyes glittered with excitement.

"It has never been discovered," Sayyid replied meaningfully.

"Did the tablet say anything more about where at Amarna the tomb might be found?" Zeinab demanded.

"I don't know," Ellie admitted. "I was only able to pick out part of the first line."

"Will your brother be able to read the rest of it?" Zeinab pressed.

Ellie glanced from Sayyid to Adam. "His Akkadian isn't as strong as mine, but he's familiar enough with it that I think he could manage, if he had a few books on hand."

"And Dawson travels with a library… and tea sets. Cutlery. Special outfits. What?" Adam protested when everyone turned to look at him. "The guy had a carpet in his tent!"

"Then if the tablet does contain further information about where to find the tomb, your Mr. Forster-Mowbray will go after it," Zeinab concluded grimly.

A veiled and cloaked woman hurried into the church, escorted by one of the young nuns. She dashed to Umm Waseem and Zeinab, exchanging a few low words in Masri.

"We know where they have taken Dr. Fairfax and Miss Tyrrell," Zeinab announced as the messenger darted back outside.

"Where?" Ellie felt a sharp prick of worry at the notion of her hapless brother trapped in Julian Forster-Mowbray's clutches.

"They were loaded onto a great dahabeeyah anchored just north of the city," Zeinab replied.

Ellie straightened in her seat. "We will have to slip on board and free them. We can hire a smaller craft in Luxor and go in under the cover of darkness."

"Like pirates?" Jemmahor elaborated hopefully.

Sayyid groaned.

"Absolutely not," Zeinab retorted crossly. "Do you think that is not the first thing Mr. Forster-Mowbray would expect?"

"We could use a small explosion as a diversion!" Ellie countered with a hopeful look at Umm Waseem.

The old woman had closed her eyes as though deciding to take a nap.

"No explosions," Adam cut in. "And The Mustache might not expect us to play pirates, but Jacobs sure as hell will. If we're crazy enough to come, he'll be waiting for us."

"But—" Ellie began.

Adam cut her off with a meaningful look. "They took your brother with them for a reason, or they'd have left him to be skewered with the rest of us. Until Fairfax has outlived his usefulness—which I'm guessing means translating the rest of that tablet—he's probably safer than we are. Maybe he'll even be smart enough to take his time about the job. It's not like Dawson's going to figure it out first—or know what the hell to do with the information once he does. I've seen how he reads a map."

His tone was drier than the arid landscape outside.

"And Julian still thinks he's going to marry Constance," Ellie reluctantly allowed.

"Which means she's safe enough with him, as long as she doesn't show all her cards," Adam filled in.

"But she can be terribly impulsive," Ellie pushed back worriedly. "And Neil is… er…"

"I know," Adam agreed wryly. "Look, I'd feel better too if I knew there was a way to get them out of there, but from where I'm sitting it looks like they're safer with Julian—for now—than they would be in some half-cocked rescue scheme. Even assuming we convince the rest of these ladies to put their necks on the line again to help us."

"Not to give any offense, but we did not come here for you," Jemmahor pointed out with a slightly apologetic look. "We are here to stop those Englishmen from making off with the Staff of Musa."

"Or the contents of another tomb." Zeinab's green eyes were hard. "They have stolen enough of Egypt's treasures already."

"We already know where they're going to go," Adam added. "And that's the tombs at Akhenaten's capital city. We'll have a hell of a better chance reaching Neil and Constance while The Mustache is distracted with tomb hunting than we will on a boat in the middle of the Nile."

"Mr. Bates is right." Zeinab gave Adam a look of wary respect.

"But do we even know whether the staff can be found in the lady pharaoh's tomb?" Jemmahor pressed.

"I can't say for certain," Ellie admitted. "The only connections we have are the presence of a ring with the name of Moseh in Mutnedjmet's jewelry box and the inscription's mention of the Was-Scepter of Khemenu."

"But would not the staff have left Egypt with Moses?" Jemmahor pressed. "It was with him when he parted the Red Sea and afterward while the people wandered in the desert. Why would it have been returned to Egypt? What would have been left here for Musa or his followers?"

"It does not matter," Zeinab concluded flatly. "Mr. Forster-Mowbray believes that some object of great power lies in this lost pharaoh's tomb, and if there is even a chance that he is right, we must intervene."

The space after her words was thick with the question of whether anyone would object.

Jemmahor's eyes shone with excitement at the prospect.

Adam's expression was grim but determined.

Sayyid stared at his wife as though she stood on the far side of a great gulf—and had turned to walk away from him.

"Bismillah," Umm Waseem concluded without opening her eyes.

Ellie wondered how much of the exchange the older woman had understood, given that so far she hadn't uttered a word of English. Did she know she was agreeing to stop a cabal of thieves from raiding the tomb of a mysterious pharaoh? Or was she simply on board for whatever trouble Zeinab led them into?

"If we're hoping to stage an ambush, we're going to want to get there first," Adam pointed out.

"They are traveling by boat," Zeinab said thoughtfully. "If we take the train to Dayrout, we will only need to go a few miles downstream and cross the river. We would certainly outpace them that way."

"El atr 'atal fe Asyut," Umm Waseem announced pleasantly.

"What'd she say?" Adam asked.

"She says the train is out at Asyut," Jemmahor translated with a look of surprised admiration.

"And how does she know that?" Zeinab cast a narrow-eyed glance at the older woman.

"Do you really want to know?" Jemmahor shot back wryly.

Umm Waseem wheezed out a dark, happy chuckle.

"Asyut!" Zeinab bit out the word with frustration.

"From what I remember of the map, that still leaves us about fifty miles short of Tell al-Amarna," Adam noted.

Zeinab stood. "It doesn't matter. I can get us there in time."

"How?" Ellie asked, curious.

"By calling in a favor," Zeinab replied.

Her tone made it sound like a threat.

TWENTY-TWO

As THE BATTERED carriage rattled uncomfortably away from the temple at Deir al-Bahari, Constance Tyrrell made an unflinching assessment of her circumstances.

Up to now, Constance's existence had been fairly dull and predictable. Her mother, Lady Sabita, liked to go to dinner parties and meet up with friends for tea. Her father, Sir Robert, got very excited about numbers and balance sheets, to the point where they frequently distracted him from such lesser concerns as food or conversation.

Constance had been on holiday in Paris and Bruges. She had never been to India, though it constituted a quarter of her heritage, with both her mother and grandmother having been born there.

She took her tea with an excess of cream and sugar, because one needn't worry about one's figure if one simply refused to stop moving. She had recently begun jiu jitsu classes with some of the ladies in Ellie's suffrage club and had learned how to use the momentum of an opponent to toss him onto the floor. She had tried the move out in the dojo on the rebellious daughter of an MP—a girl easily twice Constance's weight—and it had worked splendidly.

She had been itching for an opportunity to practice it 'in the field,' as they say.

Constance's days were otherwise filled with the activities one expected of a young woman of good breeding and substantial fortune. She paid visits, shopped, and did a bit of charity work, mostly reading aloud to children in the recovery ward of the hospital.

Constance adored children, as they were usually willing accomplices in mischief and subterfuge—tendencies she encouraged through carefully curating the books she selected for them.

Yet she had always known the world had greater things in store for her—and that it was only a matter of time before she found her way to them. When she did, she would be sure to be ready for it. That rock-hard faith was likely why she had been drawn to Ellie. As a skinny, freckled child, Ellie had quietly blazed with a sense that she would not be confined by other people's expectations.

Joining her parents on their move to Egypt had been Constance's first real step toward the exciting life that she knew she was destined for, and she had taken hold of it with both hands. She had loved the weeks she had spent immersing herself in Cairo's unique spirit, from stumbling across a Byzantine mosaic in an old Coptic church to finding an alley that housed nothing but rows of glassblowers.

Then Lady Sabita and Sir Robert had made their devastating announcement—that she must choose a husband before her next birthday. Constance's world had abruptly narrowed as the possibilities she had dreamed of as a girl slipped away like smoke. For the first time in her life, she had tasted the threat of despair. Though she fought against it, striving for optimism, she could still feel it lurking at the periphery of her awareness like a patient demon hiding in the shadows.

Her current circumstances, at least, were far from boring—even if they were something less than salubrious. She knew she shouldn't feel *entirely* thrilled to be trapped in a decrepit carriage with a villain set on becoming her husband, but she had prepared for years for the possibility that someday a real adventure would find her—and now that time was most certainly here.

The carriage lurched beneath her. It was thoroughly run down, with its springs all but gone—if they had ever been there to begin with. The black box of it made the heat of the afternoon even thicker, which was likely why the Egyptians themselves showed no interest in carriages, preferring to ride or be carried about in a sedan chair.

The sweating, ginger-haired professor sat to her left. He studied the clay tablet greedily as he turned it in his hands, but he clearly couldn't just read the thing offhand.

Julian's two thugs sat across from her. They were obviously related—one with a scar on his cheek and the other with a missing front tooth. Both kept glancing sideways at Neil, apparently determining him to be the most likely source of trouble.

Constance resisted the urge to roll her eyes at the notion that Stuffy was the greatest threat in the carriage. Meanwhile, she had two knives secured about her person and a set of lockpicks hidden in a special pocket in her corset. She was fairly certain that, if necessary, she could use the ribbon belting the waist of her lawn dress as a garrote.

Sandwiched between the two mercenaries, Neil looked absolutely rotten. Constance had little sympathy for him. He really *ought* to feel rotten. He had sold out his allies in the hopes that a bit of abject groveling would save his job with a batch of fellows that anyone could see were up to no good. Admittedly, Neil had never picked up an adventure novel in his life, so perhaps he really was *that* ignorant of how these things worked, but she was still thoroughly furious with him.

Julian occupied the space to Constance's right. As Constance glanced at him, he flashed her a nervous smile. He seemed desperate to present their current situation as perfectly chummy and not-at-all something Constance ought to feel worried about.

"This isn't quite the excursion I might have planned for us," Julian said, "but I hope you don't feel terribly… er, inconvenienced."

Constance slipped into a role that she was very good at playing—that of the pretty young thing who hadn't a clue what was going on but was still quite certain of the consideration and charm that were her due. She mustered up an appropriately indignant glare.

"I should say that it is all very irregular!" she declared. "I never expected to find you running about with a bunch of fellows who use guns and fisticuffs!"

Julian had the grace to blanch at her words. "There was this wretchedly complicated incident at the Saqqara dig the other day, my dear," he explained awkwardly. "And so it seemed prudent to bring along a little additional… personal security?"

Constance was grateful that Julian still hadn't the foggiest notion that she had actually been in Mutnedjmet's tomb when he had ordered his thugs to shoot at her friends. She was tempted to share that interesting fact with him, if only to enjoy the horrified look on his face. Sadly, prudence dictated that she keep it to herself—for now.

She felt a snap of worry for Ellie, Adam, and Sayyid. They had been in an admittedly tight spot when she had left, for all that Adam had urged her onward when she had posed her silent question to him about insinuating herself into Julian's retinue. Constance had wondered if she ought to stay behind herself instead and try to use her knives and jiu jitsu skills to even the odds—but that would have left Neil entirely at Julian's mercy.

Not that he really *deserved* to be rescued, after acting like such a dolt.

There was also the mysterious tablet Neil and Ellie had found in the temple to consider. Constance assumed it must be a map that would lead the villains directly to the location of the lost pharaoh's tomb. No one had bothered to say as much during the confrontation in the sun chapel—but really, what else could it be?

Constance couldn't allow Julian to keep it and get his hands on the Staff of Moses. She hadn't been a particularly attentive Sunday School student, but she did recall the plagues of the Exodus, as they fed into her admittedly Gothic tastes. Leaving the power to unleash death, disease, and darkness on the world in the hands of the self-important grandson of a duke was simply out of the question. At the moment, she was the person best positioned to stop that from happening.

She had to trust that Ellie and the others would find a way out of their predicament while she focused on her own mission.

Steal the tablet. Save the dolt—if she was feeling generous. And maybe see if she could squeeze more information out of Julian about who was really pulling the strings of this whole affair.

Because if Constance knew one thing for certain, it was that Julian Forster-Mowbray would never have come up with something like this on his own.

The carriage jolted to a stop at a rickety wharf on the broad bank of the Nile. Julian helped Constance down. Neil lingered behind her, sunk in a gloomy reverie. The gap-toothed thug snapped him out of it with a kick, and Neil scrambled down, flashing a guilty look at Constance.

Dawson followed with his eyes still glued to the tablet like a child gloating over a prize.

They filed onto a little launch, where an Egyptian fellow in a ragged galabeya and turban rowed them out into the river. The boat bounced over the gently rippling water to the stern of the elegant dahabeeyah that Constance had seen earlier that morning, anchored just downriver from the Luxor docks. The ship was perhaps sixty feet in length with a twenty-foot beam. Sparkling windows lined the sides, opening into rows of cabins, while the upper floor was taken up by an expansive open-air salon shaded by a red-and-white-striped canvas awning.

Their ferry steered up to a small platform that extended from the rear of the boat. A pair of crewmen caught them there, holding the launch in place as they disembarked.

Neil lingered beside Constance after he stumbled onto the landing. He was slump-shouldered with guilt. The two bored-looking mercenaries hovered at his back.

"Connie, I…" he began.

"Not now," Constance snapped impatiently under her breath.

"Welcome to the *Isis*," Julian announced grandly as he turned back to her—though his eyes revealed a flash of nervousness over his elegant mustache.

"It's very nice," Constance said dismissively, slipping into her role. "But is there any lemonade?"

"Lemonade! Yes, of course!" Julian hurriedly assured her. "You there! Reis!" he called out to an older, better-dressed fellow who had stopped to speak to the other crewmen—the ship's captain, based on the title Julian had used for him, however condescendingly.

The reis schooled his features into an expression of barely tolerant courtesy.

"We need a suite prepared for my guest," Julian rattled authoritatively. "And see that she is brought some lemonade. On ice, this time! I don't know why anyone would think it acceptable to present a glass of lemonade without it."

He turned to Constance, picking up her hand and planting a dry kiss on the back of it. "I shall be with you shortly, my dear, after I have taken care of the tiniest little bit of business. Dry stuff, but needs must. Dawson, have those Al-Saboors escort Fairfax to the study and see that he's settled."

Dawson looked up from the tablet and shot a panicked look from Julian to the two thugs. "But I don't speak any—"

Julian cut him off, already walking away and clearly not really listening. "And do be sure to provide any… *encouragement* that Fairfax might require to be helpful with the translation."

Neil went over even more pale, throwing Constance a panicky look. She returned it with a glare that she hoped communicated something along the lines of *quit mucking about and play along until I say otherwise.*

"Er… Come? Go?" Dawson attempted awkwardly as the two thugs stared at him.

"You could try 'yalla,'" Constance offered tiredly.

"Yalla?" Dawson echoed hopefully.

The scarred fellow shot his gap-toothed cousin a look. The cousin shrugged, and the pair plucked Neil up by his arms and propelled him into the hall, Dawson scurrying ahead of them.

"Sitt el Kol?" one of the remaining crewmen prompted with nervous courtesy. He gestured into the hallway, presumably toward the room being readied for her.

Wood creaked behind her. Constance glanced back to see the ferry rowing slowly to the shore.

She refused to let the sight intimidate her. Instead, she felt the subtle pressure of the knife against her thigh, the lockpicks between her bosoms, and the capable strength of her own bare hands. No, she had not been deserted here. She was a threat these men had just unwittingly carried on board—and she would not forget it.

"Do lead on, my good fellow," she declared firmly, and followed him into the gloom.

TWENTY-THREE

$\mathcal{N}$EIL FAIRFAX SAT in an elegantly appointed gentleman's study, complete with fine Turkish carpets, cozy armchairs, and piles of books—and wondered if he had ever felt quite so abjectly awful in his entire life.

He was trapped on a boat in the middle of the Nile, surrounded by casually murderous thugs. He had left his sister, his best friend, and a colleague that he had come to care about very deeply in the hands of the most intimidating and obviously violent person he had ever encountered. Now he was charged with translating a clue to one of the most important mysteries in Egyptian history so that his villainous boss could try to steal from it.

And it was all his fault.

He should have trusted Ellie when she told him that Julian Forster-Mowbray was up to no good. Instead, Neil had stubbornly insisted on living in a different world—one where the designated representative of a respected scholarly organization would never have turned out to be capable of kidnapping and murder. One where people laughed at the notion of reasonably sane gentlemen committing acts of violence in the name of chasing down an object everyone knew to be a myth.

But Neil couldn't blame all of this on his ex-employer. His own stupid, stubborn decisions had led him to be imprisoned in a well-lit library on Julian's graceful dahabeeyah, ill with worry over what might have happened to his sister and his friends. He was the one who had written that stupid, foolish note to Julian at Saqqara, slipping a coin to one of Sayyid's neighbors' children to deliver it to the excavation.

He had been so worried about his blasted job and his academic reputation. Of course, it had *seemed* like an entirely reasonable course of action at the time—but he'd been wrong. Julian Forster-Mowbray really had been in league with a batch of artifact-thieving villains, and Neil had led them right to the tablet—and to the people he cared about.

Memories tormented him—of Ellie, slight and freckled, popping up beside his desk to pepper him with questions about Persian etymologies. Of Adam at Cambridge, the brash American cowboy who tossed viscounts into rivers and befriended a bespectacled scholarship student as though it were the most natural thing in the world.

And what about Sayyid? The man was a brilliant Egyptologist, a deeply skilled conservator, and a natural leader. They had worked side-by-side, debating techniques and challenging each other's scholarly conclusions for two years now. Sayyid had come to be far more than just a foreman to him, and so Neil was only a little surprised to realize that he was just as twisted up in knots about the man as he was about Adam.

He tried to find some way to quell the racing, helpless panic inside his chest. Adam was rather good in a fight, after all… but that might not hold when he had his hands tied behind his back. Ellie was extraordinarily clever… but there were only so many ways out of a sunbaked box when one was unarmed and outnumbered.

He grasped for even more desperate threads of hope.

The baddies might all succumb to sun stroke. Sayyid might turn out to have been hiding a knack for the martial arts. Perhaps Mr. Jacobs had a trick knee.

Neil thumped his head down onto the table, feeling queasy again.

He was fairly certain Mr. Jacobs did not have a trick knee.

Not that Neil could do anything to help them from where he sat, even though the room was reasonably comfortable for a prison. In addition to the Turkish carpets and the cozy armchairs, the study was furnished with a sturdy wooden work table and a window open to let in the breeze from the Nile. Beyond the rippling brown water, Neil could make out the sandstone columns of the Temple of Karnak, gilded by the afternoon sunlight.

Books were stacked on every surface. More of them spilled out of a pile of sturdy trunks. They did not appear to be very well organized, for all that there were a great many of them—archaeological treatises, Greek epics, and translations of the Book of the Dead mingled with bound copies of respectable academic journals.

Neil would normally be quite pleased to find himself in such a space—if he weren't locked inside it wondering if the people he loved were still alive.

The only thing Neil had power over in this wretched situation lay on the table in front of him.

The clay tablet sat amid a mess of papers and books, taunting him with its tidy rows of cuneiform symbols. The object was over three thousand years old. It possibly held paradigm-shattering clues about the identity of the most mysterious pharaoh of the Eighteenth Dynasty.

And Neil was fairly certain that he needed to smash it to pieces.

The secret of Neferneferuaten's identity wasn't what made the tablet so dangerous. It was the mention of a tomb at the Horizon of the Sun, Akhenaten's ruined capital at Tell al-Amarna.

If the rest of the text contained specific clues as to where in the Amarna necropolis the tomb lay hidden, it could lead Julian Forster-Mowbray straight to the most important find in the history of Egyptology.

Neil couldn't let that happen. The tomb of Neferneferuaten had escaped looting for the last three thousand years. The artifacts housed inside of it would offer priceless information about life in the New Kingdom and the late Eighteenth Dynasty—and reveal the true story of the fall of Akhenaten's monotheistic experiment, a secret that had beckoned to Neil for years.

Julian would strip it bare and sell it all off to the highest bidders. All of that knowledge would be lost—permanently.

The notion was unconscionable… but was it worth dying for?

Neil was forced to ask himself the question… because if he did destroy the tablet, it would almost certainly cost him his life.

Of course, Neil couldn't yet be certain that the tablet pointed the way to the tomb. If he destroyed it without being sure, he would lose his life—and turn a priceless three-thousand-year-old document into dust—for no good reason.

The conundrum of it twisted inside of him like a snake.

He was still wrangling painfully with the decision when the door thudded open behind him, and Professor Dawson came back into the room.

Neil thought he might have heard the man's name before. A monograph on early Greek vase motifs came to mind, one that Neil had found both unoriginal and unconvincing. He didn't have the foggiest notion why this lackluster academic should have been recruited into aiding Julian's efforts. The fellow was clearly less than pleased to have Neil around, as though his presence was a personal affront to Dawson's capabilities.

Dawson gave him an irritated look as he returned to his seat at the table. The clay tablet lay between them. On Dawson's side, the table was covered in scribbled notes and several opened volumes on Akkadian cuneiform.

Neil had been astonished to discover that Dawson traveled with more than *one* volume on Akkadian cuneiform.

Neil's half of the table was decidedly less cluttered. In fact, it held only a mostly blank page. He beheld it with a little twist of panic. He needed to at least appear to be making himself useful—or risk being tossed overboard like so much extra ballast.

Of course, he wasn't the only one on the boat at risk of being tossed overboard. What had Constance been thinking, volunteering to go along with Julian?

Unless skipping into the arms of the enemy actually had been the more clever choice, when the alternative was perishing violently with Ellie, who might even now be lying in a ditch beside the mortal remains of Neil's best friend and the kind-hearted, intelligent gentleman with whom he had worked closely and companionably for the last two years.

The thought made Neil want to collapse into a hysterical puddle.

At least Constance must have *some* notion of what she had gotten herself into. The now alarmingly grown-up danger gnome had proved herself both frighteningly clever and perfectly amenable to situations of mortal danger. Neil could still recall the sharp poke of her dagger at his kidney, evidence that she had no qualms about using violence when necessary to achieve her aims.

She was also desperately pretty.

Neil startled at that last thought, nearly dropping his pencil. Why was he thinking about how pretty Constance was? She had always been an absolute magnet for trouble, and Neil disliked trouble immensely. In fact, there was little he wanted more in the world than to wave goodbye to all the trouble that currently surrounded him and go back to the predictable, boring pattern that had been his life before Ellie dropped into his tomb.

Well—perhaps the one thing he wanted more was to know that his sister and his friends were safe.

He pictured the pale oval of Ellie's face, stark with a look of betrayal. The flash of hurt and anger in Sayyid's brown eyes. The sight of Adam Bates on his knees, bruised and bleeding with his hands bound behind his back.

His stomach twisted again.

"Muzzazū…" Dawson muttered, breaking into Neil's thoughts. "Muzzazū, muzzazū… Why aren't any of these words where they are supposed to be in the dictionary?"

The professor's tones were laced with frustration.

"Probably because of conjugations?" Neil offered lamely.

"Conjugations!" Dawson sniffed disapprovingly, then fixed Neil with a glare. "You really ought to start making yourself more useful—in as much as one can expect from a boy barely out of Cambridge."

"I have a doctorate!" Neil protested, momentarily feeling the loss of his mustache… though admittedly, the facial hair hadn't done much to help him look his age.

Dawson didn't seem to hear him. "Check some of these other books, at the very least." He flapped a dismissive hand at the pile of tomes on the desk. "You haven't any notion of the very delicate politics involved in all of this. Matters have been tense since our last expedition went slightly *awry*— due to circumstances entirely outside of our control, of course," he added quickly. "However unjustly, we are still in something of a state of probation, as you had best remember."

"Remember?" Neil echoed disbelievingly. "I'm… I'm locked in here with you. I haven't the foggiest notion what you're on about!"

"A footman, maybe?" Dawson mused, ignoring him, and then brightened. "Ah—here it is! Muzzazū. A tax collector."

"It's not talking about a tax collector!" Neil shot back, his patience breaking. "You've transcribed the bloody word wrong. That's the symbol for 'er,' not 'az.' It's *muzzerrū*."

Dawson blinked at him in surprise as though just realizing that Neil was actually speaking. "Hmm," he grunted shortly, and then turned the page of his dictionary. "Ah. *Muzzerrū*. Means 'enemies.'"

Neil stifled the urge to groan. Had he actually just used his half-rate knowledge of Akkadian to *help* the intolerable rotter translate the tablet? He shouldn't be correcting Dawson's transcriptions! He was supposed to be deciding whether to snatch the artifact from under Dawson's nose and throw it out the window into the Nile… sentencing himself to certain and painful death in the process.

The queasiness threatened to return. Neil did not think he would be very good at dying. He certainly wouldn't go about it with noble aplomb. He was far more likely to faint or melt into a sobbing puddle.

He supposed he could at least wait to see whether the threat posed by the tablet was genuine. He likely had a bit of time in which to manage that. For all his books, Dawson was an idiot when it came to ancient Semitic languages. Neil might not have Ellie's skill, but if he had a quiet hour with a notepad and a few of Dawson's books, he stood a solid chance of deciphering the text.

He just had to manage it without Dawson catching on. Then he could decide if the artifact was a harmless if fascinating New Kingdom relic… or something worth dying for.

Unfortunately, Neil was incapable of working through the Akkadian without writing it all down—which even a dolt like Dawson couldn't help but notice.

He glanced over at what Dawson had so far scribbled into his notebook.

And this is the will of Moseh, that his legacy, the gift of Neferneferuaten, be not misused, or fallen into the hands of enemies...

Those words—*gift of Neferneferuaten*—echoed uncomfortably through Neil's mind.

The inscription in Mutnedjmet's jewelry box—found with a ring engraved with the name of Moseh—had claimed Neferneferuaten was the last bearer of the Was-Scepter of Khemenu.

The Bible was not at all ambiguous about the fact that Moses had been raised as an Egyptian. If an Egyptian had wished to work some great magic on the world, Neil had little doubt that a was-scepter was precisely the ritual object he would use to do it.

All of which meant that Neil was finding it increasingly plausible that the *gift of Neferneferuaten* might actually be the legendary staff of one of history's most important prophets.

"Look here!" Dawson said excitedly, oblivious to Neil's wretched state beside him. "Isn't this the logogram for tomb?"

Neil kept his mouth closed, anticipating what must come next with a rising sense of dread.

"*The tomb at...* What is that word? *Nab... Nabtû.* Nabtû, nabtû..." Dawson mused, flipping through the pages of his books. "Ah! There it is—horizon. *The tomb at the horizon... of... the... sun.*" He turned to Neil with a superior smirk. "Don't feel too bad about not figuring it out first. I have had several more years' experience to bring to bear on the translation. I was tenured at St. Andrews, you know."

Neil knew. Dawson had mentioned it four or five times since he had been locked into this room.

"Horizon of the sun..." Dawson mused thoughtfully. "It must mean somewhere in the west."

Neil went still. Was it possible that Professor Formerly-Tenured-at-Saint-Andrews didn't realize the connection between *Horizon of the Sun* and Akhenaten's former capital city at Tell al-Amarna?

A new set of footsteps, firm and confident, sounded from outside the study door. The lock clicked, and the panel swung open to reveal the lean form and cold eyes of Mr. Jacobs.

Dawson startled in his chair, fumbling his pen. "It's about time you showed up," he complained. "Do you know, I had to knock and shout for one of those Al-Saboors a few minutes ago just to relieve myself? I don't see why I have to be locked in here like I'm also a…" He trailed off, casting an awkward look over at Neil—obviously realizing he was about to spill out the word *prisoner*.

The professor cleared his throat. "What I mean is, someone ought to give me a key!"

Jacobs gave Dawson a tired, disdainful look. "He'd just take it off you." He slid an assessing glance over Neil. "Maybe," he modified flatly.

Neil felt both indignant and intimidated at the same time.

Did Jacobs' reappearance mean that Ellie and the others had been sent on their way? Or had they managed to best the man and his fellows in a fight?

He looked for some sign that Jacobs had been on the wrong end of Adam's fists, but couldn't find any… perhaps because there hadn't been any fight, and Jacobs had simply murdered all of them.

The demand to know rose into Neil's throat—and choked there.

"What have you found?" Jacobs demanded.

Dawson went over a bit sniffy. "We are still working on the translation. This is a particularly challenging form of Middle Akkadian and requires a great deal of—"

"So far," Jacobs cut in with exaggerated patience.

Dawson swallowed thickly. "The tablet mentions a tomb at the horizon of the sun, which clearly indicates a position to the west. Perhaps somewhere near the oasis of Siwa."

Neil held himself very still, making every effort not to react to Dawson's assertion.

Jacobs' gaze snapped over to him like a hawk spotting a mouse. "Do you know anything more about it?"

The question should have been simple enough to deny, but for some reason, Neil felt exposed in the face of it. "I'm, ah… I'm afraid I don't…"

"Ah." Jacobs interrupted him with a smile. It was a very *knowing* sort of smile, and the rest of Neil's words died in his throat. "But that's not precisely true. Is it?"

Why did he…? How could he possibly…? Neil's thoughts spluttered helplessly. It would be one thing if Jacobs had simply suspected he was lying, but the look in his eyes didn't *feel* like suspicion.

It felt like certainty.

Beside Neil, Dawson had gone conspicuously quiet. When Neil shot him a panicked glance, the professor was eyeing him as though he were a chicken that had just been tagged for slaughter.

Neil turned his head back to face Jacobs once more—and jolted in his chair at the realization that the man had moved closer. He had done it without making a bloody sound, like some sort of ghost. Neil instinctively pressed himself against the back of his seat as though hoping he might sink through it and escape.

"Tell me," Jacobs said evenly. "Have you any interest in the young lady upstairs?"

With a cold dart of fear, Neil realized he was referring to Constance. "She's just…" he started, choking on the words. "I barely…"

Jacobs tilted his head. "That's not what I asked you."

Neil could only blink back at him, fear stealing his voice.

"It would be a shame," Jacobs continued evenly. "If I had to hurt her to convince you to offer us your full cooperation."

The quick, visceral emotion that snapped through Neil at Jacobs' words surprised him.

By all rights, it should have been terror. After all, he was a scrawny, bookish academic who wanted nothing more in life than to translate hieroglyphs for hours. Facing the threats of a dangerously calm and extremely intimidating villain should have been far more than he could handle.

Instead, at Jacobs' implied promise of violence against Constance, a snap of anger flashed through Neil like a gust of hot wind.

She might be reckless and unpredictable—a relentless danger gnome who had spent the better part of her childhood tormenting Neil in every way imaginable—but she was *his* danger gnome. And he would be damned if he sat back and quivered while the cold-eyed bastard in front of him threatened to use her like a sacrificial goat.

All of which led Neil to make a response that was perhaps less prudent than he might otherwise have preferred, given the circumstances.

"What sort of abject coward uses threats against an innocent woman to get what he wants?" Neil burst out, pushing up from his chair to stand toe-to-toe with Jacobs. "You won't bloody touch her! And even if you wanted to—you can't," he added with a burst of angry inspiration. "Your boss has an interest in her. He won't *let* you."

Jacobs had not stepped back by so much as a breath when Neil rose— which left him very close indeed. Neil quailed a bit at the realization as the rest of his brain had a moment to catch up with what the angry part was doing.

Jacobs' near-black eyes flashed with dark frustration.

Riling up a man like Jacobs was a terrible idea. Neil's more prudent instincts screamed for him to sit back down—or cower abjectly under the desk—but his anger refused to give way to it. He was angry at Jacobs for threatening to hurt Constance. He was angry at Julian Forster-Mowbray for turning Neil's comfortable existence into an entirely unwelcome adventure. He was angry at the self-important professor currently gaping at him with a look of surprised horror for… well, just being an utter prat, really.

As he faced off against Jacobs, he knew he was doing something irrevocably stupid, but he couldn't bring himself to care the way he ought to. The words kept spilling out of him regardless.

"But if you *were* going to threaten to hurt innocent people to compel me to assist you, shouldn't you be starting with my sister?" he demanded. "She's the most obvious choice, after all. But you haven't—which makes me wonder if perhaps she and my friends got the better of you after all!"

Frustration and rage flickered across Jacobs' features, breaking his air of unrelenting competence. The look lasted only a moment before Jacobs pulled it back behind a veil of icy control.

"Or maybe I've already killed her," he replied, continuing to stand just a few claustrophobic inches away, "along with all the rest of them."

The words clenched around Neil's heart like a vise.

A wave of guilt and grief threatened to overwhelm him. He fought back against it, scrambling for a lifeline—something, *anything,* that would keep him from falling apart.

Curious hazel eyes peering over the edge of his desk. A spray of freckles over a delighted grin. A head of chestnut hair drooping against his shoulder as his baby sister dozed off over her Cicero.

His hand reaching out to brush warm fingers over the little crease between her brows.

What are you doing?

Just rubbing the worry out.

"No," Neil burst out wildly. "You *can't* have!"

A new emotion flashed through Jacobs' expression at Neil's words—one that looked oddly of both surprise… and *fear.*

Jacobs grabbed the front of Neil's shirt, hauling him closer as his eyes blazed with threat. "How could you possibly know—" he began.

"Hold on!" Dawson piped in, blinking with surprised excitement. "The tablet isn't talking about Siwa. The Horizon of the Sun—that's Akhetaten! It is quite an obscure connection to make, of course," Dawson rattled on. "One could hardly expect it of a young fellow barely out of Cambridge. I have always said the Cantabrigian education is sadly—"

"And where is this Akhetaten?" Jacobs pressed with tired patience.

His fist remained suspended in front of Neil's face.

"Oh! Right." Dawson startled as if just remembering that he was sitting beside an imminent pummeling. "The ruins are at Tell al-Amarna, about two hundred and fifty miles north of here along the river."

Jacobs lowered his hand—though he continued to fix Neil with a gaze that simmered with threat. "Do keep at it, then," he ordered calmly.

He finally released his grip on Neil's shirt and left, the door snapping shut behind him.

Neil heard the soft click of the lock turning and slumped back into his chair. His hands were shaking even as his mind whirled with panicked confusion.

How could you possibly know…

Know what? Neil wondered frantically. What had Jacobs thought he had known?

Dawson scribbled beside him, the light scratch of his pencil on the paper the only sound in the room. "It's best not to lie to him."

The quiet, awkward words snapped Neil from the maelstrom of his thoughts and back to where he was—locked in a room with an arrogant professor and three-thousand-year-old clue while a murderer stalked outside the door.

The pencil scratched a little more, then paused.

"He always knows," Dawson added without looking up.

"But how…" Neil's voice was tight as the fury that had fueled him crumbled, making way for an abysmal well of fear. "How is that possible?"

"I don't know." Dawson refused to meet Neil's eyes. "But it's true… and it makes him very, very dangerous."

Neil's gaze shifted to the closed door as though he could look through it—and the walls and deck—to wherever Jacobs currently stood.

Dawson pulled over one of his tomes. "Best get back to work."

As Dawson's lead scratched across the page, heavy footsteps and creaking ropes sounded from the deck above. The boat shifted, and the temple outside the window began to slide away.

The *Isis* was moving.

Neil hoped it wasn't leaving his chances of surviving all this behind.

TWENTY-FOUR

$\mathcal{C}$ONSTANCE GREETED THE movement of the dahabeeyah with a burst of excitement. For the last hour, she had been lying on her bed in the stateroom Julian had ordered hurriedly made over for her, tapping her fingers restlessly. She had tried the door as soon as they left her, of course, and had found it unlocked—but another Al-Saboor had been lingering outside of it, obviously posted there to trail her should she decide to go exploring. Constance could have overcome him easily enough—even if he hadn't sported a black eye and had his arm in a sling—but doing so would blow her cover.

She resigned herself to waiting, albeit impatiently and with frequent requests for more lemonade.

At least she was feeling less worried about Ellie, Adam, and Sayyid. She had caught a glimpse of the launch when it had returned to the *Isis* carrying Jacobs and the rest of Julian's hired thugs. The remaining Al-Saboors had looked fairly shamefaced, and there'd been an air of simmering frustration in Jacobs' quick pace. Just that would have been enough to tell Constance that Ellie must have managed to escape, but Julian's quite audible outburst a few minutes later had put a pin in it.

"What do you mean, you were overcome by a batch of women?!"

Constance was admittedly a little miffed. It was hardly fair that Ellie had kept something as deliciously exciting as a secret getaway strategy involving a cadre of mysterious accomplices to herself!

But at least now, she need only concern herself with accomplishing her own mission—interrogate Julian, steal the tablet, and rescue the idiot who had given their position away to the enemy in a desperate ploy to reclaim his old life.

Constance would have a thing or two to say about that once she had safely whisked Stuffy off the boat.

They were tasks sure to require all her skills of deception, espionage, and—one might hope—a dash of physical violence.

———

Unfortunately, she had to wait another three hours before she could do it. Constance was seething with impatience when a crewman finally turned up to show her to dinner.

She trailed behind her escort down the hall, tuning her senses to the row of cabins to either side of her. In front of the third one down, she heard the scrape of a chair on the floor and a rustle of papers that sounded distinctly scholarly.

It had to be Neil. Constance certainly couldn't imagine any of the Al-Saboors reading a book. Satisfied, she filed the information away and hurried after the sailor.

He led her to where Julian waited in the open-air salon at the top of the boat. It ran the full length of the cabins and had been loosely organized into a dining area with a fine mahogany table, a bar, and a parlor furnished with couches and overstuffed armchairs. The deck was bordered only by a low rail, offering a stunning view of the Nile to every side.

Constance glanced up at the canopy, which offered a more sinister sort of scenery. "Goodness! Is that a crocodile?"

The ten-foot-long reptile was suspended within the rafters over the bar, its dark green leather offset by rows of yellowing teeth. As taxidermy went, it was not the finest specimen Constance had ever seen.

"Oh, that!" Julian strolled over to join her. "Relic of a past rental, I gather. Do you want me to have it removed?"

"To where?" Constance pictured the stuffed creature bobbing on the Nile like raft.

"Ha ha ha!" Julian chuckled forcefully. "Well, you know how things are in these godforsaken outposts. One can't be too choosy, can they?"

Constance bristled a bit.

Her complexion was a soft hue of light brown, which had led older ladies to scold her about spending too much time in the sun. Her hair was a rich, glossy black that curled into charming little waves if left to dry properly, and her lashes were much longer and thicker than those of most English ladies. Constance liked that she could see these little hints of India in her mirror. How could she feel anything but proud of that part of her heritage when it was shared by someone as regal and brilliant as her Aai—a royal princess of the ancient kingdom of Nandapur, educated like a scholar in the family palace?

She was fairly certain Julian would categorize Nandapur as one of those 'godforsaken places' as well.

Though Constance made no secret of her Indian blood, people around her seemed to find it easy to forget, especially when they began airing their personal opinions about the ignorance and rebelliousness of colonial peoples.

Normally, Constance would find a clever way to turn such a comment around on the speaker, subjecting them to a subtle but razor-edged verbal skewering that left people like Julian Forster-Mowbray feeling vaguely humiliated for reasons they couldn't quite put a finger on.

That was another skill she had inherited from her remarkable Aai.

Refraining from pulling the intellectual rug out from under Julian now took a palpable effort—but then, Constance was committed to a bigger game.

The thought of how Julian would feel when she foiled all his plans made her smile in a way akin to that of the stuffed crocodile overhead.

"How very clever you are!" she assured him airily. "But aren't you going to invite me to sit?"

It took roughly three courses for Julian to forget to be nervous around her. He spent most of the soup and the fish angling in a patently obvious manner to determine whether Constance had sensed anything suspicious about the fact that his thugs had ambushed her and her friends, threatening them at knife and gunpoint. Constance played along by complimenting the roast pigeon and sympathizing with his complaints about the wine until he had tossed back three or four glasses of it—which warmed him up nicely for interrogation.

She wasn't sure whether Julian's willingness to believe her *that* oblivious to his nefarious purposes said more about his desperate ambitions for her dowry—or his low opinions of the intelligence of females in general.

Most likely, it was a bit of both.

Constance made her first parry as they retired to the couch to sip little glasses of pastis.

"How far downriver shall we be going, then?" she asked, taking a sip of the sweet, pungent liquor.

The sun had declined into evening, painting the sky with the startling hues of an Egyptian sunset. Pink and orange shifted to a richer violet in the east, just speckled with the first emerging stars. The landscape they sailed gracefully past was decidedly rural—just bands of green fields interspersed with small villages, giving way to the golden sprawl of the desert. The *Isis* was making quick progress, her big white sails taut with the river breeze.

Julian gave a guilty little start. "Oh! We have a spot of business a day or so north of here. Nothing you need to worry about."

Constance's attention sharpened. She had no doubt this 'business' to the north had to do with the tablet from Hatshepsut's temple.

The time had come for her first gambit. Her blood hummed with excitement at the prospect of truly opening the game. She had long suspected that she had a natural gift for espionage, though she had rarely had an opportunity to put it to the test.

Well, she would test it here, applying all her feminine wiles and rhetorical weaponry to lure Julian Forster-Mowbray into revealing his secrets.

Constance scooted a little closer to him on the settee—and got to work.

"You know, Julian… you've been holding out on me," she scolded playfully.

"Have I?" Julian returned, looking nervous.

"You most certainly have!" Constance wondered whether she was laying it on a bit thick with her blatantly flirtatious tones—but she was betting Julian was far too self-absorbed to consider that she might be selling him a pile of lemons. "Here you are dashing about Egypt with the most dastardly-looking characters. You can't possibly expect me to believe it's just imports-and-exports or something equally drab." She let her face show a touch of disappointment. "Unless it really is that dull."

Julian was obviously torn. After all, he clearly wanted to impress her, and brushing off his current activities as nothing worth talking about would only make him look boring.

As Constance had hoped, he couldn't resist the chance to at least *hint* at being involved in something that made him sound more mysterious and important.

"Perhaps it isn't *quite* so dull as that," he confessed, leaning in closer and flashing her a conspiratorial smile.

Constance plucked a sporting magazine from the nearby coffee table and batted Julian on the arm with it. "Now you are teasing me!"

"It's only that the business is terribly—well, *sensitive*. I'm not supposed to talk to anyone about it."

"I must admit, Julian—I had no idea you could be involved in something so… *intriguing.*" Constance ended the word on a breathy note, leaning forward and blinking up at him.

Julian ate it up with a spoon—just as she had planned.

She really was rather good at this.

"There are many things you don't know about me, Connie," he assured her, slinging his arm over the back of the settee.

"But surely you could give me just the tiniest little hint," Constance pressed. "Seeing that we're…"

She pretended to catch herself and pushed a becoming little blush into her cheeks. It was a trick she had practiced at some length in her vanity mirror, in case she should ever need to put her charms to work to foil an enemy.

"Connie!" Julian exclaimed. "Dare I hope that you have developed a tendre for me?"

"Oh, you will embarrass me utterly!" Constance hid her face behind the sporting magazine.

That way he couldn't see her grin.

"By no means!" Julian assured her. "I should be the last one to blame you for such a thing. How could you help it?"

Constance dropped her carefully assumed persona, her eyebrow cocking at the sheer self-absorption of his response. Thankfully, Julian had turned to gaze off into the distance as he said it, which gave her a vital moment to fix an expression of brainless admiration on her face before he noticed anything.

She certainly had her fish on the hook, at any rate… Now to reel in her catch.

"Though I did wonder about our compatibility when you presented yourself at the house back in Cairo," she mused thoughtfully.

"You did?" Julian echoed, clearly bewildered. "But my grandfather is a duke!"

Constance fought the urge to roll her eyes. "Not because of that!" She batted him again with the magazine—perhaps just a hair harder than she needed to. "I only mean that… Well, discovering that you are involved in something so important—and perhaps just a little dangerous?—makes me see you… *differently.*" She trailed the magazine down his sleeve, dropping her voice a husky octave.

"I see!" Julian burst out.

"I am afraid I am quite drawn to men of *action,*" Constance emphasized.

She gave his arm a little squeeze—and had to hide a dart of surprise. His triceps were more solid than she had suspected for someone who presumably spent most of his time lounging about reminding people of his prestigious family tree.

Julian puffed up a bit. "It's not something I can share openly, of course," he told her confidently. "I must allow the rest of the world to think me a mere sportsman."

"That must be hard for you." Constance leaned her cheek against her hand and blinked up at him admiringly.

With another target, it might have been a bit much—but Constance didn't put much stock in Julian Forster-Mowbray's powers of discernment.

"Not really," Julian declared regally, casually studying his manicured nails. "One grows used to living a double life when it is required of you."

Constance wanted to snort. Really, she deserved an accolade for this performance. It was a pity her only audience was a stuffed crocodile.

"Have you been doing that for very long?" she pressed.

"Well, I would say that this is my first truly *critical* mission," Julian admitted a little uncomfortably. "Such things don't exactly come up all the time. One must simply be ready for them."

Constance leaned closer. The shift took her in range of a heady nose of Julian's cologne, which he must have applied liberally before dinner. It nearly made her sneeze.

"Is it so great a matter as all that?" she prompted breathlessly.

Julian was briefly torn by indecision—and then crumbled like a wall made of biscuit. "I suppose I can show you just a little something."

He popped up from the couch and crossed to a trunk beside the bar, where he opened the lid and pulled out a slender bundle wrapped in dusty velvet. Returning to the settee, he laid it on the coffee table and pushed the fabric aside.

The sun had set as they talked, dropping the world around them into the gloom of dusk. One of the crew had come through a few minutes beforehand to light the lamps that were liberally suspended from the posts and rafters of the canopy. They cast a warm illumination over the salon—and the object that Julian had just revealed.

Nestled amid the velvet was a leather scabbard, cracked with age. The hilt of a sword protruded from the top of it, wrought from yellowed bone inlaid with gold filigree.

This was not what Constance had been angling for, of course. She had been hoping to prompt Julian into a further confession about the nature of his business in Egypt—but perhaps the sword could still lead her there. To her admittedly inexpert eye, it looked like the sort of crusty old thing that

Ellie would go mad for.

"Goodness!" she exclaimed, a bit at a loss. "It's very… large?"

She winced at the word, which she might not have chosen had she had a bit more time to think about it.

"Ha ha," Julian laughed nervously. "And excessively old, of course. In fact, I'm told it likely dates back to the sixth century."

"The sixth century!" she echoed—as though very impressed by this.

"Go ahead and pull it out," Julian told her.

Constance started a bit at his instruction. "You want me to… er, remove it from the scabbard?" she prompted carefully.

"I'm afraid odd things happen when I touch it," Julian replied with a chuckle.

Constance gave him a hard look to see if he had intended to make a double entendre. He clearly hadn't the foggiest idea.

"Fair enough," she concluded with a shrug, and then tugged at the hilt of the sword. It slid easily from the scabbard.

"The metal looks… different," she noted with a frown of genuine interest.

The oiled surface was twisted through with rippling lines of lighter and darker metal.

"That's because it's iron," Julian replied. "They didn't exactly have steel in the sixth century!"

Constance bit her tongue, as she was fairly sure she'd heard Ellie rambling on about the long and storied history of steel manufacture in places like China and the Middle East, which went back at least so far as that. She doubted educating Julian on the subject would aid her cause.

"But where did you get it?" she asked instead.

"It's been in the family for centuries," he replied. "One of my noble ancestors acquired it in Cumbria when he was granted land there by Henry I. Found it tucked into a pile of hay in a byre after he'd subdued some local laird up there, as the story goes. It's Dyrnwyn."

"What's a Dyrnwyn?" Constance demanded.

"The sword. That's its name," Julian elaborated. "It's one of the Thirteen Treasures of Britain. Or was it twelve?" he questioned, frowning. "Well, I hardly suppose it matters, anyway."

Constance knew very little about the Twelve—or Thirteen—Treasures of Britain, but she was fairly certain Ellie would have been horrified to learn that one of them was stashed in Julian Forster-Mowbray's travel trunk rather than an institution of learning.

"It's very… er, impressive," Constance hedged. "But what does it have to do with your dangerous and exciting double life?"

Julian's expression went over a bit canny. "Legend has it that when a worthy or well-born man wields Dyrnwyn, the sword bursts into holy flames."

Constance's mind went blank. She hadn't the foggiest notion how to respond to that.

"You think I'm having you on," Julian filled in for her, lounging comfortably on the settee, "but it's entirely true. I would show you right now, only I'm afraid it would throw the crew into a panic. They're very particular about fire."

Probably because the *Isis* was a floating tinderbox, Constance thought exasperatedly.

More surprisingly, she found that she believed him—perhaps because she had recently watched Ellie light up a rooftop with a wing bone and had spent the last few days chasing down the Staff of Moses.

"But why do *you* have it?"

The words spilled out of her before she could think better of them. Julian's face flashed with irritation as he jolted the sword back into the scabbard. "My older brother Heathcliffe isn't interested, so I've the loan of it for now," he retorted a bit crossly.

Constance sensed her misstep. She had obviously stumbled into a sore spot. She worked quickly to correct it. "Oh no—I mean, *of course* you have it. You are the expert swordsman, after all," she said soothingly, quickly pulling up that useful tidbit from Julian's droning over dinner back in Cairo. "What I meant was—why did you bring it here to Egypt?"

"Oh, that," he said, relieved. "I convinced my father that it might be useful, given what I'd been sent here to do."

"But what has Lord Aldbury to do with it?" Constance pressed eagerly, sensing she was getting closer to the nub of things.

Julian didn't immediately answer. Clearly, she had reached a point at which he began to wonder whether he was giving away too much.

She needed to push him over that edge before he wised up and closed his mouth.

"I mean," she modified a little shyly, tracing the magazine along his knee in a tantalizing manner. "You must have been given a very *big* responsibility for your father to have trusted you to take such a dangerous and important treasure along with you."

Julian had sharpened with an avid interest, his eyes on the place where the bundled pages brushed along his trousers.

Constance decided to throw it all in.

"I only wish I could appreciate the full extent of your burden." She gazed up at him with a look of abject admiration.

A further bat of her black lashes apparently did the trick.

Julian puffed out his chest. "Well, *someone* needs to step up and take care of things," he asserted self-importantly. "And the rest of that lot are hardly clamoring to get out into the field. They'd all rather sit around back in London and let a dressed-up gutter rat like Jacobs do the work for them."

That lot, Constance noted carefully. She was getting closer now—and she knew just how to lure Julian into giving away the rest.

"Why, they sound like a bunch of old fuddy-duddies!" she commented with a careless laugh.

"They really are!" Julian exclaimed, chuckling with her. "Prendergast can barely lift a box of papers, never mind a flaming sword. Yardborough's just a stuffed shirt who loves the sound of his own voice. Northcote might stab a bloke in the back, but he wouldn't do it himself—he'd hire someone else while he sipped sherry in his club over the papers. The only one who truly intimidates me is Lady Hastings—but as she's older than my grandmother, she's hardly about to go gallivanting about the globe."

Constance absorbed the spill of information with a blink, her mind whirling. Julian had revealed so much more than she had hoped. He had given her names!

Prendergast sounded familiar, though she couldn't place it. Lord Yardborough was a senior Conservative who sat on the Privy Council. The Northcotes were a wealthy family of bankers with ties to the East India Company before it was subsumed into the Raj.

Lady Hastings was a countess suo jure. Now in her early seventies, she was a perfect terror of the ton, making men or destroying lives at a whim by pulling on the strings of her extensive network of noble relations and the political figures who owed their careers to her influence.

So far as Constance knew, the only thing all of them had in common was wealth and power—but clearly the connection went deeper.

The beginnings of a theory tickled at the back of her mind. She thought she might even be able to lure Julian into confirming it—but it would require a leap. If she was wrong, her next words might throw him off the game entirely.

She decided to take the chance. She couldn't know when she might get another one—not when she still had a daring escape to accomplish.

"What an utterly pretentious bunch!" she said happily. "Don't tell me, but they must have some dreadfully pompous name for themselves."

"Oh, they do!" Julian was laughing hard enough now that he had to wipe a tear from the corner of his eye. He paused, clearly torn between the secrecy he had been sworn to maintain and the opportunity to laugh at his betters with a pretty and admiring woman.

Constance could not be too surprised at which side ended up winning.

"The Order of Albion!" he blurted out helplessly, pitching his tones to a parody of stuffy self-importance.

Got you, Constance thought with a burst of exultation. There *was* some sort of secret organization.

Now she only wanted a motive.

"Goodness, but that is ponderous!" she agreed with a giggle. "What, then—are they all looking to bulk up their curio cabinets?"

"Oh, no," Julian assured her, going over more serious. "It's not like that. They've a good reason for it, even if they are rather full of themselves. After all, we really can't just leave all these magical what-nots lying around the globe for any heathen revolutionary to get his hands on, can we? It wouldn't do! It really is best that we set about collecting them and putting them somewhere safe."

"Like where?" Constance asked with a bat of her eyelashes, deciding to press her advantage one step further.

"Oh, no!" Julian wagged an admonishing finger at her. "I've already said far too much. You're going to have to pretend you haven't heard any of that!"

Then Julian dropped to his knees in front of her, and Constance felt a snap of alarm.

"You know I've only shared as much as I have because we have—well—a certain *understanding* between the two of us," Julian insisted ardently. "Don't we, my dear girl?"

He leaned in, and with a jolt, Constance realized he was about to kiss her.

Her position on the settee didn't amend itself to any of her jiu jitsu maneuvers. She briefly considered going for one of her daggers, but stabbing Julian Forster-Mowbray—even in a spot that wasn't particularly deadly—hadn't been part of her plan.

She fumbled for a less lethal weapon she might use. She settled on the sporting magazine and whacked him with it.

The blow landed on his upper arm. Julian's eyes widened with surprise and a shock of pain.

Constance forced out an airy laugh as she slid out from beneath him, escaping the confines of the settee.

Julian's expression had gone dark and angry, leading Constance to wonder if she had just set a trap for herself. If she refused to allow her nose to be tickled by Julian's mustache—and who knew what else beyond that—he might think better of all the beans he had just spilled to her, which could put her in a tight spot indeed.

She had no interest at all in making Julian Foster-Mowbray her lover, even for the purpose of espionage. She scrambled for a way out.

The only one that presented itself to her was admittedly a bit of a stretch—but if one must bluff, one might as well do it wildly.

"Julian!" she exclaimed. "You know I don't believe in doing such things until one is properly and legally wed!"

Julian stared at her with shock. "You... what?"

"Reverend Spencer has been quite clear about it," Constance lied authoritatively. "A woman's lips are for prayer alone until she is in a state of legal and holy matrimony."

Julian opened his mouth to reply but was clearly at a loss. "I... had no idea that you were so... er, spiritual," he offered awkwardly.

"Oh yes." Constance widened her eyes in a manner she hoped looked suitably devout. "I really am."

Julian's gaze had turned distinctly skeptical, and Constance began to feel just a little bit nervous.

She was saved by the sound of a voice from the stairwell.

"Amir?"

"What is it?" Julian shot back irritably at the thin crewman who hovered at the edge of the salon.

"Reis Hassan wished me to inform you that we will stop for the evening in one hour, after the bridge at Nagga Hammadi," he replied.

"What do we need to stop for?" Julian complained. "I told you that we needed to reach our *destination* as quickly as possible."

He cast an awkward look over at Constance, who tried to appear as though she was contemplating something holy.

"But it is not safe to run the ship in the dark, Amir," the crewman returned a little desperately.

"Why not?" Julian retorted petulantly. "The river's enormous and we're just going along with the current. Surely we can keep that up by moonlight. Put some lamps in the bow."

The crewman cast a nervous look down the stairwell. Constance suspected that the reis himself likely hovered there, having wisely preferred not to subject himself directly to Julian's whining.

"We would certainly need to slow beyond the bridge for the cliffs at Gebel Tukh," the crewman pressed. "The river narrows there and it would be foolish to attempt the passage in the dark at full speed."

"Fine," Julian said with an impatient wave of his hand.

The crewman made a hurried bow, obviously eager to get away. Constance more or less agreed. She had best extricate herself from the situation before Julian questioned her spiritual awakening. She really would prefer not to have to stab him.

"Goodness, would you look at the time?" She put on a yawn. "All of this *traveling* is so very exhausting! I'm off to bed. Brunch al fresco in the morning?"

Julian stared at her, not quite managing to keep up. "Brunch? I mean— certainly, darling. Whatever you like."

"Aren't you a dear?" Constance assured him—and bolted for the stairs.

She had come dangerously close to endangering her virtue—which, to be fair, she had been eager to throw to the wind regardless. But not to Julian Forster-Mowbray!

Her lips-are-for-prayer excuse wouldn't stand for long—but it didn't have to.

Constance had no intention of sticking around for brunch.

TWENTY-FIVE

$\mathcal{E}$LLIE STEPPED FROM the train into the smoldering heat of late afternoon that hovered over the dusty platform at Al Mutiah, just south of the broken line at Asyut. She had to fight her way through a crowd of farmers carrying chickens and wealthy travelers frantically organizing mountains of baggage. Piles of freight—most of it bales of raw cotton—were stacked in towers around the station as those charged with their transport wrangled loudly with the drivers of donkey carts and wagons.

The sight of all those stranded travelers made her worry about just how they were going to get to Tell al-Amarna in time to stop Julian Forster-Mowbray from finding Neferneferuaten's tomb. If the train line was out, and they could not hope to catch up to him by boat—what other option remained to them?

She supposed she would find out once they made their way through the packed chaos of the platform. The disruption to Egypt's major railway had clearly wreaked havoc—as Ellie suspected it had been meant to.

The thought made her take a closer look at the sturdy, black-cloaked figure of Umm Waseem, whom Jemmahor had described as Zeinab's 'munitions expert.' The squat older woman wore her black abaya and headcloth, blending in with dozens of other sun-weathered farmer's wives crowding the platform.

Ellie wondered just how much Umm Waseem knew about the use of incendiary materials. The thought was desperately intriguing—though as the old smuggler didn't speak any English, Ellie would require the cooperation of a translator if she was to pick her brain for any useful tips.

Not that she planned on blowing anything up. Her questions would be prompted purely by scholarly interest.

If Ellie did happen to spot an appropriate situation for the use of a small detonation, she wondered if she would need to inform Adam before setting it off. Back in British Honduras, she had technically promised to check with him before exploding anything. That had been weeks ago, but strictly speaking, he had not yet released her from the commitment.

Umm Waseem was carrying her black canvas satchel slung across her back. Ellie gave it a surreptitious study, trying to determine whether there might be anything explosive inside. She wondered how heavy such things were. Her only previous contact with dynamite had been Padre Kuyoc's breastplate back in British Honduras. As she recalled, the garment had been rather hefty.

Umm Waseem didn't seem to struggle under her burden—which could mean the bag held nothing more than some spare clothes and a toothbrush. Ellie knew she would have relished having those items along for herself.

"Want me to carry that for you?" Adam offered.

Umm Waseem snorted in lieu of reply, otherwise ignoring him. Ellie tried to determine whether that indicated the presence of TNT or extra stockings. She couldn't be sure.

"This way," Zeinab ordered, finding a gap in the crowd and leading them out into the relative quiet of the thoroughfare.

They took a ferry across the river to the eastern bank, where only a narrow band of fields lined the Nile before the ground rose steeply up to a scrubby desert plateau. Ellie began to weary as they hiked to the top—but after all, hunting for ancient clues, narrowly avoiding being murdered, and escaping with a band of revolutionaries did tend to wear one out.

She stepped off the path into a sprawling wilderness. Nearer to hand, little shrubs and wind-blasted trees clung to the stony ground, but beyond them lay open desert interrupted only by a distant, hazy range of mountains tinted peach by the setting sun.

Zeinab led them along a dusty track. Around a bend lay a cluster of low, broad tents of black wool secured by well-tied ropes. They glowed with the light of hanging lanterns and crackling cookfires. Fluffy white sheep grazed on tufts of desert grass nearby, looking plump and well-fed.

The still evening air resounded with the sound of barking, and a pack of long-legged, fawn-hued dogs came bounding toward them from the camp. Ellie stopped with an instinctive wariness at the sight of them.

"Don't worry," Adam said, coming to her side as he watched the animals approach.

"Don't worry?" Ellie echoed skeptically.

Adam looked down at her. His eyes were bright. "Those are happy dogs."

"They are?" Ellie frowned. "How on earth do you know that?"

"Just look at them," he replied as though the answer were obvious.

Then the pack was upon them, and Adam stepped out to meet it. The dogs slammed into him—and immediately turned into a mess of wiggling tails and lapping tongues as the animals wrangled to get closest to him.

"Awww—who's a good boy?" Adam cooed happily, reaching down to scratch every available ear. "You're a good boy! And you are!"

Ellie watched with surprise, Sayyid hanging back at her side.

"Is he always this fond of dogs?" Sayyid asked.

"I'm not actually certain," Ellie replied with a little jolt of surprise. "This is the first time I've actually seen him with any."

Two of the dogs jumped up, knocking Adam back. He collapsed under a pile of them, roaring out a delighted laugh. "Ouch! Ow! Watch the ribs! Aww—come here, you!"

A few figures rose from the fire in front of the largest tent, looking toward Ellie's party. They wore elegant quftans over their galabeyas, and their heads were draped with banded scarves instead of the usual turbans.

"Are those Bedouin?" Ellie asked with a spark of interest.

"The Ibn Rashid clan of the Hamadyiin," Zeinab confirmed.

Ellie had read about Egypt's Bedouin, the nomadic people who herded their flocks across the desert that lay between the Nile and the Red Sea.

"But why are we going to the Arabs?" Sayyid pressed, clearly unsettled by the notion.

"Because they owe me a favor," Zeinab replied shortly. "But the Hamadyiin keep the harem. I will need you to entertain Sheikh Mohammed while I speak with his wife."

Ellie gathered that 'keeping the harem' meant the men and women would be in separate tents, and that their party would therefore be split accordingly. That would leave Sayyid and Adam charged with acting the part of gracious guests for a Bedouin chief—a prospect Sayyid did not look particularly happy about.

Ellie couldn't tell what Adam thought about it, as he was currently covered in a mass of joyful dogs—a situation he appeared to be enjoying thoroughly.

She felt a pang of sympathy for Sayyid. He and Zeinab still hadn't had a chance to talk about her revolutionary activities—a revelation that had clearly come as a shock to him and which would certainly require discussion. Entertaining a Bedouin sheikh would likely put that off for a while longer.

The two fellows who had risen from the campfire intercepted them.

"Salâmu 'alaykum," Zeinab said, stepping forward to meet the greeting party.

"Salâm," the older of the two men returned.

The greeting was courteous, but his eyes flashed with a note of caution—until they fell to where Adam was extracting himself from under a mass of wagging tails.

"Stop! Enough!" he laughed, stumbling back and pushing down on more wet noses as the dogs tried to leap up to him.

The Bedouin took in Adam's bruised face, split lip, and dog-licked hair. He raised an eyebrow.

"He's an American," Zeinab said, as though that explained everything. "I have come to see Nur Hanim al-Rashidi. May we share your fire?"

"Ahlan wa sahlan," the Bedouin replied. "You are welcome. Please, follow."

Their arrival at the tents was more unambiguously warm. Sheikh Mohammed—a large man with a luxuriant silver beard—greeted Sayyid with open arms and kisses to his cheeks as though they were the oldest of friends, though Jemmahor quietly informed Ellie that they had most certainly never met before.

Sayyid and Adam—trailed by a few hopeful dogs—were compelled over to the fire where the men of the family were gathered, and a great show was made of setting out a pan to roast beans for coffee. The nutty aroma soon filled the air.

Ellie found herself caught up in a mass of veiled and cloaked women who hurried her and the other ladies over to another tent. The space was warmly lit by hanging lanterns of pierced copper, while the ground was covered with brightly patterned carpets and soft cushions.

The black coverings fell away as they came inside, revealing colorful galabeyas and hijabs. The tent was packed with women who eyed the new arrivals with curiosity, from young girls whose heads were not yet covered to wrinkled great-grandmothers gossiping on comfortable pillows.

Zeinab crossed over to a plush seat where an elegant lady roughly Umm Waseem's age held court. She sparkled with gold from the ring in her nose to the anklets that jangled at her feet. Her chin was decorated with three blue-inked lines Ellie realized were not paint but tattoos.

The lady rose as Zeinab approached, greeting her warmly and kissing her cheeks.

"That is Nur Hanim al-Rashidi," Jemmahor whispered in Ellie's ear. "She is the first wife of Sheikh Mohammed."

"*First* wife?" Ellie's eyebrows rose. "Is there a second?"

"There is a *third*," Jemmahor informed her. "And he keeps them all very well, from what Ostazah Zeinab has told me. She delivered Nur Hanim's grandsons in Cairo—twins, and a most difficult birth, but both were born healthy and the mother is well, praise be to God! It is Nur Hanim who will make the arrangements for us."

"And what arrangements are those?" Ellie had been excited to find herself among the famous Bedouin, but now they had arrived, her worries about Julian Forster-Mowbray, her missing loved ones, and the lost tomb had all returned.

"Who knows?" Jemmahor shrugged. "But in the meantime, we can eat. I smell lamb!"

Ellie was handed a cup of sweet mint tea and settled by a great platter covered in rice, herbs, and roast meat, from which everyone ate neatly with their hands, plucking up morsels with little pieces of soft, flat bread.

By the time dinner was through, the sun was setting. The children flooded outside, racing through the open space by the sheep pen in a game, their voices high and bright in the evening air. The women washed up and made their evening prayer as Ellie watched from a little apart. Jemmahor, who remained behind as well, had acquired one of the many babies in the family and cheerfully tickled him, eliciting happy chirps and giggles.

As the ladies returned to the tent, one of the women took up a drum, tapping out a happy rhythm on it as others began to sing. Several of the women got up to dance, and the atmosphere devolved into that of a party.

It grew rather raucous for a group who forbade themselves so much as a drop of alcohol, and Ellie eventually discerned that one young woman with kohl-lined eyes and a softly rounded face had been picked out as the focus of much of the attention.

"There will be a wedding in two days," Zeinab informed her, finally dropping down onto a pillow by Ellie's side after talking with Nur Hanim all evening. "For one of the sheikh's grand-nieces, Fatimah. She is to be married to Nur Hanim's sister's grandson, as was arranged."

"Arranged?" Ellie echoed pointedly.

Zeinab flashed her a dry look. "You don't approve?"

"Of a woman being bartered for like property?"

Ellie felt a little bad once the words had left her mouth. After all, she knew that the arrangement of marriages was considered a perfectly reasonable way to go about things in many parts of the world—including this one.

Zeinab didn't respond right away. Instead, her gaze lingered on the figure of the soon-to-be bride. "The engagement was set for the length of a year. If the bride decided at the end of that time that she still did not want the match, the families would have found a way to call it off gracefully."

"And is that always the case?" Ellie demanded. "That the girl is free to decide?"

"Not always." Zeinab flashed Ellie a pointed look before returning her attention to the bride.

The girl was a little on the shorter side and adorably plump. She giggled as she danced, shooing at a few of her teasing cousins.

"Nur Hanim said Fatimah was opposed at the start," Zeinab continued, her eyes still on the young woman and her friends. "But after a little while, she found the prospect of a kind and reliable cousin more charming than perhaps she had thought."

She picked up her cup of mint tea and took a slow sip.

"Marriage is complicated," she added quietly. "Choosing a partner who sets your blood on fire does not make it less so."

"I suppose that must be true," Ellie allowed, thinking of a laughing man covered in dogs, the fierce spark of passion she felt every time she was near him, and the host of unsettled questions that entailed. "Was your match to Sayyid arranged?"

Zeinab snorted. "Not until after we had already set our minds on it."

Ellie fought the urge to pry further. She was aided in that effort by the sudden arrival of a hefty burst of guilt.

"I'm sorry I dragged you and Sayyid into this," she spilled out.

Zeinab stiffened, fixing her with a glare. "You did not drag me into anything. I am here for Egypt, not for you."

Her words were harsh, but Ellie didn't find herself offended by them. After all, what did Zeinab owe her? Certainly not the dangerous rescue that she had executed that afternoon, however much Ellie had reason to be grateful for it.

"But I would not have known about the threat at all, had you not brought it to my attention," Zeinab allowed. "And so I thank you for that."

"You still might have preferred your husband had stayed out of it instead of being used for shooting practice," Ellie noted a little ruefully. "If I hadn't asked Sayyid to come, you might not be having such trouble in your marriage now."

Zeinab sighed, setting down her cup. "My husband was made to pour over books and dig things from the sand. He is not a revolutionary. I kept my activities secret from him because I knew he would worry over it like an old woman—but it would never have been up for negotiation," she added fiercely. "I will not betray what I know to be right—not even for someone that I love."

Ellie's thoughts turned to her own situation. Adam had made it clear he didn't want her to change her mind about marriage—but where did that leave them when any alternative ran straight up against his complicated sense of honor?

"But how do you manage it all, then?" she pushed back a little helplessly.

"We will sort it out," Zeinab asserted. "We have been through hard times before."

"*How* hard?"

Ellie's question carried a note of desperation. Zeinab flashed her a thoughtful look.

"I am barren," Zeinab replied.

Surprise quieted Ellie's voice. "I… I'm sorry."

"A barren midwife," Zeinab elaborated with a dark twist of her lip—and then slumped a bit, exhaustion showing in the lines at the corners of her eyes. "I believe it may stem from a fever I had as a girl. But who knows? There is no power but Allah. I did not learn it until after we had been wed. I offered Sayyid a divorce."

"You can do that?" Ellie cut in, surprised.

Zeinab smiled wryly. "Our Muslim laws on the matter are less barbaric than your English ones. He refused, of course." She paused, and a flash of old pain made her hard features vulnerable. "He would have been a very good father."

Ellie's heart twisted in unexpected sympathy. She hadn't the least interest in children herself, but to have that choice taken away before you could make it for yourself seemed like a terrible burden. She found herself vividly imagining years of disappointed hopes, followed by the wrenching grief of realizing the truth—and the fear Zeinab must have felt as she bravely tried to offer her husband an honorable way out.

She was struck by an unexpected urge to reach out and take the other woman's hand. Constance would have done it—but that sort of thing had never come naturally to Ellie. She settled for a few bracing words instead.

"Perhaps he would have been a good father—but he most certainly *is* an excellent husband," Ellie asserted firmly.

"Yes," Zeinab agreed, and there was a softness in her voice that Ellie had not heard before. "He is."

"I am certain that the two of you will sort this latest trouble out," Ellie declared—and then hedged uncomfortably. "But have you any notion *how*, by any chance?"

Zeinab arched an eyebrow, regarding Ellie thoughtfully.

"In a manner that will be messy, awkward, and imperfect," she replied. "And yet it will work, nonetheless."

"It will? But what does that even look like?"

Zeinab gave a dark laugh. "Perhaps I will let you know—when I find out."

She rose in a fluid, graceful motion.

"The sheikh will loan us a guide and transportation to cross the desert," she announced. "By traveling along the most direct route, we will cut thirty miles off our journey. That should allow us to arrive at Tell al-Amarna ahead of Mr. Forster-Mowbray—or near enough to it. We will leave before dawn. You should get some sleep."

"Of course." Ellie stood and brushed off her skirts. "And… thank you. I mean—I know you aren't doing any of this for me. But I want you to know that I am grateful for your aid, all the same."

Zeinab accepted her words with a careful nod, then walked away.

Sleeping turned out to be easier said than done, as the pre-wedding celebrations continued late into the evening. When Ellie slipped away from the nosy aunts and the never-ending piles of pastries for a breath of fresh air, she caught sight of two figures silhouetted against the twilight purple of the sky, near to where the scrub land gave way to desert.

She recognized the solid set of Sayyid's shoulders and Zeinab's noble bearing as the pair of them slowly walked together. Zeinab's hands gestured strongly. Sayyid shook his head in response.

Then he stopped her, turning her to face him under the blanket of the emerging stars. He stilled her hands by catching them gently in his own, then leaned down to speak to her with a heartfelt intimacy that Ellie could feel even from where she stood in the shadows outside the tent.

Zeinab slipped her fingers from his grasp. She raised them to the sides of his bearded face with an aching tenderness—and Ellie quickly looked away, only to realize that Jemmahor had come to stand beside her.

"Good," Jemmahor said softly, gazing out toward the couple. She turned to glance down at Ellie, her eyes damp but happy, and said the word again with even more feeling. "*Good.*"

The tall young apprentice hooked her arm through Ellie's elbow, hauling her back to the lights and music of the tent. "Now let's go find some cake."

TWENTY-SIX

Night had fallen. Dawson was snoring… and Neil worked furiously to complete the translation of the clay tablet.

The *Isis* was sailing for Tell al-Amarna. By Neil's admittedly inexpert estimation, they would reach the site of Akhenaten's ruined capital by the following evening.

Of more immediate concern was the steady progress Dawson had been making with the Akkadian text. The professor owed his success more to the stack of books he had brought along with him to Egypt rather than any innate ability on Dawson's part—of which there was very little, as far as Neil could tell.

At least Neil hadn't actually needed to help him. Muttering the odd agreement and nodding along seemed to be sufficient evidence of his cooperation, at least so far as Dawson was concerned.

But it would not take Dawson much longer to reach the end of the tablet. Neil had to get there first. He had to know what was truly at stake—and then decide what to do about it.

When Dawson's head dropped back, his jaw falling open as the pen slipped from his fingers, Neil had seized his chance, frantically putting his wretched grasp of the ancient language to work to try to decipher the final lines.

So far, he had found three more instances of feminine verb endings—all of which Dawson had unsurprisingly overlooked. They clearly indicated that Neferneferuaten had been none other than Akhenaten's queen, Nefertiti. It was a revelation that would throw the scholarly world into an uproar, but it made perfect sense to Neil when he stopped to think about it. He had been studying Akhenaten for years, after all, and had seen the manner in which his relationship with Nefertiti was depicted in the art of the period. She stood side-by-side with the pharaoh as his partner in faith, life, and authority. Why wouldn't he have left her his crown, in the absence of a male heir with a legitimate claim on the succession?

He was actually feeling a bit chagrined that the idea had never occurred to him before. He was sure Ellie would have a thing or two to say about that.

Not that he had much time to dwell on it now. He scanned the remaining text on the tablet, painfully conscious of Dawson's precarious napping position in the chair beside him.

If the snoring professor fell over, he'd certainly wake up, and Neil's opportunity to get ahead on the translation would be lost.

He wished Ellie were here. Based on how easily she had picked out some of the words and logograms during her brief examination of the cuneiform at Hatshepsut's temple, she would have made short work of the rest of the translation with the added help of Dawson's library. Neil was reduced to scrambling through pages as he racked his brain for the few bits and pieces of the language that he had picked up over the years.

Neil pushed up his spectacles to pinch the bridge of his nose, fighting through his panic for an ounce of clarity.

As he let his glasses fall back into place, the text turned from a mushy blur to tidy clarity before him—and a symbol leapt out from among the tightly packed lines and wedges.

𒌋

Neil stared down at it with a sense of vague recognition and rising unease. He snatched up one of the volumes on the table from beneath Dawson's disorganized notes and flipped through the pages hurriedly, already half terrified of what he would find.

There it was—𒌋 was the Akkadian symbol for the cubit, one of the fundamental units of measurement used in both the Egyptian and Ancient Semitic worlds.

Units for measuring *distance*.

Neil ignored the rest of the text, setting frantically to work on the words around the cubit logogram.

The meaning—and its dire implications—spilled out across his hurriedly scribbled page.

Valley to the east… 120 rods… South branch… 815 cubits.

He stared down at the tablet, feeling ill. No—not a tablet, he corrected himself with a rising sense of horror. The clay slab wasn't just a clue to the location of Neferneferuaten's lost tomb.

It was a bloody *map*.

Beside him, Dawson's snores hitched. The professor stirred, smacking his lips… and tilted as his balance in the chair shifted.

On a panicked impulse, Neil reached out and caught him.

He braced the dozing professor as Dawson's breathing settled, becoming regular again.

Neil's spectacles had fallen down his nose. He wanted to push them back into place, but his hands were both occupied with holding up a lightly snoring twit. Instead, he tried wildly to think through his options.

There weren't many of them.

Ellie had pushed them all into this adventure with stories of magical artifacts and dire consequences—none of which Neil could bring himself to truly credit. As much as he respected his sister's intelligence, basing his decisions on fairy tales about spooky mirrors and plague-bringing staffs was simply a bridge too far.

But he didn't need a magic staff to recognize the vital importance of Neferneferuaten's tomb. It was the key to the greatest mystery of the Eighteenth Dynasty—a priceless and irreplaceable trove of knowledge that would be utterly lost if Neil allowed it to fall into Julian Forster-Mowbray's hands.

Add to that the possibility that the tomb might hold some connection to the true identity of the prophet Moses and the real story behind the Exodus… and Neil's decision became painfully clear.

He couldn't let Julian have the tablet.

He would have to destroy the text and pay the price for foiling Julian's plans… which was certain to be death.

Neil wondered how he would do it. A firing squad, perhaps? Or would he be shoved off the boat into a swarm of hungry crocodiles?

Of course, Julian wouldn't be the one pulling the trigger—or enticing the crocodiles. It would be that man Jacobs who did the dirty work.

The thought of Jacobs reminded Neil of Dawson's words earlier that evening.

It's best not to lie to him.

A few hours earlier, Neil would have scoffed at that sort of assertion… but he had seen the cool certainty in Jacobs' eyes when he had tried to deny any further knowledge about the translation of the tablet.

Jacobs hadn't just guessed that Neil was lying. He had been sure.

He always knows.

As the phrase echoed through Neil's brain, it triggered an even more dire realization.

If Neil destroyed the tablet, Jacobs wouldn't just kill him. He'd first ask what Neil knew about the tablet's contents… and Neil would be unable to lie to him.

Already, the coordinates from the translation were burned into his brain, whether Neil liked it or not. He couldn't erase the knowledge from his mind. Jacobs would cheerfully beat him—or worse—until Neil finally coughed it out.

Which he would, he admitted with a sinking sense of dread. Because he was a boring, lily-livered academic, not a stoic hero out of some adventure novel.

If he truly wanted to stop his former supervisor from ravaging the tomb of Neferneferuaten and all the precious knowledge it contained, Neil had to destroy every reference to those cubits and rods… even the ones in his own head.

Neil wasn't going to have to wait for Jacobs to subject him to a painful demise. He had to do the job himself.

The panic of the realization nearly made him drop the professor that he was still frantically bracing with both hands.

Neil fought the urge to laugh hysterically, biting his lip. It came out as a groan instead.

How was he to do it? He was locked in a study on a boat. There was no convenient sword to fall on—or even so much as a dagger. It was too much to hope that there might be a convenient dose of cyanide lying around.

All he had was a pen, the nib still warped from when Ellie had used it to pry up the stones of Hatshepsut's sun altar.

Could he kill himself with a bent pen?

Neil pictured the various places he might try to stab himself and fought back a wave of queasiness.

He was still reeling from all of it when he heard the doorknob turn.

He startled, losing his grip on Dawson's side. The professor began to fall, and Neil caught at him again, his spectacles dropping to the floor in the process. With a burst of desperate inspiration, he set his shoe to the leg of Dawson's chair and shoved, spinning the seat a quarter-turn. The maneuver put Dawson's lean in the direction of the table, where Neil lowered him—as gently as he could while fighting the urge to shriek like a schoolgirl.

"Pleased to accept…" the professor mumbled sleepily, "…great honor, Your Majesty…"

To Neil's immense relief, Dawson settled, his cheek puddling against a Sumerian lexicon as he fell back into a soft, gurgling snore.

Whoever was at the door had come up against the lock, but a rather ominous scratching sound now rose from the wooden panel.

Neil fought a rising panic. What should he do—smash the tablet before they came in or stab himself with the pen? He wouldn't have time to do both, and failure on either front would leave Julian with the keys to find the tomb.

Only one other course of action remained to him—he must try to disable whoever was coming into the room, which would hopefully leave him time to do away with both the tablet and his pathetic self before anyone else arrived.

He felt frantically around the blurry objects on the table for something that might serve as a weapon. His hands closed around the girth of a thick, heavy tome. Was it the bound *Transactions of the Royal Historical Society* or *The Hittites and Their Language*?

It didn't matter. The lock clicked, and Neil was out of time.

He scurried to the space behind the door, raising the book over his head and preparing to strike at whatever threat stepped inside... which he wouldn't be able to see very well, as he'd neglected to retrieve his spectacles.

He contemplated going back to fumble for them under the table, but before he could act on it, the door swung carefully, quietly inward.

Hefting the book, Neil drew in a shaky breath—and swung wildly at the figure that slipped into view in front of him.

He only had time to notice that the intruder was smaller than he had anticipated before it grabbed him, twisted like a snake, and tossed him onto the floor.

Neil landed with a wind-stealing impact, sprawled across the Turkish carpet with the book in his hand and something firm and shapely straddling his chest.

A blurry face hovered over him, light brown in hue and framed by a halo of dark hair.

"Were you really trying to brain me with the *American Journal of Philology?*" the face hissed irritably in a voice Neil recognized.

"Connie?!" he blurted out. "But how on earth did you—"

"Oh, that was my jiu jitsu," Constance said cheerfully. "I have been practicing that maneuver for some time, so I'm chuffed I finally had a chance to put it to practical—"

She cut off as Dawson's snores hitched. The fuzzy shape of the professor raised its head from the table.

Neil froze. Constance went still as well... with her thighs braced around his torso, Neil realized with a dawning sense of both heat and dismay.

Danger gnome, he thought furiously as his body threatened to respond. *Stolen socks. Scorched textbooks. Just a menacing… curvy… chest-straddling…*

He choked back a groan, and Dawson's head drifted back to the desk with a mutter about commencement addresses.

Constance's hand clamped around Neil's arm, and she levered him upright, demonstrating a strength Neil never would have expected a woman of her stature to possess.

"Well?" she prompted in a harsh whisper once he was on his feet. "We haven't got all evening."

"Tablet," Neil blurted in reply, blinking at her blurry form as he waved vaguely in the direction of the table.

Constance quickly studied the surface. She snatched up the tablet, shoving it into Neil's arms—then bent down and plucked something from the floor.

She pushed it toward his face. Neil instinctively flinched back until the familiar weight of a pair of wire frames slipped over his ears.

The room came into focus in a sprawl of papers across the desk, a sleeping professor—and Constance's irritated glare, framed by thick black locks that were making an admirable effort to escape from their pins.

"You're… I'm…" Neil stammered, blinking down at her. "We're… Why…?"

"It's a bloody rescue, you nitwit!" Constance hissed.

Then she planted a leg on the table, whipped up the froth of her white gown, and exposed the smooth, muscular curve of her calf.

Neil's mind went blank of everything but *leg*—until Constance slipped a dagger from her garter.

He fumbled the tablet, nearly dropping it to the floor.

"Stay behind me and keep quiet," Constance ordered, grabbing him by the sleeve and hauling him through the door into the dark, silent hallway. "There's a rowboat tied to the landing platform at the stern. We'll use that—unless you can swim?"

"We did summer occasionally at the lake, and I went for the odd… Hold on—why would we need to swim?" Neil demanded in a tight hush.

"It would be a stealthier means of escape than the launch." She made the conclusion sound as though it were the most reasonable thing in the world.

"You want us to throw ourselves into the Nile?" Neil protested, barely remembering to keep his panicked voice low. "What about crocodiles?"

"We can deal with the problem of crocodiles if it arises," Constance replied with a dismissive wave.

"How does one simply deal with *crocodiles*?" Neil burst back incredulously.

"You are talking too much!" she hissed in reply.

She grabbed his arm, dragging him down the hallway. The opening to the landing was a rectangle of softer darkness against the thick gloom.

A figure stepped into the middle of the space—an Al-Saboor with his right arm wrapped in a sling, a cigarette glowing from between the fingers of his left.

He stared at them with surprise. Neil stared back.

Another Al-Saboor popped into the opening beside him, his face framed by a pair of enormous ears.

"El aganeb beyehrabo!" he called out sharply.

The words rang out like bells through the silence of the boat. Neil's Arabic was far from excellent, but he was fairly certain the words meant something along the lines of *that scrawny Englishman is getting away.*

"Drat," Constance cursed—and let her knife fly.

The big-eared mercenary and his companion stumbled back onto the platform to avoid the blade.

With the pair out of view, Constance shoved Neil through the nearest doorway.

He found himself nose-to-nose with the contents of a linen closet, and only just managed to turn around before Constance slammed into him and shut the door.

The space between the shelves and the threshold was tight. Neil was sandwiched between piles of sheets and the lush frame of the danger gnome.

The darkness was absolute. Constance's soft curls tickled at his nose, and her breath puffed against the thin fabric of his shirt. The rhythm of her exhalations was perfectly regular, as though racing through a boat packed with violent thugs was the sort of thing she did every day.

Neil tried to figure out where to put his hands. The only sensible option seemed to be holding them over his head—which felt patently ridiculous.

Not that it made any difference to his anatomy. He was feeling pathetically turned-on. How could he be turned on by Ellie's unruly schoolmate, of all people?

Though she wasn't Ellie's schoolmate anymore. She was an intimidatingly gorgeous force of nature who had just thrown a dagger at a pair of dangerous criminals.

The force of nature began to wriggle.

"What are you doing?" Neil breathed desperately, certain that his involuntary state was about to become humiliatingly apparent.

"Trying to access my other blade," she retorted in a hiss.

"Where is it?" Neil recalled the intimate location of her first dagger and felt a jolt of alarm.

"In a special sheath sewn into my corset," she replied.

Cloth rustled in a terrifying manner from somewhere around the level of Neil's abdomen.

"Why would you put a knife in your corset?" His voice was strangled, and he was beginning to sweat.

"For emergency situations, of course," Constance retorted. "Ah!"

A sliver of light through the narrow gap in the frame of the door glinted against her blade. Voices sounded from outside, calling to each other in frustrated Masri.

They passed, and Constance silently yanked Neil back out into the hall.

She glanced at the landing, but Neil could hear some of the Al-Saboors shuffling out there, obviously on guard. Constance hauled him toward the bow instead, only to pivot sharply at the sound of angry voices from the forward deck and shove Neil into a narrow stairwell.

They hurried up, twisting around a sharp turn and emerging into the broad, open-air salon that occupied the upper deck of the boat.

The space was softly illuminated by scattered lanterns hung from the pillars of the canopy, their wicks lowered to a glimmer. The golden glow mingled with the silvery moonlight to paint the mahogany dining table and the well-appointed bar.

Beyond the rail, sand-blasted cliffs soared up against the eastern side of the river, looming over them in fantastical pillars and billowing shapes. They were tall enough that their upper reaches were out of view behind the canopy of the salon.

Neil glanced down at the bow. The crew were awake, making a careful adjustment to the sails as the reis shouted orders. The *Isis* was moving at a quick clip, white-capped foam roiling to either side of the boat as it rushed along with the current of the narrow, fast-moving river.

"This way." Constance tugged Neil hurriedly across the night-haunted stillness of the salon.

They stopped at the low railing that bordered the back of the deck. It hung over the landing platform at a height of perhaps twelve feet, though all Neil could see from his current angle was the frothing chop of the river and the lightly bobbing rowboat.

"Take off your coat," Constance ordered in a whisper.

"Why?" Neil asked even as he shrugged out of the garment and handed it to her.

"We'll use it to climb down, take out those two Al-Saboors, and steal the boat," Constance replied, crouching down to tie the tweed sleeve around a banister.

"Take out two Al-Saboors?" Neil returned in a hiss, ducking down a bit as he heard the voices of the pair of thugs rise in another exchange below.

"Connie?" a new voice called out from across the salon.

Julian Forster-Mowbray stood at the top of the stairs, his profile gilded by one of the low-burning lanterns. His expression shifted from confusion to dismay as his gaze moved to Neil. "But what are you doing here? With *him?*"

Constance straightened as she faced him. "I am sorry, Julian. But needs must."

"Needs must what?" Julian pressed back. "I thought we had an *understanding!*"

Constance rolled her eyes. "I was using an established method of interrogation!" she retorted. "It's nothing personal. Just a classic case of espionage."

"Espionage?" Neil echoed with skeptical surprise.

"Be quiet, Stuffy!" Constance retorted crossly.

Julian's expression hardened. "I see," he said tightly. "Then I suppose I am sorry as well."

He reached down to snatch something from the coffee table nearby. Neil vaguely recognized the leather bundle as a belt and scabbard.

"If you'll forgive us, we'd prefer not to overstay our welcome." Constance held out her dagger in one hand. With the other, she shoved Neil back until the low railing bumped against his thighs.

Holding the tablet to his chest, Neil looked down over the back of the boat.

The Al-Saboor below him—a third who had joined the original pair—flashed him a gap-toothed grin and waggled his sword in a friendly wave.

Neil jolted back upright, his heart leaping into his throat as the railing pressed into the back of his legs.

"Connie, please be reasonable," Julian pleaded. "I'm sure we can talk this through! We're going to be married!"

"When did I ever give you the impression that I was going to marry you?" Constance retorted with a note of exasperation.

"But why wouldn't you?" Julian returned, obviously bewildered. "My grandfather was a duke!"

"Nobody cares!" Constance shot back.

Julian's expression hardened, and he set his hand to the bone-white hilt protruding from his scabbard. "I'm afraid I can't let you make off with my tablet."

"I'm not asking for your permission," Constance asserted stoutly.

She shifted into a posture of dangerous readiness that reminded Neil of his recent encounter with the floor, and he realized this was very likely going to end in a fight—one that he was utterly unqualified to take part in.

Then the official representative of the British Athenaeum for Egyptological studies pulled out his weapon—and Neil's world tipped upside-down.

In the space of a breath, his scholarly brain automatically registered that the sword his former employer now held in his hand was an excellent example of Anglo Saxon iron twist welding.

His scholarly brain stopped registering things as the sword burst alight with a whirl of blue flame.

Constance raised her dagger. Julian stepped forward. The flickering glow of his patently supernatural weapon danced over the gleaming surface of the bar and drew Neil's eyes up to something that loomed in the rafters above him.

He found himself staring up into the leering yellow grin of a ten-foot-long crocodile.

When he lowered his gaze again, it halted on the even more terrifying sight of Mr. Jacobs.

He stood at the top of the stairs, a gloom-shadowed presence behind Julian's shoulder. He did not look cross or even particularly determined. His expression was rather one of tired exasperation as he took in the scene—and pulled a pistol from the flap of his coat.

Clasping the cuneiform tablet to his chest, Neil felt his options wink out, one after the other, until only a single possible course of action remained.

He hated absolutely everything about it.

"Want us?" Constance sang out boldly, making a little come-hither flap of her hand. "Come and get us!"

Julian raised his blade.

Jacobs aimed the gun at Constance's head.

"Bugger," Neil said—and hocked the tablet across the salon with an uncharacteristically neat snap of his wrist.

The hunk of clay flew at Jacobs' head, forcing him to flinch back. He recovered quickly, swinging the pistol around again—but Neil had already hooked his arm around Constance's waist.

He clasped her to him as he threw himself at the rail... and launched both of them into the Nile.

TWENTY-SEVEN

*T*HE WATER THAT closed over Neil's head was colder than it had any right to be. It moved fast, whipping him into a twisting current that threatened to pull Constance from his arms.

No, he thought with furious desperation, clutching at her dress to catch her even as his lungs began to scream.

Constance writhed in his grip. She caught his wrist and hauled Neil powerfully toward the surface. He kicked after her, pulling wildly with his free hand.

They burst through the water. Neil gasped for air, spluttering as he blinked at a sloshing world of blurry darkness. It took him a moment to realize that his spectacles were still on his face, though being repeatedly drenched with water, they were more or less impossible to see through.

Neil yanked the glasses off and shoved them into the pocket of his trousers, nearly submerging himself again in the process. Constance grabbed at him, her face a pale oval against the tumultuous darkness.

The current had already carried the *Isis* ahead of them. Cries of angry frustration echoed over the river from the boat. Even without his spectacles, Neil could see the rough form of the decks and the cold, shimmering glow of Julian Forster-Mowbray's impossible sword.

The flames illuminated a lithe, dangerous shape that joined his former employer in the stern. Neil vaguely recognized it as Jacobs before it raised a hand, pointing the pistol at them from across the water.

"Get down, you idiot!" Constance snapped—and shoved him into the Nile.

Neil was swallowed by a chilling blackness, his body rushed by powerful surges that tossed him around like a cork as Constance held on to him, her fist twisted solidly into his shirt.

They surfaced again a moment later, shoved up by another pulse of the river. The *Isis* had moved further away. Neil picked out snippets of Julian's furious orders to drop sails and turn around.

The reis hollered back—something about *cliffs, current*, and *not losing my boat to some idiot ingilyzy*.

The boat was not the only thing moving. The Nile carried Neil and Constance along the looming cliffs at an alarming speed.

Another wave sloshed over his head. He came up from it spluttering.

"This way!" Constance ordered.

She tugged at him and began to swim, arrowing capably through the water. Neil hauled himself after her, grateful that he had already abandoned his coat when he had thrown them to their possible doom.

They were moving closer to the cliffs, which rushed past Neil even faster now that they were nearer by. The sheer face of stone was painted a subtle silver by the light of the crescent moon, save for a few places where his poor eyesight detected dark abscesses in the surface of the rock.

He flinched against the assault of another wave and realized that the black spots were actually a pockmarking of rectangles that were certainly not natural in origin. Geography and years of research clicked together in his brain.

"Hold on!" he called out with a spark of scholarly interest. "Isn't this Gebel Tukh?"

"Shut up and keep swimming!" Constance retorted.

The current shoved them into the base of the cliffs. Constance caught hold of a low ledge and snatched at Neil's waistcoat as the river threatened to push him past her. She scrambled up, then hauled him from the water. The pair of them spilled onto the narrow surface of the rock.

The ledge was worn smooth by centuries of the cycle of the inundation. The surface slipped under Neil's dripping body as he lay there entangled with Constance, gasping like a beached fish.

His mind reeled with the utter madness of what he had just done— jumping off a boat in the middle of the night next to an eighty-foot cliff. Dodging bullets. Tossing a three-thousand-year-old tablet of inestimable historical importance across a salon.

He groaned, dropping his head back against the stone.

Constance shoved at him as she tried to extricate herself. The narrowness of their perch just above the racing surface of the water didn't leave her much room to maneuver, and Neil found himself shockingly aware of every limber inch of her muddy efforts.

He lurched away and nearly fell off the ledge. Constance caught him and yanked him to his feet.

They balanced there, bracing each other's arms, until Constance abruptly released him.

"Why did you throw the tablet?" she demanded angrily.

"He was about to kill you!" Neil shot back.

She grabbed his shirt, shaking it with furious agitation. "Will it tell them where to find the tomb?"

The blood drained from Neil's face. He couldn't answer her.

Constance shoved him loose with a growl of disgust. The move nearly sent him sliding back into the river. He found a handhold on the cliff that rose beside him, using it to steady himself as his knees threatened to give out.

Neil couldn't feel guilty for what he had done. He had been willing to die to keep the tablet and its secrets out of Julian Forster-Mowbray's hands.

He hadn't hesitated to sacrifice it to save Constance's life.

She eyed the cliffs, her mouth tight with lingering frustration. "We need to find someplace less exposed in case they turn back the boat."

"They can't turn back the boat." Neil's voice was hoarse. He cleared his throat. "The current is too strong, and the wind is against them. They could only reverse course by offloading the crew and dragging the boat upriver by rope, and they can't do that along these cliffs."

"Well, that's something, at least." Constance grimly eyed the steep rocks that rose around them. "This way."

She didn't wait for him to answer. With the sturdy confidence of a goat, she picked out a path up the ragged face of the mountain. Neil struggled after her, torn between his terror of being left behind and his fear of losing his grip and plummeting into the river. Both outcomes felt entirely plausible.

He followed her to one of the square-cut openings in the rock. The doorway was barely tall enough to clear Neil's head. Beyond it lay a narrow chamber cut into the face of the cliff, empty of anything but a scattering of rubble.

The ridge at Gebel Tukh was known to be peppered with rock-cut tombs, none of them considered to be of particular archaeological interest. All had been looted in antiquity, and their relative inaccessibility, suspended as they were above one of the most dangerous sections of the river, had deterred both casual explorers and professional excavators.

Neil's eyes slowly adjusted to the gloom. If there had ever been a burial in this tomb, it was long gone now—not that he could make out much more about the place when it was all a blur. He fumbled for his glasses, taking them from his pocket and making a futile attempt to dry them on his soaked shirt.

He settled for blowing on them for a bit before slipping them back onto his face.

The world came back into focus—as did Constance.

Her hair had come loose, falling in damp waves around her shoulders. Her fashionable lawn dress was streaked with slime from their landing on the ledge. The fabric clung mercilessly to her well-proportioned figure.

Neil's mouth went a bit dry, even as he considered with mortification how disheveled he must look himself.

That consideration vanished as Constance began picking at her buttons. She wriggled out of a sleeve.

"What… What are you…" Neil stuttered, panic rising.

"Stop gaping and take off your clothes," she ordered.

"My *what?!*" Neil squawked, fumbling to catch his glasses, which threatened to slide off his damp nose.

"They'll dry better if you lay them out, and you'll be less likely to catch a chill," Constance clarified with barely concealed irritation.

She shoved her dress down over her hips and stepped out of it. Plucking it from the ground, she expertly twisted it into a knot, wringing it out.

Neil stared at the strong curve of her hip where it pressed against the fabric of her chemise. His mind blanked.

She rolled her eyes. "Stop looking so horrified. It's not like I have any designs on your virtue. I had been considering it, but you scuppered any chance of that when you turned out to be such a lily-livered snitch."

"I know," Neil blurted back abjectly. "I was an utter…" His brain skidded to a halt as the full implication of Constance's words cut through the fog of his shock.

I had been considering it…

Constance released the ties of her corset with a neat tug. She popped the clasps at the front of the lacy garment and tossed it down beside her wrung-out gown.

A strangled sound emerged from the back of Neil's throat.

"Just take off your trousers already," Constance snapped. "Or don't, and freeze. It hardly makes any difference to me."

She plopped down onto the ground in her chemise and drawers, crossing her arms over her chest and glaring out into the night.

Neil was starting to shiver. The Egyptian night was reasonably warm, but the water had been fairly bracing, and standing in a stone box while wearing soaked clothes was bound to leave one feeling a chill.

It's fine, he told himself numbly as he struggled free of his clinging waist-coat, mortification burning through him. *It isn't like it means anything,* he thought as he tugged his shirt over his head, the fabric sticking against his arms.

They were in desperate circumstances, and it was only Constance, he reminded himself as he squirmed free of his undershirt. He'd known her since she was in pinafores. It wasn't as though… She was practically his…

I had been considering it…

His hands froze on the buttons of his trousers as the room started to spin.

"I can't," he blurted out, his face hot as a frying pan. "I'm sorry."

"Suit yourself," Constance retorted without looking at him.

Neil slumped down against the wall and let the exhaustion and humiliation wash over him.

"Who do you think they were?" Constance asked.

Neil opened his eyes to see her looking at a pair of statues carved into the wall near the tomb's entrance. They were deeply weathered, the soft sand-stone reduced to little more than the most basic forms of a man and a woman standing side-by-side in the thin silver moonlight.

"Old Kingdom," Neil blurted automatically, resting his head back against the rough-cut stone. "Some minor Eighth Nome official and his wife."

"How can you know that?" Constance pressed with a mix of irritation and curiosity.

Neil shifted uncomfortably. His wet trousers clung unpleasantly to his thighs. "The carvings on the wall are sunken relief rather than bas relief. That usually means Old Kingdom."

"What about the Nome?" Constance studied him narrowly through the gloom. "What's that, and what makes you think this fellow was part of one?

Nomes, Neil thought distractedly, her question brushing past him like a rogue butterfly. *Nomes and gnomes.*

He almost giggled. Apparently, a slight edge of hysteria was the natural outcome of a surplus of terror, shock, and mortification. "A Nome is an Ancient Egyptian administrative unit. And who else would he be?"

"Hmm." Constance frowned as she continued to pin him with a thought-ful gaze.

The burst of manic energy faded, letting Neil's rational mind slowly reassert itself—not that it remotely liked what it saw when it did.

"Mr. Forster-Mowbray's sword was on fire," he said, the words spilling involuntarily from his lips.

"You don't say," Constance huffed in reply.

Neil closed his eyes. "It was a flaming sword. An Anglo Saxon twist-welded flaming sword."

"Julian called it Dyrnwyn," Constance reported tiredly.

"Dyrnwyn?" Neil echoed, feeling as though the ground beneath him was sliding away even further. "As in the sword of Rydderch the Generous, King of Strathclyde? Dyrnwyn of the Thirteen Treasures of Britain?"

"He said it would only flame up for someone well-born or worthy. I'm not sure he realizes that those aren't necessarily the same thing," Constance added dryly.

"The flaming sword of Rydderch Hael is real." Neil enunciated each word carefully, as though hearing them aloud would make them easier to accept. "And it flames. With fire." He closed his eyes again. The stone box of the tomb swam around him.

"So *now* you believe it!" Constance retorted. "The thing the rest of us have been trying to tell you this *entire* time!"

"But you were talking about magic!" Neil pushed back wildly.

"Of course we were!" Constance threw up her hands. "What else do you think has been going on?"

Despair washed away Neil's last shreds of indignation. He dropped his head to his arms where they were crossed over the soaked knees of his trousers. "I have been an enormous ass," he mumbled mournfully into his lap.

"I suppose it's something that you're able to admit it," Constance allowed. "That's more than I can say for Julian Forster-Mowbray. At least Ellie, Adam, and Sayyid managed to escape with that batch of mysterious women."

Neil's head shot back up, his eyes widening with a mixture of hope and alarm. "They escaped? They're all right? But how do you know?"

"I did a bit of eavesdropping." Constance smiled a little viciously. "The look on Mr. Jacobs' face when he gave Julian the news was quite satisfying."

Relief crashed through Neil like a bucket of water. The impact was staggering, momentarily stealing his breath. When he finally spoke, his voice was hoarse and uneven. "I... I didn't let myself really think of what might have... I couldn't, or I would have..." A wash of overwhelming feeling choked off the words—and then Neil's head shot up with a jolt of aching panic. "But are you *certain*?"

Constance's expression softened at the urgency of his tone. "I'm certain."

Neil yanked off his spectacles and put his face in his shaking hands. "They all might have been..." His throat tightened on the word, cutting it off. He forced out the rest, the confession spilling from him in a desperate rush. "And Ellie told me—she *told* me that Julian was an unreliable rotter. She told me to *trust her*, only I couldn't! No—I *wouldn't*, because I wanted so badly for things to go back to the way they were! It was a stupid, stubborn, selfish impulse, and all three of them might have…"

He couldn't bring himself to say the rest. It still hurt too much, shooting a wrenching fear through him that left him feeling as though he was tearing down the middle.

"It would have been my fault," he finally choked out, pressing the heels of his trembling hands to his eyes.

A sigh carried to him softly from across the room. Something plopped down next to him. Warmth radiated against his damp skin as Constance settled against his side.

"You made a mistake," Constance declared.

"A mistake?" Neil's head jerked up. "I could have gotten all of them killed!"

"Give Ellie and Adam a little more credit than that," Constance returned dryly.

"But I should have listened!" Neil pushed back.

"Yes," Constance calmly agreed.

"I should have trusted all of you!"

"That, too. And I am still furious at you for it," she added pointedly.

Neil stared at her helplessly.

Constance picked his spectacles up and slipped them over his ears. Her face came back into focus. She looked at him steadily. "But we're all idiots every once in a while."

Neil's cheek was wet. He swiped at it awkwardly.

"You'll do better next time," Constance finished.

The easy confidence in her tone caught at something inside Neil's chest and gave it a wrench. It hurt, and he found himself deeply, quietly grateful for it.

Constance comfortably leaned back against the wall beside him as Neil roughly pushed another tear from his cheek with the palm of his hand. It took him a few moments before he could speak again.

"What about this batch of mysterious women?" he asked once he felt like his voice would come out somewhat steady.

"I haven't the foggiest idea." Constance put on a slightly martyred tone. "If Ellie had something up her sleeve, she didn't let me in on it. I can only guess that they were a band of rogue lady revolutionaries who caught wind of our mission and interceded to prevent the Staff of Moses from falling into the hands of Egypt's enemies."

Neil blinked, lost for words in the face of her fantastical theory.

"The important thing is that our co-conspirators are no longer in Julian's clutches," Constance continued. "Though we cannot rely on them to prevent that rogue from accomplishing his criminal mission. I am afraid that will be up to us."

"Us?" Neil echoed with a snap of unease.

Constance cocked an eyebrow. "Frogs," she recited neatly. "Locusts. Gnats. Pestilence. Boils. A thunderstorm of hail and fire. Water turning into blood. The slaughter of the firstborn. Am I missing anything?"

Neil swallowed thickly. "Three days of darkness," he replied. "And lice."

"And would you like to abandon the legendary staff that caused all of that to an avowed villain?" Constance prompted.

"No," Neil moaned in response, resisting the urge to curl up into a ball. "But how are we supposed to stop him? There are only two of us!"

"And I lost my last dagger when we fell into the river." Constance pouted. "I am rather cross about being deprived of *both* of my knives. I had to go to some lengths to acquire them in the first place. I can hardly rely on finding yet another means of blackmailing the butler."

Neil felt a pang of sympathy for the head of the Tyrrell household staff.

"I'm not like Bates," he warned carefully. "Or Ellie. I'm not a hero. I'm just a..."

He trailed off. A few days ago, he might have finished that sentence with the word 'scholar'—but how could he call himself a scholar when he had been so blind to such an enormous truth about the world of the past? He had just discovered that the magic of the old stories wasn't fantasy but as true to life as the dusty genealogies and battle records on which he had based his life's work.

Only one word felt right in his current circumstances, and it wasn't 'scholar.'

"Fool," Neil finished flatly. "I'm just a fool." He put his fingers to the bridge of his nose, fighting a rising headache. "I don't know how to do any of this. But it's my mess. The least I can do is try to clean it up."

"How much of the tablet were you able to translate?" Constance asked.

"Enough," Neil replied.

"Will it tell them where to go?"

Neil's shoulders slumped. "If I didn't manage to break it when I threw it at Mr. Jacobs, then it will give them the exact coordinates of the tomb of

Neferneferuaten at Tell al-Amarna." He winced, forcing himself to continue. "Where I think it increasingly likely that the Staff of Moses, or the Was-Scepter of Khemenu—whatever the dashed thing really was—has been hidden for the last three thousand years."

"Well. I suppose that settles that, then." Constance shifted, lying down on the stone floor with her arm tucked under her head. "Try to sleep. You'll need the energy for tomorrow."

"What happens tomorrow?" Neil asked uneasily as he flattened himself uncomfortably on the hard ground beside her.

"We find a way off these cliffs, steal a boat, and go after Julian," Constance returned authoritatively.

"Why do we have to steal a boat?" Neil protested, hesitant to add *piracy* to the list of frightening activities in which he was apparently to be engaged. "Haven't you a wad of cash in your..."

The word 'bosom' stuck in his throat.

"I suppose I do." Constance sounded disappointed.

Neil felt very far from capable of fixing the problems that faced them— problems that *he* had made—but as he lay on the cold ground of the tomb, he realized he was going to try.

He only hoped he wouldn't be as much of an abject failure at it as he'd been at so many other things in his life.

"Goodnight, Stuffy," Constance said, closing her eyes.

Neil's gaze lingered on the elegant curve of her hip under the still-damp fabric of her chemise.

"Goodnight, Connie," he said tightly, then rolled over to put his back to her.

His wet trousers clinging uncomfortably to his legs, Dr. Neil Fairfax resigned himself to an utterly miserable night.

TWENTY-EIGHT

THE WOMEN'S TENT at the camp of the Ibn Rashid was swathed in the softer gloom of the hour before sunrise when Ellie was shaken awake.

"It is time," Zeinab ordered, then moved away without further ceremony.

Ellie forced herself up from her pillow, still groggy. She tidied herself quickly and silently before slipping out of the tent to where Zeinab and the other ladies waited in their black abayas and headscarves.

Adam and Sayyid stood beside them. Adam was still without a jacket, which Ellie knew he did not mind in the least. That he had kept on his braces seemed like a minor concession to propriety.

He was holding something in his hand, flipping it distractedly in his fingers as he gazed out at the desert. It winked gold as it caught a fragment of the low lamplight from the entrance to the tent, and Ellie recognized it as Adam's compass. The case was dented and scratched, the hinges dulled with a hint of rust.

She recalled the engraving she had seen inside the lid back in British Honduras.

To A—May you always know your path. GB

GB. George Bates.

"How did you sleep?" she asked.

He turned to her, and the pensive creases at the corners of his eyes were replaced by a smile like a slowly dawning desert sun.

"Great," he replied with a look that felt like a caress. "You?"

His sun-stained hair stuck out at odd angles, and his jaw was darkened by a day's growth of beard. He appeared... well, delectable, really. Ellie's cheeks heated a bit at the sight.

"Very well, thank you," Ellie managed to reply.

One of the leggy gold-hued dogs from the evening before sat at Adam's feet, gazing up at him adoringly as it panted. Adam gave it a happy rub between the ears as he looked back over the camp. "I like this place."

Ellie followed his gaze. A cluster of Bedouin men were roasting beans for another pot of coffee. A few of the dogs chased around the open ground beside them. Quiet laughter rose from the women's tent nearby.

Ellie flashed him a warm smile. "They probably have splendid sunsets," she noted meaningfully.

Adam met her eyes. "You remember that, huh?"

The echo of his words sang through her mind, coming to her as readily as a note from an old book.

When I get to the end of the day, I just want to take off my boots and watch the sky change for a little while.

"I remember," Ellie replied simply, looking up at him.

Zeinab cast an assessing gaze over the group, which included both Jemmahor and Umm Waseem, who was just finishing up her dawn prayer.

Her eyes lingered for an extra breath on the figure of her husband.

"Yalla," she ordered. She picked up a bundle of gear that included ropes, lanterns, and an iron crowbar, then set off across the desert.

They walked across the dry, flat ground of the plateau for about half a mile, the dog trotting happily in their wake. As they approached a low, stony ridge, Ellie startled at a strange sound from around the corner ahead of them. It was a distinctly animal noise somewhere between a grunt and a yawp, utterly unlike anything she had heard before.

"What was that?" she demanded with a dart of alarm.

"Our transportation," Zeinab replied.

They rounded the ridge, revealing a scrubby patch of grass where a herd of lumpy, intimidatingly large animals grazed contentedly.

Adam's eyes lit up with delight. "Camels!"

The dromedaries were decked out in double-horned saddles covered in thick, colorful blankets. Tassels dangled from their harnesses, giving them a festive air that did nothing to offset the deep misgiving that Ellie felt as she looked at them. The beasts looked taller even than horses, with the added complication of their enormous humps. Where was one supposed to sit when a great big mound stood in the way?

"Sheikh Mohammed has granted us the use of his caravan for the journey to Tell al-Amarna," Zeinab reported. "His younger son Mustafa and nephew Yusuf will guide us."

Ellie pulled her gaze from the intimidating animals to the two Bedouin gentlemen who accompanied them.

They were possibly the most attractive men she had ever seen.

Yusuf was tall and broad, with a luxuriant mustache. Even through the flowing cut of his quftan, he was obviously of an exceptionally robust build. A rifle hung across his back, while a pair of wicked daggers were tucked into either side of his belt. They were at least as long as Adam's machete but thinner and dangerously curved.

Mustafa, the sheikh's son, was shorter than his cousin, with the fit grace of a panther. His rich bronze complexion contrasted strikingly with a pair of sharp gray eyes that reminded Ellie of the inescapable focus of a hawk. His haughty, angular features were perfectly accented by an elegantly trimmed beard.

While Yusuf stood with his feet braced and his hands on the hilts of his daggers, Mustafa lounged against a rock with his scimitar at his side, his posture mingling confident repose and a natural authority.

Neither fellow could have been older than Ellie, but they looked fully capable of taking on a small army—should they have deigned to do so.

Ellie did not realize that she had fallen into a line of women gaping at the two cousins until she was startled by the distinct tones of Umm Waseem's wheezing chuckle.

"Allâhu 'akhbar," the older woman commented wickedly before walking on.

"What did she say?" Ellie asked a little distractedly, watching transfixed as Mustafa rose from his rock to gaze out across the desert, the breeze rippling the silk folds of his quftan.

"God is great," Jemmahor replied with a sigh. "And He really is."

The younger woman followed the rest of the party, forcing Ellie to hurry after her—though she found herself less than eager to approach the grunting, yawning flock of camels. The sheikh's caravan admittedly looked majestic with their saddle bells jingling softly in the pale light of imminent sunrise, but Ellie could barely manage a donkey.

The camels looked both larger and significantly less stable than donkeys.

Mustafa called out an order, and with a groan, one of the beasts lowered itself down to sit on the ground.

Zeinab hopped nimbly onto the saddle, folding her legs beneath her with practiced ease.

The Bedouin gave another order, and the camel rose—but not all at once. In a manner that seemed designed to toss one to the ground, first the front half of the animal straightened, tilting the saddle to an alarming angle before the rear end deigned to join in.

Zeinab rode it all out with no apparent trouble.

Umm Waseem set her black satchel on the back of the saddle of her mount. Ellie studied the bag carefully. Would the stout older woman have tossed it up there quite so casually if it were full of explosives?

Ellie's own camel waited placidly in front of her. She eyed it with unease.

Clearly intent on pressing its advantage, the creature made an even more unsettling noise, then extruded a wet glob of spit, which landed in the sand near her boots.

"Perhaps I can simply walk to Tell al-Amarna," Ellie offered reasonably as Adam joined her.

"Want a hand up?" Adam offered, eyes twinkling with amusement.

The camel ground its teeth, which were far too close to Ellie's face. The sound was terrifying.

"I would really rather not go up at all," Ellie admitted.

"Who's a beautiful girl?" Adam said warmly.

Ellie realized that he was addressing the remark to the camel. She wondered how he could be sure that the creature was female—until she glanced past it at the beast that Mustafa was riding and noted the presence of an enormous and very obviously male set of accouterments dangling between its legs.

"That's right, gorgeous," Adam continued happily. "Now, how about you sit down? Hoosh!"

Yusuf had used the word a minute earlier for Jemmahor's ride. Adam accompanied it with a tap to the camel's knee—and with a groan and an awkward lurch, the monster knelt.

Of course, he had already figured out how to wrangle the beasts. Why wouldn't it take him more than five minutes to do it?

He was Adam Bates.

Adam held out his hand. "This is the part where you climb on, Princess."

The sun chose that moment to breach the horizon. The first rays of dawn fell across his rugged profile, gilding it with light. His eyes were warm and happy as he gazed down at her.

Words burst from Ellie's lips on a wave of pride and affection. "You really are magnificent, you know."

Adam stilled as though her remark had struck him like a dart. A grin slowly lit up his face.

"You saying that to be nice?" His tone shifted from a rich warmth to wryness. "Or to put off getting in this saddle?"

The tease was casual—but the brightness in his eyes was real. The glow of it filled Ellie up like the light of dawn spreading across the sky.

Jemmahor's laugh cut through the air, and the camel brayed, reminding Ellie that she wasn't alone. She glanced over at the rest of their party.

Umm Waseem waited nearby with implacable patience. Sayyid exchanged a quiet word with his wife while Jemmahor let Yusuf help her onto her camel, obviously enjoying the attention. Mustafa watched over them with his hand on the pommel of his sword, looking as though he were posing for a painting.

"What do you think we're going to be up against once we get to Amarna?" Ellie asked.

"A glorified antiquities thief and a bunch of hired thugs." Adam flashed her a smile. "Nothing we haven't handled before."

A familiar worry flashed through her. "What about Neil and Constance? Do you think they're all right?"

"I think Connie is more than capable of handling herself," Adam returned confidently.

"And my brother?" Ellie prompted more dryly.

"He's gotta stick around for me to give him hell about that stupid note of his, doesn't he?" Adam let the wry twist fall from his lips. He reached out and touched her face. His thumb brushed comfortingly over her cheek. "We'll get them out when we get to Amarna, if they haven't found a way to escape already."

"It's my fault that either of them got involved," Ellie insisted with a dart of guilt.

"Nah," Adam replied.

"Excuse me?"

"You didn't hold anybody's feet to an iron," Adam pointed out. "They chose to come along."

Ellie studied his face in the soft light of the early morning. "And you?" she asked solemnly.

His blue gaze burned down at her. His hand slipped to the back of her neck, his fingers tangling lightly in her hair. "I chose it too. And I'd do it again in a goddamned heartbeat." His mouth quirked into another smile. "But now you're definitely just stalling."

Ellie cast an exasperated and skeptical look back at the waiting camel. "How do you know it's not going to try to eat me?"

"She's a vegetarian." Adam more or less picked her up and set her on the saddle. He tapped the camel's flank. "Qūm! Up you get!"

Ellie flailed out to grasp the horn of the saddle as her mount thrust up its front legs, throwing her against the rear of the seat. She bit back an instinctive yelp, and then the rear half of the animal was rising, lurching her forward.

At last it was done. Ellie found herself clinging to a perch that was far higher from the ground than it had any right to be.

"Keep both your legs on one side," Adam instructed her as he easily mounted his own camel, his body instinctively shifting along with the animal's movement as it rose. "You'll be more comfortable."

"Nothing about this feels comfortable!" Ellie shot back.

"You look great up there," Adam countered wickedly. "Yalla!"

The camel lurched into a trot, and Ellie clung to it as it bounced after Zeinab, Sayyid, and the others, the yellow dog dashing along in their wake with a happy bark.

TWENTY-NINE

ℭONSTANCE CONTEMPLATED THE sleeping form of Dr. Neil Fairfax in the morning light that streamed into their tomb, a pot full of river water in her hands.

She had found the pot in another rock-cut tomb when she went out to investigate their situation an hour earlier. The neck had been broken off, but enough volume remained for her to scoop up a bit of the Nile and carry it with her to where Neil lay dozing.

She hesitated before executing the rest of her plan. Neil looked better than he had any right to. He was still stripped down to his trousers, allowing Constance a more thorough opportunity to appreciate his torso than she'd had the night before. He really must have been doing more than reading excavation reports these last few years. While he wasn't quite of the proportions of someone like Adam Bates, he had certainly filled out from the scrawny boy Constance had known as a child.

Not that it mattered. She had quite set aside her notions of taking Neil as her lover. Really, the whole idea had been nonsensical! As he had indelibly proved over the last few days, he might have developed a respectable set of biceps, but he was still Stuffy. He would probably respond to Constance's amorous attentions by blurting out bits of Latin poetry. He'd fumble his glasses, and the tips of his ears would turn red.

She frowned. The images were less off-putting than she might have liked.

At any rate, it was time matters went back to the way they were supposed to be—with Neil complaining about how unsafe things were and Constance finding creative uses for ropes and fire.

Or river water.

Neil muttered uneasily in his sleep, rolling onto his back. His soft brown hair had dried at odd angles. Little creases tugged at the corners of his mouth, as though he were still worrying about something even while he dreamed.

She *could* smooth those out with a kiss, Constance thought distractedly.

Instead of kissing, she tipped the broken pot and let a stream of Nile water splash down onto Neil's face.

He woke up spluttering and flailing. "Who…?! Where…?!"

"It's time to go," Constance informed him, setting down the now-empty pot.

Still in her chemise and drawers, she crossed over to pluck her corset from the ground and give it a thorough shaking out. Behind her, Neil fumbled at his pocket for his spectacles.

He slipped them on and blinked at her.

The tips of his ears turned a distinct pink.

Serves him right, Constance thought pertly and fixed her corset into place with a practiced tug at the cords.

Her lawn dress was looking a bit worse for its recent adventures, but she hardly needed to worry about that. No one could see it at the moment but Neil Fairfax.

She pulled it on over her head, popping her arms back into the sleeves.

Neil had scrambled to gather up his own clothes, tugging on his shirt as though it were a hole he could dive into and hide. He was still working on the buttons when his eyes lit on Constance's broken pot.

He snatched it from the ground and turned it with an air of urgent examination.

"This is Fatamid-era Minis lusterware!" Neil burst out. "Where did you get this? Was there any more of it? Did you see any nearby inscriptions or graffiti?"

"Leave off about the lusterware and finish getting dressed," Constance retorted. "Unless you're content to climb over a mile and a half of cliffs as you are. It hardly makes any difference to me."

Neil looked down at his half-buttoned shirt. He clamped his hand on it, then turned and hurried into his waistcoat.

"Where are we going, anyway?" he asked.

"There's a bit of farmland on this side of the river at a break in the cliffs to the south," Constance reported. "We'll head there and see if we can acquire that boat."

"Right." Neil ran a distracted hand through his hair as though to tidy it. The gesture didn't really help.

Constance gave an impatient huff and batted his hand away, running her fingers through the cropped brown length herself. It was still damp from her wake-up call.

"There," she concluded, satisfied with the results.

Neil swallowed thickly and pointedly looked past her shoulder. His eyes widened. "Well, there you are! *Blessings of Hathor upon Nihkayankh, steward of the nomarch of Ta-Wer!*"

"What are you on about?" Constance demanded with a note of exasperation.

Neil pushed past her to the statues by the mouth of the tomb. He pointed to a few lines of hieroglyphs that it had been too dark to see the night before.

"An Eighth Nome official," he declared proudly, "and his wife."

Constance narrowed her eyes thoughtfully. "That was quite the lucky guess, then," she noted, remembering his comments about the ancient couple from the night before.

"It wasn't a guess," Neil retorted crossly.

"Then how did you know this was an Eighth Nome official before you could read any of the words?" She waved a hand at the hieroglyphs.

Neil crossed his arms. "I just... used a bit of intuition."

A new and unexpected suspicion popped to life in the back of Constance's mind. She contemplated it as she studied him.

"What?" Neil frowned at her. "Why are you staring at me?"

"No reason," Constance replied, filing the bizarre and intriguing thought away for later.

Neil frowned at her skeptically before his gaze was drawn back to the inscription on the wall—and then he was pushing past Constance to kneel down in front of it.

"Thinis!?" he exclaimed.

"Sorry?" Constance returned, confused.

Neil jabbed an urgent finger at the hieroglyphs. "Nihkayankh, steward of the nomarch of Ta-Wer, *who sealed the royal tombs of Thinis!* Do you have any idea how important this is?"

He sprang to his feet, pacing across the entrance to the tomb as he continued. "Thinis is the ancient lost capital of Egypt's First Dynasty. Maspero theorized that it was located somewhere in the vicinity of Girga, though Brugsch and Mariette have argued for Kom el-Sultan or el-Tineh. But we know it was very likely somewhere in the Eighth Nome, and really when you consider..."

Constance stared at him.

"I'm... I'm rambling. Aren't I?" he offered awkwardly.

"Yes." Constance softened. "Though to be fair, I would normally be quite happy to discuss mythical cities, especially if it means there might be clues to undiscovered ancient ruins full of forgotten treasure knocking about. But at the moment, we already have a legendary tomb to find and a bevy of villains whom we must assume are already several hours ahead of us. We cannot rely on the booby traps holding them off forever."

"Booby traps?" Neil echoed. "What booby traps?"

"The ones in Neferneferuaten's tomb, of course."

"But tombs don't have booby traps," Neil protested.

"Of course they do," Constance corrected him.

They paused at the mouth of their rock-cut chamber. Neil contemplated the climb with an expression of tired resignation, then cast Constance an awkward look. "I never thanked you for last night."

"Which part of it?" Constance asked.

"The part where you broke me out of that study. Herded me through a boat full of criminals." He nodded at the stone cavern behind them. "Found us a place to hide."

"You would have done the same thing," Constance said dismissively.

"Would I?" Neil returned with obvious skepticism.

"Well—maybe not *quite* the same thing," Constance allowed. "But you did save both our hides when you threw us off the boat. That was a good bit of quick thinking."

"But I left them the tablet," Neil pointed out glumly.

Constance gave his arm a reassuring pat. "You can't expect to get it all right on the first try."

Neil's expression drew into lines of resigned dismay. "How many more tries do you expect we're going to have?"

Constance flashed him a sympathetic smile and refrained from answering. Why give him the bad news now? He'd only worry over it the rest of the way up the Nile.

Neil took in her expression and groaned.

Constance cast a final look at the age-worn sculptures in the wall—the steward of the nomarch of Ta-Wer and his wife, their features worn away by the millennia. Her gaze dropped to where the fingers of the two statues were still delicately entwined.

"They're holding hands," she observed with a pang of surprise.

"Yes." Neil's tone was a little solemn and awkward. "They do that sometimes."

Even though the sculptures were deeply weathered with age, obscuring much of their detail, the time-worn gesture was oddly poignant.

"How long do you think they have been like that?" Constance pressed.

"Around four thousand years."

Constance's heart squeezed with a poignant sympathy. "He must have loved her very much," she said with feeling.

Neil frowned as he adjusted his spectacles.

She grabbed his hand and gave it a tug. "Now come along. We have a boat to steal."

"Don't you mean *buy?*" Neil pleaded, stumbling after her.

Constance tucked up her skirts as she set off along the cliffs. The ragged landscape was not as impenetrable as it had looked from the boat. A little scrambling over the rocks and a shuffle along a few narrow ledges brought them near the top of the escarpment, where a perfectly serviceable goat path wended across the heights. There were only a few places where she had to leap across a small chasm along the way.

Haranguing Neil into following her took rather more effort.

She steered them to the narrow, low-lying band of green farmland that lay at a dip in the ridge to the south. The cotton fields were broken up by a cluster of humble houses and a rickety dock that ran out into the water, where Constance had picked out the shape of a tidy little single-sail felucca.

The boat looked somewhat less tidy as they drew nearer to it. The hull had not been painted in some time, and the sail was patched in places. The craft was also listing a bit to port.

Constance spotted the farmer in a field near the dock, his blue galabeya tucked up around his knees.

"I don't suppose you speak any Masri?" she asked as Neil joined her.

"A bit?" Neil replied, huffing from the exertion of the climb. "I mean— I've picked up a few things, but Sayyid is always telling me that my pronunciation is—"

"It'll do." Constance hooked her arm through his elbow and dragged him over to the farmer.

The fellow was only a few years older than Constance, with wide brown eyes and sun-weathered skin. He straightened as they approached, staring at them as though he half suspected they were a mirage.

The way Neil stared back at him was hardly better.

"Say hello." Constance nudged him with her elbow.

"Right," Neil squeaked nervously. "Er… salâmu 'alaykum!"

"Waleikum as-salâm," the farmer replied skeptically.

"Tell him that he has a very nice farm," Constance prompted.

"Why?" Neil retorted, clearly bewildered.

"You can't just start right into bargaining. You have to soften him up first!"

"Bargaining?" Neil echoed with alarm. "Who said anything about bargaining?"

"How else do you think we are going to acquire the boat, if we are not stealing it?" Constance threw up her hands.

"But I'm awful at bargaining!" Neil protested.

"*You* aren't going to do it," Constance retorted. "*I* am. You are merely a necessary instrument. Now say something nice!"

Neil appeared singularly unhappy with her instructions, but he drew in a breath to brace himself and swung into a halting stream of Masri.

The farmer appeared confused, offering a few polite if unenthusiastic answers.

Neil breathed out a sigh. "I have ascertained the well-being of his sons, his cattle, and the likelihood of bad weather between now and the end of the inundation. Is that sufficient?"

"I suppose," Constance allowed. "Now you may ask him about the boat—but don't sound too interested yet! If he doesn't think you're set on buying it, he won't try to gouge you." She hesitated, taking in Neil's pale complexion, river-stained shirt, and slightly panicked expression. "Maybe," she amended.

Neil looked miserable but waded back into his negotiations with the farmer.

Constance had only been in Egypt for a few weeks, but she had always had an ear for languages—and Neil's Masri sounded distinctly off.

The farmer stared at him in shock.

"Hold on," Constance cut in. "Did you ask him about his felucca—or his *falaka*?"

"Aren't those the same thing?"

"A felucca is a sailboat," Constance retorted impatiently. "A falaka is…" She reconsidered the word she was about to use as she absorbed Neil's already rattled sensibilities. "One's posterior region."

"*Oh God!*" Neil moaned, his expression falling into lines of abject mortification.

"Best clear that up," Constance helpfully suggested.

Neil managed to recover from the blunder, but even with the right vocabulary to hand, Constance could sense that it was a frankly pathetic performance. The farmer himself looked a little disappointed by it. After all, one did have to appreciate the opportunity to engage in a bit of skilled haggling—and Stuffy was falling quite short of that.

"He says that the boat belonged to his father and is therefore extremely dear to him, but that he might be willing to part with it for the right price," Neil finally reported. He was sweating.

"His father's boat, my left foot," Constance assessed. "Offer him five ginehs."

The farmer made an elaborate reply.

"He says he cannot possibly part with it for less than ten ginehs," Neil translated, "as the boat is actually on loan from his cousin and—"

"Ten ginehs for that floating bathtub?" Constance caught herself and pasted on a polite smile. "Tell him that it is a very fine boat, but you can only possibly offer him six and a half ginehs."

Neil winced, but trudged back into it.

"He says because it is such a fine boat, he can't possibly give it to us for six and a half ginehs. The lowest he can go is eight," Neil pleaded, looking haggard.

"Tell him seven and a half." Constance kept her gaze on the farmer, who looked back at her with a similar expression of happy competition.

"He accepts." Neil's shoulders sagged with relief.

Constance plunged her hand into her corset to pluck out a bundle of cash, which was still a little damp from its plunge into the Nile. She peeled off the notes.

"Here," she said, holding them out.

Neil stared at the bills as though taking them would be equivalent to rubbing his hands over her bosom.

Constance snapped her fingers. Neil jolted, snatched the money, and shoved it at the farmer.

Another exchange of Masri had him looking decidedly peaked.

"He's insisting we stay for tea!" Neil protested, near panicking.

"Tell him that is a very kind offer, and we shall certainly return to take him up on it, but right now your mother is expecting you for lunch," Constance neatly rattled off.

"My mother?" Neil echoed. "But my mother's in—"

"Just tell him!"

Neil looked queasy as he delivered the message, but the farmer accepted it with a shrug. A great deal of handshaking followed before Neil was freed to follow her to the boat.

Constance stepped inside. The weathered deck wobbled under her boot.

It was not a very large boat, but there was no sign that it was actively leaking—which meant it would do.

"I'm so glad that's over!" Neil burst out.

"Can you sail?" Constance demanded.

Neil stiffened a bit. "I can, as it happens."

"Good. Then I needn't do it all myself," Constance concluded. "Free the lines, would you?"

Neil loosed them from the dock and then hurriedly leapt into the boat before the current could tug it free. The felucca tilted precariously, forcing him to spin his arms to maintain his balance.

"This is a terrible idea!" he exclaimed.

"Hoist the sail," Constance replied, taking hold of the tiller. "We have villains to catch."

THIRTY

With its large sail and light hull, the felucca turned out to be reasonably river-worthy as it skimmed across the water, carried by a steady breeze from the south. There were only a handful of moments when Neil was convinced they were going to drown.

They sailed through the length of the day, stopping only once for food. As the sun declined in the west, turning the deserted landscape a deeper gold, Constance asked Neil about the contents of the cuneiform tablet.

Twenty minutes later, he was still talking.

"And so you see, Genesis is full of references to other gods," he explained as the Nile breeze tousled his hair. "Which begs the question—what *caused* the shift from monolatry to monotheism among the proto-Hebrews? There are strong indications that the Hebrews themselves attributed the change to the time of Moses, who by all accounts was raised as an Egyptian. And then we have the roughly contemporaneous cult of Akhenaten—a clear early case of monotheism, whatever Flinders Petrie might have to say about it…"

"Come about to starboard," Constance ordered with a vague wave of her hand.

It was the only comment she had made since Neil had begun giving her a detailed summary of his theories on the relationship between the Exodus story and the history of the Eighteenth Dynasty. Neil did not let that bother him overmuch, continuing his lecture as he adjusted the rigging.

"The only thing we have been missing is an explicit link between the Hebrews and the Atenists. But if hard evidence exists that Moses was an official in Akhenaten's court—"

"Are you an atheist, then?" Constance asked abruptly.

"I… What?" Neil squirmed in the face of her renewed attention.

"It is only that you keep talking about the Egyptians inventing God—

which is a very clever theory, of course," she allowed in conciliatory tones. "Only it does make one wonder whether you actually believe in God after all. Not that I would be bothered about it one way or another. My Aai has a shrine to Durga in her suite that is hardly a secret to anybody. I have not ruled out becoming a Hindu myself."

"Can you just… do that?" Neil asked, bewildered.

"Whyever not? Being a Hindu sounds altogether more interesting than attending services at St. Matthew's Bayswater. Reverend Spencer gives the most abominably dull sermons."

She flashed him a considering look, and Neil realized that she was still waiting for an answer to her question.

"I don't know that the Egyptians invented God, as such," Neil replied carefully, feeling as though he were stepping out onto ground as fragile as porcelain. "One might just as easily suppose that Akhenaten came to acknowledge something that was already there."

"Oh! Like a prophet, you mean," Constance concluded easily.

Neil tried not to choke. "I am not sure that most people would find that equivalence… er, entirely inoffensive."

Constance's eyes narrowed. "Are *you* offended by it?"

"No!" Neil blurted out in reply.

"Then why would you worry about what most people think?"

"Because…" Neil began automatically, then caught himself. He drew in a breath. "Because I am not as brave as you are, Connie."

Constance considered Neil quietly. "I am not sure you have ever called me brave before. There's been reckless, menacing, 'a short and holy terror,'—"

"That was when we were children," Neil cut in nervously, "and you were trying to use my spectacles to burn holes in the carpet."

"Which never did work," Constance complained.

"That's because I'm nearsighted," Neil automatically explained. "Near-sighted vision is corrected by concave lenses, and concave lenses spread light out rather than focusing it."

Constance's look grew a little more thoughtful—and a touch more intense. Neil felt the weight of it like a prickling electricity.

"I would have told you that, if you had asked first," he finished awkwardly.

"I shall keep that in mind for next time," Constance replied.

Silence lingered. The hull of the ragged boat creaked beneath them as they glided along with the current. The waters of the Nile lapped softly at the boards. In the reeds on the shoreline, an ibis startled, lifting into great-winged flight.

"I am still cross with you," Constance noted.

"I am still rather cross with myself," Neil admitted.

"And you are an abysmally bad haggler," she added.

"Yes," Neil agreed. "Nor do I have any wish to get better at it. It makes me extremely uncomfortable."

"I will say, I was surprised that someone like Mr. Bates would choose to be friends with you," she mused, and then caught herself. "Sorry. I think that might have come out wrong."

There had been nothing particularly vicious in her words. Neil still stiffened with a quick, reflexive hurt—perhaps because the question she had just voiced was one that he had wondered about himself on more than one occasion.

"Sometimes I think he just adopted me out of pity, like a three-legged cat," he offered a little glumly.

Constance studied him quietly from her place by the tiller. Her dark curls were gilded by the falling sunlight. Neil was once again struck by how extraordinarily lovely she had become, and for perhaps the first time since she had skidded into his tomb at Saqqara, he met her eyes without feeling like he had to steel himself to it.

The moment stretched like a held breath, woven through with the creak of the lines and the soft rhythm of the rippling water.

"For a scholar, you have quite a few things left to learn," Constance finally said, her voice surprisingly soft. "Though do tack us to port, please, before we run into that rock."

"Oh, bugger!" Neil swore, hurrying to tug the lines.

An hour later, the landscape opened into a broad, flat plane. Beyond a fringe of green marsh, the arid ground was painted orange with the decline of evening and peppered with crumbling ruins.

Though Neil had never been there, he still recognized the lines of those ancient foundations from dozens of sketches and reports. He was looking at Tell al-Amarna, home to the dusty remnants of Akhenaten's empire.

Little was left of the heretic pharaoh's once-great capital. The palaces and temples had been reduced to low, ragged boxes on the ground, punctuated by the lonely sentinel of the odd surviving column.

The gleaming white length of Julian Forster-Mowbray's dahabeeyah was tied up at a wharf below a small mud-brick village that crouched at the edge of the plain. The *Isis* was alight with lanterns, silhouetting the figures that moved across the deck.

Neil crouched lower into the felucca, hoping the sun at his back would help shadow his features.

"That's Reis Hassan and some of the crew," Constance said, lowering herself a bit as well. "But I don't see Julian or his mercenaries, and there are fewer crewmen than there ought to be."

"I suppose it was too much to hope that they might have rested for the night before going after the tomb," Neil grumbled.

"But where will they have gone?" Constance demanded.

Neil pointed across the rubble-strewn plain to where the sunset painted a ragged ridge in hues of mauve and ocher. "See that gap in the cliffs? That's the entrance to the royal wadi, where the tombs of Akhenaten and his chief ministers are located. The tablet said the tomb of Neferneferuaten will be on a branch about three miles up."

Past the *Isis*, the shoreline thickened with palm trees and tangled shrubs. Constance steered the felucca into a gap in the growth. The prow caught up against the muddy earth.

"Then we'd best start walking," she declared.

They climbed the steep, slippery bank, pushing through scratchy young acacia trees. Beyond the brush, the fertile land gave way to an arid expanse of sand and stone.

Neil looked out over a landscape peppered with tumbled fragments of the city Akhenaten had raised from the virgin desert as a tribute to his revolutionary god.

He had planned to come here before, of course. How could he not wish to visit a place that had loomed so large in his studies for the better part of a decade? Somehow, even after two years in Egypt, he hadn't found the time. The excavation at Saqqara had eaten up nine months out of the year, and then there had been visits to home and reports to make.

Little of the city's former splendor remained. Akhetaten had not been built of great limestone slabs like the pylons of Thebes, but of smaller talatat blocks and mud-brick. Later pharaohs had ravaged the place for materials for their own monumental projects, leaving nothing behind but low rubble, the sand-swept platform of a road, and the bases of shattered columns, all whispering of ghosts.

Neil didn't realize that he had stopped until Constance turned back to look at him.

"Is something wrong?" she asked.

Neil struggled for the words to answer her. How could he possibly explain what it meant to him to be standing here in the ruins of a city that had loomed so large in his imagination for so long?

A rogue breeze stirred the sand by Neil's boots as he stepped forward. He looked down and realized that he was standing on the weathered paving stones of an ancient courtyard.

That he had stepped into Akhetaten.

An electric chill shivered through him, along with a scent of ozone like the breath before a storm. Neil raised his head—and Akhetaten rose around him.

Monumental buildings soared over clean-swept boulevards, their walls painted with bold murals. Silk curtains bloomed from palace balconies. Pools shimmered coolly in palm-shaded courtyards.

The Temple of the Aten was visible to the north, crowned by the smoke of offering fires. To the south lay the records office and the police barracks beside the house of the high priest.

He smelled incense and roasting lamb. Heard chariot wheels clatter over paving stones.

Women laughed in gardens lined with lemon trees. Flower petals drifted from an open window, dancing to the rattle of a sistrum.

"It's beautiful," Neil breathed, awe and wonder washing over him until he felt like he would break.

"Neil?" Constance asked carefully.

Neil blinked, and his gaze fell across a field of rubble, colorless and still.

"What's beautiful?" Constance pressed, standing beside him at the edge of the ruins. "What were you looking at?"

"Nothing." His voice was rough in his throat. "Just… imagining things."

That was all it had been, of course. Years of research and the shock of finally being in this place that he had studied for so long must have combined into something like a hallucination.

The reaction was perfectly natural… and should not have left Neil feeling as though something had been taken from him when it winked out of view.

Constance eyed him thoughtfully as a dry wind tugged softly at her dark curls.

"We should keep going," she finally said, her voice uncharacteristically solemn.

"Right," Neil agreed tightly. "Of course."

They picked their way through the vast plain of debris, the rubble silent save for the crunch of their boots against the ground and the quick scurry of a mouse. A scarab beetle clicked its wings, suddenly taking flight.

The disk of the sun slipped below the line of the horizon as they reached the edge of the ruins. A mile of rocky desert lay between them and the entrance to the Royal Wadi—the steep, bone-dry canyon that split the high face of the ridge like the jagged cut of a knife.

The eastern sky, which lay over the ridge ahead of them, dropped into a rich violet-blue. The moon had just slipped above the hills, a pale sliver that offered fair illumination through the still, clear air.

"We'll need to be quiet from here," Constance said. "They might have left someone behind to watch the entrance to the wadi, and we can't know how sound might carry against the cliffs. If there's anything you need to say, best say it now."

Constance likely meant for Neil to share his questions or thoughts about their plans, but something else spilled out of his lips in a desperate torrent.

"If I don't make it out of there, I want you to tell Ellie and Bates that I'm sorry," he burst out. "I… also want to beg you to stay here and let me go on without you, but I know you wouldn't do it, and I know how utterly ludicrous it would be for me to even try, as you are far more capable of handling whatever we might encounter in there than I am. I am not at all sure what use I can possibly be in all this, and I'm very afraid that is going to get me or someone I care about killed."

The storm of words petered out. Neil drew in a long, unsteady breath, then carefully let it back out again.

Constance's gaze flashed with sympathy.

"What do we do when we find Julian and the others?" Neil asked more calmly.

Constance tipped up her chin, eyeing the wadi with determination. "Whatever we must."

A realization swept through Neil in the wake of her declaration.

"I used to think you were mad, you know," he blurted, and then caught himself. "Or reckless, at least. Utterly blind to all the things that could go wrong. But that isn't it at all."

Constance startled, her eyes wide and just a little vulnerable.

"You're too clever not to know what we're walking into," Neil went on. "You know perfectly well how dangerous it's going to be. You're just… *choosing* to be courageous, over and over again, even when the whole world rises up against you. Aren't you?"

Constance had gone very still. The silvered moonlight painted her features. Neil could see the ghostly echo of the girl he'd known in the angle of her chin and the line of her nose—but changed, merged into the elegant form of the woman who stood before him.

"I don't know how to be like that." Neil looked away from her, the weight of her liquid gaze becoming too much to bear. "But I admire it—a very great deal."

A hand slipped into his own—slender but strong, holding him with a tender determination.

"Thank you," Constance said quietly.

"For what?" Neil replied with a choking laugh.

In answer, she gave his hand a squeeze.

They stood together in silence as they faced the looming shadow of the ridge and the shadowy gap of the wadi.

"Are you ready?" Constance finally asked.

The answer rose through the rock under Neil's boots, putting steel into his spine.

"Yes," he said and stepped forward.

Millions of years ago, ancient waterways had come together in the hills above Amarna to empty into the larger river that carved out the plain. Those waters had dried up long before Akhenaten had set the first stone of his capital city into place, leaving behind only the dry, silent gorges they had rent in the earth.

Steep cliffs rose to either side of the entrance to the ancient canyon that the heretic pharaoh had chosen for his royal cemetery. Moonlit rock formations towered over Neil in fantastical shapes that reminded him of hulking sphinxes or hungry crocodiles.

The wadi was broader up close than it had looked from a distance. Constance kept to the edge where the shadows ran deeper. Neil joined her there, even though the footing felt more treacherous. He kept his steps light, painfully conscious of every scrape or rattle of shifting stones against the exquisite silence.

His brain screamed with the possibility that at any moment, a cry of alarm and a blast of gunfire would see both him and Constance perish in a spray of blood on arid stone.

He tried not to think about it too much.

It took them nearly an hour to reach the branching canyon mentioned in the tablet inscription. As it came into view, the breeze that tugged at Neil's hair began to ring with the sound of metal clanging on stone.

Constance tucked herself against the ragged cliff that framed the entrance.

Neil leaned out from behind her as she peered around the corner. Light spilled down into the chasm from somewhere ahead.

"Julian has set up on a ledge about forty feet high," Constance reported in a whisper. "The whole thing is lined with lanterns."

"Have they found something?" Neil demanded, his nerves tightening.

"There's no way to see from down here." Constance looked up, nearly bumping into Neil's chin. He took a quick step back. "But I think I know how we can find out. Follow me."

She led him to a spot where the wall of the canyon had been softened by an ancient spill of water. The path formed a rough trail that wound up the side of the ridge.

Constance climbed it confidently. Neil struggled after her, biting back a yelp as loose rocks shifted under his boots.

At the top, the path decayed into a scramble up a steep wash. As Neil painstakingly scaled it, he glanced back at the way they had come.

It was a mistake. Though their path had looked reasonable from the floor of the canyon, it revealed itself to be sheer madness when viewed from above.

Neil tore his eyes away, forcing himself to breathe as visions of plummeting to his doom danced through his mind. He set his boot carefully to another foothold—which promptly crumbled beneath him. The loosened stone tumbled down the cliff with a racket like a peppering of gunfire.

Constance shot him a warning look.

Sorry, Neil mouthed.

Several terrifying minutes later, he collapsed onto the top of the mountain with blissful, shaking relief. He rolled, flipping onto his back to better relish in the feeling of being on solid ground.

He gazed up at a sprawling blanket of stars. They pierced the ebony fabric of the sky in astonishing quantity, stealing his breath—the same stars Akhenaten might have seen had he slipped from his palace out into the desert to gaze up at the firmament that had given him his god.

"I've... It's..." Neil started in a hoarse whisper, unable to find the words.

"Entirely lovely," Constance agreed, glancing up. "But do refrain from nattering on about it, lest we get ourselves shot."

Neil slammed back to earth, turning over to squirm forward on his elbows to where Constance crouched at the edge of the cliff.

From their perch, Neil could see Julian's work site halfway up the wall of the wadi in perfect detail. Several crewmen from the *Isis* were digging out a section of the hill that was buried in loose rubble. A smattering of Al-Saboors were positioned at various places around the excavation. Neil counted three rifles and a pistol among them, along with an assortment of swords, cudgels, and knives.

The weapons were all held loosely. The men were obviously bored.

"I don't see any sign of the tomb entrance," Constance whispered as she studied the site. "They must not have reached it yet. We'll have to find a way to thwart them before they do. Perhaps if we…"

A creeping sensation flared at the back of Neil's neck. He turned—and found himself staring at the point of a large sword.

The blade was steadily held by a bearded man whose layered robes fluttered elegantly in the ghostly breeze that winged across the cliffs. The kaffiyeh scarf on the stranger's head suggested he belonged to one of the Bedouin tribes who roamed Egypt's deserts in search of pasture—or things to raid.

The man was gray-eyed, hawk-nosed… and possibly the most objectively attractive person Neil had ever seen.

"C-Connie…" Neil stammered softly, flailing out a hand to bat at her without taking his eyes off the sword.

"Just a minute, Stuffy," she retorted crossly. "I'm thinking."

"But there's, ah…" Neil swallowed thickly. "There's a very nice gentleman here with a large… er, sharply pointed…"

Constance whirled. Instead of flattening herself to the rocks like a bug—as Neil had done—she whipped into a dangerous-looking crouch, her hands raised for battle.

Her aplomb faltered as she stared at their assailant with surprise. "Goodness! That fellow is unreasonably good-looking."

"Emshi," the sword-bearing Bedouin ordered flatly.

"He is strongly implying that we should go with him," Neil translated.

He was still the one at the wrong end of the Bedouin's sword, which struck him as rather unfair. Constance was by far the more substantial threat out of the two of them.

"He doesn't look like one of Julian's people," Constance noted thoughtfully.

"Yalla," the Bedouin elaborated.

The point of his sword descended a bit closer to Neil's throat.

"Perhaps we ought to…?" Neil squeaked.

"Oh, fine," Constance allowed.

She raised her hands peacefully and stood. Neil inched himself from beneath the sword and joined her.

Constance's gaze drifted over the gentleman's admittedly fine figure. "Do you think he might be a sheikh?"

"How should I know?" Neil protested. "And why does it matter?"

"Just an idle thought," Constance replied in a manner that did not sound at all idle. "Shall we, then?"

Without waiting for Neil to answer, she confidently set out across the cliff.

THIRTY-ONE

$\mathcal{E}$LLIE HID IN the lee of a boulder at the top of the ridge, looking down into the steep, ragged cut of the wadi where Julian Forster-Mowbray was searching for Neferneferuaten's tomb.

Her caravan had arrived just after sunset, finding their way to this particular gorge by following the echoing clamor of hammers and calling voices—sounds which had traveled with remarkable clarity through the still, clear air of the desert.

Night had fully fallen. Stars pricked out in a wild array from the black velvet of the sky overhead. The other members of Ellie's party were scattered around her. Zeinab lay on her belly at the edge of the cliff, gazing down at the ledge where Julian was digging. The area was brashly illuminated by a ring of paraffin lanterns.

"I count a dozen," she murmured. With her black abaya and headscarf, she looked like a patch of deeper shadow against the stones.

"Thirteen," Adam corrected flatly from where he crouched beside her, watching the ledge with hawk-like focus.

Julian's site sat about halfway down the opposite wall of the canyon. It buzzed with activity, the air ringing with the impact of picks on stones. Besides the thugs from the sun chapel, he had brought along others that Ellie assumed must be part of the crew of his boat. They served as workers, digging out rubble and carting it off to dump into the canyon.

Even if the men below had numbered only twelve, it would still have been too many. With only the three Egyptian ladies, Adam, and Sayyid, Ellie's side was vastly outnumbered.

Not that it mattered. If it looked like Julian was close to finding the entrance to Neferneferuaten's tomb, they would have to intercede anyway—regardless of what it cost them.

For now, Zeinab simply watched, exchanging the occasional low observation with Jemmahor as the two women quietly schemed.

Somewhere behind their perch, the flat, dark expanse of the Amarna plain lay sleeping. Ellie had caught only a glimpse of it when they had approached the wadi that evening, just enough to pick up the general impression of rubble strewn across packed earth beside the flat ribbon of the Nile. She would have given her right foot for a chance to trek down and explore the ruins of ancient Akhetaten.

So far, there had been no sign of Constance or Neil. That most likely meant that Julian had left them back on the boat—unless they had already escaped… or been ruthlessly murdered.

Ellie refused to let her thoughts linger on that last possibility. Adam had been right back at the Coptic convent. Julian had a use for both Constance and Neil—at least until he could be certain he'd found the tomb.

Adam pushed back from his place beside Zeinab at the edge of the ridge. He staggered over to Ellie and slid down against the boulder beside her. His long legs sprawled out in front of him as he closed his eyes.

"Didn't *think* I was looking that far down," he commented a little queasily.

"Zeinab will keep watch," Ellie assured him sympathetically. "And you'll probably feel better if you open your eyes again."

"I think I'm half afraid if I do, the world will still be spinning." Adam cracked an eye, peering over at where Sayyid sat opposite them, worriedly watching his wife. "Still a little jerky," he concluded, closing it again.

Ellie poked him lightly in the ribs.

"Those are still bruised, you know," Adam remarked.

"Open," Ellie ordered.

With a sigh, Adam obeyed.

"Does Zeinab have a plan?" Ellie asked.

His lip twisted wryly. "What makes you think Zeinab's the one with the plan? Why couldn't I have a plan?"

"You never make plans."

"That's not *entirely* true," Adam protested.

"Do you have a plan now?" she prompted dryly.

Adam turned a sharp gaze over to the lights and noise of the dig—though he made no move to go back to the cliff. "Odds aren't great. We could try coming down at them from above, but height's not that much of an advantage when all you've got for weapons are a bunch of knives and one beat-to-hell Enfield."

He nodded to their single rifle, which Jemmahor had packed with her after stealing it from one of the Al-Saboors in Hatshepsut's temple.

"Could we stage a distraction?" Ellie suggested. "Draw some of them away?"

"Maybe," Adam allowed. "But then we'd be splitting our forces—and we don't have that many of them to begin with."

"He will have a weakness," Zeinab cut in, her gaze still locked on the canyon. "And I will find it."

"Woman's got ears like a cat," Adam grumbled. He nodded at Ellie's hand. "How's your project going?"

Ellie had been working to assess the damage to her firebird arcanum. The bone was carved in Glagolitic, a script invented by St. Cyril in the ninth century to transliterate the ancient Slavic tongue. Ellie's knowledge of it was limited, as she had studied it only briefly before hurrying on to a deeper dive into Old French. Now she wished she hadn't been in such a rush to read *La Chanson de Roland*.

She held the bone out in front of her, trying to catch more of the pale moonlight that washed over the ridge. "It's this first character that was chipped. I can see that it's something including a single circle. That means it must be either the Izey, the Omega, or—no, no. That character was hardly ever used. The Fert, perhaps? Or the Slovo… Blast it, that's still too many possibilities."

"Izey and Fert," Adam echoed. "I think I played cards with those guys once."

Ellie shot him a dry look, and he grinned at her.

She returned her attention to the bone and decided to read the possibilities aloud, hoping one of them might ring a bell. "Ivĕtŭ," she muttered. "Fvĕtŭ. Svĕtŭ."

"Bless you," Adam offered.

"Don't make me poke your ribs again," Ellie threatened darkly. "Svĕtŭ… Isn't that a bit like śvetá, the Sanskrit word for white? White, bright…" She perked up. "*Light!* Svet is the root of the cognates for light in the Slavic languages. It must be the Slovo!" Ellie flapped an impatient hand at Adam. "Give me your machete."

"What do you want my machete for?" Adam asked.

"I need to fix the inscription."

"You're gonna try to etch that tiny bird bone with my eighteen-inch knife?" Adam pressed skeptically.

"I need something sharp!" Ellie protested.

"That's a whole lot of sharp for one little bone."

Zeinab hissed at them warningly from where she crouched at the edge of their hiding place.

Sorry, Ellie mouthed back with a wince.

"Anybody else here got a knife?" Adam asked in a whisper.

Umm Waseem, who reclined against her black canvas bag with her hands folded comfortably on her round belly, revealed a wickedly curved fish gutter.

Jemmahor lifted her stolen rifle. She gave an apologetic shrug.

"You are not using my scalpels," Zeinab said flatly without looking back at them.

With a sigh, Sayyid pulled a little folding penknife from his pocket.

The rest of their party—namely the extremely persistent dog and their two remarkably handsome Bedouin guides—had hung back with the camels, which Ellie could hear grunting contentedly in the near distance.

"Thanks," Adam said, accepting the penknife.

He held out his hand for the bone, a waiting expression on his face. Ellie drew it back protectively.

"You don't know Glagolitic." She gave him a thoughtful look. "Do you?"

"Not a word," Adam replied. "You can draw it for me. I mean, it's basically a picture, right?"

"Oh, very well," Ellie conceded, handing him the bone.

She flattened a little well of sand that lay between them and used her index finger to shape the lines of the Glagolitic Slovo.

"It starts with this equilateral triangle, and then the circle is inscribed on top," she explained—remembering to keep her voice low at another warning glare from Zeinab. "But the tip of the triangle should pierce the bottom of the circle. And make sure it's in exactly the same place as the old one!" she added, leaning over Adam's shoulder like a worried mother hen.

He paused, cocking an eyebrow at her. "I got it."

Ellie made no further protest, even as her throat tightened with worry. Trying to carve an ancient Slavic rune into the delicately rounded surface of a centuries-old bird bone by moonlight was madness. She wouldn't have dared chance it—except she imagined that an arcanum that could sponta-neously erupt with a substantial burst of fiery light might prove useful in whatever dangers the rest of the night held in store.

She bit her lip to keep from offering more helpful advice to Adam and tried not to twitch with nervousness.

He whistled a quiet tune as he set the tip of the penknife to the bone in a manner that struck Ellie as dangerously confident. Rather than hover and anticipate disaster, she turned her attention to Sayyid.

He looked exhausted. Sayyid was much like Ellie's brother in temperament, far better suited to a comfortable routine of hard work and intellectual stimulation than a life of uncertainty and danger.

Those traits would have made Neil and Sayyid natural friends, and indeed, Ellie had sensed an easy, affectionate rapport between the two men when she had first popped into the tomb at Saqqara. She liked to think of Neil being friends with someone like Sayyid—someone clever and good-hearted who shared Neil's intellectual interests and wasn't afraid to challenge him when he acted like a stick-in-the-mud.

She had watched that relationship grow more strained as Neil had stubbornly clung to the crumbling remnants of his old life. Nor had she missed the look of shocked betrayal on Sayyid's face when he had learned about Neil's note to Julian Forster-Mowbray back at Hatshepsut's temple. Ellie wondered how heavily that breach of trust weighed on Sayyid alongside his worries about his wife's revolutionary activities and the substantial risks of their current mission.

Rubble crashed down into the canyon as Julian's workmen emptied their buckets. The sound of picks echoed out through the still night air that blanketed the ridge.

"Can't be easy finding out your wife is a secret revolutionary," Adam said quietly, noticing the direction of her attention. "Why do you think she didn't tell him?"

"I think she was trying to protect him," Ellie murmured back. "That she knew he would be terribly worried about it, but she was going to do it anyway."

"That's a big part of yourself to hide from the person you love," Adam noted.

Ellie soaked up the way the pale moonlight silvered the line of his jaw. She had never hidden her principles from Adam... but she hadn't realized how they would run up against his own.

The chaos of Julian's ambush and their race to the wadi hadn't left them any time to address the questions about their future that still hung over them. They felt like a knife that threatened to drive them apart.

Adam held out the firebird bone. "One Slovo."

Ellie took the arcanum from him and studied the newly carved Glagolitic character. She tried to remember if it had looked the same before. "What if I was wrong?" she asked in an uncomfortable whisper.

"You weren't," Adam assured her confidently.

"But I thought you didn't know Old Church Slavonic," Ellie protested. "How can you be sure?"

Adam met her gaze with a look that warmed her bones. "I'm sure."

His assurance—and that heated look—both settled her and sent an electric hum of awareness buzzing through her veins.

"I suppose I will simply have to test it," Ellie conceded. "Though perhaps not when we are hiding from a batch of mercenaries."

She slipped the arcanum back into the cigar tube, returning it to her pocket—and then reached out to take hold of Adam's hand.

He flashed her a look of surprise but allowed her to turn his palm until it caught the pale light washing down from the crescent moon. She traced her finger gently along the straight red line that marred his palm.

She could remember the sound of his blood softly splattering against the stones and the quick, panicked fear that had tightened her chest at how easily it might have been so much *worse*.

"I'm afraid this is going to leave a scar," Ellie observed quietly.

"I'll add it to the collection," Adam returned with a note of wry humor.

She let her thumb graze over his work-roughened skin. "It cut right through your life line—if one were to give any credence to that sort of superstitious nonsense," she added curtly.

"That sounds about right," Adam replied easily.

Ellie frowned. "It does?"

"Changed my life, didn't it?"

"What—getting your hand sliced open?" she countered crossly.

His other hand rose to her chin, gently turning her face up to look at him. His gaze was steady through the gloom. "Finding you, Princess."

The words shivered through her—and then Ellie startled at the scuff of leather on stone from behind.

Adam surged to his feet with a deceptive ease, his hand going to the hilt of his machete. Ellie more awkwardly whirled to see an absurdly good-looking Bedouin slip around the corner with the silent grace of a desert fox—prodding a pair of shadowy captives ahead of him with the point of his scimitar.

"Spies," Mustafa said in richly accented tones that flowed from his lips like water. "English."

The cloud passed, and moonlight spilled once more over the ridge—revealing the faces of Mustafa's prisoners.

"Neil!?" Ellie gasped.

"Peanut?" her brother blurted back, blinking with surprise through the round frames of his spectacles.

He let out an *oomph* as Ellie crashed into him, squeezing him around the ribs.

"You're all right!" she exclaimed, breathless with the relief that washed over her.

His arms came around her and tightened. His cheek pressed against her hair.

"I'm all right," he assured her quietly.

"And you, too," Ellie added, releasing her brother and reaching for Constance.

"Don't tell me you were worried!" Constance scolded, squeezing her back. "Stuffy and I had the situation fully under control the entire time."

Neil's face blanched. "I wouldn't say that's quite…"

He bit back the rest as Constance shot him a warning look.

Adam joined them.

"Bates," Neil said awkwardly, facing him.

"Fairfax," Adam replied—and then yanked him into a hug. "Damned good to see you in one piece."

"Rather glad of that myself," Neil confessed tightly. "It's very good to see you as well—all of you." He cast a meaningful look at Sayyid, who had come to his feet beside them, and his face fell into lines of pained dismay. "I owe you all the most abject—"

"Yes, yes." Constance cut him off with a wave of her hand. "There will be plenty of time for groveling later. I want to know how the three of you managed to escape Julian's thugs in Hatshepsut's temple!"

"The three of us had very little to do with it," Ellie admitted frankly. "We were rescued by Mrs. Al-Ahmed and her band of lady revolutionaries."

Neil's face blanked with surprise. He cast a startled look at Constance. "Revolutionaries?" he echoed numbly.

Zeinab rose with a fluid shift of shadowy black cloth and regarded Neil through narrowed eyes. Jemmahor gave him a cheerful wave, the rifle balanced across her knees.

Umm Waseem looked to be napping again.

"Told you," Constance commented smugly.

"But however did the pair of you escape the boat?" Ellie pressed.

"It was simple enough, really," Constance replied. "I waited until dark, picked the lock, hauled Neil out—and lost both of my knives evading our pursuers," she added grumpily. "Then Neil tossed the pair of us into the Nile."

Ellie turned wide eyes on her brother. "You jumped out of a boat into the Nile? In the middle of the night?"

"It was awful." Neil paled at the memory.

"We sheltered in an ancient cliff tomb, and the next morning I purchased a felucca at an extortionate price from a local farmer so that we could follow Julian and his villainous cohort here," Constance finished. "We were captured by your extremely handsome Bedouin accomplice, and there you have it."

Adam made a choked sound from behind her. He either had sand in his throat, or had made an only moderately successful attempt not to burst out laughing and thereby reveal their position to the excavators below.

"Who is that fellow, anyway?" Constance pressed with canny interest as she cast an appreciative look over at Mustafa. "Is he a desert prince here to aid our cause?"

The dashing Bedouin had stepped aside as soon as it was clear that his captives were friends rather than enemies. He stood on a ledge that fell away to the ragged, wadi-crossed landscape of the plateau, his noble figure swept with pale moonlight.

"He is here to watch the camels with his cousin," Ellie replied a little reluctantly.

"Camels, is it?" Constance tore her gaze from the gorgeous Bedouin with obvious effort. "So what is the plan for stopping Julian and his henchmen? Are we well stocked with firearms?"

"I have this," Jemmahor offered, waggling her rifle.

"That's a bolt-action Enfield," Adam elaborated. "It's almost as nice as a Winchester repeater, but it doesn't help much if you don't have any rounds for it."

"I have rounds," Jemmahor retorted.

"You've got two," Adam corrected her. "I checked the magazine."

Jemmahor pouted.

"I used to have a Winchester repeater," Adam added in a deceptively casual tone.

"Where is it now?" Jemmahor asked hopefully.

Adam flashed Ellie a smirk. "Ellie dropped a cave on it."

"We don't need firearms." Ellie tried to suppress an embarrassed flush. "We have... er, the element of surprise."

"Hmm," Constance mused, clearly unimpressed.

"Either of you happen to know why The Mustache picked this spot to dig?" Adam jerked a thumb back at the lights and noise of Julian's excavation. "Because it'd be real nice to find out he's doing it all on some posh whim."

"Neil threw the map at him," Constance replied.

Neil groaned, setting his face in his hands.

"Why were you throwing maps at people?" Ellie demanded.

"It was on the tablet," Neil reported through his fingers.

Ellie gaped at Neil. "You *threw* a three-thousand-year-old document of immeasurable historical importance at Mr. Forster-Mowbray?"

"No!" Neil protested. His shoulders slumped. "I threw it at Mr. Jacobs."

"It was actually quite well done," Constance offered helpfully. "That villain had just produced a firearm and was about to riddle us with bullets, only Neil launched the tablet at him and then knocked both of us over the railing into the river."

She flashed Neil a conciliatory smile.

"Might've been well done, but it left the damned thing in Fusty Mothball's hands," Adam pointed out.

Neil straightened with effort, forcing himself to wade in. "There were measurements in the final line of the Akkadian. Something about eight hundred and fifteen cubits past the entrance to this wadi."

"Guess that's where they're digging." Adam cast a grim look back at the glow of the excavation.

"Which cubits?" Sayyid cut in.

The others turned to him in surprise. Sayyid had been oddly quiet throughout the reunion. Ellie could still see an edge of anger in his eyes as he looked at Neil.

"Of course!" Neil bit out the words like a curse. "How could I have missed that?"

"Explain," Zeinab ordered sharply.

"In the Ancient Egyptian measurement system, there are two types of cubits," Sayyid elaborated. "There is the small cubit, the meh nedjes—that works out to approximately forty-five centimeters in length. And then there is the meh nisut—the royal cubit. That is a bit longer, at five-two centimeters."

"Well—more or less," Neil hedged as if he couldn't quite help himself. "The cubit rod that Lepsius found in the tomb of Maya came in at exactly fifty-two-point-three centimeters. But then Maspero found a cubit rod box at Lisht that indicated a measurement of closer to fifty-two-point-nine, so you see it isn't entirely clear that the standard remained consistent between the Old Kingdom and—"

Zeinab interrupted him. "Which cubit would Mr. Forster-Mowbray use?"

"Not Mr. Foster-Mowbray," Ellie modified. "It would be Professor Dawson who did the calculations."

Sayyid frowned thoughtfully. "If he was classically trained, he will most likely know the cubit through the Roman system of measurement—which aligns with the Egyptian meh nedjes. The small cubit."

Ellie felt a buzz of excitement. "But it was the *royal* cubit that served the standard unit of measurement in Ancient Egypt, wasn't it?"

"It's what was used to lay out the dimensions of the pyramids at Saqqara and Giza," Neil confirmed quickly.

"So Dawson's unit is off by seven centimeters!" Ellie concluded.

"Seven centimeters?" Constance echoed, unimpressed.

"Seven centimeters times eight hundred and fifty," Adam clarified. "Which works out to about a hundred and ninety feet." He met Ellie's eyes significantly. "Hundred and ninety feet can make a hell of a difference."

Ellie glanced back at the glow and racket of Julian's dig. "They're in the wrong place!"

"Should we simply let him be, then?" Jemmahor suggested.

"We cannot be sure that he would give up if he does not find what he is looking for in the first place he digs," Zeinab declared firmly. "And it is possible that your professor might realize his mistake."

"I… can't rule that out," Neil admitted uneasily. "He's not entirely ignorant of Egyptology. Just excessively sure of himself."

"That's one way of putting it," Adam added dryly.

Zeinab looked down at her sandals as her mind worked furiously. When she raised her head again, her eyes spoke of a decision. "I would like to know whether there is anything at the true location for him to find."

"Right." Adam sighed resignedly. "Hell. Fairfax, grab the back of my shirt."

"Your shirt?" Neil hurried after Adam as he moved across the ridge. "Why?"

"In case I pass out," Adam replied, stepping up to the edge of the cliff.

Zeinab joined him there, moving like a wisp of shadow.

Adam studied the opposite wall of the canyon. "Hundred and ninety feet's gonna take you right… about… there."

He pointed across the gap to a spot that looked like a bowl scooped out of the face of the ridge. The geological feature was framed on three sides by a crown of ragged stone and blocked from Julian's dig site by a narrow outcrop.

"How can you be sure that is the spot?" Zeinab demanded.

Adam met her gaze evenly. "I'm a surveyor. This is what I do." His expression shifted, his mouth tightening greenly. "And now I'm gonna lie down for a second."

He staggered back from the drop and collapsed onto the ground.

Zeinab shot Ellie a questioning look.

"He's… not overfond of heights," Ellie explained.

Zeinab studied the spot Adam had indicated. Her brow wrinkled with concentration. "It is possible we might examine the area without being seen—if we are very careful and *very* quiet."

Ellie felt a thrill of danger at the idea. Things would quickly go bad if they were discovered… but if any truth lay behind the text on the tablet, then an exploration of that ledge might reveal the true location of Neferneferuaten's tomb—and perhaps solve the mystery of the lost pharaoh's connection to the man the world knew as Moses.

"We'll need to cross about a quarter mile down and then backtrack," Adam commented from behind them, where he continued to lie flat on his back on the stones. "That's the only way to make sure those sentries don't spot us."

"Is there no chance that extremely attractive Bedouin and his cousin might join us?" Constance asked hopefully.

Ellie wasn't sure whether she was more eager for the assistance—or the view.

"No," Zeinab replied flatly.

She trudged off toward the hollow behind their perch, where Ellie could hear the occasional grunt and bray from the herd.

Ellie gave her brother a more thorough examination. Neil's waistcoat was missing a button, and his soft brown hair was in a state of disarray. "How are you, really?"

Neil hesitated before he replied. "Your Mr. Jacobs is terrifying."

"Yes." Ellie's skin chilled with the memory of her past encounters with the man.

"That professor, Dawson… he claimed that Jacobs always knows when someone is lying." Neil met Ellie's gaze with a wide-eyed trepidation. "And I… I think I actually believe him. Is that mad?"

Ellie found herself washed over with memories—of Jacob's icy confidence in the hotel in Belize Town. His tired, resigned certainty in the wilderness of the Cayo. The uncanny, impossible feeling that he simply *knew*.

Ellie forced the answer out. "No. I don't think you are."

"How is that possible?" Neil demanded. "To *always* know? I mean, I can see where a fellow might have a particular sense for the thing, which when looked at from a certain angle—"

"But it's more than that," Ellie cut in quietly.

Neil shook his head. "I don't understand any of this."

"Don't have to." Adam hauled himself back to his feet.

"Then what am I supposed to do?" Neil pushed back helplessly.

Adam clamped a hand on his shoulder, giving it a squeeze. "Stop the bad guys. Stay alive."

Zeinab returned in a swirl of black cloth, the ropes, lantern, and crowbar slung over her shoulder.

"If you are here to be useful," she declared authoritatively, "then come."

Without waiting for answers, she set out across the cliffs, a scrap of fluttering shadow slipping through the darkness.

Sayyid stared after her, his face drawn with worry. He glanced back at the rest of them, his eyes drifting from Constance and Adam to Ellie.

They stopped at Neil, and for a moment his gaze hardened, flashing with something that Ellie was startled to realize she recognized.

It looked like hurt.

He stalked after his wife without another word.

Neil hadn't noticed, lost in his own uneasy thoughts. "Is it possible to be both excited and abjectly terrified at the same time?"

"We might very well be on the verge of discovering the final resting place of one of the most important women in Egyptian history," Ellie replied. "And we are doing it under the noses of your villainous ex-employer, a batch of mercenaries, and an unflinchingly ruthless killer who can detect lies."

"So pretty much just your average day," Adam concluded.

"What are you all waiting for? Christmas?" Constance hissed as she hurried past them.

Neil cast a forlorn look up at the stars. "I miss books," he moaned and trudged after her.

Jemmahor hopped over the rocks like a long-legged gazelle. Umm Waseem swung her ubiquitous satchel over her shoulder and trundled after her.

Adam lingered at Ellie's side. The two of them stood alone together under a cobalt sky sparkling with a thousand stars. The wind that danced over her skin smelled of dust and time.

"I won't try to talk you out of coming along," Adam commented quietly. "I'm aware that would go over about as well as a sack of bricks. Even though there's a good chance this whole business could end with all of us being shot." Heat mingled with worry in his gaze. "But I'd appreciate it if you'd do whatever you could to stay alive for the rest of the night."

"I will if you will," Ellie replied softly.

The shadow of a smile tugged at his lip. It fell away as he glanced out across the canyon. "You really think the Staff of Moses is over there?"

"I think if there is even a chance," she replied deliberately, "then it is worth any cost to protect it."

Adam's calloused thumb smoothed gently over the curve of her cheek. "Suppose we'd better be getting on, then."

Ellie gazed up at him, memorizing the familiar lines of his face in the slender moonlight. "I supposed we had."

They set out across the ridge.

THIRTY-TWO

$\mathcal{N}$EIL FOLLOWED THE black-cloaked form of Sayyid's wife down the mountain, hoping he wasn't about to plummet to his doom. The path Zeinab picked along the steep face of stone would barely have accommodated a cat. It followed the line of an ancient washout rife with loose stones and slender ledges that fell straight down to the hard floor of the wadi.

The light from Julian's lanterns washed over the walls perhaps two hundred yards ahead, which still felt far too close. Voices echoed from the excavation site, laughing heartily or calling out orders before another spill of spoil was tipped over the ledge to rattle down into the gorge.

Neil's calves ached. His boots found every loose stone with an uncanny accuracy. He lost track of the number of times someone glared back at him in a silent imprecation to keep quiet.

He *was* keeping quiet. The cliff was making all the noise.

When they finally reached the ground, Neil breathed out a sigh of relief—one that cut short when he looked up at the wall of sheer, ragged stone that they now needed to climb on the opposite side.

Sayyid's wife led them up another precarious route of steep runnels and narrow perches that wound them back in the direction of Julian's excavation. The sounds of the dig grew louder as they neared it. Neil flinched at the bark of a rough cough and the crack of the pickaxes.

They rounded another turn, and Neil faced a moonlight-washed depression that looked as though it had been scooped out of the top of the ridge by the hand of a giant. The ledge was framed on three sides by steep, high walls of stone. On the fourth, the land fell away precipitously to the canyon floor.

The rest of the group tucked themselves into hiding places behind the boulders as they surveyed the terrain. Only Neil lingered—until Adam's hand clamped onto his shoulder and yanked him behind the cover of a ragged crust of limestone.

"Where does your hundred and ninety feet take us, exactly?" Zeinab demanded of Adam in a low murmur.

Adam crept forward to join her, keeping to the shadows with the grace of a jaguar. "Right there." He pointed a little beyond the center of the hollow curve of the rock, near to where Julian's lights spilled up from beyond a slight rise in the landscape.

Neil regarded the spot as his heart leapt, thudding powerfully at the base of his throat. Was it really possible that somewhere among those scattered boulders and pools of wind-blown sand lay the final resting place of one of the most mysterious and important pharaohs in Egyptian history?

The answers to so many puzzles must lie in Neferneferuaten's tomb—not the least of which was the true identity of the pharaoh herself. If Akhenaten's queen, Nefertiti, had indeed risen to rule in her own right after the death of her husband, her origin story remained rife with mysteries. No one knew who her parents had been. She had arrived in Egyptian royal life seemingly out of nowhere, rising from obscurity to claim first the love of a king, then the most powerful position in the empire.

Zeinab frowned with wary displeasure as she regarded the place Adam pointed out. "What are we looking for?"

"If there is a tomb here, the entrance would most likely have been dug into the cliff and then covered in rubble," Sayyid replied from where he hid a little further back under the shadow of the looming cliff.

Ellie crept forward to peer down into the barren, silent hollow. "I don't see much rubble."

"The Egyptians were very clever about disguising their tomb entrances," Sayyid returned. "We might have to look from exactly the right angle to see it."

"Then we will spread out and search," Zeinab declared.

Nobody questioned her order. The others—even the gangly young apprentice and the stout old fishwife—slipped down the rest of the steep, awkward distance to the floor of the depression.

As they reached the bottom, Constance set her hands on her hips and studied the curved wall of stone that framed their perch. The crown of the ridge rose perhaps forty feet overhead. "Someone really ought to scale the cliffs. There's no reason the Egyptians couldn't have dug their tomb a little further up."

"I'm good," Adam demurred flatly.

Constance's gaze shifted deliberately to Neil.

"I… uh…" Neil started uncomfortably.

"I will do it," Jemmahor cut in, adjusting the strap of the rifle that hung over her back before striding away. Neil watched the young woman find a grip on the stones and haul herself up.

"I'll take the side by the bad guys." Adam glanced over at Ellie as she let out a soft huff of irritation. "What?"

"Of course you are. And I'm going with you," she replied, and the pair set off.

Zeinab moved along the base of the cliffs like a flicker of black shadow. Constance started off toward another section, then stopped to glance back. "Aren't you coming?"

"I…" Neil turned his head to realize that Sayyid had wandered away from them, lingering at the place where the ground fell away into the canyon. "I'll join you in a moment."

Neil crossed over to his foreman—or was that his *former* foreman? The thought carried a healthy burst of guilt along with it. He looked down over the drop into the wadi. Even though the ledge stood only a little over halfway up the height of the ridge, the floor of the canyon still looked very far away.

It should have been easy to break the silence that lingered as he and Sayyid stood beside each other, but Neil found himself struggling to open a conversation. Everything that came into his mind sounded painfully awkward. The truth was, he hadn't the foggiest notion of what he *should* say to Sayyid. Should he apologize for the way his sister had come barreling in to overturn the man's life? Or for that wretched note he had sent to Julian Forster-Mowbray?

He wanted to tell Sayyid how much he wished he could go back to those months in Saqqara where they had worked side-by-side together in such comfort… but sensed the declaration wouldn't be entirely welcome.

"The bottom of the wadi looks oddly flat, doesn't it?" Neil offered instead.

Sayyid frowned down at the pale surface of the canyon floor. "I suppose," he distantly agreed.

They both kept their voices low. Neil was still painfully conscious of the lamplight spilling into the canyon from Julian's dig, which was just around the bend from where they stood.

"It almost looks like a road," Neil mused.

Sayyid opened his mouth to respond, and the furrow in his brow cleared, his eyes widening. "It *is* a road," he observed wonderingly.

Neil felt a spark of scholarly excitement. "And that slight rise in the grade over there? I mean, it could just be a natural declination—but one might almost imagine it to be a ramp of some sort."

"But why build a ramp in the middle of a canyon?" Sayyid returned carefully. "This hardly seems the place for chariot races."

"Maybe they were dragging something along," Neil replied a little absently. Something about the notion felt right.

Sayyid finally turned to look at him, his eyes narrowing with interest. "And what might they have been dragging?"

Ellie popped into place between them, leaning out over the ledge. "Goodness! Doesn't that look rather like the road at the quarry of Hatnub?"

Neil blinked at her in surprise while Sayyid raised his eyebrows.

"That ramp there would have been for dragging larger cuts of stone. Look—you can see the stairs cut to either side of it," Ellie elaborated.

She pointed, and Neil realized that he *could* see them. The steps were pale lines of light and shadow marking out a narrow space to either side of the softly graded ribbon of packed earth.

"But what do they need steps for?" Neil had to work to keep his voice down.

"For pushing along large slabs by pole and sledge, of course," Ellie returned. "Didn't you read Griffith and Newberry's report on the tombs at El Bersheh?"

"Of course I did," Neil retorted. "But I don't remember anything about poles and sledges."

"Well, it was more of a passing mention," Ellie said dismissively. "Only it does suggest the most intriguing theory about how the Egyptians might have used similar technology to raise blocks high enough to build the pyramids."

Only Ellie would manage to file a passing mention in an obscure excavation report away in her brain like a neatly coded library card, ready to pull out at the slightest peripheral reference. She had always had a prodigious knack for recalling anything that she had read.

That skill would have made her a formidable archaeologist in the field… had such a position ever been open to her.

She planted her hands on her hips, turning around to survey the cliff-ringed bowl with a frown. "We have been all the way around the walls, and there are no substantial piles of rubble to speak of—only boulders and sand. I cannot see anywhere that someone might have concealed a royal tomb."

Neil wondered if he ought to feel disappointed.

He was not immune to dreams of finding the lost tomb of an important pharaoh. What Egyptologist didn't hope to make the sort of discovery that would revolutionize the entire field? But Neil had always imagined himself doing it the proper way—in the broad light of day with an official concession from the government granting him permission to excavate.

First, there would be weeks of careful survey. When he finally uncovered the entrance to the tomb, he would be surrounded by government officials and newspaper reporters—along with his sponsors, of course. He could envision the speech he would have given.

I am honored to recover this lost evidence of Egypt's noble history, and I look forward to the wisdom and enlightenment that its careful study can grant to the scholars of the world.

Instead, he was creeping through the dark with a band of lady revolutionaries.

"I might have been wrong about the cubits," Sayyid admitted with a frown.

"I honestly don't think you were," Ellie insisted, then twitched the fabric of her skirt. "Oh! I seem to have acquired a passenger."

She shifted the folds of gray poplin, exposing the shining black carapace of a very large beetle clinging to her hem.

"Aeerrggh!" Sayyid exclaimed, taking an instinctive, panicked step back—which put him very near to tumbling off the edge of the cliff.

Neil caught him by the sleeve of his coat.

"It's just a scarab," Ellie protested.

The insect was the length of Neil's index finger, fat and glossy in the moonlight. Even he had to admit that it was larger than the usual type.

"But are there any more of them?" Sayyid pressed urgently. "Are any of them trying to climb my trousers?"

"I don't see any on your trousers." Ellie gave the fabric of her skirt a neat shake. In response, the scarab spread its wings and buzzed loose.

Sayyid ducked. "Where did it go?"

"It's all right," Ellie assured him. "It flew off that way."

She pointed across the depression in the vague direction of the continuing rattle and clanging of Julian's dig.

"Alhamdulillah," Sayyid noted with a fervent sigh of relief.

Neil was only half listening to him. He was still staring in the direction where the scarab had flown as something tickled at the back of his brain. The uncomfortable itch reminded him of the feeling he'd had when he first stood on the plain at Saqqara and looked at the place Sayyid had flagged out for their dig.

Not there, he had thought automatically. An irresistible tug had pulled at him from thirty meters to the southwest, where he could picture pylons and painted walls rising from the sand. *There.*

There, something whispered at him again as he gazed out over the still, moonlight-washed landscape. It felt like a flicker of movement—the soft slap of sandaled feet on sun-dry stone. Skin brushed with dust. Exhaustion mingling with purpose.

Neil followed it without quite realizing that he was moving.

"Where are you going?" Ellie demanded behind him.

"I just…" Neil trailed off distractedly—and then kept walking.

Sayyid's eyes narrowed thoughtfully. He cast Ellie a questioning look, and she frowned, but the pair fell into step behind Neil as he picked his way across the hollow.

He stopped in front of a large, flat boulder that hung suspended over the ground, the opening beneath it taking the form of a thin black gap. The shiny carapace of the scarab glittered against the surface of the rock. The bug wiggled its antennae at his approach before skittering over the stone and disappearing beneath it.

"Neil?" Ellie asked in a low and fairly urgent whisper. "What are we doing here?"

The sound of her voice pulled Neil out of a fog. He realized where he had come to stand—just below the natural wall that separated the hollow from Julian Forster-Mowbray's dig site. He was close enough that he could see where the yellow glare of Julian's lanterns painted the top of the stones. Individual voices emerged from the murmuring clamor of activity—Dawson's peevish complaints distinguishing themselves from the laughter of a pair of Al-Saboors.

Neil startled, coming back to himself sharply. This was the *last* place he wanted to be. Should anyone from Julian's excavation wander uphill, he would be immediately visible to them, spotlit like a bug under a looming shoe.

"I… I don't…" He trailed off as something about the boulder beside him tugged irresistibly at the back of his mind—then blurted out the rest, both embarrassed by the words and utterly certain that they were true. "There's something here."

Sayyid's gaze was quietly thoughtful.

Ellie raised a skeptical eyebrow. "There's no rubble here that could conceal a tomb entrance."

She was right. Constructing a tomb was a massive undertaking. Any entrance would have needed to be large and accessible enough for transporting hundreds of tons of spoil carved from the core of the mountain, never mind the myriad grave goods that would accompany a royal burial.

His mind still rang quietly with the sound of sandaled footsteps.

With a burst of irrational determination, Neil crawled beneath the boulder.

The ground sloped softly downward, forming a little cave just high enough for Neil to move from wriggling on his stomach to a crouch. The space was black as pitch.

"Does anyone have a light?" he asked awkwardly, whispering back at the pale line of the gap he had crawled through.

He heard rustling cloth and quick, soft footsteps. A moment later, Ellie's hand thrust into the opening, holding one of Zeinab's shuttered lanterns. She lowered her face down to peer in at him.

"Are you all right?" she asked.

Neil's first instinct was to brush her off, but the careful concern in her tone held him back. He realized what she must be seeing—her rational, cautious brother crouching in a claustrophobic hole for no apparent reason.

Was he fine?

"I just… want to take a look," he returned awkwardly.

He carefully slid open the shutter on the lamp.

Golden light flooded the space around him, revealing the jagged underbelly of the boulder… and a small army of shining black scarabs.

"Oh bugger," Neil bit out, then threw himself down as the insects took flight, whizzing furiously around the tight space.

They shot around him in a hissing storm… and then spilled into a dark, ragged crack in the ground nearby.

"What was that?" Sayyid demanded nervously from outside.

"Er… nothing?" Neil offered back unconvincingly.

He crawled to his knees, moving over to the edge of the fissure. The dark opening zigzagged across the stone like a bolt of black lightning, widening to perhaps eighteen inches before thinning to a jagged line.

A lingering black scarab crawled over the side of the gap and disappeared.

Neil had never been particularly bothered by bugs, unlike his foreman. He still found that he had to steel himself against an instinctive sense of horror in order to carefully lower the lantern into the hole.

A beetle flew out of the fractured stone, buzzing at Neil's face. He shooed at it furiously with his free hand, biting out a curse. Then he brought the lantern lower and the flickering light washed over what lay inside the ragged fissure.

He was only vaguely aware of rustling of cloth behind him. A moment later, Ellie slid into place at his side.

"What is it?" she asked.

Neil stared into a cavity that went down, down, down into the heart of the mountain, its lamplight-washed walls peppered here and there with the iridescent bodies of lingering scarabs.

"We need to go in there," he declared, his voice tight with both certainty and unease.

THIRTY-THREE

THE SPACE UNDER the boulder had grown crowded. Zeinab had arrived a few moments before, immediately taking charge. She crouched over the fissure in her black abaya, carefully withdrawing the lantern.

Neil was squished in between her and Ellie. The others hovered outside—all except for Sayyid, who had displayed no interest in getting a turn under the rock.

"I have no desire to crawl into a scarab nest," he declared firmly.

A coil of rope spilled through the gap, sliding to a stop near Neil's boots. Adam lowered his face into view behind it. "We've tied it off," he reported. "You should be all set."

"Dr. Fairfax?" Zeinab prompted impatiently.

Neil quailed—but he was the one who had found the opening in the rocks and insisted on investigating it. Who else did he expect would squeeze into the fissure to see where it led?

"Shouldn't Bates do it?" he blurted out hopefully.

"I've got about thirty pounds on you, buddy," Adam replied from outside.

"Maybe I should go," Constance eagerly suggested, dropping down beside him to peer in at Neil and the others. "I'm the smallest of us, and if there are any wild animals down there, I have a better chance of overcoming them than he does."

"How's that?" Neil returned with a note of panic. "Why would you be better at dealing with wild animals than I would?"

"Isn't it obvious?" Constance returned.

"Dr. Fairfax goes," Zeinab ordered. "Preferably quickly, before someone from that dig hears all of the talking you are doing."

She punctuated the remark with a glare at the rest of the party, who quickly clammed up.

Neil stared down at the dark mouth of the fissure. The opening looked barely wide enough for him to squeeze into, which begged unpleasant thoughts of what might happen to him if he got stuck.

"Dr. Fairfax goes," Neil echoed in a wretched whisper. "And why wouldn't he? Who else is qualified to descend into a pit full of beetles?"

But even as he loathed the notion of lowering himself into an unknown scarab-lined hole in the mountain, another part of him was drawn toward the fissure like a moth to the moon.

Yes, his instincts urged. *This is right.*

He faced the descent with a new sense of determination. "Pass me the lamp."

"You are not taking the lamp," Zeinab replied.

"What?!" Neil exclaimed.

"You cannot climb down a rope while you are carrying it. I will lower it down to you once you are inside."

Neil imagined climbing forever until the rope simply ran out. Or perhaps he might get caught in the increasingly tight space until he was no longer able to move.

Or the gap in the floor might open into a labyrinthine and inescapable cave system where Neil would slowly die of thirst.

"Couldn't you drop the light down there first?" he suggested hopefully.

"Who would untie it so that we could bring the rope back up for you?" Zeinab returned. "And what if you kicked it over when you landed? We only have two lanterns. We cannot risk one getting broken."

"I'm not going to kick it over!" Neil protested.

Zeinab answered him with a raised eyebrow.

With a resigned lurch in his gut, Neil took off his spectacles, tucking them carefully into the pocket of his waistcoat. He shuffled awkwardly around the two women until he was positioned above the fissure.

He slid his legs into the opening, then took the rope in both hands, pulling to test it. It held firm against whatever Adam had tied it to.

In all probability, there was very little chance that it would come loose and plummet him into an impenetrable abyss from which he would never escape.

"Get on with it already!" Constance hissed through the entrance slightly above him. "Some of us would like to know what's down there before we die of old age!"

Neil flushed with embarrassment and lowered himself into the gap.

The space was tight. Stone scraped at the back of his waistcoat as he slid inside. He struggled to find footholds, as there was barely any room to maneuver his legs. He tried to brace himself with his back and his knees instead, quickly earning a few new scrapes.

A scarab took flight near his ear, buzzing an inch from his nose as it dove past him. The surprise of it nearly made him lose his grip on the rope.

He fell, skidding down the fissure. The fibers of the rope rasped against his palms as he tightened his grip and lurched to a stop.

A spill of dust showered down on him from above. The back of his waistcoat snagged against the rock.

He sneezed.

"Keep quiet!" Zeinab hissed.

She glared down at Neil from above, her sharp features lit by the soft glow of the lantern he had left behind. Constance joined her, her face framed by tendrils of dark hair that had come loose from her Gibson.

She frowned. "All I can see is Stuffy!"

"He'll get out of the way in a minute," Zeinab replied.

Little stones peppered his face as Neil dropped himself lower—and swung his boot out into nothing. It waved there helplessly, his efforts to find a foothold utterly failing.

He nearly let go of the rope in shock and dismay. He managed to stop himself after another short slide, his palms burning.

Neil's other foot reached the nothingness. He flailed until he caught the rope between his boots, which took some of the weight from his aching shoulders.

Thick, silent darkness surrounded him.

His arms made another fiery protest, and he forced himself to climb, sliding awkwardly down until his soles struck the ground.

Neil planted them there, terrified to move lest he step over the edge of some hidden abyss and plummet to his doom.

"What is happening?" Zeinab demanded impatiently.

Neil could just make out her face overhead. "I think I found the bottom."

"Then will you release the rope?" she pressed dryly.

Neil realized that he had been clinging to it like a lifeline. He hurriedly let go, and the rope slithered up in front of him like a quick-moving snake.

His eyes began to adjust. Just enough distant light filtered down through the fractured stone to let him make out the vaguest form of the space around him. He instinctively fumbled at his pocket for his spectacles and slid them on… which made absolutely no difference at all. He was left with only the dim impression of a still, silent space that had more in common with a grave than anywhere else.

He brushed his burning palms on his trousers and waited, trying not to feel utterly abandoned in the dark.

A soft glow rose from above him. Neil breathed a shuddering sigh of relief as he looked up to see the lantern bobbing down through the fissure.

As it reached the bottom, illumination spilled over the space that surrounded him. It burst into startling color—blue, green, and gold leaping out at Neil from the walls.

Palm trees bent over stands of papyrus flowers. Courtiers rode on barges rowed by lines of slaves with glossy, curling hair. Spears flashed over charging chariots while leopards lunged toward waiting prey.

A mother held a child to her breast. Worshipers piled up offerings under a golden sun.

Neil wasn't in a cave. He was standing in a gallery—a long hallway painted in rich color from floor to ceiling.

"Well?" Ellie's urgent tones echoed down to him from above. "What do you see?"

"Everything," Neil replied, his voice thick with wonder.

The images were bold and pristine as if someone had just paused working on them to step out to lunch—as if Neil might turn and find a paintbrush discarded on the floor, its tip still wet with rich red ocher.

His gaze stopped on an image of the sun. Some of the plaster below had broken away with the weight of time, taking part of the artwork with it, but Neil could still see the myriad rays that fell down from the golden disk, ending in delicately cupped hands. One of them caressed the remains of a linen-clad shoulder. Another brushed against the distinct curve of a crown—the white hedjet of Upper Egypt.

"It's a tomb," Neil forced out through the shock and awe that had paralyzed him, his voice hoarse. "An Amarna period tomb."

A whispered, excited consultation sounded from atop the fissure, and Sayyid's wife called down again.

"Does it look as though it is about to fall in on you?"

Neil tore his attention from the paintings to answer her question. He skimmed past the art to look at the walls themselves, picking out the fine lines in the plaster before he raised his gaze to the ceiling.

It was covered in glittering golden stars. The sight of them stole his voice.

"There are hairline fractures," he reported when he was able to speak again. "I can see two places where some of the plaster has broken away. And the fissure in the ceiling goes another several yards down the hall."

He thought nervously of just how much stone must be pressing down on that crack from above. Neil swallowed thickly. "But nothing appears to be actively unstable."

Neil startled as a pair of sandaled feet slipped through the gap above him, and Zeinab slithered down the rope like a gymnast.

A small pile of rubble lay by Neil's boots, fragments of the ceiling that had crumbled to the ground with whatever minor seismic activity had opened the crack in the first place. Neil skipped around it to make way as Zeinab landed.

She automatically stepped aside, the line of her mouth tightening with worry as she studied the murals.

Ellie descended behind her. Her eyes went wide as soon as she dropped past the ceiling. "I see archers!" she exclaimed. "And wine makers! And a temple dancer!"

The rope spun her in a lazy circle as she craned her neck to try not to lose her view.

"Bet you can see it better from the ground, Princess," Adam called down wryly.

Ellie slid the rest of the way down and hurried over to a portrait of nobly dressed hunters pursuing a diverse array of water birds. She gazed at it with an expression of pure joy, raising her hand to where a heron swept up from the clustered reeds, each feather depicted in perfect detail. Her fingers hovered above the ancient pigments as she drew in a careful, uneven breath, her eyes glistening.

"Aw hell," came the sound of Adam's voice from above.

Ellie forced her attention away from the paintings to call up to him. "Are you stuck?"

"Just… a little… tight…" Adam grunted, and a scattering of stones came loose to join the rubble under the fissure. "Got it. Guess I should've laid off the extra kofta."

He dropped from the opening, his battered boots landing solidly on the ground. As he straightened, his broad shoulders took up most of the span of the hallway.

"I don't think the kofta are the problem," Neil commented a little weakly.

Adam's expression sobered as he took in the wonder around them. He crossed over to where Ellie lingered, her eyes shimmering with joyful tears as she studied the vivid artwork.

"It's… I…" she began, helpless to find the words.

Adam slipped an arm around her shoulders. "Yeah," he agreed softly.

Neil was feeling shaky himself. The images that lined the hall were beautifully rendered snapshots of life in Egypt three thousand years ago, from the farmers in their fields to warriors flying into battle.

One figure in particular began to leap out at him from the murals—a woman with high cheekbones, fine almond-shaped eyes, and generous lips. The gold-wrapped cylinder of a false beard extended from her chin, a masculine kilt wrapping her curved hips. Her elegant head carried the weight of all the various crowns of Egypt—the double pschent, the striped and cobra-topped nemes headdress, and even the broad blue kephresh, worn when the pharaoh marched to war.

She was everywhere—holding her hands out over ripe fields of wheat as the rays of the Aten brushed her shoulders. Riding into battle with a lance in her hand, feet braced on the floor of her chariot. Raising up offerings to her god or playing with infants on her knee. She stood over every aspect of life in Egypt, from the pressing of grapes to the raising of monuments, her slender hands outstretched to offer bounty or serve justice.

"It's her, isn't it?" Ellie breathed from beside him as Neil stared at an image of the woman scattering seeds while washed by the compassionate rays of her sun. "It's Nefertiti."

"Neferneferuaten," Neil countered, his voice still numb with awe. "She isn't a queen here. She's pharaoh." His gaze drifted along the hall, every inch of which was rich with color. "This is *Neferneferuaten's* story."

"She must have been extraordinary," Ellie softly said with a reverent look at the noble figure on the wall.

Neil found himself struck by the significance of Ellie's observation. Even if Nefertiti had been named heir by her husband before his death, women in Egypt did not come to hold the throne without exerting a great deal of power, cleverness, and determination. There would have been rivals to overcome, generals to woo, courtiers to manipulate—and then the immense challenge of ruling itself. The pharaoh of Egypt had led an empire that stretched from the Mediterranean to the mountain forests of Punt, a distance of over two thousand miles.

That Neferneferuaten's name had fallen into obscurity—nearly disappearing into the cracks of history—spoke more to the enemies who had come after her than it did to the scale of her accomplishments.

That, and the unusually short length of her reign.

The reminder that the elegant, powerful woman depicted on the walls of the hallway had ruled for only three or four years before succumbing to some unknown fate was sobering.

"Oh, it's beautiful!" Constance exclaimed as she released the rope and stepped into the tomb, looking around with wide-eyed wonder.

Sayyid descended behind her and immediately hurried from place to place along the murals. "But there are the offerings being made at the Great Temple of the Aten! And a depiction of the pharaoh as sphinx—and there's the royal family in the Window of Appearances!"

His eyes sought Neil from across the hall, alight with a shared understanding of the immensity of the discovery as he instinctively looked for the person he knew would understand its significance. Neil beamed back at him, warmed by it—until the light flickered, then shuttered entirely as Sayyid quickly turned away.

"That is all of us. Jemmahor and Umm Waseem will stay above to keep watch."

Zeinab's words were a splash of cold water. In his excitement over the painted hall, Neil had nearly forgotten that he wasn't entering this extraordinary place as part of a proper scientific expedition. This survey was happening under the noses of a batch of ruthless villains who would happily shoot the lot of them.

"But where did all of those bugs go?" Constance wondered.

"Good question," Adam commented, pulling his focus from the paintings to look more carefully around the hall.

"One might expect them to have scurried away under cover," Ellie suggested, lifting one of the larger pieces of debris piled under the fissure with the toe of her boot.

A cluster of shiny black scarabs scurried out from beneath it. Sayyid skipped back with a gurgled noise of protest as they raced past him, darting to the end of the hall, which still lay in relative gloom.

"Could I have the light?" Neil distractedly asked.

Zeinab handed Neil a lantern.

The shadows fled as he pressed forward, revealing a door made up of two narrow panels framed by carved posts and a stone lintel. The scarabs shimmied through the bottom corner, where the ground had shifted over the centuries to open a narrow gap.

The panels were carved with the dim forms of a pair of noble figures. As Neil drew closer, the soft glow of the lamplight fell more fully across the carvings.

The material of the door captured the illumination and shone with it as though from within.

"Goodness!" Ellie said as she joined him. "Is that alabaster?"

"I... think it is," Neil returned wonderingly.

The stone was subtly translucent, shining with a pale ivory hue. The glow made the images carved on its surface flare to astonishingly vivid life.

On the left stood the woman who appeared in so many other places in the hall—the pharaoh Neferneferuaten, who had once been Queen Nefertiti.

Facing her, hand extended, was a tall man with sharp cheekbones and a long jaw, his figure lanky save for the soft droop of a potbelly.

His face was one that Neil knew almost as well as his own.

"Isn't that…" Ellie began.

"Akhenaten," Neil finished for her, his voice tight.

The visionary pharaoh who had revolutionized Egyptian life. Who had birthed a new faith, one whose influence might very well still be felt across the world. Genius or tyrant, prophet or heretic—the views on who he was and what he meant to history were as varied as the stars.

Akhenaten's reign was known for its hyper-realistic artistic style, one that may have even over-emphasized the physical imperfections of its subjects. In the glowing panels of the alabaster door, Neil could see the crow's feet accenting Neferneferuaten's eyes. Her husband had the body of a scholar rather than the warrior's physique imposed upon most other pharaonic images of the New Kingdom, regardless of how well they actually fit the men being depicted.

The flaws only made the two figures feel more real—more *human* as they glimmered magnificently from the rare and precious stone.

Sayyid hung back a step, torn between his desire to examine the panels and his trepidation about the possibility of more scarabs.

"There are a few Old Kingdom alabaster quarries to the south of here," he noted. "The builders of the tomb might have mined the material there and carried it to the wadi."

Sayyid's revelation did not come as a surprise to Neil. Egypt was riddled with quarries. How else could the Egyptians have built their massive monuments and temples? They had sought out places in the hills and mountains framing the Nile where particular varieties of stone could be found, then either scooped them out like taking fruit from a bowl or cut straight into cliffs to carve out what they wanted.

Alabaster was perhaps the most sought-after and precious stone in the Egyptian world. These two doors alone were masterpieces.

"It's terribly sad, though. Isn't it?"

Neil startled at the sound of Constance's voice. He had been so absorbed in the discovery that he hadn't noticed her arrival.

She was standing very close to him. The hallway was narrow, and they had to avoid brushing against the delicate artwork on the walls. Her proximity triggered an involuntary flush.

It was a silly physical reflex, and Neil rallied himself against it. She might be a lovely young woman, but she was still *Connie*. He hardly needed to act like a stammering adolescent just because she came nearby.

"Sad?" he echoed in purely professional tones.

"When the door opens, it will pull them apart," Constance pointed out.

Neil felt a less-than-entirely-professional pang at her words.

Constance was right, of course. When the doors parted, Akhenaten and the pharaoh who had once been his queen would be torn from each other—just as death had divided them three thousand years before.

The poignant twist in his heart surprised him. He was a scholar, after all, not a romantic.

Perhaps the notion hit him harder because so much of the art of the Amarna period showed the royal family together in such ordinary ways—celebrating, worshiping, or playing with their children. It made Akhenaten and his queen feel like people that Neil had actually known.

He glanced down at Constance. Her eyes were wide and liquid with sympathy.

"But *can* it be opened?" Zeinab demanded impatiently from behind them.

Neil straightened, trying to shake off the unexpected wave of emotion and act like the scholar he was supposed to be. "New Kingdom tomb entrances were typically blocked up with rubble and then sealed over with plaster from the outside—not that we can usually see much of it. It's always been ripped away by looters."

"How do you know that this is the entrance?" Zeinab pressed. "And not a passage deeper into the tomb?"

Neil opened his mouth to answer—and realized he didn't have one.

"Well, it's…" he began. "I mean, obviously…"

Sayyid shot him another of those impenetrable, thoughtful looks. "I think Dr. Fairfax is correct. The entrance to the tomb is typically where one would expect to find these imprecations against disturbing the burial."

He gestured to a block of hieroglyphs on the wall.

"You mean curses?" Constance brightened with interest. "I was hoping for a good curse! It really wouldn't be a proper tomb without one."

Neil peered over Sayyid's shoulder and smirked with a hint of old mischief. "Looks like it's your favorite. *Keper… wanam'ef… san.* 'It is the scarab who will eat him,'" he finished cheerfully.

"*Khep*er," Sayyid corrected him automatically, making the guttural, distinctively Arabic sound at the back of his throat.

"If this is the front door, why'd they build it into the middle of the mountain?" Adam asked, frowning absently as he brushed some of the dust from his hair.

Neil turned to stare at him, as did the others.

"Based on how far we are from that fissure, this oughta be sitting right in the middle of the ridge," Adam clarified with a wave at the alabaster panels.

Ellie looked from the crack in the ceiling to where they stood. "Of course! How very odd."

"Perhaps it's a false door," Neil suggested.

"A false door?" Mrs. Al-Ahmed prompted.

"They are a common feature in tombs of this period," Sayyid explained. "They are generally believed to serve as a means of communication between the mundane world and the afterlife. But one usually finds them in burial chambers, not corridors."

"If it's false, why does it have hinges?" Constance countered.

She pointed up at the top corner of the alabaster slab, where a round bronze peg was just visible through the slight gap between the glowing stone panel and the bedrock.

"That… admittedly looks very much like a hinge," Neil conceded, blinking at it with surprise.

Ellie plucked a pin from her hair. She slipped it carefully into the thin crack between the two sides of the door, prodding gently. "There is something blocking the far side."

"Rubble, perhaps?" Neil suggested. "Or the seals of the necropolis?"

"Or the mountain," Adam offered dryly.

"Why don't we just open it and see?" Constance suggested.

Neil stiffened, a posture he saw echoed in Sayyid's red cheeks and Ellie's sudden stillness.

"I'm sorry, but that isn't strictly—" he began.

"Connie, one must really ensure that the context has been fully documented before—" Ellie started.

"The stone would need to be thoroughly inspected and stabilized—" Sayyid hurriedly offered.

Zeinab silenced them with her authoritative tones. "It does not matter. If it is blocked from the other side, then it is not the entrance to the burial chamber—and that means it is not where we need to go."

Without waiting, she turned and stalked back up the corridor, her black abaya swirling magnificently around her ankles.

Ellie lingered by Neil's side as the others followed. "Though one does have to wonder… if this opens into the middle of a mountain, then where did those scarabs go?"

Her words rang through Neil's mind with a strange significance as he stared at the softly glowing images of the two kings—husband and wife, separated by a thin black line that led to who-knew-where.

THIRTY-FOUR

$\mathcal{P}$RIESTESSES SHAKING SISTRUMS, papyrus stalks heavy with white blooms, children playing in the halls of a palace—Adam was surrounded by a vanished world.

The hallway was a revelation. The three Egyptologists in their party were gasping over references to rituals or courtly activities they'd all read about in books. Adam might not have known what a Sed festival was, but he was fully capable of appreciating the paradigm-shattering importance of the artwork that surrounded him.

He just wished they weren't exploring it with a ticking clock looming over them.

The Mustache wasn't going to dig into a random piece of the mountain forever. Eventually, he'd figure out that he was in the wrong spot—and start looking for the right one. Adam had no illusions that the two ladies upstairs, Jemmahor and Umm Waseem, could hold off a small army of Al-Saboors. If Julian's men realized Ellie and the others were down here, the best possible scenario was that one of the two Egyptian ladies managed to get through the fissure in time to warn them before the bad guys showed up.

That still left them all cornered in a hole in the ground with only one way out.

Past the crack in the ceiling through which they'd entered, the hallway sloped gently down, tunneling deeper into the mountain. The timeless stillness and the scent of old stone reminded Adam of another piece of lost history he'd stumbled into not so long ago—namely the caves beneath the city of Tulan.

Those tunnels had concealed secrets that had turned Adam's world upside down—and nearly cost him and Ellie their lives.

The painted passage ended at another doorway. This one was completely covered over in plaster.

"It's intact!" Ellie's tone was bright with excitement. She whirled to Adam. "Don't you see? If the plaster is unbroken, it means no one has been down here since the pharaoh's body was laid to rest somewhere beyond this barrier. We could be looking at an untouched royal Amarna burial!"

Adam eyed the yellowed material. It still showed ridges in places from the movements of an ancient trowel. "That's not all the same stuff. The discoloration is slightly off here in the middle. Looks to me like it's a different compound or something put on a bit more recently."

Neil moved in for a closer look, adjusting his spectacles. "You're right. There's a swath of newer plaster in the center. You can see where it overlaps some of the royal seals."

"If a tomb was looted during antiquity, it was sometimes closed up again by the priests of the necropolis." Sayyid frowned thoughtfully. "But the necropolis here at Amarna would have been abandoned during the reign of Ay, if not even earlier, in Tutankhamun's time. That is a very narrow window of time for a looting and official restoration."

"So maybe it wasn't official," Adam offered.

Sayyid contemplated his suggestion with a raised eyebrow. "I don't see any seals on the newer plaster. Had it been a ritual closing, the priests would have stamped it again."

"So was the tomb looted or not?" Constance demanded.

Adam met Ellie's eyes. He could see the worry in them, and it struck a pang through him. He knew damned well what it felt like to stumble across a forgotten part of the past, only to find out somebody else had already come along and torn it to pieces. That was why he'd stopped putting the Mayan sites he'd found on the maps he was paid to draw.

This place—and this woman, this Neferneferuaten—were obviously important to Ellie. The notion that they might come this far only to find a bunch of rubble on the other side had to be killing her. It was killing him a little, and he hadn't been wondering over the mysteries of the Amarna period for the last ten years.

"Somebody came down here after the burial was closed," Neil reasoned. "But what sort of thief robs a tomb and then closes it up again nicely afterward?"

"Maybe they weren't thieves," Adam cut in with a spark of inspiration— and a dart of relief. "Thought we were here because someone might've come along and put something *in* this tomb—not taken things out."

"*And this is the will of Moseh,*" Neil recited softly, his eyes on the broken seals, "*that his legacy, the gift of Neferneferuaten, be not misused or fallen into the hands of enemies.*"

"But why would Moses put his staff here?" Ellie wondered urgently. "In the tomb of an Atenist pharaoh?"

"Enough talking," Zeinab fixed them all with a green-eyed glare. "Or have you forgotten that there are men above who mean to take this tomb's secrets for themselves, no matter if they need to kill us all to do it? We must know what is here that is worth protecting."

Ellie cast an aching look back at the beautiful artwork that lined the hallway. "But *all* of it needs to be protected!"

Adam slipped a hand over her shoulder. "Sometimes you can't save all of it," he said, the words rougher with feeling than he'd intended. "Sometimes you just save what you can."

Ellie met his eyes. Her gaze softened, and Adam knew she was thinking of that other cave in the Cayo—the one where he'd fallen to his knees before a pile of shattered pots and ravaged bones.

Zeinab stepped forward with the crowbar in her hands. Neil shifted to make way for her. Only Sayyid lingered, gazing mournfully at the layered plaster on the door.

"This is not the way we should be doing this," he said quietly.

The hardness in Zeinab's face fell away, her eyes darkening with sympathy. "I know, ya habibi," she replied softly. "Wallah, I wish we lived in a world where you could open this tomb with all the tenderness of a mother—but the imperialists have left us no room for that. We may only stand by to watch as they take what is ours… or fight back however we can."

She touched his face, fingers brushing gently against the dark hair of his beard as Sayyid drew in a heavy breath.

"Let me do it," he said.

Zeinab stepped back.

"Mr. Bates—could I use your knife?" Sayyid asked sadly.

Adam pulled the machete from the sheath at his waist, flipped it expertly in his hand, and extended the hilt to him.

Sayyid set the tip of the blade to the plaster—and then drew it down, scoring a deep line through the length of the doorway. Dust trickled over his shoes.

He offered the machete back to Adam. "You keep your blade sharp," he commented sadly.

Adam silently took the knife back.

"The crowbar." Sayyid held out his hand.

Constance passed it to him with uncharacteristic reverence.

He pushed the iron hook into the slender gap revealed by the scored plaster. He held it there for a moment, leaning forward and closing his eyes.

A dua for forgiveness fell from his lips, and he wrenched the iron back.

The scrape of stone echoed up the passageway. Plaster popped around the top and sides of the panel, spurting out little clouds of white powder.

Sayyid set down the crowbar and gripped the exposed edge of the door. "Mr. Bates?" he prompted.

Adam joined him and hauled back against the stone. It pivoted on another concealed hinge, opening onto a steep, narrow staircase. Lamplight spilled over the first few steps. The rest descended into darkness.

"Who should go first?" Ellie eyed the shadowy tunnel with both excitement and trepidation.

"Whoever it is, they had best watch for booby traps," Constance piped in helpfully, rising up onto the toes of her boots to peer over Ellie's shoulder.

"There is no such thing as booby traps," Neil countered impatiently. "They're a ludicrous invention of adventure novelists."

"That's not entirely accurate," Ellie countered. "There are contemporary documents that indicate the First Qin Emperor of China was entombed in an enormous mausoleum threaded through with rivers of mercury and crossbows that would shoot at anyone who stepped in the wrong place."

"But no one has ever excavated the tomb of Qin Shi Huang!" Neil complained. "That's just propaganda to deter thieves!"

"Ancient Egyptians used curses to protect their tombs," Sayyid offered. "Promises of untold pain and eternal suffering that would be inflicted on anyone who violated their rest."

The rest of the group regarded him with various degrees of unease.

"But not—ah—booby traps," he finished uncomfortably.

"I'll go," Neil declared irritably and stalked out onto the first stair.

The rock promptly gave way beneath his shoe, and Neil dropped like a stone.

Sayyid was a step ahead of Adam. He dove as Neil plummeted, throwing his arms around Neil's chest and catching him just before he disappeared through the collapse.

Sayyid slid across the floor as Neil's weight dragged him down.

Adam threw himself across Sayyid's legs. Grasping him by the ankles, he pivoted, slamming his boots up against the stone to either side of the door.

"Fiddlesticks!" Ellie burst out.

Behind her, Zeinab took one look at the scene and raced up the hallway.

Adam could hear her shouting through the fissure to the women above.

"You are heavier than you look," Sayyid complained, his voice tight with strain.

"I'm not trying to be!" Neil called back in a panic.

He'd fallen completely through the hole in the stairs. Only Sayyid's tenacious grip kept him from plummeting down to whatever lay below.

Hopefully not a pit full of razors, Adam thought ruefully.

"Neither of you are a piece of cake," Adam bit out, adjusting his sliding grip on Sayyid's feet.

"Perhaps if I just… swung my leg up here…" Neil offered helpfully.

Chips of stone from the edge of the hole broke away as he moved, pinging down into the black abyss.

"No!" Adam and Sayyid shouted simultaneously.

Zeinab skidded back to them with a coil of rope in her hands. "Apologies, habibi," she said, and then clambered unceremoniously across Sayyid's back.

He let out an *oof* of protest as she leaned over him and whipped the rope around Neil's body.

She scrambled back, digging a knee into Adam's thigh, and threw the other end of the rope to Ellie.

"Pull!" Zeinab ordered, and the two women hauled at their lines. Constance rushed to join them, the heels of her kid boots digging against the ground. The tension in Sayyid's body started to shift—and suddenly everything was moving.

Neil spilled across Adam and Sayyid, the three of them tumbling into a tangled mess of limbs. Adam found himself staring up at the ceiling with somebody's ankle propped on his shoulder.

Constance's face appeared above him, eyes bright with excitement. "That was splendid!"

Ellie appeared beside her, lines of worry creasing her brow. "Are you all right?"

"I would be," Neil gasped thinly in reply, "if Sayyid would take his elbow out of my diaphragm!"

"Think that might be my elbow," Adam replied, shifting the limb in question.

Neil groaned with relief.

A sturdy hand clasped Adam's arm, helping to lever him to his feet. He rose to face Sayyid's wife and cocked an impressed eyebrow.

"I'll haul Stuffy out," Constance announced, hooking her hands under Neil's shoulders.

He popped free and flopped over while Sayyid staggered upright.

"Was it a bottomless pit, then?" Constance asked hopefully.

"Ancient Egyptians did not build bottomless pits!" Neil's spectacles had gone a bit sideways. He adjusted them, which resulted in them skewing wrong the other way. His brown hair was glazed with dust.

"Tell that to the one that just tried to swallow you," Constance countered. "But how shall we get past it?"

Adam moved over to the doorway, peering down at the collapse. "Anybody got a light?"

Ellie pushed a lantern into his hand. He extended it over the opening, and the glow spilled down into a pit.

"Not bottomless," Adam declared. "Looks about twenty-five feet deep."

"I think I would rather not have known that," Neil returned queasily.

Adam was feeling a little queasy himself. Twenty-five feet might not be bottomless, but it was just far enough to make his head spin.

He forced himself to stick around for another breath as he examined the interior of the hole. "It's all just rock," he reported. "Walls look oddly regular for a cave, though."

He pulled back as another wave of dizziness threatened to overwhelm him. "The edge of it lines up with the left half of the stairs. Should be able to go along all right if we stick to that side."

Adam tried not to think about how much his suggestion sounded like walking along an ancient tightrope.

"I'll lead the way," Constance happily offered, hopping over the gap.

They descended the stairs without falling into any more deadly pits. The passage was close and low enough that Adam had to duck to navigate it. There were no paintings on the walls, only roughly carved stone that seemed to grow thicker and heavier as they moved deeper into the heart of the ridge.

The steps stopped at another doorway. Instead of hinged panels like the others they had found, this one was closed off with only an ancient slab of wood.

"Not quite as elaborate as the one upstairs, is it?" Constance mused, eyeing it a little critically.

"Perhaps this stairwell was considered a less important part of the tomb," Ellie offered.

"Or it was not finished." Sayyid nodded at the stone lintel. "There are holes drilled there as though meant for another set of stone doors."

"Neferneferuaten only ruled for a short time," Neil reminded them as he stared at the dusty boards.

"Perhaps they didn't have enough time to complete her tomb before she needed to use it," Ellie filled in.

"Was she very old when she became the king?" Constance asked.

"No," Neil replied. "She would not have been old at all."

"Begs the question of what did her in," Adam noted soberly.

He didn't know a fraction of the Egyptian history that Ellie, Neil, and Sayyid did, but he recognized that a woman stepping into the role of king would have been fairly revolutionary—even if she hadn't been part of some crazy new faith that her husband had imposed on the entire country. Maybe she'd died of the same plague that Neil had said killed Akhenaten… but it seemed to Adam that a lady like that would have accumulated plenty of enemies.

The thought made him a little sad.

"We should move it carefully," Sayyid said with a tired sigh as he studied the wooden screen that blocked their way.

"I'll help," Neil offered.

The two Egyptologists each took a side, carefully lifting the slab and shifting it gingerly to the wall. As they moved, the glow of Zeinab's lamp spilled into the space that lay beyond.

Light flared back from within. For a moment, those sparkling glimmers were all Adam could discern. Then his vision adjusted—and the wonders inside came into focus.

The chamber was packed. Elegant furniture crowded the space, rich with lapis blue and ruddy ocher—chairs accented with gold leaf and cabinets stuffed with gray bundles that would once have been fine linens.

Statues watched them with jewel-like glass eyes beside tables piled with urns and vases.

Though jammed full like a rummage sale, everything looked carefully arranged in tidy stacks and piles.

"Not looted," Adam concluded, numb with awe.

"It would seem not," Ellie replied in shock-strangled tones.

They stepped inside. Only a narrow ribbon of the floor was clear, turning from the entrance to the far corner of the room, beyond the heavy bulk of a wardrobe. Everything else was stuffed with historical objects. Jeweled scarabs and colorful faience collars winked in the lamplight from atop desiccated carpets and painted boxes. Glass bowls and crystal cups sat cheek-by-jowl with stacked leather sandals, blackened with age. Woven baskets rose in towers to the ceiling, marked with the hieroglyphs for ox bones, bread, or dates.

Adam spotted a gilded bed with a base of braided ropes. A model dahabeeyah rested atop it, the shape remarkably similar to the vessels he'd just seen docked at Luxor.

Ellie stopped short in front of a cabinet packed with rows of diminutive mummy-shaped figures, which gleamed Caribbean blue in the lamplight.

"Shabtis!" she breathed out admiringly. "And look—you can see how each of them is unique. Possibly modeled on the actual royal servants who were part of the pharaoh's retinue."

Adam gave the little blue figurines a closer look. The notion that each of their placid faces might represent a real person who had lived and died three thousand years ago caught his breath. And they would've been ordinary people—not the famous rulers who appeared all over the place. The people who carved the furniture and wove the linens that were stacked up around him. People whose names nobody was going to find in any textbooks.

"There's so much!" Constance exclaimed behind him, gazing at the room's treasures.

"Everything a pharaoh would need for an eternity in the Field of Reeds," Sayyid replied reverently.

"But what are we looking for?" Constance bent over to peer around a pile of footstools. "I always imagined the Staff of Moses to look something like a shepherd's crook."

Her words brought Adam firmly back to earth. The contents of the room raised the stakes of a situation that had already been pretty damned tense. They weren't discovering the tomb's wonders in a vacuum. They were huddled here under the noses of a self-absorbed thief and a small army of mercenaries. Everything that Adam saw around him looked important, from the glittering gemstones to the humble straw of a fly-whisk. It all deserved to be saved from The Mustache and his cronies—but Adam could hardly pick it all up and haul it out of here.

They needed to focus on the most dangerous part of this puzzle—the one thing in this tomb that might have the power to unleash hell on earth in the wrong hands. After that, they would do whatever they could to keep Julian from getting inside to ravage the rest of it. Stage a distraction, maybe— though that would be a risky mission for whoever took it on.

Which would be Adam, of course. Because he'd be damned if he'd let anyone else here do it.

"The jewelry box of Mutnedjmet mentioned a was-scepter," Ellie recalled firmly. "If that is the staff we're looking for, it will take the form of a Set beast—something like a dog with an elongated snout and long pointed ears on top, finishing in a forked tail."

"It could be made of anything from wood to faience or bronze," Sayyid added, still gazing with shock at the bounty of the room.

"How big is it?" Constance pressed, peering into a quiver full of arrows.

Ellie threw a questioning look at Sayyid as she answered. "Was-scepters are usually depicted as being similar in height to the bearer's chin. But I believe there are examples that are shorter, perhaps as little as twelve to eighteen inches in length."

"So we're looking for something that could be anywhere from five feet to twelve inches long and made of just about any material other than paper." Adam cast a rueful glance around the tightly packed piles of treasures. "That sure narrows it down."

"There is another door," Zeinab cut in sharply.

Adam realized what had been itching at the back of his mind since they'd stepped into the room. The place was full of everything a pharaoh might need to enjoy a damned fine time in the afterlife… but was distinctly absent any sign of the woman it had all been put here for.

"No coffin," he pointed out significantly, meeting Ellie's gaze.

They gathered behind Zeinab at the turn of the path, and Adam found himself facing a dark rectangle cut into the wall of the chamber. The doorway opened onto a short passage that turned sharply before he could glimpse what lay beyond it.

"I suppose it might be worth seeing what is there," Ellie offered carefully. "Before we come back and make a more systematic survey of the artifacts."

"I agree," Zeinab declared. She plucked up a lantern and strode forward.

Adam lingered behind, casting a wary glance back at the stairwell. He wished he could see through it to whatever was happening above ground, but the space around him remained still as the grave. Only the faces of the dead gazed back at him in a silence that felt complicit.

Find the staff, he thought grimly. *Then get out and try like hell to save the rest.*

Adam set his hand to the hilt of his machete and strode after the others.

THIRTY-FIVE

$\mathcal{E}$LLIE FELT LIKE she was walking through a dream. The halls and chambers around her whispered with the story of the woman who had become king.

She had read about Nefertiti before, of course. What self-respecting lady scholar of ancient history wouldn't have paid special attention to a queen who was depicted on near equal footing with her husband, present at his side through everything from worship to war? Now she was faced with irrefutable evidence that the same woman had also ruled Egypt in her own right, guiding an empire with benevolence under the blessings of a compassionate sun.

A discovery like that destroyed paradigms and revolutionized entire schools of thought. To find the tomb at all would have been life-changing. To discover it untouched, with all its treasures left exactly where ancient hands had set them three thousand years ago, was nothing short of awe-inspiring.

Neil was a numb presence beside her, blinking with shock behind his spectacles. Sayyid had looked close to tears in the hallway above, where Ellie herself had been fighting the urge to break down into helpless, joyful laughter. Even Constance was caught up in the spell of the tomb, gazing with wide-eyed wonder and childlike excitement at each new secret it revealed.

Zeinab kept a grim set to her mouth, the lines of her body tense as a cat deciding whether to pounce or flee.

Adam, too, seemed more subdued rather than swept up in the excitement of the discovery. The wary glances he kept casting back the way they had come were a sobering reminder of their circumstances. Ellie couldn't afford to stop and translate every line of hieroglyphs or carefully catalog each packed hoard of funerary objects. They had stumbled into this revolutionary discovery more or less under a gun, and she was deeply uncertain how much of it they would be able to save before this was all over.

Those worries crowded against the awe flooding her mind as Ellie turned the corner of the narrow corridor and found herself at the threshold of the final chamber.

Like the room before, the space was packed with grave goods. Gold shone at her from every corner of the massed artifacts that were piled halfway up the walls, chests and statues mingling with shining piles of jewels.

In the center of it all lay the sarcophagus.

Neferneferuaten's resting place was a box of rare red granite, polished to a subtle sheen. The sides were carved with the many-handed disk of the Aten while winged goddesses stood sentinel on each corner, their arms held out in a gesture of protection.

The mortal remains of the larger-than-life figure who had decorated the paintings above lay inside—and stopped Ellie short. She was struck by the painful sense that this entire complex had been meant to remain inviolate, waiting for the moment when Neferneferuaten would answer the call of her god and join him in eternity.

The pharaoh-queen wasn't a figure in a textbook anymore. She was a being of real flesh, blood, and feeling, who now lay in dusty silence amid the ancient relics of her life.

Ellie forced herself to examine the rest of the burial chamber. Between what was here and the inventory back in the treasure room, the tomb contained an absolute trove of priceless information about royal life in the late Eighteenth Dynasty. A full team of archaeologists could spend a lifetime cataloging, stabilizing, and analyzing it all.

She had absolutely no idea how they were going to locate a single was-scepter in the midst of it.

Her gaze rose from the grave goods to the walls. Like the hallway above, these were decorated with beautiful artwork. The paintings ran only three-quarters of the way around the room. They stopped at a bas relief that was only partially painted.

The murals had obviously been meant to continue. The pharaoh must have died too soon, forcing the royal artists to abandon the work while only partway complete.

Ellie stepped closer to the first panel, which sat nearest to the entrance. It depicted a group of captives kneeling before the looming figure of a conquering king.

"Amenhotep the Third." Neil nodded to the cartouche by the pharaoh's knee as he joined her. "Akhenaten's father."

"These look like members of a Semitic group," Ellie said, noting the curled hair, bearded faces, and paler skin of the kneeling prisoners. "But they're not all warriors. There are women and children here."

"They still might have been war captives. Prizes taken after battle," Neil pointed out.

"Slaves," Sayyid clarified bluntly, stepping to Ellie's other side.

Neil went still. "There's a name here." He lifted a hand, pointing to a cluster of hieroglyphs below the prisoners.

Ellie carefully leaned forward over the jumble of furniture that sat between her and the wall, squinting to read the phonetic symbols. "Ha... pi... ru." She straightened, frowning. "Hapiru?"

Sayyid looked over at her sharply, his eyebrows rising. "The Hapiru was the name given by the Egyptians and the Akkadians to the nomadic people who roamed the deserts of the Sinai and the Red Sea."

"Like the Bedouin," Ellie filled in.

"Like the *Hebrews*," Neil corrected her, his voice a little strangled. He was still staring at the image. "The Hapiru are considered a plausible candidate for the people who would evolve into the tribes of the Hebrews."

Sayyid and Neil locked eyes.

"You realize what this means," Neil began urgently. "An Egyptian depiction of a group of people who might well have been early Hebrews captured and enslaved by a New Kingdom pharaoh..."

Sayyid clearly did realize what it meant. His eyes were wide with a shock and wonder that mirrored the expression on Neil's face.

Academics and archaeologists had been searching for years for evidence that the Hebrews might actually have once been enslaved in Egypt, as the Bible claimed.

Now they were looking at exactly that.

The shared awe between Sayyid and Ellie's brother lasted only for a moment. Then Sayyid's expression closed, and he looked away.

In the painting, the Aten shone down from the sky above the captives... but oddly, its rays didn't center on the noble figure of the pharaoh, as they usually did in Amarna-period portraits featuring royalty. Instead, the long beams with their delicate hands brushed against the slight form of a child who knelt among the mix of captive warriors and their families. The little girl had high cheekbones, straight brows, and a generous mouth—features that Ellie recognized, because she had seen them over and over again in the hallway above.

"That's Nefertiti!" she blurted out, pointing to the girl. "That's her among the prisoners! But why would she be there? Unless…" The epiphany swept over Ellie, making her feel dizzy. "Could she possibly have been a slave herself?"

"Of course!" Neil burst out. "Why hadn't I considered that before? It's right there—it's right in her name!"

"What are you talking about?" Ellie pushed back.

"Nefertiti," Sayyid cut in solemnly, his eyes locked on the girl in the mural. "That is what it means. 'The Beautiful One From Afar.'"

The beautiful one from afar… The significance shocked Ellie to silence as she gazed at the slender child who sat straight-backed under the benevolent rays of her god.

Constance pressed in, drawn by their outbursts. "But who's that fellow beside her with the rest of the little hands on him?"

Ellie was startled to realize that Constance was right. Another figure sat beside the future queen, a boy whose body was half-obscured by her own. His shoulders were also graced by the soft, brushing touch of the rays of the Aten.

The features of the two children looked remarkably similar. Ellie wondered if perhaps that was just a shortcut taken by the ancient artist who had carefully chiseled their forms out of the plaster covering the walls… but none of the rest of the assembled captives had those same high cheekbones and full lips.

Sensing a deeper story, Ellie looked at the next image.

The child Nefertiti sat on the ground between two noble figures who loomed in throne-like chairs to either side of her. A cat rolled lazily at her feet, sleekly gray and dotted with black spots.

The boy from the previous scene was there as well. Once more, his form was almost obscured by that of his sister—but Ellie could just pick out the lines of his profile where he sat behind her like a shadow. He held a tablet and stylus in his hands in the pose of a young scholar.

Sayyid pointed to the hieroglyphs by the man and woman who framed the two children. "These are Ay's names and titles. Ay and his wife Tey."

Ellie felt a little chill. She was looking at an image of the same Ay who had been a leading courtier during the reign of Akhenaten before placing Tutankhamun on the throne… only to rule Egypt himself after the boy-king's mysterious death.

And then undo all Akhenaten's accomplishments, right down to chiseling his face from monuments across Egypt.

"Nefertiti was *Ay's* slave?" Ellie guessed tightly.

Sayyid shook his head, pointing to another cluster of hieroglyphs. "Not just his slave. This says that she was his daughter."

"How is that possible if she was a war captive?" Ellie demanded.

"Egyptian families sometimes adopted slaves as their full legal children, especially if they had none of their own to honor their funerary rites after they died," Sayyid explained.

"But what about the boy?" Ellie asked.

Sayyid frowned as he studied the glyphs that surrounded the painting. "I don't see a name."

"It's obviously Moses," Constance said with a dismissive wave of her hand.

Neil went still beside her. "But… that almost fits. I mean, it isn't a perfect parallel—Tey wasn't an Egyptian princess, but she *was* a very high-ranking aristocrat in Akhenaten's court."

"Only he was captured instead of washed up in a basket," Constance filled in cheerfully.

"It is a more likely story anyway," Zeinab offered as she stuck her head under a table for a better look at a pile of jumbled relics. "What mother in Egypt would set her child into the Nile in a basket? You would be asking for the baby to be eaten by crocodiles."

"Well, there you have it, then," Constance concluded. "Moses was obviously Nefertiti's brother."

"Her brother?" Ellie protested.

"Just look at them," Constance countered with an airy wave of her hand.

Ellie did—and found herself once more taking in the remarkably similar features of the two captive children.

Constance didn't wait for a response, perfectly comfortable with her conclusions, whether the scholars in their group agreed or not. "This one looks like a wedding," she mused as she reached the next mural.

Nefertiti had grown in this depiction, appearing as a lovely young woman. She faced the distinct, lanky figure of Akhenaten, gazing up at him with an affection that Ellie could sense across the centuries as the rays of the Aten fell down over their shoulders.

"The Egyptians didn't have weddings," Neil countered a little crossly. "Marriages were most likely arranged through an exchange of gifts."

"They're holding hands," Constance countered authoritatively.

"I didn't say that meant they couldn't like each other!" Neil protested.

"They look happy," Constance concluded as though that was the end of the matter, leaving Neil to gape at her helplessly.

In the scenes that followed, the royal couple held up offerings to their god and played with a growing cluster of children. They were moments of warmth and intimacy, offering a glimpse into the life of the woman who now lay behind Ellie in that gleaming granite sarcophagus.

"Oh!" Constance exclaimed softly. "Everyone is dying in this one!"

Ellie joined her at the next panel.

In the vivid colors on the wall, Nefertiti wept over a funeral bier. Three bodies lay on top of it. Sayyid quietly pointed out the hieroglyphs identifying them. "The Great King's Mother Tiye. His daughter Meketaten. And the Horus of Gold, King of Upper and Lower Egypt, Neferkheperure Waenre Akhenaten."

"Her mother-in-law, her daughter… and her husband," Ellie quietly filled in.

"It was the plague," Neil elaborated solemnly as he gazed at the mural beside her. "It swept through Egypt near the end of Akhenaten's reign, perhaps brought in by a party of foreign diplomats. Thousands of people died."

In the detailed, realistic style of the ancient artist, Nefertiti's grief looked raw. Tears coursed down her cheeks as she extended her arms in a gesture of despair.

The rays of the Aten spilled softly down onto her bowed back, tiny hands brushing the length of her spine.

The last image was unfinished. The woman it depicted was no longer Nefertiti but rather the pharaoh Neferneferuaten. She stood in royal proportions over the massed people of Egypt, who were depicted in hues from soft copper to midnight black. The pharaoh was kilted like a man with the double crown of Egypt on her brow and a false beard on her chin—but her face was still the same, with those elegant cheekbones and wide-set eyes.

To her left, she raised up a hand to the rays of the Aten. To her right, she reached down to the people crowded by her sandaled feet. An assemblage of otherworldly figures clustered in her palm—blue-faced Osiris and hawk-beaked Horus mingling with Hathor, Isis, and even Amun with his crown of soaring plumes.

Some of the people below the pharaoh reached out to accept the deities while others held up their hands to the greater god that rose over Neferneferuaten's head.

"Why is she handing them those strange little dolls?" Constance asked.

"Those are the old gods of Egypt," Ellie replied slowly as the significance of the image dawned. "I… think she's giving them back."

"Akhenaten didn't strictly ban the worship of other gods, but he removed all royal patronage from their temples," Neil explained. "And certainly no one who admitted allegiance to another cult would have been granted a position in his court."

"She must have been trying to change that," Ellie said, following a sense of intuition that tugged at her from the noble figure on the wall. "To show some grace to those of her subjects who found their solace in the other deities, even as she remained loyal to her own god."

"But why is it only half painted?" Constance asked.

"I… think she must have died before it could be completed," Ellie replied uneasily.

"From the plague?" Constance pressed.

Ellie found herself turning to look back at the other wall—at the stern face of the grand courtier Ay. Any man who would eventually rise to the position of pharaoh must have possessed a great deal of ambition. Just how far might Ay have gone to consolidate his own grip on power? Would he have eliminated his own adopted daughter if she stood in his way?

"Oh, but there's one more!" Constance exclaimed, moving a little further along. "It's very small, though."

She leaned over a beautifully preserved model of the great solar barque—a long, narrow boat lined with dozens of tiny oars. It sat atop a carved wooden table painted and shaped like a roaring leopard.

A smaller carving marked the wall above the ship. Beside it, the plaster split in a dark, thin fracture like a lightning bolt that darted from the ceiling to disappear under the piled artifacts on the floor.

It certainly wasn't unusual to see faults in the stone of a space that had rested in the earth for three thousand years, Ellie reminded herself—but she also couldn't help but think of the bigger gap through which they had all climbed into the tomb to begin with.

A trail of unease crept through the back of her mind at the thought.

The image beside the crack was of a very different nature than the grand royal portraits Ellie had just been studying. Instead of an elegant bas relief, it looked like a rough caricature scraped into the virgin plaster with the tip of a dagger.

The style of the work was also entirely different from that of the other tomb art. The eyes of the roughly drawn figures were too large, their noses prominent and angled.

In fact, to Ellie's eyes, it did not look Egyptian at all.

"This is clearly a later graffito," Sayyid commented. "Something you might expect to find if the tomb had been looted."

Despite the artistic differences, Ellie could pick out the figure meant to represent Neferneferuaten. A rough approximation of the double crown had been slashed into the plaster atop her head, and something about the noble lift of her chin reminded her of the other portraits she had seen.

In the graffito, the pharaoh held her hand out over a cluster of smaller figures who faced away from her, walking toward the rising disk of the Aten.

"Hold on!" Neil burst out. "There's cuneiform here!"

Ellie had taken the marks he pointed to as natural defects in the plaster—but realized that he was right. She leaned further over the exquisitely formed oars and sails of the solar barque for a better look.

"Those phonemes sound out *Hapiru*." She pointed at a cluster of lines and wedges. "And this is… *durāru*. Hmm."

She cast a questioning glance at Neil, who shrugged helplessly.

"Durāru… roaming?" she offered with a frown. "Converging? No, no—that's not it. Freedom!" she concluded triumphantly. "Durāru is freedom."

"What about this one?" Constance asked.

She pointed to a smaller cluster of cuneiform. The symbols hung over the head of the tallest of the people in the group that departed under Neferneferuaten's hand—the only figure turned to gaze back at the pharaoh. The man carried a staff, the object primitively represented by a line topped with a few jagged slashes. Even though the drawing was primitively done, sadness marked the rough lines of his features.

Ellie's brain automatically picked out the sounds indicated by the Akkadian characters.

"Moseh," she said, her voice tight as she stared at the figure scratched into the wall. "It says *Moseh*."

Neil paled beside her. He whirled back to the other portraits. "This… this is all of it. The whole story." He pointed a shaking finger. "The taking into captivity. The plague. The pharaoh who freed the slaves. It's all here—the entire bloody Exodus is on these walls!"

"Allâhu 'akhbar," Sayyid breathed, his eyes wide as he looked over the murals. "You mad fool—you were actually right!"

Neil lifted his hands to his head, swaying a little. "I… I think I need to sit down."

He plopped onto the floor, bracing his forehead against his palms.

Ellie's mind spun with the implication of the evidence before her—that the prophet of three of the world's great faiths had found some part of his inspiration in Akhenaten's religious revolution.

It was all right here, where it had lain in secret for three thousand years.

The impact of that made her wonder if she ought to sit down as well.

Adam's voice cut through the spell. "I hate to break up the party, but I'm counting over seventy-five staffs in this chamber alone. And that's just what I can see—not what's likely buried behind all the rest of this stuff. If we wanna find this arcanum before the sun comes up and makes sneaking out of this place a whole lot more complicated, we need to narrow things down."

Ellie raised her eyes to the dagger-carved sketch of the prophet on the wall—and the significance of those scratched lines at the top of the rod he carried in his hand clicked into place.

The angular line like an elongated snout. The two upward dashes like pointed ears.

The man in the graffito, gazing back at his royal sister, was holding a was-scepter in his hand.

THIRTY-SIX

"We NEED TO look for something with the head of a Set beast," Ellie burst out urgently.

"I've been looking for Set beasts," Adam replied patiently. "Haven't seen any yet. I checked all the rods I could see for cuneiform too, just in case that mattered. There's nothing but Egyptian."

He cast a narrow-eyed gaze over the tightly packed mountain of artifacts. "There's a lot more here that we can't see, but if we start hauling through it at random, we're going to make one hell of a mess—never mind that it might take a month."

"Would whoever put it here really have gone to the trouble of digging out a place for it behind all this stuff and then putting it all back again?" Constance waved an expressive hand over the stacks of gilded chests and alabaster vases.

"We need to look in the sarcophagus," Zeinab declared firmly.

The granite box took up the center of the chamber. It was longer than Adam was tall and roughly three feet wide. The lid stood at about the height of Ellie's waist. The polished, rose-hued granite shone softly in the light of the lantern.

Ellie fought an unexpected urge to protest. Of course, she knew as a scholar that any scientific survey of the tomb would eventually include a careful emptying of the sarcophagus and the layers of coffins encased within it. Still, the notion of exposing what lay inside the box of pale red granite felt oddly sacrilegious.

She stared down at the rows of hieroglyphs carved into the surface of the stone.

Oh sole god, like whom there is no other, she read silently. *You created the world according to your desire.*

"Why there?" she burst out tightly. "The staff could be anywhere!"

"But whoever went to the trouble of returning it to this tomb must have known it was an object of unimaginable importance," Neil cut in uneasily. "If he was bringing it back here to rest with Neferneferuaten, it makes sense that he would put it as close to her as he could."

"How could he have lifted the lid?" Ellie shot back, waving a hand at the massive slab of granite that closed the sarcophagus. "It must weigh five hundred pounds!"

"You're probably pretty close," Adam said with an assessing gaze at the stone. "But he wouldn't have had to lift it. He just had to slide it off one of the corners." He frowned down at the box. "Problem is, we don't know which corner. We'll need to take the whole thing off."

"It would be easy enough to push it free," Constance offered.

"But it might break when it hits the floor!" Neil protested.

"We would be best lowering it down," Sayyid admitted uncomfortably.

Neil closed his eyes with a wince, clearly torn. "It's solid granite."

"Five hundred pounds," Adam repeated. "There's six of us. That's less than a hundred pounds apiece."

"How often do you run around lifting a hundred pounds!?" Neil demanded.

"I mean, I lift *me* all the time," Adam countered. "And I'm pretty close to two hundred."

"You take your two hundred, then," Zeinab ordered as she grabbed the fluted edge of the lid. "And the rest of us will split the difference."

They circled the sarcophagus, each taking hold of the rosy granite slab that covered it. Ellie joined them with a wrench of guilt. The stone was cool under her hands.

Sayyid picked up the crowbar from Zeinab's bundle of gear. With an expression of solemn resignation, he wedged it carefully under the lid. "On my count. One… two…"

Ellie lifted along with the others, her shoulders already protesting at the weight.

Beside her, Zeinab crouched down to put her shoulder to the fluted edge. Ellie did the same, and the granite unsteadily rose.

"Tip it our way!" Adam barked.

"Our way!?" Neil echoed from beside him in obvious panic.

Ellie slid a little closer to Zeinab and shoved up on her end of the stone. The enormous slab tilted. She was facing away from the lower end and could only hear the commotion that followed.

"Sweet… holy…" came Adam's groaning voice.

"I'm going to lose my fingers!" Neil cried.

"Get the corner down—No, the other corner!"

"I am lowering the other corner!"

"Sure as hell doesn't feel like it!"

Ellie heard a firm tap of stone on stone, and the weight against her back released.

"Slide it down—no, the other way!" Adam ordered.

She turned to see him sandwiched between Sayyid and Neil as they worked the rest of the long edge of the lid down onto the floor of the burial chamber, leaning it against the side of the sarcophagus… which now lay open.

Ellie stared down at a golden coffin. The gilded image of the pharaoh gripped a crook and flail in its hands, accented by pieces of rich blue lapis and sunset-hued quartz. It was crowned with a striped nemes headdress and uraeus cobra.

A face was carved into the fine-grained wood. Ellie recognized the noble visage from the walls brought to full, three-dimensional life. The pharaoh's lips were softly open as though about to draw a breath. Her wide-set almond eyes gleamed softly with an inlay of ivory and onyx that showed from under delicate golden lids.

The entire splendid construction stood out in stark glory against a background of the fine, blood-red sand that filled the rest of the sarcophagus.

"She's lovely!" Constance exclaimed wonderingly.

"She is," Ellie agreed reverently.

Sayyid rose from the far side of the coffin, red faced and still huffing—and then raised his arms in a desperate warning. "Wallah—stop moving! All of you! Stay exactly where you are! Do not even breathe if you can help it!"

"What's wrong?" Zeinab held herself in a tense, ready stillness.

"That powder," Sayyid rasped urgently. He barely dared to nod toward the interior of the sarcophagus.

"The sand?" Constance pressed.

"It is *not* sand," Sayyid replied, sweat beading on his brow. "It is powdered hematite!"

Zeinab's eyes flashed with fear.

"Hematite?" Ellie frowned down at the substance even as she kept her body frozen. The red powder filled the box right up to the level of the top of the gilded coffin. "What's wrong with hematite?"

"Nothing when you are using it in a stabilized form as a pigment for artwork," Sayyid replied with careful, terrified patience. "But when inhaled in sufficient quantity, it brings on vomiting and convulsions."

"Metal poisoning," Zeinab filled in sharply, staring at the powder as though it were a cobra flaring for a strike.

"Hell," Adam breathed, the lines of his mouth firming with recognition.

Zeinab's eyes flashed to the rest of them, grim and urgent. "It will kill us all, if enough of it is aerosolized."

"But how do you know it's hematite?" Neil's tone was pleadingly skeptical.

A mix of emotions flickered across Sayyid's features—a quick sadness and hurt followed by a flare of anger. They were gone a moment later, forced back under a wall of careful self-control. "A tomb outside Qena was entered by a group of looters six years ago. They described finding the floor covered thickly in a fine red powder." He paused. "Within two years, all of them were dead."

"I never heard of that," Neil protested.

"Why would you have heard of it?" Sayyid retorted.

Neil flinched at the sharpness of his tone.

"How do *you* know of it?" Ellie pressed more carefully.

Sayyid drew in a breath as though forcibly controlling his racing emotions. "Their relatives came to me for help. They knew I had experience with tombs and hoped that I would know of a cure."

"But there is no cure for metal fever," Zeinab cut in sharply. "The body can only clear it on its own… or not, if the exposure is too great."

"Saw the end result once in some miners out of Colombia." Adam's gaze locked with Ellie's across the sarcophagus, dark with worry. "It wasn't nice."

Ellie held herself perfectly still as she studied the fine red dust. It filled the sarcophagus in soft waves, a crimson sea framing the golden figure of the pharaoh. "What if we masked ourselves?"

"The effectiveness of a mask would depend on the material and how fine the particles are," Zeinab replied.

"Hell of a risk if you got it wrong," Adam noted flatly.

"Then how do we open the coffin?" Neil pressed.

The obvious answer rose into her mind. *Maybe we shouldn't.*

"We would have to stabilize the powder so that it did not come into the air when disturbed," Sayyid said. "Perhaps with an oil—adding it slowly so that it turned the hematite to paste. Something that would not dry and allow it to stir back up again." He frowned thoughtfully. "You might minimize the damage the oil causes to the coffin by inserting panels around it—but of course, you would have to do so with the utmost care."

"We've got a little oil in the lamps," Adam pointed out. "But not much. And we'd be left in the dark if we used it."

Beside Adam, Neil was no longer looking at the coffin and its nest of deadly powder. His eyes had wandered to something beyond Ellie's shoulder with an air of puzzled distraction.

Ellie glanced back, seeing only the model solar barque with its delicate oars and sails and the cuneiform graffito, which they had already examined.

"Neil," she began. "What are you—"

Her words cut off as she turned back around—and watched Julian Forster-Mowbray step into the carved doorway of the burial chamber.

"But this is absolutely splendid!" he happily observed with a greedy look around the room. "Look at all this treasure!"

Adam turned with slow menace, the machete sliding into his hand. Zeinab's posture was one of still, dangerous readiness.

Constance rolled her eyes. "It's not treasure, you dolt! It's history!"

"Why can't it be both?" Julian protested, looking a little hurt.

He had changed into a khaki sporting suit like a gentleman heading out for a spot of game hunting—save for the oddity of the old leather scabbard he wore around his hips. A bone hilt protruded from the sheath, the material gently yellowed with age.

Julian cheerfully surveyed Neferneferuaten's grave goods as though he had turned up to shop at an exceptionally good rummage sale. His thugs filed into the room behind him. Ellie counted five Al-Saboors, variously armed with knives and—most worryingly—a pair of rifles.

"How are you even here?" Constance demanded impatiently.

"One of the Al-Saboors climbed the ridge to—er, answer the call of nature—and spotted your rope," he replied. "Though he rather took his time getting the word back to us."

He cast an irritated look back at the cluster of menacing cousins as though trying and failing to pick out which of them had been responsible for the lack of alacrity.

The men glanced at each other in confusion. The one with the big ears shrugged, then quickly stepped aside as a shadowy figure approached the doorway.

Jacobs entered the room, his hand twisted into the back of Jemmahor's cloak.

He shoved the apprentice midwife to her knees and swung up her stolen Enfield, pressing the barrel to the back of her neck as the young woman's dark eyes flashed with frustrated fury.

Julian grimaced awkwardly. "Look—I am sorry it's come down to this. The whole situation seems to have gotten entirely out of hand, but I'm sure we can settle things like reasonable people."

"Reasonable people don't generally point guns at each other," Adam noted in a deceptively lazy tone. The blade of his machete gleamed in the lamplight as he held it ready at his thigh.

"This is just a precaution!" Julian protested with a wave at Jemmahor, who glared at him like an angry cat. He whirled to Constance. "This has all been a wretched misunderstanding. I don't know what these people told you, but I'm not the villain here! We're all on the same side!"

"We are not on the same side," Zeinab spat back, her green eyes flashing with quiet rage.

"Well, maybe not *you*," Julian amended. "But the rest of you are civilized people. That's all we're doing here—protecting civilization!"

Ellie took in the pleading expression on Julian's face—framed as it was by the skeptical, bored, or greedy expressions of his hired mercenaries—and realized that the fool actually *believed* what he was saying.

A familiar voice rose in self-important tones from behind the clustered thugs. "Excuse me! Coming through! Let the expert through, please!"

Dawson shuffled into the room, squeezing past the bulk of an enormous, thickly muscled Al-Saboor. "Please refrain from touching anything—this must all be left to the professionals," he ordered. "A little-known pharaoh and the entirety of his grave goods is a find of unprecedented importance!"

Ellie's patience burnt out like a fuse. "Not 'his.'" She jabbed a finger toward the gilded woman in the sarcophagus. *"Hers!"*

"Ha ha ha!" Dawson laughed. "What a silly notion."

"We can split the rest of it. Fifty-fifty." Julian cast another greedy look at the glittering funerary hoard. "Or sixty-forty, maybe—just so long as we get what we came here for. Where is the staff?"

"Haven't found it yet." Adam's tone was casual—but a ready tension quietly infused his frame.

"Search them," Jacobs flatly suggested. A thin thread of impatience wove through the words.

"Well, I… I suppose that would be a sensible precaution," Julian admitted.

Zeinab lifted her hands. "No one move! If the powder in this sarcophagus is disturbed, everyone here will die in a mess of vomit and convulsions!"

Julian stiffened with surprise. "What's that?!" He cast a bewildered glance at Dawson. "Is she serious?"

"There is no such thing as booby traps," Dawson authoritatively retorted.

"Right," Julian concluded with a weary sigh. "Best get on with it, then."

Jacobs' eyes narrowed thoughtfully. "Best not."

Ellie's pulse skipped. Nothing in Jacobs' expression had changed. He still held the rifle to the back of Jemmahor's neck as she knelt on the ground before him, her hands clenched into fists.

Julian looked back at Jacobs with obvious surprise. "Why?"

Jacobs' gaze shifted over to Ellie. "Call it a feeling."

At his words, a chill slipped over her skin.

"Though perhaps if you shoot a few of them, the rest will fall into line. And there isn't much movement needed for that." Jacobs' eyes remained locked on Ellie as a low buzz of fear rose in her ears. "Start with the Egyptians. There's less likely to be much bother about them."

Adam's stillness took on a new, ready edge. Ellie could feel the silent fury simmering off of him—along with a sense of dangerous calculation.

Julian's gaze ping-ponged between Jacobs and Constance. "Surely we can come to *some* sort of compromise without resorting to shooting anyone," he offered hopefully.

Ellie wondered whether all of their fates actually rested on Julian Foster-Mowbray's lack of spine.

Constance's foot shifted back as she slipped into one of her jiu jitsu poses. With a look of mingled terror and determination, Sayyid's eyes dropped to the iron crowbar that rested against the sarcophagus beside him.

Adam glanced incongruously at a nearby leopard-footed Eighteenth Dynasty chair.

Neil inched away from the sarcophagus, backing toward a cabinet stuffed with bolts of ancient linen that stood before the jagged crack in the chamber wall.

Ellie studied the fracture more closely. It actually started on the ceiling of the chamber—a thin black line that zigzagged across the stone, thickening as it descended the wall until it disappeared behind the cabinet.

She recalled the way the stairs had given out during their descent through the tomb. Unease itched at the back of her mind.

The Al-Saboors cast their leader questioning looks, their weapons held loosely in their hands. The elder Al-Saboor shrugged.

"Amir?" he prompted uneasily.

"I am thinking!" Julian protested.

Jacobs' lip curled with contempt.

Ellie glanced down. A thin, dark line snaked out from between her brother's boots as he lifted them to take another step.

The itch in her mind coalesced into certainty.

"Neil, *no!*" she called out.

He set down his foot, and the ground collapsed beneath him.

The wall fell with it. Bundles of linen and delicate palm-leaf fans crashed into chairs and a mummified crocodile, all of it spilling through the black hole that had just opened in the floor of the tomb. Neil teetered at the edge of the precipice, waving his arms wildly for balance.

"Not again!" he groaned—and tipped backward into darkness.

THIRTY-SEVEN

$\mathcal{N}$EIL PLUMMETED DOWN a near-vertical face of rock at a speed only slightly short of a free-fall.

Artifacts tumbled around him. He smashed into an Eighteenth Dynasty table, bursting it into splinters. He scrabbled for some sort of foothold, his boots kicking out against nothing but sheer stone that scraped his back through his waistcoat.

Neil had just enough time to wonder if he would die instantly when he hit the ground or only mortally injure himself—and then one of his flailing hands snagged a grip. He jerked to a painful stop against a ridge of rock no wider than his fingertips, his arm wrenching against his shoulder.

Muscle screamed. His fingers were raw. He very much did not want to look down. Instead, he turned his face up to where a ragged opening glowed with lamplight from the burial chamber.

It looked uncomfortably far away.

Sayyid rushed into the center of the gap with an expression of quick, potent worry, holding the crowbar in his hand.

"Fairfax, are you well?" he called down urgently.

"Not… particularly…" Neil's voice strained as his burning, painful hold on the ledge began to slip.

Everything that came next happened rather quickly.

Zeinab snapped into view beside her husband. She took in Neil's situation with a glance.

Shouts rose from behind her, along with the crack of a gunshot.

Zeinab's green eyes flashed down to Neil, tightening with a sudden calculation—and she shoved her husband through the hole in the wall.

Sayyid spilled onto the impossibly steep slope with a yelp. The crowbar flew from his hand, bouncing against the stones with a clear, resonant ping.

Neil had only a moment to register a snap of horrified dismay before Sayyid smacked into him, knocking him from his precipitous perch.

He flew back, feeling a strange gravity-defying lurch in his gut as he plummeted through the air.

He smacked into a lumpy mound that pulverized into dust at the impact. It felt only marginally less hard than rock. Neil coughed and wheezed as the air filled with clouds of rotted linen. He rolled over, his boots sliding for purchase through the slippery remnants of three-thousand-year-old fabrics.

His hand landed on something round and solid that rolled under his palm. On instinct, Neil tugged it from the debris.

He found himself staring at a human skull. His thumb was stuck through an eye socket.

Neil choked on a scream, dropping the skull and scrabbling back from it through the tattered mess of decayed cloth and broken furniture until he bumped into something warmer and softer.

Sayyid answered the impact with a groan as he shoved Neil off of him and sat up.

Finally staggering to his feet, Neil took in his situation. He was in a high chamber as deep and narrow as a well. The walls were unnaturally smooth save for semi-regular cuts that formed tiny, narrow ridges along their surfaces, like the one he had caught to break his fall.

And it was a good thing he had caught that hold. His neck craned back as he looked up at the light spilling through the opening to the burial chamber. It had to be at least thirty feet over his head.

Zeinab was still visible in the opening. The biggest of the Al-Saboors had snagged an arm around her waist, and the midwife kicked against him viciously, railing out a stream of Masri imprecations against his father, his donkey, and his testicles. Other voices clamored down from beyond her, the sounds violent but muffled by distance.

Zeinab was snatched away, and Ellie threw herself into the opening, shoving at some unseen assailant.

"Neil!" she shouted down. "Shake it!"

Her arm snapped out. Something flew from her hand—a small, narrow object that landed on the hard stone floor with a bright, clear *ting*.

Ellie was yanked away, biting out ferocious protests.

Sayyid struggled to his feet beside Neil. He had recovered the crowbar, but it hung in his hand uselessly. The tool obviously wouldn't help them climb up a thirty-foot cliff.

The next figure to move into the light of the burial chamber was Mr.

Jacobs. He gazed down at them calmly from above, and Neil felt uncomfortably sure of what the implacable man must see—two soft scholars standing in a pile of rubble at the bottom of an oubliette.

Julian stepped into place beside him. His tie had gone askew, and a tuft of his blond hair puffed up at a strange angle. He looked awkward as he blinked down at Neil and Sayyid.

Jacobs turned to Julian—and as the light glazed his profile, Neil saw naked contempt flash across his features.

"What should we do about them?" Julian asked uncertainly. "Can they get out of there, do you think?"

Jacobs' gaze moved to something at Neil's feet. Neil glanced down and saw the skull.

His stomach lurched.

"I doubt it… but we ought to shoot them anyway," Jacobs concluded flatly. "This lot have a bad habit of popping back up out of caves where they rightfully should have rotted."

Julian's eyes found Neil's across the pit, and Neil recalled all the times he had met this man before—over drinks at Shepherd's or a light lunch at a café around the corner. Signing a few friendly papers or passing off a progress report. Julian bidding him a cordial 'cheerio' before going off to practice at the gym.

"Fine," Julian replied tightly.

His former employer walked away, and time turned to water around Neil.

His pulse slowed. He watched Jacobs issue a calm order to someone just out of view. Heard Ellie's distant, ferocious shout mingling with an angry protest from Constance.

A big-eared Al Saboor took Jacobs' place in the ragged tear of light. He raised his rifle.

"Move, you idiot!" Sayyid shouted, barreling into Neil from the side.

Neil bolted as bullets cracked off the stones behind him. The toe of his boot snapped against something on the floor—a narrow object that spun over the stone before it came to rest ahead of him with another soft *ping!*

On a quick, desperate instinct, Neil snatched it from the ground as he flew by.

A bullet chinked against the wall where his head had been a moment before. Chips of debris sprayed over the back of his neck.

Sayyid grabbed the sleeve of Neil's shirt and yanked him through a dark, square opening in the wall.

Neil was swallowed by darkness as the world around him dropped into a starless midnight as thick as ink. He stumbled to a stop, terrified of taking the wrong step and plummeting into another endless hole in the ground.

"Sayyid?" Neil was slightly humiliated to find that his voice vaguely resembled that of a bleating sheep.

"Quiet!" Sayyid hissed from nearby.

Neil oriented himself to the sound, which had come from behind him. A ghost of illumination faintly limned the edges of a rectangular doorway—and the lines of Sayyid's face as he pressed himself to the wall to peer back the way they had come.

In the silence, Neil picked out the sound of distant, angry voices.

"Are they coming after us?" he asked in a careful whisper.

"That Jacobs fellow wants to," Sayyid reported back, low and tense. "But I think Mr. Forster-Mowbray is refusing."

"Why?" Neil demanded—even though it came as a relief.

Sayyid glanced back at him. Neil could just make out the frustration and contempt that briefly tightened his features. "Because he's quite certain we haven't any way out of here."

Neil recalled the impossible height of the sheer rock face that led to the burial chamber, where a horde of villains waited for them.

The surrounding darkness began to feel thicker and closer.

"Let's not wait around to see who wins," Sayyid determined. "Come on."

He stalked past Neil, brushing roughly against his shoulder as he moved ahead into the darkness.

"But how?" Neil burst out in panic.

He heard Sayyid's footsteps stop, accompanied by a heavy sigh. "Keep your hand to the wall and test where you step before you put your foot down."

Sayyid's voice was thin with irritation. Neil's shoulders slumped. In the excitement of discovering the tomb, he had nearly forgotten how angry Sayyid was at him. He wondered whether he should apologize, but when he tried to form the words, everything he thought of felt inadequate.

Instead, he picked his way along in Sayyid's wake. His fingers trailed over the oddly flat surface of the wall. He tried not to choke on his own abysmal fear with every step he took.

Now that they had moved away from the oubliette, the darkness had become complete. Neil couldn't even see his hand when he held it up in front of his eyes. He felt as though the world around him had ceased to exist, leaving behind only a dull, echoing, dust-scented oblivion that he would wander through for eternity.

The thought threatened to throw him into an even deeper state of panic. Neil kept reaching up with his free hand to adjust his spectacles as though that would make some kind of difference—which seemed very close to insanity.

The frames were bent, making them sit slightly crooked on his nose, but otherwise they had survived his fall into the pit… probably because he had landed on the back of his head.

It still smarted, as did most of the rest of him, from his aching shoulder to his scraped fingers.

The darkness loomed thicker, closing in more tightly around him. He fought back against the claustrophobic terror, forcing himself to attend to his other senses.

Sayyid's boots scraped softly against the ground ahead of him, which was remarkably flat for an uncharted cave system. The air was dry and smelled of stone.

It helped—but only a little.

"It's too bad we didn't think to fall through that hole with a light," Neil joked weakly.

Sayyid stopped ahead of him—though Neil only knew it by the scuff of his boot.

"What did your sister throw at you?" Sayyid pressed.

"Peanut?" Neil had to think, confused by the abrupt change in subject.

His hand went to his pocket, and he pulled out the object he'd picked up from the floor of the cave. He felt a length of smooth metal, warm from the heat of his body, and a round screw top. "I think it's that cigar tube of hers. The one where she keeps the…"

His voice trailed off as he finally put it together.

"Firebird bone?" Sayyid filled in dryly.

"But that's just a load of superstitious…" Neil stopped, catching himself with a wince.

He could hardly call Ellie's bone *superstitious nonsense* when he'd seen Julian Forster-Mowbray swing around a flaming sword.

Suppressing a sigh, he unscrewed the lid. He tipped the tube carefully, and the bone slid into his hand.

The world around him remained dark and uncomfortably silent.

"But what do I do with it?" Neil startled at the echo that rang back at him. It spoke of being surrounded by a vast, low, empty space.

"In the tunnel at Saqqara, your sister tried some sort of motion with her hand," Sayyid recalled.

Shake it! Ellie had shouted down at him from above.

Neil swallowed the feeling of being unutterably foolish—reminding himself that no one could actually *see* him—and gave the bone a quick little shake.

A soft, sputtering blue flashed against the darkness, momentarily illuminating Sayyid's face a few steps away before it vanished.

The blackness that closed back in around Neil felt even thicker.

"I must have done it wrong," he said, panic lacing his words.

"How hard did you try?"

"I don't know!" Neil protested wildly. "A mild shake?"

"As though you were rolling dice in a cup or preparing a soda canister?" Sayyid pressed.

"More like the dice?" Neil hedged awkwardly.

"So give it a right shake, then!" Sayyid snapped.

His mouth twisting against the utter lunacy of what he was doing, Neil gave the bone a right bloody shaking.

A wild, impossible light blazed to life in his hand.

The glare was somehow both pale and hot, a fiery white-gold like a burning star. Neil's eyes watered against the abrupt intensity of it, forcing him to squint as he thrust the bone out in front of him.

"Wallah! Can't you turn it down?" Sayyid threw up an arm to shield his eyes.

"It's a bone! It doesn't have a bloody wick!" Neil flapped an urgent hand at Sayyid. "Give me one of your socks!"

"*My* socks?" Sayyid shot back. "What do you want one of *my* socks for?"

"Oh, dash it anyway!" Neil cursed.

He shoved the bone at Sayyid, who accepted it with fumbling hands, nearly dropping his crowbar. Hopping on one foot, Neil pried off one of his boots and then yanked his sock free.

With a wincing squint, he snatched the bone from Sayyid's hand and dropped it into the tube of argyle knit, which was looking significantly worse for wear after being dunked in the Nile and trudged halfway across Egypt.

Through the muddy filter, the light softened from the glare of a comet to the moderate glow of a paraffin lamp. With the change, Neil's watering eyes could finally adjust—and see what the illumination revealed of his surroundings.

He stood at the edge of a broad, low cavern supported by countless pillars roughly hewed from the stone. It sprawled far beyond where the light of the sock-encased firebird bone could reach—a cool, silent, and uncannily still cathedral carved from the earth.

The hairs on the back of Neil's neck rose at the sight.

"I knew it!" Sayyid cried out, shattering the quiet. "I *knew* there was a quarry! The road in the wadi made me suspect it, and then when I saw the regularity in the shape of the walls where we fell—"

"This is a quarry?" Neil cut in, still reeling with astonishment at the sight of the bone-lit underground fairy kingdom.

"A cave quarry," Sayyid clarified. "Cut right into the mountain rather than dug out. Old Kingdom, based on the size of the blocks they were cutting. Just look at the ridges in this wall—these weren't talatat stones." His gaze roamed over the rest of the cavern. "It appears to be fine-grade limestone, mostly—though I should not be surprised to find traces of alabaster. It is clearly an extensive works. Comparable to Tura, at the very least. Of course, it begs the question of whether the builders of Nefertiti's tomb knew of the quarry and used its proximity deliberately, or whether…"

Sayyid stopped, catching himself. His jaw tensed as though he had just recalled that he was supposed to be angry at Neil—not rattling on to him about the development of stone-cutting techniques as though they were still working comfortably side-by-side in Saqqara.

Neil felt a sharp pang—but he could hardly blame Sayyid for it. He cleared his throat awkwardly. "Would you mind taking the bone while I put my boot back on?"

Sayyid startled uncomfortably. "Oh! Of course."

He accepted the sock with a distinct lack of enthusiasm, eyeing it with disdain. Neil could hardly blame him for that, either. It was hardly in a fine fettle. He wasn't all that excited about wearing it on his foot, never mind carrying it around in his hand.

Neil tugged his boot back on. The leather stuck against his bare, clammy skin. He hoped he wouldn't end up with blisters.

The light flickered, growing weak. Both Neil and Sayyid looked at it with alarm.

"I think it needs to be shaken again," Neil guessed urgently.

Sayyid let out a sigh of resignation. With a grimace, he took hold of the bone through the sock and gave it a vigorous jiggle.

The bone flared up, casting its pale glow over the silent, marching columns of stone.

Sayyid thrust the sock back at him, then surreptitiously scrubbed his hand off on his waistcoat.

Neil's companion looked a mess. His beard was lightened with a layer of dust, while the collar of his shirt was smudged with dirt. He had lost his fez in the fall, leaving his head bare.

Not that Neil would be looking much better. His glasses were bent, and his sockless foot stuck a bit against the leather of his boot. The buttons of his waistcoat had torn off in the fall, leaving it hanging open over his battered shirt.

"What now?" he asked.

"We need to find the way out." Sayyid gazed through the maze of pillars.

"*Is* there a way out?" Neil pressed nervously.

"There must have been," Sayyid returned. "How else could the quarrymen have taken out all this stone?"

"That was *five thousand years ago*. Archaeologists and looters have been scouring these hills for a century now, and nobody's ever reported finding a way into something like this!" Neil waved a wild hand around the vast space before them.

"That does not mean it isn't there," Sayyid insisted stubbornly.

He set off without looking back to see if Neil would follow. Neil did follow, of course. The notion of being left behind in that silent, eerie cavern frankly terrified him, even if he was the one holding the light.

They moved through the lines of pillars, the blocky towers of stone pale in the muffled glow of the firebird bone. The quarry felt as mummified as the bones of a pharaoh. Neil suspected that if he stopped to conduct a proper survey, he would quickly stumble across frozen remnants of the lives that had passed through this space before—an ancient length of rope, a lost sandal, the point of a tarnished copper chisel. In this stable underground environment, those objects would likely look much as they had the moment some quarryman had dropped them thousands of years before.

He was looking for signs of any such artifacts when the pillars abruptly stopped.

Where the next row should have been, Neil faced a wall. It was not the smooth, even-cut stone that had framed every other side of the quarry. This was a ragged, tumbling avalanche of crushed boulders—the debris of an ancient, long-forgotten collapse.

Neil regarded it in the flickering light of the firebird bone with a growing sense of horror.

"This is it, isn't it?" he choked out. "This is the entrance to the quarry."

Sayyid stared at the barrier, looking pale. "I think… that it is very possibly the entrance to the quarry," he agreed weakly.

A subtle fear had been stalking Neil since they fell into the dark. In the face of the piled stones before him, it tightened, gaining focus. "But is there a way through it?"

Sayyid glanced from the collapse to the dimming sock in Neil's hands. His expression was grim. "I know how we might find out."

"How?"

"Let the light go out." Sayyid met his eyes uneasily.

The notion of plunging back into that utter, complete darkness filled Neil with dread—but Sayyid was right. If they eliminated their light and gave their eyes time to adjust, they might pick out any cracks or openings to the moonlit night outside.

Swallowing thickly, Neil turned from Sayyid to face the blockage. The firebird bone flickered, sputtering like a guttering candle—and then snuffed out.

Midnight, thick and oppressive, closed around him. Neil forced himself not to panic as he steeled his eyes at the pile of boulders… and waited… and waited.

The darkness remained complete, an impenetrable wall that wrapped him up like a blanket.

"Do you see anything?" Neil asked hopefully. His voice sounded like it came from somewhere else, disembodied in the dark.

"No," Sayyid replied tightly after a moment.

Neil closed his eyes. It made not the least bit of difference. He could feel the vast, dry expanse of the cavern lurking behind him with a weighty, patient silence.

"Perhaps we should bring back the light," Sayyid finally suggested, the words small.

Neil absorbed them with a chill, then vigorously shook the bone. Light boomed to life behind the argyle of his sock. It spilled across the impenetrable barrier of rubble that lay before him, and he felt dizzy.

"Maybe there's…" He stopped, his throat dry. "Perhaps there's another…"

Sayyid wasn't listening. He frowned down at something on the ground near his boots. It was the base of another pillar—one that Neil could see lying in pieces beside the squarish, stubby protrusion from the ground.

There were more of them, marching along in parallel to the thick-packed boulders of the collapse—tumbled columns of stone resting by their truncated stumps.

"Did those all fall down?" he asked.

"They did not fall down. They were removed." Sayyid looked along the length of the butchered row. "They were *all* removed. Someone did this deliberately to compromise the structural integrity of the quarry."

"You mean they *wanted* it to cave in?" Neil demanded, aghast. "But how would they have even known how many to take?"

"I very much doubt that they did," Sayyid returned. "I imagine they simply kept going until it fell."

"But then how would whoever had done it esc—" Neil cut himself off as his throat closed with horror. "There were bones—in the room where we fell. There was a… a skull… on the floor…"

He desperately looked to Sayyid, hoping that he would find some hint of reassurance in his expression—*something* that belied the terrible conclusion Neil was rapidly coming to.

He didn't.

"We're going to die in here," Neil blurted out. "We're going to die in here and dry up like old sandals. Aren't we?"

Sayyid met his desperate gaze… and then slowly looked away.

It was all the answer Neil needed.

THIRTY-EIGHT

$\mathcal{N}$EIL FOUGHT THE urge to collapse into hysterics, unsure whether it would emerge as laughter or sobs. Instead, a heavy sense of guilt settled into place in his chest.

He dropped down to one of the shattered stone stumps, putting his head in his hands. "This is… this is all because of me. I should have listened to Ellie from the start. You told me that she was right about those…" He paused, at a loss for the word, and waved awkwardly at the sock-enclosed firebird bone.

"Arcana," Sayyid filled in without looking at him.

Arcana—from the Latin *arcanus,* Neil thought automatically. Most likely derived from the Latin word *arca*—a chest or box.

For the things that were secreted away. A shared root with the word *ark*.

Ark. Arcane. *Arcana.*

He wondered if he was losing his mind. He forced his thoughts back to the present—and to the dusty, tired man who had been trapped in this inescapable cavern with him.

"I know you're upset with me," Neil admitted quietly. "You have every right to be. I was an idiot to write that note to Mr. Forster-Mowbray. If I'd simply left well enough alone…"

Sayyid stared at him incredulously. "*That* is why you think I am upset with you?"

"Isn't it?" Neil flushed with bewilderment.

Sayyid clamped his mouth firmly shut. He stalked along the shadowy line of the pillars.

Neil hurried after him. "If it's something else I've done, please tell me! I can't possibly make it right if I don't know what it is!"

Sayyid whirled back to him, throwing up his hands. "Has it not occurred to you that perhaps you *can't* make it right?"

The blood drained from Neil's face. "Of course it has. My little sister is up there, along with one of my oldest friends. And Constance, who I… that I…" He couldn't quite find the right words, struggling onward without them. "Your wife and her apprentice and that frankly intimidating old lady! None of them are safe! And whatever those villains do to them is on my conscience, because I'm the one who told them where to find us—like an utter, bloody fool!"

"Why did you tell them?" Sayyid took a quick, angry step closer. "Why?"

"I don't know. I…" Neil caught himself with a wince. He owed Sayyid more than that. "Because I didn't *want* it to be true. I wanted it to be some mad flight of fancy that Ellie had dreamed up. I wanted everything to go back to the way it was when you and I were stabilizing artwork and sorting out finds. Arguing about the semantic changes from Middle to Late Egyptian—even though you were always right about those," he added in a grumble.

He closed his eyes, washed by a powerful sense of hurt and loss. "I *liked* things the way they were. I didn't want them to change. Didn't you?"

The anger in Sayyid's face drained away, leaving him drawn. "It isn't that simple."

Neil barked out a hysterical laugh, running a hand through his already wild hair. "Of course it isn't—since the representative of the British Athenaeum has turned out to be a murderous artifact thief!"

"You really don't get it, do you?" Sayyid burst out. "None of that was ever real! The Athenaeum, the semantics… the two of us working together like we were—"

His words choked off, swallowed by the thick, waiting silence that surrounded them. The silence lingered, pressing down on Neil as the rows of frozen pillars marched away at his back.

"Like we were what?" Neil tentatively prompted, his chest tight.

Sayyid answered him with a glare. "I've been an utter fool," he concluded and marched away through the hollow quarry.

"What? Why?" Neil stumbled after him.

Sayyid halted so abruptly, Neil almost crashed into him. "And you don't even know!" he exclaimed with a note of hysteria. "You still have absolutely no idea!"

"Then tell me!" Neil shot back, fear and frustration sharpening his voice.

"I suppose I must," Sayyid retorted. "It is not as though you would ever figure it out for yourself!"

The words stung like the crack of a whip.

Sayyid dropped his head, exhaustion slumping his shoulders. He put his fingers to the bridge of his nose and drew in a long, uneven breath.

The air of the quarry went even more still. The firebird bone flickered again, threatening to plunge them once more into that abysmal darkness. Neil forced himself to give the bone another energetic shake, even as his cheeks flushed with shame.

When Sayyid finally looked at him, his face was drawn into lines of tired sadness. "Before you, I was just a foreman. Sometimes all I could do was staff the dig—ensure that everyone arrived on schedule, oversee dismissals, and administer pay. On other excavations, I might do more—run the washing stations. Set procedures for sifting spoil. Stabilize artifacts before their removal and transport. Whatever the archaeologist in charge didn't want to be bothered with."

His expression tightened. "I know how to document finds. Record texts and artwork. Analyze stratigraphy and context. To the other men I have worked for, those skills were a convenience—like finding a dog who already knows how to fetch your slippers."

Sayyid's voice snapped with an old bitterness. "My father was not a pasha. I could never have gone to one of your universities. But even if I had, it would not have mattered—because I am not an Englishman. I am an Egyptian, and Egyptians are not archaeologists—no matter that it is *our* history the world is digging up. *Our* language on the walls. *Our* ancestors in the sarcophagi. I could only—ever—be *the help*." He flung the words out like stones. "The best I could hope to do was correct the foolish, stubborn errors of my 'betters' without letting on that I knew more than they did—which would see me fired from my position for *forgetting my place*. Then *you* come along."

He jabbed an accusing finger at Neil, who flinched back from it.

"You, who are so fresh-faced at all of this that it is laughable—but you don't even *pretend* to know what you are doing!" Sayyid burst out. "You just throw yourself onto my mercy, asking me a thousand questions—'Sayyid, what about suffix pronouns? Which adhesive do I use to stabilize plaster? Where should we site the spoil heap?' And before I know what is happening, I am working alongside you as though I was your...."

He stopped short, choking on what would have come next.

So Neil said it for him.

"Partner," he filled in quietly.

Sayyid dropped onto one of the broken pillars, putting his head in his hands. "But I am not your partner!" he bit out, his voice uneven. "Perhaps you actually listen to me when we get into an argument. You might even admit that you're wrong and then laugh about it like it means nothing for me to have corrected you. You stand back and let me lead on excavation procedure and conservation—but you are still the Englishman. You are the one with the university education, and the letters after your name, and the concession that grants you permission to excavate." He looked up, his eyes glistening. "My father had a university degree and letters after his name. But it did not matter, because he was still an Egyptian. And that killed him. Slowly, quietly… a little bit day after day until there was nothing left of the great man—only an old shadow who faded away."

Sayyid looked down at his hands—brown and strong, worn with callouses and capable of enormous delicacy. A tear slipped down his cheek, disappearing into the dark curls of his beard. "I thought it would be easier if I simply kept myself from expecting anything more… but you ruined that."

Neil's heart wrenched with a pain that felt like falling—like the lurch of finally realizing just how much of a fool he had been.

How could he not have seen it? He had been perfectly well aware of both Sayyid's brilliance and the enormous gulf between their stations—and their opportunities. Why hadn't he *realized?*

Because he hadn't been paying attention… just as he'd failed with Ellie. Only with Ellie, at least Neil had recognized that she *did* dream of more— even if he guiltily relegated it to the realm of the impossible.

He had never stopped to imagine what Sayyid might have dreamed of, even after working side-by-side with him for two years. He had been too swept up in the joy of putting his skills and knowledge into practice alongside someone whose intellect so perfectly matched and challenged his own.

"I wanted to pretend it didn't matter," he said softly, feeling the ache of regret like a hollow space inside of him. "It was easier to pretend it didn't matter—because I was happy. Working with you like that made me happy."

Neil drew in a breath and made himself confess the rest of it.

"Thinking of you as my friend made me happy." He lifted his gaze to Sayyid across the dry, still distance that separated them. "Was I just lying to myself?"

Sayyid stared down at his hands. "No," he replied hoarsely.

Neil blinked. There were tears in his eyes. He pushed one away with the back of his hand, his throat tight. "Well, this is embarrassing."

He had been aiming to sound reasonable and collected but didn't entirely succeed. The tears kept coming, and a deeper fear twisted inside his chest until the truth finally spilled from his lips. *"How can I fix it?"*

Sayyid finally looked up at him. "Join the revolution?" he suggested with a shadow of his old wry humor.

Neil coughed out a laugh. "You've been listening to your wife."

A sad twist of a smile crossed Sayyid's face. "Not enough, apparently."

The silence that followed whispered from between the endless rows of marching columns. Neil remembered that they were going to die here—he and Sayyid both—while the people they loved faced who-knew-what dangers on the mountain above. Dangers that Neil had brought down on them with his own foolish choices.

Frantic worry and guilt-laden helplessness rose inside of him until he thought he would choke, and Neil pushed to his feet.

"We have to help them! There must be *something* we can do!" He threw his hand out over the softly glittering stumps of limestone. "Couldn't we take out more of the pillars? Bring the whole mountain down?"

"How are we supposed to do that? With a crowbar?" Sayyid held up the tool in question, which didn't look like it stood much of a chance against the thick, sturdy columns of stone.

"There must be another way!" Neil pressed desperately.

Sayyid made a cross retort. "Well, let me know when you think of—"

He cut off as he leapt to his feet with a yelp, stumbling away from the column he'd been sitting on.

"What is it?" Neil demanded. "What's wrong?"

"Nothing," Sayyid replied in strangled tones, making a distinguished effort to straighten his waistcoat. "Just thought I imagined… Yeeeearrggh!"

He danced, hopping from foot to foot in a wild panic, then kicked out his leg.

Something flew from the cuff of his trousers, landing with a little click against the fallen stone column.

Sayyid went still. "Was that a beetle?"

Neil stepped over to investigate.

The fat, glittering form of a black scarab lay on its back in the shadow of the toppled pillar, skinny legs wriggling in the air.

"Er… yes?" Neil offered awkwardly.

Sayyid closed his eyes, shuddering. "It was on my trousers. On. My. Trousers."

The scarab rocked, then flipped itself. Legs once more on the ground, it skittered off into the shadows beyond the glare of the firebird bone.

Something tickled at the back of Neil's mind as he stared after it. "Beetles," he said absently. "Down here. In the quarry."

"I sincerely hope not," Sayyid replied fervently, twisting to get a look at the back of his legs.

The pieces suddenly clicked into place. Neil took hold of Sayyid's shoulders and gave them a shake. "Beetles in the quarry!" he repeated urgently.

"Why?!" Sayyid wailed.

The question was rhetorical rather than a direct inquiry, but Neil answered it nonetheless. "Because they went under the door—the door that Bates said must open into *the middle of the mountain!*" He gave Sayyid another shake. "The beetles went under the door, Sayyid! And now they are here in the quarry!"

Sayyid's eyes widened. "They built the tomb into the quarry. That's why no one ever found it. They built the tomb into the quarry and then collapsed the entrance!" He gave out a wild laugh. "Those clever devils!"

"Which means that somewhere down here, we will find the other side of the entrance to the tomb!" Neil added.

Sayyid's expression firmed with determination. "Yes."

He slipped from Neil's grasp and hurried into the columns, walking with quick purpose. Neil scurried after him.

"If we can get into the tomb, we can climb back out through the fissure and try to help the others," Neil reasoned, a little breathless at trying to keep up with Sayyid's quick pace. "We might still be able to *do* something! But… where are we going?"

Sayyid pointed into the gloom beyond the illuminated columns. "Over there. That is where the entrance must be."

"How do you know?" Neil demanded, bewildered.

Sayyid arched an eyebrow, shifting his arm to the right. "Because we fell into the quarry over there, from the burial chamber. The tunnel from the treasury turned ninety degrees to the left, then up the stairs and around another thirty-degree left before the painted hall."

He traced out the route with his finger as though drawing it onto the impenetrable darkness that surrounded them. "Haven't you been paying attention?" he finished impatiently.

Neil stared at Sayyid as a tumult of emotion roiled inside of his chest—then threw his arms around him. "Thank you," he said, giving Sayyid a fervent squeeze before awkwardly releasing him.

Sayyid stared at him with surprise.

Neil hurried onward, calling back to Sayyid as he went. "If we're quick enough, we might still reach the others in time to make a difference!"

"We would make far more of a difference if we found that staff," Sayyid grumbled. "But it would be like looking for your needle in a haystack."

"Not really," Neil replied automatically.

Sayyid stopped short. "Not really? What do you mean by that, precisely?"

Neil frowned at his urgent tone. "Oh! Only that I had a bit of an idea where it might be. Not that I know anything for certain," he protested at the intent look in Sayyid's eyes. "It was just a little notion that popped into my head right before Mr. Forster-Mowbray came in. It's probably nothing. It wouldn't really have made any sense, anyway."

Sayyid did not look convinced by Neil's disclaimers. He crossed his arms, planting himself firmly in their path forward. "You do realize that your notions about the past have an uncanny habit of turning out to be correct?"

"What?" Neil gave an awkward laugh. "Don't be silly."

"I am not being silly." Sayyid's eyes narrowed. "How did you find the tablet in Hatshepsut's temple?"

"I didn't find it!" Neil protested. "Ellie did!"

Sayyid rolled his eyes. "And how did Ellie find it?"

"Well, she spotted one of the little hands of the Aten on the surface of the sun chapel altar, after I…"

Neil's voice trailed off.

"After you what?" Sayyid prompted.

"After I… might have had the notion that the altar had been rebuilt and expanded in antiquity," Neil finished weakly.

"And did you see something on the altar to make you think of that?" Sayyid pressed. "Or did that notion just pop into your brain as well?"

Neil didn't answer him.

"I watched you find the location of Horemheb's funerary chapel by looking at an empty stretch of desert." Sayyid jabbed a finger up at the mountain over their heads. "Less than an hour ago, I saw you locate the way into Neferneferuaten's tomb by crawling under a boulder that looked like ten others scattered across the ridge."

"That wasn't…" Neil started, spluttering. "You can't possibly be suggesting… You're making it sound like…"

Sayyid raised an eyebrow.

"This isn't *magic!*" Neil burst out. "It's scholarship! And maybe a bit of… lucky guessing!"

"You were not guessing at Saqqara when you relocated our entire excavation plan thirty meters to the southeast without having found so much as a single pot shard to support the change," Sayyid returned stubbornly.

"I am not magical!" Neil shouted.

The words resounded hauntingly through the pillared darkness of the quarry… and Neil remembered the moment he had stepped into Akhetaten and watched the city come alive around him as though he had fallen through a hole in time.

Magical, the quarry echoed back at him. *Magical.*

"I suppose we'll find out," Sayyid declared relentlessly and dragged Neil onward.

THIRTY-NINE

THE STARLIT HOLLOW of the ridge blared with paraffin lanterns and clattering tools. The crew of the *Isis*—a mix of Egyptian, Greek, and Sudanese sailors—worked with a hurried clamor by the boulder that covered the entrance to the tomb. The men had used a heavy iron jack to lever up the enormous stone a few crucial inches, widening the space below enough to set a winch over the fissure and start lowering in equipment.

Ellie watched them from where she sat with her back resting against the steep bluff that had once separated them from Julian's misplaced excavation. Her hands were bound behind her back. She wiggled her fingers as the crewmen threw her and the other prisoners uncomfortable looks.

She highly doubted anyone had asked those simple sailors if they minded assisting in a criminal enterprise.

The Al-Saboors were scattered about the ledge. Two of them lingered nearby with rifles slung over their shoulders, while others guarded the entrance to the tomb or barked orders to the workers.

There was no sign of Mr. Jacobs.

Ellie burned with frustration. It appeared she was going to be forced to sit and watch as Julian looted possibly the most important discovery in the history of Egyptology.

"I hope you are documenting all of the objects in situ before removing them, you barbarians!" she shouted across to the tomb entrance.

"You tell 'em, Princess," Adam commented easily from beside her.

He had a new bruise on his cheek, and his split lip was bleeding again.

On Ellie's other side, the row of prisoners continued with Jemmahor and Zeinab, who wore a gag and had her ankles bound. Her green eyes flashed furiously above the strip of fabric, leading Ellie to suspect that something harsher than a critique of improper archaeological procedure might cross her lips, were she free to use them.

The big, heavily muscled Al-Saboor rounded the corner. The petite and wildly kicking figure hanging across his shoulder railed out a string of colorful insults.

"Put me down, you meathead!" Constance shouted.

The big fellow unceremoniously dumped her at the end of the row of prisoners and walked away.

Constance tugged furiously against the ropes that bound her hands behind her back.

"You'll chafe your wrists that way," Ellie called helpfully across the line of women.

After all, she had some experience with the matter.

"And to think that I was actually entertaining accepting that prat for a suitor!" Constance kicked her heels angrily against the stones. "I will tell you one thing, Eleanora—I am modifying my qualifications for potential husbands going forward. And they are going to include not being an utter villain!" She raised her voice, shouting across the ridge. "*Did you hear that, you pigeon-livered ratbag!?*"

Though Julian was still down in the tomb, Ellie thought he actually might. Constance was certainly exerting sufficient volume.

After Neil had fallen through the collapsed floor of the burial chamber, the room had erupted into chaos. Zeinab had the presence of mind to use the distraction of Neil's fall to throw a beautifully painted three-thousand-year-old wooden room divider over the open sarcophagus, which was likely the only thing that saved them all from a bout of iron poisoning. Then she had shoved her husband into the pit, clearly calculating that his chances in a mysterious hole in the ground were better than his odds of surviving if he stayed in the tomb. She likely would have gone after him herself if that big, muscled Al-Saboor hadn't snatched her around the waist and carted her off.

Zeinab had unleashed a string of Masri imprecations that would have burned a sailor's ears, then bit the man for his trouble—which was how she had acquired the gag and extra bindings.

Ellie had managed to throw Neil her firebird bone as Adam hocked an Eighteenth Dynasty chair at Jacobs—which was not a tactic Ellie approved of, even under the circumstances. It had been a very fine piece with ebony inlay and lion-footed legs. Thankfully, the object was of exceptionally robust construction and held up even against the hard head of the gap-toothed Al-Saboor that Jacobs had ducked behind.

Jemmahor had used the distraction to dive behind the sarcophagus, while two more Al-Saboors had tackled Adam into a pile of walking sticks.

All in all, it had been an entirely uncivilized rout.

Ellie had been waiting for Jacobs to conduct a tidy series of executions once they were all subdued. Surely, whatever had made him hesitate to shoot them back at Hatshepsut's temple must now be outweighed by all the trouble they continued to cause him. If it had been Julian holding him back, he certainly ought to have given up on his notion of convincing Constance to marry him by now—even if the rotter did consider being the grandson of a duke more important than something as trivial as moral character.

But they hadn't been shot. Instead, Jacobs had ordered them bound and tossed into a helpless row against the rocks, where they were forced to watch the raid on Neferneferuaten's tomb.

At least the thieves had taken Zeinab's warning about the dangers of the hematite seriously. For the last quarter-hour, workers had been reeling up buckets of blood-red sludge from the tomb, which they then carried to the far end of the ridge and dumped over the side. Julian was clearly working to remove the deadly powder before he searched it—or the coffin that it protected—for the arcanum.

There had still been no word of Neil or Sayyid. Ellie's stomach twisted with worry. She had been able to see that both men had survived their fall into the pit more or less intact, but it had been very clear there would be no climbing back out without the aid of a rope. Wherever they had gone to escape the bullets, they were trapped there unless they found some other way out of those mysterious caverns.

That left only one member of their party unaccounted for. There had been no sign of Umm Waseem when they emerged from the tomb, and a whispered question to Jemmahor revealed that the older woman had already vanished when 'that dead-eyed devil' Jacobs ambushed her. Ellie wondered whether the older woman's absence indicated some hope of a rescue... and what form it might take.

She was still very curious about the contents of Umm Waseem's black canvas bag.

Their two designated Al-Saboor guards idly chatted as they smoked, clearly bored by their assignment.

"Quick!" Ellie whispered in a low hiss. "Does anyone still have a blade?"

All of them had been searched for weapons when they had been captured. For the most part, those had been sadly lacking, other than Adam's machete. The big knife had been confiscated in a process that resulted in several more bruises—both for Adam and for the unfortunate Al-Saboor that had been tasked with relieving him of his beloved knife.

Ellie spotted the big-eared man slumped against a rock on the other side of the ledge, holding a wet cloth to his head and groaning. The fellow beside him had his arm in a sling and kept casting dirty looks over at Adam.

"I lost mine back on the *Isis*." Constance scowled. "I knew I should have equipped myself with more than two!"

"I only had the rifle," Jemmahor said—glaring at the firearm in question, which was slung over the shoulder of the limping Al-Saboor.

"Ralph's got mine," Adam said darkly.

"Ralph?" Ellie echoed in confusion.

"You know—the one with the horsey teeth." Adam nodded at an Al-Saboor giving orders to the workers.

Zeinab mumbled at them furiously from behind her gag, wiggling her fingers and jerking her head toward her back.

"Ostazah?" Jemmahor prompted, brow furrowing with confusion.

"Maybe a bug crawled into her galabeya," Constance offered helpfully.

Zeinab rolled her eyes, knocking the heels of her shoes against the rocks in frustration as she made another frantic gesture with her head.

"It is not a bug!" Jemmahor realized excitedly. "She is telling us that they did not take her scalpels!"

"Mmmph!" Zeinab agreed.

"She keeps them in a roll tucked into her belt, under her abaya," Jemmahor translated.

Constance looked sharply at their two guards. The pair were rolling more cigarettes.

She scooted behind Zeinab, pulling up the other woman's cloak—no easy task with her hands bound behind her back, even if Zeinab did try to help her by bouncing on her rear and offering terse instructions through the gag—which nobody could make out.

Constance wriggled her hands under the folds of black fabric as the Al-Saboors, ten yards away, searched their pockets for a light.

"I have it!" she whispered triumphantly, tugging a slender leather bundle out from the back of Zeinab's belt. "Now just hold still and I'll—"

With her bound hands, Zeinab swatted Constance's fingers away from the opened roll of medical instruments.

"Oh, very well!" Constance hissed back irritably, pushing her bound wrists at the midwife. "They are your scalpels, after all. But do it quickly!"

Zeinab gave Constance a withering look that clearly said *if I do it quickly, I might slice one of your fingers off.*

She set to work, and a moment later, Constance's ropes fell away. She shook out her arms with obvious relief, then hurriedly plucked the scalpel from Zeinab's fingers and set to work on the other woman's bindings. Zeinab whipped her hands free and immediately yanked down the gag, spitting violently onto the rocks.

The Al-Saboors had found a book of matches and were lighting their cigarettes. They stiffened, coming to sudden attention as Mr. Jacobs crawled out from the entrance to the tomb.

"Jacobs!" Ellie hissed in warning.

His head snapped in her direction.

She froze as she met his gaze, forcing herself not to look down the line at the other women. Even a glance in their direction might give Constance and Zeinab away.

Jacobs' eyes narrowed. He crossed over to speak to the two smoking cousins, who looked less bored and more nervous now Jacobs was there.

Ellie risked a glance at her companions. Constance leaned innocently against the rocks with her hands behind her back, whistling a little. Zeinab glared mutinously out over the ridge with her gag back in place.

Ellie let out a slow, silent breath of relief—then spotted the edge of Zeinab's scalpel roll peeking out from under the black fall of her abaya.

She looked quickly back to Jacobs, her pulse thudding at the thought that he might turn back to them and notice.

A flicker of movement from beyond the cluster of armed men caught her eye. It flashed from the top of the curved ridge that framed the bowl where they sat—little more than a quick wisp of blacker shadow against the star-speckled night sky.

Ellie wondered if she had imagined it… until Jacobs' head snapped up, his gaze zeroing in on the place where the shadow had been.

He frowned, heading for the ridge.

"Stop him!" Zeinab ordered in an urgent rasp, her gag pulled down once more. "Now!"

Ellie's throat went dry with an instinctive panic. Her mind whirled for a solution that wouldn't get them all killed. "How?"

"You could pretend to faint," Constance offered helpfully.

"Or throw a rock at his testicles," Jemmahor countered darkly.

Everyone stared at the apprentice midwife in surprise.

"What?" she shot back unapologetically. "You do not think that he deserves it?"

Ellie considered the options—with a pang of yearning over the lack of any potentially incendiary materials on hand.

Her train of thought was rudely interrupted by the bruised, dashing American beside her as he shouted across the night at the top of his substantial lungs.

"Hey, you cold-blooded bastard! How about you and I have a word?"

Everyone froze, from the crewmen carrying buckets of red sludge to the Al-Saboors with their rifles.

Jacobs stopped at the base of the cliff he was about to climb—and slowly turned back.

"Are you mad?" Ellie hissed to Adam. "Or have you forgotten that your hands are bound and you have no machete!"

"It worked, didn't it?" Adam replied.

Ellie wasn't so sure. Jacobs had hesitated, but he was still at the base of the ridge. He narrowed his eyes as though considering Adam's request.

He turned away and began to climb.

"Not even about what you saw in that damned mirror?" Adam called after him boldly.

Jacobs went very, very still.

A chill crept over Ellie's skin.

What you saw in that mirror…

There was only one mirror that mattered—the one that had lurked in the darkness beneath Tulan. A mirror that did not show reflections. A mirror that Ellie had destroyed.

Her own dark memories of that obsidian eye swirled up from the place where she had tried to bury them.

The soft plink of water in a pristine washroom. A gold-eyed woman with a scar on her cheek.

The history of an empire spilling into her brain like a rain of fire.

Tell me what you want.

"But Jacobs never used the mirror," Ellie pressed unsteadily.

Adam replied without looking at her. His eyes were locked on Jacobs, who stared at him with dangerous focus from across the ledge. "I made him bleed. It's how I knew where to find my knife—but Jacobs got a face full of that smoke as well."

Blood. Mirror. Smoke. Ellie knew what that trinity had meant inside the hollow space beneath the city of the gods.

"But what would he have seen?" Ellie gasped, reeling.

Even as she asked the question, the answer echoed in her ears, murmuring in the voice of a mischievous old priest.

It seeks the answer in your heart—in your desire.

What desire did someone like *Jacobs* hide in his heart?

Then another implication of Adam's revelation snapped into place.

"Hold on!" Ellie exclaimed, forgetting to keep her voice down. "Are you telling me that your deepest and most fervent desire was to get your blasted knife back?"

"I wanted a way to beat Jacobs!" Adam protested. "It's not my fault if the best way to do that just happened to involve me getting hold of my machete."

Ellie gazed at the familiar lines of his bruised, stubble-shadowed face. Warmth fluttered to life inside her chest. "You are…"

She wasn't quite sure what she meant to say next. Incorrigible? Magnificent?

Before she could find out, Jacobs was there.

He loomed over them, the glare of the paraffin lamps scattered about the hollow throwing his shadow across the place where Ellie and Adam sat.

Jacobs cast a look back over his shoulder. All the rest of the men who had been blatantly gaping at him, from guards to crew, quickly went back to doing whatever it was they were supposed to be doing.

Ellie was painfully conscious of her bound hands. She was utterly powerless sitting on the ground at Jacobs' feet.

In the corner of her eye, she saw Zeinab's gaze flash once more to the crown of the ridge. Her mouth firmed into a fierce, determined line.

Ellie couldn't know what she saw up there—but she hoped it was worth the terrible risk she and Adam had just taken.

Jacobs looked down at the two of them thoughtfully before his eyes shifted to Adam. "By all rights, the pair of you ought to have been dead three times over."

A hint of frustration seethed through his words. A twist of fear wrenched in Ellie's gut.

Adam leaned back against the rocks. "I'd say more like four or five, but who's counting?"

Ellie forced herself to wade in, even though the thought of deliberately provoking Jacobs' ire made her feel ill.

"So what is your innermost desire, Mr. Jacobs?" she asked, forcing a light tone. "Being set loose to murder anyone who irritates you?"

His expression was as calm and implacable as always—but Ellie thought she saw something else flash through his black gaze. Something… *complicated.*

"And why do you want to know, Miss Mallory?" Jacobs demanded.

Ellie's pulse thudded with a rising sense of danger. She forced herself not to look away, even as she could feel the other prisoners watching her worriedly.

She had to keep him talking for a while longer—no matter how she managed it. In that moment, she could think of only one thing to say that would be sure to hold his attention.

She swallowed thickly against a suddenly dry throat.

"I supposed I had better think on how I answer that," she replied carefully. "Given that you will know if I am lying."

Jacobs' habitual stillness deepened, turning into something darker. His focus on her intensified until she could feel the weight of it like a stone against her chest.

"Will I, then?" he asked in a voice like black silk.

Ellie fought against the urge to sink into the wall and disappear. "I therefore propose a deal," she went on carefully. "I will answer your question, Mr. Jacobs, if you answer mine."

Jacobs' black gaze was as cold as the end of the earth. "You are awfully sure of yourself for a woman tied up on the floor," he noted in a dry, flat drawl.

Adam stiffened beside her at Jacobs' words. She deduced that he was fighting the urge to do something extraordinarily stupid. She hurried on before his anger won out over his good sense, agonizingly conscious of his bound hands and missing knife.

"You can't kill us," Ellie retorted quickly. "Mr. Forster-Mowbray won't let you."

Jacobs… *laughed.*

The sound was bizarre—a note of helpless, involuntary humor threaded through with dark frustration.

The reaction made not the least bit of sense.

It lasted for only a breath before his eyes flashed with fury, and his cool facade slid back into place.

"This is a waste of my time," he determined.

He turned away. Zeinab coughed pointedly, and Ellie made another desperate jab.

"You despise him, don't you?" she called out. "And yet you keep doing whatever he tells you to do, even when you disagree. It can't be because you need the work. You are obviously very competent at your—er, particular area of expertise. I'm sure there are other ne'er-do-wells you could ally yourself with if you chose. Yet you keep bowing to Mr. Forster-Mowbray's whims, even when it obviously infuriates you. I wonder why that is?"

Jacob's attention was like a dagger. Ellie braced herself against it even as a cool line of sweat trickled between her shoulder blades.

"Careful, Miss Mallory," Jacobs' tone was light—and dangerous. "I don't think you want to make this personal."

"*Make* it personal?" Ellie burst back, startled into frankness. "You have already tried to kill me four times!"

"Was it four?" Adam's tone was casual, but his blue gaze was like ice as he studied Jacobs. "I was counting three."

Ellie bit back a huff of exasperation. "First, he planned to murder me at the hotel in Belize Town," she listed. "Then he threatened to flay me to force you to cooperate when we were caught on the trail. He tried to shoot us both when we were fleeing from the temple. And then there was that attempted stabbing when he caught me by the mirror. That is four!"

"I dunno if I'd count the flaying," Adam hedged. "That was more of a bluff than an actual murder attempt."

"Are you saying you didn't mind that one?" Ellie shot back, infuriated.

"Of course, I minded it!" Adam returned. "I minded it a lot!"

Jacobs pinched the bridge of his nose as though fighting a rising headache—then with a smooth, practiced motion, he grabbed hold of Constance's hair, dragged her to him, and set a dagger to her throat.

The blade seemed to have slipped into his hand out of thin air.

"Unhand me, you reprehensible, loutish—" Constance snarled.

"Connie!" Ellie pleaded.

Constance closed her mouth, though her eyes still blazed with fury.

Ellie's throat tightened with fear… and a curious, buzzing question.

Why *Constance?* Jacobs must have a far better sense of what Adam meant to her, and he was sitting right beside her. Why the friend he'd barely seen her with as opposed to the man he must know she cared deeply for?

"You rotten bastard—" Adam started, the words a growl of outrage as his arms tensed against the ropes binding his wrists.

"What is all of this about, Miss Mallory?" Jacobs' voice was taut with impatience and barely suppressed ire.

She was exquisitely conscious of the impossibility of putting Jacobs off with a lie—and of just how easily Jacobs might snap his blade and leave Constance to bleed out on the stones.

Constance held herself still—for now. She hadn't yet revealed that her hands were untied, keeping them at her back. She had likely calculated that even her more advanced jiu jitsu maneuvers couldn't help her when someone had a knife at her throat.

"Answer my question, and I will tell you," Ellie pushed back in a desperate gambit. "What did the mirror show you?"

"You are hardly in a position to bargain," Jacobs pointed out.

"I am if I have something worth telling you," Ellie retorted, glad her hands were behind her back so that Jacobs could not see them shaking.

Jacobs stilled. When he spoke, every word rang with a clear, deliberate comprehension. "And do you?"

"I do," Ellie replied, glaring up at him with all the certainty and fortitude she could muster.

Something flickered through Jacobs' black eyes—something that looked like a flash of grudging respect.

"What did you see, then, Mr. Jacobs?" Ellie carefully, deliberately prompted. "What is your innermost desire?"

The knife in Jacobs' hand was steady. His look never broke.

"Justice, Miss Mallory," he replied. "I want *justice*."

Ellie wondered if the world had just turned inside out. "*You* want justice?" she burst out. "Justice for *what?*"

His expression closed. "Your turn."

Ellie had run out of moves. She only hoped that she had played the game out long enough for whatever Zeinab had been hoping to accomplish.

She forced herself to speak calmly as she gave the only answer she could to a man who could sense every falsehood. "I am trying to distract you from whatever is happening on the ridge."

Jacobs' face flattened with surprise. He whirled to the crown of stone that rose around them, dropping the knife from Constance's throat.

The mountain bloomed gold with fire.

FORTY

ʜair askew, waistcoat open, and spectacles in place, Neil gazed at the entrance to the tomb of Neferneferuaten in the eerie glow of the sock-obscured firebird bone. The plaster that covered the doors was unbroken, still stamped with the pharaoh's royal seal and the seal of the Amarna necropolis.

Whoever had entered the tomb three thousand years earlier to return the staff had not come this way. The only ones using this portal were the scarabs.

The alabaster that lay on the other side of the plaster was visible here and there where the ancient compound had crumbled away. The stone glowed softly in the light from the bone. Instead of the portraits of Akhenaten and Nefertiti, the outside of the rosy slabs was covered in tiny columns of hieroglyphs.

"The seals are intact," Neil noted uncomfortably. "I'm not sure anyone has ever found a completely intact royal tomb entrance before."

"No." Sayyid stared at the doors, his shoulders slumped morosely. The crowbar dangled limply at his side.

"This is… this is an extraordinary find." Neil's stomach twisted. "Couldn't we just… Might there not be another…"

Sayyid didn't answer.

They should have been removing the plaster carefully, scoring through the unmarked portions and delicately lifting it from the door. He and Sayyid should have been arguing about the right methodology, possibly over a matter of days and many cups of sweet, minty tea.

"It is us or the seals," Sayyid reasoned with a pained wince.

"Not just us," Neil added, rubbing a hand over his exhausted features. Worry for his sister and friends was a growing, nagging buzz at the back of his mind.

He closed his eyes as two opposing forms of guilt fought wretchedly inside his chest.

Sayyid gave a long, eloquent sigh—then jammed the crowbar into the doors.

He wrenched back on the iron, and ancient plaster popped and burst into the air around them. Neil turned his face to avoid being peppered by it, coughing against the dust that suddenly filled the air.

Sayyid yanked again, and the massive panel of alabaster scraped against the stone of the quarry floor until Neil could see a dark gap opening into the interior.

A trio of scarabs raced through it, scurrying across the ground. Sayyid danced back from them with a strangled yelp, nearly dropping the crowbar.

Neil's nerves jangled against the silence that followed. "Do you think anyone heard that?" he asked in a whisper.

Sayyid flashed him an uneasy look, and by silent consensus, the two men eased up to listen at the finger-thin opening.

The hall beyond the door was quiet. As Neil held his breath, tuning his ears even more carefully to the silence, he could just make out the murmur of distant voices.

"I think they're down in the—" Neil began.

The rest of his words were cut off by a deep, resonant thunder that drummed through the stillness of the quarry.

Neil pressed himself against the doors as the sound boomed around him. Chips of stone shivered down from the cavern ceiling, cracking softly against the ground as they fell.

The rumble faded into a low echo before drifting back into silence.

"What…" Neil swallowed against a dry throat. "What was…"

Sayyid had flattened himself against the wall. He looked up nervously. "It sounded like firecrackers. Extremely loud, very powerful firecrackers?"

A few more bits of stone pinged down by Neil's shoes. "Is the quarry going to collapse?"

The question ended in a somewhat humiliating squeak.

"I truly, sincerely hope not," Sayyid replied fervently.

Neil jolted at the sound of voices through the crack in the alabaster doors. They were coming from much closer than before, and one of them was most distinctly that of Mr. Forster-Mowbray.

Neil couldn't make out Julian's words, but the high-pitched reply came to him in the tones of Professor Dawson.

"Attack?!" Dawson echoed wildly. "From whom? We'll be cornered down here!"

Neil quickly looked at Sayyid, who was still prudently plastered to the wall. Sayyid raised an eyebrow.

A rush of harsh whispers followed, and then Neil heard the creak of a winch.

After that, everything went quiet.

Neil met Sayyid's eyes with an unspoken question. Sayyid drooped with a distinct lack of enthusiasm, then nodded. Peeling himself from the wall, he hefted the crowbar like a cricket bat and waited.

The firebird bone flickered, reminding Neil that he was more or less carrying a beacon. He shoved it into his pocket, dropping them in a deep, thick gloom, then felt his way to grip the rough edge of the cracked door.

The heavy stone slab ground against the floor with a noise that sounded like the groan of a giant to Neil's paranoid ears. He forced himself to keep pulling, knowing that leaving the door half-open at this point would only invite some burly, well-armed enemy to set up an ambush.

Sayyid rushed inside, the crowbar raised. Neil followed him, lifting his fists… for all the bloody good that would do him.

The hallway was empty. A lone paraffin lantern sat under the hole in the ceiling like a neglected relic. A rope sling dangled down from the opening, clearly a more elaborate system for lifting people and gear than what Neil and the others had managed an hour before.

Sayyid's favorite scarab curse decorated the wall beside him, reminding Neil of the divine punishments intended for those who violated tombs.

Fear tugged at him—not of curses, but of the possibly murderous thugs who might lurk around every corner.

His worry about Ellie and the others outweighed it. As quietly as possible, he crept up the hall to where the fissure opened in the ceiling. There were no more explosive sounds, but he could hear the bark of angry voices.

Sayyid held the crowbar uneasily. "Have they all gone?" he whispered.

"I… think our people must have been taken outside." Neil glanced up at the hole.

"How can you be certain?" Sayyid demanded.

"I think we would hear them if they were still here," Neil pointed out. "None of them are particularly quiet."

"That is true," Sayyid acknowledged.

"Should we go up?" Neil looked anxiously to Sayyid.

"And defeat them with a crowbar?" Sayyid retorted in a hiss, waving his questionable weapon.

He grabbed the sleeve of Neil's shirt and hauled him forward.

They picked their way down the precarious stairwell. Someone had lain boards over the place where Neil had nearly fallen through. He still preferred not to test them, keeping to the safer edge.

Moving silently, they peered into the treasure room and found it empty. Neil stepped inside—and heard the rush of low voices from the burial chamber.

With a thrill of fear, Neil threw Sayyid a questioning look. Sayyid frowned down at the crowbar in his hand uncomfortably.

Neil didn't even have a crowbar. He made a wild survey of the treasure room for something he might use to defend himself. A finely carved alabaster shabti? A faience vase?

The notion of using any of those precious historical objects to bash someone on the head horrified him on multiple levels.

The timbre of the voices rose in urgency and speed, like the crest of an argument.

It ended, and quick footsteps approached down the corridor.

Neil didn't have time to think. He simply snatched up the nearest thing that came to his hand from the jumbled pile of grave goods by his boots and raised it up over his head.

Two unfamiliar Egyptians hurried through the door—and then froze, gaping at Neil and Sayyid. They threw up their hands, stammering in quick and obviously conciliatory Masri. Neil struggled to keep up.

Following orders… Please don't kill us…

The pair were clearly crewmen from the *Isis* rather than Al-Saboors, but Neil was still surprised at how easily he and Sayyid had managed to cow them.

Then he glanced up and realized that he was holding an enormous scimitar over his head.

"Oh bugger!" he exclaimed, fumbling his grip on the weapon and nearly dropping it. He just managed to catch it again before it hit the floor.

Thankfully, he had grabbed it by the hilt. The bronze blade still looked wickedly sharp.

Sayyid burst out in stern Masri, jabbing a finger at the two crewmen. Neil picked up the gist of it even as he worked to stop his heart from pounding.

Looting your own history… Have you no shame… What would your mothers say?

He finished it off with a particularly pointed remark, and the two men startled, then burst out into a round of abject apologies. Neil struggled to keep up.

We are so sorry, uncle! Wretched… tricked… By God, we did not mean…

Sayyid cut in. "La ilâha illa Allâh." He waved impatiently toward the door. "Yalla!"

"Shukrân, ya 'amm!" they exclaimed, inching around Neil and Sayyid nervously. "Shukrân!"

Once clear, the crewmen hurried up the stairs.

Holding the scimitar limply in his hand, Neil looked wide-eyed to Sayyid. "What did you say to them?"

"I told them they were working for an English bandit and that the police would be here momentarily with the Antiquities Service," Sayyid replied. "And that if they did not wish to be imprisoned, they had best tell their reis and take the boat as far from here as possible."

Neil straightened, impressed. "Well done!"

"Enough standing about." Sayyid pulled him into the burial chamber.

The space around Neferneferuaten's sarcophagus was empty of threats, save for the red powder around the coffin. A wet canvas covered most of it, while a half-full bucket of red sludge sat at the foot of the granite box.

Sayyid peered at it with a thoughtful frown. "They are dampening the hematite and removing the stabilized mud." He sniffed a bit. "It is not the worst idea, but they should have better protected the coffin first."

Across the room, Neil could see the ragged hole in the floor where he and Sayyid had fallen. Broken artifacts dangled over the black edges.

He realized he was still holding the scimitar. He set it down awkwardly beside the sarcophagus.

"I can see the seam of the coffin lid." Neil tentatively bent down closer to the covered hematite for a better look. "Should we open it?"

He was uncomfortable with the suggestion. Part of Neil itched for the chance to examine the mortal remains of a woman he had studied for most of his life… and yet something about it felt surprisingly wrong.

It was not a feeling he had ever had when examining a mummy, which he had done a half-dozen times before. Perhaps that was because this mummy wasn't just an anonymous find or a priest or courtier with little more than a name attached to it. This was Neferneferuaten, who had been Nefertiti—a woman who had played a critical role in a religious revolution, who had ruled with her husband through one of the most profoundly transformative periods of Egyptian history. Neil felt like he *knew* her… and the idea of disturbing the eternal rest of someone who was quite a bit more to him than a name made him feel desperately uncomfortable.

"I don't know," Sayyid retorted with a pointed look. "Should we?"

A flush came into the tips of Neil's ears. He knew what Sayyid was asking him—but it was impossible.

"This is ridiculous," he said aloud, trying to let the sound of the words comfort him. "I don't know where to find the Staff of Moses. I haven't known where to find any of these things! They've all been informed, scholarly hypotheses, each of which I've investigated in a perfectly rational, orderly manner."

"That is not what you did when you found Horemheb's tomb," Sayyid countered stubbornly.

"Of course it is!" Neil protested wildly. "My brain just has… a bit of a knack for putting those hypotheses together without me needing to sit down and spell out every little step. There's nothing supernatural about that. It's… neurology," he finished awkwardly.

Sayyid looked both impatient and unimpressed. "Well, then, what does your *neurology* tell you about where the staff has been hidden?"

Neil automatically looked over at the solar barque.

The model boat was roughly two feet in length, executed in exquisite detail with a shaded canopy and a cluster of little plaster sailors. But it was what lay beneath it that tugged at his attention like a fishhook, just as it had in the moments before Julian Forster-Mowbray had entered the tomb.

The object was a simple, slender whitewashed wooden box.

He tore his gaze from it quickly—only to find Sayyid staring at him.

"It's nothing!" Neil protested. "It's just… I only…"

Sayyid's mouth firmed into a determined line. He grasped Neil by the shoulders, spun him, and marched him over to the model boat.

Neil faced the whitewashed box as though it were crocodile-headed Ammit rising up to devour him.

"It's a cubit box," he blurted uncomfortably, recognizing the little cluster of hieroglyphs stamped on its surface. "It doesn't make any sense that the staff would be in cubit box. A cubit rod has absolutely no relevance to the Atenist faith or early Judaism. And anyway, it's too small. The staff wouldn't fit. Well—I mean, it *could* fit, if it isn't as big as we think it is, but then the Hebrew terms used to refer to it would be…"

Neil trailed off as Sayyid continued to stare at him.

"That's all very sensible," Sayyid replied calmly. "Except that the cubit rod is on the floor."

He pointed to the distinct, blocky shape of the Egyptian ruler, which was leaning against a bundle of reed arrows.

Neil closed his eyes as dismay and a mild, gut-clenching terror washed over him.

"But the solar barque must be extremely fragile," he pleaded, starting to sweat. "We couldn't possibly risk moving it."

"I can move it." Sayyid picked up a piece of scrap wood that Julian's men had dropped on the floor of the tomb. He set it parallel to the cubit box. "Hold this."

Out of sheer habit, Neil obeyed. After all, he'd been following Sayyid's orders when it came to matters of conservation for two years now.

Sayyid expertly eyed the three-thousand-year-old boat, slipped delicate fingers under either end of it, and shifted it onto Neil's board. He set it down carefully on the floor nearby, then rose to fix Neil with a waiting, implacable look.

The cubit box lay before them.

"I don't want to open it," Neil confessed tightly. "I don't..." He drew in a breath, feeling dizzy.

Somewhere on the mountain above them, his sister was in danger. His best friend. Sayyid's wife. And a woman who had grown from a nerve-wracking hellion into someone he found he cared very much for.

"You do it," Neil blurted helplessly. "You're... better with wooden pieces than I am."

Sayyid absorbed Neil's plea, then set his expert hands to the box.

The front panel slid free on grooves that had remained straight and true through three thousand years of rest. Inside lay two pieces of elegant bronze, green with a rich layer of verdigris.

One was shaped with the slender head and pointed ears of the Set beast. The other formed a forked tail.

They were hollow at the ends, made to slip over a staff of wood.

"It's..." Neil's throat was as dry as the sands that stretched out over the world above them.

"A was-scepter," Sayyid filled in, his voice thick with wonder. Tears gathered at the corners of his eyes. "Wallah—*it is a was-scepter!*"

The two bronzes in the cubit box were covered in etched rows of tiny hieroglyphs. The carved eyes of the Set beast were blankly serene.

A lingering part of Neil's brain wanted to protest—to muster a thousand reasons why the object before him must be simply another artifact. A misplaced relic no different from the hundreds of others that surrounded him.

His gaze rose to the roughly etched graffito on the wall—to the long-eared rod in the hands of the solemn-faced figure leading his people toward the benevolent rays of the rising sun.

The excuses and pleas fell away like sand. Neil knew what he was looking at. He knew it with a feeling in his bones like music.

The Staff of Moses. The instrument of one of the world's greatest prophets. The manifestation of holy power that had guided a people out of slavery and into history.

And Neil had known exactly where to find it.

His thoughts flew back to the moment when he had stood beside Sayyid on a sprawl of rubble-strewn ground at Saqqara. He had *felt* the wrongness of the place already marked off by stakes and lines.

He thought of the other little leaps of intuition that had come to him like a tingling electricity in his brain. The change in the size of the sun court altar. The identity of the sculptures in the tomb where he and Constance had sheltered after escaping Julian's boat. His haunted sense of some lone traveler approaching the boulder above that had led them to Neferneferuaten's tomb.

Over the years before that, there had been myriad little leaps of what he had always thought of as *intuition,* which came to him as he turned the pages of journal articles and excavation reports.

But that's not quite right, is it? Neil would think mildly and scribble a correction into the margins.

And finally, Akhetaten—living and breathing around him in the rattle of a sistrum and the tang of incense in the evening air.

All of it was linked by the past, whether through Neil's presence in the places where history had happened or a vaguer tugging sense of *wrongness* as he poured through his books and papers.

"I'm a scholar," he protested weakly. "I'm an academic. I can't be a…"

He trailed off, utterly at a loss for the right word.

"Wali?" Sayyid offered awkwardly.

"What's a wali?" Neil asked.

Sayyid winced, flashing him a sympathetic look. "It is more or less a saint."

Neil absorbed this with a groan—and thought once more of his sister and their friends, dealing with who-knew-what danger out on the ridge. "But the staff is in pieces! What are we supposed to do—just add them to any stick we like?"

"Assuming it is the right size, I suppose," Sayyid replied uneasily. He glanced around the room and picked up a long, straight rod from among a pile of walking sticks and bows. "Tamarisk. It's more likely to have resisted decay. Here—hold it."

Neil grasped the stick more or less because Sayyid thrust it at him.

With careful reverence, Sayyid gently lifted the headpiece from the cubit box. He turned it in his hands to line the hollow end up with the top of the tamarisk rod.

He drew in a breath, closing his eyes. "La ilâha illa Allah," he prayed—and pressed the bronze into place.

Sayyid snatched his hands away, eyeing Neil warily. "Do you feel anything?"

"Like what?" Neil replied. "You mean—does it feel like it's about to fall off?" He gave the staff a very careful wiggle. "Doesn't seem loose."

"Let's try the other bit," Sayyid prompted nervously.

Neil turned the rod, presenting him with the bottom end.

Sayyid delicately lifted the forked tail from the box. He carefully lined it up with the other end of the tamarisk stick, then pushed it on with a neat twist of his wrist.

A quick pain buzzed through Neil's palms, stinging like a hive of bees.

"Ow!" he shouted, bouncing the staff in his hands. "It bit me!"

"What do you mean, it bit you?" Sayyid took a hurried step back.

"I don't know!" Neil juggled the wood, torn between his protesting nerves and his terror of dropping the instrument of God on the floor.

"Is it still biting you?" Sayyid pressed.

Neil forced himself to hold the thing long enough to find out. "It's more a... highly unpleasant tingle."

"Well, you should be able to manage that," Sayyid concluded. "How does it work?"

"How should I know?" Neil protested, still wincing at the subtle sting against his palms.

Sayyid cocked an eloquent eyebrow.

"What?!" Neil quailed. "You can't seriously expect that I'll just... *magic* the answer out of it!"

"You magicked learning where it was hidden," Sayyid returned easily.

"That's different!"

"See?" Sayyid shot back triumphantly. "You are admitting it was magic!"

"I haven't admitted anything!" Neil burst out.

"Hmph," Sayyid countered skeptically. "Well, the carving on Mutnedjmet's jewelry box referred to it as the Was-Scepter of Khemenu," he continued blithely. "Khemenu was the center of the cult of Thoth. I am sure that means it must be blessed by one of the god's priests before it can work."

"Of course it doesn't," Neil retorted crossly.

Sayyid's lip curled into a smirk, and Neil clamped a hand over his mouth.

"Perhaps it has something to do with language, then," Sayyid suggested cannily. "As Thoth was the scribe of the old Egyptian gods."

A sense of rightness hummed in the back of Neil's mind. It felt like moving his hand closer to the top of a stove with his eyes closed.

"Maybe?" he returned weakly.

Sayyid's brown eyes flashed with satisfaction. "But it would not be just any language. In the Book of the Dead, the incantations used to protect and guide the deceased through the afterlife are described as being gifted to priests by the gods themselves."

"Like… spells?" Neil rallied himself with a burst of desperate rebellion. "What are you getting at—that we're supposed to wave the staff around while we say the magic words?"

The sense of heat—of *rightness*—flared through his brain like an igniting match, and Neil's jaw dropped with dismay.

Sayyid clamped a sympathetic hand down on his shoulder. "It cannot be that bad to be a wali. I am sure we can sort it out later, after we save our people."

He glanced from his iron crowbar to the discarded scimitar by the sarcophagus. With a grimace of distaste, Sayyid picked up the sword—and promptly hurried through the exit.

Neil panicked.

The staff's power hummed through his arms, burning across his chest like a warning. Neil sensed its potential. The truth of it whispered through the same part of his mind that had made the cubit box itch at his awareness like a bite he couldn't scratch. He *knew* in a space beyond doubt that the staff in his hands was capable of both miracles and nightmares—that the potential for both hummed inside of it, buzzing like a horde of insects hidden just beneath the earth.

All it waited for was the key—for a whisper that would unleash it on the world.

The realization that he had been left holding it slammed into Neil like a pile of bricks.

He raced after Sayyid, catching up to him on the stairs. "Hold on! You can't run off! *You're* the one who has to use it!"

"Me?" Sayyid reared back from him in horror. "Absolutely not! You're the one who found it! You use it!"

"I can't!" Neil called back as they reached the hall.

"Why not?" Sayyid dropped his voice to a hoarse whisper as he cast a nervous glance at the fissure in the ceiling.

The answer washed over Neil with a strange and impossible certainty.

He started to laugh. The laugh was wheezing and slightly tortured, which at least kept it relatively quiet.

"What's going on?" Sayyid pleaded. "Why are you laughing?"

"Because it has to be in Egyptian," Neil replied, his voice still strangled with hysteria. "The spells. You have to say them in Egyptian."

"How can you possibly know that?!" Sayyid burst out.

"How do you think?" Neil choked back, wiping at the helpless tears escaping the corners of his eyes.

Sayyid's face collapsed into lines of dismay. "I could tell you what to say!" he pushed back desperately. "You could just repeat it after me!"

"I can't repeat it after you!" Neil wheezed, holding his aching gut. "I can't say your bloody *khaa*!"

"But you could…" Sayyid started. "If you tried a little…"

"Kaaaagch," Neil demonstrated. "Aaeercgh."

Sayyid grimaced. "That isn't even close."

"Awrrrchghk," Neil offered.

"Just stop," Sayyid pleaded, wincing.

"I'll stop when you take the bloody thing from me!" Neil pushed the staff at him. "Krraaguuuff!"

Sayyid stumbled back from the arcanum and jabbed an accusing finger. "Wielding it would be a violation of the sacred tenets of my faith that forbid the use of magic!"

"It's not magical—it's holy!" Neil threw back. "It belonged to one of your prophets! Rauuuuch!" he added for emphasis, his throat gurgling. "Haaacgh-htk!"

"Khalas!" Sayyid burst out—incidentally providing a perfect demonstration of the proper vocal fricative. He snatched the staff from Neil's hand. "Just stop butchering my consonant!"

"Thank you," Neil said with obvious relief, shoulders slumping as he shook out his tingling hand.

Sayyid awkwardly fumbled the staff, bouncing it from arm to arm while still wrangling the bronze scimitar. "It stings! Why didn't you tell me it stings?"

"I did!" Neil protested.

"Well, does it ever stop?"

"Maybe?" Neil hedged awkwardly.

"What am I supposed to say?" Sweat beaded Sayyid's forehead. "I can't just shout anything and expect it to work—not if you are right about needing ritual words! Something from the Coffin Texts, perhaps? Or one of the prayers to Anubis? Or what about—"

"Just use the bloody curse from over there!" Neil pointed down the hall to the alabaster doors, which still hung ajar.

"The bug curse?" Sayyid protested with obvious horror.

"Do you have a better idea?"

"Anything would be better than bugs!" Sayyid insisted.

"Well, you work on that, then," Neil growled.

"Fine. But you take this." Sayyid shoved the scimitar at him. "If I must wield the power of Allah while muttering in Middle Egyptian, then you will keep the villains off me."

"Me?" Neil squawked, awkwardly clutching the ancient blade.

Sayyid had already turned, stalking toward the ropes at the fissure with the Staff of Moses in his hand. "Hurry up!"

Neil made a noise of dismay in the back of his throat that sounded remarkably like an accurately pronounced 'khaa'—and ran after him.

FORTY-ONE

Shock blanked Adam's mind as explosions lit up the ridge like a volley of artillery, the stone heights blazing with fire.

It was impossible, but that hardly mattered. It was happening—which meant that Ellie was in danger.

"Get down!" Adam shouted, tackling her to the stone.

They weren't the only ones diving for cover. Half the Al-Saboors had hit the ground as well—except for Hobbles and Scarface, the two cousins assigned to guard the prisoners, who had been watching Ellie's tête-à-tête with Jacobs like a music hall show. They gaped at the fireworks with their cigarettes hanging from their lips, guns limp in their hands.

Jacobs skidded into the lee of a boulder.

"Take cover, you idiots!" he screamed out at the other men. *"Inzil!"*

Hobbles and Scarface finally hit the dirt. A cluster of men from the boat, gathered near the edge of the drop to the canyon, flinched down, and bolted for the path off the ridge.

Jacobs sprinted from his hiding place, darting through the shadows toward the heights where pale streams of smoke now ghosted up into the sky.

Adam wrenched at his hands, trying to break the ropes that bound his wrists by sheer force of desperation. "Get me out of these!"

Zeinab skidded into place behind him, her scalpel glittering in her hand. She sliced through his bindings and Adam threw them aside.

"Yalla," a rough voice grumbled from behind him.

He whirled, fists ready, and barely held back from throwing a punch at the stout, sun-wrinkled figure who stepped from the shadows.

Adam recognized the smuggler, Umm Waseem. Her clever eyes glittered above the black fall of her niqab.

Zeinab had moved to Ellie, who yanked her hands free of her own ropes with a groan—and a spark of delighted interest.

"You *were* carrying explosives in your bag!" she declared triumphantly. "I knew it! But what was it? Dynamite? Black powder? TNT, perhaps? You made it look exactly as though someone had put a half-dozen Howitzers on the ridge!"

"I'm sure she'll tell you all about it later." Adam hauled Ellie to her feet. "After we get the hell out of here."

Umm Waseem and Zeinab held a quick exchange before the midwife turned back to the rest of them, her green eyes sharp with urgency.

"She has set more charges on the cliffs," Zeinab reported. "Enough to bring them down and bury this place."

Adam's gaze shot to the forty-foot high crown of stone that framed the depression where they sheltered.

"Definitely TNT," Ellie concluded in an awed voice.

"That'd bury us," Adam pointed out flatly.

"Why do you think she hasn't blown it yet?" Zeinab snapped.

Adam's ears were still ringing from Umm Waseem's first round of explosions as he turned to take in their situation.

Julian and Dawson cowered behind a boulder not far from the entrance to the tomb. The Al-Saboors, on the other hand, seemed to have realized they weren't actually being shot at. Hobbles and Scarface had staggered back to their feet—and were now looking over at their clearly unbound and conspiring prisoners with alarm.

George Bates had berated Adam for his failure to make plans or think through the consequences of his actions. He had done everything he could to burn those words—*reckless and ill-considered*—into Adam's heart.

But if there was one bright side to being reckless, it was that it never took Adam long to make a decision when it mattered.

"Go," he ordered. "All of you—get the hell out of here."

"All of *us?*" Ellie pushed back sharply. "What about you?"

Adam met her gaze. "I'm going to buy you some time."

Her eyes widened with horrified understanding—and then narrowed with angry determination.

Adam knew what that look meant.

He took hold of her, one hand grabbing her back while the other slid into her hair, forcing her to face him. "No, Ellie," he said firmly. "Not this time. This time, you let me be the hero."

There was too much more he wanted to say—*needed* to say. He didn't have time for any of it.

All he could do was show her.

Knowing the consequences—and not giving a damn about them—Adam kissed her. He did it hard and fast, catching her to him and aching with how much she meant… how much he *needed* her.

Then he pushed her back into Constance, who caught her instinctively.

"Take her and get clear of the ridge," Adam barked.

Ellie opened her mouth to protest, even as Constance stared at him with wide-eyed understanding.

Adam didn't wait for her to speak. He wasn't going to listen anyway. Instead, he launched himself at the Al-Saboors.

Scarface hesitated, still thrown by the shock of the explosion and clearly unsure how to react to Adam's drive at them in the absence of any clear orders from the men supposed to be in charge. Hobbles took an instinctive—and pained—step back, still flinching from his last encounter with Adam at Deir al-Bahari.

That was all the opportunity Adam needed.

Hobbles went down like a cut tree, dropping his rifle to grab the leg Adam had already injured as he howled. Adam whirled to Scarface, driving a fist into his gut. The mercenary fumbled his rifle as the wind came out of him, falling to his knees.

Adam made a grab for the gun, then toppled as someone barreled into him from the side. He rolled to find a thick black beard tickling his nose.

Adam sneezed, and Beardy whipped a dagger from his sleeve. Adam caught his arm as he drove the knife down, grunting with the effort of holding it at bay.

He snapped his head forward, driving it into Beardy's face.

The Al-Saboor lurched back, clutching his bleeding nose. Adam took the opportunity to shove him off.

Beardy landed on Scarface, who was just staggering to his feet.

Adam scrambled upright. Out of the corner of his eye, he glimpsed Umm Waseem's stout black-cloaked figure dashing across the ridge with the speed of a house cat. She blew past Ears and Lefty, who both ignored her, busy gaping at Adam instead.

Not that those two bruised Al-Saboors showed any sign of jumping in to help the cousins that he was currently pummeling. They were obviously feeling a little hesitant to join the fray while still nursing the damage from the last couple rounds.

A battle cry sounded from across the ledge. Ralph raced toward Adam, holding a familiar blade up over his head.

That's my damned machete, Adam thought with a burst of indignation.

Zeinab was halfway across the ridge with Jemmahor in tow. The apprentice skidded to halt, then snatched a rock from the ground and whipped it at the charging Al-Saboor.

Ralph ducked with a yelp, fumbling his knife.

Zeinab grabbed Jemmahor's arm and hauled her back into a sprint.

Adam lashed out at Scarface with a kick, and he went back down. Then Ralph was on him.

Adam dove under a blow from his own damned blade, taking Ralph in the ribs with his shoulder instead. He swung an arm around the man's legs, catching them and flipping the skinny thug over his back.

Ralph landed with a stream of curses, and Adam skidded against the ground. Spinning around, he clutched at a handful of sand and whipped it back at Scarface. The mercenary had reclaimed his rifle, but dropped it again to cover his eyes with a scream.

Adam used the breath of time that bought him to look for Ellie—only to find her still lingering by the remnants of their cut ropes as Constance tugged at her arm.

"Come on, Ellie!" she urged.

"Get out of here!" Adam roared.

"I will not leave you!" Ellie shouted back, her voice raw.

Adam wrenched the rifle from Scarface's hands—and looked up to see that Gaps, stationed by the tomb, had finally noticed the melee. He was darting toward them, his own gun raised.

There was no time for Adam to swing the rifle around and aim.

He threw the gun itself at Gaps instead.

The rifle hit him in the face, and Gaps went down.

Beyond him, Adam picked out Jacobs' lean figure at the base of the ledge, where he had run to investigate the explosion. He was no longer looking at the crown of rocks above them. His eyes were on Adam. He took in the groaning pile of Al-Saboors at Adam's feet with a cold glance… before his gaze snapped to Adam's left.

Adam followed it—and saw a pair of dusty figures stagger out from under the boulder hiding the entrance to the tomb.

Neil's glasses were skewed, his face smudged with dirt. His waistcoat had lost its buttons. He was holding an actual goddamned sword in his hand— though not in a way that indicated he had any idea what to do with it.

But he was alive.

Beside him stood a bareheaded, battered Sayyid, his beard pale with dust.

As he straightened after crawling out from under the boulder, Adam realized he was also carrying something with him.

Wooden stick. Long-eared head. Forked tail.

For a moment, the night seemed to hold its breath. The desert breeze whispered and the stars sprawled overhead… as Sayyid held a legend in his hands.

"Well, hell," Adam breathed with quiet wonder. "They actually found it."

"Neil!" Ellie shouted, her voice tight with relief and fear.

Her cry echoed across the ridge, bouncing off the high walls of the cliffs that surrounded them.

Julian lurched from behind the shelter of one of the boulders scattered around the tomb entrance, his blond hair in disarray and the sleeve of his khaki jacket torn.

Dawson peered over the top behind him, took in the scene, and promptly dropped from view again.

"Forget the rest of them!" Julian jabbed a finger toward Sayyid as his voice rang out across the ledge. "That Egyptian has my staff!"

Grasping the aged bone hilt at his side, Julian whipped out a sword. The blade caught the moonlight for the space of a breath—and then burst into cold blue flames.

Julian charged at Neil, who flinched back, bringing up the ancient scimitar in his hand more on instinct than out of any real technique.

The blades clashed in a burst of sparks.

Hobbles scrabbled free of the pile of his cousins at Adam's feet and bolted across the ridge—or hurriedly staggered, rather. Scarface rolled over with a groan, and Ralph lurched to his feet.

Adam yanked his attention from the glowing sword fight to give Ralph another kick, wrenching the machete from his hand.

The hilt fell into his grip in a way that felt beautifully right. Adam smiled— and looked up to see Jacobs running toward him.

"Parry him!" Constance screamed at Neil as Julian made another swipe. "With the sword! You have to—oh bugger it, anyway."

Constance let go of Ellie and ran toward them.

Julian swung again. The swords locked, and with an expert turn of his wrist, Julian ripped the scimitar from Neil's grip. The ancient blade clattered to the ground.

Julian raised his flaming sword, his eyes flaring with anger and disdain. "You're far more trouble than you're worth, for a bloody scholar!"

He readied himself for a killing blow—and Constance hit him.

She twisted her hands in the back of his coat, shoving a boot between his legs. With a neat and practiced pivot, she swiveled her torso—and flipped Julian over her back.

Jacobs reached Gaps, who stood in the middle of the chaos looking utterly bewildered as he juggled a pair of rifles—his own and the one Adam had recently thrown into his face. Jacobs snatched one of the guns from his grip without so much as a hitch in his pace.

Time slowed. The rifle rose in Jacobs' hands, moving with expert grace as he pivoted—turning to bring it to bear on Neil.

Adam felt the familiar slick grip of the machete in his hand and made a rapid calculation.

"Hell," he bit out, and let the knife fly.

Jacobs caught the flashing movement of it out of the corner of his eye. He twisted with the reflexes of a cat, dodging the blade—and losing his shot. Before he could line it up again, Adam hit him like a train.

They both went down as Ellie shouted his name. Adam grabbed the rifle, his hand closing on the barrel where it lay pinned between them as they rolled across the ground. Jacobs wrenched at it, but Adam gritted his teeth and kept his hold—then slammed the heel of his other hand into Jacobs' chin.

Jacobs' head snapped back in what Adam knew from personal experience was a dizzying and damned painful blow, but his hold on the gun stayed firm. He shook off the hit, his eyes blazing with fury mere inches from Adam's face.

Adam saw a cold calculation flicker through them, and Jacobs pulled the trigger.

The crack of the shot roared in Adam's ear, deafening it. The barrel of the gun flared with heat, burning through the skin of his palm.

Adam roared with pain, forced to snatch his hand away.

Jacobs kicked loose. Adam went sprawling, and Jacobs swung the rifle around to point at Adam, where he lay on the ground.

Adam went still.

So did Jacobs.

By the entrance to the tomb, Julian staggered to his feet. Constance stood between him and Neil in a posture of martial readiness.

Julian's eyes narrowed at her with furious outrage. "That's it! This engagement is over!"

"We have never been engaged!" Constance shouted back, exasperated. "What will it take for you to get that through your thick head?"

Julian's expression chilled, his mouth twisting with obvious viciousness. "This is far less civilized than the sword—but needs must."

He whipped a pistol from his coat.

Behind Constance, Neil lunged across the ground. His hand closed around the hilt of Julian's discarded sword.

He swung it up as he scrambled to his feet, pointing it at Julian by Constance's side.

The sword ignited. Blue flames illuminated the look of utter shock on Neil's face.

Julian's jaw dropped. "But you're nobody!" he exclaimed with wild disbelief. "How can you possibly make it burn!"

"Because he's worthy, you twit!" Constance shot back.

Closer by, Jacobs' expression twisted with frustration and rage as he loomed over Adam. "You and your woman have been making my life exceedingly difficult," he bit out dangerously.

Ellie had reached them. She skidded to a stop a step away, her eyes moving from Jacobs' rifle to Adam's face. He could read the naked, desperate fear in her expression.

"Then why didn't you shoot the pair of us in Luxor when you had the chance?" Adam pushed back.

Jacobs' jaw was tense. His eyes flashed with a dark, tight fury. "I am starting to wonder about that myself," he replied in a hiss. "Killing the pair of you *might* just be worth the consequences."

The uncharacteristically bald words gave Adam a spark of hope. Something *was* holding Jacobs back from murdering them. If that was the case, then there might just be a way for Adam to get him and Ellie out of this without any bullet holes… if he could guess just how far Jacobs' hesitation would extend.

Which was, quite frankly, a complete and terrifying shot in the dark.

"The consequences from your employers, you mean," Ellie retorted.

Adam suspected Ellie's taunt was aimed at reminding Jacobs of any orders he might have received to refrain from leaving a trail of bodies behind him… considering that it was most likely Adam's body that would be at the top of that list.

Jacobs moved his acid glare to her. "You think those soft, entitled dogs have any power over *me?*"

"Julian Forster-Mowbray has been reining you in all week," Ellie shot back deliberately.

The rifle barrel was a tidy black zero hovering less than a foot from Adam's head. Thirty degrees to the right, and it'd be pointing at *Ellie's* head. Which was an increasingly likely outcome if she kept on baiting the man.

"You have no *idea* what you're talking about," Jacobs seethed.

"Then why don't you enlighten us?" Adam cut in, hoping to recapture his attention. "If it's not your bosses stopping you, then what is it? Because we know it's sure as hell not your conscience."

"Not your employers. Not your conscience." Ellie murmured the words automatically.

Adam could practically see her mind whirring like a well-tuned clock—and then her eyes went wide with a clear, perfect surprise.

"The Smoking Mirror," she blurted, the words falling like stones into the night air—and the chaos of the ridge went utterly, perfectly still.

Jacobs looked as though he had been carved from ice. His gaze shifted from Adam to Ellie, pinning her with that same twisted mix of frustration and fury—only now the look was utterly unveiled, exposed against his pale features.

"Your desire—your *justice*," Ellie went on, the words spilling out of her in a torrent of horrified inspiration. "We're part of it somehow. That's why you haven't been able to kill us even though we keep getting in your way."

Jacobs didn't answer. He didn't speak. He was as still and rigid as a statue—and yet Adam could read the truth of Ellie's words in every tormented line of his body.

"Holy hell," he breathed out as shock washed over him like a wave.

On the other side of the ridge, Muscles snatched Zeinab up by the waist, forcing the scalpel from her hand with a twist of her arm.

Jemmahor ran at them, throwing rocks and screaming in Coptic, but Ears mustered a burst of courage and tackled the girl, pinning her to the ground.

Gaps fumblingly pointed his remaining rifle at Neil, shouting for him to drop the sword. Constance glared up at Julian from the ground as the pistol shook in his hand.

None of it looked good.

A deeper, wilder rage blackened Jacobs' eyes. His look hardened—as did his grip on the rifle.

"Maybe I can't kill you," he agreed in a tone that snapped with electric tension. "But I think I might like to see just how much I can make you *hurt*."

The gun shifted to Ellie.

Adam's world narrowed to a black length of iron—and the face of the woman he loved.

Thoughts cascaded through his mind in the space of a breath. Lazy evening sunsets. Stumbling across a waterfall no one had known was there. Stripping off his shirt to fall into the sea after a long, hard day. The simple, unprepossessing scope of his ambitions—to feel life with every sense, every bone. Let it wash over him like a sudden summer rain, exactly as he found it, without pushing constantly for more, more, more. He wasn't ready to let that go. He *liked* life.

But something else mattered more. It was all tangled up with the woman two steps away from him—the one who hadn't even started to show the world everything she was capable of.

Adam wanted to watch those lazy sunsets with *her*—smoking his cigar while she rattled on about the Khmer empire. Spend afternoons watching the rain fall while he just held her and nobody talked about anything at all.

She needed to see those waterfalls. Learn poker—Adam bet she could bluff like an adorably freckled terror. Feel what it was like to throw yourself into the waves and let them wash over you like a benediction.

Pain could change a person. It could break them. Adam wouldn't let Ellie get broken.

Even if that meant she'd have to do all of those things without him.

Jacobs dropped the barrel to aim at Ellie's hip… and Adam got ready to throw his stubborn, *reckless* body directly in the way.

Then the glass-tight stillness of the night shattered as Sayyid Al-Ahmed's voice rang out over the stones in the syllables of a tongue that had been lost for a thousand years.

"Nen ankh rek ty'fy wi. Kheper ir'ek her tah," Sayyid sang as he lifted the Staff of Moses in his hand. "In kheper wanam'ek san. Tem'tjen!"

Jacobs went still, his finger perfectly balanced on the trigger. Beside Julian, the Al-Saboors cast each other uncertain looks.

Dawson poked his head back out from behind the boulder he'd been cowering under, his jaw dropping.

For a breath after the echo of Sayyid's words drifted into silence, the ridge froze, an involuntary reverence keeping each of them captive under the sprawling fabric of the night.

Then the shadows began to move.

Scarabs shivered from between the narrow crevices of the rocks. Others poured over the moon-silvered line of the ridge. They came in trickles and clusters, black bodies shining in the far threads of the lamplight.

Two of them flew at Gaps. He dropped his hold on the rifle to smack at them.

Another landed on Julian. He stiffened and swatted at it, dancing back a step.

Dawson flapped his hands furiously as a trio of fat beetles whizzed at his face.

Adam drew in another breath—and the air around him came alive.

The darkness itself rose in a thousand buzzing forms. They filled the air in clouds, swooping over the lamplit ledge.

Sayyid stumbled back as the beetles flashed through the air around him. Julian waved his pistol wildly as he tried to swat at the swarming insects, which only closed in more thickly.

Ears and Scarface shouted, then burst into a sprint—or as much of one as they could manage when they were both limping. They hauled across the ledge toward their former dig site and the path down to the valley.

With a yelp, Beardy followed them, two more of his cousins close on his heels.

The rifle twitched in Jacobs' grip as he flinched at a pair of scarabs diving toward his face.

Neil still held the flaming sword, raising it over his head like a shield. The insects danced around him, whipping past the place where he and Constance crouched. They clung to Julian instead, peppering his pale suit like dark jewels as he shrieked and danced back.

He dropped the pistol and ran.

Dawson bolted after him, wailing about being left behind.

Jacobs flinched as another scarab landed on the side of his face. Three more clung to his hair. He kept his hands on the rifle—and his eyes on Adam.

But as the last of the Al-Saboors bolted past them, screaming and slapping at the horde of shining black insects that swarmed around their heads, Adam watched a familiar calculation shift through Jacobs' dark gaze.

Julian's sword still flamed in Neil's hand, for all that Neil was staring at it with an expression of mingled awe and terror. Jemmahor had snatched up one of the discarded rifles with an expression of delight.

Zeinab grasped Julian's pistol, her gaze shifting to the place where Jacobs still stood.

Behind all of them cowered Sayyid—ducking down and cursing from the whirling black storm of insects, even though the bugs refrained from coming too close.

But he did not lose his grip on the staff in his hand.

Jacobs gave a dark chuckle. It grew, collapsing into a harsh laugh twisted through with both frustration and an odd, unhappy relief.

His suit crawled with beetles. Black insects clung to his hair.

He tossed the rifle down at Adam's feet.

"Till next time," he rasped, and then walked away.

Ellie scrambled up. Adam gripped her, hauling her to his side, and watched with a wary, ready tension as Jacobs crossed to the path off the ridge… only occasionally swatting at the insects that hissed around him as he went.

FORTY-TWO

HOLDING UP A flaming sword, Neil watched the impossible swarm settle like dust after a sandstorm. Most of the insects hissed and buzzed after Julian's fleeing party. A few stray scarabs remained, clinging to the rocks or marching along in contended lines.

He looked at his hand and realized it still clung to the bone hilt of Dyrnwyn. Neil dropped it as though it might bite him, and the flames of the sword snuffed like a spent candle.

Constance punched him in the arm hard enough that he nearly staggered. "That was rather well done, you!" she declared approvingly.

Her hair had wrenched loose of its pins and spilled in an abundant, disarrayed mess around her shoulders. One of the sleeves of her white lawn dress was half torn away. Somehow, it made her look more like the unruly child he had known years before—and yet simultaneously achingly lovely.

Not that the loveliness mattered, he told himself. She was his sister's friend.

Maybe his friend, too.

Neil might very reasonably have simply asked her that sort of question—*are we friends now, too?* Something else came out of his mouth instead.

"You attacked a man who had a flaming sword."

"It was only Julian," Constance retorted dismissively.

"You... I..." Neil's voice was strangled. He closed his eyes, then forced himself to open them again. "Thank you."

Constance flashed him a look of cat-like satisfaction. "You're welcome, Stuffy."

Sayyid stood a few steps away, still holding the was-scepter. His collar was askew and the shoulder of his waistcoat was torn. His expression was blank with shock and terror.

Neil threw his arms around him. "Thank you, too," he said, his voice muffled by Sayyid's shoulder.

After a moment's hesitation, Sayyid hugged him back. "That was awful. Could you not have thought of any curses besides the one with beetles? I will be having nightmares about that experience for months."

Neil laughed, feeling slightly hysterical. He pushed back from the embrace to check on the rest of the people he cared about.

Ellie launched herself into Neil with the impact of a small rhinoceros. "Are you all right?" She shoved back to get a better look at him. "Were you hurt in the fall? Or during your fight with Julian? And how did you get out of that hole in the ground?"

"I am bruised in possibly every place that a person can become bruised, and I never want to do anything remotely like this ever again," Neil quickly told her. "But… I'm fine."

Adam came up behind her. He looked like hell. He was also staring at Neil's sister like a man who knew that he'd nearly just lost the most important thing in the world to him.

The sight of it tugged at Neil's heart in a way that took his breath.

There was nothing thoughtless or irresponsible about that look. The emotion flooding through Adam's eyes had another name—one that Neil couldn't possibly fault him for. Not in a million years.

He'd need to talk to his friend about that before too long. His sister, too. It seemed he had a bit more groveling still left to do.

The rest of their party was miraculously intact. Jemmahor lingered near the edge of the drop into the canyon. She picked up an extra rock from the ground and ceremoniously hurled it in the direction the villains had fled. "Thawra hatta'l-naśr, imperialist scoundrels!" she shouted happily.

Zeinab stood at Sayyid's side. Her face was smudged with dirt and blood, though she had managed to retain her headscarf. She smiled at her husband, then casually brushed something from his shoulder.

Sayyid closed his eyes, looking pained. "Please do not tell me what that was. I do not want to know."

He still held the was-scepter in his hand. Ellie reached out to examine the verdigris-dulled bronze with reverent fingers.

"You found it." She looked from Sayyid to Neil. "You found the Staff of Moses."

Sayyid unhesitatingly handed it to her. She took the tamarisk rod carefully, then yanked a hand back, shaking it out. "Ow! It stings! Why does it sting?"

"I have absolutely no idea!" Sayyid returned with an edge of wild laughter.

With a curious grimace, Ellie brushed her fingers gently over the lines of hieroglyphs that covered the ancient bronze.

"*Oh God who has no equal,*" she read, turning the tamarisk rod to follow the line of characters. "*Who knows a man by the words in his heart, and who makes the deed rise up against the doer.*"

A strange, powerful warmth burst through Neil as he watched her—his little sister, ragged and bruised but utterly unbowed, holding the Staff of Moses in her capable hands as she read the words inscribed on it in a language the world had tried very hard not to let her learn.

His sister the scholar—the warrior—whose determination to do what was right had brought all of them to this place and this moment, despite the most overwhelming odds.

He slowly came to recognize the feeling blooming up inside of him. He was wildly, desperately proud of her.

He was less proud of himself, but instead of making him miserable, as it had before, Neil found himself oddly… *determined.*

If he had not done things quite right in the past, then he simply needed to do better—now and for the rest of his life.

"Is that from the Hymn to the Aten?" Constance wondered.

"It's a prayer to Thoth," Ellie corrected. "But it sounds as though it could be, doesn't it?"

"Or a prayer to God," Zeinab offered solemnly.

"Buṣṣû!" a voice called from the top of the ridge.

Neil picked out the stout, sturdy figure of Umm Waseem framed against the night sky.

Buṣṣû was a simple word. Neil automatically translated it. *Look!*

Zeinab slipped from Sayyid's side. She crossed to the drop into the canyon, gazing out in the direction where Umm Waseem pointed.

Neil and the others joined her there, Ellie still carrying the staff.

The view opened out across the royal wadi to the broad, moonlit Amarna plain. Halfway to the pale, tumbled columns of the ruined city, an odd, dark shadow hovered over the ground like a shifting, slow-moving cloud.

He stood too far away to make out any details… but Neil found himself oddly certain that he was looking at a swarm of insects harrying a cluster of quickly retreating figures.

"I suppose it's a good thing those bugs aren't actually carnivorous," he said a little weakly.

"Why is that?" Ellie asked, her eyes on the fleeing mercenaries.

"That's the precise translation of Sayyid's curse," Neil replied. "'In kheper wanam'ek san.' It is the scarab who will eat you."

Sayyid swallowed thickly beside him, looking a little queasy.

"What do they eat, then?" Constance asked, curious.

"They're dung beetles," Adam replied. "So they eat… er, what you'd more or less expect."

Ellie repressed a laugh. It came out as a snort.

"One would think that lot might have qualified." Jemmahor punctuated the remark with a rude gesture at the fleeing party of villains. "Well! At least Umm Waseem did not have to blow the ridge down on us!"

"What?!" Neil exclaimed, his stomach lurching.

"Don't worry," Jemmahor assured him. "It was only a last resort." She paused, frowning thoughtfully. "Though I suppose we did come rather close to that, didn't we?"

Neil vividly imagined several thousand tons of exploded rock cascading down the mountain to crush them. He thought he might be ill.

Umm Waseem hopped down from the rocks nearby, moving with a nimbleness that defied her advanced age. Her black canvas bag was slung over her shoulder. Neil regarded her with a deep and extremely wary respect.

Ellie gave the was-scepter a final longing look and held it out to Sayyid. "Here."

Sayyid blanched. "Absolutely not. I will be quite happy never to touch that thing again, thank you."

"Is that it, then?" Neil asked hopefully.

"Not entirely." Constance shoved a long, heavy bundle at him, wrapped up in a piece of canvas.

Neil fumbled it as he caught it, and a bit of the fabric fell away, revealing a hilt of gold-wrapped bone.

"Dyrnwyn?!" He immediately tried to shove it back at her. "Why are you giving this to me?"

"You won it in a fair battle," Constance replied as though the matter should have been obvious.

"I did not!" Neil protested. "Mr. Forster-Mowbray just dropped it when you knocked him over! That's not winning anything! And anyway, I haven't the foggiest notion of how to use it! Bates should have it!" He jabbed a finger at his broad-shouldered friend.

"I'm good with my knife," Adam replied comfortably.

"Sayyid?" Neil pleaded hopefully.

"Absolutely not," Sayyid returned stoutly.

Neil's ire rose at the utter lack of support he was receiving. "Well, then I don't see why we can't leave it right here on the mountain."

"Isn't it an object of enormous historical importance?" Constance reminded him with an innocent blink of her exceptional eyelashes. "One of the Thirteen Treasures of Britain or some such thing?"

Ellie fixed Neil with an outraged glare. "You want to leave one of the Thirteen Treasures of Britain on a mountain?!"

"What else am I supposed to do with it?" Neil burst out.

"Bring it back to England and give it to an institution of public learning, perhaps?" Ellie returned impatiently. "It's one of our own this time—you can do that."

"Except if he does, Julian's high-and-mighty forebearers will probably just show up to claim it again," Adam reasoned.

"Well, then, I suppose Neil will just have to hold on to it for a while," Ellie conceded.

"I don't want to hold on to it!" Neil shouted. "It bursts into flames!"

"Only when you take it by the hilt," Constance returned comfortably. "Why do you think I wrapped it up for you?"

"And most likely when one is engaged in battle," Ellie mused.

"Oh, I don't know about that," Constance pushed back. "It's not like Julian could have been in many battles before now."

"Be kinda handy if you could just use it to spark up a campfire," Adam offered. "Or get your cigar going."

Neil stared at all of them, his jaw hanging open with shock and dismay.

Adam clamped a sympathetic hand onto his shoulder. "I'll find you a bit of rope so you can tie it on."

"There is still the matter of the tomb that must be settled." Zeinab studied their ragged party. "Mr. Forster-Mowbray knows where it is. He will come back for it, even if the staff is no longer there. Neferneferuaten's treasures would be worth a fortune to him back in England."

"Does that mean Umm Waseem should set off her charges?" Ellie suggested. "I will admit, I was hoping to see a bit more of her skills in action. Perhaps I might quiz her afterward on the relative merits of different fuse materials, if one of you is willing to translate. I have been curious about…"

The horror Neil felt at her words must have shown on his face, because Ellie trailed off as she glanced at him.

"Maybe save the fireworks tutorial for later," Adam suggested mildly as he tossed a length of rope at Neil, who caught it only by reflex, still juggling the canvas bundle of the sword.

Sayyid gaped at her. "You might collapse the entire tomb! The whole quarry could cave in! There would be nothing left of it!"

"I suppose you are right." Ellie sighed a little reluctantly.

"But what else can we do?" Neil pressed.

"Isn't it obvious?" Constance replied.

The rest of the party looked at her blankly.

"You people really haven't the foggiest notion of how these things work, do you?" Constance protested with a note of indulgent exasperation. "We have to curse the tomb!"

"Curse the tomb?" Sayyid echoed uneasily.

"But how are we supposed to do that?" Neil burst out.

Something about the look in Constance's eyes made him feel distinctly nervous.

"With the Staff of Moses, of course," she replied with a dangerously sweet smile.

FORTY-THREE

$\mathcal{E}$LLIE SAT DOWN on a rock and stretched out her legs. They ached, along with most of the rest of her. Her skirt was torn at the knee, her white blouse smudged with dirt.

She felt battered and worn-out enough to sit back and rest while Neil, Sayyid, and Zeinab argued about ancient Egyptian spells.

They were searching for the right ritual words that would protect Neferneferuaten's tomb from the very real possibility that Julian would return to loot its treasures. Any straightforward curse might have done the job, but as Zeinab pointed out, they didn't want to prevent the tomb from *ever* being studied. In a future Egypt where Egyptians controlled the rights to their own heritage, the artwork and funeral goods could provide profound insight into one of the most fascinating periods of the country's history.

Neil and Sayyid bickered over their memories of old inscriptions and papyri. Ellie could sense that something had changed between the two scholars after they fell into the quarry. The tension between them had eased, making space for them to slip back into the companionable banter that she had observed back in Saqqara.

Constance perched on a boulder just above the bedraggled Egyptologists, shamelessly eavesdropping. Ellie noticed how her eyes kept drifting over to Neil as he pushed his bent glasses back up on his nose and cited Lepsius.

Jemmahor cleaned the rifle she had claimed for herself from among the firearms left discarded on the ridge. "I always liked the plague of frogs," she offered helpfully as she pulled a twisted rag from the barrel. "But it would be even better if instead of raining, the frogs actually built up inside of you until you choked on them."

Sayyid and Neil gaped at her with horror. Umm Waseem chuckled darkly where she reclined against her black canvas bag. It looked less full than it had before, but Ellie still felt a quiet sense of awe that the cackling old smuggler was using a mound of TNT for a pillow.

Adam dropped down beside Ellie heavily, wincing at the aches and bruises that covered his body. His machete was back in the sheath at his belt.

"How are your ribs feeling now?" Ellie demanded.

"I mean—they've been better," Adam admitted with a wince. "But I gave back worse."

Ellie flashed him an admiring smile. "I am certain the Al-Saboor family will be cursing your name for generations."

His gaze flashed with amusement before growing more serious again. "Pretty sure I tried to tell you to get off that damned ridge."

Her thoughts flew back to the grim determination in Adam's expression when he had ordered them to leave, then turned to face Julian's thugs. He had known perfectly well what he was walking into and had done it anyway, throwing himself into the fire to give the rest of them a chance at escape. It had been a desperate, noble, and infuriatingly self-sacrificing move—just like the one he'd very nearly made when he prepared to toss himself into the path of Jacob's bullet.

Ellie wasn't certain whether she wanted to slap him for that or kiss him until they fell over.

Every time she closed her eyes, her mind burned with the image of Adam lying helpless on the ground with Jacobs' rifle pointed at his chest.

"That isn't fair," she bit back, fear sharpening her tone. "I don't get to order you to safety when I'm afraid of losing you. You can't ask the same thing of me."

"Maybe you could," Adam countered, "if we were up against translating an ancient manuscript before someone drops a rock on us. Or if saving our necks depends on recognizing whether a piece of pottery is Hittite or Phoenician. But if it's down to a knife fight, that's on me."

Ellie felt a quick burst of fury. "And would you honestly do it? Would you really just walk away if I had to stop an avalanche with a manuscript translation?"

Adam went quiet. His gaze burned into her as though he could capture her that way and keep her safe inside of himself forever.

"No," he said finally. "Can't say that I would."

Something inside her seemed to crack, and both the fear and the fury shivered away, leaving in their place only an aching sense of vulnerability and a wash of desperate relief. She had come so close to losing him that night, but now he was here beside her. Filthy, battered, and wearing three-day-old socks—but *here.*

She raised her hand to his face. He had collected a few new bruises. Stubble gilded his cheek. Understanding warred with worry in his eyes as he looked down at her.

"There is an obvious solution to this problem, you know," she pointed out, lightening her tone.

"And what's that?"

"You could teach me to fight with knives."

"Not a chance in hell," Adam replied easily.

"Why not?" Ellie protested. "Constance does it!"

"Never said I thought that was a good idea, either."

Ellie narrowed her eyes at him. "We'll continue this conversation later."

"Pretty sure we will," Adam agreed easily.

His arm slipped around her back, a band of warmth she could feel through the battered fabric of her waistcoat. His chin came down to rest against her hair, and he breathed in her scent. His grip on her tightened as his chest shuddered with some deep emotion.

"What about Jacobs?" Ellie asked quietly, her cheek resting against the solid heat of his shoulder. "Do you really think we're meant to... *help* him somehow?"

"That's kind of a hard sell," Adam countered with a frown.

"But he must have seen *something* to that effect," Ellie pushed back. "He very clearly would have preferred to do away with us, and he had ample opportunity to do so. I can't imagine he would have held back from that and opened himself up to so much trouble on a whim."

"'It couldn't possibly be,'" Adam recited.

Ellie glanced up at him. His expression was quietly thoughtful.

"That's what he said after he got a face-full of that smoke," Adam elaborated. "And it was just that—maybe a puff of the stuff. I can barely remember what it felt like myself. There was this sense of something old and twisted asking me what I wanted, and then knowing that if I threw my arm up at just the right angle, I'd find what I needed."

"I was... *told* that greater desires required greater sacrifices," Ellie offered carefully.

Adam didn't ask her who—or what—had told her. She found herself a little grateful for that. It wasn't that she didn't want to tell him. She had alluded here and there to some of what had passed for her during her time in the mirror, and she supposed that she would share all of it with him eventually. Adam would never judge her for it, no matter how bizarre and unscholarly it all sounded.

"There was only a drop or two of blood," Adam mused thoughtfully. "Maybe all he saw were a few hints of how he could get whatever justice he thinks he wants."

"And one of them involved… us," Ellie filled in uneasily.

Adam's mouth quirked into an uncomfortable smile. "Not sure whether that's a relief or something to be even more nervous about."

"Nor am I," Ellie agreed.

"Hold on!" Neil straightened with the force of an epiphany. "What about that vignette on the wall of the funerary chapel back at Saqqara? That bit about the Flame of Isis from the Book of the Dead. Something about *driving away enemies…*"

Ellie frowned with recognition. "You mean—*The Flame of Isis says: I surround the hidden tomb with sand and drive thy enemy away,*" she recited automatically.

Neil startled. "How do you know that?!"

"I saw it on the chapel wall before we descended into Horemheb's tomb," Ellie replied easily. "I am quite certain it is from Chapter One Hundred and Fifty-One of the Book of the Dead," she added helpfully.

"And you have it memorized?" Neil protested. "How long did you look at it for—three minutes?"

"It might have been more like five," Ellie admitted.

"You really do have a knack for that sort of thing," Constance commented. "I always said you ought to try a turn on the stage."

"Nonsense!" Ellie said. "That would be an entirely frivolous use of one's memory."

Zeinab's eyes narrowed thoughtfully. "It sounds as though that spell might simply bury the tomb in sand."

"But what if they just dug it out again?" Jemmahor protested.

"Presumably, that's where the 'drive thy enemy away' part comes in," Constance replied confidently.

Ellie felt a quick lurch of fear—and of guilt, as her memory was flooded by the image of collapsing temples and shattering white stone. "But what about in the future? We can't possibly destroy it forever. It's… It would be…"

Adam set a steady, warm hand to her back. The strength of it gave her enough fortitude to draw in a breath, forcing down the panic that threatened to choke her.

"'Drive thy *enemy* away,'" Constance emphasized. "That doesn't mean everyone. Just Sayyid's enemies."

"*Sayyid's* enemies?" Ellie echoed in confusion.

"Me?" Sayyid protested.

"Of course!" Constance returned. "You would be the one doing the spell. You're still the only one among us who speaks Egyptian."

"But who are Sayyid's enemies?" Ellie pressed.

"I should say they include Julian Forster-Mowbray," Constance replied dryly.

Adam stroked his hand along her spine. At the comforting feeling of his touch, Ellie's panic steadied enough to allow her a little space to think. "And perhaps… they might also include anyone else who wished to take Egypt's historical resources for reasons of greed or power," she added tentatively, thinking of what she knew of Sayyid's principles—as well as his anger and grief over the ravaging of his culture.

Sayyid had been looking a bit green at the notion of using the staff again, but at Ellie's words, his expression grew more thoughtful.

"Yes," Constance agreed authoritatively. "I should say it would."

"How do you know so much about all of this?" Jemmahor's narrowed eyes were both skeptical and intrigued. "Are you an expert on curses?"

"I have read a great many books about them," Constance explained.

"Novels," Neil burst out with an edge of unease. "You've read novels."

"I… do think a strict rhetorical analysis of the curse text aligns with Constance's interpretation," Ellie allowed.

"See?" Constance smiled triumphantly.

"You can't apply modern Western rhetorical analysis to Middle Egyptian!" Neil protested. "You haven't the foggiest idea of the social context!"

"Actually, I do not think it is far off, in this case," Sayyid countered.

Ellie thought once more of a world that she had watched crumble into dust—the legacy of thousands of years and countless lives collapsing into rubble at her feet. Guilt snaked up from inside of her once more. "But to bury it all in the sand…"

Adam's hand slipped over her fingers. He gazed down at her, his eyes shadowed with both sympathy and understanding. "We're not in Tulan. And… maybe some stories have to be hidden for a little while, before they can live forever."

The truth of his words washed over her. Adam was right, of course. The world wasn't ready for everything history had to teach it—not yet.

But someday, she vowed to herself with a quiet, fierce determination. Someday, it would be. Ellie would do everything she could to make sure of that.

"It is the best choice." Zeinab rose to her feet. "And it is nearly dawn."

Ellie was surprised to realize that the eastern horizon was turning a soft pink that rose to merge with the deeper violet of the desert night.

"I'm afraid I don't recall the actual Egyptian words from that excerpt," Ellie apologized.

"'I surround with sand…'" Sayyid mused, frowning. "Nuk ahu sai… teb ament?"

He glanced at Neil for confirmation. Neil flashed him a tired smile. "It sounds right to me, for whatever that's worth."

"Driving away," Sayyid continued. "Xesef-a. And the enemy…"

"Xeft," Neil offered.

"You always forget your pronouns," Sayyid automatically corrected him. "*Thy* enemy. Xeft-k."

"It sounds splendid to me." Constance hopped down from her perch with unfair energy. "But perhaps before we do any spells, we ought to cross the wadi. If we are trying to bury this tomb, we might not want to do it while we are standing on top of it."

Dawn continued to climb the eastern horizon as they hiked across the canyon. Ellie's legs ached as she picked her way along the narrow, winding track. The path was the same one that they had taken when they descended earlier that night, but it felt like a thousand years had passed since then.

By the time they reached the opposite side of the gorge, the sky was streaked with pink and gold, casting the wadi into hues of burnished red and purple.

Ellie glanced behind her to where the camels of the Ibn Rashid lingered in a sandy hollow. Most of them were sleeping, their long necks stretched out across the sand. Yusuf leaned against the rocks to watch contentedly over the flock. Mustafa gazed to the south, a soft desert breeze tugging at his quftan and headscarf as his hand rested on the pommel of his sword in a posture that would have given a Romantic painter convulsions of joy. The skinny yellow dog lay at his feet, its head resting on its paws.

"Might have been nice if they had helped out while we were being shot at," Neil grumbled beside her.

"They only care about the camels." Adam clapped a hand on his shoulder. "We're just the baggage."

Ellie turned back to the wadi. Beyond the shadowy cut that held the tomb, the ridge flattened into a broad plateau of undulating dunes that stretched out to the east, where the flame-red orb of the sun would soon slip over the horizon.

"It is time," Zeinab declared solemnly.

The rest of them quieted, gathering near the edge of the cliff—except for Adam, who remained a few prudent steps back. Sayyid drew in a breath, steeling himself, and raised up the was-scepter in his hand.

"Nuk ahu sai er teb ament," he called out in a clear, steady voice. "Xesef-a xeft-k."

The canyon caught his words and echoed them softly back and forth against its rocky walls until they faded.

All of them waited in an instinctive, reverent silence. A breeze pulled gently at the bottom of Ellie's skirt, sand rasping over the toes of her boots.

As the silence stretched, Ellie felt a pang of dismay. Had she remembered the words wrong? She didn't think she had—but then, perhaps the call to the Flame of Isis hadn't been a proper spell after all.

She tried to think of an alternative. Perhaps something else from the Book of the Dead? There were quite a few protective spells in its earlier chapters, though most of them referred to the decay of the body. But surely if she wracked her brain, she could think of *something*…

She was filing through her memories of the Spell of Going Forth By Day when the ground began to rumble.

Little stones bounced and rattled beside her feet. Ellie danced back, struck by a sudden terror that the cliff was about to collapse from beneath her.

Zeinab's hand clamped around her arm, stopping her short. "La ilâha illa Allâh," she croaked, her voice raw with astonishment.

Ellie looked up—and realized that the desert was moving.

The sands beyond the wadi shifted like the waters of an impossible golden sea, rising and falling in the fiery light of the moment before dawn. With a sibilant hiss, a wave lifted from the plateau and rolled toward them.

It grew as it approached—and *grew*. The shadow of it fell across Ellie's boots, then rose to cover her entirely as it raced at the wadi, roiling and building like an impossible tsunami.

Adam's arm tightened around Ellie's waist. He pulled her back against him, and she knew that he was also wondering if this was the last moment they would have together before the desert itself ruthlessly devoured them.

The wave fell.

A roaring cascade of sand spilled into the wadi, spraying up against Ellie and the others with a stinging heat. Adam whirled, shielding her with his body as the air filled with a maelstrom of dust and grit.

She braced herself for the impact—for the hot, suffocating crush.

The wind softened. Clouds of sand drifted down around her boots.

The air was filled with a shifting, deafening hiss. Ellie twisted in Adam's grip, far enough to look back.

The sun had crested the horizon, blazing from red to gold. It spilled a clear, wild light out over the scene that lay before her.

The wadi was gone. Where the deep cut of the canyon had once lain was only a river of dawn-gilded sand. Nothing remained of the crown of high cliffs that had cradled Neferneferuaten's tomb, save for scatter of jagged rocks that poked up here and there from the settling, drifting mass of sand.

Ellie took a careful step forward to where the ridge ended. Instead of a steep fall into the ravine, the ground dropped only a single step onto a softly whispering dune.

Neil gaped at the transformation, adjusting his spectacles as if that would make it more believable. Constance had a hand clapped to her mouth, her eyes wide with shock and wonder.

Sayyid swayed.

"I believe I might be sick," he announced flatly as his knees gave out.

Adam darted forward to catch him, softening Sayyid's collapse into an abrupt sit.

Sayyid promptly leaned forward and put his head between his knees. He held out a shaking hand, which was still holding the was-scepter. "Could someone please take this from me?" he asked a little desperately.

Zeinab stepped forward and gently removed the staff from her husband's grasp.

Gravel crunched behind them. Ellie glanced back to see Mustafa climb up from his place by the camels.

The early sunlight highlighted the perfect angles of his cheekbones. His hawk-like eyes took in the impossible change to the landscape, then dropped to the arcanum Zeinab held in her hands.

"We must return the camels," he announced imperturbably. "It is time to depart."

He left without any further to-do. The breeze tugged at his elegant layers of robes as he returned to the place where Yusuf waited with the saddled beasts, the bells of their harnesses jingling softly.

Zeinab gazed solemnly down at the relic. With a neat twist of her wrist, she plucked the bronze head from the ancient tamarisk.

She tugged the tail off as well, slipping both ends of the was-scepter into the voluminous pockets of her abaya. Her eyes lingered on the unadorned stick of ancient wood—and then rose to the newborn desert that sprawled before her.

Zeinab took three neat steps out onto the gilded river where the wadi had once been and drove the tamarisk rod into the sand.

Jemmahor carefully joined her. Without speaking, she unwrapped a black scarf from around her waist and tied it to the top of the staff.

She stepped back.

A breeze drifted over the ridge, brushing across the newly minted dune and twisting up little eddies of sand. It picked up the fine, soft fabric, setting it dancing as it pulled toward the west.

Ellie's chest tightened with grief as she realized what she was looking at—the only surviving monument to the final resting place of a woman who through love, loss, and principle had helped reshape the world.

A place now deeply, safely concealed beneath an impossible river of sand.

FORTY-FOUR

$\mathcal{E}$LLIE SLUMPED AGAINST the warm, sturdy back of her riding companion, her eyelids drooping.

"Wake up, Ellie!" Constance said cheerfully, reaching back to tap her on the shoulder. "You're about to fall off the camel."

She yanked herself upright, blinking painfully as she held loosely to Constance's waist. The day had sunk into early evening. They had been riding since dawn, returning along the same desert route that had brought them to the royal wadi of Tell al-Amarna. The addition of Neil and Constance to the party had made them two animals short, so the ladies had been paired up.

Jemmahor rode with Umm Waseem, her confiscated rifle proudly slung over her back. She kept up a running commentary in indignant Masri as they crossed the fifty miles of desert. Ellie heard the word *ingilyzy* often enough to guess that the apprentice midwife was still railing against the way in which Jacobs had used her as a hostage.

"What does 'ibn kalb' mean?" she called over to Neil.

"Er—son of a dog, I believe," Neil returned awkwardly.

Sayyid snorted. He wore a kaffiyeh scarf around his head, loaned to him by Yusuf after the Bedouin cast a sympathetic look at Sayyid's bald spot.

Adam rode up to join them. He looked perfectly at ease seated on his enormous camel. Though perhaps not quite as dashing as their exceptionally handsome Bedouin guides, with his bruises and stubble, Ellie still drank in the sight of him like water.

He caught her looking and flashed her a grin.

"We are here," Zeinab announced, bringing her camel to a stop.

Ellie pulled her gaze from Adam to see that the camp of the Ibn Rashid lay before them. Three new tents had joined the assemblage, reminding Ellie that there was to be a wedding that night. The celebrations were clearly already in full swing, based on the music and the smell of roasted lamb that drifted to her across the evening air.

Lanterns had been lit against the approaching dusk, and a band of children played in the scrubby grass beyond the tents. The clear, high sound of their laughter rang through the evening air like small bells.

The figures clustered in front of the sheikh's tent were already cast in shadow against the setting sun. One of them detached itself from the others to approach the incoming riders. Something about the tall, exceptionally well-tailored form struck Ellie as oddly familiar.

"Goodness!" Ellie exclaimed, straightening as she held onto Constance's waist. "Isn't that your grandmother's dragoman?"

"Oh drat!" Constance blurted out. "It certainly looks like him."

Mr. Mahjoud stepped into the light. His elegant ivory suit was set off by a bright red silk waistcoat—and the leather strap of a scabbard hung across his back.

"But is he wearing a sword?" Ellie asked with surprise.

"It is ceremonial. For the wedding," Zeinab explained.

"That's what *you* think," Constance returned skeptically—and then stiffened as a smaller figure stepped into the light from behind the dragoman.

The form was distinctly feminine and slightly stout with age. Folds of midnight blue silk studded with golden embroidery peered out from under a dark traveling cloak... and Ellie was fairly certain she could feel the force of a penetrating, mildly sardonic glare from across the hundred yards of desert that still separated them.

"Er..." Ellie began awkwardly. "It would appear that he is accompanied by your grandmother."

The word Constance used in response was significantly less polite than 'drat.'

A few minutes later, Ellie inelegantly dismounted her groaning camel and brushed out her skirts. She hurried over to join Constance where she stood before the petite, regal, and extremely intimidating Maharajkumari Padma Devi.

"Aai!" Constance called out with forced brightness. "What a lovely surprise to see you here!"

"And how convenient that you have arrived," Padma replied dryly, "as Mr. Mahjoud and I were just about to mount up to pursue you."

Ellie swallowed against a dry throat as Constance plastered a desperate smile on her face.

"Is that right?" Constance asked with a bit of a squeak.

"Mr. Mahjoud, do let Samir know that we shall not be requiring his assistance after all." Padma made a little wave of her hand in the direction of a trio of flawless Arabian stallions, which were being held in place by a tall, leanly muscular Bedouin gentleman in his mid-forties. His perfectly trimmed beard was spiked with silver while fine lines accented his golden eyes. Beneath his gently wind-tossed robes, his figure was straight and powerful.

He was possibly even more mouthwateringly attractive than Mustafa. He was also bristling with weapons—two daggers at his belt, a rifle over his shoulder, and a pistol in a holster under his arm.

"And who did you say that was?" Constance asked distantly as she drank up the sight.

"Samir is Sheikh Salah Mohammed's younger brother," Padma replied.

For a brief moment, Ellie wondered that Constance's grandmother was already on comfortable terms with a remote Bedouin chief... but then, nothing ought to surprise her when it came to Kumari Padma's cords of influence. Either she had already been acquainted with the sheikh through some arcane network of royal obligation, or she had simply marched up to his tent and bowled him over with her natural authority.

Mr. Mahjoud reached Samir and delivered his message. With perfect grace, Samir swung himself into the saddle and led the three horses away at a gallop.

Ellie only realized she was still gaping after him when Padma continued speaking.

"Now that's settled," she began neatly, "shall we talk about why you ran off without any word after being shot at by a pack of villains?"

"I sent a telegram!" Constance protested stoutly. "And we didn't 'run off.' We were with a party of organized professionals."

Padma raised a single eloquent eyebrow and allowed her gaze to brush over the company behind them.

Zeinab and the other Egyptian ladies were already gone, striding purposefully toward the brightly lit women's tent. Instead, there was Neil, wobbling as he stumbled free of his camel. He still wore his bent glasses and open, tattered waistcoat, his brown hair sticking out at odd angles. The canvas bundle of Julian's sword was tied awkwardly against his back with a length of rope.

Sayyid rubbed a nerve-wracked hand over his exhausted features, dark circles showing under his eyes.

Adam had slung an arm around the neck of his camel, scratching happily at its ears. "Who's a good girl?" he cooed as the camel brayed. The skinny yellow dog ran in happy circles around his legs.

Ellie's cheeks flushed. "But how did you even know where to find us?"

"When you disappeared amid flustered accounts of nefarious villains and a dash of sporadic gunfire, Mr. Mahjoud promptly reported the incident to me," Padma replied archly. "Whereupon I joined him and proceeded to track you."

Ellie's eyes shifted involuntarily to Mr. Mahjoud, who had returned to Padma's side. He crossed his arms over his chest and regarded Ellie and Constance with a seething disapproval.

She wondered how many new favors Constance must now owe her grand-mother. Somehow, Ellie felt certain that Constance would not be let off simply because Padma's rescue had not strictly turned out to be necessary.

"Now, then," Padma cut in authoritatively. "Shall you tell me what, precisely, the pair of you have been up to for the last four days?"

Padma herded Ellie and Constance to the women's tent, leaving Neil, Adam, and Sayyid to answer the enthusiastic calls of the Bedouin gentlemen gath-ered around the fires, where they were greeted like returning family.

With a great deal of laughing and chatter, Ellie was deposited beside a platter loaded with roast lamb and rice dotted with dried fruits and herbs. The Bedouin ladies were beautifully decked out in elegantly embroidered gowns and hijabs accented by layers of brightly jingling jewelry.

The bride—the sheikh's grandniece Fatimah—sat raised up over the other ladies, swathed in silk robes that glimmered with gilded embroidery as the older women fussed over her.

The food was plucked up and carried off to make room for dancing by the time Constance reached the end of her explanation.

"And so you see, Aai," Constance continued, pitching her voice louder to be heard over the oud and drums. "The entire situation was entirely under control."

"Indeed," Padma blithely agreed, sipping her tea. "Entirely under control, from the part where you were thrown off a boat to the bit where Umm Waseem nearly had to blow a mountain down on top of you."

Ellie's gaze flickered over to where the old smuggler and munitions expert had joined the dancers, shaking her hips with remarkable agility.

"Of course I would have *preferred* to inform Mr. Mahjoud of our plans,"

Constance pressed. "But we could hardly go back to Saqqara to fetch him with Julian and his mercenaries on the lookout for us! Really, we made the most sensible choices we could, given the circumstances. After all, I am not some child who requires coddling whenever things become difficult. I am nearly twenty-four!"

"I am quite aware of your increasingly advanced age, Kondi." Padma's eyes glittered dangerously. "Tell me—amid all of your adventures this week, have you made any further progress toward finding yourself a husband?"

Constance's mouth firmly closed.

"Perhaps it is worth noting that the gentleman Lady Sabita preferred for Constance turned out to be an absolute bounder," Ellie burst out testily. "And that Constance might be best left to judge any new prospects for herself in her own good time!"

Ellie had largely remained quiet during Constance's account of their recent adventures, except when she had piped in to offer her personal theories about the impact of the Pharaoh Neferneferuaten on the development of the Abrahamic religions. Padma had cut that off just when Ellie was getting rolling.

The kumari was paying very close attention to her now, which left Ellie feeling like a butterfly pinned to a museum display board. She stiffened, refusing to be intimidated.

"Marriage is not always to a woman's benefit," she observed stoutly. "In fact, I should say that as an institution, it is currently so broken that I wonder why any woman would willingly enter into it, regardless of the quality of the gentleman involved!"

Ellie's outburst came out a mite higher in volume than she had strictly intended—only so that it might be heard over the happy ululations of the Bedouin ladies trilling out the zagharit, of course.

Zeinab's head turned from within the dancers, her green eyes locking thoughtfully onto Ellie before she was carried past by the current of celebrating ladies.

Beside Ellie, Constance's face flashed with quick sympathy.

Padma's gaze was harder to read. "I would not permit my granddaughter to marry a bounder, Miss Mallory," she declared in a voice both as firm as stone and unimpeachably regal.

Jemmahor bounced over, her cheeks flushed pink. Her hair curled with a touch of well-earned perspiration at her forehead, where her hijab had fallen back a little.

"Come on, you two!" she ordered happily, holding out her hands. "You can't possibly sit and gossip through the whole party like a pair of aunties!"

Constance shot a nervous look at her grandmother, but Padma only gave them a little wave, apparently dismissing them—at least for now.

Jemmahor grasped Ellie and Constance's hands, hauling them up into the bouncing, shimmying mass of dancers, who let out a trill of delight at the new additions to their celebration.

An hour later, Ellie was herded out into the shadowy dusk to watch the men perform the Ardah. The Bedouin ladies had donned their abayas, many of which were richly decorated with silver sequins and elegant fringe. Their eyes were laughing and happy over their veils.

The gentlemen lined up outside their tent, their own wedding finery illuminated by a blaze of torches and lanterns. Each of them held some sort of weapon—mostly swords, though Ellie also spotted a few rifles.

The drum began to beat, the bass of it pulsing with the thrum of her heart as she watched from among the row of seated women. She had been separated from Constance and Padma in the rush outside but spotted them a little further down the line.

Constance was watching Ellie's brother.

The Bedouin had co-opted their guests into the display. Neil held a sword—but not the distinct twist-welded iron of his legendary blade. Ellie supposed that was for the best, as it might have an unanticipated effect on the party if it were to suddenly burst into flames. Neil held his borrowed weapon out in front of him as though afraid he was going to slice himself with it. An older gentleman beside him took pity and helped him adjust his grip.

His sword now somewhat more properly positioned, Neil's gaze rose—rather unerringly, Ellie thought—to where Constance sat among the women.

Adam stepped into place in the line, and Ellie's eyes found him just as unerringly.

He had taken out his machete. The men around him were laughing, clearly making jokes about its relatively smaller size. Someone handed him a shamshir, the curved blade gleaming in the light of the rising moon.

Another of the sheikh's remarkably attractive relations started to sing, calling out lines of poetry as the drum beat rose.

The men began to move, their swords rising and flashing as they swept out and down. The blades twisted in their hands as the song rose into the evening sky, echoing softly off the unchanging stones that framed the camp.

Zeinab dropped beside Ellie without waiting for an invitation. The light fabric of her abaya pooled on the carpet that had been set out for them. Her eyes settled on the men.

Sayyid clearly knew the dance, joining it with a smile on his face. He fit in very well, despite being a city scholar among a band of herders and warriors. One would never guess that earlier that morning, he had wielded the power of a prophet to bury a revolutionary secret beneath the sand.

Ellie wondered if he even realized how much of a hero he was.

Neil was obviously struggling to keep up, nearly fumbling his sword, but he kept at it with a slightly desperate determination. The sight warmed her heart, even as her feelings for her hapless, scholarly brother remained a bit complicated. He had done some *very* foolish things over the last few days— and some very brave ones as well.

Ellie found herself wondering whether perhaps the complications went back even further… whether maybe she had been more hurt by Neil in the past than she had allowed herself to recognize.

But to be hurt, one had to care. And over all that had happened since she arrived in Egypt, Ellie had been reminded that she cared about Neil a very great deal. That it would be worth muddling through what had gone wrong between them instead of pretending that none of it really mattered.

Her gaze shifted down the line to where Adam wielded his borrowed sword with easy instinct, the blade flashing in his hand as though he had been born to it. A lop-sided grin brightened his unshaven face.

Something wrenched painfully in Ellie's chest at the sight.

"I think I have realized why the two of you have been mooning over each other like a pair of lost puppies," Zeinab quietly observed.

Ellie startled at the sound of her voice, having momentarily forgotten the other woman was there. "Lost puppies!" she protested.

"You are in love with him," Zeinab continued relentlessly.

The pain in Ellie's chest tightened, threaded through with worry, fear, and a wild, desperate longing. The bone-deep feeling snuck up on her like a bandit with a power that threatened to overwhelm her.

Zeinab's gaze lingered on Adam as he swung his sword in the wrong direction, then corrected himself with a laugh, the men around him smiling. "But you will not marry him. Because marriage in your world is a monster."

"How did you…" Ellie's voice trailed off, and she drew in a careful, unsteady breath. "It's… we're…" She swallowed thickly. "It's *complicated*."

"*Complicated.*" Zeinab echoed the word like a curse. Her tone shifted. "Of course, marriage is far from good in Egypt. Our mullahs say that it is the will of Allah that women be subservient to men. But that is not what I read in the Quran. My Quran declares that Allah made men and women to be equals. *Waman ya'mal mina l-ṣâliḥâti min dhakarin aw unthâ wahuwa mu'minun fa-ulâika yadkhulûna l-janata,*" she recited. "'For whoever does right, whether man or woman, and is a believer, will enter Heaven.'"

The song of the men drifted to them on a night breeze scented with acacia blossoms. Stars pricked to life against the deep velvet of the twilight sky overhead.

"Tell me, Miss Mallory," Zeinab continued. "Which truth should I live? Their truth? Or the one that holds between me and my Lord?"

Her words were quiet. The Bedouin women scattered around them did not hear, comfortably wrapped up in their happy gossip as they watched the Ardah.

Zeinab waited for an answer. Ellie gave the only one she possibly could.

"Yours," Ellie replied.

"*Mine,*" Zeinab confirmed, her green eyes flashing with determination. "I know the mullahs have law and custom on their side. I know that my truth does not save the women who are forced into marriages with men who misuse them. Some might even say that it changes nothing—but they would be *wrong.*"

Ellie's heart skipped strangely in her chest. Zeinab's tone sounded *dangerous* in a way that tugged at her like a golden thread.

"Your Bates is a good man. An *honorable* man," Zeinab added meaningfully. "It is obvious to anyone with eyes to see that he is devoted to you exactly as you are, even when it is troublesome for him—and you have chosen a path with no shortage of trouble," she noted dryly. "But the trouble that this world would thrust upon you—the trouble of the choice you think you must make between this man and what you believe in… That is not *complicated.* That is *tyranny.*"

A sense of wild, strange potential whispered through Ellie, notching up the low drumbeat of her heart.

"What are you saying?" she asked, her voice careful.

"I am saying that if you wish to change the world, you must first know what you mean for it to become." Zeinab's words snapped with quiet ferocity. "When you find your own truth—yours and God's—and live it in spite of those who would confine you… *now* you are dangerous. Because you know what *ought* to be. Because you seize it for yourself from the teeth of their injustice, even as the world howls that you must not."

Ellie felt as though she were teetering at the edge of a precipice. Behind her lay the world she had known, while before her stretched… something *else*. Something she was only beginning to imagine.

She realized that her hands were shaking. She tucked them carefully around her bruised ribs.

"What could that even look like?" she asked, her breath tight.

"Only the two of you can decide that," Zeinab returned authoritatively.

"But… what if the rest of the world thinks it's wrong?" Ellie pressed back urgently.

"Do I go about telling everyone I meet that I am a revolutionary?" Zeinab scoffed. "Running up to the doors of tyranny to bang on them with your sword is a man's way of doing battle." Her eyes glittered. "Women take the hinges off."

Ellie snorted with laughter. The sound burst from her involuntarily and was loud enough that a few of the other women glanced over, their eyes warm with wry surprise over their veils.

Zeinab's gaze shifted to the figure of her husband, where he gracefully swept out his borrowed sword. "Of course, you cannot keep it from the people who truly love you. And they may worry, because they care about your happiness. But once they understand that this is your truth, they will accept it."

Ellie glanced over at Neil as he far less gracefully worked to keep up, his face brightened by a tired, involuntary grin. "Do you really believe that?"

"I do," Zeinab solemnly replied. Her expression shifted, going over more dry. "Unless they are bigots, in which case they may change their hearts or go away."

This time Ellie's laugh simply spilled out, and something loosened inside of her—a tight, heavy knot that she had been carrying around without realizing it. As it unraveled, the night around her grew wider, sprawling out across a moon-silvered desert rife with possibilities.

Her gaze locked on Adam where he danced among the line of men, tracing the graceful sweep of his arm as his sword flashed in the torchlight. "What if we want different things?"

"Do you think only suffragists have that problem?" Zeinab retorted. "That is part of every relationship, even those among friends. We work it out together as best we can. That is all we can ever do."

"Can it really be that simple?" Ellie demanded cautiously.

Zeinab rolled her eyes. "There is nothing remotely simple about it. But I think you and Mr. Bates will manage."

She stood, the black folds of her abaya shifting into place around her. She was not a large woman, but in that moment, kissed by the distant lamplight against the rich shadows of the dusk, she looked like something out of myth.

Her green eyes shone with a quiet fire as she looked down at Ellie, and her words rang with low, furious power. "The oppressors take enough from us already. Do not *dare* let them take your heart as well."

A thrill burst through Ellie's nerves with the electric force of a firework.

The men sang their ancient song of war and honor as the women laughed in the shadows. The stars glittered overhead as the wind danced across the sand-scoured verge of the desert… and everything quietly changed.

Ellie rose as though drawn by an invisible cord that pulled her toward both the awakening night and the man who danced across from her.

Zeinab's lip twisted with a warm hint of mischief. "Don't stay out too late," she warned and strolled away.

The dance was finished. At the finale, a zagharit swelled up from the line of women, their trilling celebration rising into the velvet sky.

Ellie's gaze unerringly picked out the battered, golden-haired American mingling with the crowd of victorious men. As though he could sense her across the yards that separated them, Adam turned, his blue eyes finding her among the shadows.

Though exhaustion still tugged at her, a quicksilver steel came into her spine as she lifted her head and knowingly—pointedly—tipped her chin toward the vast silence of the desert that lay beyond the warm embrace of the lamplight.

Without waiting for his reaction, she set off across the rock-strewn sand, slipping into the cobalt shadows of the dusk.

FORTY-FIVE

$\mathscr{B}$EYOND THE LOW ridge that bordered the tents, the scrubby Bedouin grazing lands softened into gently rolling dunes. The sand sifted around Ellie's boots as she walked into the dark silence of the desert. She stopped once she was safely out of view of the camp.

The sky sprawled around her, the great bowl of it arching from horizon to horizon, pierced by the countless silver pinpricks of a wild array of stars. The sheer immensity dizzied her. She gazed up at the firmament, feeling lost and overwhelmed—like a feather caught in a soaring, timeless symphony of cause and effect, past and present… and perhaps something more. Something that moved in and around those stars like the beating of great, silent wings.

There was no sound. The sand under her boots swallowed any scrape of sole or rattling pebble that might otherwise give someone away, and yet Ellie knew with a shiver that she was no longer alone. That Adam Bates was there.

She turned to face him. Between the stars and the narrow horn of the moon, she could make out every detail of his bruised, beautiful face and his lanky warrior's form.

"Not sure how we pulled it off," Adam said with a careful lightness. "But it looks like we saved the world again."

"And we didn't have to destroy an entire site to do it," Ellie replied with a pang of old guilt. "Only bury one for the foreseeable future."

"Sounds like we're getting better at this," Adam quipped.

His tone was easy, but the seriousness of his gaze spoke of something deeper and more complicated.

He suspected why she had called him out here. Now that the immediate danger of the fate of the staff had been resolved, all the old questions about their future together were bound to come roaring back to the surface. The lines of Adam's bruised, beard-shadowed face were uncharacteristically solemn.

Ellie's throat tightened. She opened her mouth to speak, but he raised a hand—a pleading look in his eyes.

"Let me start—please," he added meaningfully. "I just… want to get this out before it slips out of my brain."

Ellie bit back her own words, recognizing the tight desperation in his tone.

"I've been thinking…" Adam began. "About what happened on that ledge. About how I didn't even have to *think* to know that I was gonna put myself in the line of fire if it meant that you had a chance of getting out of there alive. I'd make the same choice again in a heartbeat, even though I know you'd be rightfully furious with me for doing it. And I've got to ask myself what that means, exactly."

His lip was still scabbed from where it had been split. His eyes were tired—but his shoulders were straight, and there was nothing uncertain in the look he gave her.

"My dad never would've made a choice like that," Adam went on. "He'd rattle off a hundred reasons why it wouldn't make any sense—which'd all more or less amount to why saving his own ass was better for the greater good. George Bates has never cared about anything enough to give up his life for it. And I'm pretty damned sure he never will."

He stepped closer to her, his voice softening as he gazed down at her through the twilight. "I told you I didn't want you to be anybody other than who you are. But… it occurs to me I've been pushing exactly the opposite of that on myself."

He lifted a tentative hand to her face, gently brushing a lock of hair back from her cheek. The gesture ached with a quiet tenderness.

"Maybe I don't know where all of this is going to go," he said, the words tight with feeling. "But I know that I'm in love with you. And even though I'm still not sure entirely why, I think you might actually love me too—just as the big, smelly, reckless lout that I am."

A storm rose inside Ellie's chest, a tumult like an untamed sea. It was too big for words—too wild, too immense, like trying to stuff a symphony into a music box.

She raised her hand and pressed it gently to the broad plane of Adam's chest instead, just over his heart. Her palm lay there softly, where she could feel the deep beat of his pulse through his shirt.

"Not reckless," she finally said when she could speak again, the words rough with feeling. "Quick-thinking. Selfless. *Brave.*"

"I haven't been feeling very brave lately," Adam admitted.

Still ravaged by the emotions swelling through her, Ellie raised her other hand to his beard-roughened face.

"We have been tying ourselves into knots over what our future ought to look like," she said, meeting his gaze. "But how could we possibly know? I want *time*. Time for us to better understand what each of us wants. What we fear. What we need. But I do know that I want us to have a future together—desperately, with every bone in my body." Her eyes narrowed, her voice sparking with a new ferocity. "And that I am never going to walk away from this, or you, no matter how hard it gets. Not without a monster of a fight. Because there is no one else in this world that I want like I want you—just you. Exactly as you are."

His eyes were damp, his face drawn into lines of aching vulnerability.

"Ellie…" he began.

She raised her hand to his lips, stopping his next words with her fingertips.

"Just you," she repeated forcefully as her own tears slipped down her cheeks. "Exactly as you are. Will you give me that, Adam Bates?"

He caught her hand, the gesture slow and careful. He took it from his lips, wrapping his warm, calloused fingers around it instead.

"Yeah," he said, the word raw and uneven as it slipped from his throat. "Yes, Ellie."

She brushed the moisture from her face and raised her chin. "Good," she declared firmly.

He pulled her closer, slowly and tenderly. His lips brushed her hair, and then his head came to rest against her own.

She felt the uneven hitch of his breath through the circle of her arms.

"It doesn't matter if we don't know yet what it will look like," she added pointedly. "We will figure it out together—in our own way. Not your father's way or the way the rest of the world tells us."

Something subtle shifted in Adam's posture as she held him. It sparked a tingling awareness in her nerves, the first whispering intimations of a new heat.

"Been thinking about that too, as it happens," Adam said, the words deceptively casual.

"You have?" Ellie pulled back to look at him, though the warmth and pressure of his hands on her waist still sent little shivering butterflies through her skin.

"About touching you," Adam clarified, the words rich with a dark warmth.

Ellie swallowed thickly. "Oh?"

"Seems to me there's two ways I could go about looking at that." His hand began to move, fingertips tracing delicately up the line of her back. "There's my father's way—which says it's a load of selfish impulse with no thought to the consequences."

"I've told you—" Ellie began.

Adam stopped her with a finger to her lips. He traced it slowly down, catching the sensitive tissue along the rough surface of his skin.

"And there's the other way," he continued, softly relentless, gazing down at her with a cobalt heat. "The way that says I'm not taking advantage of you or lining you up for hurt—but giving you the kind of worship you deserve without demanding you change yourself in order to get it."

The word—*worship*—shivered over her like another kind of touch, and Ellie's breath grew a little shorter.

"Because that's really what it comes down to, isn't it?" Adam went on, moving his hand to the line of her jaw, then gliding it back to slide into the thick waves of her hair. "It's that, or I'm just waiting for you to come around on this whole marriage thing—or settling for that goddamned 'colleagues' nonsense you tossed at me back in Luxor."

He pulled her in with a quick flex of his arm and pressed Ellie against the lean, dangerous line of his body from chest to toes. His eyes glittered with a dangerous new intensity.

"I want you in my life, Princess—any damned way I can have you," he said, the words low as a growl. "But I'd be lying to us both if I pretended I didn't want that to include feeling you come apart in my arms."

Ellie's mouth was dry. Desire sparked through her, electrifying her skin. The ache for him came roaring back, dizzying her with the sheer force of her need.

"Adam…" The word was a plea.

He tugged irresistibly at the back of her hair, then softened, a flash of the old hurt and vulnerability mixing with the heat in his look.

"I'm not done yet." The words sounded like both a warning and a plea. He closed his eyes, drawing deep. When he opened them again, Ellie saw a new kind of naked honesty in his expression. "You've told me how marriage is one kind of tyranny. But my father's voice in my head—George Bates sitting up there, telling me I'm not good enough and never will be… That's another. Even if it's personal and not a whole damned institution. He doesn't deserve to have that kind of power over us."

"Over you," Ellie corrected him, touching his face.

The old hurt tightened his expression, and he pulled her to his chest. Ellie let her head fall against his shoulder, holding him in return.

"We came pretty close to dying out there," Adam said roughly. "More than once. And that's got a way of putting things into perspective." He brushed a hand down the side of her face, turning her chin up to meet his eyes again. "I can't say how easy it's going to be for me to shake it off. I spent a lot of years hearing those words—reckless and irresponsible. But if I'm going to be the kind of man you deserve, then I need to stop being afraid of who I am."

"Who you are…" Ellie said, framing his face with her hands, "is everything that I could possibly want."

The heat in his gaze intensified. His fingers trailed along her spine once more—this time triggering a cascade of shivers across her skin. "Guess that means I have to get used to being a bit of a cad."

The words carried an air of wicked promise.

"How *much* of a cad, exactly?" Ellie pushed back hopefully.

Adam raised an eyebrow.

Ellie hurried onward. "It is only that Constance says her father has this very interesting book hidden in the bottom of his wardrobe that might offer certain… er, *creative workarounds* to the sort of practical considerations faced by a couple who choose to engage in extramarital activities."

"You talking about what I think you're talking about?" Adam returned carefully.

"I believe so?" Ellie hedged in reply.

Adam's hand rose to thread into her hair again, sparking an electric awareness that coursed through her from her fingertips to her toes. "I think maybe I could manage being that kind of cad."

"You could?" Ellie brightened.

"Worth a few tries." Adam dropped his lips to her throat. "But we're not going to need that book."

"We won't?" Ellie echoed a little numbly, her brain mostly subsumed by the exquisite sensation of Adam's beard-roughed cheek lightly scraping against her jaw.

"Nope," he confirmed easily as his mouth trailed lower—and his hands traveled up. "Because it turns out…" His lips trailed over her collarbone. "That I am very good…" His hand slid up to her breast, gliding across the curve through the fabric of her corset. "At improvising."

"Thank God for that!" Ellie said fervently—and let him carry her down to the sand.

FORTY-SIX

$\mathcal{E}$LLIE WASN'T SURE how much sleep she managed to get after finally returning to the camp of the Ibn Rashid, but it certainly didn't feel like enough. Her limbs were heavy as they made a warm departure from Sheikh Mohammed and his strikingly good-looking family—whom Ellie was fairly certain had not slept at all themselves, being too busy celebrating the wedding.

They had gained an extra member of their party in the process of their departure. When Adam had taken his leave of the scrawny yellow dog—a ritual which had involved him kneeling down on the ground and then flopping over entirely as the wriggling animal assaulted him with its tongue—the sheikh had made a declaration with a wave of his hand.

"That is your dog now," his dashing brother, Samir, had succinctly translated for them.

Ellie's stomach had sunk… but when Adam's face lit up like a rising sun, she'd found herself incapable of making any protest.

When Adam had asked for the animal's name—while vigorously rubbing at its ears as the beast gazed up at him in obvious bliss—Samir had told him *Kalb*.

"What does 'kalb' mean?" Ellie had quietly asked her brother.

"Er… Dog?" he replied awkwardly.

And so the dog—named Dog—trotted happily in their wake all the way to Al Mutiah, where Mr. Mahjoud booked them a pair of first-class compartments on the next departure up the now-repaired train line. Ellie had given in to the urge to close her eyes for a moment as they pulled out of the station—and the next thing she knew, she was blinking into wakefulness as the golden light of late afternoon streamed in through the window.

She was slumped against Adam's shoulder. For something so solid, it made a remarkably comfortable pillow. Still, she sat up with a start, conscious of Padma sitting in regal splendor on the opposite bench of their compartment between Constance and Mr. Mahjoud.

Kalb looked up at her from where he lay sprawled across Adam's boots.

"Goodness. I must have dozed off," Ellie observed as the train jerked to a stop. "What station is this?"

"Cairo," Adam replied wryly.

She looked up at him in surprise—and spotted a distinct damp spot on the pale fabric of his shirt.

"You've a bit of…" Ellie trailed off, her cheeks flushing as she realized the most likely source of the puddle on Adam's shoulder.

Not that she was typically prone to drooling in her sleep.

Adam grinned back at her mercilessly as Kalb thumped his tail against the floor.

They disembarked quickly, as they had hardly any luggage to speak of. Even Padma had traveled exceptionally lightly, proving that she was quite capable of forgoing some of her usual finery when engaging in a pursuit.

They met up with Sayyid, Zeinab, and the other ladies out in the busy forecourt of the railway station, which was crowded with carriages, donkeys, and street vendors.

Ellie spotted a burly figure in a striped galabeya beside a cart full of little blue statues. She recognized her fake antiquities vendor and gave him a friendly wave.

The man's eyes widened, and he quickly tapped his donkey, urging it into a trot that set his reproduction artifacts rattling as he made his escape.

Jemmahor sported a scrape on her chin. She wore it under her grin like a badge of honor. "You must promise you will not leave Egypt without seeing me again!" she threatened.

"Happily," Ellie assured her.

"And I have not forgotten that you promised to teach me this jiu jitsu," Jemmahor added pointedly to Constance.

"Oh, I think you will be absolutely splendid at it!" Constance assured her.

Umm Waseem stuck out her hand. "Allah yehmeeky, okhti. E'meli mashakel kteer."

Ellie clasped Umm Waseem's palm warmly. "But what is she saying?"

"She asks for God to protect you while you cause more trouble," Jemmahor cheerfully translated.

"Ilâ l-liqâ'," Umm Waseem finished with a hint of mischief.

She slung her canvas bag over her shoulder and slipped away, quickly indiscernible from the many other black-cloaked ladies that crowded the street.

"You all right?" Adam asked as Ellie watched the old smuggler go. "You look a bit like someone just made off with your puppy."

"I was hoping to quiz Umm Waseem on the finer points of working with nitroglycerin compounds," Ellie mused forlornly. "Only everything has happened so quickly."

"Aww," Adam said lightly. "What a shame."

Ellie narrowed her eyes. "You don't think it's a shame at all."

"I'm still recovering from the last time you got your hands on a pile of dynamite," Adam replied. "Now come on. I think our ride is here."

He steered her toward the Tyrrell carriage, which had pulled up to wait by the station door. They took a quick leave of Sayyid and Zeinab, who promised to rejoin them after they had checked on their home.

After all, they had a good deal to talk about.

Ellie could still feel the exhaustion in her bones as she trudged into the cool, palm-shaded courtyard of the Tyrrells' Cairo house. The fountain tinkled musically beside the clean-swept tiles under the shade of the softly rustling palms.

Lady Sabita and Sir Robert sat at one of the wrought-iron tables. Sir Robert browsed a newspaper while Lady Sabita sorted through the post. She spoke distractedly as they entered, barely glancing up.

"Oh! Are you back from your excursion already?" she asked. "Was it very nice? Maa said you were going all the way to Aswan."

Constance stopped short in front of Ellie, causing Ellie to nearly collide with her. She cast a quick and uncomfortable look over at her grandmother.

Padma had apparently taken the effort to concoct a cover story for them before setting out in pursuit.

The kumari smiled dangerously, and Constance blanched—undoubtedly considering how many more favors had just been added to her Aai's count.

"Aswan! Yes!" Constance blurted out, flashing her mother a bright smile. "Ellie's brother joined us, as you can see, and it was lovely. They had the most beautiful…"

"Temples to Ramses II and Nefertari," Ellie filled in with a mutter.

"Some very nice quarries as well," Neil added. "I have been wanting to see them. I mean—had," he corrected himself with a slightly panicked look at Ellie and Constance. "Had been wanting. Because now I *have* seen them, and they were splendid!"

At Neil's painfully awkward tone, Lady Sabita finally looked up from her letters. Her eyes immediately widened.

"But you look as though you have been through a robbery!" she exclaimed. "Has something happened?"

Ellie was conscious of the rip in her blouse and the scab on Adam's split lip. Even Neil was showing the shadow of a beard—though it paled in comparison to the scruff on Adam's jawline. They were all wearing the same clothes they had left in nearly a week before, which were looking significantly worse for wear.

They had acquired a scruffy dog.

"You wouldn't believe it, Maa!" Constance cut in quickly. "All the better carriages were full, and we had to travel third class!"

"All the way from Aswan?" Lady Sabita exclaimed with obvious horror as she rushed toward them. "You poor things! That must have been absolutely dreadful. We shall have to coddle you soundly. Come—let's get you all a change of clothes. And a wash," she added awkwardly, stopping a few steps shy and giving them an unenthusiastic sniff.

"Sounds good to me," Adam said happily. "I've been itching for another turn in that sauna."

"Thank you, Lady Sabita." Ellie forced a tired smile. "That would be lovely."

A few hours later, Ellie stepped into the meshrabiyeh-screened salon on the roof to find Constance sprawled across the cushions, shamelessly stuffing her face with dates. The tortoiseshell cat had returned as well—if it had ever left. It dozed on a pillow above her head.

Zeinab sat beside her in a fresh galabeya of midnight blue embroidered with gold, with a hijab to match. She leaned tiredly against her husband. Sayyid's fez was back in place, which he looked quite relieved about.

Neil looked far less comfortable as he tried to settle himself on the piled cushions. He had managed to shave, and his hair was still wet from a wash. Mr. Mahjoud had sent someone to fetch some of Neil's spare clothes out of storage, and so he, too, had been able to indulge in a change. Ellie couldn't be sure when it would be safe for him to fetch his things from the dig site at Saqqara—if ever.

With his crooked spectacles, he looked overwhelmed and slightly forlorn.

Ellie sat down next to him. He blinked at her as though a bit surprised to find her there.

Adam rubbed a towel through his wet hair as he stepped out from the stairwell. He had donned a clean shirt and trousers, even deigning to shrug into a pair of braces, but had foregone a coat, clearly using the extremity of their circumstances as a continued excuse to avoid putting on a jacket. Kalb trotted worshipfully at his heels.

His gaze moved unerringly to Ellie and locked there. His mouth broke into a boyish grin.

Ellie found herself grinning back—and remembering the feel of calloused hands on her skin under a sprawling desert sky.

Deliberately, Adam crossed to her side. He dropped onto the cushions… and set his arm around her shoulders.

Neil stared at the casually intimate gesture. Constance smirked a little triumphantly.

Zeinab met Ellie's gaze, her green eyes glittering with quiet approval.

The dog flopped down by their feet.

Something glowed warmly inside Ellie's chest, and she let herself settle against Adam's side.

The sky blushed with the warm rainbow of an Egyptian dusk as the call for the sunset prayer echoed musically through the close-packed rooftops. The jasmine vines twining through the meshrabiyeh screens had opened, their scent mingling with a muddy hint of the great river on the evening breeze.

"Well, then," Ellie began. "Now we are all here, I suppose it is time to tie up our loose ends."

Constance stuffed another date into her mouth. "It seems Aai has covered for us with my parents—though I am frankly terrified to think of how many favors she will add to her tally for that."

"What about the Staff of Moses?" Adam prompted.

"Julian will keep trying to retrieve it," Constance pointed out.

Ellie looked to Zeinab, who had stuffed the two bronze pieces of the was-scepter into the voluminous pockets of her abaya back in Amarna.

Sayyid let out a puff of breath. "My father concealed the arcana he discovered within the collection of the Egyptian Museum," he reminded them. "Though of course, when he did that, nobody but him realized they were anything other than ordinary artifacts."

"I'm sure the museum has an extensive collection of was-scepters," Ellie mused. "But if Julian or one of his minions got a good look at this one, it's possible they could identify it from among the others."

"Or it could be sold off," Neil admitted.

"Which would be perfectly legal," Sayyid added grimly.

"Not the museum, then," Constance concluded. "What if we brought it back to the Ibn Rashid? From what I gather, they're constantly moving about, and those men looked quite ferocious."

Her mouth widened into a dreamy smile, and Ellie knew she was thinking of what else the men of the Ibn Rashid had looked like besides *ferocious*.

"They may be quite fierce, but heaven knows what influence Julian Forster-Mowbray's masters might bring to bear on them," Ellie warned.

"Quite a bit, I should imagine." Constance reached for another date. "Considering that Lord Yardborough is one of them."

"I beg your pardon?" Ellie said, straightening with surprise.

Constance's eyes widened. "Oh, I never did mention that, did I? We were simply swept right into all the tomb raiding and daring escapes, and it completely slipped my mind. While I was on the *Isis*, I quite cleverly lured Julian into confessing who is actually behind all of this. Not that it was very hard to do—he has always been quick to brag about how well-connected he is. It's some organization that is pulling all the strings—a club of sorts who call themselves the Order of Albion."

"A *club?*" Ellie echoed, aghast.

"That matches up with what Dawson was yammering about back in Tulan," Adam offered. "He kept telling me he worked for some super-secret important organization."

"Julian rattled off a whole list of names," Constance went on. "There was Yardborough—he's Lord President of the Privy Council and quite the higher-up with the Tories. Someone by the name of Northcote, which I can only think must be one of the financial Northcotes. They've the Bank of Suffolk and half a dozen others. And he mentioned a Prendergast, who sounds like some sort of paper-pusher."

The blood drained from Ellie's face. "Henry Augustus Prendergast is the assistant to the director of the British Museum."

"And of course, Lord Aldbury must be involved—Julian's father. That's the only way I could see any of that lot coming to rely on Julian to do their dirty work for them," Constance deduced. "And then there is Lady Hastings. She's related to half the ton and likely knows the dirty secrets of the rest of them." She gave a little shudder. "You wouldn't think a five foot tall woman in her seventies would be such a terror, but she's nearly as bad as my Aai."

"But what could they possibly want with the arcana?" Ellie demanded, her mind spinning.

"Back in British Honduras, Dawson made it sound like some grand battle of good versus evil," Adam reminded her. "The good side being the oh-so-civilized British Empire and the bad side being—well, everybody else."

Ellie was still reeling at the discovery that the mysterious forces she had been battling for the last several weeks had names and identities—faces that she had seen in the newspapers.

"So our enemies are… a social club?" she filled in awkwardly. "A social club of extremely influential people united by the notion that the world's arcana should be secured for the use of the British Empire."

"I hope you realize how dangerous that sounds," Zeinab observed flatly, her frame taut with tension.

A chill crept up Ellie's arms despite the warmth of the evening. "There would be no accountability," she said carefully as she put it together. "It isn't like a branch of the government, which might conceivably be called to turn out its pockets if there was a change of administration. They would be completely free to pursue the arcana however they liked, so long as they have enough influence to deter anyone from paying attention to any… *inconvenient consequences* of their efforts."

"There will certainly be more than five of them," Constance reasoned. "Those were the names Julian gave me, but anything this juicy and exclusive is sure to attract more interest. I shouldn't be surprised to find out that half of the British ruling class is involved in some way or another, even if it is only by doing a little favor here or there. That is how things work among that lot, anyway—financiers, politicians, members of the nobility. It's all just little favors, and only when you step back to look at it do you realize that those little favors are driving the entire empire."

Neil paled. "But that's… that's absolutely terrifying!"

Ellie soaked up the significance of what Constance was describing… and quietly agreed.

Learning they were up against a single ruthless collector, however powerful, would have been one thing. Even a secret government agency devoted to rounding up the legendary artifacts of history would not have felt entirely insurmountable.

But an informal organization based on threads of obligation and influence woven throughout the highest fabric of British society… It would be hard enough to prove it even existed, never mind find an authority who could bring those involved to justice.

The authorities were likely all members.

It would be like battling a hydra—a slippery, ruthless beast that sprouted new heads everywhere you looked for it.

A great weight settled onto Ellie's shoulders. How was one lady scholar, however principled and determined, possibly supposed to go up against something like that?

The thought threatened to pull her down into despair… until her gaze drifted over the people who were gathered around her on the rooftop.

There was fearless Constance and clever Sayyid. Zeinab the warrior, battling for justice under the shadow of her abaya. Ellie's bewildered brother, who was slowly fighting his way into doing what was right even though it meant overthrowing everything he had thought he knew about the world.

And finally Adam Bates, strong and steady beside her—ready to go wherever she might lead him with complete and unflinching trust.

That was how, Ellie realized silently as a wave of warmth washed over her. She couldn't possibly hope to thwart something like the Order of Albion on her own. She could only dare to do it with the most extraordinary band of allies at her side. With *friends*.

"As to the staff," Zeinab calmly cut in as she poured herself a cup of sweet mint tea. "You needn't worry about that anymore."

"Why not?" Ellie pressed.

"Because it has already been disposed of." Zeinab sipped her tea.

Adam cocked an eyebrow. Neil's jaw dropped.

"But where have you put it?" Constance pressed.

"I gave it to Umm Waseem."

They all stared at her with surprise—even Sayyid, who blinked down at his wife where she nestled at his side.

"None of these imperialists or their mercenaries ever saw her face," Zeinab calmly continued. "They do not know her name. She is a smuggler from a family of smugglers—people who have been keeping secrets for generations. She can put the staff someplace where it will not be found until the time is right, however long that might take." She shrugged. "It seemed the obvious solution."

Ellie wondered whether she ought to be offended that Zeinab had decided the fate of an arcanum that each and every one of them had risked their lives for without so much as a word of consultation.

But she wasn't. It seemed oddly right. Why shouldn't Zeinab have decided? The artifact was Egyptian, after all—and Zeinab knew better than any of them how to hide things in plain sight.

"What if they come after us to get to her?" Neil suggested uneasily.

"What can you tell them?" Zeinab shot back. "That she is Umm Waseem?"

"It's not a legal name," Sayyid explained with a look at his wife that was both uncertain and admiring. "It just means Mother of Waseem. We call older women by the names of their sons. It is a mark of respect."

"And there are thousands of Waseems in Egypt," Zeinab finished pointedly. "We may tell them everything we know of her. Even I may do so—because it isn't very much. When Umm Waseem wants to disappear, she disappears. Nobody will be able to track her down if she doesn't wish them to."

Ellie thought of the old woman with eyes like glinting blades and her ubiquitous sack of explosives—and found that she did not doubt Zeinab's words one bit.

She cast a significant look at Adam. "So we would be able to tell Jacobs *truthfully* that we have no idea where Umm Waseem is."

"And he'll know that means harassing us for more information is a dead end," Adam filled in.

He didn't have to explain any further. They both knew perfectly well how capable Jacobs was of recognizing the truth.

"What if he just wants revenge?" Neil pressed nervously.

Adam shook his head. "I don't think that's his style. Don't get me wrong—he's a nasty piece of work. But he's not one of those guys who hurts people for the fun of it. It's just business for him."

Ellie uncomfortably considered how awful Jacobs' notion of *just business* was... and then found herself thinking of the bizarre revelations exposed by their encounter with him on the ridge.

What is it that you truly want?

Justice.

Justice that somehow—in some way—Ellie and Adam must be meant to play a part in.

It had stayed Jacobs' hand when he might otherwise have easily—and happily—killed them both. And yet, Ellie wasn't sure whether she ought to find that a relief... or an even more frightening prospect than being at the wrong end of Jacobs' gun.

His final words at the wadi drifted through her mind, sparking a chill that defied the warm air of the Egyptian night.

Till next time.

"Of course, there is also the little issue that both Mr. Al-Ahmed and Dr. Fairfax have most certainly lost their jobs," Constance helpfully pointed out, interrupting the dark turn of Ellie's thoughts.

Neil groaned at the reminder, dropping his face into his hands. "I highly doubt I'll be getting a reference," he muttered, his voice muffled by his palms.

"I would suspect not," Ellie agreed sympathetically. She looked at Sayyid. "I imagine you have quite enough experience and contacts to get other work without Mr. Forster-Mowbray's help."

"I… do." Sayyid sounded oddly unenthusiastic about the prospect.

Neil raised his head. "Or you could finish your father's book," he blurted out quickly.

Zeinab slowly set down her tea. Constance's eyebrows arched with surprise.

Sayyid frowned.

"The Egyptian lexicon," Neil elaborated. "You could do it brilliantly—you know more about the language than anyone I have ever met, and that includes the entire Cambridge History Department. If you translated what your father had already written into English and filled in whatever was missing, I know more than one publisher who would jump at the chance to get their hands on a work like that. And if you were recognized as the world's preeminent expert on the reconstructed pronunciation of Middle and Late Egyptian…" Neil's expression firmed as he put a bit more steel into his tone. "Well, it would be a little harder for the Antiquities Service to justify turning down any application you might make for an excavation of your own."

Sayyid looked torn, hope and a tired skepticism warring on his features.

"Who would fund a dig run by an Egyptian?" he pushed back in tones as careful as glass.

"Aai would," Constance replied, plucking another date from the bowl.

Everyone looked at her in surprise.

"But the expense…" Sayyid protested.

"She has thrown parties that would cost more than you do," Constance assured him. "And she has always had an interest in history." She frowned. "Among other things."

Like blackmail, espionage, and intimidation, Ellie thought quietly.

"I think it is worth considering," Zeinab declared.

Sayyid straightened. "You do?"

"At least until we have managed to overthrow the British oppressors and reclaim Egypt's heritage for Egyptians," she added in smoothly dangerous tones.

"I think we can all agree that is the ideal outcome," Ellie offered stoutly.

Adam smirked with pride.

Constance turned a curious gaze on Zeinab. "Is your revolutionary cell taking on any new members?"

"Not at the moment," Zeinab returned dryly.

Neil stared at Constance with a look of horrified admiration.

"Well, then." Constance brushed the date crumbs from her hands. "I suppose that settles things."

"Not entirely," cut in a crisp, authoritative voice from behind her.

Ellie whirled to see Kumari Padma standing at the top of the stairs, clad in a luxurious sari of richly patterned silk in hues of pink and green. Mr. Mahjoud stood at her back, giving them a quietly exasperated look that made Ellie wonder just how long he had been listening.

"There is still the matter of a few little favors you owe me." Padma's gaze shifted meaningfully from Ellie and Adam to Constance and Neil. "Perhaps now would be an appropriate time to discuss them?"

It was not really a question.

"Of course, Aai." Constance swallowed thickly as she looked nervously to the rest of them. "We would be happy to."

FORTY-SEVEN

$\mathcal{P}$ADMA LED ELLIE, Constance, Neil, and Adam into the house after they bid Zeinab and Sayyid a quick but warm goodnight. One of the household staff guided Kalb away—the dog, apparently, not being invited to join the meeting.

The kumari's suite of rooms included an elegant, high-ceilinged salon with screened windows overlooking the courtyard. The space was framed by a divan piled with cushions in colorful patterns of embroidered silk. An altar stood against the wall, draped in a beautiful cloth and hosting murtis of a handful of gods. Incense burned in front of it next to a scattering of fresh flowers.

Padma sat down in the center of the plush bench, looking regal, comfortable, and entirely in charge.

Mr. Mahjoud poured out more tea. Instead of the sweet, minty brew Ellie had become accustomed to in Egypt, this was richly creamy and spiked with notes of cardamom and clove.

Constance cast a distinctly nervous look at her grandmother, even as she clearly aimed to bluff unconcern. Adam cocked an eyebrow as he picked up on the simmering tension in the room.

Neil shifted uncomfortably until he took a sip of his tea, at which point his eyes widened with delight. "Oh! This is…" He took another sip. "This is absolutely *lovely!*"

"I am so glad that you enjoy it, Dr. Fairfax." Padma's reply was serene— and still somehow carried an air of subtle threat.

Neil's cup paused on its way back to his mouth—but after a moment, he brought it up anyway. Apparently being deeply intimidated wasn't enough to put him off his chai.

"Now that we are all nice and cozy together," Padma said with a dangerous smile, "I thought we might talk about how you will settle your debts."

Something about the subtle emphasis Padma put on the word 'your' made it sound distinctly and alarmingly *plural*.

"And how many favors are... er, owed you, exactly?" Ellie pressed carefully.

Padma waved an airy hand. "I do not think we need to be so vulgar as to mention numbers."

Constance frowned, too surprised to keep quiet. "But you always keep count, Aai."

"I think the little favor I mean to ask should settle any outstanding balances." Padma waved to Mr. Mahjoud to refill her cup.

Constance looked warily hopeful. "It would?"

"And what is the little favor, Kumari?" Ellie asked.

"Call me Auntie, Jhia," Padma replied with a frankly intimidating note of affection. "After all, we will be spending a great deal of time together over the next few weeks."

"We will?" Ellie squeaked, her nerves jolting.

Padma calmly sipped her tea. "What do you know of the Brahmastra?"

Neil and Adam gave each other a blank look. Padma shifted her gaze to Constance, who sank back against the cushions.

"Sorry, Aai," she admitted awkwardly.

Padma set down her tea before straightening regally. "The Brahmastra is perhaps the most powerful weapon of our Hindu legends and histories. It was used, among other things, by Lord Rama to overcome the demon king Ravana when he stole away Rama's beloved wife, Sita."

"Of course!" Ellie exclaimed. "You're talking about the Ramayana—one of the great Hindu epics. But... isn't Rama's weapon described as being unimaginably destructive?"

"A ball of fire that makes the mountains shatter," Padma confirmed flatly. "Where it burns, not a single blade of grass will ever grow again—not for thirty-two trillion years." She cast a serious gaze over the four of them. "And certain reputable sources back in India have informed me that the power to invoke it is at very real risk of falling into the wrong hands."

Ellie felt a thrill of danger... and a whisper of excitement.

She glanced at Adam. There was a knowing light in his eyes as he gazed back at her.

Neil, on the other hand, looked confused... until his face abruptly blanched. "Hold on. Are you asking us to go to *India?*"

Padma wore a deceptively benign look as she took another sip of her tea.

"I am not sure 'asking' is precisely the right word."

Constance brightened. "Aai, do you mean that we would be going to see Uncle Vijay?"

"Who else do you think told me about the trouble?" Padma replied.

"Uncle Vijay is Aai's nephew—my mother's cousin." Constance practically bounced in her seat with excitement. "He's the Maharaja of Nandapur and the most terribly dashing and interesting person. He has fought in duels, and once wrestled a tiger, and there was the most scandalous story about a Sikh princess… Oh, Aai! You can't really mean it!"

"I have taken the liberty of asking Mr. Mahjoud to make the arrangements," Padma said with a dismissive wave of her hand. "We will leave out of Port Said on Tuesday morning. I do hope that will give you sufficient time to pack?"

She addressed the latter question to Ellie, Adam, and Neil.

Neil looked pale and a little dizzy. "And you are saying that it is real," he pressed uncomfortably, "this weapon that can raze mountains and turn the land into desert. As real as… that other object of interest we just encountered."

"Do you doubt me, Dr. Fairfax?" Padma's eyes glinted like steel.

Neil rubbed a tired hand over his face. "No," he admitted with a wince. "No, I do not."

Constance studied Neil with a thoughtful frown. Padma saw it—and the smallest little smile crossed her lips as she took another sip of her tea.

"I'll do it," Neil replied firmly, then immediately wavered. "Though I haven't the foggiest idea what sort of use I'll be. My education is all in Egyptology and the classics. I barely know anything about Indian history."

"I am sure you will be a quick study," Padma cheerfully assured him—and cast a pointed glance over at her granddaughter.

Adam coughed suspiciously into fist, his blue eyes twinkling.

"Jhia?" Padma prompted, looking to Ellie.

Ellie felt as though she stood on the edge of a precipice. A new unknown sprawled out before her, promising untold threats—and wild adventure.

A conspiracy in India. The world-destroying power of a god on the line.

She raised her eyes to Adam.

"I'm game if you are," he declared, strong and steady at her side.

Ellie drew in a breath. She met Padma's patient, steel-hard gaze—and gave her answer.

"We should be happy to be of service," she vowed purposefully. "Auntie."

Before Ellie quite knew what was happening, Mr. Mahjoud had deposited the four of them in the hall outside Padma's suite, which fronted onto one of the balconies overlooking the courtyard.

"Would it be too much for me to request that you *not* get into any more trouble between now and Tuesday?" He gave each of them—but particularly Constance—a pointed look.

"Whyever would you feel the need to ask that?" Constance returned innocently.

"It's hardly our fault people were shooting at us," Ellie grumbled.

"I never want to do anything remotely like that again in my life," Neil blurted forcefully.

"I give it maybe fifty-fifty," Adam offered.

Neil blanched. Mr. Mahjoud gave an eloquently aggrieved sigh. "Off to bed now, if you please. Before you bring the roof down or unleash a plague of locusts."

Ellie kept her expression carefully blank. Adam coughed.

"It's not like we can do that *anymore*," Constance shot back crossly.

Mr. Mahjoud looked up to the heavens, muttered a dua, and shut the door.

"Well!" Constance said brightly, turning to the rest of them. "I should say that worked out quite splendidly. We are going to India! I have always wanted to see it for myself. Of course we will have to visit the temples and pay our respects to Lord Jagannath. I have heard there are the most splendid waterfalls, and still tigers to be found in the more remote areas of the forest... I am going to need to work on my Odia! It is absolutely wretched. Never mind all the shopping we will need to do. You and Adam barely have enough to fill a suitcase, and as for Stuffy..." She cast Neil a look, then patted him sympathetically on the arm. "I'm sure you'll manage."

Ellie gave herself a breath to absorb the whirlwind of conversation that had just changed her life.

Constance's maharaja cousin's realm lay in the region of Odisha, part of the ancient kingdom of Kalinga. That area of India was rich with history from the splendor of the Mughal Empire back to the days of the great conqueror Ashoka. The notion of seeing it for herself was desperately exciting—and deeply intimidating. If rumors were circulating of the re-emergence of the Brahmastra, Padma would not be the only one to have heard them. Ellie would very possibly find herself going up against Jacobs or other agents of the Order of Albion once again.

Till next time...

Jacobs' parting words echoed through her mind once more. Ellie swallowed her unease and turned her attention to her brother—who had never asked for any of this. "How are you feeling about all of it, Neil?"

"Well—I mean, I have lost my job," Neil returned a bit helplessly. "Then went on a madcap expedition to find the lost tomb of a woman I've studied for most of my life… which I can never actually tell anybody about. Jumped off a boat. Was nearly buried alive in an Old Kingdom quarry. Saw an entire desert move because Sayyid told it to." He drew in a careful breath. "And now it appears that I am going to India."

"I suppose that is rather a lot," Ellie admitted.

"Is this what it's going to be like from now on?" Neil demanded with a note of panic.

Constance shrugged.

Adam gave Neil's shoulder a sympathetic squeeze. "Sorry, buddy."

Neil pushed up his glasses to pinch the bridge of his nose. "Right. Well then." He dropped his hand, looking from Adam to Ellie. "The two of you. You're…"

His voice trailed off.

Ellie met Adam's gaze. A flash of guilt crossed his features—but only for a moment before it was replaced by a look of determination. He slid a hand around the small of Ellie's back and locked his eyes on Neil.

"We are," he replied simply.

Constance hung back, watching the exchange with careful focus.

Neil ran a helpless hand through his hair, hopelessly disheveling it. "I can't pretend I don't find the notion absolutely terrifying," he blurted out—then pulled up his shoulders, straightening. "But you're my sister." He looked up at Adam. "And you are one of the best men I have ever known. Whatever the two of you end up deciding this all means—you will have my support." He wavered a bit. "Even if… even if I haven't always been so good at giving it in the past."

A pang of old hurt and disappointment twinged inside of Ellie. "It's fine, Neil," she assured him quietly.

Neil let out a slightly desperate laugh. "It isn't, really. But I… I'm going to do better at it. At a lot of things. I'm… I'm quite determined about that."

His words sparked a warm burst of affection, one that was only deepened by how obviously intimidated he was by the prospect.

Changing oneself was incredibly difficult. One *ought* to be intimidated by it.

"Thank you." Pride and love warmed Ellie's words. "That means a very great deal to me."

Neil's face broke into a tired smile. It flinched into a grimace as Constance punched him in the shoulder.

"Well done, Stuffy," she declared approvingly. "Now that's settled, I'm off to bed. The rest of you had better get some sleep as well if you want to keep up with Aai. She is an unholy terror once she gets a plan in her head."

"I think I could sleep for a month," Neil moaned.

"I'm giving you seven hours," Constance replied.

His eyes widened. "Seven hours? What happens after seven hours?"

Constance flashed him a smile like a knife blade. "I suppose you'll find out, won't you?"

Ellie wondered if Constance's wake-up plan might involve Neil's socks and some degree of combustion. It warmed her to see her brother and her friend getting back to their usual affectionate repartee.

Even if there did seem to be something a little more in the looks they kept casting at each other… not that either of them would admit it.

At least, not *yet*.

The notion left Ellie feeling a little uneasy… but not entirely so.

Constance gave Neil a wave—and shot Ellie a knowing look—before darting into the haramlek, the quarter of the house where she and Ellie had their rooms.

"Goodnight, Neil," Ellie said, kissing her brother's cheek.

"You too, Peanut," he replied, hugging her back.

He started down the hall to the guest wing, where he and Adam were staying. He turned back with a puzzled look.

"Aren't you coming?" he asked Adam.

"I'll be there in a minute," Adam assured him. "You go on."

Neil's gaze shifted to where Ellie stood beside his friend. He swallowed thickly.

"Right," he muttered to himself. "Just… heading on, then."

He hurried around the corner and out of view.

Adam smiled down at her, his eyes bright with a hint of mischief. "All in all, I think that went pretty well. Found the staff. Saved the tomb. Even got your brother to loosen up a little bit. And I mostly managed to keep my shirt on."

"You needn't be too proud of that last bit," Ellie grumbled.

"Saying you don't mind the view?" Adam returned with a note of self-satisfaction.

"I think you are perfectly well aware of my thoughts on the view," Ellie returned.

She realized they had come to stand on the same balcony where she had lingered a few nights before when Adam had regaled her with his best iambic pentameter. Memories of how a few moments later, he had tossed her up against the wall and kissed her positively senseless set her pulse knocking a little harder.

Just like before, the gently lamplit garden below them was empty, quiet save for the chirp of a night bird and the soft rush of the fountain.

"Of course, it is worth noting that we have been more or less coerced into going to India." Ellie looked up at him worriedly. "I am fairly certain if you go to India, you aren't going to have a position as Assistant Surveyor General for the colony of British Honduras waiting for you when you get back."

"Probably not," Adam agreed.

Ellie felt a little dart of guilt. "Adam, I…"

"No," he cut in gently. "You don't even have to start down that road. I don't know if I could've gone back to that job, even if we weren't being blackmailed into going after some apocalyptic piece of Hindu mythology."

"Whyever not?" Ellie asked, confused.

He sighed, looking out over the courtyard—and perhaps beyond it, to where the lights of the city gave way to the vast, starlit sprawl of the unknown. "I don't know what I'm meant to be doing with my life, Ellie. And that restless feeling has been itching at my brain since long before you dropped off a balcony into my lap. I know what my dad would have to say about it," he added dryly. "But I'm choosing not to listen to that anymore. Leaves me wondering what should go in its place." He glanced down at her. "I'd be interested to hear your thoughts on that."

She felt the seriousness of his question—and the honor of what it meant that he had asked her.

"I think…" she began carefully, "that I have already seen you make a tremendous impact on the world, just by being who you are in it."

"That isn't exactly going to keep a roof over our heads—not that I'm claiming some patriarchal responsibility to support you," he added wryly. "I just… I dunno, Princess. I feel like I'm still trying to figure out who I'm supposed to be. Not for George Bates, but… maybe for you, a little. And for myself, mostly," he added quickly before Ellie could protest.

Swallows flitted overhead, delicate shadows against the purple span of the night. The fountain splashed quietly in the lamplit courtyard below.

"Do you… think that's something you could explore in India?" she asked.

Adam looked tired and a little battered—just a rough, scarred, soon-to-be-unemployed surveyor who also happened to be the bravest and most honorable man she'd ever known.

"Pretty sure I've told you this before," he replied. "But where you go, I go… for as long as you're willing to keep me around."

"For as long as I'm willing?" Ellie pushed back crossly. "What—do you think I'm going to banish you to the hinterlands for displeasing me? We've already been to the hinterlands, and as I recall it, I was quite insistent on wanting to keep you very close indeed!"

Adam's hand firmed on her back, pulling her a little nearer as a self-satisfied smile quirked his lip. "That does ring a bell or two."

The strength of his grip—and the reminder that she stood inches from six-feet-or-so of wonderful, disreputable man, pushed Ellie's thoughts in a somewhat less… *collegial* direction. "And what about tonight? Did you have any… *thoughts* on where you might like to go?"

"You mean…" Adam prompted carefully.

Ellie elaborated quickly. "Of course, we are guests under Lady Sabita and Sir Robert's roof, and I suppose it would be extremely inconsiderate of us if we were to engage in any less-than-entirely-proper activities while enjoying their hospitality. So I'd understand if you wished to… er… keep to your own devices for the evening."

"My own… devices?" Adam's words sounded tight.

"You know," Ellie clarified. "Retire with a good book."

Adam moved closer. It made him seem to loom over her, even as the heat of his body warmed her through the fabric of her blouse.

"Something on Latin conjugations, maybe?" he suggested silkily.

Ellie frowned. She was feeling a little distracted, which was making it hard to put her thoughts together. "I suppose that might be a fair option if you're looking to go directly to sleep."

"I'm not looking to go to sleep," Adam said in a low rumble.

"Oh?" Ellie appeared to be going over a mite breathless.

His fingers grazed along the line of her back. "And as it happens, I can think of a thing or two I'd rather do to pass the time than *conjugate*." His hand stilled. "If you're feeling amenable."

Ellie had not wanted his hand to still. She slipped her own palms up the front of his shirt, feeling all the firm, elegant planes and contours that lay beneath the fabric. "I believe I could be quite amenable to a bit of consummation… I mean, conjugation!" she quickly corrected, her cheeks flushing with embarrassment. "No—caddishness!"

"Caddishness?" Adam carefully pressed.

"Definitely… caddishness," Ellie breathlessly replied.

His mouth widened into a grin that bloomed like a slow summer sunrise. "Well, then," he concluded—and swept her up into his arms.

He carried her down the hall, pushing open the door to her room with a precise tap of his boot. The space beyond was dark, quiet—and full of promise.

"So what are you… thinking, exactly?" Ellie asked, sliding her hand up the back of his neck to let her fingers tangle in his hair.

"I'm not." Adam's tone was darkly wicked as he gazed down at her, limned by the soft golden light from the hall. "I'm improvising."

He was impulsive. *Reckless*… and Ellie was deeply, wildly grateful for all of it.

"Fiddlesticks," Ellie breathed with approval.

Adam grinned, carried her inside, and kicked shut the door.

A NOTE FROM THE AUTHOR

Ellie and Adam's adventures will continue in Raiders of the Arcana Book 3, *Arrow of Fortune*, coming in late 2025. To stay informed about when the book will be available for preorder, join the mailing list at JacquelynBenson.com/subscribe-to-the-newsletter.

If you enjoyed *Tomb of the Sun King*, please consider leaving a rating or review on your favorite book retailer or review site.

ACKNOWLEDGMENTS

I wrote a perfectly serviceable Raiders of the Arcana Book 2. It's not the book you just read. This book is much better, and I owe that entirely to the genius suggestions of my beta reader team. In particular, Olivia Atwater is responsible for most of the fun in Neil and Constance's dynamic, while Nicholas Atwater's casual suggestion that there might be something *more* to Neil's bursts of intuition had me going back and retconning my entire story.

(I have no regrets.)

Chris Mornick needs a special shout-out as well for finally giving me the key to unlocking Ellie and Adam's dynamic this time around. Rosalie Oaks, Matthew Dow, and Kaitlyn Huwe also lent their brilliant minds to the project, and I'm deeply grateful for all their feedback.

Hagar Moawad provided lovely insights into Egyptian life and culture, along with some desperately appreciated additions and corrections to my Masri phrases.

Big thanks also go to my Renegade Scholars for their ongoing support and enthusiasm as I utterly failed to take a month off and heedlessly blew through my deadlines in the interest of pushing even more loveliness into this story.

I continue to owe much to both the authors of the Lamplighter's Guild and the Fantasy Romance February community.

Selkkie Designs outdid herself once again with the cover for this book, and Elsa Kroese stepped in with the delightful character portraits.

Dan and the kids: Thank you for the ongoing moral support and abiding faith in me as I turned my brain to mush for several months over this story.

And finally, to the readers—knowing that you've opened your hearts to all of these characters is what keeps me coming back to the keyboard.

A brief historical note

Much of the history in this story is true. The summary of the Amarna period that I have shared in this narrative is all factual, if somewhat oversimplified. (Sorry for leaving you out of it, Smenkhkhare.) Akhenaten did indeed revolutionize Egyptian religion through the establishment of the royal cult of the Aten, though whether that constituted an early instance of monotheism or monolatry remains the subject of debate.

After dying precipitously—possibly in the same plague that killed his mother and daughter—Akhenaten was succeeded by Neferneferuaten, whose identity served as a tantalizing mystery to scholars and archaeologists for most of the 19th and 20th centuries. It has recently come to be generally accepted that this 'lost pharaoh' was most likely none other than Nefertiti.

Nefertiti's name translates to 'the beautiful one has come', which some scholars have posited indicates she may not have been Egyptian. The theory that she was a slave adopted into the family of the courtier Ay is my own— but Ay's dodgy story of eventually rising to claim the throne of Egypt for himself is all based on fact.

Hapiru was an Akkadian term also used in Egypt to refer to a diverse body of nomadic, mercenary, slave, or laboring peoples who populated parts of Egypt, Canaan, and Syria. Some scholars have speculated that the tribes who would later become the Hebrews may have been considered Hapiru by the Egyptians, though no specific reference to proto-Hebrew peoples enslaved in Egypt has yet been discovered.

My suggestion that Moses was an official in Akhenaten's court is entirely speculative, and owes much to the book *Moses and Monotheism* by Sigmund Freud.

Moving closer to the present, the British Consul General of Egypt, Lord Cromer, did indeed close or defund many institutions of higher learning out of a fear that a class of educated Egyptians would be prone to revolution.

Sayyid's father, Kamal Al-Ahmed, is loosely inspired by the early Egyptologist Ahmed Kamal. Though Kamal was educated at the short-lived School for the Ancient Egyptian Tongue, he had to fight for two decades to earn himself a position in the Egyptian Antiquities Service before eventually going on to serve as a curator at the Egyptian Museum. The routine exclusion and discrimination faced by Egyptian Egyptologists during the 19th century, which Sayyid describes in the book, is real. The discipline of archaeology is also still coming to terms with how the knowledge of local archaeological field workers is often overlooked and undervalued.

I stole the idea for the hematite in Neferneferuaten's sarcophagus from Egyptologist Zahi Hawass's excavation of the tomb of Eyuf, a provincial mayor, where he found large quantities of yellow powdered iron ore and speculated it may have been intended to deter or punish theives.

The curse of the scarab is adapted from materials in "The Process of Cursing in Ancient Egypt" by Sarah Louise Colledge. Descriptions of reconstructed Middle Egyptian phonetics are based on my own reading on the subject, and I apologize for any errors or liberties I've taken.

The spell of protection used at the conclusion of the story is based on a line from Chapter CLI of the Book of the Dead. My text for it is a bit of a mashup of E.A. Wallis Budge's translations of versions of the chapter from the Papyrus of Ani and British Museum papyrus No. 10010.

I have taken the liberty of making Ellie aware of the 4,500 year old ramp at the Egyptian quarry of Hatnub, which was not actually discovered until quite recently—purely in order for her to show up her stuffy brother. Do forgive me.

THE
RAIDERS OF THE ARCANA

*Find the magic artifacts, thwart imperialists, and fall in love with this smart,
swashbuckling historical fantasy adventure series.*

Book 0
The Stolen Apocalypse
When a manuscript goes missing in a Gothic priory, Ellie
and Constance set out to thwart the theft.

Book One
Empire of Shadows
Archivist Ellie Mallory teams up with roguish surveyor Adam Bates
in a race to find a legendary city.

Book Two
Tomb of the Sun King
Ellie and Adam race through Egypt on a quest to find a
lost tomb and protect an arcanum of Biblical proportions.

Book Three
Arrow of Fortune
Coming late 2025.

Available everywhere books are sold.